MYST: THE BOOK OF TI'ANA

ABOUT THE AUTHORS

RAND MILLER — WHO ALONG WITH HIS BROTHER ROBYN discovered and brought to life the secrets of D'ni empire in the megahit CD-ROM world MYST and the novel *Myst: The Book of Atrus* — rather enjoys his simple life . . . one that now includes a garage at his home in the Pacific Northwest. And when he has the time, he carefully practices his form and technique at his self-designed 14-hole, Certified Cross Country, Off-Road disc-golf course. On rare occasions he invites only the best of friends or employees over for a weekend disc-golf slaughtering.

David Wingrove is the author of the *Chung Kuo* series of novels, which include *The Middle Kingdom, The Broken Wheel, The White Mountain, The Stone Within,* and *Beneath the Tree of Heaven.* He also co-authored, with Brian Aldiss, *Trillion Year Spree: The History of Science,* a volume which won the prestigious Hugo and *Locus* Awards for best non-fiction work in the science fiction genre. He lives in North London with his wife and three daughters.

Chris Brandkamp, when he's not being slaughtered in disc-golf by Rand, manages Cyan's business affairs. He also enjoys all sorts of outdoor activities, for example chipping (grinding huge trees into pea-size pieces). And no, that's not what happened to his fingers!

Richard Watson is the keeper of the D'ni. His expertise in D'ni culture, language, and events is exceeded only by his skill at Mario Brothers.

Ryan Miller (a.k.a. Rand and Robyn's little brother) is the most competitive of the Miller brothers. When the Dallas Cowboys won the Superbowl, it allowed him to relax and transfer his competitive energy into working with his brothers, repairing his sewer pipe and gas line, having a kid, and writing his own novel.

Myst: The Book of Atrus is also published by Corgi and the third chronicle of *Myst, Myst: The Book of D'ni,* is now available as a Bantam Press hardback.

MYST

THE BOOK OF TI'ANA

RAND MILLER
WITH DAVID WINGROVE

CORGI BOOKS

MYST: THE BOOK OF TI'ANA
A CORGI BOOK: 0 552 14387 1

Originally published in Great Britain by Bantam Press,
a division of Transworld Publishers Ltd

First published in the United States and Canada 1996 by
Hyperion

PRINTING HISTORY
Bantam Press edition published 1996
Corgi edition published 1997

Illustrations by Tom Bowman

Set in 10.5pt Venetian301 BT
by Phoenix Typesetting, Ilkley, West Yorkshire.

Corgi Books are published by Transworld Publishers Ltd,
61–63 Uxbridge Road, London W5 5SA,
in Australia by Transworld Publishers (Australia) Pty Ltd,
15–25 Helles Avenue, Moorebank, NSW 2170
and in New Zealand by Transworld Publishers (NZ) Ltd,
3 William Pickering Drive, Albany, Auckland.

Reproduced, printed and bound in Great Britain by
Cox & Wyman Ltd, Reading, Berks.

TO DEB AND THE GIRLS

Acknowledgments

It's amazing how little we know, after all these years, about the history of D'ni and the story surrounding Myst Island. Over the years the story is revealed piece by piece, like a large puzzle waiting to be put together. It's only with the continuing effort of a core group of people that the pieces are uncovered and assembled to make a book like this possible.

It has been my pleasure to uncover these past events in D'ni history even as Robyn continues to bring the events surrounding Myst Island to its final chapter. Not having Robyn's help for this translation, the burden of discovery was taken up by Chris Brandkamp, Richard Watson, and Ryan Miller working closely with David Wingrove. Our task was large and yet the results are stunning, as for the first time the public gains a glimpse into the richness and complexity of the D'ni civilization.

So it is to these four close friends (particularly David and Chris for their long hours of work) that I extend my sincerest thanks and admiration. This story reaches you because of their dedication and brilliance.

RAND MILLER

MYST: THE BOOK OF TI'ANA

PART ONE: ECHOES IN THE ROCK

THE SOUNDING CAPSULE WAS EMBEDDED IN THE ROCK
face like a giant crystal, its occupants sealed within the
translucent, soundproofed cone.

The Guild Master sat facing the outstretched tip of the
cone, his right hand resting delicately on the long metal
shaft of the sounder, his blind eyes staring at the solid rock,
listening.

Behind him, his two young assistants leaned forward in
their narrow metal and mesh seats, concentrating, their eyes
shut tight as they attempted to discern the tiny variations in
the returning signal.

"Na'grenis," the old man said, the D'ni word almost
growled as his left hand moved across the top sheet of the
many-layered map that rested on the map table between his
knees. *Brittle.*

It was the tenth time they had sent the signal out on
this line, each time a little stronger, the echoes in the rock
changing subtly as it penetrated deeper into the mass.

"Kenen voohee shuhteejoo," the younger of his two
assistants said tentatively. *It could be rocksalt.*

"Or chalk," the other added uncertainly.

"Not this deep," the old man said authoritatively, flicking back the transparent sheets until he came to one deep in
the pile. Holding it open, he reached beside him and took a
bright red marker from the metal rack.

13

"Ah," the two assistants said as one, the carmine mark as clear an explanation as if he'd spoken.

"We'll sound either side," the old man said after a moment. "It might only be a pocket. . . . "

He slipped the marker back into the rack, then reached out and took the ornately decorated shaft of the sounder, delicately moving it a fraction to the right, long experience shaping his every movement.

"Same strength," he said. "One pulse, fifty beats, and then a second pulse."

At once his First Assistant leaned forward, adjusting the setting on the dial in front of him.

There was a moment's silence and then a vibration rippled along the shaft toward the tapered tip of the cone.

A single, pure, clear note sounded in the tiny chamber, like an invisible spike reaching out into the rock.

"What is he doing?"

Guild Master Telanis turned from the observation window to look at his guest. Master Kedri was a big, ungainly man. A member of the Guild of Legislators, he was here to observe the progress of the excavation.

"Guild Master Geran is surveying the rock. Before we drill we need to know what lies ahead of us."

"I understand that," Kedri said impatiently. "But what is the problem?"

Telanis stifled the irritation he felt at the man's bad

manners. After all, Kedri was technically his superior, even if, within his own craft, Telanis's word was as law.

"I'm not sure exactly, but from the mark he made I'd say he's located a patch of igneous material. Magma-based basaltic rocks from a fault line, perhaps, or a minor intrusion."

"And that's a problem?"

Telanis smiled politely. "It could be. If it's minor we could drill straight through it, of course, and support the tunnel, but we're still quite deep and there's a lot of weight above us. The pressures here are immense, and while they might not crush us, they could inconvenience us and set us back weeks, if not months. We'd prefer, therefore, to be certain of what lies ahead."

Kedri huffed. "It all seems rather a waste of time to me. The lining rock's strong, isn't it?"

"Oh, very strong, but that's not the point. If the aim were merely to break through to the surface we could do that in a matter of weeks. But that's not our brief. These tunnels are meant to be permanent—or, at least, as permanent as we can make them, rock movement willing!"

Still, Kedri seemed unsatisfied. "All this stopping and starting! A man could go mad with waiting!"

One could; and some, unsuited to the task, did. But of all the guilds of D'ni, this, Telanis knew, was the one best suited to their nature.

"We are a patient race, Master Kedri," he said, risking the anger of the other man. "Patient and thorough. Would you have us abandon the habits of a thousand generations?"

Kedri made to answer curtly, then saw the look of challenge in Telanis's eyes and nodded. "No. You are right,

Guild Master. Forgive me. Perhaps they chose the wrong man to represent our guild."

Perhaps, Telanis thought, but aloud he said. "Not at all, Master Kedri. You will get used to it, I promise. And we shall do our best to keep you busy while you are here. I shall have my assistant, Aitrus, assigned to you."

And now Kedri smiled, as if this was what he had been angling for all along. "That is most kind, Master Telanis. Most kind, indeed."

The excavator was quiet, the lighting subdued. Normally, the idle chatter of young crewmen would have filled the narrow corridor, but since the observers had come there was a strange silence to the craft that made it seem abandoned.

As the young guildsman walked along its length, he glanced about warily. Normally he took such sights for granted, but today he seemed to see it all anew. Here in the front section, just behind the great drill, was the Guild Master's cabin and, next to it, through a bulkhead that would seal automatically in times of emergency, the chart room. Beyond that, opening out to both right and left of the corridor, was the equipment room.

The excavator was as self-contained as any ship at sea, everything stored, each cupboard and drawer secured against sudden jolts, but here the purpose of the craft was nakedly displayed, the massive rock drills lain neatly in their racks, blast-marble cylinders, protective helmets, and analysis tubes racked like weaponry.

The young guildsman stopped, looking back along the

length of the craft. He was a tall, athletic-looking young man with an air of earnestness about him. His dark red jumpsuit fit him comfortably rather than tightly; the broad, black leather tool belt at his waist and his long black leather boots part of the common uniform worn by all the members of the expedition.

His fine black hair was cut short and neat, accentuating his fineboned features, while his eyes were pale but keen. Intelligent, observant eyes.

He passed on, through the crew quarters—the empty bunks stacked three to a side into the curve of the ship's walls, eighteen bunks in all—and, passing through yet another bulkhead, into the refectory.

Master Jerahl, the ship's cook, looked up from where he was preparing the evening meal and smiled.

"Ah, Aitrus. Working late again?"

"Yes, Guild Master."

Jerahl grinned paternally. "Knowing you, you'll be so engrossed in some experiment, you'll miss your supper. You want me to bring you something through?"

"Thank you, Guild Master. That would be most welcome."

"Not at all, Aitrus. It's good to see such keenness in a young guildsman. I won't say it to their faces, but some of your fellows think it's enough to carry out the letter of their instructions and no more. But people notice such things."

Aitrus smiled.

"Oh, some find me foolish, Aitrus, I know. It's hard not to overhear things on a tiny ship like this. But I was not always a cook. Or, should I say, *only* a cook. I trained much as you train

17

now, to be a Surveyor—to know the ways of the rock. And much of what I learned remains embedded here in my head. But I wasn't suited. Or, should I say, I found myself better suited to *this* occupation."

"You *trained*, Master Jerahl?"

"Of course, Aitrus. You think they would allow me on an expedition like this if I were not a skilled geologist?" Jerahl grinned. "Why, I spent close on twenty years specializing in stress mechanics."

Aitrus stared at Jerahl a moment, then shook his head. "I did not know."

"Nor were you expected to. As long as you enjoy the meals I cook, I am content."

"Of that I've no complaints."

"Then good. Go on through. I shall bring you something in a while."

Aitrus walked on, past the bathing quarters and the sample store, and on into the tail of the craft. Here the corridor ended with a solid metal door that was always kept closed. Aitrus reached up and pulled down the release handle. At once the door hissed open. He stepped through, then heard it hiss shut behind him.

A single light burned on the wall facing him. In its half-light he could see the work surface that ran flush with the curved walls at waist height, forming an arrowhead. Above and below it, countless tiny cupboards held the equipment and chemicals they used for analysis.

Aitrus went across and, putting his notebook down on the worktop, quickly selected what he would need from various cupboards.

This was his favorite place in the ship. Here he could forget all else and immerse himself in the pure, unalloyed joy of discovery.

Aitrus reached up, flicking his fingernail against the firemarble in the bowl of the lamp, then, in the burgeoning glow, opened his notebook to the page he had been working on.

"Aitrus?"

Aitrus took his eye from the lens and turned, surprised he had not heard the hiss of the door. Jerahl was standing there, holding out a plate to him. The smell of freshly baked *chor bahkh* and *ikhah nijuhets* wafted across, making his mouth water.

Jerahl smiled. "Something interesting?"

Aitrus took the plate and nodded. "You want to see?"

"May I?" Jerahl stepped across and, putting his eye to the lens, studied the sample a moment. When he looked up again there was a query in his eyes.

"Tachyltye, eh? Now why would a young fellow like you be interested in basaltic glass?"

"I'm interested in anything to do with lava flows," Aitrus answered, his eyes aglow. "It's what I want to specialize in, ultimately. Volcanism."

Jerahl smiled as if he understood. "All that heat and pressure, eh? I didn't realize you were so romantic, Aitrus!"

Aitrus, who had begun to eat the meat-filled roll, paused and looked at Jerahl in surprise. He had heard his fascination called many things by his colleagues, but never "romantic."

"Oh, yes," Jerahl went on, "once you have seen how this is formed, nothing will ever again impress half so much! The meeting of superheated rock and ice-chill water—it is a powerful combination. And *this*—this strange translucent matter—is the result."

Again Jerahl smiled. "Learning to control such power, that is where we D'ni began as a species. That is where our spirit of inquiry was first awoken. So take heart, Aitrus. In this you are a true son of D'ni."

Aitrus smiled back at the older man. "I am sorry we have not spoken before now, Guild Master. I did not know you knew so much."

"Oh, I claim to know very little, Aitrus. At least, by comparison with Master Telanis. And while we are talking of the good Guild Master, he was asking for you not long back. I promised him I would feed you, then send you to his cabin."

Aitrus, who had just lifted the roll to his mouth again, paused. "Master Telanis wants me?"

Jerahl gestured toward the roll. "Once you've been fed. Now finish that or I shall feel insulted."

"Whatever you say, Master!" And, grinning, Aitrus bit deep into the roll.

Aitrus stopped before the Guild Master's cabin and, taking a moment to prepare himself, reached out and rapped upon the door.

The voice from inside was calm and assured. "Come in!"

He slid back the heavy bolt and stepped inside, closing the door behind him. That much was habit. Every door in the craft was a barrier against fire or unwelcome gases. Turning, he saw that Master Telanis was at his desk looking at the latest survey chart. Facing him across the table was Master Geran. Also there were the four Observers who had joined them three days back. Aitrus took a step toward them and bowed.

"You sent for me, Guild Master?"

"I did. But if you would wait a moment, Aitrus, I must first deal with the news Master Geran has brought us."

Aitrus lowered his head, conscious that the Legislator—the big man, Kedri—was watching him closely.

"So, Geran," Telanis went on, indicating the bright red line that ran across the chart in front of him, "you recommend that we circumvent this area?"

The blind man nodded. "The fault itself is narrow, admittedly, but the surrounding rock is of low density and likely to collapse. We could cut through it, of course, and shore up on either side, but I'd say there is more to come the other side of that."

"You know that?" Kedri asked, interrupting the two.

Geran turned his blank, unseeing eyes upon the Legislator and smiled. "I do not *know* it, Master Kedri, but my instinct is that this is the mere root of a much larger igneous intrusion. Part of a volcanic system. Imagine the roots of a tree. So such things are. As excavators, we try hard to avoid such instabilities. We look for hard, intact rock. Rock we have no need to support."

Kedri looked puzzled at that. "But I thought it was your practice to support everything?"

Telanis answered him. "We do, Guild Master. As I said, we are very thorough. But if it is as Master Geran says—and long experience would tend to bear him out—we would do well to drill sideways a way before continuing our ascent. After all, why go courting trouble?"

"So how long will this . . . *detour* take?"

Telanis smiled pleasantly. "A week. Maybe two."

Kedri looked far from pleased, yet he said nothing. Relieved, Telanis looked to Geran once more.

"In the circumstances I approve your recommendation, Master Geran. We shall move back and across. Arrange the survey at once."

Geran smiled. "I shall do it myself, Guild Master."

When Geran was gone, Telanis looked across at Aitrus.

"Aitrus, step forward."

Aitrus crossed the narrow cabin, taking the place Geran had just vacated. "Yes, Guild Master?"

"I want you to place yourself at Guild Master Kedri's disposal for the next eleven days. I want you to show him how things work and explain to him just what we are doing. And if there's anything you yourself are uncertain of, you will ask someone who *does* know. Understand me?"

Surprised, Aitrus nodded. "Yes, Guild Master." Then, hesitantly. "And my experiments, Guild Master?"

Telanis looked to Kedri. "That depends upon Master Kedri. If he permits, I see no reason why you should not continue with them."

Kedri turned to Aitrus. "Experiments, Guildsman?"

Aitrus looked down, knowing suddenly that he ought not to have mentioned them. "It does not matter, Master."

"No, Aitrus. I am interested. What experiments are these?"

Aitrus looked up shyly. "I am studying volcanic rocks, Master. I wish to understand all I can about their nature and formation."

Kedri seemed impressed. "A most worthy task, young Aitrus. Perhaps you would be kind enough to show me these experiments?"

Aitrus looked to Telanis, hoping his Master would somehow get him off the hook, but Telanis was staring at the multilayered chart Geran had given him, flipping from page to page and frowning.

Aitrus met Kedri's eyes again, noting how keenly the other watched him. "As you wish, Guild Master."

The cavern in which they rested was a perfect sphere, or would have been but for the platform on which the two excavators lay. The craft were long and sinuous, like huge, segmented worms, their tough exteriors kept buffed and polished when they were not burrowing in the rock.

Metal ladders went down beneath the gridwork platform to a second, smaller platform to which the junior members of the expedition had had their quarters temporarily removed to make way for their guests. It was to here, after a long, exhausting day of explanations, that Aitrus returned, long after most of his colleagues had retired.

There were thirty-six of them in all, none older than

thirty—all of them graduates of the Academy; young guilds-men who had volunteered for this expedition. Some had given up and been replaced along the way, but more than two-thirds of the original crews remained.

Two years, four months, Aitrus thought as he sat on the edge of his bedroll and began to pull off his boots. It was a long time to be away from home. He could have gone home, of course—Master Telanis would have given him leave if he had asked—but that would have seemed like cheating, somehow. No, an expedition was not really an expedition if one could go home whenever one wished.

Even as he kicked his other boot off, he felt the sudden telltale vibration in the platform, followed an instant or two later by a low, almost inaudible rumble. A Messenger was coming!

The expedition had cut its way through several miles of rock, up from one of the smaller, outermost caverns of D'ni. They could, of course, have gone up vertically, like a mine shaft, but so direct a route into D'ni was thought not merely inadvisable but dangerous. The preferred scheme—the scheme the Council had eventually agreed upon—was a far more indirect route, cut at a maximum of 3825 *torans*—22.032 degrees—from the horizontal. One that could be walked.

One that could also be sealed off with gates and defended.

The rumbling grew, slowly but steadily. You could hear the sound of the turbine engines now.

Slowly but surely they had burrowed through the rock, surveying each one-hundred-span section carefully before they drilled, coating the surfaces with a half-span thickness of special D'ni rock, more durable than marble. Last, but not least, they fitted heavy stone brackets into the ceiling of each section—brackets that carried air from the pumping stations back in D'ni.

Between each straight-line section was one of these spherical "nodes"—these resting places where they could carry on experiments while Master Geran and his assistants charted the next stage of their journey through the earth—each node fitted with an airtight gate that could be sealed in an instant.

The rumbling grew to a roar. For a moment the sound of it filled the node, then the engines cut out and there was the downward whine of the turbines as the Messenger slowed.

Aitrus turned and stood, watching as the metal snout of the machine emerged from the entry tunnel, passing through the thick collar of the node-gate, its pilot clearly visible through the transparent front debris shield.

It was a large, tracked vehicle, its three long segments making it seem clumsy in comparison to the sleek excavators, but as ever Aitrus was glad to see it, for besides bringing them much-needed supplies—it being impossible to "link" supplies direct from D'ni into the tunnels—it also brought letters from home.

"Aitrus? What time is it?"

Aitrus turned. His friend Jenir had woken and was sitting up.

"Ninth bell," he answered, bending down to retrieve his boots and pull them on again.

Others had also been woken by the Messenger's arrival, and were sitting up or climbing from their beds, knowing there was unloading to be done.

He himself had been temporarily excused from such

duties; even so, as the others drifted across to the ladders and began to ascend, he followed, curious to see if anything had come for him.

When the last Messenger had come, three days back, it had brought nothing but the Observers—those unexpected "guests" billeted upon them by the Council. Before that it had been almost three weeks since they had had contact with D'ni. Three solid weeks without news.

The Messenger had come to rest between the two excavators. Already its four-man crew were busy, running pipelines between the middle segment of their craft and the two much larger vehicles, ready to transfer its load of mechanical parts, equipment, drill bits, fuel, and cooling fluid to the excavators.

Aitrus yawned, then walked across. The young men of the Messengers Guild were of nature outward, friendly types, and seeing him, one of them hailed him.

"Ho! Aitrus! There's a parcel for you!"

"A parcel?"

The Messenger gestured toward where one of his colleagues was carrying a large mesh basket into the forward cabin of the left-hand excavator.

Aitrus turned and looked, then hurried after, almost running into Master Telanis coming out.

"Aitrus! Why such a hurry?"

"Forgive me, Guild Master. I was told there was a parcel for me."

"Ah," Telanis made to walk on, then stopped, lowering his voice. "By the way, how was our guest?"

Tiring, he wanted to answer. "Curious," he said after a moment, keeping his own voice low. "Oh, and imaginative."

Telanis frowned. "How so?"

"It would seem we are too cautious for him, Guild Master. Our methods are, well . . . *inefficient*."

Telanis considered that, then nodded. "We must talk, Aitrus. Tomorrow. Early, perhaps, before Master Kedri has need of you. There are things you need to know."

Aitrus bowed. "I shall call on you at third bell, Master."

"Good. Now go and see what the Messengers have brought."

Master Tejara of the Messengers had commandeered the table in the chart room to sort out the post. Surrounded by shelves of bound surveys, he looked up from his work as Aitrus entered.

"Ah, Aitrus. And how are you today?"

"I am well, Guild Master."

Tejara flashed a smile at him. "You've heard, then?"

"Master?" But Aitrus's eyes had already gone to the large, square parcel—bound in cloth and stitched—that rested to one side of the table.

"Here," Master Tejara said, handing it to him.

Aitrus took it, surprised by how heavy it seemed. Unable to help himself, he held it to his ear and shook it gently.

There was a gentle chime.

"Well?" Tejara said, grinning at him now. "Are you going to open it or not?"

Aitrus hesitated a moment, then set the parcel down on the table and, taking a slender chisel from his tool belt, slit open the stitching. The cloth fell back.

Inside was a tiny wooden case, the top surface of which was a sliding panel. He slid it back and looked inside.

"By the Maker!"

Aitrus reached in and drew out the delicate, golden pair of portable scales. They were perfect, the spring mechanism of the finest make, the soft metal inlaid with tiny silver D'ni numerals. Nor were they the only thing. Setting the scales down carefully, he reached in once more and took out a flat, square rosewood box the size of his palm. Opening it, Aitrus stared openmouthed at the exposed pair of D'ni geological compasses, his fingertips gently brushing the tiny crystal magnifier that enabled one to read the tiny calibrations. For a moment he simply looked, studying the minute transparent dials and delicate adjustable attachments that overlay the simple circle of its working face, then shook his head in wonder.

"Is it your Naming Day, Aitrus?" Tejara asked.

"No," Aitrus said distractedly as he reached in a third time to lift out an envelope marked simply "Guildsman Aitrus" in an unfamiliar hand.

He frowned, then looked to Tejara, who simply shrugged. Slitting the envelope open, he took out the single sheet and unfolded it.

"*Aitrus,*" it began,

You might remember me from school days. I realize we were not the best of friends, but we were both young then and such misunderstandings happen. Recently, however, I chanced upon a report you wrote among my father's papers and was reminded of those unfortunate days, and it occurred to me that I might do something to attempt to reverse your poor opinion of me. If the enclosed gifts are unwelcome, please forgive me. But I hope you will accept them in the same spirit with which they are given. Good luck with your explorations! Yours in friendship, Veovis.

Aitrus looked up, astonished to see *that* signature at the foot of the note.

"It is from Veovis," he said quietly. "Lord Rakeri's son."

Tejara looked surprised. "Veovis is your friend, Aitrus?"

Aitrus shook his head. "No. At least, he was no friend to me at school."

"Then these gifts are a surprise?"

"More a shock, to be honest, Guild Master. Yet people change, I suppose."

Tejara nodded emphatically. "You can be certain of it, Aitrus. Time teaches many things. It is the rock in which we bore."

Aitrus smiled at the old saying.

"Oh, and before I forget," Tejara added, handing him his mail, "there are three letters for you this time."

Aitrus lay there a long time, unable to sleep, staring at the pattern of shadows on the smooth, curved wall of the node, wondering what the gifts meant.

His letters had contained the usual, cheerful news from home—chatter about old friends from his mother, word of

Council matters from his father. But his mind kept going back to the note.

That Veovis had written at all was amazing, that he had sent gifts was . . . well, astonishing!

And not just any gifts, but just those things that he most needed in his work.

Oh, there were plenty of scales and compasses he could use—property of the guild—but not his own. Nor were the guild's instruments anything as fine as those Veovis had given him. Why, they were as good as those that hung from Master Telanis's own tool belt!

When finally he did manage to sleep, it was to find himself dreaming of his school days, his mind, for some strange yet obvious reason, going back to a day in his thirteenth year when, tired of turning his back on Veovis's constant taunts, he had turned and fought him.

He woke to find Master Telanis shaking him.

"Come, Aitrus. Third bell has sounded. We need to talk."

The cabin door was locked. Master Telanis sat behind his desk, looking up at Aitrus.

"Well, Aitrus, how did you fare with Master Kedri?"

Aitrus hesitated, not sure how much to say. The truth was he did not like the task he had been given. It made him feel *uncomfortable*.

Telanis coaxed him gently. "You said he felt our methods were inefficient."

"Oh, indeed, Guild Master. He constantly commented upon how slow our methods are. How overcautious."

"And do you agree with him, Aitrus? Do you think, perhaps, that we *are* too pedantic in our ways?"

"Not at all, Guild Master. There is, after all, no hurry. Whether we reach the surface this year or next does not matter. Safety must be our first concern."

Telanis stared at him a moment, then nodded. "Good. Now let me tell you a few things, Aitrus. First, I am aware that this task is not really to your liking."

Aitrus made to object, but Telanis raised a hand. "Make no mistake, Aitrus. I realize you are not at ease looking after Master Kedri, but I chose you for a reason. The good Master seeks to sound us out on certain topics—to *survey* our attitudes, if you like."

Aitrus looked horrified at the thought. "Should I watch what I say, Master?"

"Not at all, Aitrus. I have no fear that you will say anything that might upset Master Kedri. That is why I chose you. You are like basalt, Aitrus, solid through and through. But it would help me if, at the end of each day, you would note down those areas in which Master Kedri seemed most interested."

Aitrus hesitated. "Might I ask why, Master?"

"You may. But you must keep my answer strictly to yourself." Telanis paused, steepling his fingers before his chin. "There is to be a meeting of the Council, a month from now. It seems that some of the older members have had a change of heart. They have thought long and hard about whether we should make contact with the surface dwellers or not, and a few of them now feel it might not be quite so good an idea as it first seemed. Indeed, they might even ask us to abandon the expedition."

Unable to help himself, Aitrus slammed his fist down on the desk. "But they *can't!*"

Master Telanis smiled tolerantly. "If that is their final word, then so be it. We must do what they say. We cannot argue with the Council."

Aitrus lowered his head, acknowledging what Master Telanis said. The Council was the ruling body of D'ni and their word was law. His own opinion was irrelevant—it was what the five Great Lords and the eighteen Guild Masters decided that was important.

"That is why," Telanis went on, "it is so important that we impress our guests, Aitrus, for they represent the Eighteen and the Five. What they report back might yet prove crucial in swaying the decision . . . either for us or against us."

"I see." And suddenly he *did* see. Master Kedri was not just any busybody, butting his nose into their affairs; Kedri was a potential enemy—or ally—of the expedition. All of their hard work, their patient progress through the rock, might prove to no avail if Kedri spoke against them.

"I am not sure I can do this, Master."

Telanis nodded. "I understand. Do you want to be relieved of this duty, Aitrus?"

He stared at Master Telanis. It was as simple as that, was it? And then he understood. It was like going home. He *could* go home, at any time, but it was his choice *not* to go home that gave this voyage its meaning. So with this. He could quit, but . . .

Aitrus lowered his head respectfully. "I shall do as you wish, Guild Master."

Telanis smiled broadly. "Good. Now go and eat. You have a long day ahead of you."

Four long, exacting days followed, one upon another. Aitrus was ready to go back to Master Telanis and beg to be taken from his task when news came to him that they were ready to start drilling the next section.

Master Kedri was in the refectory when the news came, and, delighted that he could at last show the Legislator something real and tangible, Aitrus interrupted him at table.

"Yes, Guildsman?" Kedri said, staring at Aitrus. The conversation at table had died the moment Aitrus had stepped into the cabin. All four of the Observers seated about the narrow table had turned to stare at him.

"Forgive me, Masters," Aitrus said, bowing to them all, "but I felt you should know at once that we are about to commence the next stage of the excavation."

There was at once a babble of sound from all sides. Some stood immediately and began to make their way out. Others began to hurriedly finish their meals. Only Kedri seemed unmoved by the news.

"Thank you, Aitrus," he said after a moment. "I shall finish my meal then join you. Wait for me at the site."

Ten minutes later, Master Kedri stepped out of the excavator and walked across to where they had set up the sample drills. The other Observers had already gathered, waiting for operations to commence.

"Let us see if I understand this correctly," Kedri began, before Aitrus could say a word. "Master Geran's 'sounding' is a rough yet fairly accurate guide to whether the rock ahead of us is sound or otherwise, correct? The next stage—*this* stage— is to drill a series of long boreholes to provide us with a precise breakdown of the different kinds of rock we are about to cut through."

Aitrus nodded, for the first time smiling at the Legislator.

"Oh, I can retain some minimal information, Guildsman," Kedri said, a faint amusement on his own lips. "It isn't only contracts I can read. But there is one thing you can tell me, Aitrus, and that's where all the rock goes to."

"The rock?" Aitrus laughed. "But I thought you knew, Master. I thought *everyone* knew! It is reconstituted."

"Reconstituted?"

"In the fusion-compounder. The machine reconstitutes the very matter of the rock, reforging its atomic links and thereby reducing its volume by a factor of two hundred. The result is *nara*."

"So that's what nara is!" Kedri nodded thoughtfully. "Can I *see* this fusion-compounder?"

Aitrus smiled, suddenly liking the man. "See it, Master? Why, you can operate it if you want!"

Aitrus took a sheet of paper and, for Master Kedri's benefit, sketched out a cross-section diagram of the tunnel.

"This," he said, indicating the small shaded circle at the

very center of it, "is the hole made by the excavator. As you can see, it's a comparatively small hole, less than a third the total circumference of the tunnel. This," and he pointed to the two closely parallel circles on the outer wall of the tunnel, "is the area that the Cycler removes."

"The *Cycler?*" Kedri looked puzzled.

"That's what we call it. It's because it cuts a giant ring from the rock surrounding the central borehole."

"Ah, then that would be the big spiderlike machine, right?"

Aitrus nodded. Only two days before they had exhaustively inspected all of the different excavating tools.

"What happens is that the Cycler removes a circular track around the outer edge to a depth of one and a quarter spans. We then fill that space with a special seal of D'ni stone, let that set, then chip out the "collar"— that is, the rock between the inner tunnel and the seal."

"Why one and a quarter?"

Aitrus sketched something on the pad, then handed it across. "As you can see, we insert a special metal brace a quarter of a span wide, deep in the cut, then pour in the sealant stone. Then, when the collar has been chipped away, we remove the brace and set up the Cycler ready to start all over."

Kedri frowned. "Forgive me, Guildsman, but once again it seems a most laborious way of going about things."

"Maybe so, Master Kedri, but safe. When we make a tunnel, we make it to last."

"Yes . . . " Kedri nodded thoughtfully. "Still, it seems a lot of effort merely to talk to a few surface-dwellers, don't you think?"

It was the first direct question of that type Kedri had

asked him, and for a moment Aitrus wondered if he might not simply ignore it, or treat it as rhetorical, but Kedri, it seemed, was waiting for an answer

"Well, Guildsman? Have you *no* opinion on the matter?"

Master Telanis came to his rescue.

"Forgive me, Master Kedri. Guildsman Aitrus might well have an opinion, but I am sure he would be the first to admit that at twenty-five he is far too young and inexperienced to express it openly. However, if you would welcome the opinion of someone of greater years?"

Kedri laughed. "Oh, I know *your* opinion, Master Telanis. I simply thought it would be refreshing to seek a different, *younger* view on things."

"Oh, come now, Kedri, do you really think our Masters on Council would be in the least interested in what a young guildsman—even one as brilliant as Aitrus here—has to say? Why, Lord Tulla is near on eleven times young Aitrus's age! Do you think *he* would be interested."

Kedri bowed his head, conceding the point.

"Then let us proceed with more important matters," Telanis continued quickly, before Kedri might steer the conversation back onto more tricky ground. "Normally we would take bore samples at this stage, but as you are so keen to see us in action, Master Kedri, I have decided to waive those for once and go direct to drilling."

The news seemed to cheer Kedri immensely. "Excellent!" he said, rubbing his hands together. "Will we need protective clothing of any kind?"

Master Telanis shook his head. "No. But you will need to be inside the second craft. When we drill, we drill!"

The node-gate was closed behind them, its airtight seal ensuring that not a single particle of rock would escape back down the tunnel. The temporary camp had been packed up and stored; the sounding capsule attached to the back of the second excavator, which now rested against the back wall of the node, slightly to the left of the bore-site. Two large observation lenses had been mounted on the ceiling to either side of the site, high up so that they'd not be hit by flying rock.

All was now ready. Master Telanis had only to give the order.

Aitrus was in the second vehicle, standing at the back of the chart room behind the Observers, who looked up at the big screen, watching as the excavator was maneuvered into place.

In operation it seemed more like something living than a machine, its sinuous, quiet movements like those of a giant snake.

Aitrus looked on with quiet satisfaction. He had first seen an excavator in action when he was four—when his father, a guildsman before him—had taken him to see the cutting of a new tunnel between the outer caverns.

Kedri, in particular, seemed impressed. He was leaning forward, staring at the screen in fascination.

"In place!" Master Telanis called out, his voice transmitted into the chart room where they sat. A moment later a siren sounded, its whine rising and then falling again.

The snout of the excavator came around and seemed almost to kiss the bore-mark on the rock face, so gentle was

37

its touch, but the great drill bit had a brutal look to it, and as they watched, they saw the cooling fluid begin to dribble down the thick grooves of the drill.

Slowly the drill began to turn, nudging blindly into the rock, the mechanical whirr of its slow spiral accompanied by a deeper, grinding sound that seemed to climb in pitch as the bit whirred faster and faster until it was a squeal, great clouds of dust billowing out from all around it.

The noise was now deafening, the vibrations making the second excavator ring like a struck bell. Slowly the great sphere of the node filled with dust, partly obscuring their view. Yet every now and then they would glimpse the excavator again, each time buried deeper and deeper into the rock, like some ferocious, feral animal boring into the soft flesh of its victim.

From time to time there would be a clang or thud as a large fragment of rock struck their craft, but there was no danger—the excavators were built to withstand massive pressures. Even a major collapse would merely trap the machine, not crush it.

After a while, Kedri turned and looked to Aitrus. "It's a fearsome sight," he said, raising his voice above the din.

Aitrus nodded. The first time he had seen it he had felt a fear deep in the pit of his stomach, yet afterward, talking to his father, he had remembered it with wonder and a sense of pride that this was what his guildspeople did.

Perhaps it was even that day when he had decided to follow his father into the Guild of Surveyors.

"Watch the tail," he shouted, indicating the screen as, briefly, the excavator came into view again. It was almost wholly in the rock now, yet even as they watched, the tail end of the craft began to lash from side to side—again like a living thing—scoring the smooth-bored wall of the tunnel with tooth-shaped gashes.

"Why does it do that?" Kedri shouted back.

"To give our men a purchase on the wall. Those gashes are where we begin to dig out the collar. It makes it much easier for us!"

Kedri nodded. "Clever. You think of everything!"

Yes, Aitrus thought, *but then we have had a thousand generations to think of everything.*

In the sudden silence, the excavator backed out of the hole, its segmented sides coated in dust, its drill head glowing red despite the constant stream of coolant. Inside the node the dust was slowly settling.

"Can we go outside and see for ourselves now?" One of the other Observers, Ja'ir, a Master in the Guild of Writers asked.

"I am afraid not," Aitrus answered him. "It is much too hot. Besides, you would choke on the dust. Even our men will have to wear breathing suits for a while. No, first they will have to spray the node with water to settle the dust. Then, once the drill bit has cooled a little, we shall start pumping air back into the node from outside. Only then will they start the clearing up process."

"And the next stage of drilling?" Kedri asked, turning fully in his seat and leaning over the back of the chair to stare at Aitrus.

"That begins almost at once, Master," Aitrus answered. "Look."

Even as he spoke, a door opened in the side of the excavator and two young guildsmen stepped out, suited-up, air canisters feeding the sealed helmets they were wearing. They were both carrying what looked like spears, only these spears were curved and had sharp, diamond tips at the end.

"They'll set the Cycler up straight away. We should be able to start the second stage of drilling as soon as that's done. Meanwhile, the rest of the men will begin the clearing up operation."

As the two suited guildsmen began to put together the great cutting hoop of the Cycler, two more stepped out, trailing flaccid lengths of hose behind them. Getting into position in the center of the platform, one of them turned and gave a hand signal. Almost at once the hoses swelled and a jet of water gushed from each, arching up into the ceiling of the great sphere. As the two men adjusted the nozzles of their hoses, the fountain of water was transformed into a fine mist that briefly seemed to fill the node.

It lasted only a minute or two, but when the water supply was cut, the node was clear of dust, though a dark paste now covered every surface.

Aitrus smiled. "If you ever wondered what we surveyors do most of the time, it's this. Cleaning up!"

There was laughter.

"You talk as if you dislike the job, Aitrus," Kedri said with a smile.

"Not at all. It gives me time to think."

Kedri stared at him a moment, a thoughtful expression in

his eyes, then he turned back, leaving Aitrus to wonder just what was going on inside the Legislator's head.

The four Observers stepped out from the excavator, their movements slightly awkward in the unfamiliar protective suits Master Telanis had insisted they wear. Kedri, as ever, led the way, Aitrus at his side as they stepped over to the tunnel's mouth.

The Cycler had done its job several times already and the cadets had already chipped out a section twenty spans in length and sprayed it with a coating of D'ni stone. Further down the tunnel, they could see the dark O of the central borehole running straight into the rock and, surrounding it like some strange, skeletal insect, the Cycler, encased in its translucent sheath.

Two brightly glowing fire-marbles the size of clenched fists were suspended from the ceiling. In their blazing blue-white light a number of cadets loaded rock onto a mobile trailer.

"This is more like it," Kedri said, with an air of satisfaction. "This is just how I imagined it."

They walked slowly toward the lamps. Surrounding them, the finished section of the tunnel had the look of permanence. Moving past the young guildsmen, they approached the rock face, stopping beneath the anchored feet of the Cycler.

They looked up, past the sleek engine of the Cycler to where its great revolving hoop was at rest against the face. The transparent sheath surrounding the Cycler was there to catch the excavated rock and channel it down into a chute that fed straight into the central borehole. From there the cadets would collect it up, using great suction hoses, and feed it into the pulverizer.

Kedri looked to Aitrus. "You remember your promise, Aitrus?"

"I have not forgotten."

"Then what are we waiting for?"

Aitrus turned and signaled to his friend, Efanis, who was working nearby. At once, Efanis came across and, positioning himself at the controls of the Cycler, gave two long blasts on the machine's siren.

Kedri made a face. "Yours must be the noisiest of guilds, young Aitrus. It seems you do nothing without a great blast of air beforehand!"

Aitrus smiled. It was true. If anyone was up there, they would surely hear them long before they broke through to the surface.

"If you would make sure your masks are kept down, Masters," he said, looking from one to another. "It should be perfectly safe, but if the sheath was to be punctured your head-gear should protect you."

"Cautious," Kedri muttered. "Ever cautious!"

Slowly the great cutting-hoop of the Cycler began to spin, slowly at first, then faster, at first only skimming the surface of the rock, whistling all the while. Then, abruptly, the whole top of the Cycler seemed to lean into the rock face, a great grinding buzz going up as if a thousand swarms of bees had all been released at once.

Chips of rock flew like hailstones against the clear, thick surface of the sheath. Slowly the arm of the Cycler raised on its hydraulics, moving toward the horizontal as the spinning cutting hoop bit deeper and deeper into the rock, carving its great O, like the outer rim of an archery target.

In less than three minutes it was done. Slowly the machine eased back, the hoop slipping from the rock, its surface steaming hot. As the Observers turned, four of the young Surveyors wheeled the great metal hoop of the brace down the tunnel toward them. They had seen already how it was mounted on the cutting hoop, then pushed into place.

So easy it seemed, yet every stage was fraught with dangers and difficulties.

As the guildsmen took over, removing the covering sheath and fitting the brace, Kedri and his fellows stood back out of their way. Only when they were finished and the brace was in place did Aitrus take them through, past the base of the Cycler and into the central borehole. It was darker here, but the piles of rock stood out against the light from outside.

Aitrus pointed to two machines that stood to one side. The first was recognizably the machine they used to gather up all the fragments of rock, a great suction hose coiling out from the squat, metallic sphere at its center. The second was small and squat, with what looked like a deep, wedge-shaped metal tray on top.

Ignoring the rock-gatherer, Aitrus stooped and, picking up one of the larger chunks of rock, handed it to Kedri. "Well, Guild Master? Do you want to feed the compounder?"

Kedri grinned and, taking the rock over to the machine, dropped it into the tray.

"What now?" he asked, looking to Aitrus.

In answer, Aitrus stepped up and pressed a button on the face of the fusion-compounder. At once a metal lid slid across over the tray. There was a low, grinding sound, and then the lid slid back. The tray was now empty.

"And the nara?"

Aitrus crouched and indicated a bulky red cylinder that rested in a mesh cage on the underside of the machine.

"The nara is kept in there," Aitrus said, "in its basic, highly compacted form, until we need to use it."

"But surely it would just . . . *solidify!*"

Aitrus nodded. "It does. The cylinder is just temporary; a kind of jacket used to mold the nara into a storable form. When we have enough of the nara, we load up another machine with the cylinders. In effect, that machine is little more than a large pressure-oven, operating at immensely high pressures, within which the cylinders are burned away and the nara brought back to a more volatile, and thus usable, state."

"The sprayer, you mean?" Kedri said, staring at Aitrus in open astonishment.

Aitrus nodded.

Kedri crouched, staring at the bright red cylinder in awe, conscious of the immense power of these simple-seeming machines, then, like a schoolboy who has been briefly let off the leash, he straightened up and, looking about him, began to gather up rocks to feed into the machine.

That night Master Telanis took Aitrus aside once more.

"I hear our friends enjoyed themselves today. That was a good idea of yours to let them operate a few of the less dangerous machines. They're bookish types, and such types are impressed by gadgetry. And who knows, even something this small may serve to sway them for the good."

"Then you think it *is* good?"

"Making contact with the surface-dwellers?" Telanis smiled. "Yes. Just so long as it is done discreetly."

Aitrus frowned. "How do you mean?"

"I mean, I do not think we should mix our race with theirs. Nor should we think of any extended relationship with them. They are likely, after all, to be a primitive race, and primitive races—as we have learned to our cost—tend to be warlike in nature. It would not do to have them pouring down our tunnels into D'ni."

"But what kind of relationship does that leave us?"

Telanis shrugged, then. "We could go among them as Observers. That is, providing we are not too dissimilar from them as a species."

"But why? What would we learn from doing that?"

"They might have certain cultural traits—artifacts and the like—that we might use. Or they might even have developed certain instruments or machines, though, personally, I find that most unlikely."

"It seems, then, that Master Kedri is right after all, and that ours is something of a fool's errand."

Master Telanis sat forward, suddenly alert. "Are those his words?"

"Something like. It was something he was saying to one

of the other Observers—Ja'ir, I think—as they were coming away from the rock face. Ja'ir was wondering aloud whether there was anyone up there on the surface anyway."

"And?"

Aitrus paused, trying to recall the conversation. "Master Kedri was of the opinion that there would be. His view was that the climatic conditions are ideal for the development of an indigenous species."

"And on what did he base this claim?"

"It seems that all four of them have seen copies of the Book."

"The Book of Earth," Telanis said, nodding thoughtfully. "It was written by Grand Master Ri'Neref himself, Aitrus, perhaps the greatest of the ancient Writers. Yet it is said that it was one he wrote as an apprentice."

"So Master Kedri also claimed. Yet most troubling, perhaps, was what Master Ja'ir said next."

Telanis's eyes seemed to pierce Aitrus. "Go on."

"Ja'ir said that whether there was a humanoid race up there on the surface or not, he nevertheless wondered whether so much time and effort ought to have been spent on such a speculative venture."

"Speculative . . . he said *speculative*, did he?"

Aitrus nodded.

Master Telanis sat back and stared thoughtfully. For a while he did not speak, then, looking at Aitrus, he asked, "And what do *you* think, Aitrus? *Is* it worth it?"

"Yes, Guild Master. To know for certain that we are sharing a world with another intelligent species—that surely is worth twice the time and effort that we have given it!"

While the excavation was in process, the young guildsmen had been permitted to return to their quarters on the ships, while the Observers had been moved into the Guild Master's cabin in the second excavator.

Aitrus returned to his bunk. Briefly he smiled, thinking of Kedri's comment, but the smile quickly faded. The endless secondary process of clearing up normally gave him time to think of his experiments, something he had little time to do these past few days. Indeed, it made him wonder how others could stand to live as Kedri so clearly lived, constantly in someone else's pocket.

Personally, he needed space, and quiet. *Yes, and an adequate supply of chemicals and notebooks!* he thought, recollecting how his mother used to tease him about his obsession with rocks and geological processes.

Unnatural, she had said, but the old cook, Master Jerahl, was right, there was nothing *more* natural for a D'ni. Stone was their element.

As he sat on the edge of his bunk, he could hear the whine of drills and the sudden crunch as rock fell to the floor. Let others think birdsong and the sound of a river flowing were natural; for him, this was the most natural of sounds.

"Young worm," his father had called him as a child, as if anticipating his future calling, and so he had become. A burrower. A seeker of passages. An explorer of the dark.

Aitrus stood, meaning to undress for sleep, when there came the sound of a commotion outside. He hurried along the corridor and poked his head out, looking about him. It was coming from inside the tunnel. The sound of a human in pain.

He heard a scuffling behind him. A moment later, Master Telanis joined him in the doorway.

"What is it, Aitrus?"

"Someone's hurt."

The two men ran across. At the tunnel's mouth, one of the young engineers met them, his face distraught.

"Who is it, Ta'nerin?" Telanis asked, holding his arms.

"It's Efanis. The cutting tip shattered. He's badly hurt. We've tried to staunch the blood but we can't stop it!"

"Fetch Master Avonis at once. I'll see what I can do!"

Letting Ta'nerin go, Master Telanis ran, Aitrus close behind. The tunnel was almost finished now. Only the last 5 spans remained uncut. There, at the far end, beneath the burning arc lamps, they could see a small group of cadets gathered—some kneeling, some standing—around one of their colleagues.

The moaning grew—an awful, piteous sound.

As the two men came up, they saw just how badly Efanis was injured. The wound was awful. The shattered tip must have flown back and hit Efanis full in the chest and upper arm. He had not stood a chance. Even as they stood there he gave a great groan. Blood was on his lips.

Pushing between the guildsmen, Master Telanis tore off his shirt and poked it into the wound. Then, looking about him, he spoke urgently, trying to rouse them from their shock. "Help me, then, lads! Quick now!" And, reaching down, he gently cradled Efanis's head even as the others crowded around, putting their hands under Efanis's shoulders and back and thighs.

"That's good," Telanis said softly, encouraging them as they gently lifted the groaning Efanis. "Now let's get him back to the excavator. The sooner Master Avonis gets to look at him, the better."

There had been accidents before, but never anything more severe than broken bones, or bruising, or rock splinters. Master Telanis prided himself on his safety record. Efanis's accident had thus come as a great shock.

When Aitrus reported to Kedri the next morning, it was to find the Legislator crouched over a desk in the chart room, writing. He looked up as Aitrus entered and put down his pen.

"I'm sorry, Aitrus. I understand that Efanis was your friend. A bad business, eh?"

Aitrus nodded, but he felt unable to speak. Efanis was not yet out of trouble.

"I'll not be needing you today, Aitrus, so take the day off. Do your experiments, if you wish. We'll carry on tomorrow."

"Yes, Master."

Leaving Kedri to his work, Aitrus went straight to Master Telanis. He found him in the tunnel, crouching beside the temporarily abandoned excavation, staring at a dark patch in the rock. At the center of that small, irregular ovoid was a tiny, slightly flattened circle of what looked like glass.

It had the look of a bruised eye staring from the rock.

"What is that?" Aitrus asked.

Telanis looked up at him. "It appears to be a pyroclastic deposit—a 'volcanic bomb' deposited in this strata hundreds of millions of years ago." The Guild Master pointed to the outer, darker area. "The outside of it is simple obsidian—a glassy basalt—but this pellucid nugget here was already embedded within it when the volcano spat it out. It looks and feels like diamond."

Aitrus nodded.

"My guess," Telanis continued, "is that the cutting tip slipped on the glassy surface, then snagged on this much harder patch here and shattered."

He sighed heavily. "I should have taken core samples, Aitrus. I was in too much of a hurry to impress our guests. And now *this* has come of it."

"You cannot blame yourself, Guild Master," Aitrus said. "The bit must have been flawed, anyway. One cannot foresee everything."

"*No?*" Telanis stood. He looked about him at the abandoned tools, his eyes, for the first time that Aitrus could recall, troubled by what he saw. "If not me, then who, Aitrus? It is *my* job to ensure the safety of my crews, *my* responsibility, no one else's. That Efanis is hurt is my fault. If I had done my job properly . . ."

Aitrus put out his hand to touch his Master's arm, then withdrew it. In a sense Telanis was right. All of their patient checks and procedures were designed to avoid an event like this.

He cleared his throat. "Master Kedri says he does not need me today, Guild Master. I came to be reassigned."

Telanis glanced at him, then made a vague gesture with his hand. "Not now, Aitrus. We'll do no work today."

"But, Master . . ."

"Not now."

Aitrus packed a knapsack for the journey and set off, walking back down the nodes to where—almost two months before—they had drilled through a small cave system.

Though they had labored long and hard in the rock, it took but an hour or so to reach his destination. For the first part the way was fairly straightforward, zigzagging back and forth in the normal D'ni way, but then it branched to the left, where they had been forced to detour around an area of folds and faults.

His way was dimly lit. Chemicals in the green-black coating of D'ni rock gave off a faint luminescence bright enough to see in. But Aitrus had packed two lamps and a small canister of luminescent algae for when he left the D'ni path.

Coming to his destination, he rested briefly, seated on the rock ledge outside the circular door that led through into the cave system, and ate a brief meal.

The sphere of this node had been peppered with openings—some tiny apertures barely large enough to poke one's hand into, others big enough to walk inside. One—the one he now sat outside—had been large enough to drive the excavator inside. Indeed, with Master Telanis's permission, they had shored up the entrance and bored almost fifty spans into the rock, widening the passageway to give access to a large cavern that lay just beyond. But time had been pressing and they had not had more than a day or two to explore the system before they had had to press on with their excavations. They had sealed the tunnel with a small gate—similar to those that linked the nodes to the lengths of D'ni tunnel—leaving the caverns for future investigation, then they had sprayed the rest of the node with a smooth coating of nara.

Aitrus had made extensive notes of the cave system at the time. Now he had the chance to go back and resume his explorations. The thought of it cheered him as, finishing his meal, he stood and, taking the protective helmet from his pack, he strapped it on and, slipping the sack onto his shoulder, walked over to the lock.

It was a simple pressure lock. Turning the wheel, he could hear the air hiss out from the vent overhead. A moment later a crack appeared down the very center of the door and the two halves of it slid back into the surrounding collar.

Inside was darkness.

In a small cloth bag he carried in his pocket he had a collection of fire-marbles. Taking one from the bag, he opened the back of the lamp mounted on his helmet and popped it into the tiny space. Clicking it shut, he waited for a moment until the fire-marble began to glow. After less than a minute a clear, strong white radiance shone out from the lamp into the darkness, revealing the smooth, uncoated walls of rock within.

Aitrus smiled, then stepped inside.

Aitrus paused to spray a tiny arrow on the rock wall, pointing back the way he had come, then slipped the canister away and walked slowly on, counting each step, all the time turning his head from side to side, scanning the walls and floor ahead of him.

After a moment he stopped again and took his notebook from his pocket, quickly marking down how many paces he had come before checking his compass again to see if the tunnel had diverged from its slow descent.

It was a narrow passageway, one they had not explored the first time he had been here. Overhead it tapered to a crack that seemed to go some way into the rock, but it was barely wide enough to walk down, and it was slowly narrowing. Up ahead, however, it seemed to emerge into a larger space—a small cavern, perhaps—and so he persevered, hoping he might squeeze through and investigate.

The rock was silent. There were no waterflows here, no steady drip from unseen heights, only the absence of sound. He was the intruder here, the noise of his own breathing loud in his ears. It was warm in the rock and he felt no fear. Since he'd been a child and his father had first taken him deep inside the rock, he had felt no fear. What he felt, if anything, was a tiny thrill of anticipation.

There was hidden beauty in the rock. Locked deep within the earth were caverns of such delicate, shimmering beauty that, to step out into them, was a joy beyond all measuring.

Taking his sack from his shoulders, he dropped it softly onto the floor of the passage, then turned and began to squeeze into the narrow space. Breathing in, he found he could just slip through.

He turned, then grabbed hold of the rock beside him. Just below him the rock fell away into a narrow chasm. To his left it climbed to meet a solid wall of rock. But to his right . . .

Aitrus grinned. To his right, just beyond the gap, the cavern opened out. Points of shimmering crystal seemed to wink back at him as he turned his head. The roof of the cavern was low, but the cave itself went back some way, a huge, pillarlike outcrop of rock concealing what lay at the far end.

Aitrus turned and, squeezing back through, retrieved his sack. By the timer on his wrist he had been gone from the base-node almost three hours, but there was still plenty of time. Securing the strap of the sack about his wrist, he edged through the gap again, standing on the lip of the entrance hole.

The gap seemed deep, but he could jump it at a stride. The trouble would be getting back, as the floor of the cave was much lower than where he stood. It would not be so easy leaping up onto this ledge.

Taking a length of rope from his sack, Aitrus hammered a metal pin into the rock beside him and tied one end of the rope fast about it. He uncoiled the rope, letting two or three spans of it hang down, then jumped down.

For a moment he looked about him, his eyes searching for a chunk of loose stone to lay upon the end of the rope to keep it in place, but there was nothing. The rock was strangely fused here and glassy. Aitrus coiled the end of the rope and rested it on the rock, trusting that it would not slip into the gap. Then, straightening up, he turned to face the cavern.

For a moment Aitrus held himself perfectly still, the beam of light from his lamp focused on the pillar at the far end of the cavern, then he crouched and, again taking his notebook from his pocket, rested it on his knee, and began to sketch what he saw.

Finished, he began to walk across. The floor was strangely smooth and for a moment Aitrus wondered if he were in a volcanic chamber of some kind. Then, with a laugh, he stopped and crouched.

"Agates!" he said softly, his voice a whisper in that silent space. "Agates in the rock!"

Taking a hammer and chisel from his tool belt, Aitrus chipped at the smooth surface of the rock just to his left, then, slipping the tools back into their leather holsters, he reached down and gently plucked his find from the rock.

The agate was a tiny piece of chalcedony no bigger than a pigeon's egg. He held it up and studied it, then, reaching behind him, popped it into the sack on his back. There were others here, and he quickly chipped them from the rock. Some were turquoise, others a deep summer blue. One, however, was almost purple in color and he guessed that it was possibly an amethyst.

Aitrus smiled broadly, then stood once more. Such agates were hypabyssal—small intrusive bodies from deep in the earth's crust that had been thrust up with the lava flow to cool at these shallow depths. In a sense they were no more than bubbles in the lava flow; bubbles that had been filled with heated groundwater. Long eons had passed and this was the form they had taken. Polished they would look magnificent.

Aitrus began to walk toward the distant pillar of rock, but he had taken no more than two paces when the floor beneath him began to tremble. At first he thought they had perhaps begun drilling again, for the source of the vibrations seemed quite distant, but then he recalled what Master Telanis had said.

We'll do no work today . . .

As if to emphasize the point, the ground shuddered. There was a deep rumbling in the rock. He could hear rock falling in the passage behind him.

Aitrus walked across. If the passage collapsed, he would be trapped here, and it might be days before anyone knew where he was. He had told no one that he was off exploring.

The rope, at least, was still where he had left it. He swung across and pulled himself up onto the ledge.

There was the faintest trembling in the rock. A trickle of dust fell from a crack above him. He looked up. If there was to be a proper quake, that rock would come down.

Calming himself, Aitrus squeezed through the gap and began to walk back along the narrow rock passage. He was halfway along when the rock shook violently. There was a crashing up ahead of him, dust was in his mouth suddenly, but the passage remained unblocked.

He kept walking, picking up his pace.

The luminous arrows he had left to mark his way shone out, showing him the direction back to the node. Coming to one of the smaller caverns near the node, he found his way blocked for the first time. A fall of rock filled the end of the cavern, but he remembered that there was another way around, through a narrow borehole. Aitrus went back down the tunnel he'd been following until he found it, then crawled through on his hands and knees, his head down, the sack pushed before him. There was a slight drop on the other side. Aitrus wormed his way around and dangled his feet over the edge. He was about to drop, when he turned and looked. The slight drop had become a fall of three spans—almost forty feet. Hanging on tightly, he turned his head, trying to see if there was another way out. There wasn't. He would have to climb down the face, using metal pins for footholds.

It took him a long time, but eventually he was down. Now he only had to get back up again. He could see where the tunnel began again, but it was quite a climb, the last two spans of it vertical. There was nothing he could do; he would have to dig handholds in the rock face with a hammer.

The ascent was slow. Twice the ground shook and almost threw him down into the pit out of which he was climbing, but he clung on until things were quiet again. Eventually he clambered up into the tunnel.

If he was right, he was at most fifty spans from the gate.

Half running, he hurried down the tunnel. Here was the tiny cavern they had called The Pantry, here the one they'd called The Steps. With a feeling of great relief, he ducked under the great slab of stone that marked the beginning of the cave system and out into the D'ni borehole.

Glancing along the tunnel, Aitrus could see at once that it had been badly damaged. The sides had been smooth and perfectly symmetrical. Now there were dark cracks all along it, and huge chunks of rock had fallen from the ceiling and now rested on the tunnel's floor.

Ignoring the feeling in the pit of his stomach Aitrus walked slowly on. He could see that the gate was closed. It would have closed as soon as the first tremor registered in its sensors. All the gates along the line, in every node, would be closed. If he could not open it he would be trapped, as helpless as if he'd stayed in the cavern where he'd found the agates.

There was a rarely used wheel in the center of the gate, an emergency pressure-release.

Bracing himself against the huge metal door, Aitrus heaved the wheel around, praying that another tremor wouldn't come.

At first nothing, then, the sound making him gasp with relief, there was a hiss of air and the door opened, its two halves sliding back into the collar of rock.

Aitrus jumped through, knowing that at any moment another quake might come and force the doors to slam shut again.

After the tunnel, the node was brightness itself. Aitrus blinked painfully, then turned to look back into the borehole. As he did, the whole of the ceiling at the end came crashing down. Dust billowed toward him. At the sudden noise, the sensors in the gate were activated and the doors slammed shut, blocking out both noise and dust.

Aitrus whistled to himself, then turned, looking about him. The walls of the great sphere in which he stood were untouched—it would take a major quake to affect the support walls—but both node-gates were shut.

He would have to wait until the tremors subsided.

Aitrus sat and took his notebook from his pocket, beginning to write down all that had happened.

It was important to make observations and write down everything, just in case there was something important among it all.

Small tremors were quite common; they happened every

month or so, but these were strong. Much stronger, in fact, than anything he had ever encountered.

He remembered the agates and got them out. For a while he studied them, lost in admiration. Then, with a cold and sudden clarity, he realized they were clues.

This whole region was volcanic. Its history was volcanic. These agates were evidence of countless millennia of volcanic activity. And it was still going on. They had been boring their tunnels directly through the heart of a great volcanic fault.

Stowing the agates back in the sack, Aitrus wrote his observations down, then closed the notebook and looked up.

It was at least an hour since the last tremor.

As if acknowledging the fact, the node-gates hissed and then slid open.

Aitrus stood, then picked up his sack and slung it over his shoulder. It was time to get back.

As Aitrus stepped out from beneath the node-gate, he frowned. The base camp was strangely silent.

The two excavators remained where he had last seen them, but there was no sign of the frenetic activity he had expected after the quakes. It was as if the site had been abandoned.

He walked across, a strange feeling in the pit of his stomach, then stopped, hearing noises from the tunnel; the faintest murmur of voices, like a ritual chant.

Coming to the tunnel's entrance, he saw them: the whole

company of both ships lined up in ranks, together with the four Observers, who stood off in a tiny group to one side. The assembly stood at the far end, where the accident had happened, their heads bowed.

At once Aitrus knew. This was a ceremony to mark Efanis's passage. He could hear the words drift back to him, in Master Telanis's clear and solemn tones.

"In rock he lived, in rock he rests."

And as the words faded, so Master Telanis lay the dead guildsman's hand upon the open linking book, moving back as the body shimmered in the air and vanished. It was now in the great burial Age of Te'Negamiris.

Aitrus bowed his head, standing where he was in the tunnel's mouth, mouthing the words of the response, along with the rest of the company.

"May Yavo, the Maker receive his soul."

Everyone was silent again, marking Efanis's passage with respect, then individual heads began to come up. Master Telanis looked across; seeing Aitrus, he came across and, placing a hand on Aitrus's arm, spoke to him softly.

"I'm sorry, Aitrus. It happened very quickly. An adverse reaction to the medication. He was very weak."

Aitrus nodded, but the fact had not really sunk in. For a time, in the tunnels, he had totally forgotten about his friend.

"Are you all right?"

"I'm fine," Aitrus answered. "I went back to the cave system. There's a lot of damage there. The quakes . . . "

Telanis nodded. "Master Geran seems to think it is only a settling of the surrounding rock, but we need to make more soundings before we proceed. There may be some delays."

"Guild Master Kedri will not be pleased."

"No, nor his fellows. But it cannot be helped. We must be certain it is nothing critical." Master Telanis paused, then. "It might mean that Master Kedri will require your services for slightly longer than anticipated, Aitrus. Would that worry you?"

Master Telanis had said nothing about Aitrus not letting anyone know where he had gone. That, Aitrus knew, was his way. But Aitrus felt guilty about the breach, and it was, perhaps, that guilt that made him bow his head and answer.

"No, Guild Master."

As Master Kedri climbed up into the Messenger, he turned, looked back at Aitrus, and smiled.

"Thank you, Aitrus. I shall not forget your kindness."

Aitrus returned the smile.

"And I shall not forget to deliver your letter," Kedri added, patting the pocket of his tunic, where the letter lay.

"Thank you, Guild Master."

Kedri ducked inside. A moment later the door hissed shut and the turbines of the craft came to life.

Aitrus stepped back, rejoining the others who had gathered to see off the Observers.

"You did well, Aitrus," Master Telanis said quietly, coming alongside as the Messenger turned and slowly edged into the tunnel, heading back to D'ni.

"Yet I fear it was not enough," Aitrus answered.

Telanis nodded, a small movement in his face indicating that he, too, expected little good to come of the Observers' report.

Unexpectedly, Master Kedri and his fellows had chosen not to wait for tunneling to recommence, deciding, instead, to return at once. All there read it as a clear sign that the four men had made up their minds about the expedition.

Efanis's death, the quakes—these factors had clearly influenced that choice— had, perhaps, pushed them to a decision.

Even so, the waiting would be hard.

"What shall we do, Guild Master?" Aitrus asked, seeing how despondent Telanis looked.

Telanis glanced at him, then shrugged. "I suppose we shall keep on burrowing through the rock, until they tell us otherwise."

Progress was slow. Master Geran took many soundings over the following five days, making a great chart of all the surrounding rock, then checking his findings by making test borings deep into the strata.

It was ten full days before Master Telanis gave the order to finish off the tunnel and excavate the new node. Knowing how close the Council's meeting now was, everyone in the expedition feared the worst.

Any day now they might be summoned home, the tunnels

filled, all their efforts brought to nothing, but still they worked on, a stubborn pride in what they did making them work harder and longer.

The advance team finished excavating and coating the sphere in a single day, while the second team laid the air brackets. That evening they dismantled the platforms and moved the base camp on.

Efanis's death had been a shock, but none there had known quite how it would affect them. Now they knew. As Aitrus's team sat there that evening in the refectory, there was a strange yet intimate silence. No one had to speak, yet all there knew what the others were feeling and thinking. Finally, the old cook, Jerahl, said it for them.

"It seems unfair that we should come to understand just how important this expedition is, only for it to be taken from us."

There was a strong murmur of agreement. Since Efanis's death, what had been for most an adventure had taken on the aspect of a crusade. They wanted now to finish this tunnel, to complete the task they had been given by the Council. Whether there was anyone up there on the surface or not did not matter now; it was the forging of the tunnel through the earth that was the important thing.

Aitrus, never normally one to speak in company, broke habit now and answered Jerahl.

"It would indeed seem ill if Efanis were to die for nothing."

Again, there was a murmur of assent from those seated about Aitrus. But that had hardly died when Master Telanis, who now stood in the doorway, spoke up.

"Then it is fortunate that the Council see fit to agree with you, Aitrus."

There was a moment's shocked silence, then a great cheer went up. Telanis grinned and nodded at Aitrus. In one hand he held a letter, the seal of which was broken.

"A special courier arrived a moment ago. It appears we have been given a year's extension!"

There was more cheering. Everyone was grinning broadly now.

"But of much greater significance," Telanis continued as the noise subsided, "is the fact that we have been given permission to build a great shaft."

"A shaft, Master?"

Telanis nodded, a look of immense satisfaction on his face. "It seems the Council are as impatient as we to see what is on the surface. There is to be no more burrowing sideways through the rock. We are to build a great shaft straight up to the surface. We are to begin the new soundings in the morning!"

The moon was a pale circle in the star-spattered darkness of the desert sky. Beneath it, in a hollow between two long ridges of rock, two travelers had stopped and camped for the night, their camels tethered close by.

It was cool after the day's excessive heat, and the two men sat side by side on a narrow ridge of rock, thick sheepskins draped over their shoulders; sheepskins that had been taken from the great leather saddles that rested on the ground just behind them.

They were traders, out of Tadjinar, heading south for the markets of Jemaranir.

It had been silent; such a perfect silence as only the desert knows. But now, into that silence, came the faintest sound, so faint at first that each of the travelers kept quiet, thinking they had imagined it. But then the sound increased, became a presence in the surrounding air.

The ground was gently vibrating.

The two men stood, looking about them in astonishment. The noise intensified, became a kind of hum. Suddenly there was a clear, pure note in the air, like the noise of a great trumpet sounding in the depths below.

Hurrying over to the edge of the rocky outcrop, they stared in wonder. Out there, not a hundred feet from where they stood, the sand was in movement, a great circle of it trembling violently as if it were being shaken in a giant sieve. Slowly a great hoop of sand and rock lifted, as if it were being drawn up into the sky. At the same time, the strange, unearthly note rose in intensity, filling the desert air, then ceased abruptly.

At once the sand dropped, forming a massive circle where it fell.

The two men stared a moment longer, then, as one, dropped onto their hands and knees, their heads touching the rock.

"Allah preserve us!" they wailed. "Allah keep us and comfort us!" From the camp behind them, the sound of the camels' fearful braying filled the desert night.

Master Geran sat back and smiled, his blind eyes laughing.

"Perfect," he said, looking to where Master Telanis stood. "I intensified the soundings. Gave the thing a real blast this time! And it worked! We have clear rock all the way to the surface!"

Telanis, who had been waiting tensely for Geran's analysis of the sounding, let out a great sigh of relief.

"Are you saying this is it, Master Geran?"

Geran nodded. "We shall need to cut test holes, naturally. But I would say that this was the *perfect* site for the shaft."

"Excellent!" Telanis grinned. For three months they had pressed on, burrowing patiently through the rock, looking for such a site. Now they had it.

"I should warn you," Geran said, his natural caution re-surfacing. "There is a large cave off to one side of the proposed excavation. But that should not affect us. It is some way off. Besides, we shall be making our shaft next to it, not under it."

"Good," Telanis said. "Then I shall inform the Council at once. We can get started, excavating the footings. That should take us a month, at least."

"Oh, at least!" Geran agreed, and the two old friends laughed.

"At last," Telanis said, placing a hand on Geran's shoulder and squeezing it gently. "I was beginning to think I would never see the day."

"Nor I," Geran agreed, his blind eyes staring up into Telanis's face. "Nor I."

The preparations were extensive. First they had to excavate a massive chamber beneath where the shaft was to be. It was a job the two excavators were not really suited to, and though they began the work by making two long curving tunnels on the perimeter, heavier cutting equipment was swiftly brought up from D'ni to carry out this task.

While this was being organized, Master Geran, working with a team of senior members of the Guild of Cartographers, designed the main shaft. This was not as simple a job as it might have appeared, for the great shaft was to be the hub of a network of much smaller tunnels that would branch out from it. Most of these were service tunnels, leading back to D'ni, but some extended the original excavation to the north.

As things developed, Master Telanis found himself no longer leading the expedition but only one of six Guild Masters working under Grand Master Iradun himself, head of the Guild of Surveyors. Other guilds, too, were now steadily more involved in the work.

Aitrus, looking on, found himself excited by all this frenetic activity. It seemed as though they were suddenly at the heart of everything, the very focus of D'ni's vast enterprise.

By the end of the third week the bulk of the great chamber had been part-cut, part-melted from the rock, a big stone burner—a machine of which all had heard but few had ever seen in action—making the rock drip from the walls like ice before a blowtorch.

The chamber needed supporting, of course. Twenty massive granite pillars supported the ceiling, but for the walls the usual method of spray-coating would not do. Huge slabs of nara, the hardest of D'ni stones—a metallic greenish-black stone thirty times the density of steel—were brought up the line. Huge machines lifted the precast sections into place while others hammered in the securing rivets.

A single one of those rivets was bigger than a man, and more than eight thousand were used in lining the mighty walls of the chamber, but eventually it was done.

That evening, walking between the pillars in that vast chamber, beneath the stark, temporary lighting, Aitrus felt once again an immense pride in his people.

Work was going on day and night now—though such terms, admittedly, had meaning only in terms of their waking or sleeping shifts—and a large number of guildsmen had been shipped in from D'ni for the task. The first of the support tunnels, allowing them to bring in extra supplies from D'ni, had been cut, and more were being excavated. The noise of excavation in the rock was constant.

To a young guildsman it was all quite fascinating. What had for so long been a simple exploratory excavation had now become a problem in logistics. A temporary camp had been set up at the western end of the chamber and it grew daily. There were not only guildsmen from the Guild of Surveyors here now but also from many other guilds—from the Guild of Miners, the Messengers, the Caterers, the Healers, the Mechanists, the Analysts, the Maintainers, and the Stone-Masons. There were even four members of the Guild of Artists, there to make preliminary sketches for a great painting of the works.

Food, of course, could have been a problem with so many suddenly congregated there in the chamber, but the Guild of Caterers brought up two of their Books, linked to the great granary worlds of Er'Duna and Er'Jerah, and the many were fed.

Not everything, however, was quite so simple. With the chamber cut and supported, they had begun to bring in the big cutting machines.

For five full days the tunnels were closed to any other traffic as these huge, ancient mechanisms were brought up one by one from D'ni. Dismantled in the lower caverns ready for the journey, they were transported on massive half-tracked wagons and reassembled in the base chamber, beneath the eyes of the astonished young guildsmen.

There were four of these machines in all, and with their arrival, there was a sense that history was being made. Only rarely was more than a single one of these monolithic cutters brought into use; to have all four at a single site was almost unprecedented. Not since the breakthrough to the lower caverns and the opening of the Tijali Mines, eighteen centuries before, had they been found together.

The machines themselves were, in three of the four cases, much older than that. Old Stone Teeth, as it was known, was close on four thousand years old, while Rock-Biter and The Burrower were contemporaries at three thousand years—both having been built for the broadening of the Rudenna Passage. The youngest, however, was also the biggest, and had been fashioned especially for the opening of the new mines. This was Grinder, and it was to Grinder that Aitrus and the rest of the young explorers were assigned.

Grinder arrived in stages. First to arrive was the Operations Cabin—the "brain" of the beast—itself four times the size of one of the excavators. Yet this, as it turned out, was the least impressive of its parts—at least, physically. In the days that followed, two giant, jointed legs arrived, and then, in a convoy that took several hours to enter the great chamber, the eighteen sections that made up its massive trunk.

Aitrus watched in amazement as trailer after trailer rolled in, filling the whole of the northern end of the chamber. Then, when he thought no more could possibly arrive, the cutting and grinding arms turned up—six massive half-tracks bearing the load.

The job of reassembly could now begin.

For much of the following weeks, the young guildsmen found themselves playing messenger for the thousands of other guildsmen who had suddenly appeared at the site—running about the great chamber, taking endless diagrams and maps and notes from guild to guild. The rest of the time they found themselves idle spectators as slowly the big machines took form.

It was a lengthy and painstaking process.

By the end of the third week, Grinder was complete. It crouched there, its matt black shape still and silent beneath the ceiling of the chamber, like some strange cross between a toad and a crab, its huge cutting arms lowered at its sides. Like all the great machines, it was constantly updated and modified, yet its outer form was ancient.

Standing before it, Aitrus felt, for the first time in his life, how small he was compared to the ambitions of his race.

Though the D'ni were long-lived, the rock in which they had their being was of an age that was difficult to comprehend; yet with the use of such machines they had challenged that ancient realm, wresting a living from its bare, inhospitable grip.

Grinder was not simply a machine, it was a statement—a great shout into the rock. *This* was D'ni! Small, temporary creatures they might be, yet their defiance was godlike.

Turning from it, Aitrus walked out across that vast, paved floor, stepping between the massive pillars that stretched up into the darkness, then stopped, looking about him.

Grinder lay behind him now. The Burrower and Rock-Biter lay to his left, like huge black scarabs. Ahead of him was the dull red shape of Old Stone Teeth, squatting like a mantis between the pillars and the ceiling. As a child he had had an illustrated book about Old Stone Teeth, and he could vividly recall the pictures of the great machine as it leaned into the rock, powdered rock spraying from the great vent underneath it into a succession of trailers.

And now, as an adult, he stood before it. Aitrus nodded to himself. It was only when you were up close to such machines that you could appreciate their true size and power. No illustration could possibly do justice to such machines. They were truly awesome.

That night Aitrus barely slept. Soon it would begin, and he would live to see it! This was a tale to tell one's children and one's children's children: how, in the days of old, his people had cut their way up from the depths and made a great shaft that had reached up from the darkness to the light.

The next morning Aitrus was up early, keen to start. But

his masters were, as ever, in no hurry. There were test bore-holes to be drilled, and rock analyses to be made. For the next few days the Guild of Analysts took over, their temporary laboratories filling the center of the chamber, their "samplers"— a dozen small, bullet-shaped, autonomous drilling machines — boring their way into the rock overhead.

For Aitrus the next few weeks were pure frustration. Much was done, yet there was still no word of when the main excavation would begin. Letters from home spoke of the excitement throughout D'ni, yet his own had waned. And he was not alone in feeling thus.

Returning to the excavator after a day of running messages, Aitrus was about to pass the Guild Master's cabin when he noted Telanis seated at his desk, his head slumped forward, covered by his hands. A single sheet of paper was on the desk before him.

"Master? Are you unwell?"

Telanis looked up. He seemed tired, his eyes glazed and dull.

"Come in and close the door, Aitrus."

Aitrus did as he was told.

"Now take a seat."

Aitrus sat, concern growing in him. Telanis was looking at him now.

"To answer your question, Aitrus, no, I am not unwell, at least, not physically. But to be true to the spirit of your question, yes. I feel an inner fatigue, a sense of . . . "

"Disappointment?"

Telanis's smile was weary. "I thought it would not concern me, Aitrus. I knew that at some stage the whole thing might be taken from my hands. After all, we are but servants of the Council. Yet I had not expected to feel so *useless*, so peripheral to events. Great things are happening, Aitrus. I had hoped . . . well, that perhaps it would be we few who would be the ones to make the breakthrough."

Aitrus stared at the Guild Master in astonishment. He had not even suspected that Telanis felt this way.

"It seems we were merely the pathfinders, Aitrus. Yet I, for one, had grander visions of myself. Yes, and of you crew-men, too. I saw us as explorers."

"And so we were, Master."

"Yes, and now we are redundant. Our part in things is done."

"So why do they not simply send us home to D'ni?"

In answer Telanis handed him the paper. Aitrus quickly read it then looked up, surprised. "Then it is over."

"Yes," Telanis said quietly, "but not until the day after the capping ceremony. They want us there for that. After all, it would hardly be right for us *not* to be there."

The slight edge of bitterness in Telanis's voice again surprised Aitrus. He had always viewed Guild Master Telanis as a man wholly without desire; a loyal servant, happy to do whatever was required of him. This tiny fit of pique—if pique it was—seemed uncharacteristic. Yet Telanis clearly felt hurt at being brushed aside.

"They will surely recognize your contribution, Guild Master."

"Maybe so," Telanis answered distractedly, "but it will not be you and I, Aitrus, who step out onto the surface. That honor will be given to others."

For a moment Telanis was silent, staring down at the letter on the desk between them. Then he looked back at Aitrus.

"Forgive me. I did not mean to unburden myself on you, Aitrus. Forget I ever said anything."

Aitrus bowed his head. "As you wish." Yet as he stood, he felt compelled to say something more. "It was not your fault, Guild Master. You led us well. None of us will ever forget it."

Telanis looked up, surprised, then looked back down again, a dark shadow appearing in his eyes. Clearly he was thinking of Efanis.

"The excavation begins tomorrow. The capping ceremony will take place a week from now. Use the time well, Aitrus. Observe what you may. It may be some time before you return here."

The next morning the major excavation work began. First into action was Old Stone Tooth, the picture-book illustrations coming to life for Aitrus as he watched the huge jaws of the machine lean into the ceiling, gnawing hungrily at the dark surface, a great fall of fine-ground rock cascading from three vents in its long, segmented underside into a massive open trailer that squatted beneath the ancient machine, the gray-black heap in its giant hopper neither growing nor diminishing as the minutes passed.

The noise was deafening.

For three long hours it labored, its long legs slowly stretching, its shoulders gradually disappearing into the great hole it was making in the roof of the chamber. Finally, with a deafening hiss, the great hydraulic legs began to fold back down. It was Grinder's turn.

As the grand old machine backed slowly into the shadows at the north end of the chamber, its massive chest stained black, its great cutting jaws still steaming, Grinder eased forward.

As the huge machine hissed violently and settled into place beneath the hole, its maintenance crew hurried across, Aitrus among them, small half-tracks bringing up the six massive stone brackets that would secure Grinder to the floor of the chamber.

In an hour it was ready. The crew moved back behind the barriers as the five-man special excavation team—their stature enlarged by the special black protective suits they wore—crossed the massive floor of the great chamber, then climbed the runged ladder that studded Grinder's huge curved back.

Another five minutes and Grinder's great engines roared into life. Grinder raised itself on its mighty hydraulic legs, like a toad about to leap, its four circular, slablike grinding limbs lifted like a dancer's arms. Then, without warning, it elbowed its way into the rock.

If Old Stone Tooth had been loud, the noise Grinder made was almost unbearable. Even through the thick protective helmet and ear-mufflers he was wearing, Aitrus found himself grimacing as the high-pitched whine seemed to reach right inside him.

Slowly the jointed arms extended as the rock was worn away, until they formed a giant cross that seemed to be holding up the roof of the chamber even as it ground away at its edges. Reaching a certain point it stopped and with a huge hiss of steam the arms retracted inward.

The relief from that constant deafening noise was sweet, but it was brief. In less than a minute it started up again, as Grinder lifted slightly, repositioning its limbs, then began to cut another "step" just above the one it had already made.

And so it went on, until the great hole Old Stone Tooth had made had been extended to form a massive vault. Not that it was finished even then: There was a great deal more rock to be cut from the walls before the shaft could be clad with nara and supported with cross-struts. Before Rock-Biter and The Burrower were brought in, they had first to build a platform two-thirds of the way up the partly completed shaft. Once that was in place, Old Stone Tooth and Grinder would be lifted up onto it by means of massive winches.

And then it would begin again, the two main excavating machines taking turns carving out the main channel, while below them the two slightly smaller machines finished the job they had begun, polishing the shaft walls and cutting the steps that would spiral up the walls of the giant well.

As guildsmen from the Guild of Engineers moved into place, ready to construct the platform, the young Surveyors began to drift away, their part in things finished for a time.

Aitrus was the last to go, looking back over his shoulder as he went. Their camp was a long way down the line, and walking back, through node after node crammed with guild tents and equipment, past endless troops of guildsmen coming up from D'ni, and units of the City Guard, whose job it was to keep the traffic flowing down the tunnels, Aitrus found himself sharing Master Telanis's feeling of disappointment that things had been taken from their hands. In the face of such awesome preparations, he saw now just how peripheral they really were to all of this.

Yes, and in six days they would be gone from here.

Aitrus sighed. His fellow Surveyors were now some way ahead of him; the murmur of their talk, their brief but cheerful laughter, drifted back to him down the tunnel. They, he knew, were keen to go home. Whether it was they or someone else who made the breakthrough to the surface did not trouble them; at least, not as it troubled Master Telanis and himself.

Yet Master Telanis was right. One *ought* to finish what one had begun. It seemed only fitting. And though their whole culture was one of finely drawn guild demarcations and task specialization, there had to be some areas in which pure, individual endeavor survived—and if not in the Guild of Surveyors, where else?

Stepping out under the node-gate and onto the platform where their camp was situated, Aitrus looked across at the excavators where they were parked against the north wall and smiled fondly. He was almost of a mind to ask to serve on an excavator crew again. That was, if there *were* to be any new explorations after this.

Seeing Aitrus, Master Telanis summoned him across, then quickly took him into his cabin. He seemed strangely excited.

"Aitrus," he said, even before Aitrus had had a chance to take his seat, "I have news that will cheer you greatly! The Council have reconsidered their decision. They have permitted a small contingent from the exploration team to accompany the Maintainers for the breakthrough!"

Aitrus grinned broadly. "Then we *shall* get to finish the job!"

Telanis nodded. "I have chosen six guildsmen to accompany me. You, of course, shall be among their number."

Aitrus bowed his head. "I do not know how to thank you, Guild Master."

"Oh, do not thank *me*, Aitrus. Thank your friend Veovis. It seems it was his intervention that swayed them to reconsider."

"Veovis?" Aitrus shook his head in amazement. He had written to Veovis weeks back, thanking him for the gifts, but there had been nothing in his letter about the Council's decision. "I do not understand."

Telanis sat, then took a letter from the side of his desk and handed it to Aitrus. "It appears that your friend and benefactor, Veovis, has been an active member of the Council these past two months, since his father's illness. It seems that he has the ear of several of the older members. His suggestion that a token body of men from the Guild of Surveyors should be included was apparently unopposed." Telanis smiled. "It seems we have much to thank him for."

"I shall write again and thank him, Master."

"There is no need for that," Telanis said, taking the letter back. "Veovis will be here in person, six days from now. Indeed, we are to be honored by the presence of the full Council for the capping ceremony. I am told that every last cook in D'ni has been engaged to prepare for the feast. It should be some occasion! And all from the seed of our little venture!"

The next few days passed swiftly, and on the evening of the sixth day, at the very hour that the Guild of Surveyors had estimated, the great shaft was completed, the last curved section of nara lining bolted into place, the eighty great ventilation fans, each blade of which was thrice the length of a man, switched on.

It was an awesome sight. Standing on the floor of the great chamber, Aitrus felt a tiny thrill ripple through him. The great floor stretched away on all sides, its granite base paved now in marble, a giant mosaic depicting the city of D'ni at its center, the whole surrounded by a mosaic hoop of bright blue rock that was meant to symbolize the outer world that surrounded their haven in the rock. Yet, marvelous as it was, the eyes did not dwell on that but were drawn upward by the great circle of the walls that climbed vertiginously on every side, the spiral of steps like a black thread winding its way toward the distant heights.

Aitrus turned full circle, his mouth fallen open. It was said that some twenty thousand fire-marbles had been set into the walls. Each had been placed within a delicately sprung lamp that was agitated by the movement of the fans. As the great blades turned, the fire-marbles glowed with a fierce, pure light that filled the great well.

He lowered his eyes and looked across. Already the Guild of Caterers was hard at work, whole troops of uniformed guildsmen carried into the chamber massive wooden tables that would seat twenty men to a side, while others tended the ovens that had been set up all along the southern wall, preparing for the great feast that would take place the next day.

Old Stone Tooth had been dismantled and shipped back down the line to D'ni two days back. Grinder had followed a day later. While the guildsmen set up the tables and began constructing the massive frames that would surround the central area where the feast was to be held, members of the Guild of Miners were busy dismantling Rock-Biter and Burrower on the far side of the great chamber. By tomorrow they, too, would be gone.

Aitrus, freed from all official duties, spent his time wandering on the periphery of all this activity, watching what was happening and noting his observations in his notebook. He was watching a half-track arrive, laden high with fine linen and chairs, when two strangers approached.

"Aitrus?"

He turned. A tall, cloaked man was smiling at him. Just behind was a second, smaller man, his body partly hunched, his features hidden within the hood of his cloak.

"Forgive me," said the taller of the two, "but you are Aitrus, no? I am Veovis. I am pleased to meet you again after all these years."

Veovis was a head taller than Aitrus remembered him and broad at the shoulder. His face was handsome but in a rather stark and monumental manner—in that he was very much his father's son. As Aitrus shook the young Lord's hand, he was surprised by the smile on Veovis's lips, the unguarded look in his eyes. This seemed a very different person from the one he'd known at school all those years ago.

"Lord Veovis," he said, stowing his notebook away.

"It seems I have much to thank you for."

"And D'ni has much to thank *you* for." Veovis smiled. "You and your fellow guildsmen, of course." He turned slightly, introducing his companion, who had now thrown back his hood. "This is my friend and chief adviser, Lianis. It was Lianis who first brought your papers on pyroclastic deposits to my attention."

Aitrus looked to Lianis and nodded, surprised to find so ancient a fellow as Veovis's assistant.

"Lianis was my father's adviser, and his father's before him. When my father fell ill, it was decided that I should keep him on as *my* adviser, so that I might benefit from his experience and wisdom." Veovis smiled. "And fortunately so, for he has kept me from many an error that my youth might otherwise have led me into."

Aitrus nodded, then looked to Lianis. "My paper was but one of many submitted from the expedition, Master Lianis, and hardly original in its ideas. I am surprised it attracted your attention."

Lianis, it seemed, had a face that did not ever smile. He stared back at Aitrus with a seriousness that seemed etched deep into the stone of his features. "Good work shines forth like a beacon, Guildsman. It is not necessarily the originality of a young man's work but the clarity of mind it reveals that is important. I merely marked a seriousness of intent in your writings and commented upon it to the young Lord's father. That is my task. I claim no credit for it."

Aitrus smiled. "Even so, I thank you, Master Lianis, and you Lord Veovis. I have found good use of the equipment you were so kind in giving me."

"And I am glad it has found good use . . . though I never doubted that for an instant."

The two men met each other's eyes and smiled.

"And now I am afraid I must go. My father's guildsmen await me. But I am glad I had a chance to speak with you, Aitrus. I fear there will be little time tomorrow. However, when you are back in D'ni you must come and visit me."

Aitrus bowed his head. "My Lord."

Veovis gave the faintest nod, then, with a glance at Lianis, the two walked on, their cloaked figures diminishing as they crossed the great floor.

Aitrus stared a moment, then, with a strange sense of something having begun, took his notebook from his pocket and, turning to that day's entries, wrote simply:

Met Veovis again. He has changed. The man is not the child he was. He asked me to visit him in D'ni. He paused, then added. *We shall see.*

Closing the book, he slipped it back into his pocket, then, turning on his heel, hurried across, heading for the bright circle of the exit tunnel.

The great feast to celebrate the cutting of the great shaft was almost over. Young guildsmen from the Guild of Artists looked on from the edge of events, hurriedly sketching the scene as the great men said their farewells to each other.

It had been an extraordinary occasion, with speeches and poems in honor of this latest venture of the D'ni people. A year from now a whole series of new canvases and tapestries would hang in the corridors of the Guild House back in D'ni, capturing the occasion for posterity, but just now the Grand Masters talked of more mundane affairs. Matters of State stopped for no man and no occasion—even one so great as this—and there was ever much to be discussed.

It was not often that one saw all eighteen major Guilds represented in a single place, and the colorful sight of their distinctive ceremonial cloaks—each Guild's color different, each cloak decorated with the symbols that specified the rank and status of the guildsman who wore it—gave Aitrus an almost childish delight. Such things he had only glimpsed in books before now.

Aitrus's own cloak, like those of all young guildsmen without rank, had eight such symbols, four to each side, beneath the lapels, whereas those of the great Lords had but a single one.

Looking on from where he sat on the far side of the feasting circle, Aitrus saw Veovis rise from his seat to greet one of the Great Lords, his friendly deference making the old man smile. Four of the Five were here today, the fifth—Veovis's father—being too ill to come. All eighteen of the Grand Masters were also here, to represent their guilds, along with several hundred of their most senior Masters, every one of them resplendent in their full Guild colors.

To a young guildsman, they seemed an impressive host. Lord Tulla, it was said, was 287 years old, and his three companions—the Lords R'hira, Nehir, and Eneah—were all well into their third century. Veovis, by comparison, was a babe—a glint of sunlight against dark shadow. Lord Tulla, in particular, looked like something carved, as if, in the extremity of age, he had become the rock in which he had lived all his life.

One day, perhaps, Aitrus too might become a Grand Master, or perhaps even one of the Five, yet the road that led to such heights was long and hard, and some days he wondered if he had the temperament.

If this expedition had proved one single thing to him it was that he was of essence a loner. He had thought, perhaps, that such close proximity to his fellows, day in, day out, might have brought him out of his shell—rounding off the hard edges of his nature—but it had not proved so. It was not that he did not get on with his fellow cadets—he liked them well enough and they seemed to like him—it was simply that he did not share their pursuits, their constant need for small distractions.

You were born old, Aitrus, his mother had so often said. *Too old and too serious.* And it had worried him. But now he knew he could not change what he was. And others, Master Telanis among them, seemed to value that seriousness. They saw it not as a weakness but a strength.

Even so, he wondered how well he would settle back into the life of the Guild House. It was not the work—the studying and practicals—that concerned him but the personal element. Watching the great men at the feast had reminded him of that, of the small, personal sacrifices one made to be a senior Guildsman.

Given the choice, Aitrus would have spent his whole life exploring; drilling through the rock and surveying. But that, he understood, was a young man's job, and he would not be a young man all his life. In time he would be asked to take charge; of small projects at first, but then steadily larger and larger tasks, and in so doing he would have to deal not with the dynamics of rock—the certainties of weight and form and pressure—but with the vagaries and inconsistencies of personality.

He looked across, catching Telanis's eye. The Guild Master smiled and raised the silver goblet he was holding in a toast. Aitrus raised his own uncertainly but did not sip. Many of his companions were drunk, but he had not touched even a drain of the strong wine he had been served.

Indeed, if the choice had been given him, he would have left an hour back, after the last speech, but it was not deemed polite for any of them to leave before their Masters. And so they sat, amid the ruins of the feast, looking on as the old men went from table to table.

"Look!" someone whispered to Aitrus's right. "The young Lord is coming over here!"

Aitrus looked up to see Veovis making his way across. Seeing Aitrus, Veovis smiled, then turned to address Telanis. "Master Telanis, might I have a word in private with Guildsman Aitrus?"

"Of course," Telanis answered, giving the slightest bow of respect.

Aitrus, embarrassed by the sudden attention, rose and made his way around the table to where Veovis stood.

"Forgive me, Aitrus," Veovis began, keeping his voice low. "Once more I must rush off. But Lord Tulla has given me permission to stay on an extra day. I thought we might talk. Tomorrow, after the breaching."

The "breaching" was a small ceremony to mark the commencement of the breakthrough tunnel.

Aitrus nodded. "I'd welcome that."

"Good." Briefly Veovis held his arm, then, as if he understood Aitrus's embarrassment, let his hand fall away. "Tomorrow, then."

That evening they winched the excavator up onto the platform at the very top of the great shaft. Aitrus, standing beside Master Telanis, watched as it was lowered onto the metal grid, feeling an immense pride at the sight of the craft. Its usefulness as a cutter was marginal now—other machines, much larger and more efficient were already in place, ready to cut the final tunnel from the rock—yet it would serve as their quarters in this final leg of their journey.

Earlier, Master Telanis had given a moving speech as he said farewell to those cadets who would be returning to D'ni in the morning. Only Master Geran, Aitrus, and five others remained; their sole task now to represent their Guild when finally they broke through to the surface.

"How long will it take?" he asked, looking to Telanis.

The Guild Master's attention was on the excavator, as strange hands removed the winch chains and began to lift the craft so they could extricate the great cradle from beneath it. His eyes never leaving that delicate task, Telanis answered Aitrus quietly.

"A week. Maybe less. Why? Are you impatient, Aitrus?"

"No, Master."

"Good. Because I would hate you to be disappointed."

"I do not understand, Master."

Telanis glanced at him. "The tunnel will be cut. But whether we shall ever step out onto the surface is another matter. There will be one final meeting of the Council to decide that."

Aitrus felt a strange disturbance—a feeling almost of giddiness—at the thought of coming so close and never actually stepping out onto the surface of the world.

"I thought it had been decided."

Telanis nodded vaguely. "So did I. Yet it is an important matter—perhaps the most important they have had to debate for many centuries. If they are wrong, then D'ni itself might suffer. And so the Council deliberate until the last. Why, even today, at the feast, they were still discussing it even as they congratulated one another!"

"And if they decide not to?"

Telanis turned and met his eyes. "Then we go home, Aitrus."

"And the tunnel?"

"Will be sealed. At least, this top part of it. It is unlikely that the surface-dwellers have the technology to drill down into the shaft, even if they were to locate it."

"I see."

"No, Aitrus. Neither you nor I see, not as the Great Lords see. Yet when their final word comes, whatever it may be, we shall do as they instruct."

"And what do *you* think, Master? Do you think they will let us contact the surface-dwellers?"

Telanis laughed quietly. "If I knew that, Aitrus, I would be a Great Lord myself."

That night Aitrus woke to find the platform trembling, as if a giant gong had been struck in the depths. All about him people slept on drunkenly, unaware of the faint tremor. After a while it subsided and the platform was still again. For a moment Aitrus wondered if he had imagined it, but then it came again, stronger this time, almost audible.

Aitrus shrugged off his blanket and stood, then walked across until he stood close to the edge of the great drop. The whole shaft was vibrating, and now there was the faintest hum—a deep bass note—underlying everything.

For close on three months, the earth had been silent. Now, even as they prepared to leave it, it had awoken once again.

Aitrus turned, looking back to where the guildsmen were encamped beside the excavator, but they slept on, in a dead sleep after the feast. He alone was awake.

Hurrying across, he bent down beside Master Geran and gently shook him. At first the old man did not wake, but then his blind eyes flicked open.

"Aitrus?"

Aitrus did not know how the old man did it, but his senses were infallible.

"There's movement," he said quietly. "The shaft was vibrating like a great hollow pipe."

Master Geran sat up, then turned to face the center of the tunnel. For a moment he was perfectly still, then he looked up at Aitrus again. "Help me up, boy."

Aitrus leaned down, helping him up.

"How many times?" Geran asked as he shuffled over to the edge of the shaft.

"Three so far. That is, if the one that woke me was the first."

Geran nodded, then dropped into a crouch, the fingertips of his right hand brushing gently against the surface of the platform.

For two, maybe three minutes they waited, Aitrus standing there at his side, and then it came again, stronger—much stronger—this time and more prolonged. When it had subsided, Geran stood and shook his head.

"It's hard to tell the direction of it. The shaft channels its energy. But it was powerful, Aitrus. I wonder why I was not woken by it."

Aitrus looked down, a faint smile on his lips, but said nothing. He had seen how much of the strong D'ni wine Master Geran had drunk. The only real surprise was that he had woken when Aitrus had shaken him.

"Should we wake the others, Master?" he asked. But Geran shook his head.

"No. We shall leave it for now. The final survey will show whether there is any risk. Personally I doubt it. We have come far to the north of the isopaches we identified earlier. If there is any volcanic activity, it is far from here. What we are hearing are merely echoes in the rock, Aitrus. Impressive, yes, but not harmful."

Geran smiled, then patted his arm. "So get some sleep, eh, lad? Tomorrow will be a long day."

Reassured by Master Geran, Aitrus settled back beneath his blanket and was soon asleep once more. If the ground shook, he did not notice it. Indeed, he was the last to wake, Master Telanis's hand on his shoulder, shaking him, returning him from the dark stupor into which he seemed to have descended.

"Come, Aitrus. Wash now and get dressed. The ceremony is in half an hour!"

They lined up before the cutter, alongside men from the Guild of Maintainers, whose task it would be to oversee this final stage of the journey to the surface.

The Maintainers were one of the oldest guilds, and certainly one of the most important, their Grand Masters—alongside those of the Guild of Writers, the Miners, the Guild of Books and the Ink-Makers—becoming in time the Lords of D'ni, members of the Five. Yet this was a strange and perhaps unique task for them, for normally their job was to ensure that the D'ni Books were kept in order, the Ages correctly run, and that the long-established laws, laid down countless generations before, were carried out to the letter. They had little to do with excavations and the cutting of tunnels. Indeed, guildsmen from some of the more physical guilds—those who dealt constantly with earth and rock and stone—would, in the privacy of their own Guild Halls, speak quietly of them, in a derogatory fashion, as "clean-handed fellows." Yet these guildsmen had been specially trained for this purpose and had among their number guildsmen drafted in from the Guild of Miners, and from the Surveyors.

They now would carry out the final excavation, and if any surface dwellers *were* found, it would be the Maintainers who would first establish contact, for this was a most delicate matter and it was held that only the Maintainers could be vouchsafed to undertake *that* task properly.

Few of the Guild Masters who had been at the feast the day before had remained for this final little ceremony; yet in the small group who now stepped forward were no less than two of the Great Lords, Lord Tulla and Lord Eneah. Standing just behind them, among a group of five Grand Masters, was Veovis.

Lord Tulla said a few words, then stepped forward, pulling down the lever that would set the great cutter in motion. As he did, Veovis looked across at Aitrus and gave the tiniest nod.

Were these, Aitrus wondered, the faction in the Council who were in favor of making contact with the surface-dwellers? Or was that a misreading of things? Had the rest, perhaps, simply been too busy to attend?

As Lord Tulla stepped back, the engines of the cutter thundered into life and the circular blade began to spin, slowly at first, then, as it nudged the rock, with increasing speed.

The simple ceremony was concluded. The great men turned away, ready to depart. At a signal from Master Telanis, the Surveyors fell out.

Aitrus could see that Veovis was busy, talking to the Grand Master of the Guild of Messengers. Content to wait, he watched the machine, remembering the noises in the night.

Master Geran had been up early, he had been told, making a new survey of the rock through which this final tunnel was to be dug. His soundings had shown nothing unusual, and the vibrations in the earth had ceased. Both Geran and Telanis were of the opinion that the quakes had not been serious, but were only the settlement of old faults. Aitrus himself had not been quite so sure, but had bowed to their experience.

"Aitrus?"

He turned, facing Veovis.

The young Lord smiled apologetically. "You must forgive me, Aitrus. Once again I must be elsewhere. But I shall return, this evening, after I have seen Lord Tulla off. I did not think he would stay for the ceremony, but he wished to be here."

"I understand."

"Good." And without further word, Veovis turned and hurried across to where Lord Tulla was waiting.

Aitrus watched the party step into the special carriage that had been set up on a temporary track down the wall of the shaft, then stepped up to the edge, following its progress down that great well until it was lost to sight.

It was strange. The more Veovis delayed their talk, the more uncomfortable Aitrus found himself at the thought of it. Veovis wanted to be his friend, it seemed. But why? It made little sense to him. Surely Veovis had friends enough of his own? And even if that were not so, why him? Why not someone more suited to his social role?

Perhaps it would all come clear. Yet he doubted it. The rock was predictable. It had its moods, yet it could be read, its actions foreseen. But who could say as much of a man?

Aitrus turned, looking back across the platform. Already the cutter was deep in the rock, like a weevil burrowing its way into a log. Crouching, he got out his notebook and, opening it, laid it on his knee, looking about him, his eyes taking in every detail of the scene.

This evening, he thought. Then, dismissing it from his mind, he began to sketch.

Aitrus was reaching up, his hands blindly feeling for the scales, when the shock wave struck. He was thrown forward, his forehead smacking against the bulkhead as the whole craft seemed to be picked up and rolled over onto its side.

For five long seconds the excavator shook, a great sound of rending and tearing filling the air.

And then silence.

Struggling up, Aitrus put a hand to his brow and felt blood. Outside, on the platform, a siren was sounding. For a moment the lights in the craft flickered dimly, then the override switched in and the emergency lighting came on. In its sudden light, he could see that the excavator had been completely overturned. It lay now on its back.

Pulling himself hand by hand along the tilted corridor, he climbed out onto the side of the craft and looked about him.

Guildsmen were running about, shouting urgently to one another. On the far side of the platform a huge section of the metal grid had buckled and slipped from its supports and now hung dangerously over the shaft. Behind it a dark line snaked up the wall of the shaft.

Aitrus's mouth fell open in surprise. *The shaft was breached! The nara stone torn sheet from sheet!*

The quake must have been directly beneath them.

Looking across, he saw that the mouth of the new tunnel was cracked. A large chunk of rock had fallen from the arch and now partly blocked the tunnel. The cutter, deep inside the tunnel, was trapped.

As he stood there, Master Telanis came over to him and, grasping his arm, turned Aitrus to face him.

"Aitrus! Get on protective gear at once, then report back to me. We must secure this area as soon as possible. If there's another quake, the platform could collapse."

Too shocked to speak, Aitrus nodded, then ducked back inside, making his way to the equipment room. In a minute he was back, two spare canisters of air and a breathing helmet lugged behind him. If the air supply to the shaft had been breached, breathing might soon become a problem, particularly if any of the great ventilation fans had been damaged.

Seeing him emerge, Telanis beckoned him across. Several of the guildsmen were already gathered about him, but of Master Geran there was no sign.

Calmly, the simple sound of his voice enough to steady the frayed nerves of the young men, Master Telanis organized them: sending some to bring powerdrills, others to sort out protective clothing. Finally, he turned, looking to Aitrus.

"Master Geran has gone, Aitrus," he said quietly. "He was standing near the edge when it hit. I saw him go over."

The news came like a physical blow. Aitrus gave a tiny cry of pain.

"I know," Telanis said, laying a comforting hand on his

shoulder. "But we must look after the living now. We do not know the fate of the cutter's crew yet. And there were Maintainers with them. If the tunnel came down on them we may have to try to dig them out."

Aitrus nodded, but he was feeling numb now. Geran gone. It did not seem possible.

"What should I do?" he said, trying to keep himself from switching off.

"I have a special task for you, Aitrus. One that will require an immense amount of courage. I want you to go down and make contact with whoever is in the lower chamber. I want you to let them know how things are up here: that the shaft wall is cracked, the cutting team trapped. And if they *can* send help, then I want it sent as soon as possible. You have that, Aitrus?"

"Master."

But for a moment he simply stood there, frozen to the spot.

"Well, Aitrus?" Telanis coaxed gently.

The words released him. Strapping one of the cylinders to his back, he pulled on the helmet, then hurried across to the head of the steps.

They were blocked. A great sheet of nara had fallen across the entrance. He would have to find another way down.

He went back to where the temporary track began. With the steps blocked, there was only one way down, and that was to climb down the track, hand over hand, until he reached the bottom.

For a moment he hesitated, then, swinging out over the gap, he grabbed hold of the metal maintenance ladder that ran between the broad rails of the track. Briefly his eye went to the metal clip at the neck of his uniform. If another big quake struck, he would have to clip himself to the ladder and pray it did not come away from the shaft wall.

And if it did?

Aitrus pushed the thought away and, concentrating on the task at hand, began the descent.

Aitrus was almost halfway down when the second quake struck.

Clipping himself to the metal strut, he locked both arms about the ladder, then dug his toes into the gap between the rung and the wall.

This time it went on and on, the whole shaft shaking like a giant organ pipe, things falling from the platform overhead.

The metal track beside him groaned and for a while he thought it was going to prize itself from the wall as the metal studs strained to come away from the rock—if he wasn't shaken from the ladder first!

How long it was he could not tell, but it seemed a small eternity before, with an echoing fall, the shaking stopped.

The sudden silence was eerie. And then something clattered onto the marble far below.

Aitrus opened his eyes. Across from him the shaft wall gaped. Cracks were everywhere now. The great molded sections were untouched, yet there were huge gaps between them now, as if the tunnel wall behind them had slipped backward. The outer wall of the spiral steps had fallen away in many places, and several of the huge securing rivets had jiggled their way out of the rock.

The sight made his stomach fall away. It had all seemed so sound, so *permanent,* yet one more quake and the whole shaft could easily collapse in upon itself.

Unclipping himself, Aitrus resumed his descent, ignoring the aches in his calves and shoulders, pushing himself now, knowing that time was against him. But he had not gone far when he stopped dead.

There had been a shout, just below him.

He leaned out, trying to see where it had come from, and at once caught sight of the carriage.

Some forty, maybe fifty spans below him, the track bulged away from the shaft wall, pulled outward by the weight of the carriage.

As Aitrus stared, the shout came again. A cry for help.

"Hold on!" he shouted back. "Hold on, I'm coming!"

The floor of the shaft was still a good five hundred spans below, and looking at the way the track was pulled away from the wall, he knew he would have to climb along the track and over the top of the carriage if he was to help.

A length of rope would have come in handy, but he had none. All he had was a canister of air.

Making sure his grip on the ladder was good, Aitrus reached across and grabbed hold of the rail.

Just below where he had hold of it, the bolts that had pinned the track to the shaft wall had been pulled out. The question was: Would his extra weight bring a further length of track away from the wall and send the carriage tumbling down to the foot of the great shaft?

He would have to take a chance.

The outer edge of the track was grooved to match the teeth in the track that ran up one side of the carriage. The great guide wire that ran through the carriage had snapped, so that tooth-and-groove connection was all that prevented the carriage from falling. If *that* went . . .

There was the faintest rumble, deep in the earth. Things fell with a distant clatter onto the marbled floor below. The metal of the carriage groaned.

Now, he told himself. *Now, before there's another quake.*

Counting to five, he swung over onto the track, his fingers wrapped about the toothlike indentations in the rail, then he began to edge backward and down, his feet dangling over the abyss.

The track creaked and groaned but did not give. He moved his hands, sliding them slowly along the rail, left hand then right, his eyes all the while staring at the wall just above him, praying the bolts would hold. And then his toes brushed against the roof of the carriage.

He swallowed deeply, then found his voice again. "Are you all right?"

There was a moment's silence, then, in what was almost a whisper. "I'm badly hurt. I've stopped the bleeding, but . . ."

Aitrus blinked. That voice.

"Veovis?"

There was a groan.

It *was* Veovis. He was certain of it.

"Hold on," Aitrus said. "It won't be long now."

There was a hatch underneath the carriage. If he could climb beneath it and get into it that way, there was much less chance of him pulling the carriage off its guide track.

Yes, but how would he reach the hatch? And what if he could not free the lock?

No. This once he had to be direct. He would have to climb over the top of the carriage and lower himself in, praying that the track would bear the extra weight.

Slowly Aitrus lowered himself onto the roof, prepared at any moment for the whole thing to give.

He was breathing quickly now, the blood pounding in his ears. The straps from the cylinder were beginning to cut into his shoulders and for a moment he wondered if he should slip it off, together with the helmet, and let it fall, but it seemed too much effort. If he was going to die, the cylinder would make no difference. Besides, he was almost there now. He had only to slip his legs down over the edge of the roof and lower himself inside.

It was easier said than done. With his legs dangling out over the roof, he realized that he was just as likely to fall out into the shaft as he was to slip inside, into the relative safety of the carriage. Yet even as he thought it, he lost his grip and slipped. With a cry, he reached out and caught hold of the metal bar above the carriage door. His whole body was twisted violently about and then slammed against the side of the carriage.

The pain took his breath for a moment. For a full second his feet kicked out over the gap as he struggled to hold on. Then, with a grunt of effort, he swung himself inside.

The carriage creaked and groaned as it swung with him. There was the sound of bolts tearing from the wall. One by one they gave with a sharp pinging sound. With a sudden jolt the carriage dropped, throwing Aitrus from his feet, then, with another jolt, it held.

Aitrus lay on his back, the cylinder wedged under him. He felt bruised all over, but he was alive. Turning his head, he looked across the narrow floor of the carriage.

Veovis lay there, not an arm's length from him, his eyes closed, his breathing shallow. His flesh, which had seemed pale before, was now ash white, as if there were no life in him.

Moving slowly, carefully, Aitrus got himself up into a sitting position, then edged across to where Veovis lay.

Veovis looked badly hurt. There was a large bruise at his temple, and blood had seeped through the makeshift bandage he had wrapped about his upper arm, but that would have to wait. His breathing had become erratic. Even as Aitrus leaned over him to listen to his chest, Veovis's breath caught and stopped.

For a moment Aitrus wasn't sure. Then, knowing that every second counted, he reached behind him and pulled the cylinder up over his head, laying it down at Veovis's side before removing his helmet.

Precious seconds were wasted making sure the airflow was working properly; then, satisfied, he lifted Veovis's head and slipped the helmet on, before rolling him over onto his back.

The carriage swayed then settled.

Nothing was happening . . .

Aitrus blinked, then felt down at the wrist for a pulse. Veovis's heart had stopped.

Leaning over him, Aitrus pressed into his chest, leaned back, then pressed again. Veovis groaned, then sucked in air.

Aitrus sat back, knowing that he had done as much as he

could. Veovis was in no condition to help himself, and on his own, Aitrus knew that he would not be able to lift the dead-weight of Veovis out of the carriage and back down to the floor of the shaft.

There was a faint rumble. Again the carriage shook.

Slowly the rumbling grew, stronger and stronger until Aitrus was sure that the carriage would shake itself free from the restraining track. Slowly the light faded, as if a great shadow had formed about them. Then, with a sound of rending metal, the carriage was torn from the track.

It tilted sharply forward. Aitrus caught his breath, waiting for the fall, but the carriage had stopped in midair. Slowly, the walls on either side of him began to buckle inward.

"Noooo-oh!"

The buckling stopped. With a hiss of hydraulics the carriage jerked forward, then began slowly to descend with a strange jogging motion.

Aitrus began to laugh. Relief flooded him.

It was a cutter. A cutter had climbed the shaft walls and plucked them from the track. Now, holding them between its cutting arms, it was slowly carrying them down.

Aitrus leaned across, checking that Veovis was breathing steadily, then sat back, closing his eyes, his head resting against the buckled wall.

Safe.

The Council ordered the shaft repaired, the top tunnel completed, and then they sealed it. There was to be no breakthrough, no meeting with the surface-dwellers. That was decided within the first ten minutes of the meeting. Whether the quakes had happened or not, they would have decided thus. But there was the matter of D'ni pride, D'ni expertise to be addressed, hence the repairs, the drive toward completion.

It would not be said that they had failed. No. The D'ni did not fail. Once they had decided upon a course of action, they would carry it through. That was the D'ni way, and had been for a thousand generations.

In the future, perhaps, when circumstances differed, or the mood of the Council had changed, the tunnel might be unsealed, a form of contact established, but for now that was not to be.

And so the adventure ended. Yet life went on.

It was two weeks after the Council's decision, and Aitrus was sitting in the garden on K'veer, the island mansion owned by Lord Rakeri situated to the south of the great cavern of D'ni.

Rakeri's son, the young Lord Veovis, was lounging on a chair nearby, recuperating, his shoulder heavily bandaged, the bruising to his head still evident. The two young men had been talking, but were quiet now, thoughtful. Eventually, Aitrus looked up and shook his head.

"Your father's offer is kind, Veovis, and well meant, yet I cannot accept it. He says he feels a debt of gratitude to me for saving your life, yet I did only what any other man would have done. Besides, I wish to make my own way in the world. To win honor by my own endeavors."

Veovis smiled. "I understand that fully, Aitrus, and it does you credit. And if it helps make things easier, I, too, would have turned down my father's offer, though be sure you never tell him that."

Aitrus made to speak, but Veovis raised a hand.

"However," he went on, "*I* owe you a debt, whatever you may say about this mythical 'anyman' who might or might not have helped me. Whether that is so or not, you *did* help me. And for that I shall remain eternally grateful. Oh, I shall not embarrass you with gifts or offers of patronage, dear friend, but let me make it clear, if there is ever anything you want—*anything*—that is in my power to grant you, then come to me and I shall grant it. There, that is my last word on it! Now we are even. Now we can both relax and feel less awkward with each other, eh?"

Aitrus smiled. "You felt it, too?"

"Yes. Though I don't know which is harder, owing a life or being owed one."

"Then let us do as you say. Let us be friends without obligations."

"Yes," Veovis said, rising awkwardly from his chair to grasp both of Aitrus's hands in his own in the D'ni fashion. "Friends, eh?"

"Friends," Aitrus agreed, smiling back at the young Lord, "until the last stone is dust."

PART TWO: OF STONE AND
DUST AND ASHES

ANNA STOOD AT THE CENTER OF THE STRANGE CIRCLE of rock and dust and looked about her, her eyes half-lidded.

She was a tall, rather slender girl of eighteen years, and she wore her long auburn hair, which had been bleached almost blond by the sun, tied back in a plait at her neck. Like her father, she was dressed in a long black desert cloak, hemmed in red with a broad leather tool belt at the waist. On her back was a leather knapsack, on her feet stout leather boots.

Her father was to the left of her, slowly walking the circle's edge, the wide-brimmed hat he wore to keep off the sun was pulled back, a look of puzzlement on his face.

They had discovered the circle the previous day, on the way back from a survey of a sector of the desert southwest of the dormant volcano.

"Well?" she asked, turning to him. "What is it?"

"I don't know," he answered, his voice husky. "Either someone spent an age *constructing* this, sorting and grading the stones by size then laying them out in perfect circles, or . . ."

"Or what?"

He shook his head. "Or someone shook the earth, like a giant sieve." He laughed. "From *below*, I mean."

"So what *did* cause it?"

"I don't know," he said again. "I really don't. I've never

107

seen anything like it in over fifty years of surveying, and I've seen a lot of strange things."

She walked over to him, counting each step, then made a quick calculation in her head.

"It's eighty paces in diameter, so that's close on eight hundred square feet," she said. "I'd say that's much too big to have been made."

"Unless you had a whole tribe working at it."

"Yes, but it looks natural. It looks . . . well, I imagine that from above it would look like a giant drop of water had fallen from the sky."

"Or that sieve of mine." He narrowed his eyes and crouched a moment, studying the pattern of stones by his feet, then shook his head again. "Vibrations," he said quietly. "Vibrations deep in the earth."

"Volcanic?"

"No." He looked up at his daughter. "No, this was no quake. Quakes crack stone, or shatter it, or deposit it. They don't grade it and sort it."

"You're looking tired," she said after a moment. "Do you want to rest a while?"

She did not usually comment on how he looked, yet there was an edge of concern in her voice. Of late he had tired easily. He seemed to have lost much of the vigor he had had of old.

He did not answer her. Not that she expected him to. He was never one for small talk.

Anna looked about her once more. "How long do you think it's been here?"

"It's sheltered here," he said after a moment, his eyes taking in every detail of his surroundings. "There's not much sand drift. But judging by what there is, I'd say it's been here quite a while. Fifty years, perhaps?"

Anna nodded. Normally she would have taken samples, yet it was not the rocks themselves but the way they were laid out that was different here.

She went over to her father. "I think we should go back. We could come here tomorrow, early."

He nodded. "Okay. Let's do that. I could do with a long, cool soak."

"And strawberries and cream, too, no doubt?"

"Yes, and a large glass of brandy to finish with!"

They both laughed.

"I'll see what I can rustle up."

The Lodge had been named by her father in a moment of good humor, not after the hunting lodge in which he had spent his own childhood, back in Europe, but because it was lodged into a shelf between the rock wall and the shelf below. A narrow stone bridge—hand-cut by her father some fifteen years ago, when Anna was barely three—linked it to the rest of the rocky outcrop, traversing a broad chasm that in places was close to sixty feet deep.

The outer walls of the Lodge were also of hand-cut stone, their polished surfaces laid flush. A small, beautifully carved wooden door, set deep within the white stone at the end of the narrow bridge, opened onto a long, low-ceilinged room that had been hewn from the rock.

Four additional rooms led off from that long room: three to the right, which they used as living quarters, and another, their laboratory and workshop, to the left.

Following him inside, she helped him down onto the great sofa at the end of the room, then ducked under the narrow stone lintel into the galley-kitchen at the front.

A moment later she returned, a stone tumbler of cold water held out to him.

"No, Anna. That's too extravagant!"

"Drink it," she said insistently. "I'll make a special journey to the pool tonight."

He hesitated, then, with a frown of self-disapproval, slowly gulped it down.

Anna, watching him, saw suddenly how pained he was, how close to exhaustion, and wondered how long he had struggled on like this without saying anything to her.

"You'll rest tomorrow," she said, her voice brooking no argument. "I can continue with the survey on my own."

She could see he didn't like the idea; nonetheless, he nodded.

"And the report?"

"If the report's late, it's late," she said tetchily.

He turned his head, looking at her. "I gave my word."

"You're ill. He'll understand. People are ill."

"Yes, and people starve. It's a hard world, Anna."

"Maybe so. But we'll survive. And you *are* ill. Look at you. You need rest."

He sighed. "Okay. But a day. That's all."

"Good. Now let's get you to your bed. I'll wake you later for supper."

It was dark when she heard him wake. She had been sitting there, watching the slow, inexorable movement of the stars through the tiny square of window.

Turning, she looked through to where he lay, a shadow among the shadows of the inner room.

"How are you feeling now?"

"A little better. Not so tired anyway."

Anna stood, walked over to where the pitcher rested in its carved niche, beside the marble slab on which she prepared all their meals, and poured him a second tumbler of cold water. She had climbed down to the pool at the bottom of the chasm earlier, while he slept, and brought two pitchers back, strapped to her back, their tops stoppered to prevent them from leaking as she climbed the tricky rock face. It would last them several days if they were careful.

He sipped eagerly as she held the tumbler to his lips, then sank back onto his pallet bed.

"I was dreaming," he said.

"Were you?"

"Of mother. I was thinking how much you've come to look like her."

She did not answer him. Six years had passed, but still the subject was too raw in her memory to speak of.

"I was thinking I might stay here tomorrow," she said, after a moment. "Finish those experiments you began last week."

"Uhuh?"

"I thought . . . well, I thought I could be on hand then, if you needed me."

"I'll be okay. It's only tiredness."

"I know, but . . . "

"If you want to stay, stay."

"And the experiments?"

"You know what you're doing, Anna. You know almost as much as I do now."

"Never," she said, smiling across at him.

The silence stretched on. After a while she could hear his soft snoring fill the darkened room.

She moved back, into the kitchen. The moon had risen. She could see it low in the sky through the window.

Setting the tumbler down, Anna sat on the stone ledge of the window and looked out across the desert. What if it wasn't simple tiredness? What if he was ill?

It was more than a hundred miles to Tadjinar. If her father *was* ill, there was no way they would make it there across the desert, even if she laid him on the cart. Not in the summer's heat.

She would have to tend him here, using what they had.

Her head had fallen at the thought. She lifted it now. It was no good moping.

Flowers. She would paint him some flowers and place the canvas in the doorway so he would see them when he woke in the morning.

The idea of it galvanized her. She got up and went through to the workroom, lighting the oil lamp with her father's tinderbox and setting it down on the stone tabletop on the far side of the room.

Then, humming softly to herself, she took her mother's paintbox down from the shelf and, clearing a space for herself, began.

Anna?

"Yes, father?"

What do you see?

"I see . . . " Anna paused, the familiar litany broken momentarily as, shielding her eyes, she looked out over the dusty plain from the granite outcrop she stood upon. She had been up since before dawn, mapping the area, extending her father's survey of this dry and forlorn land, but it was late morning now and the heat had become oppressive. She could feel it burning through the hood she wore.

She looked down, murmuring her answer. "I see stone and dust and ashes."

It was how he had taught her. Question and answer, all day and every day; forcing her to look, to *focus* on what was in front of her. Yes, and to make those fine distinctions between things that were the basis of all knowledge. But today she found herself stretched thin. She did not *want* to focus.

Closing the notebook, she slipped the pencil back into its slot, then crouched, stowing the notebook and her father's compass into her knapsack.

A whole week had passed, and still he had not risen from his bed. For several nights he had been delirious, and she had knelt beside him in the wavering lamplight, a bowl of precious water at her side as she bathed his brow.

The fever had eventually broken, but it had left them both exhausted. For a whole day she had slept and had woken full of hope, but her father seemed little better. The fever had come and gone, but it had left him hollowed, his face gaunt, his breathing ragged.

She had tried to feed him and look after him, but in truth there seemed little she could do but wait. And when waiting became too much for her, she had come out here, to try to do something useful. But her heart was not in it.

The Lodge was not far away, less than a mile, in fact, which was why she had chosen that location, but the walk back was tiring under the blazing desert sun. As she climbed up onto the ridge overlooking the Lodge, she found herself suddenly fearful. She had not meant to be gone so long. What if he had needed her? What if he had called out to her and she had not been there?

She hurried down the slope, that unreasonable fear growing in her, becoming almost a certainty as she ran across the narrow bridge and ducked inside into the cool darkness.

"Father?"

The pallet bed was empty. She stood in the low doorway, breathing heavily, sweat beading her brow and neck and trickling down her back. She turned, looking out through the window at the desert.

What if he'd gone out looking for her?

She hurried through, anxious now, then stopped, hearing a noise, off to her right.

"Father?"

As she entered the workroom, he looked around and smiled at her. He was sitting at the long workbench that ran the full length of the room, one of his big, leather-bound note-books open in front of him.

"This is good, Anna," he said without preamble. "Amanjira will be pleased. The yields are high."

She did not answer. Her relief at seeing him up and well robbed her of words. For a moment she had thought the very worst.

He had the faintest smile on his lips now, as if he knew exactly what she was thinking. Anna wanted to go across to him and hug him, but she knew that was not his way. His love for her was distant, stern, like an eagle's love for its chicks. It was the only way they had survived out here without her mother.

"Anna?"

"Yes?"

"Thank you for the painting. How did you know?"

"Know what?"

"That those flowers were my favorites."

She smiled, but found she could not say the words aloud. *Because my mother told me.*

He continued to improve the next few days, doing a little more each day, until, a week after he'd got up from his bed, he came out from the workroom and handed Anna the finished report.

"There," he said. "Take that to Amanjira. It's not precisely what he asked for, but he'll welcome it all the same."

She stared at the document, then back at her father. "I can't."

"Why not?"

"You're not strong enough yet. The journey would exhaust you."

"Which is why I'm not going. You know the way. You can manage the cart on your own, can't you?"

Anna shook her head. She could, of course, but that wasn't what she meant. "I can't leave you. Not yet."

He smiled. "Of course you can. I can cook. And I don't need much water. Two pitchers should see me through until you return."

"But . . ."

"No buts, Anna. If Amanjira doesn't get that report, we don't get paid. And who'll pay the traders then? Besides, there are things we need in Tadjinar. I've made a list."

Anna stared at him a moment, seeing how determined he was in this. "When do you want me to go?"

"This evening, immediately after sundown. You should reach the old volcano before dawn. You could take shelter in the cleft there. Sleep until the evening."

It was what they always did, yet in reiterating it like this it almost seemed as if he were coming with her.

"Aren't you worried?"

"Of course I am," he answered. "But you're a tough one, Anna. I always said you were. Just don't let those merchants in Jaarnindu Market cheat you."

She smiled at that. They were always trying to cheat them. "I'll fill the pitchers, then."

He nodded, and without another word returned inside.

"To Tadjinar, then," she said quietly, looking down at the report in her hands. "Let's hope Lord Amanjira is as welcoming as my father thinks he'll be."

Amanjira was in good humor. He beamed a great smile at Anna, gestured toward the low chair that rested against the wall on one side of the great room, then he returned to his desk and sat, opening her father's report.

As Amanjira leaned forward, his dark eyes poring over the various maps and diagrams, Anna took the chance to look about her. This was the first time she had been inside the great man's house. Usually her father came here while she stayed at the lodging house in the old town.

The room was luxuriously decorated in white, cream, reds, and pinks. Bright sunlight filled the room, flooding in through a big, glass-paneled door that opened out onto a balcony. There was a thick rug on the floor and silk tapestries on the wall. And on the wall behind Amanjira was a portrait of the Emperor, given to him by the Emperor himself.

Everything there spoke of immense wealth.

Anna looked back at the man himself. Like herself, Amanjira was a stranger in this land, a trader from the east who had settled many years ago. Now he was one of the most important men in the empire.

Amanjira's skin was as dark as night, so black it was almost blue, yet his features had a strangely Western cast; a well-fleshed softness that was very different from the hawkish look of these desert people.

As if a dove had flown into a nest of falcons.

But looks deceived sometimes. This dove had claws. Yes,

and a wingspan that stretched from coast to coast of this dry and sandy land.

Amanjira made a tiny noise—a grunt of satisfaction—then looked across at her, nodding to himself.

"This is excellent. Your father has excelled himself, Anna."

She waited, wondering what he would say next; what he would give her for this information.

"I shall instruct the steward to pay you in full, Anna. And tell your father that, if his findings prove correct, I shall reward him with a bonus."

She lowered her head, surprised. So far as she knew, Amanjira had never offered them a bonus before.

"You are too kind, Lord Amanjira."

Anna heard him rise and come across to her. "If you wish," he said softly, "you might stay here tonight, Anna. Share a meal, perhaps, before you return home."

She forced herself to look up. His dark eyes were looking at her with a surprising gentleness.

"Forgive me," she said, "but I must get back. My father is not well."

It was not entirely the truth. She wanted to stay this once and explore the alleys of the old town, but duty had to come first.

"I understand," he said, moving back a little, as if sensitive to the sudden defensiveness in her attitude. "Is there anything I can do for him? Potions, perhaps? Or special foods? Sheep's brain is supposed to be especially nutritious."

Anna laughed at the thought of her father eating sheep's brain, then grew serious again, not wanting to hurt Amanjira's feelings. "I thank you for your concern, Lord Amanjira, and for your kind offer of help, but we have all we need."

Amanjira smiled, then gave a little bow. "So be it. But if you change your mind, do not hesitate to come to me, Anna. Lord Amanjira does not forget who his friends are."

Again the warmth of his sentiments surprised her. She smiled. "I shall tell him what the Lord Amanjira said."

"Good. Now hurry along, Anna. I am sure I have kept you far too long."

The journey home was uneventful. Making good time, Anna arrived at the Lodge just after dawn. She had been away, in all, seven days.

Leaving the cart in the deep shadow by the ridge, she climbed up onto the bridge and tiptoed across, meaning to surprise her father, but the Lodge was empty.

Anna returned to the doorway and stood there, looking out over the silent desert.

Where would he be? Where?

She knew at once. He would be at the circle.

Leaving the cart where it was, she headed east across the narrow valley, climbing the bare rock until she came out into the early sunlight. It made sense that he would go there at this hour, before the heat grew unbearable. If she knew him, he would be out there now, digging about, turning over rocks.

Her father's illness had driven the circle from her mind for a time, but coming back from Tadjinar, she had found herself intrigued by the problem.

It seemed almost supernatural. But neither she nor her father believed in things that could not be explained. *Everything* had a rational reason for its existence.

Coming up onto the ridge, Anna saw her father at once, in the sunlight on the far side of the circle, crouched down, examining something. The simple physical presence of him there reassured her. Until then she had not been sure, not *absolutely* sure, that he was all right.

For a time she stood there, watching him, noting how careful, how methodical he was, enjoying the sight of it enormously, as if it were a gift. Then, conscious of the sun slowly climbing the sky, she went down and joined him.

"Have you found anything?" she asked, standing beside him, careful not to cast her shadow over the place where he was looking.

He glanced up, the faintest smile on his lips. "Maybe. But not an answer."

It was so typical of him that she laughed.

"So how was Amanjira?" he said, straightening up and turning to face her. "Did he pay us?"

She nodded, then took the heavy leather pouch from inside her cloak and handed it to him. "He was pleased. He said there might be a bonus."

His smile was knowing. "I'm not surprised. I found silver for him."

"*Silver!*" He hadn't told her. And she, expecting nothing more than the usual detailed survey, had not even glanced at

the report she had handed over to Amanjira. "Why didn't you say?"

"It isn't our business. Our business is to survey the rocks, not exploit them."

She nodded at the pouch. "We make our living from the rock."

"An honest day's pay for an honest day's work," he answered, and she knew he meant it. Her father did not believe in taking any more than he needed. "Enough to live" was what he always said, begrudging no one the benefit from what he did.

"So how are you?" she asked, noting how the color had returned to his face.

"Well," he answered, his eyes never leaving hers. "I've come out here every morning since you left."

She nodded, saying nothing.

"Come," he said suddenly, as if he had just remembered. "I have something I want to show you."

They went through the gap between two of the converging ridges, then climbed up over a shoulder of rock onto a kind of plateau, a smooth gray slab that tilted downward into the sand, like a fallen wall that has been half buried in a sandstorm.

Across from them another, larger ridge rose up out of the sand, its eroded contours picked out clearly by the sun. The whiteness of the rock and the blackness of its shadowed irregularities gave it the look of carved ivory.

"There," he said, pointing to one of the larger patches of darkness near the foot of the ridge.

"A cave?" she asked, intrigued.

"A tunnel."

"Where does it lead?"

"Come and see."

They went down, crossing the hot sand, then ducked inside the shadowed entrance to the tunnel. They stopped a moment, letting their eyes grow accustomed to the darkness after the brilliant sunlight outside, then turned, facing the tunnel. Anna waited as her father lit the lamp, then held it up.

"Oh!"

The tunnel ran smoothly into the rock for fifteen, twenty paces, but that was it. Beyond that it was blocked by rock fall.

Undaunted, her father walked toward it, the lamplight wavering before him. She followed, examining the walls as she went.

"It looks lavatic," she said.

"It is," he answered, stopping before the great fall of rock. "And I'd say it runs on deep into the earth. Or would, if this rock wasn't in the way."

Anna crouched and examined a small chunk of the rock. One side of it was smooth and glassy—the same material as the walls. "How recent was this fall?" she asked.

"I can only guess."

She looked up at him. "I don't follow you."

"When I found no answers here, I began to look a bit wider afield. And guess what I found?"

She shrugged.

"Signs of a quake, or at least of massive earth settlement, just a few miles north of here. Recent, I'd say, from the way the rock was disturbed. And that got me thinking. There was a major quake in this region thirty years back. Even Tadjinar was affected, though mildly. It might explain our circle."

"You think so?"

"I'd say that the quake, the rockfall here, and the circle are all connected. How, exactly, I don't yet know. But as I've always said to you, we don't know everything. But we might extend our knowledge of the earth, *if* we can get to the bottom of this."

She smiled. "And the surveys?"

He waved that away. "We can do the surveys. They're no problem. But this . . . this is a once-in-a-lifetime opportunity, Anna! If we can find a reason for the phenomena, who knows what else will follow?"

"So what do you suggest?"

He gestured toward the fallen rock. "I suggest we find out what's on the other side of that."

After they had eaten, Anna unpacked the cart. She had bought him a gift in the Jaarnindu Market. As she watched him unwrap it, she thought of all the gifts he had bought her over the years, some practical—her first tiny rock hammer, when she was six—and some fanciful—the three yards of bright blue silk, decorated with yellow and red butterflies that he had brought back only last year.

He stared at the leather case a moment, then flicked the catch open and pushed the lid back.

"A chess set!" he exclaimed, a look of pure delight lighting his features. "How I've missed playing chess!" He looked to her. "How did you know?"

Anna looked down, abashed. "It was something you said. In your sleep."

"When I was ill, you mean?"

She nodded.

He stared at the chessboard lovingly. The pieces—hand-carved wood, stained black and white—sat in their niches in two tiny wooden boxes.

It was not a luxury item by any means. The carving was crude and the staining basic, yet that did not matter. This, to him, was far finer than any object carved from silver.

"I shall begin to teach you," he said, looking up at her. "Tonight. We'll spend an hour each night, playing. You'll soon get the hang of it!"

Anna smiled. It was just as she'd thought. *Gifts,* she recalled him saying, *aren't frivolous things, they're very necessary. They're demonstrations of love and affection, and their "excess" makes life more than mere drudgery. You can do without many things, Anna, but not gifts, however small and insignificant they might seem.*

So it was. She understood it much better these days.

"So how are we to do it?"

He looked to her, understanding at once what she meant. Taking one of his stone hammers from the belt at his waist he held it up. "We use these."

"But it'll take ages!"

"We have ages."

"But . . . "

"No buts, Anna. You mustn't be impatient. We'll do a

little at a time. That way there'll be no accidents, all right?"

She smiled and gave a single nod. "All right."

"Good. Now let me rest. I must be fresh if I'm to play chess with you tonight!"

In the days that followed, their lives fell into a new routine. An hour before dawn they would rise and go out to the tunnel, and spend an hour or two chipping away at the rockfall. Anna did most of this work, loathe to let her father exhaust himself so soon after his illness, while he continued his survey of the surrounding area. Then, as the sun began to climb the desert sky, they went back to the Lodge and, after a light meal, began work in the laboratory.

There were samples on the shelves from years back that they had not had time to properly analyze, and her father decided that, rather than set off on another of their expeditions, they would catch up on this work and send the results to Amanjira.

Late afternoon, they would break off and take a late rest, waking as the sun went down and the air grew slowly cooler.

They would eat a meal, then settle in the main room at the center of the Lodge to read or play chess.

Anna was not sure that she liked the game at first, but soon she found herself sharing her father's enthusiasm—if not his skill—and had to stop herself from playing too long into the night.

When finally he did retire, Anna stayed up an hour or so afterward, returning to the workroom to plan out the next stage of the survey.

No matter what her father claimed, she knew Amanjira would not be satisfied with the results of sample analyses for long. He paid her father to survey the desert, and it was those surveys he was interested in, not rock analysis—not unless those analyses could be transformed somehow into vast riches.

In the last year they had surveyed a large stretch of land to the southwest of the Lodge, three days' walk away in the very heart of the desert. To survive at all out there they needed to plan their expeditions well. They had to know exactly where they could find shelter and what they would need to take. All their food, water, and equipment had to be hauled out there on the cart, and as they were often out there eight or ten days, they had to make provision for sixteen full days.

It was not easy, but to be truthful, she would not have wanted any other life. Amanjira might not pay them their true worth, but neither she nor her father would have wanted any other job.

She loved the rock and its ways almost as much as she loved the desert. Some saw the rock as dead, inert, but she knew otherwise. It was as alive as any other thing. It was merely that its perception of time was slow.

On the eighth day, quite early, they made the break-through they had been hoping for. It was not much—barely an armhole in the great pile of rock—yet they could shine a light through to the other side and see that the tunnel ran on beyond the fall.

That sight encouraged them. They worked an extra hour before going back, side by side at the rock face, chipping away at it, wearing their face masks to avoid getting splinters in their eyes.

"What do you think?" he said on the walk back. "Do you think we might make a hole big enough to squeeze through, then investigate the other side?"

Anna grinned. "Now who's impatient?"

"You think we should clear more of it, then?"

"I don't know," she answered, walking on. "I think we should think about it."

That afternoon, in the workshop, he talked about it constantly and, come the evening, rather than debate it further, she gave in.

"All right," she said, looking up from her side of the chessboard. "But only one of us goes through at a time. And we use a rope. We don't know what's on the other side. If there's more quake damage it might be dangerous."

"Agreed," he said, moving his Queen. "Check." Then, smiling up at her. "Checkmate, in fact."

It took them two more days to make the gap wide enough. It would be a squeeze, but to make it any bigger would have meant another week's work at the very least.

"We'll prepare things tonight," he said, holding his lamp up to the gap and staring through. "You won't need much."

Anna smiled at that "you." She had thought she might have to fight him over it. "So what am I looking for?"

He drew the lamp back and turned to face her. "Anything unusual. A volcanic funnel, perhaps. Vents. Any pyroclastic deposits."

"You still think this is part of a larger volcanic system?"

"Almost certainly. These vents and boreholes are only part of it. There would have been a great basin of lava—of magma—deep down in the earth. In fact, the deeper it was, the wider spread these surface manifestations will be. The super heated lava would have found all of the weakest routes through the rock, fault lines and the like. That's all this is, really."

"Like the roots of a tree?"

He nodded, smiling faintly at her. Anna had never seen a tree. Not a *proper* tree, anyway. Only the shallow-rooted palms of Tadjinar. Most of what she knew of the world had come out of books, or had been told to her. That was the worst of living here—the narrowness of it.

Walking back with her, he raised the subject, the two of them speaking, as they always did, with their heads down, not even glancing at each other.

"Anna?"

"Yes?"

"Do you regret living here?"

"Do you?"

"I chose it."

"And you think if I had a choice, I'd chose differently?"

"Sometimes."

"Then you're wrong. I love the desert."

"But you don't know anything else."

"I'd still want to be here."

"Are you sure?"

"I'm sure."

"Mind the rope, Anna, it's getting snagged."

Anna paused, edging slightly to one side, then tugged gently at the rope. It came free. She was halfway through the gap in the rockfall and finding it a tighter squeeze than she'd imagined. She had managed to shrug her shoulders through the narrow hole, but her hips were another matter altogether. Nor could she see anything properly. The tiny slivers of light that peeped through the narrow gaps between her and the wall served more to emphasize how stuck she was than help her.

She could always try and heave herself through, of course, but then she'd most likely tumble down onto the floor on the other side, and it was quite a drop. Besides, only her left arm was free; the other was still wedged between her and the wall.

"Turn yourself about, Anna. Until you're facing the ceiling. The channel's wider than it's tall."

"We should have waited another week," she said, trying to do what he said.

"Maybe. But you're almost there now. Try and edge back a little. Yes . . . that's it."

Slowly, very slowly, she wriggled her way back, until she

could feel that her head and shoulders were out over the gap. Now she had to try and free her arm. She tried to bring it up, but there wasn't room. She'd have to turn again.

"Hold my feet," she said.

Anna felt his hands grip the ankles of her boots firmly.

"Good. I'm going to try to turn onto my front now. At the same time I'm going to try to free my right arm."

"All right."

It was difficult. It felt as if the rock was trying to crush her—to pop her bones—but slowly she managed to turn herself, until she was facing the floor.

Anna could not see anything. The darkness in front of her seemed absolute. Not that the darkness itself worried her; she simply did not want to fall onto anything sharp.

"All right," she said, as she finally freed her arm. "Now lower me slowly."

The rock seemed to come up to touch her hands. Above her, light slowly spilled into the tunnel.

"That's it," she said. "Slowly now."

She began to take her own weight, reaching forward slightly with her hands.

"All right. You can let go now. I'm down."

Anna felt his fingers relent, his hands move back, away from her ankles. There was a faint noise from him, a grunt.

She scrambled up, then turned, brushing herself down. "Are you okay?"

He made a small noise of assent. "Just winded a little. Just give me a moment to get my breath."

Anna went to the hole and looked back through. The lamp was on the floor by his feet where he had left it. He himself was leaning against the wall, slumped slightly, one hand on his chest.

"Are you sure you're all right?"

He nodded and looked up at her. "I'll be okay. I didn't realize how heavy you are, that's all."

"You're sure?"

"Yes. Now get on. Tie the rope about your waist. I'll pass you through the lamp."

She stooped and picked up the rope, fastening it tightly about her waist. It was a thin, strong rope, and they had some five hundred feet of it. That should be plenty for this preliminary exploration. Satisfied, she turned and, leaning through the gap, took the lamp from him.

"This, too," he said, handing her his protective hat.

She put the lamp down, then tried on the hat, expecting it to be too big for her, but it was a perfect fit. She fastened the leather strap under her chin, then turned, lifting the lamp so that he could see her.

"Good," he said, his eyes shining in the lamplight. "I'll give you an hour, then I'll call you back. But keep your eyes open, Anna. And don't take chances."

"I won't."

"You've got the notebook?"

Anna patted her top pocket.

"All right. Then get going. It's cold here."

She smiled then turned, facing the darkness, the lamp held up before her.

The library overlooked the darkened lake, its long, latticed windows giving a distant view of D'ni, the city's lamplit levels climbing the great wall of the cavern.

A fire had been lit in the great fireplace. In its flickering light four men could be seen, sitting in huge armchairs about the fire, their faces thrown into sharp contrasts of gold and black. They had eaten an hour ago, now, as it grew late, they talked.

"I don't know how you can say that, Veovis. Not with any certainty, anyway. Where's your proof?"

Veovis turned to face his friend, his wineglass cradled in both hands, the light from the fire winking at its ruby heart.

"But that's just it, Fihar. I need no proof. The matter is axiomatic. You argue that those races we have knowledge of, on those Ages to which we have linked, behave morally. I agree. But they do so because we have made it our business to encourage them to do so. Their morality is not innate, but taught. And we, the D'ni, were the ones who taught it to them. So much we have known for *thousands* of years."

Veovis turned slightly, looking to another of them. "You, Suahrnir. You are a Maintainer. Is it not so? Is it not one of your prime duties to encourage a stable and moral social framework among the natives of the worlds to which we link?"

Suahrnir was in his middle years and a senior member of his guild. He had already served as Keeper of the Prison Ages and was currently in charge of disposing of all failed or unstable Ages. He pondered Veovis's words a moment, then shrugged.

"It is, yet even so I have some sympathy with Fihar's view. We cannot say with certainty until we have seen for ourselves. That, surely, is the scientific method?"

"Nonsense!" Veovis said, leaning forward, his face suddenly animated. "Without D'ni influence and D'ni guidance, those Ages would, without a shred of doubt, be nasty little backwaters, peopled by savages! Have you not instances enough in your own experience, Suahrnir, of such backsliding? Do we not need to be constantly vigilant?"

"We do," Suahrnir agreed.

"Imagine then, up there on the surface. If there *are* people living up there, then they have developed now for several thousand years without any moral guidance. They will, most certainly, be savages, little more than animals, subservient to their most basic needs. And we have seen, all of us on many Ages, how wild animals behave!"

Aitrus, who had been listening silently, now spoke up. "Unless, like the D'ni, they have an innate morality."

Veovis smiled and turned to his friend. "I would say that the chances of that were exceedingly small, wouldn't you agree, Aitrus?"

"I . . . guess so."

"There!" Veovis said, as if that capped it. "You know, it makes me shudder to think of it. A whole society governed by lust and violence!"

"And the threat of violence," Fihar added, clearly half-convinced now by the argument.

"Exactly! And where, in such a society, would there be room for the development of true intelligence? No. The most we might expect from the surface-dwellers is a surly, grunting species, a pack of jackals who would as soon bay at the moon as hold a decent conversation!"

There was laughter at that.

"Then you think the Council should reaffirm their decision?" Aitrus asked, returning the conversation to the place where it had begun. "You believe we should have nothing to do with the surface-dwellers?"

"I do indeed," Veovis said emphatically. "And to be honest with you, I would not have simply sealed the end of the tunnel, I would have destroyed the whole thing altogether!"

"I see."

"Oh, Aitrus," Veovis said, leaning toward him. "I realize what sentimental feelings you have toward that expedition, and I admire you for it, but the venture was a mistake. The Council were wrong even to consider it!"

Aitrus said nothing. He merely sipped his wine and stared into the fire.

"And now I've hurt your feelings." Veovis stood. "Look, I apologize. It was, perhaps, insensitive of me."

Aitrus looked up at him, smiling sadly. "No, Veovis. You spoke as you saw, and I admire you for that. Besides, I have come to feel that maybe you were right after all. Maybe it *was* a mistake."

Veovis smiled back at him. "Then you will vote with me in Council this time?"

Aitrus shrugged. "Who knows?"

Less than a hundred paces down, the tunnel was blocked again, a second rockfall making it unpassable. Yet to the left of the fall, like a grinning dark mouth, was a crack in the tunnel

wall, large enough for Anna to step into, if she wished.

Anna stood on the rim, her left hand holding the edge of the wall, and she leaned into it, the lamp held out.

The crack was deep. Its floor went down steeply into the dark, from which a faint, cold breeze emanated. She could hear the sound of water, muted and distant, far below, and something else—a kind of irregular knocking. A tap, tap, tap that was like the weak blow of a chisel against the rock.

Anna turned, looking back the way she had come, then, deciding that the slope was not *too* steep, she clipped the lamp to the top of her hard hat and stepped down, steadying herself against the walls with both hands and digging her heels in, so that she would not fall.

The crack was not as long as she'd imagined. After twenty paces it leveled out. For a moment she thought it was a dead end, for the rock seemed to fill the crack ahead of her, but just before that it twisted to the side again, almost at ninety degrees. As she turned that corner, she gave a little cry of surprise.

"It's a cavern!" she yelled, not knowing whether he could hear her or not. "A huge cavern!"

That tapping noise was close now and the sound of flowing water much stronger.

Stepping out onto the floor of the cavern, Anna turned, looking about her. The lamp illuminated only a small part of space, yet she could see, at the edge of the light, what looked like a tiny stream, its surface winking back at her.

Water. The most precious thing of all here in the desert. More precious than the silver her father had found for Amanjira.

Anna walked over to it, conscious of the rope trailing out behind her. The stream was crystal clear. She stooped down beside it, dipping her hand into the flow, then put her fingers to her lips.

Ice cold, it was, and pure. Much better than the water in the pool.

She grinned, looking forward to telling her father of her discovery, then she turned and looked up at the ceiling, twenty yards or so overhead.

There it was! The source of the tapping noise. It looked like a bright red hanging of some kind, marble smooth yet thin, the tip of it swollen like a drop of blood. And where it hung in the breeze it tap-tap-tapped against the roof of the cavern.

Anna frowned, then turned, looking for the source of the breeze. The cavern narrowed at its near end, becoming a kind of funnel. The breeze seemed to come from there.

She sniffed the air, surprised by how fresh it was. Usually there was a stale, musty smell in these caverns. A smell of damp and stone. But this was different.

Unclipping the lamp again, she held it up, trying to make out what the red stuff was. It seemed to be trapped in the rock overhead, or to have squeezed through the rock and then congealed.

She took out her notebook; settling it on her knee, she began to write, noting down not merely what she could see but her first notions about the cavern. Such, she knew from experience, could prove important. One might notice something that one afterward overlooked, or simply forgot. It was best to jot down *everything*, even if most of it proved subsequently to be ill-founded.

Putting the notebook away, she took hold of the rope and pulled a length of it toward her, making sure it was not snagged in the crack. It came easily. Reassured, she walked on, toward the near end of the cavern, toward the "funnel," glancing from side to side, keen not to miss anything.

Thirty paces from it, she stopped, the slight sense of wrongness she had felt earlier now welling up in her.

There, facing her, filling the whole of one end of the narrowed cavern, was a huge sheet of the red stuff. It looked like a thick, stiff curtain, except that it jutted from the rock like a lava flow.

But it wasn't lava. Not of any kind she knew, anyway.

It made her think of the circle on the surface. Somehow

these two things were connected, but just how she didn't know.

She could not wait to tell her father of it.

Anna walked over and stood before it, lifting the lamp. It was blood red, but within that redness was a faint vein of black, like tiny worm-threads.

Perhaps it *was* a kind of lava.

Clipping the lamp to her hat again, she took one of the hammers from her belt and, kneeling beside the wall, tried to chip a small chunk of the stuff away.

After a moment she looked up, puzzled. The hammer had made no impression. The stuff looked soft and felt soft. It *gave* before the hammer. But it would not chip. Why, it wouldn't even mark!

Not lava, then. But what precisely *was* it? Unless she could get a piece for analysis, there was no way of telling.

Anna stood back a couple of paces, studying the wall, trying to see if there might not, perhaps, be a small piece jutting from the rest that would prove more amenable to the hammer, but the stuff formed a smooth unvarying surface.

She turned, looking about her, then laughed. There, only a few paces from her, lay a line of tiny red beads, like fresh blood spots on the gray rock floor. She looked up, seeing how the red stuff formed a narrow vein overhead, as if, under great pressure, it had been squeezed between the lips of the rock.

And dripped.

Anna crouched and, chipping this time into the rock *beneath* the red stuff, managed to free four samples of it, the largest of them the size of her fist.

As she went to slip the last of them into her knapsack, she turned it beneath the light, then squeezed it in her hand. It was almost spongy, yet it was tougher than marble. Not only that, but it seemed to hold the light rather than reflect it.

It was time to get back. They would need to analyze this before they investigated any further.

Anna slipped the sack onto her shoulder, then, taking the rope in her right hand, began to cross the cavern again, coiling it slowly as she headed for the crack.

The others were gone. Only Veovis and Aitrus remained. They stood in the broad hallway of the Mansion, beneath the stairs, the great stone steps and the tiny harbor beyond, visible through the glass of the massive front door.

"Stay the night, Aitrus. You can travel back with me in the morning. The meeting does not start until midday."

"I would, but there are some people I must see first thing."

"Put them off. Tell them you have to prepare for the meeting. They'll understand. Besides, I'd really like to talk to you some more."

"I, too. But I must not break my word."

Veovis smiled. "I understand. Your word means much to you, and rightly so. But try and come to me before the meeting. I shall be in my office in the Guild Hall. I would feign speak with you again before you cast your vote."

Aitrus smiled. "I have decided already, old friend. I shall abstain."

"Abstain?"

"I feel it would be for the best. I am not convinced by

either argument. It may be as you say, and that my hesitancy is only sentiment, yet I still feel as if I would be betraying Master Telanis should I vote *against* the motion."

"Then so be it. Take care, dear friend."

The two men clasped each other's hands.

"Until tomorrow."

"Until tomorrow," Aitrus echoed, smiling broadly. "And thank you. The evening was a most pleasant one."

"As ever. Now go. Before I'm angry with you."

"I've no idea," he said, lifting his eye from the microscope.

"I've never seen anything like it. It looks . . . *artificial.*"

"Impossible," Anna said, stepping up beside him and putting her own eye to the lens.

"So tell me what it is, then. Have you ever seen stone with that kind of structure before? There's not a crystal in it! That wasn't formed. At least, not by any *natural* process. That was *made!*"

She shrugged. "Maybe there are processes we don't know about."

"And maybe I know nothing about rock!"

Anna looked up and smiled. "Maybe."

"Well?" he said, after a moment. "Don't you agree?"

"I don't see how you could make something like this. The temperatures and pressures you'd need would be phenomenal. Besides, what would the stuff be doing down there, in the cavern? It makes no sense."

"No . . ."

She saw the doubt creep back into his face. He looked tired again. They had been working at this puzzle now for close on ten hours.

"You should rest now," she said. "We'll carry on with this in the morning."

"Yes," he said, but it was clear his mind was still on the problem. "It has to be obvious," he said, after a moment. "Something we've completely overlooked."

But what *could* they have overlooked? They had been as thorough with their tests as anyone could be. Had they had twice the equipment and ten times the opportunity to study it, they would still have come up with the same results. This stuff was strange.

He had been cheerful that night. More cheerful than he'd been in quite some time. He had laughed and joked. And in the morning he was dead.

She had woken, remembering the dream she'd had of flowers. Blue flowers, like those she had painted for him. Getting up, she had gone through into the galley kitchen and set out their bowls and tumblers, staring out of the window briefly, conscious of how different everything looked in the dawn light. It was only then that she found him, slumped on the floor beside the workroom bench. She knew at once that he was dead, yet it was only when she actually physically touched him that it registered on her.

His flesh was cold, like stone.

For a moment she could not turn him over. For a moment there was a blankness, a total blankness in her mind. Then she blinked and looked down at him again, where he lay.

He must have come here in the night. Unheard by her. And here he had died, silently, without a word to her.

She groaned and closed her eyes, grief overwhelming her.

The front lobby of the great Guild Hall was in turmoil. Aitrus, arriving late, looked about him, then, seeing Veovis to one side of the crowd of senior guildsmen, hurried over to him.

"Veovis. What's happening?"

"It is Lord Eneah. He was taken ill in the night."

Lord Eneah was Lord Tulla's replacement as head of the Council. Without his presence, or the appointment of a Deputy, the business of the Council could not be carried out.

"Then there will be no vote today."

"Nor for a week or two if the rumors are correct. It seems the Great Lord is at death's door."

"Ill tidings, indeed," said Aitrus.

While none of the D'ni elders could be considered jovial in any way that the young could recognize, Lord Eneah had maintained a sense of humor well into his third century and was wont to control the Council by means of wit rather than chastisement. If he were to die, the Council would indeed lose one of their finest servants.

"What are we to do?" Aitrus asked, looking about him at the crowded vestibule.

"Disperse, eventually," Veovis answered, "but not until our business here is done. Now, if you would excuse me, Aitrus, I would like to take the chance to talk to one or two waverers."

Aitrus nodded, letting Veovis go. Unlike Veovis, he had no strong political ambitions, and though he had been appointed to the Council young—as the junior representative of his Guild—it was not because he had pushed for that appointment.

He had moved swiftly through the ranks, becoming a Master in his thirty-eighth year—the youngest in almost seven centuries—and then, three years ago, he had found himself elected to the Council by his fellow guildsmen; an unexpected honor, for there were men almost twice his age, which was fifty five, who had been put up as candidates against him.

And so here he was, at the very center of things. And though his word meant little yet, and his vote was but a tiny weight on the great scales of D'ni government, he was not entirely without influence, for he was a friend of Lord Veovis.

Watching Veovis from across the pillared hallway, seeing how easily the young Lord moved among his peers, how relaxed he was dealing with the high and mighty of D'ni society, Aitrus found it strange how close they had grown since their reunion thirty years ago. If you had asked him then who might have been his closest friend and confidant in later years, he might have chosen anyone but Lord Rakeri's son, but so it was. In the public's eyes they were inseparable.

Inseparable, perhaps, yet very different in their natures.

And maybe that was why it worked so well, for both had a perfect understanding of who the other was.

Had they been enemies, then there would have been no late-night debates, no agreements to differ, no grudging concessions between them, no final meeting of minds, and that would, in time, have been a tragedy for the Council, for many now recognized that in the persons of Veovis and Aitrus were the seeds of D'ni's future.

Their friendship had thus proved a good omen, not merely for them but for the great D'ni State.

"Aitrus? How are you? How is your father these days?"

Aitrus turned to greet his interrogator, smiling at the old man, surprised—ever surprised—to find himself in such high company.

"He is well, Grand Master Yena. Very well, thank you."

All was done. The cart was packed, her last farewells made. Anna stood on the far side of the bridge, tearful now that the moment had come, looking back into the empty Lodge.

This had been her home, her universe. She had been born here and learned her lessons in these rooms. Here she had been loved by the best two parents any child could have wished for. And now they were gone.

What remained was stone. Stone and dust and ashes.

Those ashes—her father's—were in a tiny sealed pot she had stowed carefully on the cart, beside another that held her mother's ashes.

She turned away, knowing she could not remain. Her future lay elsewhere. Tadjinar, perhaps, or maybe back in Europe. But not here. Not now that he was dead.

Her heart felt heavy, but that, too, she knew, would pass. Not totally, for there would be moments when she would remember and then the hurt would return, yet the grief she now felt would lessen. In time.

She clambered down. The cart was heavy and Tadjinar was far, yet as she leaned forward, taking the strain, beginning to pull it up the shallow slope, the harness ropes biting into the leather pads on her shoulders, she recalled her father's words:

A journey of a thousand miles begins with a single step.

That much remained of him, at least. The memories, the words, and the great wisdom of the man.

She wiped the wetness from her cheeks and smiled. He was in there now, in her head, until she, too, was dust or ashes.

What do you see, Anna?

As she climbed the narrow slope that led out of the valley, she answered him, her voice clear in the desert's stillness.

"I see the endless desert, and before me the desert moon, rising in the last light of the dusk. And I see you there, everywhere I look. I see *you* there."

The way to Tadjinar did not take her past the circle, yet she felt compelled to see it. If her future path lay elsewhere, she would at least take the memory of it with her.

Leaving the cart hidden in a narrow gully, she set off

across the sand toward the circle, the full moon lighting her way. In the moonlight it seemed more inexplicable than ever. What on earth could have caused it?

Or what *in* earth.

Anna crouched at the center of the circle, thinking of what her father had said that first time. It was indeed as if the earth beneath had been not just shaken but *vibrated*. And what could do that? Sound was pure vibration, but what sound—what mighty echo in the rock—could possibly account for this?

Perhaps the answer was in the cavern. Perhaps it was there and she had simply not seen it.

It was madness even to think of exploring again, especially alone, yet the thought of walking away, of never having tried to find an answer, was impossible. She had to go and look.

In the knapsack on her back she had all she needed. In it were her father's hard hat, his lamp and tinderbox, the rope. As if she'd known.

Anna smiled. Of course she'd known. It was compulsion. The same compulsion to know that had driven her father all his life.

And if you find nothing, Anna?

Then she would know she had found nothing. And she would go to Tadjinar, and wherever else afterward, and leave this mystery behind her.

The tunnel was dark—a black mouth in the silvered face of the ridge. The very look of it was daunting. But she was not afraid. What was there to fear, after all?

Anna lit the lamp then walked into the tunnel. The rock fall was where they had left it, and the gap.

She studied it a moment, then nodded to herself. She

would have to douse the lamp then push the knapsack through in front of her. It would not be easy in the dark, but she had done it once before.

Taking the hard hat from the sack, she pulled it on, tying the straps securely about her chin, then snuffed the lamp. The sudden darkness was intense. Stowing the lamp safely at the bottom of the sack, she pulled the drawstrings tight, then pushed it through the gap, hearing it fall with a muffled clatter.

Remembering how difficult it had been, this time she went into the gap face down, her arms out before her. Her problem last time was that she had misjudged how wide the gap was. With her arms outstretched it was much easier. The only problem now was lowering herself on the other side.

Emerging from the gap, she let her hands feel their way down the irregular surface of the rock face, her feet hooked about the edges of the gap. Then, when she was confident that the drop was not too great, she pulled herself forward, letting her legs slide into the gap, her head tucked in to her shoulders as she rolled.

In the dark, the drop seemed a lot farther than she remembered it. There was a moment's inner panic, and then she hit the floor hard, the impact jolting her badly.

She lay there a moment, the knapsack wedged uncomfortably in her lower back. Her wrists ached from the impact and the back of her head and neck felt bruised, but there seemed to be no serious damage.

Anna sat up, reaching behind her for the bag, then winced as a sudden pain ran up the length of her left arm from the wrist to the elbow. She drew the arm back, then slowly rotated the wrist, flexing her fingers as she did so.

"Stupid," she said, admonishing herself. "That was a very stupid thing to do."

Yes, but she had got away with it.

Only just, a silent voice reminded her.

She turned herself around, organizing herself, taking the lamp from the knapsack and lighting it.

In its sudden glow, she looked back at the blockage and saw just how far she had fallen. It was four, almost five feet in all. She could easily have broken her wrists.

She had been lucky.

Clipping the lamp onto the hat, Anna slung the bag over her shoulder then eased herself up into a standing position.

She would have one good look around the cavern, and that was it.

And if she found something?

Anna turned, facing the darkness of the borehole, noticing the faint breeze in the tunnel for the first time.

She would decide that if and when. But first she had to look.

To the left of the wedge, on the shoulder of that great flattened mass of redness that protruded from the ordinary rock, was a gap. Eight feet wide and two high, it was like a scowling mouth, hidden from below by the thick, smooth lip of the strange material.

Anna had found it late in her search, after scouring every

inch of the cavern, looking for something that clearly wasn't there. Only this—this *made* lavatic rock—was different. Everything else was exactly as one would have expected in such a cave.

Unclipping the lamp from her hat, she leaned into that scowling mouth, holding it out before her. Inside, revealed by the glowing lamp, was a larger space—a tiny cave within a cave—its floor made entirely of the red material, its ceiling of polished black rock, like the rock in the volcanic borehole. Seeing that, she understood. Whatever it was, it had once been in a molten state, like lava, and had *flowed* into this space, plugging it. Or almost so.

She squeezed through, crawling on her hands and knees, then stood. The ceiling formed a bell above her. She was in a pocket within the rock.

It was like being inside the stomach of some strange animal.

At the far end, the ceiling dipped again, yet did not entirely meet the floor. There was another gap.

Anna walked across, then crouched, holding out the lamp.

The gap extended into the rock, ending some ten yards back in a solid wall of the red material.

Yet there was a breeze, a definite breeze, coming from the gap. She sniffed. It was air. Pure, unscented air.

It had to lead up again, to the surface. Yet that didn't quite make sense, for this did not smell like desert air. She knew the smell of the desert. It left a scorched, dry taste in the mouth. This air was moist, almost sweet in its lack of minerals.

And there was something else. The light was wrong.

Dimming the lamp almost until it guttered, she set it

down behind her, then looked back. Despite the sudden darkness, the wall in front of her still glowed. That glow was faint and strangely dim, as if the light itself was somehow *dark,* yet she was not mistaken.

There was light somewhere up ahead.

Picking up the lamp again, Anna raised the wick until the glow was bright. Then, getting down on her hands and knees, she crawled into the gap, pushing the lamp before her. Sure enough, the red stuff filled the tunnel's end, yet just before it, to the left, another crack opened up. She edged into it, following its curving course about the swollen wall of red to her right. That curve ended abruptly, yet the crack continued, veering off at ninety degrees to her left. She followed it.

The breeze was suddenly stronger, the scent of sweet, fresh air overpowering. And there was a noise now, like the hiss of escaping gas.

The crack opened up, like the bell of a flower. To her right the red wall seemed to melt away. Ahead of her was a cave of some sort.

No, not a cave, for the floor was flat, the walls regular.

She climbed up, onto her feet, then held the lamp up high, gasping with astonishment at the sight that met her eyes.

Alone in his rooms, Aitrus pulled off his boots, then sat down heavily in his chair. It was a typical guild apartment, like all of those given to unmarried Masters. Sparsely furnished, the walls were of bare, unpolished stone, covered here and there with guild tapestries; thick woven things that showed machines embedded in the rock. Broad shelves in alcoves covered three of the four walls, Aitrus's textbooks—specialist Guild works on rock mechanics, cohesion, tacheometry, elastic limit, shear strength and permeability, as well as endless works on volcanology—filling those shelves.

There were a few volumes of stories, too, including an illustrated volume of the ancient D'ni tales. This latter lay now on the small table at Aitrus's side, where he had left it the previous evening. He picked it up now and stared at the embossed leather cover a moment, then set it down.

He was in no mood for tales. What he wanted was company, and not the usual company, but something to lift his spirits. *Someone*, perhaps.

It seemed not a lot to ask for, yet some days he felt it was impossible.

Aitrus sighed then stood, feeling restless.

Maybe he should take a few days off to visit his family's Age. It was some while since he had been there and he needed a break. It would be several days at least before the Council met again and his work was up straight. No one would blame him for taking a small vacation.

He smiled. Pulling on his boots again, he went over to the door and summoned one of the house stewards. While the man waited, he scribbled a note, then, folding it, handed it to him.

"Give this to Master Telanis."

The steward bowed, then turned and disappeared along the corridor.

Aitrus turned, looking back into the room, then, without further ado, pulled the door closed behind him.

The cavern, which had at first glance seemed small, was in fact massive. What Anna had first taken as the whole of it was in fact only a kind of antechamber. Beyond it was a second, larger chamber whose walls glowed with a faint, green light.

And in that chamber, dominating its echoing central spaces, rested two massive machines, their dark, imposing shapes threatening in the half-dark. Like sentinels they stood, their huge limbs raised as if in challenge.

Indeed, it had been a moment or two before she had recognized them for what they were. Her first irrational thought had been that they were insects of some kind, for they had that hard, shiny, carapaced look about them. But no insect had ever grown *that* large, not even under the blazing desert sun. Besides, these insects had no eyes; they had windows.

Anna walked toward them, awed not merely by their size but by the look of them. She had seen steam-driven machines in her father's books—massive things of metal plate, bolted together with huge metal studs—but these were very different. These had a smooth, sophisticated look that was quite alien to anything she had ever seen before. These were sleek and streamlined, the way animals and insects were, as if long generations of trial and error had gone into their design.

There were long flanges running along the sides of the nearest craft and studded oval indentations. Long gashes in its underside—vents of some kind?—gave it a strange, almost predatory air.

The closer she got to them, the more in awe she felt, for it was only this close that she came to realize the scale on which their makers must have worked. The dark flank of the nearest machine, to her left, rose up at least five times her height. While the second, tucked back a little, was bigger yet.

She also saw now just how different the two were. As if each had a separate purpose. The nearest was the simpler of the two, its four great limbs ending in cone-shaped vents. The other was much more sinister and crablike, its segmented body heavily armored.

Standing beneath the first of them, she reached out and touched its dark, mirror-smooth surface. It was cool, rather than cold. Unexpectedly her fingers did not slip lightly over its surface, but caught, as if they brushed against some far rougher, more abrasive material.

Anna frowned and held the lamp close. Instead of reflecting back her image, the strange material seemed to hold the light, to draw it into its burnished green-black depths.

Out of the corner of her eye she noted something, down low near the floor of the right-hand machine. She crouched, reaching out to trace the embossed symbol with her finger.

Symbol, or letter? Or was it merely decoration?

Whichever, it was not like any written language she had ever seen.

Taking the notebook from her sack, she quickly sketched it, placing the finished sketch beside the original.

Yes. Just so.

She slipped the notebook away, then lifted the lamp, turning slowly to look about her. As she did, she tried to place the pieces of the puzzle together.

What did she have so far? The circle of rock and dust. The strange red "sealing" material. This other, green-black stone, which gave off a dim but definite light. And now these machines.

Nothing. Or, at least, nothing that made sense. Were these the remains of an ancient race that had once inhabited these parts? If so, then why had nothing else been unearthed? So great a race as this would surely have left many more traces of its existence. And why, if these were long-lost relics, did they look so new?

She stared up the huge, smooth flank of the machine toward what seemed to be a control room of some kind. There was a long, slit window up there, certainly, the upper surface of that window flush with the roof of the craft, the lower part of it forming part of the craft's nose.

The rope was in her pack. If she could throw it up over the top of the machine and secure it on the other side, perhaps she could climb up there and look inside?

Anna slipped off her pack and took out the rope. Walking around to the front of the machine, she crouched down, holding the lamp out as she studied the chassis. Some ten, fifteen feet in, there were several small teatlike protuberances just beneath what looked like an exhaust vent. She would tie the rope to one of those.

She walked back, slowly uncoiling the rope in one hand. She really needed a weight of some kind to tie about the end of it, but the only suitable objects she had were the lamp and the tinderbox, and both were much too valuable to risk breaking.

Her first throw merely glanced against the side of the

machine and fell back to the floor. Her second was better but had the same result.

Taking the end of the rope she knotted it time and time again, until there was a palm-sized fist of rope at the end of it. Satisfied, she tried again.

This time the rope sailed over the machine, the lightweight cord whistling through the air as it fell to the other side.

Laying her pack on the remaining coil, Anna walked around and collected the other end of it, then got down and crawled under the machine, winding the rope around and around one of the small protuberances until the thick end of it was wedged tightly against the machine.

Edging back, she stood, then tested the rope, tugging at it hard, leaning her full weight back on her heels. It held.

So far, so good. But the most difficult part was next, for the rope was far from secure. If it were to slip to the side as she was climbing, she could easily find herself in trouble.

Pulling the rope taut, she placed one booted foot against the hull of the craft and leaned back, taking the strain, feeling the sudden tension in the muscles of her calves and upper arms.

She began, leaning slightly to her right as she climbed, away from the front of the strange craft, keeping the rope taut at all times, ready at any moment to let go and drop back to the floor if it were to start slipping. But the rope held, almost as if it were glued in place. Perhaps some quality of the material, that abrasiveness she had noticed, helped, but as she continued to climb her confidence grew.

As she came up onto the broad back of the craft, she relaxed. The top of the great slit window was just in front of her now, some ten or twelve feet distant. Beyond it the nose of the craft tapered slightly, then curved steeply to the floor.

Getting down onto her hands and knees, Anna crawled slowly toward the front of the craft, until the edge of the window was just in front of her. Leaning forward carefully, she looked down, through the thick, translucent plate, into the cabin of the craft.

In the oddly muted light from the oil lamp, the cabin seemed strangely eerie, the wavering shadows threatening.

She frowned, trying to understand exactly what she was looking at. There were two seats—or, at least, they looked like seats; tubular, skeletal things with a kind of netting for the seats—and there was a control panel of some kind just in front of that, but she could make neither head nor tail of the controls, if controls they were.

The panel itself was black. There were indentations in that blackness, and more of the strange symbols, but nothing in the way of levers or buttons, unless such things were hidden.

Anna eased forward a little, trying to see into the back of the cabin, but there was only a bulkhead there, not even a door. Whoever, or whatever, had operated this must have entered the cabin through this window.

That sudden thought, that the makers of this machine might have been other than human—might have been strange, alien creatures of the rock—sent a tiny ripple of fear through her. Until that moment her awe at her discovery had kept her from thinking what these machines might mean. But now her mind embraced that thought.

What if those strange webbing seats were designed not for two, but for a single creature: one huge, grotesque being, multilimbed and clawed, like the machines it made?

No, she told herself. *Whoever made this is long dead and gone. It only looks new.* But that moment of fear, of vivid imagining, had left its shadow on her.

She edged back slowly, then, taking hold of the rope again, climbed down.

Retrieving the rope, Anna stowed it away, then turned to face the second machine. If the function of the first machine was masked from her, this one was self-evident. The great drills at the end of each huge, jointed limb gave it away. This was a cutter.

Anna walked over, stopping just in front of it.

A question nagged at her. Why would someone go to such trouble to cut tunnels in the earth and then seal them? Had they found something down there?

Or was it a tomb?

The thought of a tomb—a royal tomb, surely, for why else go to all this bother?—excited her. Maybe she had stumbled onto the burial vault of some great ancient emperor. If so, then who knew what was down here? If they could build machines like these, then what riches—what curiosities—might lay buried with him?

She walked slowly to the right, circling the machine, her eyes going up, searching its massive flanks, taking in every aspect of its brutal yet elegant form. It had the look of a living thing: of something that had been bred in the depths of the rock. Here and there the material of which it was made seemed folded in upon itself, like the wing-casing of an insect. Yet if it had been based on any insect that existed, it was of a strange, muscular, hydraulic kind. And there were blisters—

large swellings on the hull, two or three feet in length—that had no apparent purpose.

Anna stopped. Just beyond the machine, low in the great wall of the chamber, was a hole: a perfect circle of blackness in the green-black material of the wall. She walked another few paces. Just beyond the first hole was another, and a third. Tunnels. Undoubtedly tunnels.

But leading where?

Her heart pounding, she went over to the first of them. It was a small tunnel, barely large enough to walk within, but made, not natural. The same green-black stone lined the walls. It went down, into darkness.

The second tunnel was the same. The third, to her surprise, was not a tunnel at all, but a storeroom of some kind. Broad, empty shelves lined both sides of that excavated space.

Anna stepped out then looked across.

So which was it to be? The first tunnel or the second?

Neither, she decided. Or not now, anyway. Not without first preparing for the journey. That was the proper way of going about things: the way her father had taught her.

But that would mean squeezing through the tiny gap in the rock fall once again, then walking across the desert to where the cart was hidden. That last part alone was a two-hour journey, which was fine in the moonlight, but would be an ordeal under the desert sun.

And for what? She wasn't going to go that far in. She only wanted to see if they led anywhere.

Five hundred paces. That was all she would allow herself. And if it did not look to be leading anywhere, she would come straight back.

Okay. But which?

Without making a conscious decision, her feet led her into the right-hand tunnel.

One, two, three, she counted, her left hand steadying her against the wall as she began the steady descent. *Seven, eight, nine.*

Five hundred. It wasn't far.

Ahead of her the darkness stretched away, running deep into the rock, forever just beyond the bright reach of her lamp.

Eighty-two, eighty-three, eighty-four . . .

Having traveled much farther than her planned five hundred paces, Anna found that she was lost. She did not want to admit it to herself, but she was lost. After that last left-hand turn she had doubled back, but she had come out in a place she hadn't been before. Or, at least, she couldn't remember having been there. It was a kind of cavern, only it was small and perfectly spherical.

She had lost count an hour ago. Two hours, maybe. Who knew down here? All she knew was that the map she had been following in her head had let her down. She had made one wrong turn and everything had seemed to slip away.

It was a labyrinth—a perfect maze of interlinked tunnels, all of which looked the same and seemed to lead . . . nowhere.

A tomb. It had to be a tomb. And this was part of it, this maze in which she was now inextricably lost.

She would die down here, she was certain of it now.

The thought made her stop and put her hand out to steady herself. Her head was pounding.

Think, Anna. Think what you're doing.

Anna looked up. The voice was clear in her head, almost as if he had spoken.

"I can't think," she answered. "I'm frightened."

Fear's the enemy of thought. Think, Anna. Consider what you ought to do.

She let her head clear, let the fear drain from her mind. Slowly her pulse normalized. She took one of the hammers from her belt and held it up.

"I need to mark my way."

Slipping the hammer back into its holster, she slipped the pack from her shoulder and took out the notebook.

"I'll make a map."

It was what she should have done to begin with, but it was too late now. The best she could do now was to slowly chart her way back to that first straight tunnel, before the way had branched. How long that would take she did not know, but if she was methodical, if she marked each tunnel wall, each branch of it with a letter and a number, then maybe, after a while, she would see the pattern of it on the page.

It was a slender chance, but her best.

Anna turned, looking about her. The tunnel sloped down. Just beyond her it forked. She walked across and, slipping her notebook into her tunic pocket, took the hammer and chisel from her belt.

The first blow was solid—she could feel the way the hammer hit the handle of the chisel squarely and firmly—but the wall was unmarked. She stared at it in astonishment, then repeated the blow. Nothing. There was not even a scratch on the green-black surface.

It was just as before, when she had tried to take the sample.

Anna groaned. It had been her only hope. Now she really was lost.

Paper wraps stone. So use paper. Squares of paper.

Of course! She could tear pages from her notebook and leave tiny squares of paper on the floor beside each entrance. It would have exactly the same effect. At once she tore a page from the book and tore it in half, then in half again. Four pieces. It wasn't enough. She'd soon work her way through her stock of paper. She would have to leave much smaller pieces. She tore them in half again, and then a fourth time.

There. That should do it. She had about fifty pages—that ought to be enough.

Crouching, she began to write on them—A1 to A16. She would allocate two pages to each letter, and then move on to the next. That way she would hopefully chart "areas" of the labyrinth. And if she came back to one of them, say C, she would know exactly where she was on her map, and be able to turn away in a different direction, until she knew exactly how it all fit together.

Anna looked up, smiling grimly. She wasn't beaten yet.

The Guild House was in the oldest part of town, surrounded by the halls of all the major guilds. From its steps one could look out over the great sprawl of D'ni to the harbor and the great arch named after the legendary prince Kerath.

Turning from the steps through a row of fluted marble pillars, one entered a massive vestibule of irregular shape. Here, set into the floor, was a great mosaic map of the main cavern of D'ni, while the floors of the smaller rooms, leading directly off the vestibule, displayed similar mosaic maps of the lesser caverns.

The ceiling of the vestibule was not high—barely twice the height of a standing man—yet it had a pleasant look to it. Great arching beams of pale mauve stone thrust out from the walls on every side, thinning to a lacelike delicacy as they met overhead.

On the right-hand side of the main room was a great arched door. The carved stone fanned about the doorway had the look of trees, forming a natural arch in some woodland glade. Beyond it was the great Council chamber.

It had long been a standing joke that the D'ni would never excavate to the east of the main cavern, lest they had to redesign the Guild House, but the truth was that the rock to the east was home to a stable reservoir of magma, slowly cooling over the millennia, from which they had long tapped energy.

Stepping through the massively hinged doors—each door a great slab of stone three feet thick and ten high—one entered the most impressive of D'ni's many chambers. The great dome of the ceiling seemed far overhead, eighteen huge pillars reaching up like massive arms to support it. Broad steps, which also served as seats, led down into a circular pit, in the midst of which were five huge basalt thrones.

The great shields of the guilds hung on the outer walls, along with their ancient banners.

Today the thrones were occupied, the great steps filled with seated members, here to debate whether the edict banning contact with the "outsiders," the "surface-dwellers" as they were otherwise known, should be lifted.

For six hours they had sat, listening to the arguments for and against, but now the debate was finally coming to a close. The young Lord Veovis was speaking, standing at his place on the second steps, just before the thrones, summing up the case for maintaining things as they were, his confident eloquence making many of the older members nod their heads and smile.

As Veovis sat, there was the sound of fists drumming on the stone—the D'ni way of signaling approval. He looked about him, smiling modestly, accepting the silent looks of praise.

Across from him, just behind the thrones and to the right, some six steps up, Aitrus looked on, concerned now that the time had almost come. Veovis still thought he was going to abstain. Indeed, he was counting on it, for the matter was so finely poised that a vote or two might well decide it. But he could not abstain, and though he knew it might well damage their friendship, he had to do what he believed was right.

But knowing that made it no easier.

There was a brief murmur in the chamber, and then Lord Eneah slowly raised himself up out of his throne, his frail figure commanding the immediate attention of all. Silence fell.

Lord Eneah had been gravely ill, and his voice now as he spoke seemed fatigued; yet there was still a strength behind it.

"We have heard the arguments, Guildsmen, and many among you will have already decided what you think. Yet this is a grave matter, and before we take the irrevocable step of a vote, I feel there should be the opportunity for a more *informal* debate of the matters raised. We shall come to a vote in an hour, but first we shall adjourn this sitting and retire to the vestibule."

If some were disappointed by this, they did not show it, while others nodded, as if the decision were wisdom itself. The D'ni were a patient race, after all, and many matters that might have been decided "hastily" in the chamber had been resolved in the more informal atmosphere of the vestibule.

The remaining Lords rose to their feet and made their way out, followed a moment later by the other members of the great Council.

If the great chamber had been all solemnity and dignity, the vestibule was buzzing with talk, as members went from group to group, attempting to persuade others to their cause.

Rarely in recent years had a single issue raised so much heat and passion, and now that a vote was but an hour off, both camps made great efforts to win last-minute converts to their causes.

Aitrus, who had drifted into the vestibule alone, stood beneath the great arch a moment, looking across to where Veovis stood beside Lord Eneah, who sat in a chair that had been brought out especially for him. Veovis was addressing a small crowd of elder members, undaunted by the fact that many there were a century or two older than he. Such confidence impressed Aitrus, and he knew for certain that Veovis would one day sit where Lord Eneah had sat today, in the central throne.

It was not the right time, not just now, when Veovis was among such company, yet he would have to speak to him, to tell him of his change of mind, before they returned to the great chamber.

Aitrus made his way across, smiling and greeting other guildsmen as he went. Yet he was barely halfway across when he noticed a disturbance on the far side of the vestibule.

He craned his neck, trying to see. The door guards were arguing with someone. Then, abruptly, it seemed, they stood back, allowing the newcomer to pass. It was a senior guildsman from the Guild of Messengers. In one hand he clutched a sealed letter.

As the Council members began to realize that there was an intruder among them, the noise in the vestibule slowly died. Heads turned. Guildsmen turned to face the newcomer as he made his way between them, heading directly to where Lord Eneah sat.

The vestibule and chamber were normally sacrosanct. To permit a Messenger to enter while they were in session was almost unheard of. This had to be a matter of the greatest urgency.

By the time the Messenger stepped out before Lord Eneah, a complete silence had fallen over the vestibule. Kneeling, the man bowed his head and held the letter out.

At a gesture from Lord Eneah, Veovis took the letter and, breaking the seal, handed it to the elder. Eneah slowly unfolded the single sheet, then, lifting his chin and peering at it, began to read. After a moment he looked up, a faint bemusement in his eyes.

"Guildsmen," he said, "it appears the decision has been made for us. We have a visitor. An outsider from the surface."

There was a moment's stunned silence, followed by a sudden uproar in the chamber.

PART THREE: FAULT LINES

For the rest of that day the high council—the five Great Lords and the eighteen Grand Masters—sat in special session to decide what should be done.

While they were meeting, rumors swept the great city in the cavern. Many concerned the *nature* of the intruder, speculating upon what manner of creature had been taken by the Maintainers. While most agreed that it was humanoid in form, some claimed it was a cross between a bear and an ape. Other rumors were wilder yet. One such tale had it that a whole tribe of outsiders—heavily armed savages, intent on trouble—had come far down the tunnels, trying to force entry into D'ni, and that it had taken the whole garrison of Maintainers, backed up by the City Guard, to fight them off.

Such "news," Aitrus was certain, was completely unfounded, yet in the absence of hard fact even he found himself caught up in the games of speculation—so much so, that as evening fell and the lake waters dimmed, he left his rooms and set out through the narrow alleyways of the upper town, intending to visit the Hall of the Guild of Writers where his friend Veovis dwelt.

If anyone outside that central group of Lords and Masters knew what was happening, Veovis would.

Arriving at the gate of the ancient hall, Aitrus waited in the tiny courtyard before the main doors while a steward was sent to notify Veovis of his presence.

Several minutes passed, and then the steward returned.

Aitrus followed him through, between high, fluted pillars and along a broad mosaic path that bisected Ri'Neref's Hall, the first of five great halls named after the greatest of the guild's sons. Like most of the ancient Guild Halls, the Hall of the Guild of Writers was not a single building but a complex of interlinked buildings and rooms, some of them cut deep into the face of the great cavern. As Aitrus ventured farther into the complex, he climbed up narrow flights of ancient steps, the stone of which seemed almost to have been melted over time, like wax, eroded by the passage of countless feet over the six millennia of D'ni's existence.

Here, in this great sprawl of ancient stone, two thousand guildsmen lived and ate and slept. Here they were educated, here went about the simple daily business of the guild. Here also were the book rooms and great libraries of the guild, the like of which could be found nowhere else in D'ni.

Walking through its ancient hallways, Aitrus felt the huge weight of history that lay behind the Writers Guild. Though the Writers claimed no special privileges, nor had a greater voice than any other on the Council, it was held to be the most prestigious of the Eighteen, and its members had a sense of that.

To be a Writer, that was the dream of many a D'ni boy.

The steward slowed, then stopped before a door. Turning to Aitrus, he bowed again. "We are here, Master."

Aitrus waited while the steward knocked.

A voice, Veovis's, called from within. "Enter!"

The steward pushed the door open a little and looked inside. "Forgive me, Guild Master, but it is Master Aitrus, from the Guild of Surveyors."

"Show him in."

As the steward pushed the door back, Aitrus stepped forward. Veovis was in his chair on the far side of the big, low-ceilinged study. Books filled the walls on every side. A portrait of Rakeri, Veovis's father, hung on the wall behind a huge oak-topped desk. In tall-backed chairs close by sat two other men—one old, one young. The elder Aitrus recognized as Lianis, Veovis's tutor and chief adviser, the younger was Suahrnir, Veovis's Maintainer friend.

"Ah, Aitrus," Veovis said, getting up, a broad smile lighting his features. "Welcome, dear friend."

Aitrus heard the door close quietly behind him. "Forgive me for intruding, Veovis, but I wondered if you had any news."

Veovis came over and took his hands, then, stepping back, gestured toward the chair beside his own. "It is curious that you should arrive just at this moment. Suahrnir has just come from the Guild House. It seems the High Council has finished deliberating. A notice is to be posted throughout the city within the hour."

"So what *is* the news?"

Veovis sat. The smile had gone from his face. "There are to be special Hearings, before the Council."

Aitrus sat, looking to his friend. "Hearings? What kind of Hearings?"

Veovis shrugged. "All I know so far is that the outsider is to be interrogated, and that we, as Council members, will be allowed to witness the interrogation. My assumption is that the questions will have to do with the nature of life on the surface."

175

"He speaks D'ni?"

"Not a word. And it is not a he, Aitrus. The outsider is a female."

Aitrus blinked with surprise. "A woman?"

"A girl. A young girl, so I am told, barely out of infancy."

Aitrus shook his head. It was difficult to believe that anyone, let alone a young girl, could have made her way down from the surface. He frowned. "But if she speaks no D'ni, then how are we to question her?"

"Who can say?" Veovis answered, the slightest hint of irony in his voice. "But it appears she is to be handed over to the Guild of Linguists. They are to try to make sense of her strange utterances. That is the idea, anyway. Personally, I would be surprised if she does more than grunt for her food when she wants it."

"You think so?"

"Oh, I am quite certain of it, Aitrus. Word is that she is a rather large-boned animal, and totally covered in hair."

"In *hair*?"

Veovis nodded. "But I guess that, too, is to be expected, no? After all, one would need some kind of special covering to protect the body against the elements, wouldn't one?"

"I suppose so."

"And besides, some creatures find that *attractive,* or so I am told."

There was laughter, but Aitrus was silent, wondering just what circumstances would force a young girl—whatever her species—to venture down the tunnels. It was not, after all, what one would expect.

"Is there any way I could see her?" Aitrus asked.

"I doubt it," Veovis answered. "Word is she is being kept on an island in the cavern of Irrat. The Linguists will have her locked away for months, no doubt. You know how *thorough* they are!

"Besides," Veovis went on, "it is unlikely any of us will get a glimpse of her before the Hearings. If what Suahrnir says is true, almost half of the High Council were in favor of shipping her out to a Prison Age straight away, and having done with the matter. Only Lord Eneah's personal intervention prevented such a course."

"But she's only a girl."

"Sentiment, Aitrus," Suahrnir chipped in. "Pure sentiment. A girl she may be, but she is not D'ni. We cannot attribute her with the same intelligence or sensitivity we D'ni possess. And as for her being *only* a girl, you cannot argue that. Her mere existence here in D'ni has thrown the people into turmoil. They talk of nothing else. Nor will they until this matter is resolved. No. Her arrival here is a bad thing. It will unsettle the common people."

Aitrus was amazed by Suahrnir's vehemence. "Do you really think so, Suahrnir?"

"Suahrnir is right, Aitrus," Veovis said quietly. "We might joke about it, but this issue is a serious one, and had my own opinion been sought, I, too, would have advocated placing her somewhere where she can trouble the public imagination as little as possible."

Aitrus sighed. "I hear what you are saying. Maybe it *will* unsettle people. Yet it would be a great shame, surely, if we did not attempt to discover all we can about conditions up there on the surface?"

"We know now that it is inhabited. Is that not enough?"

Aitrus looked down. He did not want to be drawn into an argument with his friend over this issue.

"Still," Veovis added, when he did not answer, "the matter is out of our hands, eh, old friend? The High Council have decreed that there shall be Hearings and so there shall, whether I will it or no. Let us pray, then, that the Linguists—good men though they are—fail to make sense of the creature this one time."

Aitrus glanced up and saw that Veovis was smiling teasingly. Slowly that smile faded. "Nothing but trouble can come of this, Aitrus, I warrant you. *Nothing* but trouble."

Guild Master Haemis locked the door to the cell, then turned, facing his pupil. She sat there behind the narrow desk, quiet and attentive, the light blue robe they had put her in making her seem more like a young acolyte than a prisoner.

"And how are you, this morning, Ah-na?"

"I am well, Master Haemis," she answered, the slight harshness in her pronunciation still there, but much less noticeable than it had been.

"Thoe kenem, Nava," she said. How are you, Master?

Haemis smiled, pleased with her. They had begun by trying simply to translate her native speech, to find D'ni equivalents for everyday objects and simple actions, but to his surprise she had begun to turn the tables on them, pointing to objects and, by means of facial gesture, coaxing him to name them. The quickness of her mind had astonished them all. By the eighth week she had been speaking basic D'ni phrases. It was baby-talk, true, but still quite remarkable, considering where she came from.

Twenty weeks on and she was almost fluent. Each day she extended her vocabulary, pushing them to teach her all they knew.

"Is it just you today, Master Haemis?"

Haemis sat, facing her. "Grand Master Gihran will be joining us later, Ah-na. But for the first hour it is just you and I." He smiled. "So? What shall we do today?"

Her eyes, their dark pupils still disturbingly strange after all this time, stared back at him. "The book you mentioned . . . the *Rehevkor* . . . Might I see a copy of it?"

The question disconcerted him. He had not meant to tell her about the D'ni lexicon. It was their brief to tell her as little as possible about D'ni ways. But she was such a good pupil that he had relaxed his guard.

"That will not be easy, Ah-na. I would have to get permission from the Council for such a step."

"Permission?"

Haemis looked down, embarrassed. "I should not, perhaps, tell you this, but . . . I should not have mentioned the existence of the *Rehevkor* to you. It was a slip. If my fellow Masters should discover it . . ."

"You would be in trouble?"

He nodded, then looked up. Anna was watching him earnestly.

"Then I will say nothing more, Master Haemis."

"Thank you, Ah-na."

"Not at all," she said softly. "You have been very kind to me."

He gave a little nod, embarrassed once more, not knowing quite what to say, but she broke the silence.

"Will you answer me one thing, Master Haemis?"

"If I can."

"What do they think of me? Your fellow Masters, I mean. What do they *really* think of me?"

It was a strange and unexpected question. He had not thought it would have bothered her.

"To be honest, most of them saw you at first as some kind of grinning primitive animal."

Haemis glanced at her and saw how she digested that fact; saw how thoughtful it made her look.

"And you, Master Haemis? What did *you* think?"

He could not look at her. Even so, there was something about her that compelled his honesty. "I thought no differently."

She was quiet a moment, then, "Thank you, Master Haemis."

Haemis swallowed, then, finding the courage to look at her again, said quietly, "I do not think so now."

"I know."

"I . . . I will speak for you at the Hearings, if you wish."

Anna smiled. "Once more, your kindness does you great credit, Master Haemis. But I must speak for myself when the time comes. Else they, too, will think me but an animal, no?"

Haemis nodded, impressed by her bearing, by the strength that seemed to underlie every aspect of her nature.

"I shall ask," he said quietly.

"Ask?" She stared at him, not understanding.

"About the *Rehevkor*."

"But you said . . ."

"It does not matter," Haemis said, realizing that for once it mattered very little beside her good opinion of him. "Besides, we cannot have you going unprepared before the Council, can we, Ah-na?"

Anna stood by the window of her cell, looking out across the cavern she had been told was called Irrat. The bleakness of the view did little to raise her spirits. The sill into which the great iron bars were set was four feet thick, the view itself of rock and yet more rock, only one small, rust red pool creating a focal point of contrast in that iron gray landscape.

Master Haemis had been kind to her today, and she sensed that maybe he was even her friend, yet he was only one among many. For all his small kindnesses, she was still alone here, still a prisoner in this strange, twilight world where the days were thirty hours long and the seasons unchanging.

Anna sighed, a rare despondency descending upon her. She had tried her best to learn their language and find out something that might help her—she had even enjoyed that task—yet where she was or who these people were she still did not know.

She turned, looking across at the door. Like all else here it was made of stone. Her bed was a stone pallet, cut into the rock of the wall. Likewise, a small shelf-table had been cut from the stone. On the bed was a thin blanket, folded into squares, and a pillow; on the table was a jug of water and a bowl.

Anna walked across and sat on the edge of the stone pallet, her hands clenched together between her knees. For a time she sat there, staring blankly at the floor, then she looked up.

The door had opened silently, unnoticed by her. An elderly man now stood there; tall, dignified, in a long dark cloak edged with the same shade of burgundy the guards who had captured her had worn.

His eyes, like theirs, were pale. His face, like theirs, was tautly fleshed, the bone structure extremely fine, as if made of the most delicate porcelain. His long, gray-white hair, like theirs, was brushed back neatly from a high, pale brow.

But he was old. Far older than any of those she had so far seen. She could see the centuries piled up behind that thin-lipped mouth, those pale, cold eyes.

She waited, expecting him to talk, but he merely looked at her, then, as if he had seen enough, glanced around the cell. Behind him, in the half shadows of the passageway, stood Master Haemis and one of the guards. He took a step toward the door. As he did, Anna stood, finding her voice.

"Forgive me, sir, but might I draw you?"

He turned back, a look of surprise in those pale, clear eyes.

"My sketch pad," she said. "It was in my knapsack, together with my charcoal sticks. It would help me pass the time if I had them."

There was the slightest narrowing of his eyes, then he turned and left the cell. The door swung silently shut.

Anna sat again, feeling more depressed than ever. She had

seen the unfeeling coldness in the old man's face and sensed that her fate had been sealed in that brief moment when he had looked at her.

"So what now?"

She spoke the words quietly, as if afraid they would be overheard, yet she had little more to fear now. She let her head fall, for an instant or two sinking down into a kind of stupor where she did not need to think. But then the image of the old man's face returned to her.

She recalled his surprise, that narrowing of the eyes, and wondered if she had somehow made a brief connection with him.

"Miss?"

Anna looked up, surprised to be spoken to after so lengthy a silence. Again there had been no warning of the woman's presence before she had spoken.

"Here," the woman said, stepping across and placing a tray onto the table at Anna's side. The smell of hot soup and fresh-baked bread wafted across to Anna, making her mouth water.

As the woman stepped back, Anna stood, surprised to see that instead of the usual sparse fare, this time the tray was filled with all manner of foods; a tumbler of bright red drink, another of milk, a small granary loaf. And more.

Anna turned to thank the woman, but she was gone. A guard now stood there in the doorway, expressionless, holding something out to her. It was her sketch pad and her charcoals.

Astonished, she took them from him, nodding her head in thanks. She had asked a hundred times, but no one had listened to her. Until now.

The door closed behind the woman.

Anna put her things down, then, taking the tray onto her lap, began to eat.

He listened, yes, but what does that mean?

Was this simply the courtesy they extended to every prisoner? And was this to be her life henceforth, incarcerated in this bleak stone cell?

And if so, could she endure that?

At least she had the sketch pad now. She could use the back of it, perhaps, to write down all her thoughts and observations, something she had sorely missed these past six months. And then there were always the sessions with Master Haemis to look forward to—her struggles with that strange, delightful language.

For a moment she sat there, perfectly still, the food in her mouth unchewed. That face—the old man's face. If she could draw *that*, then maybe she would begin to understand just who he was and what he wanted of her. For the secret was there, in the features of a man, or so her mother had once said.

Stone-faced, he'd seemed. Yet if she could chip the surface stone away and see what lay behind.

Anna set the tray back on the table, then yawned, feeling suddenly tired, in need of sleep.

She would make the sketch later, when she woke.

Unfolding the blanket, Anna stretched out on the pallet and lay it over her, closing her eyes. In a moment she was asleep.

The captain paused a moment, studying the sketch, impressed despite himself that she had captured the old man's face so perfectly. Then, closing the sketch pad, he turned and handed it to her, before pointing toward the open doorway.

"Come. It's time to go."

Gathering up her charcoals, Anna tucked them into her pocket, then looked across at him. "Where are you taking me?"

He did not answer, merely gestured toward the door.

Anna stepped outside, letting the guards fall in, two to the front of her, two just behind. This time, however, no one bound her hands.

As the captain emerged, they came smartly to attention, then set off at a march, Anna in their midst, hurrying to keep pace.

A long stairway led down through solid rock, ending in a massive gateway, the stone door of which had been raised into a broad black slit in the ceiling overhead. They passed beneath it and out onto a great slab of rock, still within the cavern yet outside the stone keep in which Anna had been kept. She looked back at it, surprised by the brutality of its construction.

They slowed. Just ahead, the rock fell away almost vertically into a chasm on three sides, a chain bridge spanning that massive gap, linking the fortress to a circular archway carved into the far wall of the cavern. Stepping out onto the bridge, Anna looked down, noting the huge machines that seemed to squat like black-limbed fishermen beside dark fissures in the earth. Machines, no doubt, like those she had found up near the surface. There were buildings down there, too, and chimneys and huge piles of excavated rock, like a giant's building blocks, all far below the narrow, swaying bridge. She was not afraid of heights, nor of falling, but even if she had, the guards would have paid no heed. They moved on relentlessly, nudging her when she was not quick enough.

The arch in the far wall proved to be ornamental. Just beyond the great carved hoop of stone lay a wall of solid rock; black marble, polished smooth. She thought perhaps they would stop, but the captain marched on, as if he would walk straight through the rock itself.

As they passed beneath the arch, however, he turned abruptly to the right, into deep shadow. More steps led down. At the foot of them was a door. As he unlocked it, Anna looked to the captain, wanting to ask him where they were taking her and what would happen there, but he was like a machine, distant and impersonal, programmed to carry out his tasks efficiently and silently, his men mute copies of himself, each face expressionless.

She understood. They did not like her. Nor did they wish to take the chance of liking her.

Beyond the door the passage zigzagged through the rock, small cresset lamps set into the stone. And then they were "outside" again, in another cavern.

Anna stepped out, looking about her. A great bluff of rock lay to her right, obscuring the view. To her left, just below her and about a hundred yards or so away, a broad coil of water cut its way through a steep-sided chasm. It was not as dark here as in the first cavern. She did not understand that at first. Then, to her surprise, she saw how the water gave off a steady glow that underlit everything.

They went down the bare, rocky slope, then along a path that led to a stone jetty. There, at the foot of a flight of steep, black basalt steps, a long, dark, elegant boat was anchored, the chasm walls towering above it. Four burgundy-cloaked oarsmen waited patiently on their bench seats, their oars shipped. A burgundy-colored banner hung limply from the stern of the boat, beside the ornamental cabin, a strangely intricate symbol emblazoned in gold in its center. Anna stared at it as she clambered aboard, intrigued by its complexity.

"Where are we?" she asked.

The captain turned to her, giving her a cold, hard look, his eyes suspicious of her. For a moment she thought he would not answer her, then, curtly, he said:

"We are in D'ni. This is the main cavern."

"Ah . . ." But it did not enlighten her. *Duh-nee.* That was what it had sounded like. But where was *Duh-nee?* Deep in the earth? No, that simply wasn't possible. People didn't *live* deep in the earth, under the rock. Or did they? Wasn't that, after all, what she had been staring at every day for these past six months? Rock, and yet more rock.

The securing rope was cast off, the oarsmen to her left pushed away from the side. Suddenly they were gliding down the channel, the huge walls slipping past her as the oars dug deep in unison.

Anna turned, looking back, her eyes going up to the great carved circle of the arch that had been cut into the massive stone wall of the cave; a counterpart, no doubt, to the arch on the far side. The wall itself went up and up and up. She craned her neck, trying to see where it ended, but the top of it was in shadow.

She sniffed the air. Cool, clean air, like the air of the northern mountains of her home.

Outside. They *had* to be outside. Yet the captain had said quite clearly that this was a cavern.

She shook her head in disbelief. No cavern she had ever heard of was this big. It had to be . . . *miles* across. Turning, she looked to the captain. He was standing at the prow, staring directly ahead. Beyond him, where the channel turned to the right, a bridge had come into view—a pale, lacelike thing of stone, spanning the chasm, the carving on its three, high-arched spans as delicate as that on a lady's ivory fan.

Passing under the bridge the channel broadened, the steep sides of the chasm giving way to the gentler, more rounded slope of hills, the gray and black of rock giving way to a mosslike green. Ahead of them lay a lake of some kind, the jagged shapes of islands visible in the distance, strangely dark amid that huge expanse of glowing water.

At first Anna did not realize what she was looking at; then, with a start, she saw that what she had thought were strange outcrops of rock were, in fact, buildings; strangely shaped buildings that mimicked the flowing forms of molten rock. Buildings that had no roofs.

That last made a strange and sudden sense to her. So they *were* inside. And the water. Of course . . . Something must be in the water to make it glow like that.

As the boat glided out onto the lake itself, Anna took in for the first time the sheer scale of the cavern.

"It's magnificent," she said quietly, awed by it.

The captain turned, glancing at her, surprised by her words. Then, as if conceding something to her, he pointed to his right.

"There. That is where we are headed. See? Just beyond the bluff. It will come into sight in a moment."

There was a pillar of some kind—a lighthouse maybe, or a monument—just beyond the great heap of rock that lay directly to their right, the top of it jutting up above the bluff. Yet as they rounded the headland, she saw, with astonishment, that the pillar was not as close as she had presumed. Indeed, it lay a good two or three miles distant.

"But it's . . . "

"Over three hundred and fifty spans high."

Anna stared at the great column of twisted rock that lay at the center of the glowing lake. Three hundred and fifty spans! That was over a mile by her own measure! Somehow it didn't seem natural. The rock looked as if it had been shaped by some giant hand. Looking at it, she wasn't sure whether it was hideous or beautiful; her eyes were not trained to appreciate so alien an aesthetic.

"What is it called?"

"The ancients called it Ae'Gura," he answered, "but we simply call it The Island. The city is beyond it, to its right."

"The city?"

But it was clear that he felt he had said too much already. He looked away, falling silent once again, only the swish of the oars in the water and the creak of the boat as it moved across the lake breaking the eerie silence.

Veovis sat in the corridor outside Lord Eneah's study, waiting, while, beyond the door, the elders finished their discussion.

He had been summoned at a moment's notice, brought here in the Great Lord's own sedan. That alone said much. Something must have happened—something that the elders wished urgently to consult him about.

Veovis smiled. He had known these men since childhood. He had seen them often with his father, in both formal and informal settings. They ate little and spoke only when a matter of some importance needed uttering. Most of what was "said" between them was a matter of eye contact and bodily gesture, for they had known each other now two centuries and more, and there was little they did not know of each other. He, on the other hand, represented a more youthful, vigorous strain of D'ni thinking. He was, as they put it, "in touch" with the living pulse of D'ni culture.

Veovis knew that and accepted it. Indeed, he saw it as his role to act as a bridge between the Five and the younger members of the Council, to reconcile their oft-differing opinions and come up with solutions that were satisfactory to all. Like many of his class, Veovis did not like, nor welcome, conflict, for conflict meant change and change was anathema to him. The Five had long recognized that and had often called on him to help defuse potentially difficult situations before push came to shove.

And so now, unless he was mistaken.

As the door eased open, Veovis got to his feet. Lord Eneah himself stood there, framed in the brightly lit doorway, looking out at him.

"Veovis. Come."

He bowed, his respect genuine. "Lord Eneah."

Stepping into the room, he looked about him, bowing to each of the Great Lords in turn, his own father last of all. It was exactly as he had expected; only the Five were here. All others were excluded from this conversation.

As Eneah sat again, in the big chair behind his desk, Veovis stood, feet slightly apart, waiting.

"It is about the intruder," Eneah said without preamble.

"It seems she is ready," Lord Nehir of the Stone-Masons, seated to Veovis's right, added.

"Ready, my Lords?"

"Yes, Veovis," Eneah said, his eyes glancing from one to another of his fellows, as if checking that what he was about to say had their full approval. "Far more ready, in fact, than we had anticipated."

"How so, my Lord?"

"She speaks D'ni," Lord R'hira of the Maintainers answered.

Veovis felt a shock wave pass through him. "I beg your pardon, Lord R'hira?"

But R'hira merely stared at him. "Think of it, Veovis. Think what that means."

But Veovis could not think. The very idea was impossible. It had to be some kind of joke. A test of him, perhaps. Why, his father had said nothing to him of this!

"I . . ."

"Grand Master Gihran of the Guild of Linguists visited us earlier today," Lord Eneah said, leaning forward slightly. "His report makes quite remarkable reading. We were aware, of course, that some progress was being made, but just how much took us all by surprise. It would appear that our guest is ready to face a Hearing."

Veovis frowned. "I do not understand . . . "

"It is very simple," Lord Nehir said, his soft voice breaking in. "We must decide what is to be done. Whether we should allow the young woman to speak openly before the whole Council, or whether she should be heard behind closed doors, by those who might be trusted to keep what is heard to themselves."

"The High Council?"

His father, Lord Rakeri, laughed gruffly. "No, Veovis. We mean the Five."

Veovis went to speak then stopped, understanding suddenly what they wanted of him.

Lord Eneah, watching his face closely, nodded. "That is right, Veovis. We want you to make soundings for us. This is a delicate matter, after all. It might, of course, be safe to let the girl speak openly. On the other hand, who knows what she might say? As the custodians of D'ni, it is our duty to assess the risk."

Veovis nodded, then, "Might I suggest something, my Lords?"

Eneah looked about him. "Go on."

"Might we not float the idea of *two* separate Hearings? The first before the Five, and then a second—possibly—once you have had the opportunity to judge things for yourselves?"

"You mean, promise something that we might not ultimately grant?"

"The second Hearing would be dependent on the success of the first. That way you have safeguards. And if things go wrong . . . "

Eneah was smiling now, a wintry smile. "Excellent," he said. "Then we shall leave it to you, Veovis. Report back to us within three days. If all is well, we shall see the girl a week from now."

Veovis bowed low. "As you wish, my Lords."

He was about to turn and leave, when his father, Rakeri, called him back. "Veovis?"

"Yes, father?"

"Your friend, Aitrus."

"What of him, father?"

"Recruit him if you can. He's a useful fellow, and well liked among the new members. With him on your side things should prove much easier."

Veovis smiled, then bowed again. "As you wish, father." Then, with a final nod to each of them in turn, he left.

Eneah sat at his desk long after they had gone, staring at the open sketch pad and the charcoal image of his face. It was some time since he had stared at himself so long or seen himself so clearly, and the thought of what he had become, of the way that time and event had carved his once familiar features, troubled him.

He was, by nature, a thoughtful man; even so, his thoughts were normally directed outward, at that tiny, social world embedded in the rock about him. Seldom did he stop to consider the greater world within himself. But the girl's drawing had reminded him. He could see now how hope and loss, ambition and disappointment, idealism and the longer, more abiding pressures of responsibility, had marked his flesh. He had thought his face a kind of mask, a stone lid upon the years, but he had been wrong: It was all there, engraved in the pale stone of his skin, as on a tablet, for all who wished to read.

If she is typical . . .

The uncompleted thought, like the drawing, disturbed him deeply. When he had agreed to the Hearings, he had thought, as they had all thought, that the matter was a straight-forward one. The savage would be brought before them, and questioned, and afterward disposed of—humanely, to a Prison Age—and then, in time, forgotten. But the girl was not a simple savage.

Eneah closed the sketch pad, then sighed wearily.

"If she is typical . . . "

"Veovis?"

Veovis looked up, no sign of his normal cheeriness in his face. He looked tired, as if he had not slept.

"Ah, Aitrus. I'm glad you've come."

Veovis gestured to the chair facing him. They were in the great Common Room in the Writers Guild Hall. The huge, square room was filled with big, tall-backed armchairs. It was a favorite place for guildsmen to come and talk, but few of the chairs were filled at this early hour of the day.

Veovis smiled faintly, then looked at him. "Lord Eneah summoned me last night."

"And?"

Veovis lowered his voice. "And they want me to help them."

"In what way?"

"They want to cancel the Hearings."

Aitrus sat forward. "But Lord Eneah announced the Hearings before the full Council. He cannot simply *cancel* them!"

"Exactly. And that is why he hopes I can persuade individual members to let the matter drop."

"Is that why I am here? To be persuaded?"

"No, old friend. You will decide as you decide. But my father wanted me to speak to you, and so here you are."

"I don't follow you, Veovis."

"He wants you to help me. He thinks you might."

"And what did you say to him?"

"I said I would speak to you. No more."

Aitrus laughed. "Come now. No games. Do you want my help or don't you?"

Veovis smiled. "I'd welcome it. If you'd give it."

"Then you had better tell me everything."

That evening Aitrus did not return to his rooms in the Guild Hall, but went back to the family home in the Jaren District, which was in the upper northeast of the city, overlooking the Park of the Ages. His mother was delighted to see him, but it was his father, Kahlis, he had come to see.

Stepping back from her embrace, Aitrus looked toward the polished stone stairway that led up to the second floor.

"Is Father in his study?"

"He is, but he is very busy, Aitrus. He has a report to finish for the morning."

Kahlis looked up as Aitrus entered the big, book-lined room, and smiled wearily at him from behind a great stack of papers he was working on. "Ah, Aitrus. How are you?"

"Can I speak with you, Father?"

Kahlis glanced at the paper before him, then, setting his pen back in the inkstand, sat back.

"It is important, I take it?"

Aitrus stepped across and took a seat, facing him. "This matter with the intruder bothers me."

"How so?"

"I went to see Veovis early this morning. He asked me to call on him at his Guild Hall. His mood was . . . strange. I asked him what it was, and he said he had been asked to undertake a task, on behalf of the Five, and that he needed my help."

"And you promised you would help him?"

"Yes."

"So what exactly is the problem?"

"I do not like what I am doing, Father. I gave my word before I understood what was involved."

"That is most unlike you, Aitrus."

"Perhaps. But Veovis is my friend. To refuse him would have been difficult."

"I understand. But what exactly is it that you find so difficult about the 'task' the Five have given you?"

Aitrus stared at his father. "You have heard nothing, then?"

"What ought I to have heard?"

"That the girl now speaks fluent D'ni."

Kahlis laughed. "You jest with me, Aitrus. Word was she could barely grunt her own name!"

"Then word was wrong."

Kahlis took that in, his expression sober suddenly. "I see. Then the Hearings will be soon, I take it."

"That is just it," Aitrus said. "The Five no longer want to hold such hearings—not before the full Council, anyway. They want the sessions to be held in private, with only themselves in attendance. And they have charged Veovis and myself with the job of persuading members of the Council to that viewpoint."

Kahlis stared at him. "I am glad you came to me, Aitrus, before any damage could be done. Lord Eneah made a promise to the full Council, and that promise must be upheld."

Kahlis stood and came around his desk. Aitrus also stood, turning to face his father. "So what will you do?"

"I will go and see Lord Eneah, now, before this matter goes any further. I will tell him that I have heard rumors and that I want his confirmation that they are untrue."

"Then you will say nothing of my part in this?"

"Of course." Kahlis held his son's arms briefly. "Do not worry, Aitrus. I understand the delicacy of your predicament. If Veovis thinks you came to me, he will blame you for whatever trouble follows. But I shall make sure that Lord Eneah does not get that impression."

"Yet he might guess . . . "

Kahlis smiled. "Between guessing and knowing is a long dark tunnel. I know it is not in your nature to deceive, Aitrus, but it might be kinder on your friend—yes, and on yourself— if you kept this meeting with me to yourself."

Aitrus bowed. "I had best go, then."

"Yes. And Aitrus, thank you. You did the right thing."

Lord Eneah was already in bed when his servant knocked on the door.

"Yes, Jedur, what is it?"

A face only a degree or two less ancient than his own poked around the door and stared at him.

"It is Grand Master Kahlis, my Lord. He knows the hour is late, but he begs a meeting. He says it is of the gravest importance."

Eneah sighed, then slowly sat up. "Ask Master Kahlis to allow me a moment to refresh myself, then I shall come and speak with him."

"My Lord." The wizened face disappeared.

Eneah slid his legs around and, throwing back the single cotton cover, put his feet down on the cold stone of the floor. There had been a time when he had enjoyed the luxuries his post had brought him, but nowadays he embraced simplicity in everything.

He walked across to the washstand in the corner of his spartanly-furnished bedroom and, pouring water from a jug into a bowl, washed his face and hands, drying himself with a small cloth.

His cloak of office hung on a peg behind the door. He took it down and pulled it on, buttoning it to the neck.

"There!" he said, smoothing one hand over what remained of his ash white hair, staring at his face in the small mirror he had had placed on the wall only two days ago. "Now let us see what Master Kahlis wants."

Kahlis was waiting in the study. As Lord Eneah entered the room, he stood hastily, bowing low.

"Forgive me, Lord Eneah . . ."

Eneah waved the apology away. "What is it, Kahlis? Has it to do with the plans for the new cavern?"

He knew it wasn't. Kahlis would hardly have got him from his bed for such a matter. No. He knew already what it was. In fact, he had half expected one or other of them to come to see him. The only surprise was that it was so soon.

As Eneah sat, Kahlis stepped forward, standing at the edge of his desk.

"No, my Lord, it has nothing to do with the plans for the new cavern. Rather, it is to do with certain rumors that have been circulating throughout the day."

"Rumors?" For a moment longer he played innocent, staring back at Kahlis hawkishly. "You wake me to talk of *rumors*, Master Kahlis?"

"I would not have bothered you with such, Lord Eneah, were they not concerned with a matter of the gravest importance."

"And what matter would this be?"

"The matter of the hearings." Kahlis hesitated, then. "Word is that the Five wish to hold the hearings in secret, behind locked doors. Is that so, my Lord?"

For the first time, Eneah smiled. "It is so."

Kahlis, who had clearly steeled himself for a denial, blinked. Then, "Might I ask why, my Lord?"

Eneah gestured to a chair. "Take a seat, Master Kahlis, and I shall try to explain. It might indeed help us were you to understand our thinking on this matter."

Aitrus was seated at his desk in the corner of his study, trying to catch up on his work before he left for the Guild House, when there was a sharp rapping on his door. He stood, then went across and opened it. It was Veovis. Brushing past him, Veovis stormed across and threw himself down on the padded bench, his face dark with suppressed anger.

"Have you heard?"

"Heard? Heard what?"

"The Hearings. They are to go ahead, after all. The Five have changed their minds. They will take place a week from now."

"Before full Council?"

Veovis nodded, but he was not looking at Aitrus; he was staring straight ahead of him, as if recalling the meeting he had just come from. "It is a mistake. I told Lord Eneah it was a mistake. And they will rue it. But he was adamant. A promise is a promise, he said. Well, I would not argue with that, yet circumstances change."

"You think it might be dangerous, then, to let the girl speak?"

Veovis glanced at him. "Is there any doubt? No, the more I think of it, the more certain I am. The girl has a natural cunning. It is that, more than anything, that has allowed her to master our tongue."

"You think so?"

"Oh, I know it. And I fear that she will use that same native cunning to try to manipulate the Council. Why, I have heard that she has beguiled several of those who were sent to study her, weedling information from them when they least suspected it. And her audacity!"

201

Aitrus sat, facing Veovis. "Go on."

Veovis sat forward, staring down at his hands where they were clenched in his lap. "It seems one of the Linguists, thrown off-guard by her act of youthful innocence, mistakenly mentioned the existence of the *Rehevkor* to her. She, it seems, elicited from him a promise to show her a copy of it."

"But that is not allowed."

"Precisely. Which is why a certain Guild Master Haemis has been removed from the study team."

"Why did you not mention this to me before now?"

"Because I did not know until this morning."

Aitrus sighed, then shook his head. "You must feel . . . let down."

Veovis looked up at him, then nodded.

"So what will you do now?"

"Do?" There was a bitterness now in Veovis's face that had not been there before. "I can do nothing. I must act the perfect son and sit upon my hands and bite my tongue."

"Has your father instructed you so?"

"Not in so many words. But how else am I to interpret this?" He shook his head. "But they will rue it, I guarantee you, Aitrus. The girl is cunning."

"You have seen her?"

"No. And yet I know her by her work. She is a savage, after all, and savages have no morality, only cunning. Her words, I fear, will poison many ears, persuading them to courses they would otherwise have shunned."

"Then you must set your voice against hers."

Veovis stared at Aitrus a moment; then, smiling, he nodded. "Yes. Yes, of course. It *must* be so. My voice against hers.

Truth against trickery." And now he grinned. "As ever, you are wisdom itself, Aitrus, yes, and a pillar to me in my despair!"

Veovis stood and came across, and embraced Aitrus, "Here, let me hug you, old friend. I came here despondent and you have filled me with new hope. It shall be as you said. I shall be the voice of reason, a fierce, strong light shining in the darkness."

Veovis stood back, smiling into Aitrus's face. "And you, my friend? Will you speak out with me?"

"I shall speak the truth as I see it," Aitrus said. "I can promise you no more."

"Then let that be enough. For you will see, Aitrus, I promise you. Do not be blinded by her seeming innocence; think rather of the cunning that lies behind that mask. And as you see, so speak."

"I shall."

"Then good. I'll leave you to your work. And Aitrus?"

"Yes?"

"Thank you. You are the very best of friends."

The narrow alleyways of the lower city were crowded with onlookers as the procession made its way up that great slope of fashioned rock toward the Great Hall of the Guilds. A small troupe of the City Guard forced a way through, keeping the more curious from the huge palanquin that eight young guildsmen—Maintainers all—carried between two long poles.

From within the partly curtained palanquin, Anna sat in

her chair, looking out at the sea of faces that had gathered to see the so-called outsider taken to the Hearings. Some called out to her in their strange tongue that she had yet to fully master, yet few of them seemed hostile. It was more as if she were a curio, an exotic beast captured in some foreign clime and brought back to be displayed before the court.

Anna looked about her, at the men, women, and children that had gathered simply to stare. There were thousands of them, yet every face had that same strange elongation of the features, that almost-human fineness to the bones that she had slowly grown accustomed to these past six months. Indeed, looking in a mirror last night, it had been her own face she had found strange, and looking now she wondered how they saw her. Did they find her nose and mouth too thick and coarse, her cheekbones much too heavy, too *pronounced*, in her face?

Beyond the gate the crowds thinned out. This was a richer district, the citizens who stood outside their doors dressed opulently now, their curiosity if anything much fiercer than the people of the lower city. And the path, too, was suddenly much broader. A marble path, worn by a million feet to a melted smoothness, winding its way between huge roofless houses that were as different from one another as the houses of the lower city were similar.

Anna noted those differences and nodded inwardly. So it was with societies. For the poor uniformity, of dress and housing, for the rich . . . well, *anything*. So her father had pointed out to her years ago when she was still a child, his disillusionment with empires at its darkest ebb.

And today she would face the might of this small empire head on. It was a daunting thought, yet the days alone in her cell on the island had prepared her well for this. They could do their worst and she would still be herself, unbroken and unrepentant. For what *should* she repent, except that she lost her way? No, it was as her father had always taught her: If she believed in herself then it did not matter what the greater world thought of her. If she could square her conscience with herself then all was well.

And, thinking that, she heard his voice clearly for the first time in long months, encouraging her; saying what he had always said to her:

Be brave, Anna, but before all, be true to yourself.

She would not flinch away from what lay ahead. Whatever was said, whatever they decided, she would bear herself with pride, no matter what.

A welcoming party of senior guild officials waited before the next gate, a massive pile of stone with flanking guard towers and huge, twenty-foot doors.

Anna recognized few of them, but the three who stood at the front of the party were well known to her by now.

"Step down, Ah-na," Lord Eneah said, approaching the palanquin and putting out a hand to her courteously, "you must walk from here on."

She let herself be helped down, then stepped between the elderly Gihran and his fellow guildsman, Jimel. Now that she had to trust to her own legs she felt suddenly less confident. Her pulse had noticeably quickened; her heart fluttered briefly in her chest. They were almost there now. She sensed it.

Beyond the gate the street opened out into a square, the ground tilted steeply, as everywhere here in D'ni. Anna looked about her, realizing that she had seen this open space from her cell window many times but never understood its significance—until now.

The Guild House lay ahead of her now, a massive building fronted by huge, six-sided basalt pillars, its massive, tiered roof reaching up toward the ceiling of the great cavern. Standing before it she did not need to be told what it was, for the shields of the different guilds betrayed its function. Guildsmen crowded the covered paths surrounding the great square, young and old, all of them wearing the various-colored cloaks—burgundy, yellow, turquoise, crimson, emerald green, black, pale cream, and royal blue—of the guilds.

As Lord Eneah came alongside, she glanced at the old man, noting how hard and expressionless his face was. Yet she knew him now to be fair if not kind. If anyone would save her, it was he. Master Gihran, she knew, did not like her, and Master Jimel had as good as told her that he thought she should be locked away for good. Only Master Haemis had been kind, and he had been replaced.

At a gesture from Lord Eneah, the party walked on, Anna in their midst.

At least they have not shackled me again.

But then, why should they? What would she have done? Run away? No. For there was nowhere to run to. She stood out, like a goat in a sheep pen.

As they came to the great marble steps that led up into the hall, Gihran leaned close and whispered to her:

"You must keep absolutely silent, unless you are directly requested to speak, you understand, Ah-na? If you speak out of turn, Lord Eneah will order you gagged."

Anna turned, astonished, to look at him, but the old man merely nodded.

"Our codes of behavior must not be flouted," he continued, his words almost inaudible as they began to climb the steps. "You must do precisely what you are told, and you must answer every question as it is put. All right?"

Anna nodded, but she suddenly felt anything but all right. The tension that had been in her stomach all the while now threatened to unnerve her. She fought against it; fought against the instinct to let her knees buckle and her head go down.

Her throat was dry now. Her hands trembled.

She stopped dead, straightening her head and clenched her fists into tight balls, controlling the nervous spasm. It was only a hearing, after all, not a trial. She would speak clearly and answer every point, exactly as Master Gihran said. And maybe they would see that she was telling them the truth. For why should she lie?

The Great Hall was huge, much bigger than she would have guessed from the outside of the building. A series of steps followed the contours of the walls, at the top of which was a broad marble plinth. On the plinth was a line of massive basalt thrones. Cloaked guildsmen, more than a hundred in number, sat in those great chairs, thick golden chains of office hung about their necks.

There were only two breaks in that great square of thrones: the entrance she had come through and a second door set deep into the rock on the far side of the hall. Lord Eneah led the party on, across that great mosaic floor, then stopped, turning to face Anna.

"You will stand there, Ah-na," he said commandingly.

She nodded, then watched the old man walk across and take his place on the great throne facing her. Tense now, she looked about her. Most of the seated guildsmen were old—graybeards like Lord Eneah, if not as ancient—but one or two seemed young by D'ni standards. Two in particular caught her eye. They sat side by side, just to the left of Lord Eneah, the first's black cloak trimmed in bright red, the second's in a pale blue.

She glanced at their faces, expecting to see there the same indifference that was on Lord Eneah's features, then looked again, surprised to see how intently each of them looked at her: one curious and one with clear hostility.

Seeing that look, Anna shivered, her blood suddenly cold. There was no mistaking it; whoever he was, the young guildsman clearly hated her.

But why?

"Ah-na!" Lord Eneah said, his voice booming in that great space between the pillars.

"Yes, my Lord."

"You know why you are here?"

She spoke out clearly, letting her voice fill with a confidence she did not entirely feel. "To answer questions, Lord Eneah."

"Good. But you will keep to the point. You will not stray from the question you are asked. You understand?"

"I understand, my Lord."

"Good. Then let us begin. We have many questions to get through before we have finished here today."

As she climbed up into the sedan and pulled the curtain across, Anna felt a great weariness descend on her. For almost five hours she had stood there, without a break, answering their questions.

She sat down heavily in the cushioned seat, remembering.

Who was she? Where was she born? Who were her parents? What did her father do? To whom did he make his reports? What was Tadjinar like? What form of government did it have? Were there wars where she came from? Did they have machines? What power sources did they use? Were the men of her race honest?

Some of the questions were easy to answer. Others, like the last, were far more difficult. *Were* men honest? Some, like her father, were. But what of the traders in Jaarnindu Market? What of the inspectors and middlemen who worked for Lord Amanjira? She could hardly claim that *they* were honest. But the guildsman seemed to want a single answer to the question.

It was the young Guild Master, the one who had glared at her at the outset, who had been so insistent on this matter.

"Well, girl? *Are* all men honest?"

"No, my Lord. Not all men are honest."

"Then men are dishonest by nature?"

"Not all men."

"Come. You cannot have it both ways. Either they are—by nature—or they are not. Which is it?"

"Are all men in D'ni honest by nature, my Lord?"

There had been a sudden tension in the chamber. Lord Eneah stood, seeming suddenly a figure of great power.

"You are here to answer questions, not pose them."

She had bowed her head, and Lord Eneah, glaring at her, had signaled to his fellow Lords, ending the session. But there was to be another, tomorrow, and a further one if necessary— until she was bled dry of answers.

Anna slumped back against the cushion and closed her eyes as the sedan lifted and began its gentle rocking motion.

With her eyes closed she could see the young man vividly. Veovis, his name had been. He was a handsome, princely man, yet she had noted just how closely he had watched her throughout, the light of suspicion in his eyes at all times.

The other, who sat beside him, had often leaned toward Veovis, to catch a whispered word and sometimes nod. He seemed an ally of Veovis's, yet his eyes had never once held even the smallest hint of criticism of her. Nor had he asked a single question.

How strange, she thought, seeing his face clearly. A long, severe-looking face; not unattractive, yet not as obviously handsome as Veovis's. He seemed a studious type. But then, weren't all the D'ni studious?

The movement of the carriage lulled her. For a moment she dozed, then woke again, not knowing for an instant where she was.

Remembering, she found herself for the first time wondering just what use they would make of the answers she had given. She had seen the tunnels to the surface, and knew they were interested in what went on up there, but she could not make out just what they planned to do with the information she had given them. Some things seemed to have interested them more than others. For instance, they had seemed extremely interested in her answer as to whether her people were warlike or not. Did that mean they planned, perhaps, to invade the surface? Was that why the tunnels were there?

More to the point, did she really care? Lord Amanjira aside, she did not feel close to anyone in Tadjinar—no, nor in the entire empire. Those she had loved were dead. So did it matter?

Of course it matters, the voice inside her answered. *The weight of your words could determine the fate of empires. Besides, war of any kind is bad. Think of the suffering, Anna.*

The thought of it troubled her. Ought she, perhaps, to refuse to say anything more? Or had she said too much already?

The trouble was, she knew so little about these people. Whereas she had answered every question, they had taken great care to keep as much as possible from her. As if she were a spy.

Anna let out a long, sighing breath. Was that what they thought? That she had come to spy on them?

Were it not so serious a matter, she might have laughed. A spy! Why, the idea of it!

Yet even as she thought of it, she recalled the hostility in the young guildsman's face and wondered whether that might not be the cause.

They think I threaten them.

The thought was sobering. And suddenly, for the first time since those early days on Irrat, Anna began to wonder if her life was not possibly in danger.

"Well?" Lord Eneah asked later that evening when the Five were finally alone together, "Do you still think she is a threat, Nehir?"

Nehir, who had just taken a seat on the far side of the desk to Eneah, looked up, his pale eyes challenging.

"Not her, Eneah, but what she says. Personally, I think we have heard enough."

"I agree," Rakeri said, leaning forward in his chair. "What she is in herself does not concern us here; it is the threat that contact with her people might entail."

"You feel there is a genuine threat, then?"

Rakeri met Eneah's eyes and gave a single nod. "As you know, I did not agree with Veovis at first, but I feel my son's views have been fully vindicated. If what the girl says is true—and I believe it is—then the surface-dwellers are a backward, warlike, immoral race, whose every action is motivated by greed."

"You read that much into her words?"

"I did indeed. Why, her every utterance spoke of a deep corruption in their natures!"

"I agree," R'hira said quietly, speaking from his seat in the corner of the room. "I think we need hear no more. It would be folly even to think of establishing contact with the out-siders."

"And you, Sajka?"

Sajka, the most recently appointed of the Five, simply nodded.

"Then, so we shall propose." Eneah looked about him. "I shall summon the full Council to session tomorrow at tenth bell. There is, however, one small matter that still needs to be settled, and that is what to do with the girl."

"Send her back," Rakeri suggested.

"Far too risky," R'hira countered. "It is unlikely, I admit, but someone might believe her tale and come looking for us."

"Then maybe we should place her on a Prison Age," Nehir said. "It need not be a harsh one. Somewhere pleasant, possibly. We could even make a new one for her, if need be."

"Pleasant or otherwise, do you think that would be just reward for her honesty with us, Nehir?" Eneah's eyes went from one to another of their faces, silently questioning each in turn, then he nodded.

"So it is. The girl will stay here, in D'ni. We shall find a home for her, temporarily, until it is decided fully. Agreed?"

"Agreed."

"Agreed."

"Agreed."

Sajka, who had not spoken until then, looked about him, a wintry smile on his thin lips, and nodded. "Agreed."

Veovis was ecstatic. That evening he threw a celebratory party at an inn down by the harbor. Aitrus, who had never found time to visit such places, tried hard to make his excuses, but Veovis would have none of it.

And so Aitrus found himself wedged into a corner of a

huge dining room packed with busy tables, while all about him a dozen young guildsmen—some familiar to him, others only "faces"—dipped their goblets into the great central vat that rested at the table's center and drank to the young Lord's success.

"It was that final question that did it," Suahrnir said, his face glowing with excitement. "After that, it was a mere formality."

"Maybe so," Veovis said, standing up and looking to Aitrus across the table, "but let me say one thing that has not been said. I was wrong about the girl."

"Wrong?" several voices said as one.

Veovis raised his hands, palms out. "Hear me out, gentlemen! Before the hearing I was quite clear in my mind what kind of creature she would prove to be, and if you recall I was not hesitant in saying so!"

There was laughter at that and a great deal of nodding.

"However," Veovis went on, "I *was* wrong, and I am not too proud to admit it. Whatever the merits or otherwise of her race, the girl spoke well. Yes, and honestly, I warrant. I think we all sensed that."

There was a murmur of agreement and more nodding of heads.

"Word is," Veovis continued, "that she is to stay in D'ni. Now, whether that is for the common good or not remains to be seen, but so our Masters have decided, and I feel we should, this once, wait and see. That said, we must remain vigilant."

"What do you mean?" Veovis's constant companion, Lianis asked from where he sat to the left of the young Lord.

"I mean we ought not to let the girl become a focus for

any movement to reverse today's decision. No contact ought to mean exactly that. No contact."

"And if she proves such a focus, Veovis?" Suahrnir asked.

Veovis smiled and looked about him confidently. "Then we should act to have her removed from D'ni to some more suitable place."

Aitrus, who had been listening closely, frowned. A Prison Age, that was what Veovis meant. Yet he could not deny that his friend was being as fair as he could be, considering his views.

Aitrus reached out and took his goblet, cradling it to his chest. He was pleased that Veovis was so happy, yet he could not share their jubilation at today's decision. Perhaps it was as Veovis said, that he was letting sentiment cloud his better judgment, but part of him was still back there in the rock, making his way up to the surface, with Master Telanis and Jerahl and all the others who had gone on that youthful venture. Whatever he had become these past thirty years, he could not shed that earlier self.

Watching the girl speak, it had finally crystallized in him. He knew now that he wanted contact: wanted, more than anything, to stand up there and see, with his own eyes, what the surface was like.

But how could he say that to Veovis and remain his friend? For to Veovis the very idea of it was anathema.

"Guild Master Aitrus?"

The voice cut through the general babble of voices at the table. Aitrus looked up, expecting it to be one of the young guildsmen, then saw, just behind Lianis, a cloaked guildsman from the Guild of Messengers.

Silence fell around the table. Aitrus set down his goblet, then stood. "What is it?" he asked.

"An urgent message, Master," the Messenger answered, drawing off one of his gloves, then taking a sealed letter from his tunic pocket. "I was told to ensure that you act upon its contents immediately."

With a smile, Veovis put out a hand. "Here. I'll hand it to my friend."

The Messenger looked to Aitrus, who nodded. With a small bow to Veovis, he handed the letter to him, then stood back, pulling on his glove again.

Veovis turned back, then handed the letter across. "Urgent business, eh, old friend? That looks like Lord Eneah's seal."

Aitrus stared at the envelope a moment. Veovis was right. It was Lord Eneah's seal. But when he opened it, the note was not from Lord Eneah, but from his father.

He looked up. "Forgive me, Veovis, but I must leave at once."

"Is there trouble?" Veovis asked, genuinely concerned.

Aitrus swallowed. "It does not say."

"Then go," Veovis said, signaling to the others about the table to make way. "Go at once. But let me know, all right? If there is anything I can do . . ."

Aitrus, squeezing past his fellow guildsmen, gave a distracted nod. Then he was gone.

Veovis sat, staring across the crowded room, his face briefly clouded. Then, looking back at the others about the table, he smiled and raised his goblet. "To D'ni!" he exclaimed.

A dozen voices answered him robustly. *"To D'ni!"*

Kahlis stood in the entrance hall, pacing up and down, await-ing his son. It was midnight and the city bell was sounding across the lake.

As the last chime echoed into silence, he heard the outer gate creak back and hurried footsteps on the stone flags out-side. A shadow fell across the colored glass of the door panels.

Kahlis stepped across and drew the bolt, pulling the door open.

Aitrus stood there, wide-eyed and breathless. From the look of him he had run the last half mile.

"What's happened?" he said, looking past his father.

Kahlis closed the door. "Come upstairs, Aitrus."

They went up, into his study. Closing the door quietly, Kahlis turned to him.

"I have been asked to look after the outsider for a time. Lord Eneah summoned me this evening and asked me if I would take the girl, Ah-na, into my household, as a temporary measure. Until better arrangements can be made. He asked me because he understood my concern for the young woman."

"And you want me to agree to this?"

"Yes."

"Then I agree."

Kahlis went to speak again, then realized what his son had said. "You agree?"

"I take it Mother has agreed. And you must have, else you would not be asking me."

In answer Kahlis went over to the door and opened it, then called down the steps. "Tasera!"

His mother's head and shoulders appeared at the foot of the stairs.

"Tasera," Kahlis said, "bring the young lady. I wish to introduce her to our son."

As she stepped into the book-filled study, Anna looked about her warily.

"Aitrus," Kahlis said, "this is Ah-na. She is to be our house guest for a time."

Aitrus bowed his head respectfully. "I am glad you will be staying with us."

"Thank you," she said, their eyes meeting briefly as he lifted his head again. "I am grateful for your kindness in letting me stay."

"You are welcome," Tasera interrupted, coming across to take Anna's arm. "Now if you would excuse us, I must see Ah-na to her room."

The brevity of the welcome surprised her; yet she turned and followed the woman out and down the corridor.

"Here," Tasera said, opening a door and putting out an arm. "This will be your room."

Anna stepped inside, surprised. Compared to the Lodge, it was luxurious. Anna turned and bowed her head.

"You are too kind, Tasera. Much too kind."

Aitrus was walking across the open space between the main Guild House and the Great Library when Veovis stepped from a group of guildsmen and made to intercept him. It was more than a week since they had last met, in the inn beside the harbor.

"Aitrus! Did you get my note?"

Aitrus stopped. "Your note . . . Ah, yes. I have been busy."

Veovis smiled, putting out his hands to Aitrus who took them in a firm grip.

"So what is she like?"

"She seems . . . polite. Well mannered."

"Seems?"

Aitrus found himself oddly defensive. "It's my impression."

"Then you think she is genuine?"

"Didn't *you*? I thought you said as much?"

Veovis smiled, defusing the situation. "That was *my* impression, I grant you. But then, I am not living with her—day in, day out. If there are any cracks in that mask of hers, you would see them, no?"

"If there were."

"Oh, I am not saying that there *are*. It's just . . . "

"Just what?"

"Just that we ought to be totally certain, don't you think?"

For some reason the idea of checking up on the girl offended Aitrus.

"She seems . . . unsettled," he said, after a moment, wanting to give Veovis something.

"Unsettled? How?"

"Maybe it is just the strangeness of everything here. It must be hard to adapt to D'ni after living under an open sky."

"Does she miss her home?"

"I am not sure. To be honest, I have not asked her."

Veovis laughed. "What you really mean is that you have not spoken to her yet."

"As I said, I have been busy. Helping my father, mainly."

Veovis stared at Aitrus a moment, then reached out and held his arm. "You should take a break some time, Aitrus. And when you do, come and visit me, on K'veer. And bring the girl."

"That would be nice."

"Soon, then," Veovis said, and without another word, he turned and walked away.

Aitrus watched Veovis a moment—saw him return to the group he had left earlier, greeting them again, at ease among them—then smiled to himself as he walked away. To be honest, he had dreaded meeting Veovis again, knowing how Veovis felt about the "outsider." He had thought, perhaps, that his friend would be angry that the girl was staying with his family, but his fears, it seemed, had been illusory.

His smile broadened as he hastened his pace, knowing he was late now for his meeting.

K'veer. It would be nice to take the girl to see K'veer.

The room was a workroom or lab of some kind. Anna hesitated, looking behind her at the empty corridor, then slipped inside, pulling the door closed.

You should not be in here, Anna, she told herself, yet that old familiar compulsion to explore was on her. Besides, she would not stay long, and she would not disturb anything.

There was a long, stone-topped bench along the left-hand side of the room, a big low table in the middle, complete with sinks and gas taps. On the far wall a number of small shelves held all manner of jars and bottles. To the right of the room, in the far corner, was a desk and a chair, and on the wall above a set of shelves on which were many notebooks.

She put her hand out, touching the cool, hard surface of the bench. It had been scrubbed clean and when she lifted her hand, she could smell a strange scent to it. What was that? Coal tar? Iodine?

Slowly she walked about the room, picking things up then placing them back. Most of the equipment was familiar, yet there were one or two things that were strange to her. One in particular caught her attention. It was a small bronze jar with eight lips, beneath each of which was a tiny bowl. A bronze ball sat on a tiny stand at the very center of the jar, balanced above all else.

Anna crouched down, onto its level, staring at it for a time, then walked on, over to the far corner of the room.

Only two things were on the surface of the desk; an elaborately decorated inkstand made of fine blue jade and, just beside the stand, a pair of glasses.

Anna picked them up and studied them. The lenses were thick and seemed to be constructed of several very fine layers that acted as light filters of some kind. About each of the lenses was a tight band of expandable material which, in turn, was surrounded by a thick leather band, studded with tiny metal controls. She adjusted them, noting how they changed the opacity of the lenses, and smiled to herself. Then, on a whim, she tried them on. Strange. They were very tight. Airtight, probably, on the person for whom they were designed. And, wearing them, it became very dark.

Again she adjusted the controls, varying the light.

Taking them off, she set them down again, wondering what precisely they were used for. Mining? To protect the eyes against chips of rock? But if so, then why the varying opacity?

Anna half-turned toward the door, listening for a moment, then, turning back to face the shelves, she reached up and took one of the journals down. Inside the pages were filled with strange writing, totally unlike any script she had ever seen before. Flicking through a few pages she stopped, staring in admiration at a diagram on the right-hand page. There were more farther on, all of them intricately drawn, the lines fine yet dark, the shading subtle. They spoke of a highly organized mind.

She closed the journal and set it back in its place, then, with a final look about her, hurried from the room.

It was no good. She would have to do something or she would die of boredom.

Distracted, she almost bowled into Aitrus.

"Come," he said quietly. "We need to speak."

Anna followed him, surprised. He had barely said a word to her all week. She was even more surprised when he led her along the corridor and into the workroom she had been exploring.

Did he know? Was that what this was about?

Inside, Aitrus closed the door, then gestured for her to take the chair beside the desk. He seemed awkward.

"Here," he said, turning to reach up and take down one of the books that were on the topmost shelf. He offered it to her. "That is a history of D'ni. It is a child's book, of course, but . . . "

Aitrus stopped. She was staring at the pages blankly.

"What is it?"

She looked up at him, then, closing the book, handed it back to him. "I cannot read this."

"But I thought . . . " He shook his head, then, "You mean, you learned to *speak* D'ni, but not to read it?"

Anna nodded.

Aitrus stared at the book a moment, then set it down and turned, searching among the bottom shelves until he found something. It was a big, square-covered book with a dark amber leather cover. He pulled it out from among the other books; turning, he offered it to Anna.

"Here. This is the key to all."

Anna took it, studying the beautifully tooled leather cover a moment before opening it. Inside, on heavy vellum pages, were set out columns of beautifully intricate figures—more like designs than letters.

She looked up at him and smiled. "Is this what I think it is? Is this the D'ni lexicon?"

"The *Rehevkor*," he said, nodding.

She looked back at the page, smiling sadly now. "But I do not know what they mean."

"Then I shall teach you," Aitrus said, his pale eyes watching her seriously.

"Are you sure that is allowed?"

"No," he answered, "but I will teach you anyway."

Anna sat at the prow of the boat as it approached the island, Aitrus just behind her, standing, his right hand resting lightly on the rail.

"So that is K'veer," she said quietly. "I saw it once before, when they brought me from Irrat."

Aitrus nodded. "It has been their family home for many years."

"I remember thinking how strange it was. Like a great drill bit poking up from the bottom of the lake."

He smiled at that.

"So who is this Veovis?"

"He is the son of Lord Rakeri, Grand Master of the Guild of Miners."

"And he, too, is a Miner?"

"No. Veovis is a Master of the Guild of Writers."

"You have a Guild of Writers? Are they important?"

"Oh, very much so. Perhaps the most important of all our guilds."

"*Writers?*"

He did not answer her.

She looked back at him surprised. Slowly the island grew, dominating the view ahead of them.

"Has Veovis many brothers and sisters?"

"None. He is an only child."

"Then why so huge a mansion?"

"Lord Rakeri often entertains guests. Or did before his illness."

Anna was quiet for a time as they drifted slowly toward the island. There was a small harbor directly ahead of them now, and beneath a long, stone jetty, a dark, rectangular opening.

"Does your friend Veovis dislike me?"

The question surprised Aitrus. "Why do you ask?"

"I ask because he stared at me throughout the hearing."

"Is that so unusual? I stared."

"Yes, but not as he did. He seemed hostile toward me. And his questions . . . "

"What of his questions?"

She shrugged, then, "Did he ask you to bring me?"

"He invited you specifically."

"I see."

Yet she seemed strangely distant, and Aitrus, watching her, wondered what was going on in her head. He wanted Veovis and her to be friends. It would be so easy if they were friends, but as it was he felt awkward.

"Veovis can be outspoken sometimes."

"Outspoken?"

"I thought I ought to warn you, that's all. He can be a little blunt, even insensitive at times, but he is well meaning. You should not be afraid of him."

Anna gave a little laugh. "I am not afraid, Aitrus. Not of Veovis, anyway."

They spent hours, it seemed, just going from room to room in the great mansion that was built into the rock of K'veer, Veovis delighting in showing Anna every nook and cranny.

At first Anna had been wary, but as time went on she seemed to succumb to the young Lord's natural charm, and Aitrus, looking on, found himself relaxing.

As they climbed the final flight of steps that led onto the veranda at the top of the island, Aitrus found himself wondering how he could ever have worried about these two not getting along.

"The stone seemed fused," Anna was saying, as they came out through the low arch and into the open again. "It is almost as if it has been melted and then molded."

"That is *precisely* what has happened," Veovis answered her with an unfeigned enthusiasm. "It is a special D'ni process, the secret of which is known only to the guilds concerned."

They stepped out, into the center of the veranda. There was a tiled roof overhead, but the view was open now on all four sides. All about them the lake stretched away, while in the distance they could see the great twisted rock of Ae'Gura and, to its right, the city.

They were high up here, but the great walls of the cavern stretched up far above them, while overhead there were faint clouds, like feathered cirrus. Anna laughed.

"What is it?" Veovis asked.

"It's just that I keep thinking I am outside. Oh, the light is very different, but . . . well, it's just so big."

Veovis looked to Aitrus and smiled, then gestured toward a group of lounging chairs that rested at one end of the veranda.

"Shall we sit here for a while? I can have the servants bring us something."

"That would be nice," Anna said, looking to Aitrus and smiling.

As Veovis went to arrange refreshments, Anna and Aitrus sat.

"He's very pleasant," she said quietly. "I can understand why he is your friend."

"So you've forgiven him?"

"Forgiven him?"

"For scowling at you."

"Ah . . . " Anna laughed. "Long ago."

Aitrus smiled. "I'm glad, you know."

"Really?"

"Yes. I wanted you to be friends. It would have been hard otherwise."

Anna frowned. "I didn't know."

"I . . . "

He fell silent. Veovis had returned. The young lord came across and, taking the chair between them, looked from one to another.

His eyes settled on Anna. "Can I be honest with you, Ah-na?"

Anna looked up. "Honest? In what way?"

Veovis grinned. "We are alike, you and I. We are both straightforward people." He looked pointedly at Aitrus. "*Blunt*, some call it. But let me say this. I was not disposed to like you. Indeed, I was prepared to actively *dislike* you. But I must speak as I find, and I find that I like you very much."

She gave the smallest little nod. "Why, thank you, Lord Veovis."

"Oh, do not thank me, Ah-na. I did not *choose* to like you. But like you I do. And so we can be friends. But I must make one or two things clear. I am D'ni. And I am jealous of all things D'ni. We are a great and proud people. Remember that, Ah-na. Remember that at all times."

Anna stared at him a moment, surprised by that strange and sudden coldness in him, then answered him.

"And I, my Lord, am human, and proud of being so. Remember *that*," she smiled pointedly, "at all times."

Veovis sat back, his eyes studying Anna thoughtfully. Then, more cheerfully than before, he smiled and slapped his knees. "Well . . . let us forget such somber stuff. Aitrus . . . how go the plans for the new cavern?"

On the journey home Anna was silent, locked in private thoughts. Aitrus, sitting across from her, felt more than ever how alien their worlds were. What, after all, did they really know about each other?

"Ah-na?"

She looked up, a deep melancholy in her eyes. "Yes?"

"What would you like to do?"

Anna turned her head, staring out across the lake. "I'd like to understand it all, that's what. To know where all the food comes from. It mystifies me. It's like something's missing and I can't see what it is."

"And you want me to tell you what it is?"

She looked to him. "Yes, I do. I want to know what the secret is."

He smiled. "This evening," he said mysteriously, sitting back and folding his arms. "I'll take you there this evening."

Aitrus unlocked the door, then stood back.

"You want me to go inside?"

He nodded.

Anna shrugged. She had noticed the door before now. It had always been locked, and she had assumed it was a store cupboard of some kind. But inside it was a normal room, except that in the middle of the floor was a marble plinth, and on the plinth was an open book—a huge, leatherbound book.

Anna looked to Aitrus. "What is this room?"

Aitrus locked the door then turned to her again. "This is the Book Room."

"But there is only one book."

He nodded, then, with a seriousness she had not expected, said, "You must tell no one that you came here. Not even my mother and father. Do you understand?"

"Are we doing something wrong?"

"No. Yet it may be forbidden."

"Then perhaps . . . "

"No, Ah-na. If you are to live here, you must understand. You have too simple a view of who we are. It . . . *disfigures* your understanding of us."

Disfigures. It was a strange word to use. Anna stared at him, then shook her head. "You frighten me, Aitrus."

Aitrus stepped up to the plinth and stared down at the book fondly.

Anna stepped alongside him, looking down at the open pages. The left-hand page was blank, but on the right . . .

Anna gasped. "It's like a window."

"Yes," he said simply. "Now give me your hand."

Anna felt the surface of her palm tingle, then, with a sudden, sickening lurch, she felt herself drawn into the page. It grew even as she shrank, sucking her into the softly glowing image.

For a moment it was as if she were melting, fusing with the ink and paper, and then, with a suddenness that was shocking, she was herself again, in her own body.

Only she was no longer in the room.

The air was fresh and heavy with pollen. A faint breeze blew from the shelf of rock just in front of her. And beyond it . . .

Beyond it was a vividly blue sky.

Her mouth fell open in astonishment, even as Aitrus shimmered into solidity beside her.

He put his hand out, holding her arm as a wave of giddiness swept over her. She would have fallen but for him. Then it passed and she looked at him again, her words an awed whisper.

"Where are we?"

"Ko'ah," he said. "This is my family's Age."

Anna stood on the top of the escarpment, looking out over a rich, verdant landscape that took her breath away, it was so beautiful. Flat, rolling pasture was broken here and there by tiny coppices, while close by the foot of the hill on which she stood, a broad, slow-moving river wound its way out across the plain, small grassy moundlike islands embedded like soft green jewels in its sunlit surface.

To her right a line of mountains marched into the distance, birds circling in the clear blue sky above them.

Sunlight beat down on her neck and shoulders; not the fierce, destructive heat of the desert but a far softer, more pleasant warmth.

"Well?" Aitrus asked, from where he sat, just behind her, staring out through the strange, heavy glasses that he now wore. "What do you think of Ko'ah?"

Anna turned, looking back at him. "I think you have enchanted me. Either that or I am still in bed and dreaming."

Aitrus reached out and plucked a nearby flower, then handed it to her. She took the pale blue bud and lifted it to her nose, inhaling its rich, perfumed scent.

"Are your dreams as *real* as this?"

She laughed. "No." Then, more seriously, "You said you would explain."

Reaching into his pocket, Aitrus took out a small, leather-bound book. He stared at it a moment, then handed it to her.

"Is this another of those books?" she asked, opening it and seeing that it contained D'ni writing.

"It is. But different from the one we used to come here. This book links back to D'ni. It is kept here, in the small cave we went to.

"The words in that book describe the place to which we link back—the study in my family's mansion in D'ni. It was *written* there. Without it we would be trapped here."

"I see," she said, staring at the thin volume with new respect. "But where exactly are we? Are we in the pages of a book, or are we actually *somewhere?*"

His smile was for her quickness. "There is, perhaps, some way of calculating precisely where we are—by the night-time stars, maybe—but all that can be said for certain is that we are elsewhere. In all likelihood, we are on the other side of the universe from D'ni."

"Impossible."

"You could say that. But look about you, Anna. This world is the Age that is described in the book back in the room in D'ni. It conforms *precisely* to the details in that book. In an infinite universe, all things are possible—within physical limits, that is—and any book that *can* be written *does* physically exist. Somewhere. The book is the bridge between the words and the physical actuality. Word and world are linked by the special properties of the book."

"It sounds to me like magic."

Aitrus smiled. "Maybe. But we have long since stopped thinking of it as such. Writing such books is a difficult task. One cannot simply write whatever comes into one's head. There are strict rules and guidelines, and the learning of those rules is a long and arduous business."

"Ah," she said. "I understand now."

"Understand what?"

"What you said about Writers. I thought . . . " Anna laughed. "You know, Aitrus, I would never have guessed. Never in a thousand years. I thought you D'ni were a dour, inward-looking people. But this . . . well . . . you are true visionaries!"

Aitrus laughed.

"Why, the great cavern in D'ni is like a giant skull, filled with busy thoughts, and these books—well, they are like the dreams and visions that comes from such intense mental activity!"

Aitrus stared at her a moment, then shook his head. "You are amazing, Ah-na. Why, I have lived in D'ni more than fifty years and never once have I thought of such a thing!"

"Different eyes," she said, looking pointedly at him, "that's all it is. Sometimes it takes a total stranger to see the obvious."

"Perhaps so."

"But tell me, Aitrus. You spoke of the book's special properties. What exactly did you mean?"

He looked away. "Forgive me, Ah-na, but perhaps I have already said too much. Such things are great secrets. Grave and greatly guarded secrets, known to only the Guilds."

"Like the Guild of Ink-Makers?"

Aitrus glanced at her, then smiled. "Yes, and the Guild of Books who manufacture the paper . . . and, of course, the Guild of Writers."

"And the writing in the books . . . is it different from the writing you have been teaching me?"

"Yes."

For a moment Anna stared at the book in her hands; then, closing it up, she handed it back to him.

She turned, looking about her once again, savoring the feel of the cool and gentle breeze on her arms and neck. Her hand went to her neck, drawing back the fine silk of her long, lustrously dark hair.

"It must have been cruel for you," Aitrus said, watching her, a strange expression coming to his eyes, "being locked up."

"It was." She glanced around at him, then smiled—a bright smile, full of the day's sunlight. "But let's forget that now. Come, Aitrus. Let us go down to the river."

That evening neither Aitrus nor Anna spoke a word about their visit to Ko'ah. But later, in her room, the impossibility of it struck Anna forcibly. She sat on the edge of the bed, her mouth open in astonished recollection.

In that instant after she had "linked," she had never felt more scared. No, nor more exhilarated. And the world itself. *Ko'ah.* Sitting there, she could scarcely believe that she had really been there. It had seemed so strange and dreamlike. Yet in a small glass vase on the table at her side was the pale blue flower Aitrus had given her.

Anna leaned close, inhaling its scent.

It had been real. As real as this. The very existence of the flower was proof of it. But how could that be? How could simple words link to other places?

On their return from Ko'ah, Aitrus had shown her the Book, patiently taking her through page after page, and showing her how such an Age was "made." She had seen at once the differences between this archaic form and the ordinary written speech of D'ni, noting how it was not merely more elaborate but more specific: a language of precise yet subtle descriptive power. Yet seeing was one thing, believing another. Given all the evidence, her rational mind still fought against accepting it.

Beside the Book itself, Aitrus had gone on to show her the books of commentary—three in all, the last containing barely a dozen entries. All Books, he said, were accompanied by such commentaries, which were notes and observations on the Ages. Some of the more ancient Ages—like Nidur Gemat—had hundreds of books of commentary.

She had asked him about it.

"Nidur Gemat?"

"It is one of six worlds belonging to Veovis's family."

"Ah, I see. And do all the D'ni own such Ages?"

"No. Only the older families own such Ages. The rest—the common people of D'ni—use the Book Rooms."

"You mean, there are common worlds, that everyone can visit?"

"Yes. In fact, until my father became Grand Master of our guild, we did not have our own Age. Ko'ah was written for my father twenty years ago."

"And before that?"

"We would visit the Guild Ages. Or Ages owned by friends."

Anna had smiled at that. "That is some incentive."

"Incentive?"

"To work hard and make one's way in the guild. Is there no resentment among the common people?"

Aitrus had shrugged. "Not that I know of. The Common Ages are free to everyone. It is not as if they are denied."

"No, but . . . " She had let the matter drop, returning her attention to the first of the books of commentary. "What is this?" she had asked after a moment, looking up at him, again.

There had been a stamped impression on the page, beneath a paragraph of small, neat writing in a bright green ink.

"That is an inspection. By the Guild of Maintainers. They ensure that all Ages are maintained according to Guild laws."

"And if they are not?"

"Then the Book can be confiscated and the owner punished."

"Does that happen often?"

"Not often. All know the penalty for misdemeanors. To own an Age is an immense responsibility. Few are trusted."

"And yet you took me there."

He had hesitated, then looking at her directly, he had nodded. "Yes, I did," he said.

Anna slept well that night, and if she dreamed she did not recall it when she woke. Refreshed, she sat up, looking across at the delicate blue flower in its vase beside her bed, her mind at once filled with the wonder of what she had witnessed the day before.

Aitrus was not at breakfast, and at first she thought that maybe he had left early to go to the Guild Hall, but then, at the last moment, as she was finishing her meal, he rushed into the room in a state of immense excitement.

"Anna! Wonderful news! Veovis is to be given a *Korfah V'ja!*"

She stared at him uncomprehendingly.

He laughed. "I'm sorry. The Korfah V'ja is a special ceremony to mark the Guild's acceptance of his Book—his first Master work, that is. It is a momentous event. Few guildsmen are ever given one, and Veovis is immensely young to have been granted such an honor!"

"And Veovis . . . he *wrote* this Book? Like the Age we went to?"

Aitrus nodded. "Only much better. Incomparably better."

The thought of that made her reassess Lord Veovis. She had thought him merely a rich man's son, a politician. She had not even considered that he was also a "creator," let alone a great one.

"Then it will be a great occasion, no?"

"The greatest for many a year. All of D'ni society will be there. And you must come with us, Anna!"

She looked down. Usually she hated social occasions, but the thought of seeing all of D'ni society—and of meeting Lord Veovis once again—filled her with a strange excitement.

"When is to be?" she asked, looking back at Aitrus.

237

"A week from now," he answered. "On the anniversary of Kerath's home-coming."

It was a small ceremony. The six Assistant Grand Masters and the Grand Master, Lord Sajka himself, stood in a half circle on the great platform, while the celebrant, Veovis, stood before them, his Book, the work of sixteen long years, on the podium before him.

The day was bright and springlike, the blue sky dotted with clouds. In the distance, snow-capped mountains marched toward the south and the great ocean. Below them the great plains stretched away to east and west and south, while to the north the ancient settlement of Derisa was tucked into a fold of hills.

This was the oldest of the guild's many Ages—the Age of Yakul, made by the first great Writer of the Guild, Ar'tenen, and here, traditionally, the first official ceremony took place.

There would be a second, more public, ceremony later, on Veovis's own world of Ader Jamat, at which this moment would be reenacted for all to see, but this seemingly low-key event was by far the more important.

Each of the seven senior members of the guild had read the great work that was today accepted into the guild's own canon, and each had given their separate approval for this ulti-mate recognition of the young Guild Master's talent. It was 187 years since the last Korfah V'ja and it would be many years before another. Only ninety-three Books had been accepted into the canon in the whole of the long history of the guild—among them the Five Great Classics of D'ni—and only four guildsmen had ever received this honor younger than the man who now stood before them. Among those four was the legendary Ri'Neref.

A faint breeze gusted across the open space, rustling their cloaks, as Lord Sajka, Grand Master of the Guild of Writers, stepped forward and, in a tongue as distinct from the common speech of D'ni as that of the surface-dwellers, pronounced the Words of Binding.

And then it was done. As Veovis bowed his head to his peers, Lord Sajka smiled and, in the common speech, said:

"Well done, Veovis. We are all immensely proud of you."

Veovis looked up and smiled, conscious of the great honor being accorded him.

"My Lord, Guild Masters . . . I hope to prove worthy of your approval. It is a great privilege to be a member of the Guild of Writers, and I count myself blessed the day I chose to enter it."

And so it was done.

As, one by one, the elders linked back to D'ni, Veovis turned and looked about him at the ancient world of Yakul, and wondered if, one day, several thousand years hence, some other guildsman would stand on an Age he had written and wonder, as he now wondered, what kind of man it was whose imagination had wrought the connections to such a world as this.

He turned and walked over to the Linking Book. It was time to return to D'ni, to pause and reflect before beginning the next chapter in his life. For his next work would be something other, he was determined on it; not just a great work but a classic.

But before all, celebration. For today was his day. Today he became a great man, honored before all D'ni.

Veovis placed his hand against the glowing panel and linked, a smile appearing on his lips even as his figure shimmered and then faded into the air.

On the boat across to K'veer, Anna began to have second thoughts about meeting so many strangers at the ceremony.

With Aitrus it was fine, for it was only the two of them, as it had been with her father, but with all others, even with Aitrus's parents, she felt ill at ease. She was not by any means a social creature. How she should act and what she should say, these things were a complete mystery to her.

It does not matter, Aitrus had said to her. *They do not expect you to behave as they behave.*

Now, as the island grew nearer and she could see the great host of boats queuing to enter the tiny harbor, she felt her nervousness return.

Last night, before her conversation with Aitrus, there had been a strange little scene in Kahlis's study. Knowing that his father knew nothing of their ventures into Ko'ah, Aitrus had had his father "explain" about Books to Anna, and she, schooled by Aitrus in what to say and how to react, had pretended that it was all completely new to her.

Kahlis had clearly been concerned; not only at Anna's

possible reaction but by the problem of just how *much* to tell her. Aitrus, however, had convinced him that had Lord Eneah not meant her to know, then he would have given explicit instructions to that effect. Kahlis would, indeed, have gone to see Lord Eneah had the great man not taken to his bed again with a recurrence of his illness.

And so Kahlis had "prepared" her, telling her that she must expect a great surprise, and that she was not to be afraid, for all that she would experience was quite normal. And she, prompted by Aitrus, had feigned that she understood, even though she would barely have recognized the process of "linking" from the description Aitrus's father had given her. It had been vague almost to the point of willfulness.

As their boat joined the great queue of boats, Anna could see, on the decks, endless guildsmen and their wives and sons and daughters, all of them dressed in their best finery. Looking at them, Anna felt her spirits sink again. She should never have come. Then her father's voice sounded clearly in her head.

Don't worry, Anna. Just be yourself.

It was almost an hour before their boat drew up alongside the stone jetty and they climbed the dark granite steps, up onto the marble-flagged forecourt. Facing them was the carved stone gate that surrounded the massive doorway.

Anna had seen K'veer by day and it had seemed a strange yet pleasant edifice, but at night it seemed a wholly forbidding place. As they approached the doorway, Aitrus came alongside her.

"Forgive me, Ah-na," he said quietly, "but we must conform to certain formalities. When we are inside, you will draw back and wait a moment while my father and I are greeted. Then it will be your turn."

Inside the great atrium, Anna did as she was told, holding back beside Tasera as Aitrus and his father stepped forward and were presented by the Chief Steward to Rakeri and his son.

Anna saw once more that curious taking of both hands that was the D'ni way of greeting, the fingers linked; witnessed the smiles, the easy banter between the two sets of men, and knew that this was a world she would never enter, book or no book.

As Kahlis turned, Tasera nudged her gently. "Ah-na."

Veovis was smiling pleasantly, his attention half on what was being said, half on greeting the next guests. As he looked across and his eyes met hers, the smile faded. There was a moment's consideration and then he turned to Kahlis.

"Forgive me, Master Kahlis, but might I have a word with you, in private?"

Kahlis looked to his son, then shrugged. "Of course, Veovis."

Veovis turned and bowed to Rakeri. "If you would forgive us a moment, Father? I shall not be long."

Tasera and Anna had stopped, yards distant of Lord Rakeri. As Veovis and Kahlis walked away, Aitrus stared after them, perturbed. Rakeri himself was simply mystified.

There was an embarrassed silence. Rakeri looked to Tasera and smiled weakly. Aitrus simply stared at the door through which Veovis and his father had passed. A moment later the two men returned, his father clearly embarrassed by something. Coming over to Aitrus, he drew him aside.

"It seems there has been a misunderstanding," he began. "I took the invitation to include our house guest, Ah-na, but it was not meant so."

Aitrus, who had been listening to his father's words, glanced over at Veovis, who stood beside his father, wearing a determined look.

"A misunderstanding?" Aitrus tried to keep calm, tried not to let his anger show.

"Yes," Kahlis said. "Ah-na can stay here, in the house. Veovis has promised that his servants will make sure she has everything she wants. But she cannot go through into Ader Jamat."

"Why not?"

Kahlis raised a hand, bidding him be silent. "Because she is not D'ni."

Aitrus felt the anger boil up inside him. Keeping his voice low, he leaned close to Kahlis. "This is not right, Father."

"Maybe," Kahlis conceded, "but it is Lord Veovis's decision who enters his Age, not ours, and we must respect that."

"I see."

"I'm glad you do. Now will you tell her, Aitrus?"

Aitrus stared back at him a moment, then looked down. "You must forgive me, Father. I respect you deeply, and love you, but in this I must disobey you. This is wrong."

"Aitrus . . ."

But Aitrus turned and walked across to where Rakeri and Veovis stood. "Forgive me, Lord Rakeri, but I have been suffering from an illness these past few weeks. It has left me feeling rather weak . . . light-headed." He glanced at Veovis, who was watching him hawkishly now. "I feel it coming on now, and beg you to excuse me."

Rakeri, who had no idea what was going on, gave a tiny bow of his head. "I commiserate, Aitrus, but maybe my house surgeon could help?"

"That is kind of you, my Lord, but I really ought to go home."

Rakeri shook his head, a look of disappointment in his eyes. "I am sorry about that. I had hoped to talk with you."

Aitrus bowed low, then turned to Veovis. "And may good fortune shine down on you, Veovis. I am sorry that I cannot be there for the celebration of your Korfah V'ja."

There was a black anger now behind Veovis's eyes, yet if he felt like saying something, he kept it well in check. He nodded curtly.

Aitrus stood there a moment longer, wondering whether something more ought to be said; then, knowing that the situation was irreparable, he turned on his heel and walked across to where Anna stood beside his mother.

"Aitrus," Tasera said, her curiosity almost overwhelming her by now, "what is going on?"

"Ah-na and I are leaving," he said, making no attempt to explain how things were. "Ask Father."

Anna was staring at him now, bemused. "Aitrus? What's happening?"

"Later," he said, then took her arm and turned her, leading her out through the gathered ranks of guildsmen and their families, heading back toward the boat.

Aitrus was standing at the stern of the boat, chewing on a thumbnail and staring back at the great rock of K'veer as it slid into the darkened distance.

"You do not want to know."

Anna, sitting just below him, let out an exasperated sigh. "I am not blind, Aitrus. I saw how Veovis looked at you."

"There was a misunderstanding."

Anna waited, conscious of how pained he was by all this. After a moment he spoke again.

"He said you were not invited."

"Ah . . . I see."

"He said it was because you were not D'ni."

"That much is undeniable."

Aitrus was silent a moment, then, "It was an impossible situation, Ah-na. He made me choose."

"And you chose me?"

"Yes."

"Why?"

"Because he was not right to make me choose."

Anna was dressing the next morning when there was a hammering on the door downstairs. It was still very early and it was unusual for anyone to call at this hour. Going over to her door, she opened it a crack, listening.

There was a murmured exchange between Kahlis and his steward. Then,

"Here? Are you sure?"

There was silence for a moment, then:

"Lord Veovis! Welcome! To what do we owe this most pleasant surprise?"

"I have come to see your son, Master Kahlis. Is he at home?"

"He is. I shall go and see if he has risen. If you would take a seat, meanwhile. I'll not be long."

A hand briefly brushed her arm. She turned, her heart thumping, and found herself staring into Aitrus's face.

"Aitrus!"

"Will you come down with me, Ah-na?"

She hesitated, then shook her head. "This is between you two."

"No. This is about *you*, Ah-na. You ought to be there."

Veovis stood as they stepped into the room.

"Aitrus," he said, coming across the room, both hands extended. "Will you forgive me?"

Aitrus took his hands, tentatively at first, then with a greater firmness.

"That depends."

"I understand. I handled things badly. I know that, and I am sorry for it." He looked past Aitrus to where Anna stood. "And you, Ah-na. I owe you an apology, too."

"You do, indeed," Aitrus said sternly.

Veovis nodded, accepting the rebuke. "Yes. And that is why I have brought you a present. To try to make amends."

He turned and, going back across, picked up a box and brought it back, handing it to Anna. It was a small, square box with tiny airholes in one side of it.

She stared at it a moment, then untied the bright red ribbon and lifted the lid . . . and then looked up at Veovis, laughing.

"Why, it's beautiful! What is it?"

Carefully, cupping it in one hand, she lifted out a tiny creature—a veritable fur ball, its long silky coat the dark, brown-black of rich loam. Its large, cobalt-colored eyes stared up at her.

"It is a reekoo," Veovis said. "It comes from Ader Jamat."

Aitrus, who had turned to look, now smiled. "Thank you. It was a kind thought."

Veovis sighed, then, somberly. "I am sorry you were not there last night, Aitrus."

"And I. Yet we must resolve this matter, no?"

Anna, who was stroking the rippled, leathery neck of the tiny creature, looked up, glancing from one to the other. So it was not settled, even now.

Veovis took a long breath, then nodded. "Tonight," he said. "Come to my rooms. We'll talk about it then."

It was very late when he came back that night. Anna waited up, listening as his footsteps came up the stairs. As he made to pass her room, she opened the door and stepped out.

"Aitrus?" she whispered.

Aitrus turned. He looked weary.

"Is everything all right now?"

He stared at her, then, "You had better come to my study, Ah-na. We need to talk."

The words seemed ominous. Anna nodded, then followed him down the long corridor and into his room.

"Well?" she asked, as she took a chair, facing him.

Aitrus shrugged. "I am afraid Veovis is intractable."

"Intractable? In what way? You are friends again, are you not?"

"Perhaps. But he will not bend on one important matter."

"And that is?"

Aitrus looked down glumly. "He says that as you are not D'ni, he will not countenance you going into an Age, no, nor of learning *anything* about D'ni books. He claims it is not right."

"Then you said nothing of our visit to Ko'ah?"

Aitrus hesitated, then shook his head.

"Can I ask why? It is unlike you to be so indirect."

"Maybe. But I had no will to fight Veovis a second time."

"So did you promise him anything?"

"No. I said only that I would consider what he said."

"And was that enough for him?"

"For now."

She stared at him a moment, then, "So what *have* you decided?"

His eyes met hers again. "Can I hide nothing from you, Ah-na?"

"No. But then you have had little practice in hiding what you feel from people, Aitrus."

Aitrus stared at her for a long time, then sighed. "So you think I should abandon my plan?"

"Your plan?"

In answer, he opened the top right-hand drawer of his desk and took out a big, leather-bound book. It was a *book*—a D'ni book—she could see that at a glance. But when he opened it, there was no box on the front right-hand page, and the inside pages were blank.

She stared at it. "What is it?"

"It is a *Kortee'nea,*" he said. "A blank book, waiting to be written."

Anna looked up, her mouth falling open slightly.

"I have had it for a year now," he answered. "I have been making notes toward an Age. One I myself am writing. And I thought ... well, I thought that perhaps you might like to help me. But now ... "

She saw what he meant. There was a choice. Defy Veovis and lie about what they were doing, or go along with Veovis's wishes and deny themselves this.

"And what do you want, Aitrus?" she asked quietly, her dark eyes probing his. "What do you *really* want?"

"I want to teach you everything," he said. "Everything I know."

In the months that followed, the relationship between Aitrus and Veovis was strained. As if both sensed that all was not well between them, they kept much to themselves. It was a situation that could not last long, however, and a chance remark to Veovis by a young man from the Guild of Maintainers brought things to a head once more.

Aitrus was in his rooms at the Guild Hall, when Veovis burst in upon him unannounced.

"Is it true?" Veovis demanded, leaning across the desk.

Aitrus stared at his old friend in amazement. Veovis's face was suffused with anger. The muscles stood out at his neck.

"Is *what* true?"

"The girl . . . the outsider . . . are you teaching her to Write? How could you, Aitrus! After all you promised!"

"I promised nothing. I said only that I would consider your words."

"That's pure sophistry, and you know it! You lied to me, Aitrus. You lied and deceived me. And not only me, but D'ni itself!"

"Now come," Aitrus said, standing.

"You are a traitor, Aitrus! And you can be sure I shall be taking this matter before the Council!"

And with that Veovis turned and stormed from the room. Aitrus stood there a moment, half in shock, staring at the open doorway. Since the Maintainers inspection two weeks back he had feared this moment. Veovis wouldn't go to the Council, surely? But he knew Veovis. His friend was not one to make idle threats.

Anna sat in the window of her room, the tiny reekoo asleep in her lap as she gazed out over the ancient city and the harbor far below.

They had come that morning—six uniformed guards from the Guild of Maintainers and the great Lord R'hira himself. Kahlis and Aitrus had greeted them at the door, then stood back as Guild Master Sijarun walked through and opened the door to the Book Room, removing both the Book of Ko'ah and the new, uncompleted book that had no name.

The decision of the Council had been unanimous—Kahlis and his son were given no voice in the matter. It had been ruled that there had been a serious breach of protocol. In future, no one who was not of D'ni blood would be allowed to see a Book or visit an Age. It was, Veovis had argued, important that they set a precedent. And so they had.

Anna sighed. It was all her fault. And now Aitrus was in despair. Even now he sat in his study, wrestling with the question of whether to resign his seat on the Council.

She had seen Kahlis's face, and Tasera's. To lose a Book, Aitrus had once told her, was a matter of the gravest importance, but to have one taken forcibly, by order of the Council, was far, far worse. And she had brought that upon them. She groaned softly.

There was no way she might make amends. No way, unless . . .

The old man looked across at Anna, staring at her through half-lidded eyes, then, pulling his cloak about him, he answered her.

"I do not know," he said, shaking his head sadly. "I really do not know. Even if we find something . . . "

"They will listen. They *have* to listen."

Kedri, Master of the Guild of Legislators, lifted his shoulders in a shrug. Then, with a sad smile, "All right. I shall try my best, young Ah-na. For you, and for my dear friend Aitrus."

He sat there for a long time after she had gone, staring straight ahead, as if in a trance. It was thus that his assistant, Haran, found him.

"Master? Are you all right?"

Kedri slowly lifted his head, his eyes focusing on the young man. "What? Oh, forgive me, Haran. I was far away. Remembering."

Haran smiled and bowed his head. "I just came to say that the new intake of cadets is here. A dozen keen young students, fresh from the academy. What shall I do with them?"

Normally, Kedri would have found them some anodyne assignment—an exercise in dust-dry law, overseen by some bored assistant or other—but the arrival of this new intake coincided perfectly with his need.

If he *was* to search back through the records, he would need help—and what better help than a dozen keen young men, anxious to impress him? At the same time, he needed to be discreet. If word of his activities got back to the Council, who knew what fuss might ensue, particularly if young Lord Veovis got wind of it? By assigning these cadets to the Guild Age of Gadar—to search among the legal records stored in the Great Library there—he could split two rocks with a single blow, as the old saying went.

"Take them to the Book Room," he said. "I'll address them there. I have a task for them."

Haran stared back at him a moment, surprised, then, recollecting himself, he bowed low and quickly hurried away.

It was strange that the girl, Ah-na, had come to him this morning, for only the evening before he had dreamt of the time he had spent with the Surveyors thirty years ago. It was then that he had first come to know young Aitrus. Aitrus had been assigned to him—to show him how things worked and answer his every query. They had got on well from the start and had been friends ever since.

As far as Ah-na was concerned, he had met her only once before, when Aitrus brought her to his house, but he had liked her instantly, and saw at once why Aitrus was fascinated by her. She had a sharp intelligence and an inquisitive mind that were the match of any guildsmen. It had crossed his mind at once that, had she been D'ni, she would have made young Aitrus the perfect bride.

Even so, it surprised him still that she had come and not Aitrus, for he had half-expected Aitrus to pay him a call.

Kedri sat back, stretching his neck muscles and then turning his head from side to side, trying to relieve the tension he was feeling.

What he had agreed to do would not make him a popular man in certain circles, yet it had been a simple choice: to help his young friend Aitrus or abandon him.

Kedri sighed heavily. The Great Library of Legislation on Gadar contained a mass of information stretching back over six thousand years—the handwritten minutes of countless Council meetings and hearings, of guild committees and tribunals, not to speak of the endless shelves of private communications between Guild Masters. It would be like digging for one specific tiny crystal in the middle of a mountain.

And he had two weeks and a dozen keen young men to do it.

Lord Eneah sat at his desk, Aitrus's cloak of office lay folded on the desk before him. It had come that morning, along with that of Aitrus's father, Kahlis. Eneah had dealt with Kahlis, sending the cloak back to the Grand Master of the Surveyors. Whatever the rights or wrongs of the issue, Kahlis was clearly not to blame. But Aitrus's conduct was a different matter entirely.

It was fairly simple, really. Either he accepted Aitrus's resignation now and ended the rumors and speculation, or he left matters to the Guild of Surveyors, who, so he understood, had already instigated investigations into the conduct of their representative.

Whatever happened now, the damage was already done. The vote in Council had betrayed the mood of the guilds. In teaching the outsider D'ni, and in showing her an Age, Aitrus had not merely exceeded his brief, but had shown poor judgment. Some even claimed that he had been bewitched by the young girl and had lost his senses, but Eneah doubted that. Those who said that did not know Aitrus.

Yet Aitrus had been injudicious.

Eneah straightened slightly. He had not slept at all last

night and every joint ached as if it had been dipped in hot oil, but that was not unusual. These days he lived in constant pain.

With a small, regretful sigh, he drew a sheet of paper to him and, taking a quill pen from the inkstand, quickly wrote an acceptance letter then signed his name. Once the remaining Lords had set their names to it, the letter would be sealed and incorporated into the public record. In the meantime, a notice would be posted throughout D'ni, advising the citizens of this news.

And so ended a promising career.

Eneah reached across and rang his summons bell. At once a secretary appeared at the door.

"Take this to Lord R'hira at once."

Anna stood before the three of them.

"So you wish to leave?" Kahlis asked.

"No," she answered. "You have all been kind to me. Yet I feel I ought to. I have brought so much trouble to this household."

"The choice was mine," Aitrus said. "If anyone should leave, it should be me."

"That would be wrong," Anna said. "Besides, I shall be comfortable enough at Lord Eneah's mansion."

"Nonsense!" Tasera said, speaking for the first time since Anna had summoned them to this meeting. "I will not hear of it! Lord Eneah is an old man! No. You will stay here!"

Anna stared at Tasera, astonished. She had thought

Tasera most of all would have wanted her gone. Since the Council's meeting she had been practically ostracized. Yet Tasera seemed by far the most indignant of the three.

"Then it is settled," Kahlis said, smiling proudly at his wife, "Ah-na stays here, as family."

It was an ancient book, great whorls of faded color dotting the pale gray of its musty leather cover like dusty jewels. Looking down at it, Guild Master Kedri found himself smiling. Until yesterday it had remained unread upon its shelf for close on nineteen hundred years.

Kedri looked up at Anna, who sat to one side of the desk, then addressed the young man. "Forgive me, Guildsman, but how exactly did you find this? It is not as if this lay directly on the path of our main search."

The young man bowed his head nervously, then spoke. "It was something you said, Master Kedri. Last night, at supper. You know, about trying to identify possible factors in the search."

"Go on."

"It got me thinking, Master, asking myself just what kind of person might be granted access to an Age. That is, what kind of non-D'ni person, naturally."

"And?"

"Well . . . my first thought was that such a person would have to have the ear of someone important—someone very important, indeed, perhaps even one of the Five. And so I went to the list of clerks . . ."

"Clerks?"

"To the Five."

"Ah . . . and what did that give you?"

The young man smiled. "Six names."

Already Kedri was ahead of him. "Names that were not D'ni, I presume."

"Yes, Master. There was a time when some of the more talented natives—from Guild Ages and the like—were permitted to come here, into D'ni itself."

Kedri raised an eyebrow. "Now *that* I did not know."

"No, Master, for it was a very long time ago, very shortly after the Council was first set up in its present form, not long after the Age of Kings."

"I see. And these clerks . . . were they restricted to D'ni, or were they granted access to other Ages?"

The guildsman nodded at the book before Kedri. "I have marked the relevant passages, Master. I am sure there are further entries in the other books."

There was a small pile of books on the floor behind the young guildsman.

Anna felt a tingle of excitement pass through her. She stood and, crouching, lifted one of the books and opened it, sniffing in the scent of great age as it wafted up to her off the page.

It was an old script, different in several ways from its modern counterpart, yet easily decipherable. In several places the ink had faded almost to nothing, yet the meaning of the text was quite clear.

Anna looked across at Kedri and nodded, a feeling of deep satisfaction flooding her at that moment.

"It is not too old then, Master?" the young guildsman asked. "I thought, perhaps, that its age might possibly invalidate it."

"A precedent is a precedent," Kedri said, looking to Anna, then reading the passage once again. "We shall find further sources to verify this, no doubt—and further instances, I warrant."

He closed the book, then nodded. "You have done well, Guildsman."

"Thank you, Master," the young man answered, bowing low, a great beam of a smile on his face.

"Thank *you*, Guildsman . . ."

"Neferus, Master. Guildsman Neferus."

What had taken the full vote of the Council to decide, took but a single signature to revoke.

As Lord Eneah pushed the document away, he felt a great weight slip from him. He was glad Master Kedri had found what he had found, for he had never felt quite at ease with the decision, yet looking up, he saw in his mind the closed face of Lord Rakeri, and knew that all the Five were not as pleased as he.

The Books would be returned to Master Kahlis, and Ahna would be free to travel in them. Yet all was not quite as it had been. Aitrus still refused to take up his vacated role as representative of the Guild of Surveyors. He said he had had enough of votes and meetings, and maybe he was right. And as for Veovis . . .

Eneah dropped the pen back into the inkstand and leaned back, weary now that it was all over.

Young Veovis had called on him earlier that day, determined to have his say. He had not been rude, nor had he challenged in any way the validity of Master Kedri's discoveries, yet it was clear that he resented the Legislator's intrusion in Council matters, and was dead set against allowing Ah-na entry into any D'ni Age. He had ended by begging Lord Eneah to set the ancient precedent aside and endorse the Council's decision, but Eneah had told him he could not do that.

The law *was* the law, after all. Precedent was precedent. It was the D'ni way and had been for a thousand generations.

And so Veovis had left, under a cloud, angry and resentful, and who knew what trouble would come of that?

But so it is, Eneah thought, *looking about him at the empty study. No single man, however great or powerful, is more important than D'ni.*

He smiled, knowing that soon he would be little more than a name, another statue in the Great Hall of the Lords.

"So it is," he said quietly. "And so it must be. Until the end of time."

And with that he stood, walked across the room and out, moving slowly, silently, like a shadow on the rock.

PART FOUR: GEMEDET

ANNA WAITED, CROUCHED JUST IN FRONT OF AITRUS IN the narrow tunnel, looking out into the bottom of the well. Just below her, the surface of the tiny, circular pool was black. Slowly, very slowly, sunlight crept down the smooth, black wall facing her, a pure light, almost unreal it seemed so bright, each separate shaft a solid, shining bar in that penumbral darkness.

It was cool and silent, yet overhead, far above the surface, the sun approached its zenith.

"Wait . . . " Aitrus said softly. "Just a moment longer."

The sunlight touched the still, curved edge of the water. A moment later the water's depths were breached, the straight beam bent, refracted by the clear liquid.

Anna gasped. It was beautiful. The well had a solid wooden lid, but Aitrus had cut an intricate design into the wood. As the sun climbed directly above the well, so each part of that design was slowly etched upon the dark circle of the pool, until the whole of it could be seen, burning like shafts of brilliant fire in the cool, translucent depths of the water.

The D'ni word Shorah. *"Peace."*

Anna smiled and turned to look at Aitrus, seeing how the word was reflected in the black centers of his pupils.

"So that's what you were doing," she said quietly. "I wondered."

She turned back, knowing, without needing to be told,

that its beauty was transient, would be gone just as soon as the sun moved from its zenith and the sunlight climbed the wall again.

"I made it for you," he said.

I know, she thought. Aloud, she said, "Thank you. It's beautiful."

"Isn't it?"

They watched, together in the silence, until, with a final, glittering wink, the brightness in the pool was gone.

Anna stared into the blackness and sighed.

"What are you thinking?" he asked, after a moment.

"I was thinking of my father."

"Ah . . . " He was silent a long while, then, "Come. Let's go back up."

Anna turned and followed, half-crouched as she walked along the tiny tunnel, then straightening to climb the twisting flight of steps that had been cut from the rock. Aitrus had worked weeks on this. And all for that one small instant of magic.

A tiny shiver passed through her. She watched him climb the steps ahead of her, noticing how neatly his hair was clipped at his neck, how strong his back and arms were, how broad his shoulders, and realized just how familiar he had become these last few years.

As familiar almost as this Age they had slowly built together.

Stepping out into the sunlight beside Aitrus, Anna smiled. It was so green. All she could see was green. Forest and grasslands, wood and plain. Why, even the slow, meandering rivers were green with trailing weed.

Only the sky was blue. A deep, water-heavy blue. In the distance a great raft of huge white clouds drifted slowly from right to left, their movement almost imperceptible, casting deep shadows on the hills and valleys below.

It had all seemed strange at first, after the desert landscape she had known all her life. So strange, that she had spent hours simply staring at the clouds, fascinated by them.

She looked to Aitrus. He was wearing his D'ni glasses now, to protect his eyes against the glare of the sun. They all wore them when not in D'ni. Only she did not have to.

"We should go north next," she said. "To the mountains. I could map that area beyond the lake."

Aitrus smiled. "Perhaps. Or maybe that long valley to the northeast of here."

She looked down, smiling, knowing exactly why he was interested in that area. They had passed through it several weeks ago on their way back from the peninsula and had noticed signs of long-dormant volcanic activity. She had seen the tiny gleam of interest in his eyes.

"If you want."

They walked on, talking as they went, continuing the discussion they had begun earlier that day. Wherever they went, they talked, making observations on the physical signs of this world, and debating which small changes to the words and phrasing might have caused this effect or that.

Sometimes Aitrus would stop, crouch down with the notepad balanced on his knee, and would write down something he or she had said, wanting to capture it, ready to enter it in the book of commentary they had begun six months back. Already they had filled half the great ledger with their observations, and each day they added to it, with words and maps and drawings.

A long slope led to the encampment, which was sighted at the head of a verdant valley. To one side of that grassy plateau, the earth had folded and a great slab of smooth black rock jutted from the green. Just above it a slow-moving river pooled, then fell sheer two hundred feet to the valley floor in a clear, narrow curtain.

The sound of the falls was ever-present, a counterpoint to the exotic, echoing cries of birds from the wood that climbed the steep slope behind them. To the north were mountains, to the south the great ocean.

It was a beautiful place.

Aitrus's tent was to the left of the camp, its long frame of green canvas blending with the background. A smaller, circular tent, its canvas a vivid yellow, stood just beside and was used for stores. Until a week ago there had been a third tent, the twin of Aitrus's, but now that the cabin was habitable, Anna had moved in. It was not finished yet—Aitrus had yet to cut and fit the wooden floor—but the roof was on and it was dry. Beside Anna's section, which was screened off, Aitrus had set up a temporary lab, which they planned to use until they had built a proper, permanent laboratory a little way farther up the slope.

They walked across. A trestle table stood just outside Aitrus's tent, in the shadow of the canvas awning. On top of it, its corners held down by tiny copper weights, was the map Anna had been working on earlier, a clear thin cover of D'ni polymer laid over it in case of rain.

The map was remarkably detailed, a color key on the right-hand side of the sheet making sense of the intricate pattern of colors on the map itself. Areas of the sheet were blank, where they had not yet surveyed the land, but where they had, Anna had provided a vivid guide to it—one that not only made sense of its essential topography but also gave a clue to the types of soil and thus vegetation that overlay the deeper rock formations. It was all, she said, using one of her father's favorite terms, "a question of edaphology."

Maybe it was because she *was* from the surface, but her grasp of how the kind of rock affected the visible features of the land was far more refined than his, almost instinctive. Often she did not have to analyze a rock sample but knew it by its feel, its color and its texture. His instinct was for the pressures and stresses within the rock that provided what one saw with its underlying structure.

At first it had astonished Aitrus that she had known so

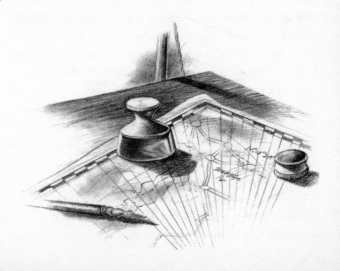

much of rocks and minerals and the complex art of mapping the rock, and even when he learned more of her father and how she had helped him, he was still amazed that she had grasped quite so much in so brief a time. Yet as the weeks went on, his surprise had turned to delight, knowing that here at last was someone with whom he might share his lifelong fascination with the rock.

It was not long before he had begun to teach her the D'ni names for the different types of rock and the terms his people used to describe the various geological processes. Anna learned easily and was soon fluent enough to hold those conversations which, through to today, had never ceased between them. After a while Aitrus had begun to push her, testing her, as if to find the limits of her intelligence, but it seemed there were no bounds to what she was capable of.

Right now, however, the two of them stood beside the trestle table. Aitrus studied the half-completed map a moment then tapped an area in the top left corner with his forefinger.

"We could start here, Ah-na, where the river bends and drops. It would give us the opportunity to map all of this area to the west of the river. That would take, what? Two days?"

Anna studied the blank area on her map and nodded. "Two. Three at most."

"Three it is. We could take the tent and camp there. Then we could spend a day or two exploring the valley. There are cave systems there. Did you see them?"

Anna smiled. "I saw."

"Good. And once we've finished there, we could come back here and spend a couple of days writing things up."

"Can the guild spare you that long?"

"If they need me urgently, they'll send someone. But I doubt it. Things are slow at present, and until the Guild of Miners present their report on the new excavation, that is how it will remain. We might as well use the time fruitfully."

"Aitrus?"

"Yes?"

"Can we set out a little later tomorrow? In the afternoon, perhaps?"

"You want to see the well again?"

Anna nodded.

"All right. I guess it will take most of the morning to pack what we need, anyway."

She smiled. That was so like Aitrus. Rather than admit to indulging her, he would always find some excuse to let her have her way.

"And Aitrus?"

He turned, clearly distracted. "Yes?"

"Oh, nothing . . . Nothing important, anyway."

That evening it rained; a warm, heavy rain that thundered on the roof of the cabin and filled the valley like a huge, shimmering mist of silver.

Anna stepped out into the downpour, raising her arms, her head back, savoring the feel of the rain against her skin.

Just across from her, Aitrus peeked out from his tent and, seeing what she was doing, called out to her.

"Ah-na! What are you doing? You'll be soaked to the skin!"

Laughing, she turned to face him, then, on whim, began to dance, whirling around and around, her bare feet flying across the wet grass.

"Ah-na!"

She stopped, facing him, then put a hand out.

"Come, Aitrus! Join me!"

Aitrus hesitated, then, reluctantly, yet smiling all the same, he stepped out. Almost instantly he was soaked, his hair plastered to his head.

He took her hand.

"Come!" she said, her eyes shining brightly, excitedly, "let's dance!" And without warning, she began to whirl him around and around beneath the open sky, the light from the hanging lanterns in front of the cabin turning the fall of rain into a cascade of silver.

Exhilarated, Aitrus whooped loudly, then stopped dead. He was laughing, his whole face alive as she had never seen it before.

"Isn't it *wonderful?*" she asked, almost shouting against the noise of the downpour.

"Marvelous!" he shouted back, then, unexpectedly, he grabbed her close and whirled around and around again, until, giddy from their circling, he stopped, swaying and coughing and laughing.

Anna, too, was laughing. She put her head back, drinking in the pure, clean water from the sky. Rain! The wonder of rain!

270

Anna stood behind the wooden partition, toweling her hair. Outside, the rain still fell, but now it could be heard only as a gentle, murmuring patter against the roof. Soon the storm would pass.

She had changed into a dry, woolen dress of cyan blue, her favorite color, fastened at the waist with a simple cord.

Folding the towel, she dropped it onto the end of her pallet bed then turned full circle, looking about her. There were books wherever she looked, on shelves and surfaces, and, on the narrow wooden table in the corner, scientific equipment, the polished brasswork gleaming in the lamplight.

Anna sighed, feeling a real contentment. For the first time in a long, long while, she was happy.

To be honest, she had never worked so hard, nor felt so good. Before Aitrus had asked her to work with him on the creation of this Age, she had felt useless, but now . . .

Now she had a problem.

Anna sat on the edge of her low bed, staring at the bare earth floor. Perhaps it was the dance. Perhaps it was that glimpse of Aitrus, happy just as she was happy. Was that an illusion? Was it a transient thing? Or could it last?

And besides . . .

There was a knock on the door of the cabin. Anna looked up, startled. It was Aitrus's habit to spend an hour at this time writing up his journal for the day.

"Come in."

Aitrus stepped inside, his right hand drawing his dark hair back from his brow.

"I wondered if you were all right."

She smiled up at him. "I'm fine. It was only rain."

Aitrus stood there a moment, hesitant, not sure just what to say, then: "Would you like a game of *Gemedet?*"

"All right."

He grinned, then nodded and turned away, returning to the tent to bring the grid. Smiling, Anna stood, then went across to clear a space on the table.

Gemedet, or six-in-a-line, was the most popular of D'ni games. She had seen a close variant of the game in Tadjinar, played by the Chinese merchants, but the D'ni version was played not on a two-dimensional board but on a complex three-dimensional grid, nine squares to a side.

It was, she thought, the perfect game for a race embedded in the rock, whose thinking was not lateral but spatial.

Aitrus returned a moment later, setting the grid down on the table. It was a beautiful thing, of hand-carved lilac jade, as delicate-looking as a honeycomb yet strong. Strong enough to have survived a thousand games without a single chip or blemish.

The base of the grid was a polished hemisphere of topaz on which the grid revolved smoothly. Long, silver tweezers, called *re'dantee,* were used to slip the playing pieces into place, while the pieces themselves were simple polished ovoids of green tourmaline and dark red almandine.

Both the re'dantee and the "stones" were kept in a velvet-lined box, which Aitrus now opened, placing it on the table beside the grid, so that both of them could easily reach it.

Anna smiled. She had fallen in love with the set at first sight.

They sat, facing each other across the table. As ever, Anna went first, slipping her first "stone" into place, deep in the heart of the grid, giving herself the maximum of options.

For an hour or more they played, in total silence, each concentrating on the pattern of the stones. After a while the patter of rain on the roof stopped. Night birds called in the darkness of the woods outside. Inside the game went on, beneath the lantern's light.

Finally, she saw that she had lost. Aitrus had only to place a single stone in the bottom left-hand corner and there was no way she could stop him making six.

Anna looked up and saw, by his smile, that he knew.

"Another game?"

She shook her head. Was now the time to speak? To tell him what she had been thinking earlier?

"What is it?" he asked gently.

Anna looked down. "I'm tired, that's all."

"Are you sure?"

She gave a single nod. It had been a good day—an almost perfect day—why spoil it?

"Shall I pack the game away?" he asked, after a moment.

"No," she said, looking up at him and smiling; content now that she had decided. "I'll do that in the morning. Besides, I want to see how you managed to beat me."

Aitrus grinned. "Experience, that's all."

At that moment, there did not seem to be so many years' difference in their ages. In human terms, Aitrus was old—as old, almost, as her father—but in D'ni terms he was still a very young man. Why, it was quite likely that he would live another two centuries and more. But was that also why she was afraid to speak of what she felt?

"I'll leave you, then," he said, standing, the lamplight

glinting in his fine, dark hair. "Good night. Sleep well, Ah-na."

"And you," she said, standing.

He smiled. And then he left, leaving her staring at the door, the words she wanted so much to say unsaid, while outside the night birds called, their cries echoing across the darkness of the valley.

The valley was a deep gash in the surrounding land, cut not by a river but by older, far more violent processes. Bare rock jutted from the slopes on either side, the folded pattern of its strata long exposed to the elements so that the softer rocks had been heavily eroded, leaving great shelves of harder rock. At one end of the valley, in the shadow of a particularly long shelf, were the caves. It was there that they began their survey.

Anna knew what Aitrus was looking for, and it was not long before he found it.

"Ah-na! Come here! Look!"

She went across to where Aitrus was crouched in the deep shadow of the overhang and looked.

"Well?" he said, looking up at her triumphantly.

It was old and worn, but there was no doubting what it was. It was the puckered mouth of a diatreme—a volcanic vent—formed long ago by high pressure gases drilling their way through the crustal rocks.

For the past two days they had kept coming upon signs that there was a volcano somewhere close by. Volcanic deposits had been scattered all about this area, but this was the first vent they had found.

From the look of it the volcano was an old one, dormant for many centuries.

"I thought we'd made a stable world."

He smiled. "We did. But even stable worlds must be formed. Volcanoes are part of the growing process of an Age. Even the best of worlds must have them!"

"So where is it?" she asked.

He stood, then turned, pointing straight through the rock toward the north.

"There, I'd guess."

"Do you want to go and look for it?"

Aitrus shrugged, then, "If you wouldn't mind."

Anna laughed. "Why should I? It's a volcano. *Our* volcano. Our first!"

He grinned, as if he had not thought of that, then nodded. "Come then. If I'm right, it can't be far."

The caldera was still visible, but time and weather had worn it down. Trees covered its shallow slopes and filled the great bowl of the volcano, but here and there the thin covering of soil gave way to fissures and vents whose darkness hinted at great depths.

It was old. Far older than they had first thought. Not thousands, but millions of years old.

It was this part that Anna had taken a little while to grasp.

The Ages to which they linked were not made by them, they already existed, for the making of worlds was a process that took not months but long millennia. Aitrus, trying to make things absolutely clear to her, had summed it up thus:

"These Ages are worlds that do exist, or have existed, or shall. Providing the description fits, there is no limitation of time or space. The link is made regardless."

And so, too, this world of theirs, their Age, which they had called Gemedet, after the game. It, too, existed, or had existed, or would. But where it was or when they did not know.

Not that it mattered most of the time, but on occasion she did wonder just where they were in the night sky, and when—whether at the beginning of the universe or somewhere near the end of that vast process.

The very thought of it humbled her, made her understand why her father had believed in a Maker who had fashioned it all. Having "written," having seen the great skill and subtlety involved merely in creating a *link* to these worlds, she now found herself in awe of the infinite care that had gone into the making of the originals to which their templates linked.

Personally, she could not believe that blind process had made it all. It was, for her, quite inconceivable, bearing in mind the complexity and variety of life. Yet in this, if nothing else, Aitrus differed from her. His was, or so he claimed, a more rational approach, more *scientific*—as if understanding the product of such processes were a key to understanding the why of them existing in the first place.

Aitrus had walked down the tree-strewn slope, making his way between the boulders, until he stood beside one of the larger vents. Resting his chest against the sloping wall of the vent, he leaned out, peering into the darkness. For a moment he was perfectly still, then he turned his head, looking back at her through his D'ni glasses.

"Shall we go in?"

Anna smiled. "All right, but we'll need to bring a rope from the camp."

Aitrus grinned. "And lamps, and . . . "

". . . your notebook."

A look of perfect understanding passed between them. It was time to explore the volcano.

They got back to the encampment three days later than they had planned, to find that a message had been delivered from D'ni. It lay upon the map table in its dark blue waterproof wrapping.

While Anna began to stow away their equipment, Aitrus broke the seal of the package and took out the letter. He knew it was not urgent—they would have sent a Messenger into the Age to find him if it was—but it was unusual. Unfolding the letter, he squinted at it through the lenses of his glasses. It was from his old friend Kedri, and concerned a query Aitrus had put to him the last time they had met for supper.

He read it through quickly, then, smiling, he slipped the paper into his tunic pocket.

"Well?" Anna asked, coming alongside him. "Anything important?"

"No, but I need to go back."

"Should we pack?"

He shook his head. "No. I only need to be away an hour or two. I'll go later tonight. You can stay here. I'll come back as soon as I can."

Anna smiled. "You should have a bath when you get back to D'ni."

"A bath?" He looked mock-offended. "Are you saying I smell, Ti'ana?"

"You positively reek of sulphur!" she said, grinning now. "Like Old Beelzebub himself!"

He smiled at that. In the caves beneath the caldera, she had taught him much about the mythology and gods of the surface, including the demons whom, according to many religions, lived in the regions beneath the earth.

"If only they knew the reality of it," she had said. "They'd be amazed."

It was then that he had given her her new name—*Ti'ana*, which in D'ni meant "story-teller," as well as punning on her surface name. "Do you need me to cook you something before you go?"

"I'd rather you helped me sort those samples."

"All right," she said, her smile broadening. "I'll do the tests, you can write up the notes."

Aitrus looked about him at the tent. All was neat and orderly. His notebook was open on the small table by his bed, the ink of the latest entry not yet dry. It was time to link back.

Anna was in her cabin. He would say goodnight to her, then go.

Aitrus went outside and stepped across to the cabin, knocking softly on the door. Usually she would call out to him, but this time there was nothing. Pushing the door open a little, he saw that she was not at her desk.

"Ti'ana?" he called softly. "Are you there?"

As if in answer he heard her soft snoring from behind the thin, wooden partition. Slipping inside, he tiptoed across and, drawing back the curtain, peered in.

Anna lay on her side on the pallet, facing him, her eyes closed, her features peaceful in sleep. The long journey back from the valley had clearly exhausted her. He crouched, watching her, drinking in the sight of her. She was so different from the women he had known all his life—those strong yet frail D'ni women with their pale skin and long faces.

It had been more than two months ago, when they had made their first, and as yet only, journey to the mountains north of the camp. On the way Anna had collected samples of various native flowers for later study. Yet, coming upon the wonder of a snow-covered slope—the first she had ever seen or touched or walked upon—she had taken the blooms from her pocket and scattered their petals over the snow. He had asked her what she was doing, and she had shrugged.

"I had to," she had said, staring at him. Then, pointing to the scattered petals, she had bid him look.

Aitrus closed his eyes, seeing them vividly, their bright shapes and colors starkly contrasted against the purity of the whiteness—like life and death.

It was then that he had decided, and every moment since had been but a confirmation of that decision—an affirmation of the feeling he had had at that moment, when, looking up from the petals, he had seen her face shining down at him like the sun itself.

Aitrus opened his eyes and saw that same face, occluded now in sleep, like the sun behind clouds, yet beautiful still. The most beautiful he had ever seen. At first he had not thought so, but time had trained his eyes to see her differently. He *knew* her now.

Aitrus stretched out his hand, tracing the contours of that sleeping face in the air above it, a feeling of such tenderness pervading him that he found his hand trembling. He drew it back, surprised by the strength of what he felt at that moment. Overwhelming, it was, like the rush of water over a fall.

He nodded to himself, then stood. It was time to go back to D'ni. Time to face his father, Kahlis.

"I cannot say that I have not half-expected this," Kahlis was saying, "but I had hoped that you would, perhaps, have seen sense in time."

"I am sorry that you feel so, Father."

"Even if it is as you say, Aitrus, have you thought this through properly? Have you thought out the full implications of such a union? She is an outsider. A surface-dweller. And you, Aitrus, are D'ni—a Guild Master and a member of the Council. Such a marriage is unheard of."

"Maybe so. Yet there is no legal impediment to it." Aitrus took the letter from his tunic pocket and placed it on the desk before his father. "I asked Master Kedri to look into the matter, and that is his expert opinion."

Kahlis took the sheet of paper and unfolded it. For a moment he was silent, reading it, then he looked up, his eyes narrowed.

"And the age difference, Aitrus? Have you considered that? Right now you are the elder, but it will not always be so. Your life span is thrice hers. When you are still in your prime she will be an old woman. Have you thought of that?"

"I have," he answered. "Yet not to have her—to have never had her by my side—that would be death indeed."

"And what if I said I was against the marriage?"

Aitrus merely stared at him.

Kahlis stood, then came around his desk.

"You will not accept my advice, Aitrus. But I shall give you my blessing. That, I hope, you *will* accept."

"Gladly!" Aitrus said, then, reaching out, he took his father's hands in the D'ni way. "You will be proud of her, Father, I promise you!"

Aitrus linked back into the cave above the encampment. Stepping out, he saw that nothing had changed. In the moonlight the camp looked peaceful, the tents to the left, the cabin to the right. Beyond and to the right the waterfall was like a sheet of silver, its constant noise lulling him.

Walking down between the trees he found that he was whistling softly, an old D'ni song his mother had once sang to him. He stopped, his eyes going to the cabin. There she slept. Ti'ana. His love.

"It cannot be wrong," he said quietly.

Aitrus felt a light touch on his shoulder and started. Turning, he found Anna standing there behind him. She was smiling, as if pleased by her little trick.

"What cannot be wrong?"

He swallowed. Now that the moment had come, he was afraid of it. Yet that fear was natural, it was there to be over-come.

"You and I," he answered, taking her hands.

Her eyes went down to where their hands met, then looked up to meet his own again. "What do you mean?"

"I mean I wish to marry you."

Her eyes slowly widened. She stared at him silently, as if in wonder.

"Well?" he asked, when the waiting grew too much. "*Will* you marry me, Ti'ana?"

"I will," she said, her voice so soft, so quiet, that he felt at first he had imagined it.

"You will?"

Anna nodded, the faintest trace of a smile coming to her lips.

"You *will!*" He whooped, then drew her close and, for the first time, embraced her. Her face was suddenly close to his, less than a hand's width away. The sight of it sobered him.

"I will be a good husband to you, Ti'ana, I promise. But you must promise me something."

"Promise what?"

"That you will be my partner in all things. My helpmate and companion, by my side always, in whatever I do."

Slowly the smile returned to her face. Then, leaning toward him, she gently kissed him. "I promise."

Veovis stormed into the room, slamming the door behind him. He grabbed an inkwell from the desk beside him and hurled it across the room, shattering it into tiny fragments.

"Never!" he said, glaring across the empty room. "Not while there's breath left in my body!"

His father, Rakeri, had broken the news to him an hour back. Aitrus was to be betrothed. At first, if anything, he had been indifferent to the news. He had not even heard that Aitrus was seeing anyone. Then, abruptly, he had understood. The girl! The surface-dweller!

Veovis stomped across the room and threw himself down into his chair, gnawing on a thumbnail.

"Never!" he said again, the word hissing from him with a real venom.

His father had explained how the Five had been approached, the documents of precedent laid before them. Again that was Kedri's fault, the traitor! Aitrus need only go before the full Council now to receive their blessing, and that was a formality.

Or had been, in the past.

Veovis took a long, calming breath, then turned his head,

staring at the shattered fragments of glass as if he did not recognize the cause, then shuddered.

Never.

Aitrus stood before the Five, at the center of the great chamber. All were present. Lord R'hira had read out the formal request; now, all that remained was for the Council to ratify the document.

R'hira stared at Aitrus a moment, then looked beyond him, his eyes raking the levels of the chamber.

"All those in favor?"

There was a chorus of "Ayes," some reluctant, others enthusiastic. For six thousand years the question had been asked and answered thus.

Lord R'hira smiled.

"And those against?" he asked, the question a formality.

"Nay."

R'hira had already turned the paper facedown. He had been about to congratulate young Aitrus. But the single voice brought him up sharp. He stared at Veovis, where he sat not two spans behind where Aitrus was standing.

"I beg pardon, Guild Master Veovis?"

Veovis stood. "I said 'Nay.'"

R'hira's wizened face blinked. All five Lords were leaning forward now, staring at Veovis. This was unheard of.

"Could I possibly have your reasons, Master Veovis?"

Veovis's face was a mask, expressionless. "I need give no reason. I am simply against." And he sat, as if that was that.

As indeed it was. The verdict of Council had to be unanimous in this matter. R'hira looked to Aitrus. The young man had his head down, his own expression unreadable; yet there was a tension to his figure that had not been there before.

"Master Aitrus . . . " he began, embarrassed. "It would seem . . . "

Aitrus looked up, his pale eyes hard like slate. "I understand, Lord R'hira. The Council has turned down my request."

R'hira, marking the immense dignity with which Aitrus bore this disappointment, gave a reluctant nod. "So it is."

"Then I will trouble you no more, my Lords."

Aitrus bowed to each of the Five in turn, then, turning on his heel, walked from the chamber, his head held high, not even glancing at Veovis as he passed.

"Aitrus! Come now, open the door!"

Tasera stood before the door to her son's room, her husband just behind her in the shadows of the corridor.

When there was no answer, Tasera turned and looked to her husband. "Why did you not say something in Council, Kahlis?"

"I did," Kahlis said quietly, "but it made no difference."

"And is that *it,* then?" she asked, incredulous. "One man says nay and nay it is?"

There was the grating metallic noise of the latch being drawn back, and then the door eased open an inch.

"Forgive me, Mother," Aitrus said from within the darkness of the room. "I was asleep."

"I heard what happened in Council," she said. "We need to discuss what should be done."

"There's nothing can be done," he said. "The Council has given their answer."

No word, then, of Veovis. No individual blame. As if this were the genuine will of Council.

"Nonsense!" she said, angry now. Pushing past him, she went over to the table and lit the lamp.

Tasera turned, looking at him in the half light. Aitrus's face seemed gaunt, as if he had been ill, but he was still, beneath it all, the same strong man she had bred.

"I know you, Aitrus. You are a fighter. I also know how much Ti'ana means to you. Now, will you bow before this decision, or will you fight?"

"Fight? How can I fight? And what can I fight with? Can I force Veovis to change his mind? No. Neither he nor the Council would allow it! And as for persuasion . . . "

"Then beg."

"Beg?"

"If Ti'ana means that much to you, go to Lord Veovis and beg him to change his mind and grant you what you want. Go down on your knees before him if you must, but do not simply accept this."

"On my knees?" Aitrus stared at his mother, incredulous.

"Yes," she said, standing face-to-face with him. "What matters more to you, Aitrus? Your pride or your future happiness?"

"You want me to beg?"

Tasera shook her head. "You said yourself: He will not be forced or persuaded. What other course is open to you?"

"Aitrus is right."

Both turned. Anna was standing in the doorway.

"Ti'ana, I . . . " Aitrus began, but she raised a hand to bid him be silent. "I know what happened. Your father just told me."

"Then you must agree," Tasera said, appealing to her. "Aitrus must go to Veovis."

"Maybe," Anna said, nodding to her. Then she turned slightly, looking to Aitrus lovingly. "You know how proud I would be to be your wife, Aitrus. Prouder than any woman in the whole of D'ni. Yet I would not have you go down on your knees before that man, even if it meant we must spend our lives apart. It would be a violation, and I could not bear it. But there is, perhaps, another way . . . "

Aitrus raised his eyes and looked at Anna. For a long time he simply studied her, and then he nodded. "So be it, then," he said, "I will go to him. But I do not hold much hope."

Veovis agreed to meet with Aitrus in his father's study, Lord Rakeri a silent presence in his chair, there to ensure that things were kept within due bounds.

"So what is it that you want, Guildsman?" Veovis said, standing six paces from where Aitrus stood facing him, his hands clasped behind his back.

Aitrus met Veovis's masklike stare with his own. "I seek an explanation for your vote this morning."

"And I decline to give it."

"You do not like her, do you?"

Veovis shrugged. "As I said . . . "

". . . you decline to give your reasons."

Veovis nodded.

"You recall our meeting in the shaft all those years ago?"

"What of it?"

"You recall what happened . . . afterward? How I helped save your life?"

Veovis blinked. He took a long breath, then: "I was very grateful for your actions. But what of it? What bearing has it on this matter?"

"You made me a promise. Remember? You said then that if there was anything I wanted—*anything*—that was in your power to grant, then I should come to you and you would grant it."

Veovis stood there like a statue, his eyes like flints, staring back at Aitrus.

"*Do* you remember?"

"I remember."

"Then I ask you to keep your word, Lord Veovis, and give me your permission, before the full Council, to marry Ti'ana."

Veovis was silent for a long time. Finally he turned, looking to his father. Rakeri stared back at his son a moment, his eyes filled with a heavy sadness, then gave a single nod.

Veovis turned back. "I am a man of my word, and so your wish is granted, Aitrus, son of Kahlis, but from this day forth I wish neither to speak with you nor hear from you again. Whatever once existed between us is now at an end. All promises are met. You understand?"

Aitrus stared back at him, his face expressionless. "I understand. And thank you."

"You *thank* me?" Veovis laughed bitterly. "Just go, for I am sick of the sight of you."

PART FIVE: THE PHILOSOPHER

THE VESTIBULE WAS PACKED WITH GUILDSMEN—GRAND Masters and their assistants, great Lords, and other, humbler members of the central D'ni Council—all waiting to enter the great chamber for the debate. As ever before any momentous occasion, the place was buzzing with talk as small groups of cloaked members gathered between the fluted marble pillars to indulge in informal discussion of the new proposal.

At the center of one of the larger groups stood Aitrus, whose proposal it was. In the fifteen years since he had returned to Council, he had established himself as the unofficial leader of the more liberal faction in the House, and was often consulted by the Five on matters of policy. Today, however, he was distracted.

"Any news?" his friend Oren of the Guild of Chemists asked as he joined the group.

"Nothing yet," Aitrus answered.

"She'll be all right," Penjul, another close friend and a Master of the Guild of Legislators, said, laying a hand briefly on Aitrus's shoulder.

"I guess so," Aitrus said, but his concern was clear.

"So how will it go today?" Oren asked, looking about him at the dozen or so Masters who formed the core of their faction. "Does anyone have a clear idea?"

There were smiles. Oren, as a Chemist, always wanted a certain answer.

"Whichever way it goes, it will be close," Hamil, the eldest of their group and Grand Master of the Guild of Messengers, said, pulling at his long white beard. "Much will depend upon the eloquence of our friend here."

Oren looked to Aitrus. "Then we are lost," he said, a faint smile at one corner of his mouth. "Master Aitrus has but a single thing in his head today."

Aitrus smiled. "Do not fret, Master Oren, I shall be all right. Having to speak will distract me from more important matters."

All nodded at that. Though the proposal was important to them all there, Ti'ana's health was tantamount.

Indeed, without Ti'ana there would have been no proposal, for it was she who had taken them down to the lower city to see conditions for themselves; she who, in the main part, had drafted the proposal.

"They say Veovis is to speak for our opponents," Penjul said, looking across the vestibule to where Veovis stood, beneath the great arched doors to the main chamber, surrounded by the old men of his faction.

"Then the debate will be long and hard," Tekis of the Archivists said wryly.

"Long-winded, certainly," Penjul added, to general laughter.

"Maybe," Aitrus said, "yet I understand Lord Veovis's objections even so. He fears that this change is but the thin end of the wedge, and he is not alone in fearing this. Our task is to allay such fears, if not in Veovis, then in others who might vote with him. They must see that we mean exactly what we say and no more. Only then might we win."

There were nods all around at that.

"And if we lose?" Oren asked.

Aitrus smiled. "Then we find other ways to help the lower city. As Ti'ana has often said to me, there is always more than one way to skin a reekoo."

The chamber was silent as Veovis rose from his seat on the lowest level and, turning, looked about him at the gathered members.

"Guildsmen, my Lords . . . as you know, my task is to persuade you not to adopt this rash proposal. I do not think I need say much. As the present system of governing our city has worked for more than five thousand years, then one might argue that it *has* worked well."

Veovis paused, his eyes resting briefly on Aitrus, who sat not five spans from where he stood, watching him intently.

"Yet there is another issue here, and that is the question of who runs D'ni. Such measures as are proposed might seem innocuous, yet they are guaranteed to encourage restlessness among the common people, for having tasted power—if only of this limited kind—then would they not want greater power? Would they be content to remain thus limited?

"Besides, as we who were bred to it know to our great cost, power is but one side of the equation; responsibility is the other. Power can be given overnight, but responsibility must be taught. Long years go into its making. Do we not, then, ask a great deal of these common men, however good their intentions, in expecting them to shoulder the burden of responsibility without due preparation? Of course we do. Is it not unfair to ask them to be as wise and knowing as ourselves, when all they have known until this time is service? It is."

Veovis smiled. "And that is ultimately why I say nay to this proposal. Because of the unhappiness it would bring to those who presently are happier than us. Why give them such care? Why burden them with it? No, fellow guildsmen, let us be content and leave things as they are. Say nay as I say nay and let us be done with it. Guildsmen, my Lords, thank you."

Veovis sat, to a murmur of approval. At a signal from Lord R'hira, Aitrus stood.

"Guildsmen, my Lords . . . As you may know, my wife, Ti'ana is in labor, and so I, too, ought to be brief."

There was laughter. Even Veovis gave a grudging nod.

"However, let me just say a word or two in answer to my fellow member's comments. I understand how busy Lord Veovis is, yet if he had read my proposal thoroughly, he would see that what I am proposing falls far short of the kind of *power* he suggests we would be relinquishing. Not only that, but I find myself in profound agreement with Veovis. Power is not a thing to be given lightly. And yes, responsibility is a grave and heavy burden and ought to be something one is schooled to bear. That is the D'ni way, and I would not have it changed."

Aitrus paused, looking about him, his eyes going from face to face among the circular levels of the great chamber.

"Let me therefore say it clearly, for the benefit of all, so that there is no mistaking what I am asking you to agree to today. I am as one with Lord Veovis. All matters of policy and funding *must* remain the prerogative of this chamber. I do not contest that for a moment. My proposal is designed to give, not take—to *empower* the common people of D'ni and give them a degree of control over their lives that at present they do not have."

Aitrus smiled. "I see that some of you shake your heads at that, but it is true, and some of you have seen it with your own eyes. Our people—D'ni, like ourselves—are not poor, nor are they hard done by. They have food and shelter, sanitation and medicines if need be, but—and this is the vital point—their lot could be improved. Greatly improved."

He looked about him once again, scrutinizing face after face.

"I know what some of you are thinking. Why? Why should we be concerned about improving their lot? Well, let me give you two good reasons. First, just think of whom we speak. We are not talking of idlers and spendthrifts and good-for-nothings, but of good, hardworking people, men and women both. All of us here know a good dozen or more such people. We meet them daily and depend on them for many things. And they depend on us.

"Second, it is often said, with justifiable pride, that D'ni rules ten thousand Ages, yet a society ought to be judged not merely by the extent of its empire but by the quality of life of *all* its citizens. We are a rich people. We can afford to be generous. Indeed, I would argue that it is our moral duty to be generous, especially to our own. And that is why I ask you, fellow guildsmen, to say 'aye' to this proposal. For D'ni, and so that we might in future look ourselves squarely in the mirror and be proud of what we have done here today. Guildsmen, my Lords, thank you."

As Aitrus sat, Lord R'hira signaled to the stewards at the back of the hall. Veovis and Aitrus had been the last two speakers; now it was all down to the vote.

R'hira waited as the eight stewards took their places. It was their job to count the hands raised both for and against the proposal. When they were ready, R'hira looked to his fellow Lords, then spoke again.

"All those in favor of the motion raise your hands."

The stewards quickly counted.

"And those against."

Again the stewards made their tally.

"Thank you, Guildsmen."

The stewards turned, making their way down, forming an orderly queue before Lord R'hira. As each gave his tally, R'hira wrote it down in the great ledger before him. As the final steward turned away, Lord R'hira quickly added up the two columns of figures, then looked to either side of him. It was a protocol that the Five Lords did not vote unless a decision was so close—within three votes, usually—that their opinion could decide the matter.

"Guildsmen," he said, looking back at the rank after rank of members seated around and above him. "It appears that you are divided on this issue. One hundred and eighty-two members for, one hundred and eighty against. In the circumstances, the Five speak *for* the proposal."

Veovis was on his feet at once. "But you cannot, my Lord! For what good reason . . . "

He fell silent, then bowed his head.

R'hira stared at the young Lord a moment, then stood, signaling to all that the proceedings were over. "The Council has spoken, Master Veovis. The proposal is carried."

Suahrnir closed the door quietly behind him, then turned, looking across the lamplit room to where his friend Veovis sat in the corner chair, lost in thought.

It was some time since he had seen Veovis quite so agitated, and even though he had calmed down considerably since the Council meeting, there was still a brooding intensity to him that did not bode well.

"Would you like a drink?" he asked, going over to the great stone cupboard beneath the window and picking up one of the three crystal decanters he kept there.

Veovis glanced up, then shook his head.

Suahrnir shrugged, then poured himself a large drink. He took a swig from the glass, then turned, facing Veovis again as the warmth of the liquor filled his throat.

"There must be something we can do," Veovis said quietly, as if speaking to himself.

Suahrnir smiled. "Maybe there is."

Veovis's eyes widened with interest. "Go on."

"There is a man I know," Suahrnir said, taking the seat beside Veovis. "They call him the Philosopher. He writes pamphlets."

"Pamphlets!" Veovis made a sound of disgust. "Really, Suahrnir, I thought you were being serious."

"I am. This Philosopher is a very influential man in the

lower city. People read his writings. Lots of people. And they listen to what he has to say. More so than Ti'ana and the reformers."

"And just what does he say?"

Suahrnir sat back. "That would take too long. You ought to read one or two of them for yourself. You would like them, Veovis."

Veovis stared at his friend skeptically, then reached out and took the glass from him, taking a sip from it before he handed it back.

"And what name does this Philosopher go by?"

"A'Gaeris."

Veovis roared with laughter. "A'Gaeris! The fraudster?"

"It was never proved."

But Veovis waved that away. "The guilds do not expel their members on the strength of rumor, Suahrnir. Besides, I was there when A'Gaeris was stripped of his Guild cloak. I heard the charges that were on the roll."

"That was fifty years ago."

"It does not matter if it was five hundred years ago. The man is untrustworthy."

"I think you are wrong. I think he could help you."

"Help me? How? By writing a pamphlet about it?"

Suahrnir looked down. He had never heard Veovis sound quite so bitter. The defeat today had clearly hit him hard; more so perhaps because of who it was had swung the vote against him.

"The Philosopher has no love of outsiders," Suahrnir said, staring into his glass. "Indeed, he argues that the mixing of bloods is an abomination."

Suahrnir looked up. Veovis was watching him now. "He says that?"

"That and much more. You should meet him."

Veovis laughed sourly. "Impossible."

"Then you will just sit here and brood, will you?"

"No," Veovis said, standing, then reaching across for his cloak. "I will go home to K'veer and brood, as you clearly do not want my company."

Suahrnir put his hand out, trying to stop his friend. "Veovis . . ."

"Tomorrow," Veovis said, brushing his hand off. "I will be in a better mood tomorrow."

Suahrnir watched him go, then sighed. Veovis was in a bad mood right now and closed to all suggestions, but maybe in a day or two . . .

He smiled, then, going over to his desk, began to pen a note.

Anna sat up in bed, a huge pile of pillows at her back, cradling the newborn; a serene smile, forged out of tiredness and exultation after a difficult twenty-hour labor, on her unusually pale face.

On a chair to one side, Tasera sat forward, her fingers laced together on one knee, her features set in a permanent grin of delight as she studied her grandson. He was small—much smaller than Aitrus had been at birth—but sturdy, and the midwife said he was a healthy child.

They were on Ko'ah, and it was spring on the island. The scent of blossoms was on the air and birdsong filled the morning's sunlit silence.

"Where *is* Aitrus?"

"He will be here soon," Anna said, smiling soothingly at Tasera. "He cannot simply walk away. It *was* his proposal."

"Even so . . ."

Tasera stopped, a grin breaching her face. "Aitrus! So there you are! What took you?"

Aitrus greeted his mother, then stepped past her, looking across the room to where Anna lay, his face, at that moment, filled with wonder.

"A boy," Anna said, smiling back at him.

Aitrus went across, then knelt beside the bed, his face on a level with the sleeping child, his eyes wide at the sight of this, his son.

"Why he's . . ."

". . . like you." Anna laughed softly. "He's beautiful, no?"

Aitrus nodded, then looked up at her. "Thank you," he said quietly, then, leaning carefully across the child, he gently kissed her.

Again he stared, drinking in the sight of his child the same way he had once studied the sleeping form of Anna, that night before he had asked her to be his wife, the two moments joined like links in a chain.

"Well, little Gehn," he said, the first hint of a tender smile on his lips. "How is the world?"

They had been expecting Master Oren for some hours. He had said he would be late, but as the time went on it began to look more and more as if he would not make the celebration. And then he arrived, his face dark, his manner withdrawn.

Aitrus, about to greet him, saw how he looked and took him aside.

"What is it, old friend?"

"We are summoned, Aitrus," Oren answered, embarrassed slightly. "All guildsmen must report back to D'ni at once. Two young guildsmen from the Guild of Maintainers have gone missing. We are to search the Ages for them."

Aitrus blinked. "But that's . . . "

". . . a mammoth task, yes, Aitrus, which is why the Maintainers have asked for the help of all the other guilds. The circumstances are . . . suspicious, let us say. They were investigating something important. What it was, we do not know, but Grand Master Jadaris is concerned enough to think that they may have been kidnapped, even killed."

The news stunned Aitrus. "All right," he said. "Come in and greet my family a moment, Oren. I, meanwhile, will gather up our friends and tell them the news. Then we shall go."

Oren nodded. For a moment he gently held Aitrus's arm. "I am sorry to be the bearer of such ill news on so joyous an occasion. I hear you have a son."

A brief smile appeared on Aitrus's features once more. "Come see him, Oren. His name is Gehn and he shall be a great guildsman one day."

An hour later, Aitrus stood before Master Jadaris himself.

"Ah, Master Aitrus. I hear congratulations are in order. A son, eh? That is good news. Very good news indeed!"

"Thank you, Grand Master," Aitrus said, bowing low.

"You have been told what is happening?" Jadaris asked.

"We are to search the Ages."

"Indeed. But not all the Ages. Only those which the two guildsmen were known to have personally investigated in the last five years."

Aitrus frowned. "Master?"

"This must not be known to all, Aitrus," Jadaris said, lowering his voice slightly and sitting forward, "but a number of blank linking books have gone missing from our Halls. We suspect that the guildsmen took them to carry out their investigations."

That news was grave. Aitrus saw at once how difficult things were.

"Do we know what they were investigating, Master Jadaris?"

"We do not. But we think they may have found something on one of the Ages they were sent to look at routinely. Something very important. And they may have gone back to try to get conclusive proof, using the missing linking books."

"How many Ages are involved, Master?"

"More than sixty."

"And you suspect that a senior guildsman might be involved?"

Jadaris nodded. "That is why we are sending in teams, rather than individual guildsmen. We do not want to take the risk of losing any more of our men. I have assigned you to a team of our own Maintainers."

"I see. And where would you like me to go, Grand Master?"

"To K'veer."

"K'veer!"

Jadaris raised a hand. "Before you object, Lord Rakeri himself asked for you, Aitrus. He considers you above reproach and felt that if you were to lead the team investigating his family's Books, no possible taint would fall upon his family. As you might understand, this is a most sensitive matter."

"Of course. Even so . . . "

"It is decided," Jadaris said with a finality that made Aitrus look up at him, then bow.

"As you wish, Master Jadaris."

Lord Rakeri greeted Aitrus on the steps above the jetty. Behind the old man, the great spiral rock of K'veer blotted out all else. It was early, and the light in the great cavern was dim, but across the lake D'ni glowed like the embers of a fire.

"Aitrus, I am glad you came. And well done. I hear you have a son."

Aitrus took the old man's hands in his own and smiled. "Thank you, Lord Rakeri. The boy's name is Gehn."

Rakeri returned his smile, squeezing his hands before he relinquished them. "It is a good name. He whom he is named after, his father's father's father, was a great man. Or would have been, if time had been kind to him. But come, let us go through. This is a difficult business yet it must be done, so let us do it with some dignity."

Aitrus nodded, walking beside the old man as they went inside, the other guildsmen—six young Maintainers and one Master of the Guild—following behind.

The great mansion was still and silent. After the laughter of the party on Ko'ah, this seemed a somber, joyless place.

The huge doors to the Book Room were locked. Rakeri took a key from the huge bunch at his belt and unlocked the right-hand door, then pushed it open.

"Will you not come in with us, my Lord?" Aitrus asked, hesitating before stepping inside the room.

"I would rather not, Master Aitrus," Rakeri said, with a tiny sigh. "This whole matter is difficult. Routine inspections one can live with. They are . . . *traditional*. But this . . . this casts a bad light on all, don't you think?"

"I am sure there is an explanation, my Lord." Aitrus smiled consolingly. "We shall work as quickly and as efficiently as we can, and I shall make sure that a copy of my report is placed before you before we leave here."

Rakeri smiled. "That is kind of you, young Aitrus. Very kind."

The Book Room of K'veer was an impressive chamber, and though Aitrus had seen it often before, stepping into it once more he felt again the weight of years that lay upon its shelves.

Shelves filled three of the walls from floor to ceiling—endless books of commentary, numbered and dated on their spines in golden D'ni letters. In one place only, to Aitrus's left as he stood, looking in, were the shelves breached. There, two great windows, paned with translucent stone of varying colors, went from floor to ceiling. Through them could be seen the lake and the far wall of the great cavern.

The whole Book Room was like a giant spur, jutting from the main twist of the rock. There was a drop of ten spans between it and the surface of the lake below.

It was a daunting place for a young guildsman to enter. Rakeri and his family owned six Books in all—six ancient Ages. These massive, ancient books were to be found at the far end of the long, high-walled chamber, resting on tilted marble pedestals, the colors of which matched the leather covers of the Books themselves. Each was secured to the pedestal by a strong linked chain that looked like gold but was in fact made of nara, the hardest of the D'ni stones.

Aitrus walked across, studying each of the Books in turn. Five of them were closed, the sixth—the Book of Nidur Gemat—was open, the descriptive panel glowing in the half light of the early morning.

He had been to Nidur Gemat often, in earlier days, when he and Veovis had been friends. Standing there now, Aitrus felt a great sadness that they had been estranged, and wished he might somehow bridge the chasm that had developed between them these past fifteen years.

Aitrus turned, calling to the Guild Master. "Master Kura. Post two men on the door. We shall start with Nidur Gemat."

The Guild Master nodded and was about to talk to his

guildsmen when the door burst open and Veovis stormed into the room.

"I thought as much!" he cried, pointing directly at Aitrus. "I might have known you would have yourself appointed to this task!"

Kura went to intercede, but Veovis glared at him. "Hold your tongue, man! I am speaking to Guild Master Aitrus here!"

Aitrus waited as Veovis crossed the chamber, keeping all expression from his face, yet a tense combative urge made him clench his right fist where it rested beside his leg.

"Well?" Veovis said, stopping an arm's length from Aitrus. "Have you nothing to say?"

Aitrus shook his head. He had learned long ago that when someone falsely accused you, the best defense you had was silence.

"You couldn't keep yourself from meddling, could you? As soon as you heard . . . "

"Veovis!"

Veovis straightened up, then turned. His father, Rakeri, stood in the doorway. "Father?"

"Leave us now," Rakeri said, the tone of command in his voice one that Aitrus had never heard him use to Veovis before this hour.

Veovis bowed, then turned glaring at Aitrus, an unspoken comment in his eyes. When he was gone, Rakeri came across.

"Forgive my son, Aitrus. He does not understand how things are. I shall speak with him at once. In the meantime, I apologize for him. And I am sure, in time, he will come and apologize in person."

Aitrus gave the tiniest nod of his head. "Thank you, Lord

Rakeri, but that will not be necessary. Things are bad enough between us. Your apology is quite enough."

Rakeri smiled and gently nodded. "You are wise as well as kind, Aitrus. Yes, and I regret that my son has lost so good a friend. And no blame to you for that. My son is stubborn, just as his grandfather was."

There was a moment's awkward silence, then the old man nodded once again. "Well, Aitrus, I shall leave you once again. Do what you must. We have nothing here to hide."

Aitrus bowed his head. "My Lord . . ."

A month passed with no word or sign of the two missing guildsmen. Slowly the great sweep of the sixty Ages came to a close. Two days after the departure of Aitrus and the Maintainer team from K'veer, Veovis sat on the veranda at the top of the island, reading his father's copy of the report.

Turning the final page, he read the concluding remarks, then set the report down on the low table at his side and sat back, staring thoughtfully into the distance.

Suahrnir, seated just across from him, studied his friend a moment, then, "Well? What does our *friend* Aitrus say?"

Veovis was silent a moment, then he turned his head and looked at Suahrnir. "He was most thorough. But also fair. Scrupulously so. I may have misjudged him."

"You think so?" Suahrnir laughed. "Personally I think he feels nothing but animosity toward you, Veovis."

"Maybe so, but there is nothing in the report."

"In the official report, maybe . . . "

Veovis narrowed his eyes. "What do you mean?"

"I mean that what is written down for all to see is not always what is said . . . in private. What if Master Aitrus gave another, separate report to the Five?"

"Then my father would have heard of such, and he, in turn, would have told me."

"Or to Lord R'hira alone?"

Veovis looked down, then shook his head. "No," he said, but the word lacked certainty.

"What if he found something?"

"*Found?* What could he find?"

"Oh, I don't mean found as in really found. Yet he might *say* he found something."

"And the Maintainers?"

Suahrnir gave an ironic smile. "They could be fooled easily enough. They were, after all, but *apprentice* guildsmen."

The thought of it clearly disturbed Veovis, nonetheless he shook his head once more. "Aitrus does not like me, but that does not make him a cheat, nor a slanderer."

"Who knows what makes a man do certain things? You hurt him badly when you opposed his marriage to the outsider. It is not the kind of thing a man forgets easily. And it is a more than adequate motive to wish to seek revenge."

Veovis looked down, his whole expression dark and brooding. Finally, he raised his head again. "No, I cannot believe it of him."

Suahrnir leaned forward, speaking conspiratorially now. "Maybe not. But there is a way we could be certain."

"Certain? How?"

"I have a friend. He hears things . . . from servants and the like. If something secretive is going on, *he* will have heard of it."

"This friend of yours . . . who is he?"

Suahrnir smiled and sat back. "You know his name."

"A'Gaeris!" Veovis laughed dismissively, then shook his head. "You ask me to take *his* word?"

"You do not have to believe anything he says," Suahrnir answered. "But what harm will it do to listen? You might learn something to your benefit."

"And what does *he* want out of this?"

Suahrnir looked surprised at the suggestion. "Why, nothing. Nothing at all. The man owes me a favor. Besides, I think you will enjoy meeting him. Yes, and he you. You are both strong, intelligent men. I would enjoy watching you lock horns."

Veovis stared at his friend, then, with a grudging shrug of his shoulders, he said. "All right. Arrange a meeting. But no word of this must get out. If anyone should witness our meeting . . ."

Suahrnir smiled, then stood, giving a little bow to his friend. "Don't worry, Veovis. I know the very place."

It was D'ni night. Not the night of moon and stars you would find up on the surface, but a night of intense, almost stygian shadow. The lake was dark, the organisms in the water inactive, their inner clocks set to a thirty-hour biological cycle established long ago and in another place, far from earth.

On the roof garden of Kahlis's mansion, Anna stood alone, leaning on the parapet, looking out over the upper city. Earlier in the evening it had been a blaze of light; now only scattered lamps marked out the lines of streets. Then it had seemed like a great pearled shell, clinging to the dark wall of the cavern; now it looked more like a ragged web, strung across one corner of a giant's larder.

Out on the lake itself the distant wink of lights revealed the whereabouts of islands. Somewhere out there, on one of those islands, was Aitrus. Or, at least, he would have been, were he in D'ni at all.

Anna sighed, missing him intensely, then turned, hearing the child's cries start up again in the nursery below where she stood. For a moment she closed her eyes, tempted to leave things to the nurse, then, steeling herself against the sound, she went across and, bending down, lifted the wooden hatch that was set into the floor. Slipping inside, she went down the narrow stairs and out into the corridor that ran the length of the top of the house.

At once the sound of the crying grew much louder; a persistent, whining cry that never seemed to end; or if it did, it ended but briefly, only to intensify.

Stepping into the room, Anna saw that the nurse had been joined by her male colleague, Master Jura of the Guild of Healers. The ancient looked up from the desk in the corner where he had been writing and frowned at Anna, as if she and not the baby were the cause of the problem.

Ignoring him, Anna walked over to the cot and looked

down at her son. Gehn lay on his back, his tiny red face screwed up tight as he bawled and bawled, his mouth a jagged black O in the midst of that redness, his arms and legs kicking in a continuous mechanical movement of distress. The sight of it distressed her. It made her want to pick him up and cuddle him, but that would solve nothing; the crying would go on whatever she did.

"Well . . ." the Healer said after a moment, consulting his notes, "I would say that the matter is a simple one."

Anna saw how he looked at her, his manner cold and unsympathetic, and felt her stomach tighten.

"The child's problems stem from its stomach," the Healer continued. "He cries because he is not receiving adequate sustenance, and because he is in pain."

"In pain?"

The Healer nodded, then looked to his notes again. "If the child were D'ni it would be fairly easy to prescribe something for his condition, but as it is . . ."

"Forgive me," Anna interrupted, "but what difference does that make?"

Master Jura blinked, surprised. When he spoke again, there was a note of impatience in his voice. "Is it not self-evident? The child is unnatural. A hybrid. He is neither D'ni nor human, but some curious mixture of the two, and therein lie his problems. Why, it is astonishing that he is even viable!"

Anna felt the shock of what he had said wash through her. How dare he talk of her son as if he were some strange experiment! She looked down at the bawling child, then back at the old Healer.

"Have you *tested* him, Master Jura?"

The old man laughed dismissively. "I do not have to test him. As I said, it is self-evident. One cannot mix human and D'ni blood. To be perfectly honest with you, the child would be better off dead."

Anna stared at him, her anger rising. Then, with a calmness she did not feel, she spoke.

"Get out."

The old man had gone back to his notes. At her words, he looked up, glancing first at the nurse, to see if it were she whom Anna had addressed, and then at Anna herself.

"Yes," Anna said, her face hard now. "*You*, old man. You heard me. Get out before I throw you out!"

"Why, I . . . "

"Get *out!*" she shouted, focusing her anger on the man. "How dare you come into my house and tell me that my son would be better off dead! How *dare* you!"

Master Jura bristled, then, closing up his notes, he slipped them into his case and stood.

"I will not stay where I am not wanted."

"Good," Anna said, wanting to strike the man for his impertinence. "And you," she said, turning on the nurse. "Pack your things and go. I have no further use for you."

It was a quiet, first-floor room in a house in the J'Taeri District, overlooking the harbor. As the door closed, Veovis looked about him. It was a staid, respectable room, three large chairs resting against one wall, a large, dark-wood dresser against another. On the third, either side of the huge picture window, were two portraits. He walked across and studied them a moment. Both of the women looked stern and matronly, their clothing dark and austere—the dour uniform of respectable D'ni women for four thousand years and more.

He shook his head, then turned. The city bell was sounding the fourth hour of the afternoon. All was peaceful.

Would A'Gaeris come? And if he did, what would the old fraud have to say?

He could remember how angry A'Gaeris had been, the day of his expulsion—could remember vividly how he had glared at the Grand Master before throwing down his guild cloak and storming from the Hall.

Veovis had been but a student that day, not even a guildsman, let alone a Master. And now here he was, almost fifty years on.

The door behind him creaked open. Veovis turned, to find Suahrnir standing there.

"Has he come?"

Suahrnir nodded, then stood back as A'Gaeris entered the room. He was a tall, broad-shouldered man, but stout in girth and balding, his gray hair swept back from his pate and worn unfashionably long. He wore a simple black tunic and long baggy pants of a similar black cloth. But it was his eyes that drew attention. Fierce eyes that stared intently, almost insolently back at Veovis.

"My Lord," A'Gaeris said, the slightest sneer in the greeting.

"Philosopher," Veovis replied, matching his tone perfectly.

A'Gaeris smiled. "I was not wrong, then."

"Wrong?"

"I said you had fire in you. And I was right."

Veovis smiled sardonically. "That would be praise if from another's lips."

"But not from mine?"

"I do not know you, except by reputation."

"You have read my writings, then?"

"Not a word."

A'Gaeris barely batted an eyelid at the news. "Then that is a joy to come."

"And modest, too?"

"Need I be?"

Veovis smiled, warming to the man. "You are sharp, A'Gaeris, I'll give you that."

"Sharp enough to cut yourself on, I warrant. So why are you here?"

"To be honest, I am not sure. I was persuaded that you might help me."

"Help you?" A'Gaeris laughed, then walked to the window and stared out. "But you are a Lord of D'ni. How can I, a mere common man, help *you?*"

But there was a teasing glint in the Philosopher's eyes that intrigued Veovis.

"I do not know."

"No," A'Gaeris looked back at him and smiled. "But maybe I do."

"Go on."

"I hear things."

"So Suahrnir told me. But are they things worth hearing?"

A'Gaeris shrugged. "What would you know?"

"Something to my benefit?"

"And your foes' disadvantage?"

"Perhaps."

The Philosopher smiled. "We share one important thing, Lord Veovis. A love of D'ni, and a belief in the purity of D'ni blood."

"What do you mean?"

"I speak of your once-friend Aitrus and his ill-chosen wife."

Veovis narrowed his eyes. "What of them?"

"Only last night, it seems, the outsider woman sent Master Jura of the Healers away with his tail between his legs. And the child's nurse."

Veovis looked to Suahrnir again. This was news indeed if it were true.

"Do you know why?"

A'Gaeris grinned broadly. "It seems Master Jura suggested that it might save time and trouble were the half-breed to be peacefully done away with."

Veovis stared back at him a moment, astonished. "And what did Master Aitrus say of this?"

"What could he say? He is away. But he will know soon enough when he is back."

"It is a shame."

"Indeed," A'Gaeris agreed. "Such a union should never have been allowed."

"I did all I could to prevent it."

"I know." The Philosopher was looking at him now with sympathy and understanding.

Veovis looked down. "It seems you know what I want, Philosopher. But what of you? What do you want?"

"To be your friend."

Veovis looked up, smiling, expecting some sardonic look upon A'Gaeris's face, but those eyes were serious and solemn.

"I have missed the company of my peers," A'Gaeris said. "It is all very well preaching to the rabble, but it changes nothing. My life ended when the guild threw me out."

"They had good reason . . . "

"They had none!"

The sharpness of the rejoinder surprised Veovis.

"I was falsely accused," A'Gaeris went on. "There was no missing book. Or if there was, it was not I who took it."

"So you say," Veovis said quietly.

"So I say," A'Gaeris said, fiercely now, challenging Veovis to gainsay him a second time.

There was a moment's silence, then Veovis shrugged. "Give me a day or two to think on this, and then, perhaps, we shall meet again."

"As you wish."

Veovis nodded, then smiled. "You say she threw the Healer out?"

"She threatened him, I'm told."

"Well . . . " Veovis nodded to himself thoughtfully, then walked over to the door. "It was interesting meeting you, Philosopher."

"And you, Lord Veovis."

Darkness was rising from the lake as A'Gaeris climbed the back stairs of the lodging house where, for the past fifty years, he had stayed. Corlam, his mute assistant, watched him from the darkened window overhead, turning hurriedly to cross the room and light the lamp.

The Philosopher seemed thoughtful tonight. As he came into the room he barely acknowledged Corlam, but went straight to his desk and sat.

The room was a shrine to the Philosopher's endeavors. Apart from the door and window, there was not a square inch of the walls that was not covered in books, piled two deep on broad stone shelves. Some were reference books, others books of Council minutes and resolutions. Some—almost all of those on the shelves at the far end of the rectangular room—A'Gaeris's own journals.

For fifty years he had labored here, since the day he had been cast out of the guild, making his plans, slowly preparing for the day when he could emerge again from obscurity and become a name again. Someone *everybody* knew, and not just the rabble of the lower city.

All this Corlam knew intimately, for, having "adopted" him as a child—an orphan of the lower alleys—A'Gaeris trusted Corlam as he trusted no one else, using him as a sounding board, rehearsing his ideas and thoughts, refining his theories until Corlam knew them almost as well as he.

Corlam went across and stood behind his master, watching as A'Gaeris took his latest journal from the left-hand drawer and, laying it on the desk, opened it and began to write.

Today had been important. Corlam knew that. His master had been in a state of some excitement for days before this meeting, though why exactly Corlam could not ascertain. Lord Veovis was, he knew, an important man, but why his master should desire to meet him only A'Gaeris himself knew, for he had said nothing on this score to Corlam.

"Real books," A'Gaeris said, after a while, glancing up at Corlam. "If only I could get my hands on some *real* Books."

Corlam stared back at him. There were many Books on the shelves—most of them "liberated" from the guild libraries; for, after all, with so many books, the guildsmen rarely ever noticed one was missing—but he knew what his master meant. He was talking about kortee'nea. Blank D'ni Books. The kind one used to link to the Ages.

"I know," A'Gaeris said, smiling at him, then turning back to his journal. "You cannot help me there, Corlam. But maybe our lordship can. Besides, I have a man on the inside now. A friend who wants to help me. If I can persuade *him* to aid me, who knows?"

Corlam looked closer. His master was practicing again. Writing words in someone else's hand. Corlam squinted at the page, then tapped A'Gaeris's shoulder, nodding vigorously. It was Lord Veovis's writing, as clear as day. He had seen examples only the other day, from the records of the Council.

Corlam watched, openmouthed. Though he had watched A'Gaeris do this many times now over the years, he still found it magical the way his master could so easily copy another's hand. He had only to study it an hour and he had it.

Pushing the journal away from him, A'Gaeris yawned and stretched, then turned to face Corlam.

"You know, I had an idea today, Corlam. While I was waiting for his Lordship to turn up."

Corlam smiled, a look of attention coming to his features.

"It's like this," he went on. "I was asking myself how I could get into a place where I should not be—into a Guild strong room, say, or a well-guarded cell—and then get out again without being caught. The easiest way, of course, would be to write a specific linking book to allow me to link into that place. But to get out again I would need a second linking book, and I would have to leave it there. You follow me?"

Corlam nodded.

"So. Getting in would be easy. Getting out without being followed and tracked down by the Maintainers would be extremely hard. Unless . . ."

A'Gaeris smiled a great smile of self-satisfaction. "Unless, of course, one linked on to another Age, and then another after that. In fact, one might take three separate Linking Books into the cell with one, just to confuse things. But it would be no good having the second and third Linking Books at the place where one linked *to* each time. That would be no good at all. No. One would need to hide the Book a good hour's walk from where one linked to, so that anyone following you would have to search a wide area in order to find that second Book. Indeed, one could have three or four such Books—only one of which you would use. And when one linked the second time, again you would have an hour's walk to get to the next Linking Book. That way no one could follow you. At least, not quickly, and maybe not at all. A little preparation, two hours' walking, and one would be safe."

For a moment A'Gaeris's eyes glowed, then he looked down. "Of course, one would need a masterful writer to create Ages at will, and, say, a mole inside with access to places such as . . . cells, for example."

Anna was in the laboratory, working on the latest soil samples from Gemedet, when Aitrus came in. Gehn was in the cot on a bench nearby. As Aitrus came across, he stopped to lean over and smile at his softly cooing son before greeting Anna.

Anna looked up from the lens of the microscope and smiled. "I won't be long."

He nodded. "I have had a letter."

"Who is it from?"

"That is just it. It is not signed and the handwriting is unfamiliar."

He handed it to her, then waited as she read it.

"Destroy it," she said, handing it back to him. "And do not get involved, whatever it is."

"But what does it mean?"

"Does it matter?"

Aitrus shrugged. "It is the tone of it that bothers me. 'Something to your benefit'. And all of the secrecy. What do you think is going on?"

Anna sighed. "If it really worries you, Aitrus, hand it over to the Maintainers. Let them send a man along. But don't you get involved."

"All right," he smiled. "I'll destroy it." And having said it, he reached across and, turning on the gas tap, ignited it, and held the corner of the letter in the fine blue flame. When it was well aflame, he dropped it into the sink. "There," he said.

Behind him, Gehn began to whimper. Aitrus went over, lifted the baby from the cot, and cuddled him in the crook of his arm.

"He must be hungry," Anna said. "I'll finish here."

"No, you work on," he said. "I'll feed him."

She smiled. "Don't over feed him. That was the trouble last time. The poor little mite could barely cope!"

"I know," he said, then, as if it were an afterthought, he added. "I have to go back to my rooms later on. There's a report I have to finish. I'll only be an hour or two. I can join you for a late supper."

Anna grinned. "That would be nice. And maybe we could get away for a few days soon. To Gemedet."

Aitrus nodded. "I shall ask Master Erafir to stand in for me. It is time he took on more responsibility."

"Then go and see to Gehn. But remember, Aitrus, nothing too heavy for his stomach."

Aitrus had meant to go straight to his rooms; his feet had led him partway there, but then curiosity had overcome him and he found himself descending the steps, then walking beneath the gate and into J'Taeri District.

I do not have to get involved, he told himself. Whatever it was, he did not have to act upon it. He would observe whatever had to be observed, then leave.

The street itself was an ordinary street, the house a staid, respectable dwelling of the kind merchants often bought. The windows were dark, the door locked. Aitrus turned. The house overlooked the harbor and Kerath's arch, the top of which was almost on a level with where he stood. Across the street, between the facing buildings, was a low wall, from which one could look out over the lake. He went across and stood there, his hands resting lightly on the stone.

There was a faint mist in the cavern tonight. In the narrow streets lamps wavered as wagons moved between the houses. There was a shout from somewhere far below, and then laughter. Otherwise the night was peaceful. Aitrus turned, conscious of a faint gurgling sound. Close by a narrow culvert cut across the street, clear water running in a stream from the very top of the huge, scallop-shaped city. He bent down and dipped his hand. It was cool.

He was about to turn away and go when he heard footsteps coming along the far end of the street. Looking about him, he spied a nearby doorway and stepped into its shadows.

The footsteps came on, the slow click of leather boots on stone, then stopped. Aitrus hesitated. He was about to risk a glimpse, when a second set of footsteps could be heard, this time from his left, brisker than the first. They paused, then came on again, slower now. There was a low murmur of greeting.

Aitrus peeked out. Two men stood in the lamplight before the door of the house. One was cloaked and hooded, the other, a heavier-set man, wore nothing on his balding head. He looked familiar, but where Aitrus had seen him he could not say. He ducked back into shadow, listening.

"What do you want?" one of them asked, the voice, again, familiar.

"I have something to show you," the second answered. "Something that will interest you."

It was a deep voice, cultured yet with a strangely common edge to it. Whereas the first . . .

"You want *me* to go in there with you?" the first man asked, and as he did, Aitrus finally recognized the voice.

Veovis!

"Don't you trust me?"

"Alone, at night, in a strange house?" Veovis laughed ironically. "Would *you* trust *me?*"

"Implicitly."

There was a silence, then a huff of resignation.

"All right," Veovis said finally. "I shall trust you. But be warned. I am armed, A'Gaeris."

That name came as a shock to Aitrus. All young guildsmen knew it. No other name attracted quite such infamy. But what was he doing here in J'Taeri, a respectable district? And what was Veovis doing meeting him?

Aitrus peeked out again, in time to see the big, heavyset man place a key in the lock and turn it, then put out his hand, inviting Veovis to step inside.

"You first," Veovis said, standing back a little, his hand on the hilt of his dagger. "And put a light on. Then I shall come inside."

A'Gaeris smiled and shrugged, then stepped inside the house. A moment later a light went on in the hall.

Letting his hand fall from the hilt of his dagger, Veovis glanced to either side, then stepped into the house.

Was that it? Was that what the anonymous writer had meant him to see? And if so, why?

Aitrus was about to leave, to make his way back up to the Guild Hall, when a light went on in the ground-floor room to the left of the front door. Easing back against the wall, Aitrus watched as A'Gaeris entered the room, followed a moment later by Veovis.

Veovis, standing in the doorway, seemed ill at ease. He glanced about him, then, satisfied that it was not a trap, closed the door and walked across to where A'Gaeris was rummaging among the papers on a desk. There were a number of slender books among the papers, and A'Gaeris lifted one and handed it to Veovis.

Veovis hesitated, then opened it. He studied it a moment then looked up, his eyes wide.

A'Gaeris smiled, then gestured toward the chair facing him.

Aitrus went straight to his rooms in the Guild Hall. He had work to do, but he found he could not work. What he had seen troubled him greatly. Anna was right, of course; he ought to have gone straight to Master Jadaris and put the matter in the hands of the Maintainers, but he had not, and this was the result. Oh, he could go there now, but what proof would he have? It was his word against Veovis's.

But what was going on? Why were such strange and unlikely companions meeting in a merchant's house?

Aitrus sat still a long while, trying to fathom it, but he could make no sense of it at all.

Anna. Anna would know. Only he could not ask Anna, because he had promised her he would not get involved. He had burned the note, as if it had held no power over him. But it had. And now he had this dilemma.

Veovis. Maybe he ought to go and see Veovis and confront him openly with what he had seen.

Aitrus thought a while, then nodded. It seemed the right thing to do. No skulking about in shadows. That was not his way. He would take a boat to K'veer in the morning and have it out with Veovis, face-to-face. For there had to be an explanation.

Aitrus put away his files, then left the room, locking it behind him. *Tomorrow*, he told himself, making his way down the long, silent corridor toward the great gate. *It will all come clear tomorrow.*

Aitrus rose early the next morning. At supper the previous evening he had said nothing to Anna, nor had he hinted at what he planned. Yet even as he ate a hasty breakfast, a servant brought him in a second letter, the handwriting on the envelope the same as that on the anonymous note the day before.

Aitrus stared at the envelope a long while, then, with a sigh of resignation, slit it open with his fingernail. Inside was a brief note in the same hand as before, but with it was a letter—a letter from Veovis to one of the two young guildsmen who had gone missing thirty days back.

He read it through, then looked to the date at the top of the page. That was the day before the guildsmen disappeared.

"No," he said quietly, setting the letter aside and picking up the note once more. "It is not possible . . ."

The note read: "Come and see me if you wish to know more" and gave a time and place. That place was the merchant's house in J'Taeri.

Three choices now lay before him: to go to Master Jadaris and lay the matter before him; to go straight to K'veer and confront Veovis; or to wait until tonight and meet the author of the note.

The first was common sense; the second satisfied his sense of honor; but it was the third he would do.

Why? He could not answer why. It was simply how he was.

Forgive me, Anna, he thought, slipping the note and letter into his pocket and rising from his seat.

Veovis stood beside A'Gaeris on the great rock, looking out across the massive plain that stretched away below him and shook his head. Everything was subtly wrong. The colors were *unnatural*, the shapes of trees, even the way the hills were formed, all was wrong. Yet it existed.

He turned, looking through his lenses at A'Gaeris. "Who made this?"

A'Gaeris turned, his eyes gleaming beyond the surface of the protective glasses. "Your old friend, Aitrus."

"Impossible," Veovis said dismissively. "Aitrus and his kin own but two Ages—Ko'ah and Gemedet. Both are strictly monitored by the Maintainers. If either were anything like this . . . well, it would not be allowed."

"Yet this *is* his Age," A'Gaeris said, smiling now as he handed Veovis the Linking Book.

"No," Veovis said quietly, disbelief vying with horror as he stared at the handwriting on the pages of the Book. It *was* Aitrus's. He had seen Aitrus's hand too often to be in doubt.

"He is experimenting," A'Gaeris answered, matter-of-factly. "Secretly, of course, for he knows the guilds would frown upon his activities. The woman leads him on, of course. Without her he would never have strayed from the D'ni path. It is her insidious influence we see all about us, Veovis. The wrongness . . . that is her doing."

Veovis looked about him, then nodded, half-convinced.

"Poor Aitrus."

"You pity him?"

Veovis looked up, a flash of anger in his eyes. "He was a good man, once. As you rightly say, the outsider has bewitched him and stolen his senses." He closed the Book and shook it. "If *this* is true . . ."

A'Gaeris put his arm out, indicating their surroundings. "Can you doubt it?"

"No . . . no, it is clear to me now."

Veovis sighed heavily.

A'Gaeris stared at him, as if sympathetic. "Would you like me to leave you for a while?"

Veovis nodded, then, with a small sad smile, opened the Linking Book for the Philosopher. The square on the right-hand page glowed softly, showing a picture of a study back on D'ni.

A'Gaeris met his eyes a moment. "There *is* more."

"More?"

"Yes. This is not the only Age he made. Perhaps you would like to see a few before you make up your mind what to do."

Again Veovis nodded, clearly shocked by this news.

"Well," A'Gaeris said finally, putting out his hand, "I shall leave you now. Farewell."

His hand touched the glowing box. In a moment he was gone.

Veovis closed the Book and pocketed it, then looked up again. There was a curious beauty to this world, yet it *was* wrong.

Aitrus had to be stopped. But how? If he went to the Five with this information, Aitrus would be expelled from the Council, stripped of his guild membership, and possibly even incarcerated on a Prison Age. Such was the penalty for making illicit Ages. It would rid him of his chief opponent in Council, but that was unimportant. Besides, he wondered if he could do it if it meant destroying Aitrus and his family. Maybe the woman *was* a pernicious influence, and maybe the child *was* better off dead, but for Aitrus himself he still felt a great sympathy. Despite all their recent animosity, he could not help but remember how good and kind a friend Aitrus had once been. A true friend, unafraid to say as he saw.

Walking to the edge of the great slab, Veovis sat, his booted feet dangling over the drop. What should he do?

I'll wait, he decided, *and see what other evidence our friend A'Gaeris has to offer. And then I'll take my father's counsel.*

Veovis stood, taking the Linking Book from his pocket and opening it. Then, like a child gently leaping a stream, he jumped out, over the edge of the great rock, putting his hand to the panel as he leapt, linking—vanishing into the air—even as the Book tumbled down into the wilderness of rock and tree below.

"Wait here. My Master will see you in a moment."

As the boy left the darkened room, Aitrus walked across. What, for the briefest instant, he had taken to be a mirror was in fact a window, looking in to what appeared to be a study. A single wall lamp lit the inner room dimly.

"Strange," he said quietly, surprised to find a window in the middle of a house.

On the far side of the study was a desk. Open upon the desk, recognizable by the tell-tale glow on its right-hand page, was a D'ni book.

Aitrus stared at it, astonished to see it there. Yet even as he looked, a figure formed in the air in front of the desk, until it stood, as solid as everything about it, on the thick, red carpet.

A'Gaeris!

A'Gaeris shook himself, shrugging off the sensation of the link, then went around to the far side of the desk and opened one of the drawers, taking something from within. For a time he sat there, staring down at it, then, sensing a disturbance in the air, he looked up.

As he did, a second figure formed before the desk. Veovis.

A cold certainty swept through Aitrus at the sight. This was ill indeed.

Veovis turned, looking to his seated companion, then nodded.

"All right. You had better show me the others."

A'Gaeris stood. In his hands was another Book. He stepped around the desk and handed it to Veovis.

"There are more," he said. "This is the only one that I have here, but I can bring the others if you wish. Tomorrow night, if that is convenient."

Veovis studied the Book in his hands a while, then handed it back. "Tomorrow," he said. "I shall come tomorrow."

"At this hour?" A'Gaeris asked.

"At this hour," Veovis answered. And then he turned and left, slamming the door behind him.

A'Gaeris stared at the Book a moment, then set it down and turned to face the one-way mirror, looking directly at Aitrus.

"Aitrus. We need to talk."

"You did not believe him capable, did you?"

Aitrus looked up wearily. For more than two hours he had worked his way through a stack of letters and documents, all in Veovis's hand.

There was nothing here that was directly incriminating—in almost every case the evidence against Veovis was purely circumstantial—yet the pattern of it seemed conclusive. Enough to convince Aitrus, anyway. He looked back across the desk at the Philosopher. A'Gaeris's brow was beaded with perspiration. In the wavering candlelight he seemed much older than his eighty five-years.

"How long has he been trading in illicit Books?"

"Two, maybe three years now—that is, as far as *I* know. As I said, I was not sure of it at first. After all, he was a great Lord. A man of real substance. It seemed remarkable—unbelievable, almost—that he should be demeaning himself so."

"It still is," Aitrus said, setting the final memorandum aside. "If I had not seen all this with my own eyes." He stared at it a moment, then looked back at A'Gaeris. "Where did you get these?"

"I have sources," A'Gaeris answered. "I bought this here, that there, collecting, all the while collecting, until I had enough to be certain."

"And the Books you are selling him; where did *they* come from? I have heard nothing of missing Books."

"They were from his friend, Suahrnir."

"*Suahrnir!* But . . . "

Aitrus saw it at once. One of the duties of the Guild of Maintainers was to destroy "failed" Books—D'ni Books that, for one reason or another, had not worked, linking to unstable Ages. These were burned in special guild ovens. Or were supposed to be. And the man in charge of that task was . . . Guild Master Suahrnir.

"But why does he not deal with his friend Veovis directly?"

A'Gaeris smiled. "They are friends, yes, but neither trusts

the other. Besides . . . " he laughed, "neither knows the other is involved. Suahrnir does not know who buys the Books, and Veovis . . . "

"Does not know who supplies them, right?"

Aitrus sat back, astonished. Then, "So why are you show-ing *me* all this?"

A'Gaeris sat forward, the fire of indignation in his eyes suddenly. "Because no one would listen to me. But you, Aitrus, *you* could do something. You could even get to Lord R'hira himself."

"But *why?*"

"Because I, who was once an honest man, was barred from the guild for something I did not do, while this Lord's son, this rock-worm, can do as he will and get away with it. That's why!"

A'Gaeris's face was dark with anger. "You must under-stand. Veovis came to me. And they found out. They must have been watching him. That is why he killed them."

The room was silent. Aitrus stared at the Philosopher coldly.

"I do not believe you," he said, finally.

"No," A'Gaeris said sadly, "yet it *is* true." He pointed to the last thing in the pile—the Linking Book—his eyes grave. "See for yourself if you do not believe me!"

Veovis stepped from the boat onto the bottom step, then turned, looking back across the lake toward the sleeping city.

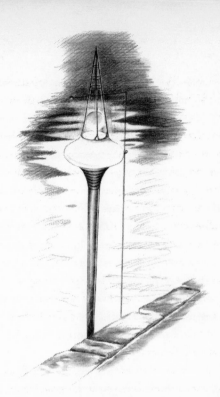

Beneath him, dark as pitch, the water lapped softly against the stone. Above and to his right, beyond the stone lip of the harbor wall, a lamp burned steadily atop its pole, reflected in the water farther out.

The great cavern was silent, as if empty of all other life. Only the faint, dull air-rhythm of the great fans could be heard, distant like a heartbeat.

Veovis stretched and yawned. He had much to think about, yet he was tired now and experience had taught him not to make decisions while in the grip of such lassitude. He would sleep on the matter, and in the morning, fresh, reflect anew upon the problem.

He climbed the steps, up onto the black stone jetty. Lianis was awaiting him there, two servants with him. As Veovis emerged, one brought a cloak and wrapped it about his shoulders, while another held up a lamp to light his way.

"Lianis," he said, greeting his advisor. "You did not have to wait up for me."

Lianis fell in beside him as they walked across the flags toward the mansion. "You have visitors, my Lord."

The news chilled Veovis. He glanced at Lianis, then looked away, troubled. Had he been watched? Had someone witnessed his meetings with A'Gaeris? For if so he would be hard stretched to explain his comings and goings.

"Where are they?" he asked, stopping as they came beneath the arch.

"In your study, my Lord. I thought it best to keep this matter discreet."

"You did well," Veovis answered, touching his arm briefly. They walked on, through the great doors and down the broad, high corridor, the servant hurrying to keep up with them, his lamp throwing their shadows on ahead of them as they approached the great staircase.

Coming to the first step, Veovis turned to Lianis again. "I will take things from here, Lianis. Send one of the servants in with wine in a brief while. I shall send for you if I need you."

"My Lord," Lianis bowed then backed away.

Veovis climbed the stairs alone. At the foot of the steps, the servant held the lamp high, lighting his way as best he could.

His study was to the left. As he stood before the door, Veovis tried to calm himself and still his swirling thoughts.

Things looked bad. He had met with a sworn enemy of the D'ni state. And why? To discredit an opponent. It was that simple, and no end of sophistry could cloud the matter. Yet against that was what he now knew of Aitrus and the illicit Ages. Was that enough? Might he claim, perhaps, that he had known before the meetings—had known and wanted confirmation?

Perhaps.

He grasped the door handle and turned it, stepping into the room, a smile forming on his lips.

"Guildsmen . . ."

The smile froze. Facing him, rising from a chair beside his desk, was the outsider woman, Ti'ana. Cradled in her arms was the half-breed child. As the door clicked shut behind Veovis, she took two steps toward him, her dark eyes accusing him.

"Where is he, Veovis? Where *is* my husband?"

Aitrus sat in his study, the Linking Book open on the desk before him. If what A'Gaeris said was true, he would find the bodies of the two young guildsmen on the other side. But could he trust A'Gaeris?

Who knew what kind of Age this really linked to? For all he knew it could be deadly, the air poisonous. On the other hand, it was, in all likelihood, the only real piece of evidence he had against Veovis—*if* things were as A'Gaeris claimed.

Aitrus reached out and closed the book. To link was too risky. If he had had a breathing mask and a second Linking Book to bring him back to D'ni, he *might* have gone . . .

If. Besides, there were Anna and Gehn to think of now.

Taking a sheet of vellum from the side, he took his pen from the inkstand and began to write, penning a note to Grand Master Jadaris of the Maintainers. He would send him the Linking Book and let him decide what should be done. In the meantime, he would take Anna and the child to Gemedet, away from things.

Aitrus signed the note then stood. He did not feel like sleep—his mind was much too filled with things for rest—yet he felt the need to see Anna and Gehn. Walking through to the bedroom he stopped in the doorway, listening for their breathing in the darkness.

Nothing. There was nothing. Slowly he tiptoed across, then crouched beside the bed, putting out his hand. The bed was empty.

He stood, then went across and lit the lamp. The bed was made. There was no sign of them in the room.

For a moment or two he could not think. When he had left, four hours ago, they had been here, asleep.

Aitrus went out, then knocked on the end door, waking his house steward.

"Were there any callers while I was gone?"

"A Messenger came," he answered, sitting up. "From the Guild House. He brought a message for you from your father. The Mistress—Ti'ana—came down and took it from me. She spoke to the man."

"Did you hear what she said?"

"No."

Aitrus thanked him, then went back to his study. There was no sign of the message, but whatever it was, he knew exactly

338

what Anna would have thought. He had told her he was going to the Guild Hall, and any message would have reached him there.

Unless he had not gone to the Guild Hall.

She would have remembered the anonymous note, and, piecing things together, would have gone after him.

Maybe. But why take Gehn? Why not go alone? Unless she had not gone to the house.

Gemedet, then? But again, why, in the middle of the night? Why not wait for him to return?

No, only her fear for him would have made her go out after him. But why should she be afraid? Unless she already knew— knew at some deeper, instinctive level—that Veovis was behind it all.

K'veer!

No sooner had the thought been spawned than it became a certainty in his mind. K'veer! They had gone to K'veer!

Whirling about, he hastened across the room and out, then ran down the corridor, not caring if he woke the house. His booted footsteps thudded on the stairs, yet as he threw open the door, it was to be greeted by the sight of men carrying lamps at his gate and, just beyond them, a dark sedan, suspended between eight uniformed runners. Veovis himself stood beside the carriage, talking to someone within its shadowed interior.

A sudden anger boiled up in Aitrus. Striding down the path, he confronted Veovis even as he turned.

"What are *you* doing here?"

Veovis stared back at him haughtily.

"Come!" Aitrus demanded. "What do you want?"

"Want?" Veovis's face hardened. "Nothing from you, Aitrus. I deal only with men of honor."

Aitrus bristled. "You dare to question *my* honor?"

"Say only that I know who D'ni's friends are, and who its enemies."

Aitrus felt a flash of hatred ripple through him. He wanted to strike Veovis. To break him as one might dash a plate against the ground.

"You had best hold your tongue, *Lord* Veovis, before I rip it from your mouth!"

Veovis's eyes flared. "It is you who should be careful, lest I teach you a lesson in manners!"

Aitrus clenched his fist, then, knowing that violence would solve nothing, forced himself to be calm. "I know to whom *my* loyalty lies well enough, Veovis. Would that I could say the same of you."

"I give my loyalty to those who deserve it," Veovis responded. "It is no *cheap* thing."

Aitrus frowned. If that was a jibe at him he did not understand it. What did Veovis mean? Changing tack, he asked the question he ought to have begun with.

"Where is my wife? Where is Ti'ana?"

Veovis's lips formed a sneer. "Do you not know, Master Aitrus? Surely it is a husband's *duty* to know where his wife is!"

Aitrus took a step closer, so that his face was but a hand's width from Veovis's. He spoke quietly, threateningly.

"Do *you* have her?"

For a moment Veovis simply stood there staring back at him, his eyes yielding nothing, then he turned and, drawing back the curtain of the sedan, reached in and, grasping her roughly by the hand, tugged Anna from her seat.

Anna glared at Veovis, then turned back, reaching in to take the sleeping child from the nurse within the sedan.

"A pretty pair you make!" Veovis said, a heavy sarcasm in his tone now. "Neither knows where the other is!"

Aitrus looked to Anna, his eyes concerned, but she shook her head, as if at some unspoken question. Cradling Gehn, she moved past Aitrus, then turned, standing at his shoulder.

"Thank you," she said, speaking to Lord Veovis. "I am sorry to have troubled you."

"No trouble," he answered, his cold eyes never leaving Aitrus's face. "No trouble at all."

"Master Aitrus. Their Lordships will see you now."

Aitrus pulled himself up off the bench, then followed the guildsman along the corridor to where two guards stood before a pair of huge double doors.

For a week he had wrestled with his conscience, not knowing what to do. It was A'Gaeris's role in things that worried him most. The man had no love of D'ni, and to bring down D'ni's favorite son, Veovis, would fit in well with any plans he had for vengeance. All well and good, yet Aitrus had seen the Book, and still had the Linking Book in his possession. That was Veovis's hand and no mistake. And A'Gaeris's indignation, that burning sense of injustice Aitrus had glimpsed the last time they had met, that, too, had seemed genuine.

Anna had begged him to go straight to Master Jadaris and

leave the Maintainers to deal with the matter, but that would have meant going behind Lord Rakeri's back, and that Aitrus would not do.

And so, eight days on, he had gone to see Lord Rakeri in his rooms in the Halls of the Guild of Miners. The old man had greeted him warmly. There, over a cup of mulled wine, he had told the old man of his son's activities.

Aitrus could see how torn the old man was. He had always treated Aitrus like a second son, even after the breach in Aitrus's friendship with Veovis, but suddenly there was a cold-ness, a distance in his manner. The old man had stared long and hard at the Linking Book, and then he had nodded.

"Leave it with me, Master Aitrus," he said, his voice cold and formal, "I shall make sure that the matter is fully investi-gated."

A long silence had followed. But now, a full month after that audience with Rakeri, the matter was to be decided.

As the doors swung back, Aitrus looked about him. Beside the five Lords who sat behind the great desk on the far side of the chamber, there were six others, seated at desks to either side of the room. To his left were three guild scribes, to his right two senior guildsmen in the Guild of Maintainers, and, slightly apart from them, their Grand Master, the elderly Jadaris.

There was no sign of Veovis.

Aitrus felt relief flood him. He had been feeling awkward enough about this, but had Veovis been there in person it would have been far more difficult.

"Take a seat, Master Aitrus," Lord R'hira said, looking up from a document.

Aitrus sat, then glanced at Rakeri. The old man was looking down, distracted, it seemed, the fingers of one hand
drumming idly on the leather cover of an official-looking file.
He did not look well these days, as if the cares of this inquiry
had fallen heavily on his shoulders.

R'hira looked directly at Aitrus. "In view of what you told
us, a unit of the City Guard was sent to the house in J'Taeri
District and a thorough search was made. Unfortunately, no
trace of any of the papers you mentioned could be found. This
is not to say that they do not exist somewhere, but without
them we have only your word. That in itself is no small thing,
Guild Master Aitrus, yet it is not evidence, as defined by D'ni
law." He paused, then, "It comes down to this. After long consideration we have decided that we cannot possibly risk using
the Linking Book. To risk a third life would be, we felt, a reckless chance, and without the direct evidence of which you
speak—that is, the bodies of the two guildsmen—then it is a
matter of your word against that of Veovis."

Aitrus blinked, surprised.

"Forgive me, Lord R'hira, but I find this situation intolerable. Either I am a liar or Lord Veovis is. If you will not send
another guildsman, I am prepared to go."

There was a moment's silence, then Lord R'hira nodded.
"It shall be as you say."

Aitrus stood, then walked across and, taking the Book
from Lord R'hira, and a Linking Book, he opened the Book in
question, placing his hand against the glowing panel.

There was silence in the room. A few moments later Aitrus
reappeared, his face ashen.

"It is true," he said. "There are bodies there."

That evening a warrant for Veovis's arrest was issued. Though the day was now advanced, K'veer still blazed with lights. Every room was lit, every lantern burned brightly. Men from both the City Guard and the Guild of Maintainers were everywhere; in every room and every corridor. It was clear that a thorough search of the island had been undertaken.

Climbing the great stairway at the heart of the rock, Aitrus began to wonder just what he had set in motion. It was true what people said about the messenger who brings ill news.

Passing the entrance to the Book Room, Aitrus saw how armed teams of Maintainer guards were waiting there, ready to link into the family Ages. That, as much as anything, told him that they had not yet taken Veovis.

So he is guilty, he thought, surprised despite all, for some small part of him still held that this was all a mistake and that an explanation would be found. But no. If Veovis was missing, then there could be but a single explanation.

Master Jadaris was waiting for him in Lord Rakeri's study, near the very top of the island mansion. It was a regular cave of a room. There were no windows; instead, huge, book-lined shelves filled every inch of the walls.

"Ah, Aitrus," Jadaris said, looking up at him from behind the great desk. The Linking Book lay before him, open, the tiny panel glowing in the half-light of the room. "We have searched high and low, but there is no sign of Lord Veovis in D'ni. In the circumstances I have given the order for the family Ages to be searched. That will happen now. But there is one other matter we must deal with."

Jadaris waved a hand over the Linking Book. "A guildsman ventured in four hours back. He found another Book at the foot of the slope. It linked back to this very room."

Aitrus nodded soberly. There was a moment's silence and then Master Jadaris stood.

"So, Aitrus. Will you link through with me?"

They linked to a cave on the eastern slope of a large, mountainous island. A cluster of smaller islands surrounded it, linked by suspended wooden bridges. It was on one of these that they finally found the two guildsmen, lying side by side in a hut beside the cliff's edge, their hands and feet bound tight. They were long dead, their cloaks stiff with their own dried blood, their throats slit from ear to ear. On the floor nearby was the dagger that had been used to kill them, lying beside its sheath as if abandoned.

It was Veovis's weapon. One he had been seen to carry often.

Aitrus saw how Jadaris stared at the dagger; saw the strange flicker in the muscles of his neck, the sudden change in his eyes, and knew that this had finally convinced him. These were *his* men who had been murdered—his young boys. To see them like this—trussed and butchered—had clearly shocked him deeply.

As a team of Maintainers arranged to bring the bodies back, Aitrus and Master Jadaris linked back to K'veer. There

they were greeted by the news that Veovis had been taken in Nidur Gemat and was being held in the Book Room down below.

They went down, Aitrus hanging back as Jadaris walked across to confront Veovis.

Veovis's hands were bound behind his back. Two guards—Maintainers—stood to either side of him, yet Veovis seemed unrepentant. His head was raised defiantly and his eyes burned with indignation.

Jadaris held the sheathed dagger out before him. "Is this yours, Master Veovis?"

"It is," Veovis said. "What of it?"

"You do not deny it, then?"

But Veovis seemed not to hear. He took a step toward Jadaris.

"What have I done to deserve this treatment, Master

346

Jadaris? Am I a common criminal to be bound and herded like an animal?"

"We found the bodies," Jadaris said.

But Veovis did not seem to be listening. "I am not normally an impatient man, but I warn you, Guildsman. Unbind me now or you shall answer to my father!"

A shiver went through Jadaris. "It was your father who ordered it."

Veovis fell silent; the words had taken him aback. "Impossible," he said. "He would never have given such an order."

"Never?" Jadaris seemed to watch Veovis a moment, then: "Do you deny the charges?"

"Charges?" Veovis laughed coldly, then tilted his head slightly. His eyes were hostile now. "I do not understand you, Master Jadaris. Of what precisely am I charged?"

"Of trading in illicit Ages. And of murder."

The look of shock in Veovis's face surprised Aitrus. For a moment Veovis seemed unable to speak, then he shook his head. "But this is ridiculous! I have done nothing."

"We have the proof," Jadaris said coldly. "But I am not your judge, Veovis. At least, not alone."

Jadaris seemed to straighten, taking on his full authority, then spoke again.

"Guild Master Veovis, you will be taken from this place to the Guild Fortress of Irrat where you will be held secure until a date is set for your trial."

"My *trial*?" Veovis's expression was one of sheer disbelief.

Jadaris nodded, yet he seemed far from triumphant. "This is a sad day for the guilds, Lord Veovis. You have brought great shame upon us, and even greater shame upon your father."

"But I have done nothing!"

Jadaris glared at him. "*Nothing?* You will be silent, Guild Master, or I shall have you gagged!"

Veovis blinked, astonished. His mouth opened, then snapped shut.

"Good," Jadaris said curtly. "Now take him from here. Before I am tempted to do to him what he did to those poor boys."

Aitrus returned home to find the blinds drawn, doctors hurrying to and fro. His mother, Tasera, greeted him in the hallway, her face gaunt, her eyes troubled. Gehn had worsened, it seemed, and almost died. It was she who had finally called in the Healers, when all else seemed hopeless.

Aitrus went through to the nursery, fearing the worst. Anna was sitting beside the cot, clearly exhausted, staring down at the feverish child as he lay there like a waxwork doll, his eyes closed, his breathing shallow. Nearby, a doctor spoke quietly, urgently to one of his colleagues, then, seeing Aitrus, came across.

"There's little we can do," he said sorrowfully. "We have tried several remedies, but the child seems unable to keep anything in his stomach. I fear it is up to the Maker now."

Aitrus thanked the man, then went over and knelt beside Anna, resting his hand lightly on her knee.

"Ti'ana? . . . Ti'ana? It's Aitrus. I'm back."

She turned her head slowly and looked down at him. "He's dying, Aitrus. Our son is dying."

The desolation in her face was unlike anything he had ever seen. "No," he said softly. "He'll come through."

But she was not to be consoled. "You did not hear him, Aitrus. The sounds he made. Such awful, dreadful sounds. And the spasms. Twice I thought I'd lost him."

"Maybe," he said, "but he's still here."

He took her hands and clenched them, looking up into her face. "Won't you fight for him, Ti'ana? Won't you help our son survive?"

Anna closed her eyes, pained by his words. "I've tried, Aitrus. The Maker knows I've tried my best. But I am so tired now. So very, very tired."

"Then rest, my love. It's my turn now."

Aitrus stood, then, bending down, lifted Gehn from the cot, holding him tightly, securely against his shoulder. The child whimpered a little, then settled against him. He was so light now; there was so very little of him. The lightest breeze would carry him off.

Aitrus shuddered, filled with an ineffable tenderness for his infant son. "Come now, little one," he said softly as he carried him from the room. "Let us see what a little sunlight can do for you."

Veovis looked up from the summary document and sighed. It was lies, every word of it, yet even he could see how convincing a case Aitrus had made against him. If the Five believed this—and why should they not?—then he would be found guilty, without a doubt.

Suahrnir. Suahrnir was the key, but Suahrnir could not be found.

Veovis's own statement lay on the desk beside his elbow— six pages in his own hand. At best it seemed naive, at worst a tissue of lies and excuses. He knew which his fellow guildsmen would think.

They had let him see the evidence against him; the books and documents and letters, all of it written, or so it appeared, in his hand. Good forgeries they were—the best he had ever seen—but forgeries all the same, for he had not written a single word of what they had shown him.

He had pointed the finger at Aitrus, but they had expected that. It was to be expected, after all. To "humor" him, and perhaps to mollify his father, they had even searched back in the guild records to see whether there might not be some earlier instance of such fraud, one that might be attributable to Aitrus, but there was nothing.

Aitrus was a clever one. None cleverer. He played the honest man. But Veovis knew better. He knew now what a snake Aitrus was.

He heard the cell door open behind him and turned to see a guard bring in a pile of clean clothes and place it on the bed in the far corner of the room. Another guard stood in the door, blocking it. The sight of it almost made him laugh, for it suggested that he might try to escape, and when did a D'ni Lord run from his fate?

Veovis turned back to the copy statement, then pushed it

away from him. It was no use. There was no way he could answer this. It was like grasping at phantoms.

He even understood it, now that he had had time to reflect upon it.

How long had Aitrus prepared this? Since he had refused to countenance the wedding, no doubt.

Veovis stood and stretched. Was that all Aitrus wanted? To bring him down? Or was there more? Was there some further part he could not see?

Veovis crossed the room and sat on the edge of the bed, beside the pile of clothes. He felt weary now and in need of sleep. Too much had happened much too quickly.

He reached out and picked up the pile of clothes, meaning to move it so that he could stretch out on the bed, but the pile was heavier than he expected. Strangely heavy, in fact. He put it down, then began to sort through it, his brows knitted.

There! Halfway down the pile his fingers closed on something hard. A book! A leather-covered Book! He drew it out and stared at it, amazed. There was no mistaking it—It was a Linking Book. He opened it. There, on the right-hand page, the tiny panel glowed invitingly.

It was a trap. It had to be, or a test of some kind. He closed the Book and set it down.

A trap. Of course it was.

But what if it was not. What if this was his father's doing? Veovis stood, then closed his eyes, wracked by indecision. This was his chance to prove himself an honest man. If he handed in the Book . . .

He groaned, then sat once more. Who was he fooling? They would find him guilty whatever. The evidence was too strong against him. And what then? Two hundred years, he'd spend, trapped on some hideous, tiny island on a Prison Age, watched every second of the day and night.

The thought was unbearable. Opening the Book again, he placed his hand against the panel . . . and linked.

Lord R'hira stepped into the empty cell and looked about him. The Linking Book lay on the bed where Veovis had left it only a moment before. He stared at it, then shook his head. A while later he heard a shout from farther down the hallway—a curse that turned into a groan.

So now you know, R'hira thought sadly. *And what will that knowledge do to you, Veovis?*

The Book had linked to an enclosed room on a different Age, in which was a table. On that table was a second Linking Book and a tank of acid. It was a classic escape maneuver, and Veovis, naturally, had seen exactly what to do.

But that second Book linked right back to D'ni—to the interrogation cell at the end of the hallway, wherein sat Master Jadaris and his guards.

R'hira sighed. Had Veovis known it was a test? Or was this simply some final piece of arrogance on his part?

He turned. Rakeri was standing in the doorway, his eyes dark with the knowledge of what his son had done.

"I'm sorry," he said quietly, but Rakeri shook his head.

"Do what you must," the old man said. "I wash my hands of him."

Aitrus woke, not knowing where he was. It was bright, too bright to fully open his eyes.

Gemedet. I must be on Gemedet.

Squeezing his eyes shut again, he searched about him with his hand until his fingers closed upon his glasses. He pulled them on, then slowly opened his eyes again. The filters in the glass made the brightness bearable.

It was morning. Or maybe afternoon. How long had he slept?

Then he remembered.

"Gehn!"

He sat up, looking about him anxiously, then relaxed. Gehn lay not three feet away from him, swaddled in a blanket where Aitrus had laid him last night. He lay there silently, his tiny glasses shielding his eyes against the light that shone in a broad band through the window just above them.

Aitrus shuffled across, then picked up his baby son, cuddling him for a moment, then putting a hand lightly to his brow.

The fever had passed.

Gehn stared back at him, curiously, his eyes placid, calm. D'ni eyes, for all the doctors said.

"You came through," Aitrus said, smiling at him, proud suddenly of his son. "Look at you, there's nothing of you, Gehn, yet you came through. You *lived!*"

There was a noise outside. Aitrus turned. Was it some forest animal, sniffing about the camp? Then he heard the soft hum of Anna's voice and smiled.

He stood, carrying the child out to her. She was standing with her back to him, looking out across the valley and the mist-wreathed waterfall. For a moment he simply stood there, watching her, conscious of how the sunlight formed a shining wreath about her long, flowing hair, then he spoke.

"Ti'ana?"

She turned, smiling at him. "I wondered when you would wake."

"Look," he said, holding out Gehn to her. "The fever's gone."

"I know," she said, coming across and taking Gehn from him. "I came in earlier and saw. I thought I'd let you both sleep."

He looked up at the sky. The sun was sinking toward the west. "It's late," he said. "How long have we slept?"

"A full day and more," she said, smiling broadly at him. "It clearly did you good."

"Yes," he agreed. Then, as if suddenly recalling something, he laughed. "You know, I had a dream last night."

"A dream?" she looked at him, intrigued. "What kind of dream? A pleasant one I hope."

He smiled. "Oh yes. I dreamed we walked the tunnels to the surface. You and I . . . and Gehn. And you took us to all of those places you have told me of in the past, even to Tadjinar itself."

"And the Lodge?"

"Yes." He nodded, staring out past her as if he really saw it. "I dreamed that we stayed there and that I sat there in the window with you, looking out across the desert. There was a full moon above us and the sky was full of stars.

And Gehn . . . I could hear Gehn sleeping in the room behind us."

"Maybe it will happen, one day."

"You think so?"

She was quiet a moment, then, "I heard what happened . . . with Veovis."

"Ah . . . " He nodded, then, "I do not know what to think, Ti'ana. The Veovis I knew would never have acted in such a fashion."

"Yet people change."

Aitrus looked directly at her. "Do they? I am not so sure, my love. What a man is, he is. Though Veovis is no friend, I would yet trust him above many who call themselves my friend. And do you forget . . . he brought you home that time."

"It was but common courtesy."

"Was it? And yet that same man is charged with callously murdering two guildsmen. Do you really think him capable of that?"

Anna looked down, troubled. "Of course . . . you have not heard, have you?"

"Heard what?" Aitrus asked.

"The Five Lords tested him. Secretly gave him a Linking Book, in his cell on Irrat. He took it and tried to escape. No honest man would do that, would they?"

Aitrus stared at her a moment, then looked down. "So it is true, after all."

"It seems so."

"And Lord Rakeri? How has he taken the news?"

"Badly," Anna said, rocking Gehn gently. "It appears he has taken to his bed. Some say he is dying."

Aitrus looked down, touched deeply by the news. "Then it is an ill day for D'ni," he said quietly. "An ill day indeed."

The narrow streets leading to the great Guild House were packed as the carriage carrying Veovis rattled through the gates, drawn by two great oxen.

After twenty days of evidence, the Council was to give their verdict. Never before had so high a public figure been on trial, and never for such heinous crimes.

To trade in illicit Books was bad enough, but to kill one's fellow guildsmen, that was unheard of. And that was why they crowded into the narrow spaces between the great houses of the upper city, straining to get a glimpse of the villain of the piece, Veovis.

Some saw him as a greedy man, for whom great riches had never been enough. Others commented on his hypocrisy and saw his protestations of innocence in the face of such a weight of fact as a sure sign of his mental instability.

This was the atmosphere in which Veovis stepped down from the carriage, and, climbing the marble steps of the Guild House, crossed the outer room and entered the great chamber to hear the verdict of his peers.

A temporary gallery had been built at one end of the chamber especially for the occasion—a temporary affair that seated those few dozen guests who had been invited by the Council to bear witness. Among these were the families of the two dead guildsmen, A'Gaeris, and Aitrus's wife, Ti'ana.

Anna was now a D'ni citizen. In a private ceremony, a week earlier, she had become by law what blood nor marriage could make her. It was a precedent, but one the Council approved.

But now the moment had come. As Veovis stepped out between the great doors, a silence fell over the great, circular chamber. From their seats on the various levels, every member turned to look.

Veovis had had his hair cut stubble short. He wore a simple one-piece of rust-red cloth. There were iron manacles about his wrists, linked by a short length of chain, and manacles at both ankles, from which two fine steel chains led back into the hands of a Maintainer guard; a big man, capable, it seemed, of holding back a team of horses.

Even so, Veovis stood there a moment with his head high, his eyes as proud, as unbowed, as an eagle's, then he began to descend the steps, passing between the great pillars.

Below Veovis, in the center of the chamber, stood the five great thrones of the Five Lords of D'ni, but today only four of them were filled. As Veovis came to a halt in the space before them, the great Lords stared at him like living statues, their dignity immense.

There was a moment's silence, tense, expectant, and then Lord R'hira spoke.

"Guildsmen. Have you decided?"

There was a resounding "Aye!" from all sides of the chamber.

"And your verdict?"

"Guilty!" 360 voices said as one.

It was done. Veovis seemed to tremble; yet his head did

not waver, nor did his eyes show even a flicker of regret. If anything he seemed even more defiant than before.

R'hira looked to him, his ancient eyes cold, no trace of compassion in them. "Before I come to your sentence, is there anything you would like to say, Guild Master Veovis?"

Veovis met the ancient's eyes, then shook his head.

"Very well. Then it is the decision of this House that you be stripped of all rank and that from henceforth your membership of the guild be annulled. Further, you will be taken from here and on the seventeenth hour fifteen days hence will be transferred to a suitable Prison Age, to be held there for the remainder of your natural life."

All eyes were on Veovis. From her seat in the gallery Anna saw how fine, how dignified he looked in this his final moment and felt the slightest flicker of doubt cross her mind. Yet he *was* guilty. She had heard and seen enough these past twenty days to know that much. Glancing across, she saw how A'Gaeris was leaning forward. What was that gleam in his eyes? Delight that justice had finally been done? Or was it simple gloating?

She looked down briefly, a shiver of distaste running through her, then looked back, her eyes seeking out Aitrus where he sat in the first row, just behind Veovis.

As Veovis turned, preparing to climb the steps again and leave the chamber, he halted briefly, right in front of Aitrus, staring down at his once-friend. Something seemed to be said, then he walked on, his bare, manacled feet climbing the stone, the big Maintainer trailing behind.

Anna waited, as the great Lords ended the session, then, as the members began to stand, a great murmur of talk rising in the chamber, she hurried quickly down the steps.

Aitrus was standing in the midst of a tiny group of other members. As she stepped into their circle they broke off their animated discussion, bowing to her respectfully.

"What did he say?" she asked, looking anxiously to Aitrus.

He hesitated, conscious of the others listening. "Not here, Ti'ana."

She frowned. "Did he threaten you?"

Aitrus shook his head, but he was awkward now. Looking about him apologetically, he stepped across the circle and, taking Anna's arm, led her away.

"Well?" she asked, when they were outside, out of the hearing of the others. "What did he say?"

Aitrus turned from her, as if he could not face her. He seemed pale now, discomfited. "He blames me."

"Is that what he said. That he blames you?"

Aitrus shook his head.

"Well, *tell* me, Aitrus. What *did* he say?"

Aitrus turned, looking directly at her. "'You should have let me fall.' That's what he said."

"But you are not to blame."

"No? I wish I could believe that. At the end there, watching him—even after all that was said and shown—do you know what I thought? I thought he was innocent. *That* is what I thought. And yet I said 'Aye' with all the rest. And sent him to his rock."

"Do you want to do something? To say something, perhaps, to the Five?"

He laughed bitterly. "What could I say? No. I must live with this, Ti'ana. Knowing I might have been wrong. Yes, and knowing that I was the one who set the wheels in motion. Those great wheels of the D'ni state that can crush a man as easily as our great hammers pound the rock."

They stood there a moment, silent, staring at each other, and then Anna took his arm and led him out. Yet even as they stepped out beneath the massive arch at the front of the Guild House, the great bell on Ae'Gura began to sound, sending its sonorous tones across the cavern.

Lord Rakeri was dead.

PART SIX: THE INK IN THE WELL

IT WAS THE FOURTH ANNIVERSARY OF GEHN'S NAMING day and a solemn ceremony was taking place in the family mansion in D'ni. Until today, Gehn had been a child, free to play as a child played, but from this hour onward he would take the first steps toward becoming a guildsman.

Looking on, Anna felt deeply for her son. Standing amid the guild officials, little Gehn looked terrified. His hair had been cut and he was wearing guild clothes—duplicates of those his father, Aitrus, and his grandfather Kahlis wore as they stood on either side of him. In front of them, behind a special trestle table that had been set up in the room, stood Yteru, the Grand Master of the Guild of Books. It was to his guild that Gehn was to be apprenticed, and the boy would join them in their halls two weeks from now.

Two days ago, knowing how much her son was dreading the occasion, Anna had gone to Aitrus in his study and asked him if Gehn really did need to join the guild just then. He was sure to miss home dreadfully, but Aitrus was adamant. It was the D'ni way, and if Gehn was to be considered D'ni and make his eventual way in the world, then he must conform to the ways of the guilds.

And so she was to relinquish him, long before he was ready to be taken from her. It would break his heart and hers, but maybe Aitrus was right. Maybe, in the long run, it *would* be best for him. Yet she had her doubts.

As the Grand Master called the boy forward, she found herself praying silently that he would remember the words she had taught him—the words of the guild oath.

Slowly, stumblingly, Gehn forced them out. As he finished, Master Yteru smiled benevolently down at the child, then, in a slow, sonorous drawl, uttered the words of acceptance.

And so it was done. Her son was now a guildsman.

Afterward, she held him, telling him how proud she was, but she could see the fear of separation in his eyes.

Aitrus had been saying his farewells to the guildsmen; now he came back. He stood in the doorway, looking in at her and Gehn. "Are you angry with me?"

She nodded.

He sighed, exasperated. "I am sorry, Ti'ana, but you know how things stand. It is the D'ni way, and we cannot afford to act differently. That would be self-indulgent. You knew that when you became D'ni."

"I know," she said, as angry at herself as at him, "but I did not think it would be so hard."

"No. But there is one thing we can do. Before Gehn goes, that is."

"You want to go to Gemedet?"

Aitrus shook his head. "I promised you once. Remember?"

At first she did not understand; then her eyes widened.

He nodded.

"Yes, Ti'ana. It's time our son saw where his mother came from."

The journey through the tunnels took two days. On the morning of the third they came to the cavern where the two great digging machines stood silently. As Anna and Gehn came up beside him, Aitrus turned to them and smiled.

"We are almost there." He pointed across at the great red wedge of rock facing them. "There is the seal. The surface must be just above."

Anna nodded. "This is where I came in. I remember it vividly. The machines . . . " She stared at them fondly, then smiled. "Do you know what I thought, Aitrus?"

"No, tell me."

"I thought I had discovered the tomb of a great king. And these . . . I thought these were the remains of some great civilization, a long-lost race of giants, perhaps, or . . . " She laughed. "Little did I know."

Aitrus looked at her fondly. "I am glad you chose to look, Ti'ana. But for that curiosity of yours, I would have been lost."

Anna looked away, a smile on her lips. "Oh, I am sure some young D'ni maiden would have found you."

He laughed. "Maybe. But let us press on now. I am impatient to see the surface."

Gehn, who had been silent until that moment, now spoke up. "Daddy? Why did we not *link* to the surface?"

Aitrus came back and, crouching before his son, began to explain. "If this were a different Age, then we might have linked to it, but the surface is in the same Age as D'ni and one cannot link to a place in the same Age."

"What, *never?*" the boy asked, wide-eyed.

"Never," Aitrus said, smiling patiently.

Gehn frowned, considering that, then looked back up at his father. "But how will we find our way back to D'ni?"

Aitrus took his notebook from his pocket and opened it. Inside, between the tanned leather covers, were page after page of maps and diagrams. Aitrus flicked through it for a while, then, coming to the page, turned the notebook so that Gehn could see.

"Look, Gehn. Here is a map of the tunnels. I have been making notes as we went along. We need only trace our way back."

It seemed to satisfy the boy. He grinned, then went across to his mother, who stood beneath one of the great machines. She put her arm about him, then looked back at Aitrus.

"When I first saw these, I was convinced that whoever had made them must be long dead, for what kind of race would make such wonderful machines then leave them in the rock?"

Aitrus smiled then walked across to her. "Was it this one that you climbed?"

She nodded.

"You climbed it, Mama?" Gehn asked, looking up at his mother in wide-eyed wonder.

"I did. And then I walked down into D'ni. Only I did not know it was D'ni. Not until long after."

They went through the gap, Anna leading the way, Gehn close behind. Reaching the pocket, Aitrus lit the lantern again.

He knew what lay ahead—Anna had already told him—but now they were so close, he felt a strange excitement. How many years now had he waited for this?

Fifty years, at least.

Anna was first to climb down. At the bottom she turned, reaching up to take Gehn as Aitrus let him down. Then they were in the cavern, where it had first begun for Anna, all those years ago. She looked to him.

"It hasn't changed."

They went on, climbing up into the tunnel and along, until the three of them stood before the rock fall.

Aitrus set the timer, then took them back to a safe distance. There was a huge bang. The whole tunnel shuddered. As the smoke cleared, Anna picked Gehn up and, following Aitrus, walked through, stepping over the rubble.

It was night. A full moon rested like a shining disk of silver in the center of the blue-black velvet sky. Surrounding it, a billion flickering stars shone down.

Aitrus stood there at the entrance to the tunnel, staring up at the moon. Beside him, Anna held Gehn against her side, her face close to his, and pointed.

"Look, Gehn. That's the moon."

"Moon," he said, snuggling in to her, tired now.

Anna smiled then turned her head, looking to Aitrus. He met her eyes and smiled.

"Come," he said, taking her hand, "let's find the Lodge."

367

They sat on the ledge of the open window, looking out across the narrow bridge toward the desert. Gehn was asleep in the room behind them.

Anna listened a moment, then smiled. Aitrus sat just behind her, his arms about her, his chin resting on the top of her head. It had been her secret dream to bring him here and sit with him like this, yet now that it was real it seemed more dreamlike than the dream—a moment wholly out of time. She pressed back against him and felt his arms tighten about her.

"Do you still miss him?" he asked softly.

"Sometimes."

She half-turned her head, looking back at him. "He speaks to me sometimes. In my head."

Aitrus smiled, but she could see he only half-believed her, or maybe thought she meant that she thought of her father and remembered his words. But it was true what she said.

She felt Aitrus sigh, a sigh of pure contentment, and turned back, letting her eyes go to the descending moon once more, the smile lingering at the corners of her mouth.

"Ti'ana?"

"Hmm?" she answered lazily.

"I know how much you loved your father, and how much you owed to him, but . . . well, what of your mother? You never speak of her."

"No."

Even the thought of it brought back the pain.

"Ti'ana?" Aitrus sat forward.

"It's all right," she said.

She began again, hunching forward as she spoke, letting the words come haltingly. "It was an accident. We were climbing. In the mountains to the south of here. My father had gone up the cliff face first, and I had followed. Mother was last, all three of us tied on the same rope. Father had walked on a little way, to inspect the cliffs we had glimpsed from below. That was why we were there, you see. We were always exploring."

Anna stopped, catching her breath. Again she saw it, vividly, as if it had happened not thirty-five years ago but yesterday—the staring eyes, the mouth open in surprise.

Anna collected herself, then carried on. "The difficult part of the climb was behind her and she was only six or eight feet from the edge. I could almost have put out a hand and hauled her up. She was smiling. And then her foot slipped. It ought not to have mattered. The rope ought to have held her. I felt a momentary tension on it, then it went, like a rotten vine. And next thing she was falling. And not a sound—just her eyes looking back at me, her mouth open in surprise.

"Father blamed himself, of course. He should have checked the rope, he kept saying, but I could see that he was devastated."

Aitrus was silent a while. "I am sorry, Ti'ana. I did not know. I should not have asked."

She turned to face him, kneeling on the ledge. Her face was streaked with tears, but she was smiling tenderly now. She reached out, her hands gently holding his cheeks. "No, Aitrus. You of all people should have known. We should have no secrets, you and I."

She kissed him then; softly, tenderly, her eyes shining in the moonlight. And as they broke from the kiss, his eyes were wide with wonder.

Gehn woke him, shaking him awake. Sunlight blazed in from the room at the front of the Lodge, so strong it stabbed into his pupils, making him shield his eyes then feel about him for his glasses.

"Mama's gone!" Gehn was saying. "Mama's gone!"

Aitrus pulled on the glasses, then sat up, putting out his arms to hold the frightened boy. "No, Gehn. She will be back. I promise you."

But Gehn was sobbing uncontrollably at the thought that he had lost his mother. Aitrus held Gehn tightly until the crying subsided, then, picking him up, he carried him out, through the room at the front until they stood in the doorway, looking out over the valley.

The heat surprised him. It could not be more than an hour since dawn, yet already it was far hotter than the hottest day on Gemedet or Ko'ah. He recalled what Anna had said about the heat; how it was the single factor that determined life here. It was not something he would have written into an Age, but someone, the Grand Master who had written the Book of Earth, had thought of it, and created the conditions for such extremes of cold and heat.

Gehn had fallen silent, yet he still clung to his father's neck as if his life depended on it. Aitrus looked at him and smiled.

"You want a drink, Gehn?"

Gehn nodded.

Aitrus took him back inside, setting him gently down on

the window ledge while he poured him a goblet of cool, clear water from the jug Anna had filled the night before.

Turning, he saw how Gehn was staring about him. "Where are we?" he asked, taking the water gratefully.

"This is where your mother lived when she was young," he answered. "This is where she grew up, with her father."

"Here?" Gehn seemed astonished. "But where are the Books?"

Aitrus laughed. "These people are human. They are not like the D'ni. They do not have Books and Ages. This is all they have."

Gehn wiped his mouth with the back of his hand, then looked up at Aitrus. "But how could they live with just this?"

Aitrus looked about him. To be honest, he had asked himself the very same question. Now that he had seen the Lodge, he wondered how Anna had survived out here.

"They made do," he answered, finally. Yet even as he said it he heard Anna's voice. She was singing. A song he had never heard before, in a tongue he did not know.

Quickly he joined Gehn at the window, in time to see Anna come over the crest of the hill, a small cart pushed before her. She was wearing a black cloak trimmed with red, the hood of which was up over her head. Seeing them, she waved, then came on again, finishing her song.

Aitrus went out onto the bridge, Gehn beside him. The heat was fierce but not yet overpowering. As Anna came up onto the bridge, she smiled and held out something for Gehn to take. He ran to her and took the strange box, then scuttled back inside, into the shade. Anna pulled back her hood, then stepped up to Aitrus.

"You should wear something on your head," she said, touching his brow. "Ten minutes in this and you will get sunstroke."

"Sunstroke?" He did not understand her.

"The heat," she said. "It will affect your brain. You will collapse and be ill."

"You are jesting with me," he said, smiling, as if he understood she was joking, but she was not smiling.

"It is very dangerous out here," she said simply. "Both you and Gehn must keep covered up as much as possible. The desert sun is unforgiving."

He nodded, then, "Where have you been? And that cart . . . "

Anna half-turned, looking across at the cart, then she turned back to Aitrus. "I went to get it. It had all my books and journals on it. And other things. Fortunately I hid it well, and the desert did the rest. It was untouched, as if I'd left it yesterday."

"And that song. What was that?"

Anna smiled. "Did you like it?" She quickly sang a verse. "It's something my mother taught me. I could not sing it before. But now . . . " Again she smiled, then took his arm, leading him back into the shadows of the Lodge.

As they came into the main room, Gehn looked up at them, his eyes wide. "What is this game?" he asked, pointing to the checkered board, the black and white pieces that were laid out beside it.

"It is called chess," she said, squatting beside him. "My father taught me how to play, and I shall teach you."

Gehn beamed. "So I am not going to go to the Guild Hall after all?"

Anna looked down. "No, Gehn. You must go. But not yet. We will stay here for a few days, yes? Just you and I and Father."

Gehn looked away a moment, struggling with his disappointment, then he nodded and, turning back to Anna, picked up the white queen. "So what is this piece and what does it do?"

"Thinblood . . ."

"Who-man . . ."

"No-dunny . . ."

The whispers surrounded Gehn in the darkness of the dormitory; endless, taunting whispers that filled the lonely nights. Gehn lay there, facing the bare stone wall, the knuckles of his right hand pressed into his mouth, trying to shut it all out, but still the whispers came.

The mattress was too thin beneath him, the blankets rough and scratchy. But worst of all was the sense of abandonment that came each evening as the great door to the dormitory was closed and absolute darkness fell.

It was awful. More awful than he had ever thought possible. They had heard him crying the first few nights and had laughed at him for it. And then the whispers had begun, playing upon his fears and insecurity, making his life even more of a misery than it already was.

At home he was used to his own room, his own smooth sheets and blankets. There, a night-light rested in the corner, warm and reassuring. And he knew that his mother was always there, next door, in case bad dreams came and disturbed his sleep. But here there was nothing. Nothing but the darkness and the endless hurtful whispers.

Why had they done this to him? Why? Had he been bad? If so, he could not remember what it was that he had done. Or did they no longer love him? For to leave him here, among these awful, spiteful boys, was surely some kind of punishment.

He could remember his father's face, unnaturally stern, as he spoke to him the night before he had come here.

"You must be brave, Gehn. It is the D'ni way. It might seem hard at first, but you will get used to it, I promise you."

So much for promises. But the worst had been the parting from his mother. He had kicked and screamed, refusing to go with them, so that eventually they had had to pick him up and carry him to the waiting carriage.

That had been two weeks ago now. Two weeks of endless homesickness, and the torment of the nights.

Yet even as the whispers multiplied, Gehn found himself thinking of the lesson earlier that day. He had begun to think himself a fool; had begun to believe that the boys were right when they called him "No-dunny" and said he had sand in his head instead of brains. But today he had begun to understand what he was doing here, for today he had seen Master Urren.

Gehn was taught in a group of eight, the eldest aged seven, the youngest himself. Most of it was basic, the kind of stuff his mother had taught him back at home, but some was specific stuff about ink and writing; today's lecture in particular.

Master Urren, the visiting tutor from the Guild of Ink-Makers, was a big, ungainly, birdlike man, with a long, thin face and huge bushy eyebrows that seemed to form a continuous line across his upper face. He had the habit of staring into the air as he spoke, as if in a trance, then looking directly at one or other of his pupils, startling them. But it was not this habit but his words that had woken Gehn this morning.

With his eyes closed, Gehn could see Master Urren now, his right hand clenched into a fist as he spoke the Ink-Maker's litany.

"What binds the Word to the World? The Ink!

"What burns the bridge between the Ages? The Ink!

"What forms the living darkness between two lights? The Ink!"

Then, to the astonishment of them all, he had brought out a great tub of ink—lifting a handful of the fine dark granules so that they could see.

"The manufacture of this is a secret. A very grave and great secret, like the secret of the paper, which in time each of *you* will learn. But you must first prove yourself worthy to be trusted with such a secret, for the making of these two things is the key to immense power—the power to make worlds!"

And there was more, the words issuing thunderously from Urren's lips, so that Gehn had found himself staring at the guildsman openmouthed, amazed by the power of the words. This, he realized, was what his father had been talking about. This was what it meant to be a guildsman. Until that moment he had thought it a senseless thing to want to be, but suddenly, in one single, blazing moment, he understood.

Gehn turned and lay upon his back, letting his hand fall onto his chest. The whispers had stopped now. Soft snoring filled the silent darkness of the narrow room.

Secrets. He was to be the heir to great and wonderful secrets. Twenty years it might take, but then he would know, as Master Urren knew, and maybe then his eyes would burn with that same ferocious knowledge, that same certainty.

Gehn shivered, then, wiping his hand across his face, formed the words silently in the darkness.

It is the D'ni way.

The ink-works were burning. Great flames curled up into the darkness, lighting the roof of the cavern almost a mile overhead. Gehn stood on the stone ledge, staring out the window across the rooftops of the upper city. Surrounding him, his fellow students jostled to see, but he stood at the very front, both hands tightly grasping the great central bar of the paneless window, looking out across the dark toward the massive blaze.

They had heard the explosion twenty minutes back, but at the time they had not understood just what was happening. Now they knew. Someone had placed a bomb in the very middle of the Ink-Works. Many were dead. Many more were missing.

For the past eight weeks there had been incidents. Senior guildsmen had been mysteriously attacked. Offices had been ransacked. In the worst of the incidents, three Kortee'nea—blank Books—had gone missing, along with a whole stock of smaller Linking Books. The Maintainers had been placed on constant alert; no one knew yet who was behind the outbreak.

And now this.

There was a shout in the corridor behind them. Gehn turned, along with the others, to see the Duty Master hurrying down the corridor toward them, his hands waving madly.

"Boys! Boys! Get down from there at once!"

They climbed down, obedient to their Guild Master, yet as Gehn went to walk away, he saw how the Master hung back at the window, staring out at the blaze, the glowing orange light reflected in his pale eyes, a look of pure fear etched in his face.

Aitrus did not wait to be summoned but went straight to the Guild House. All but two or three of the Emergency Council were already there, the others arriving very shortly after Aitrus. As Lord R'hira called the meeting to order, a Master from the Guild of Maintainers hurried in and, bowing to R'hira, gave him the latest report from the Ink-Works.

Fifteen had died. Another eight were missing. It was too early to know for certain, but it seemed that a large stock of ink had been taken.

"But how was this possible?" Master Jadaris asked, when his man had finished.

"Someone is linking to places throughout D'ni," Guild Master Jerahl answered him. "Someone with special knowledge of the guilds."

"Someone?" R'hira queried, looking about the table. "Or are there several miscreants? Look at the pattern of the attacks. Not one but six separate guilds have now been targeted. And who knows where they will strike next? The only thing these incidents have in common is that they know the intimate workings of the guilds. They know where we are vulnerable. They know precisely where to attack and when."

"Veovis?"

All eyes turned to Aitrus, who had spoken the name.

"Impossible," Jadaris said, after a moment. "He is more than safe where we have put him."

"Is he?" Lord R'hira asked, leaning toward the Grand Master. "When did you last check on him?"

"Three weeks ago. After the first of these incidents."

"But before the remainder, yes?"

Jadaris nodded. Then, shaking his head. "No. I refuse to believe it. But if my fellow guildsmen would like me to check?"

"Do so, Master Jadaris," R'hira said. "And let us know what you discover."

Jadaris bowed to R'hira and left.

R'hira looked about the table. "Whoever this is—and we must not leap to *any* assumptions without full and proper knowledge—they aim to create a climate of fear, and what better way than to engage in a meaningless sequence of violent events?"

"Do you think that is what's happening here?" Master Jerahl asked.

"I do. But there is something none of you know about. Something that has been kept a secret among the Five. In view of this latest outrage, however, we feel you ought to know of it." R'hira paused significantly, then, looking down at his hands, said, "One of the Five great Books has been desecrated. That of Master Talashar. In fact, the structure of the text was so damaged and distorted that the Age has become unstable and we fear it will shortly self-destruct."

There was horror about the table. This was one of their worst fears—that their Ages would be tampered with and destroyed. And here was news that such a thing had happened, and not just to any Age but to one of the five "Classics," those ancient, beautiful Ages made by the greatest of D'ni's Writers.

"Who would do such a thing?" Hajihr of the Stone-Masons asked, his face mirroring the shock everyone felt at that moment.

"I do not know for certain," R'hira answered, "but I am beginning to have my suspicions. If it *is* Veovis, then I'd judge he is not acting alone. And there is one other thing. The new entries were in the same hand as that of Master Talashar."

"But he died more than six thousand years ago," Jerahl said, voicing the thoughts of all.

"That is so," R'hira said. "Yet the ink on the page was barely three weeks old."

There was a stunned silence, then Aitrus spoke again. "I think we should find A'Gaeris and hold him, until his part in this is fully known."

"You think *he* is involved, then?" Hajihr asked.

Aitrus shrugged. "He may be innocent, but I think not. I begin to share my Lord R'hira's doubts."

"And Veovis?" Jerahl asked, looking across at Aitrus.

"Perhaps Lord Veovis was innocent after all."

Guild Master Jadaris paused at the outer gate, waiting as the Master of the Keys unlocked the ancient door that led down into the earth.

No part of D'ni lay deeper in the rock than this, no part of the great city in the rock was more secure. A sloping tunnel led from the inner gate down to the Gate of Traitors, ten spans into the rock. There, in a cavern that had been hollowed more than three thousand years before, lay the Cells of Entry.

Jadaris walked down the long passage between the cells. All but one were empty. So it was. For though there were fifteen cells beyond the inner gate, few were ever used, for D'ni was an orderly society and transgressions that merited incarceration on a Prison Age were rare indeed.

"He *must* be there," he muttered to himself as, standing before the solid stone door of Veovis's cell, he waited for the Master of the Keys to unlock.

But R'hira's words had rattled him. Lord R'hira did not act on whim. If *he* had a suspicion, then like as not it was the truth. Even so, he could not believe that Veovis was not in the Age.

As the door swung back, he pushed past his Key Master almost rudely, so anxious was he for confirmation one way or another.

The cell was bare, the walls plain rock. A single wooden chair and a table were the only furnishings.

The book, allowing one to monitor the Prison Age, lay on the desk, open, its glowing panel visible.

Jadaris leaned over it. The panel showed no sign of Veovis at his desk in the Prison Age.

He turned, looking back at the squad of guards who had followed him and nodded.

"We go in."

Master Jadaris appeared in a room of metal. The floor of the linking chamber was slatted black metal, the six walls a metallic blue that was almost black, undecorated and windowless, featureless almost, except for one large panel on the far wall facing him. Dim lighting panels in the ceiling gave the room an underwater feel. In the center of the floor was a hexagonal pedestal, on which rested the Linking Book. It appeared untouched.

More men were linking into the room now. Armed Maintainers, wearing sealed masks and carrying air tanks on their backs, ready for any sort of trouble.

As Jadaris stood, the armed men positioned themselves along the walls to either side of him. At Jadaris's signal, his first assistant stepped up to the panel and placed a flat "locking square" against the faint indentation in the panel, then stepped back.

There was a heavy *thunk!* as all six of the steel locking bolts retracted at once. With a hiss the door slid slowly into the floor.

Cold air flooded the room. Beyond the door a metal walkway ran on. Jadaris sniffed again, an expression of acute distaste in his face, then walked toward the doorway.

Stepping out onto the walkway he looked up. The sky was dark and glowering, a wintry sun obscured behind heavy cloud.

Facing him was the island. Jadaris stared at it, wondering what Veovis had thought the first time he had seen it, knowing that this was to be his home henceforth, until he died.

The island was a great block of black volcanic rock, its tapered shape thrusting up from a black and oily sea. Standing on top of that desolate rock was a black tower, its walls smooth and windowless. The walkway was an unsupported length of metal some five or six feet above the surface, joining the linking chamber to the island. A set of steps cut from the rock lead up from the walkway to the great door of the tower.

A cold, bleak wind blew from Jadaris's left, whipping the surface of the water and making him pull his cloak tighter about him.

"Come," he said, half-turning to his men, "let us see what is to be seen."

The great door was locked. As his Chief Jailer took the key from his belt and stepped up to fit it to the lock, Jadaris shook his head. It was not possible. It simply was not possible. Yet as they went from room to room in the tower, his certainty dissolved. In the top room was a table. On it they found a meal set out. Yet the meal had been abandoned weeks ago and lay there rotting. Beside it lay three Linking Books.

Jadaris took the first of the three Books and stared at it. He did not know how it had been done, but Veovis had been sprung.

He shivered. This whole business filled him with profound misgivings. It was hard to know just who to trust.

He opened the Linking Book and read a line or two. This

one led straight back to D'ni. Or so it seemed. It would be easy
to check—he could send one of his guards through—but that
was not the way they normally did things. It was not guild
practice to send a man through to any Age without a Linking
Book to get them back.

Jadaris sat there a moment, staring at the words, his eyes
unseeing, his thoughts elsewhere, then suddenly he stood.
Sweeping the rotting meal onto the floor, he lay the Book
down in its place and opened it to the descriptive panel. Then,
looking about him at his men, Jadaris smiled and placed his
hand down firmly on the panel.

There was the acrid taste of smoke in the air as Veovis, cloaked
and hooded, made his way along the alleyway toward the gate.
The narrow streets of the lower city were strangely crowded
for this late hour, as people stood outside their houses to
watch the guildsmen fight the great blaze farther up the city.
The light from that blaze flickered moistly in Veovis's eyes as
he walked along, but no one noticed a single figure passing
among them. Great events were happening in the cavern. They
had all heard the explosion, and rumor was even now filtering
down from the upper city. Guildsmen were dead. Some said as
many as a hundred.

Stepping out from under the gate, Veovis glanced up at
the blaze. It was still some way above him and to his left. A
muscle twitched at his cheek, then lay still. The guard at the
gate had barely glanced at him as he passed, his attention drawn

to the fire at the great Ink-Works. And so he walked on, passing like a shadow among that preoccupied crowd.

The gate to the upper city lay just ahead.

Anna pulled on her boots, then stood, looking about her at the room. A cloak. Yes. She would need to take a cloak for him.

Going over to the linen cupboard, she took down one of Gehn's cloaks. Then, knowing that if she thought too long about it she might change her mind, she quickly left the room, hurrying down the hallway and out the front door.

Outside Anna paused, her eyes going straight to the blaze. It was below her and slightly to the left of where she stood. What it meant for D'ni she did not know, but the sight of it had finally made up her mind. She was going to bring Gehn home, whether Aitrus liked it or not. This had gone on far too long.

She hurried through the streets, yet as she came into the lane that led to the Guild Hall, she found it barricaded, a squad of Maintainers keeping back a small crowd of bystanders. Even so, she went across, begging to be allowed to pass, but the guards would not let her and eventually she turned, making her way back along the street, wondering if there might not be another way to get to the Hall.

Down. If she went down to the gate and then across, she might come at the Hall by a different way.

She walked on, making for the gate, yet as she did, a man strode toward her. He was cloaked and hooded and kept his head down as he walked, as if heavily preoccupied. There was something strange about that, and as he brushed past her, she caught a glimpse of his eyes beneath the hood.

She turned, astonished.

Veovis! It had been Veovis!

No. It could not be.

Anna swallowed, then, taking two steps, called out to the man. "Sir?"

But the man did not stop. He went on, hastening his pace, disappearing into a side street.

Anna hesitated a moment, then hurried after.

Turning the corner, she thought for a moment she had lost him; then she glimpsed a shadowy figure at the end of the narrow lane, slipping into the side gate of a darkened mansion.

Anna stopped, looking about her, but the lane was empty. If she was to find out what was happening she would have to do it herself.

Slowly, almost tentatively, she approached the gate. The blaze was at her back now. In its light everything was cast in vivid shadows of orange and black. There was a padlock on the gate, but it had been snapped and now hung loose. Anna leaned her weight gently on the door and pushed.

Inside was a tiny yard, enclosed by walls. A door on the far side was open. Anna went across and stood in the doorway, listening. Again she could hear nothing. She slipped inside, into what was clearly a kitchen. The house was dark, abandoned, or, more likely, boarded up. Only the glow of the distant fire lit the room, giving each covered shape a wavering insubstantiality.

She crossed the room, her footsteps barely audible. A door

led onto the great hallway of the mansion. The body of the hall was dark, but on the far side was a huge staircase, leading up to the next floor. A great window on the landing let in the pale red glow of the blaze.

Anna listened a moment, then frowned. Perhaps she had imagined it. Perhaps he had not come in here at all. After all, it was dark, and she had been quite some distance off.

Briefly she wondered whose house this was and why it was abandoned. There were portraits on the walls, but most were in heavy shadow, all detail obscured. Only one, on the landing wall right next to the great window, could be discerned with any clarity, yet even that, in the wavering glow, seemed just a head and shoulders. It could have been anyone. Anyone at all.

Across from her, on the far side of the hallway, were more rooms. She quickly went across and peered inside, into the intense darkness, listening as much as looking. Again there was nothing.

She was about to go, to give up her fruitless search, when there was a distinct noise from the room overhead; a thump of something being put down; a heavy noise of metal and wood.

Anna felt her heartbeat quicken. She should not be here. Not alone, anyway. If it was Veovis, then he had escaped. And if he *had* escaped . . .

She was in danger—she knew that for a certainty—but she could not stop herself. Not now. The spirit of exploration was upon her. She had to know if it really *was* him, and if so, what he was doing.

She went to the foot of the stairs, staring up past the turn. Was there a faint light up there or was she imagining it?

Slowly Anna began to climb the stairs, ready at any

moment to rush down and out of the great house. There were more noises now; the sounds of someone taking things and stowing them—in a sack, perhaps, or a bag. At the turn of the stairs she stopped, glancing up at the portrait. She was about to go on, when she looked again at the painting, sudden understanding coming to her.

It was A'Gaeris, or one of his ancestors so like him as to make no difference. The figure had the same querulous eyes, the same long brow and receding hairline, the same swept-back hair.

So this was your mansion once, Philosopher. Before you fell.

The knowledge was a key. She knew now that it *was* Veovis up above, and that A'Gaeris had somehow helped him to escape. How she did not know just yet, but perhaps she would discover that, given time.

Anna climbed the last few stairs, then stopped, her hand on the top rail, listening once more. The noises were coming from a room at the far end of the hallway—to her left as she stood. All the doors to the right of the corridor were shut, so it was not the light of the blaze she had seen from below. It came, in fact, from a room just up the corridor and to the left.

Anna took a long, calming breath then began to walk toward it. But she had only gone two paces when Veovis stepped from the room at the far end of the corridor and placed a backpack down on the floor of the hallway. She stopped dead, certain he would see her, but he did not even glance her way. With a sniff he turned and went back inside.

She quietly let out a breath, then walked on.

In the doorway to the first room she stopped, staring

down the hallway to the door of the end room, certain that he would step out at that moment and see her, but then she heard him, whistling softly to himself, his footsteps clearly on the far side of the room.

She turned and looked inside. It was a study. Book-filled shelves were on every wall and a huge desk sat in the far corner. On it was a tiny lamp with a pale rose bulb of glass, lit by a fire-marble. In its glow she could see the outline of a Linking Book, the descriptive panel shining brightly.

For a moment she hesitated, then, walking across, she stood beside the desk and, putting out her hand, placed it on the panel.

Veovis crouched, tying the neck of the sack, then carried it outside. Lifting the backpack, he slung it over his shoulder then went along the hallway to the study.

All was as he had left it. He glanced about the study, then reached across and slid the catch back on the lamp, dousing the fire-marble. Slowly its glow faded. As the room darkened, the brightness of the panel in the Linking Book seemed to intensify, until he seemed to be looking through a tiny window.

Reaching out, Veovis covered that brightness with his hand, as if to extinguish it. For a moment the room was dark; then, slowly, the vivid square of light reappeared through the melting shape of his hand.

There was silence in the empty room.

Anna stood at the window, looking out at a view that was as strange as any she had ever seen. It was not simply that the sky had a heavy purplish hue, nor that the dark green sea seemed to move slowly, viscously, like oil in a bowl, it was the smell of this Age—an awful musty smell that seemed to underlie everything.

The chamber into which she had linked had been cut into the base of the island, forming a kind of cellar beneath it. Knowing that Veovis was likely to link after her, she had quickly left the room, hurrying up a flight of twisting metal stairs and into a gallery that looked out through strong glass windows on an underwater seascape filled with strange, sluggish creatures, dark-skinned, with pale red eyes and stunted fins.

Halfway along this gallery, facing the windows, was a large, circular metal hatch—wheel-operated, as on a ship. Anna glanced at it, then went on.

A second set of steps led up from the gallery into a spacious nest of rooms, at the center of which was a six-sided chamber—a study of some kind. Two of the walls were filled floor to ceiling with shelves, on which were books. Further piles of ancient, leather-covered books were scattered here and there across the wooden floor, as if dumped there carelessly. A dozen or so large, unmarked crates were stacked against the bare stone wall on one side, next to one of the three doors that led from the room. Two large desks had been pushed together at the center. These were covered with all manner of clutter, including several detailed maps of D'ni—street plans and diagrams of the sewers and service runs. In the far corner of the room a golden cage hung by a strong chain from the low ceiling. In it was a cruel-looking hunting bird. Seeing Anna it had lifted its night-black, glossy wings as if to launch itself at her, then settled again, its fierce eyes blinking from time to time as it studied her watchfully.

A long, dark corridor led from the nest of rooms to the chamber in which she stood, which lay at a corner of the island. It was a strange room, its outer walls and sloping ceiling made entirely of glass panels. Through the glass overhead she could see even more rooms and balconies, climbing the island, tier after tier.

Like K'veer, she thought, wondering if Veovis had had a hand in its design.

At the very top of the island, or, rather, level with it, she could glimpse the pinnacle of a tower, poking up out of the very center of the rock.

Anna turned from the window. Behind her were three doors. The first led to a continuation of the corridor; the second opened upon a tiny storeroom; the third went directly into the rock—perhaps to the tower itself.

She went across, opening the last of the doors. A twisting stone stairwell led up into the rock. She was about to venture up it when there was a noise from the rooms to her right. There was a thud as something heavy was put down, then the unmistakable sound of Veovis whistling to himself. That whistling now grew louder.

Anna closed the door quietly and hurried over to the middle door. She could explore the stairwell later. Right now it mattered only that Veovis not find her there.

Slipping into the storeroom, she pulled the door closed behind her, even as Veovis's footsteps came along the final stretch of the corridor and into the room beside where she hid.

Aitrus took off his cloak, then turned to face his mother.

"What is it?" he asked.

"It is Ti'ana," she answered. "I do not know where she is, Aitrus. One of the servants saw her leave an hour back."

"She went out? With things as they are?"

Tasera nodded. "I would have sent a man out after her, if I had known. But she left no message."

Aitrus frowned. "Wait here," he said, "I think I know where she might be."

"You know?"

"Not for certain, but Ti'ana has been unhappy these past few months. She has missed Gehn badly."

"We have all missed him."

"Yes, but Ti'ana has missed him more than anyone. Last week she asked me if he could come home. I think she may have gone to fetch him."

"They would not let her."

"Do you think that would stop Ti'ana if she were determined on it?"

Tasera shook her head.

"Well, I will go and see. Wait here, Mother. If she is not at the Guild Hall I shall return at once. But do not worry. I am sure she is all right."

One of the guards on the barricade remembered her.

"She was most persistent," he said, "but we had strict orders. We were to let no one pass, not even guildsmen, without special notification. She left here, oh, more than an hour ago now."

"Did you notice where she went?"

The young guard nodded, then pointed up the lane. "She went back the way she came, then turned left, under the arch. It looked as if she was heading for the western sector."

Aitrus thanked the guard then turned away. If Anna had been going home, she would have walked straight on and cut through farther up. Unless, of course, she was trying to get through to the Guild Hall by another route.

"Home," he told himself. He would check home first, just in case she had returned. Then, if she was not there, he would go to the Guild House and ask there.

Anna crouched against the wall, trying not to make a sound.

Veovis was just beyond the door. She had heard him stop and sniff the air.

"Strange," she heard him say. "Very strange."

She closed her eyes. At any moment he would pull back the door and see her there. And then . . .

His footsteps went on. She heard the door to the corridor

creak open, then close behind him, his footsteps receding.

Anna took a long breath, then pushed the door ajar. The outer room was empty now, filled with the strange mauve light from the sky. She was about to step outside again when she glimpsed, just to her right, two shelves, cut deep into the wall. She had not noticed them before, but now she stepped across, amazed by what was on them.

Books! Linking Books! Dozens of them! She took one down and examined it. D'ni! This linked to D'ni! Quickly she examined another. That, too, appeared to link to D'ni. One after another she flicked through them.

All of them on the top shelf—every last one—seemed to link back to D'ni; each at a separate location: in a specific room in a Guild Hall, or in the cellar of a house; in storerooms and servants' quarters; and one, audaciously, direct into the great Council chamber of the Guild House.

So *this* was how they did it! Veovis was behind the spate of incidents these past few weeks.

Veovis, yes . . . and A'Gaeris.

The Books on the bottom shelf were blanks, waiting to be used. She counted them. There were forty-eight.

Anna stared at them, perplexed. How had they managed to get hold of so many blank Books? Had Suahrnir provided them? And what of Suahrnir? He had disappeared five years ago, presumed dead, but was he here, too?

When she had linked through she had not been quite sure what she meant to do. To take a peek and then get back? But now that she had seen the Books . . .

I have to stop this, she thought. *Fifteen dead. That's what the guard said. And more will die, for certain, unless I act. Unless I stop this now.*

But how?

Anna stared at the Books, then nodded to herself, a plan beginning to form in her head.

Veovis stood at the end of the stone jetty, his left hand resting lightly on the plinth as he looked out over the glutinously bright green sea toward a nearby rock that jutted, purest white like an enameled tooth, from its surface. A circular platform rested on that rock, as if fused onto its jagged crown, its gray-blue surface level with where Veovis stood.

Veovis glanced at the timer on his wrist, then slowly turned the dial beneath his fingers, clockwise, then counter-clockwise, then clockwise again. He waited a moment, listening as the massive cogs fell into place beneath his feet, then pressed down on the dial.

Slowly a metal walkway slid from the stone beneath his feet, bridging the narrow channel, linking the jetty to the platform. There was a resounding *chunk!* as it locked in place.

Veovis waited, tense now, resisting the temptation to glance at his timer again. Then, shimmering into view, a figure formed in the air above the platform. It was A'Gaeris.

The Philosopher blinked and glanced up at the sky, as if disoriented, then looked across at Veovis and grinned, holding up the Linking Book that both Anna and Veovis had used; that, until five minutes ago, had rested in the study back in the boarded-up house in D'ni.

The two men met in the middle of the walkway, clasping each other about the shoulders like the dearest of friends, while behind them a third figure shimmered into being on the platform.

It was Suahrnir.

High above them, from where she stood at the north window of the tower, Anna looked on, watching the three men greet each other then turn and walk back along the jetty, Veovis and A'Gaeris side by side, Suahrnir following a pace or two behind.

She had been thinking all along of the Linking Book back on D'ni—asking herself why they should leave the back door to this Age open like that. But now she understood. A'Gaeris had come along behind Veovis and gathered up the Book, then used a second Linking Book, hidden elsewhere, no doubt, to link back to the rock.

The walkway had been retracted. If anyone now tried to link through to this Age they would be trapped on the rock, unable to get across to the island.

She stepped back, away from the window, then turned, looking about her. The big circular room seemed to be used as a laboratory of some kind. Three long wooden benches were formed into an H at the center, their surfaces scattered with gleaming brass equipment. Broad shelves on the long, curving walls contained endless glass bottles and stoppered jars of chemicals and powders, and, on a separate set of shelves, Books. *Guild* Books, she realized, stolen from the libraries of D'ni.

Anna walked across, picking things up and examining them. Coming to the window on the south side of the room, she looked out. The sea went flat to the horizon, its dark green shading into black, so that at the point where the sea met the pale mauve sky there seemed to be a gap in reality.

Just below the tower, the land dipped steeply away to meet the sea, but in one place it had been built up slightly so that a buttress of dark, polished rock thrust out into the sea. A kind of tunnel extended a little way from the end of that buttress, at the end of which was a cage; a big, man-sized cage, partly submerged.

Looking at it, Anna frowned.

She turned, looking back across the room. There was only one doorway into the room, only one stairway down. The strong wooden door had a single bolt, high up, which could be drawn from inside.

"Perfect," she said quietly, smiling to herself. "Absolutely perfect."

Back inside the study, Veovis shut the door, then walked across. A'Gaeris and Suahrnir were already deep in conversation, pointing to locations on the map and debating which to strike at next.

Veovis stared at them a moment, then walked around past them and picked up one of the two bags he had brought with him from D'ni.

"Here," he said, handing it to A'Gaeris, "I brought you a few things back this time."

A'Gaeris looked inside the bag, then laughed. Taking out the cloak, he held it up. It was a guild cloak, edged in the dark red of the Guild of Writers.

"To think I once valued this above all else!"

A'Gaeris shook his head, making a noise of disgust, then threw the cloak about his shoulders casually, preening himself in a mocking fashion and looking to Veovis as he did.

"So how *are* things in D'ni?"

Veovis smiled. "You were right, Philosopher. The destruction of the Ink-Works has unnerved them. Before now they were able to keep things close. Now all of D'ni knows there is a problem."

"That may be so," Suahrnir said, "but there is another problem: They now know that you are no longer on the prison Age."

Veovis turned to him. "They *know?*"

Suahrnir nodded. "I overheard two guards talking. It seems Master Jadaris himself took an expedition in to check that you were still there. Finding you gone, they will know that someone had to have sprung you." He turned to A'Gaeris and grinned. "And they will not have far to look, will they?"

A'Gaeris turned back to Veovis, concerned. "Then we must escalate our campaign. Until now we have had the advantage of surprise, but they will be vigilant from here on. We must identify our prime targets and hit them."

"Lord R'hira," Suahrnir suggested.

"Naturally," Veovis agreed. "But not first. First we deal with my meddlesome friend."

"Your friend?" A'Gaeris looked puzzled.

"My ex-friend, then. Guild Master Aitrus."

"Aitrus?" Suahrnir frowned. "But surely we can deal with him later?"

"No," A'Gaeris said. "What Veovis suggests makes sense. Cut off the head and the body cannot fight on. And who are the men whom we might call the 'head' of D'ni? Why, the Emergency Council, of course! Aitrus, Jadaris, Yf'Jerrej, R'hira. These are the four who are really running things right now, and so they must be our primary targets. Thus far we have unnerved the guilds. Now we must destabilize them."

"I agree," Veovis said. "But you will leave Aitrus to me."

A'Gaeris smiled. "If you want him, he is yours, my friend. But make no mistakes. And show no pity. Remember that he showed you none."

Veovis nodded. "I will not forget that easily. But come, let us formulate our plans."

Anna tiptoed partway along the corridor, then stopped. She could hear the faint murmur of their voices through the door. There was brief laughter, and then the talk went on.

Good. While they were occupied, she would move the Linking Books.

Returning to the room, she gathered up all she could carry at one go, then hurried up the tower steps. Three trips saw all of the Books removed to the big room at the top of the tower. Satisfied, Anna cleared the surface of one of the benches, then began to pile the Books up in a heap, leaving only one aside.

That done, Anna picked up the Book she had set aside and returned to the door.

The easiest and quickest way was to burn the Books—to set fire to them, then link straight back to D'ni—but the easiest was not always the best. If she was to be sure of damaging their plans, she would need to make certain that there were no more Linking Books elsewhere on the island.

Anna listened a moment, then, satisfied that there was no one on the stairs, slipped out and hurried down. She had been depending on surprise so far, but she would need luck now, too, if she was to succeed.

Her luck held. They were still there inside the study. She could hear their voices murmuring behind the door.

"All right," a voice, Suahrnir's, said angrily. "But I do not know why we cannot just kill him and be done with it!"

Anna stepped back. At any moment the door might open and she would be discovered, yet she stayed there, listening.

"I'll go right now," Veovis said clearly. "Unless you have any further objections?"

"Not I," A'Gaeris said. "But hurry back. There's much to do before the morning."

"Do not worry," Veovis answered sardonically. "I know how best to hook our friend. I shall take no longer than I must."

Aitrus sat at his desk in his rooms at the Guild Hall, in despair, his head in his hands. There was no sign of Anna. A search of the upper city had not found her. All inquiries had drawn a blank. And though Master Jadaris had agreed to make a more thorough search, Aitrus knew that they would not find her. Not in D'ni, anyway.

No. Veovis was somehow behind this. He had to be. And this was his revenge—to take Anna.

But what had he done with her?

Aitrus looked up, staring into the air, trying to think.

If he were Veovis, what would he want? Justice? No. It was far too late for justice. Vengeance? Yes, but not simply vengeance; at least, not the blind, uncaring kind that madmen seek, unless the isolation of the prison rock had sent Veovis mad.

No. He could not believe that. Veovis was stronger than that.

Perhaps, but what of A'Gaeris? What was his role in all this? And how had he persuaded Veovis to ally with him against the Guilds?

Betrayal. That was the seed A'Gaeris had planted in Veovis's mind. *Betrayal.* The guilds had betrayed Veovis, as they had once betrayed A'Gaeris. And now the guilds had to be punished.

Punished . . . or destroyed?

Aitrus stood, realizing that there was only one thing to do. They would have to search every inch of D'ni for Linking Books.

"If we can find out where he is linking back to . . . "

Aitrus looked up. Footsteps. There were footsteps farther down the hall.

He went out into the hallway.

"Ti'ana? . . . Ti'ana, is that you?"

Aitrus had barely gone two or three steps when the door at the far end of the hall swung open. He stopped dead.

"Veovis?"

Veovis stood there, smiling, a Linking Book held open in one hand.

"Yes, Aitrus, *dearest* friend. I have your wife. If you want her back, you had better follow me. And no tricks, or Ti'ana will die."

"No! Wait!"

Aitrus started toward him, yet even as he did, Veovis brought his other hand across, touching the glowing panel.

"*Veovis!*"

The Book fell to the floor.

So it was true. His darkest thoughts were thus confirmed. Walking across, he bent down and picked up the Book.

Help. Common sense told him he ought to get help.

But what if Veovis meant what he said?

Then common sense would kill his beloved wife.

"No choice," he said, as if to excuse himself. Then, sensing that only ill could come of it, he lay his hand upon the panel and linked.

Downstairs the door slammed shut. There were footsteps on the stairs. A moment later A'Gaeris appeared at the top of the stairs, looking about him. Seeing the Linking Book he smiled, then he went across and bent, picking it up. For a moment he studied the glowing panel, his smile broadening; pocketing the Book, he turned and went back down the stairs.

It was time to link back to the island.

Anna slipped through the open doorway and into the dimly lit chamber. To her right was the study. Through its thin, wooden walls she could hear the low murmur of two voices—those of A'Gaeris and Suahrnir.

She sighed. It looked as if she was never going to get the chance to search the study.

Anna turned, looking about her. There was a narrow bed in one corner of the room. Beside it, against the back wall, were a small desk and chair. A worn silk coverlet lay over the bed. On the desk were a number of thin, coverless books, like child's exercise books. She picked one up and opened it. It was one of A'Gaeris's pamphlets—one of his endless ranting tirades against the guilds that had won him notoriety, mainly in the lower city.

Putting the pamphlet aside, Anna quickly examined what else was on the surface. There was a small notebook, locked, she noted, with a tiny silver clasp. A D'ni symbol—a simplification of A'Gaeris's name—was burned into the leather of the cover. She picked it up and pocketed it. Beneath it, to her surprise, was a tiny picture in a gilded frame. It showed a young woman, barely Anna's own age by the look of her, her dark hair swept back from a stunningly beautiful face.

That, too, she pocketed.

Anna turned, looking about her once more, checking that there was nothing else—no hidden panels and no hatches in the floor. Satisfied, she hurried back across the room again, meaning to make her way back to the tower.

She had delayed too long. Every moment now increased the chance of her being discovered. Best, then, to cut her losses: to go back to the room at the top of the tower and burn the Linking Books she had.

It would be a start. Besides, she knew much now about their plans. If she could reach Master Jadaris with that knowledge . . .

There was a sudden noise behind her, a buzz of voices from the central room. Veovis had returned. She heard his voice giving hasty orders. Then there was a strange grunt and the thud of a body falling to the floor.

There were other noises—scraping and scratching noises that she could make no sense of—and then Veovis spoke again, much louder this time:

"Take him down into the cellar. We'll put him in the cage. I'll use him as bait for another, much more tasty fish."

There was laughter, unwholesome laughter, and then the sound of a body being dragged across the room.

So they had taken another guildsman.

The corridor that led to the cellar was on the other side. For the moment she was in no danger of discovery. But time was running out. It was time to prepare things. Time to bait her own trap.

Back in the top room of the tower, Anna began to search the shelves. She knew what she wanted: potassium nitrate, sulphur, carbon; some liquid paraffin, a length of wick; a tinderbox.

The bottles were labeled, each with a handwritten D'ni symbol, but she glanced at these only to confirm what her eyes already told her. She took the tiny bottles down, one after another, setting them side by side on the worktop, then took a mixing dish and a metal spoon from the side.

There were wicks in a drawer, and a polished silver tinderbox.

"What else?" she asked, her heart pumping quickly in her chest.

One bottle, set aside from all the others on the worktop, had no label. She had noticed it earlier. Its contents were clear, with a faint bluish tinge. Now, curious, she picked it up and unstoppered it, sniffing its contents.

Sputtering, Anna jerked her head back and replaced the stopper, her eyes watering. It was a horrible, noxious mixture; clearly a sleeping draught of some kind. Even a small sniff of it had taken her breath and made her head go woozy.

Anna shivered, then slipped it into her left-hand pocket, knowing that it might have a use.

A heavy iron file lay on one of the trays nearby. She took that too, tucking it into her belt. It would be useful to have a weapon of some kind.

Just in case . . .

Anna returned to the desk and picked up one of the jars, unstoppering it; yet even as she did, she heard noises from below—a single cry and a splash.

Hurrying to the south window, she looked out. Far below,

at the end of the great stone buttress, the cage was now occupied. A man was struggling, spluttering in the water momentarily; then he went still, looking about him, as if coming to a sudden realization of his fate.

As he turned toward her, Anna caught her breath, horrified.

It was Aitrus.

Veovis glanced at A'Gaeris and smiled.

"Did you hide the Book?"

A'Gaeris pulled the Linking Book from his pocket. "You mean *this?*"

The two men were halfway along the tunnel that led from the cage. They had left Suahrnir on the platform, overlooking the cage. Now it was time to carry out the next part of their scheme.

"Are you sure she will come?" A'Gaeris asked, his eyes half-hooded.

"I am certain of it," Veovis said.

They walked on. Turning a corner, they came to the narrow steps that led up to the gallery. Here they had to go single file.

"Can I ask you something?" A'Gaeris said, as he followed Veovis up.

"Ask," Veovis said, glancing back over his shoulder as he climbed out through the hatch.

"Why do you want her? I mean, she will never love

you. Not while you keep Aitrus prisoner. And if you kill him . . . "

"Vengeance," Veovis said, as A'Gaeris ducked out under the rim of the hatch and joined him in the strangely lit gallery.

"Why not simply kill them both?"

"Because I want them to suffer the way I suffered." Veovis's face was hard now, much harder than A'Gaeris had ever seen it. "I dreamed of it, when I was on the Prison Age, night after night. I want them to be tormented the way I was tormented. I want them to feel betrayed the way *I* felt betrayed."

Behind the thick glass of the gallery windows, strange fish swam slowly, menacingly, their pale red eyes unblinking.

A'Gaeris nodded. "I understand."

"Do you?"

"Yes, friend. It was not just my guild membership I lost. I was betrothed. Betrothed to the most beautiful young woman you have ever seen."

"Ah . . . " Veovis had been about to move on, to return straight to the study, but now he changed his mind. "What do you want, A'Gaeris? I mean, what do you *really* want?"

A'Gaeris did not hesitate. "To destroy it all. That is my dream."

"Then the Guilds . . . ?"

"Are only the start. I want to destroy D'ni the way D'ni tried to destroy me." A'Gaeris's whole frame seemed to shudder with indignation. "There! Does that frighten you, Veovis?"

Veovis shook his head. "No. I know now how you feel."

"You do?"

"Yes. Come . . . "

A'Gaeris had thought it was a storage cupboard of some kind, but inside was a long, high-ceilinged room, and lining the walls of that long room were rack after rack of guns and swords. Enough to start a small war.

Veovis turned, staring at the Philosopher thoughtfully. "You once wrote that it is fortunate that the common people are unarmed, for if they were armed, D'ni would fall overnight. Do you still believe that?"

A'Gaeris reached out, taking down one of the swords and examining it. He nodded, impressed. "I do," he said finally, looking to Veovis with a smile.

"Then will this do?"

A'Gaeris grinned. "I see I badly misjudged you, Lord Veovis."

Anna stood at the door, listening, then opened it and slipped out, into the adjacent room. There were voices coming from just down the corridor. Was there another chamber down there; one she had not noticed?

It seemed so. Recessed into the wall, partway along, was a door. It was open the slightest crack and she could hear Veovis and A'Gaeris talking within. Realizing that she might have only one chance, she hurried past and on into the gallery. To her surprise the hatch halfway down on her left was wide open.

She edged over to it and listened, then peeked her head around. A flight of steps went down.

She went inside, hastening down the steps, then stopped. Ahead of her, just around a turn, she could hear Suahrnir murmuring something.

The bottle containing the sleeping draught was still in her pocket, the iron file in her right hand. Taking a cloth handkerchief from her pocket, Anna wrapped it about her mouth, then took the bottle from her pocket.

With more confidence than she felt, she stepped out around the corner. Suahrnir was sitting on a platform at the end of the tunnel, overlooking the cage. He had his back to her. Calming herself, she walked on, trying not to make any noise.

She was right beneath Suahrnir when he turned, realizing that she was there. Yet even as he turned, Anna hit him hard over the head with the file. As he collapsed, she pulled the cloth up over her nose and, unstoppering the bottle, poured its contents over his face.

A cloud of thick, white fumes rose from the platform.

Anna blinked, her eyes stinging furiously, then, closing them tight, she edged around Suahrnir and climbed up onto the cage, not daring to take a breath.

The cage swayed from side to side as she moved around the outside of it, as far as she could get from the stinging white cloud. As the cage steadied, she leaned out and raised the silk, taking in a lungful of air.

"Ti'ana? Is that you?"

Aitrus was just beneath her, blinking up at her as if only half conscious. Only his head and shoulders were above the surface of the vile, dark green liquid and she could see that there was a large, dark bruise on the side of his forehead. Seeing him thus, Anna winced, her love for him making her forget her own danger. His hands were tightly bound. They had hooked them over the massive padlock to keep him from sinking down into the water. It was cruel, but it had also probably saved his life.

"It's all right, my love," she said gently. "I'll get you out. But you must be quiet. We must not alert the others."

"I was stupid," he said, his eyes flickering closed, as if he could not keep them open. His voice was faint and fading. "Veovis said he had you prisoner. I should have known. I should have brought help."

"No," Anna said, pained by the way he blamed himself for this. She took the file from her waist and, leaning across, began to try to force the lock. "You did what you thought best."

Aitrus coughed. Some of the sleeping gas was now drifting across from the tunnel. Anna could sense its stinging presence in the air. She grimaced then leaned back on the file once more, heaving at it, trying to force the lock, but it would not budge. She needed a longer piece of metal, something with more leverage.

A sudden gust of wind, coming in off the surface of the sea, swept back the drift of noxious white gas.

"Aitrus," she said, reaching through the bars, trying to touch his brow, her fingers brushing air. "Aitrus . . . I shall not be long, I promise. I'll come back for you. So hold on."

But he could not hear her. His eyes were closed, and whether it was the gas or whether he had slumped back into unconsciousness she could not tell.

Time. Time was against her now.

Taking a huge gulp of air, she pulled the cloth down over her mouth again, then turned and, scrambling back around the cage, ducked back inside the tunnel, her eyes tightly shut as she stumbled through the choking whiteness.

Veovis was sitting at a table at the end of the armory, fitting together an incendiary device. Five completed bombs lay in a row just by his elbow; long red tubes with bulbous silver ends filled with explosive chemicals. Nearby, A'Gaeris was still working his way through the racks, looking for the ideal weapon for himself.

"We should only use guns when we need to," Veovis said, looking up at him. "For what we plan, a poisoned dart is best."

"And the incendiaries?" A'Gaeris looked down the barrel of a hunting gun at Veovis, then set the gun aside. "I would have thought they would notice one of those going off."

Veovis continued to fit the device together. "These are not for use as weapons, my friend, these are to destroy the Linking Books after we have used them."

A'Gaeris stared at him. "And the Hidden Linking Books? The ones we already have in place? Did I take those risks for nothing, Veovis?"

"No, but it might be difficult to use them, now that the guilds are more vigilant. Besides, we have a whole store of Books we can use. If time were less pressing I would be less profligate, but as things are . . . "

A'Gaeris nodded. "You are quite right. And it will, at least, allow us to slip in and slip out at will." His eyes gleamed. "Think of it, Veovis! They will not know what has hit them!"

Veovis smiled and nodded, then set the sixth bomb aside, next to the others. "We shall be like shadows," he said, reaching out to take another of the incomplete incendiaries from the rack by his feet. As he set it down on the desk, he glanced across at A'Gaeris again. "Bring the map from the study. We can discuss things while we work."

As A'Gaeris stepped into the room, he saw her. Ti'ana, Aitrus's wife. She was at the center of the room, beside the table, hunched forward slightly, her back to him. She was very still, as if concentrating on something: reading, perhaps, or studying something.

The map of D'ni . . .

Smiling, A'Gaeris drew his dagger and tiptoed across until he was no more than a couple of feet from her.

"Do not move, Ti'ana," he said, a quiet menace in his voice. "I have a knife and I will not hesitate to use it."

She froze, her shoulders tensed.

"Turn slowly," he said. "Very slowly. Make no sudden movements."

She began to turn, slowly at first, very slowly; then, in a sudden rush her arms came up.

And something else. Something heavy and black that

seemed to expand into his face, screeching as it did, its sharp claws digging in deeply.

Veovis stood, turning toward the door. The first scream had made him drop the incendiary; the second startled him into action.

He ran, out of the room and along the corridor, bursting through the first room and into the study. The screaming was louder here, mixed with the bird's high, screeching call.

A'Gaeris was on the far side of the room, struggling to fend off the ferocious assault of the bird. Blood ran down his face and upper arms. Nearby the golden cage lay on the floor, the chain snapped, the door forced open.

Intruders . . .

"Help me!" A'Gaeris pleaded, putting an arm out toward Veovis. "In the Maker's name, help me!"

Veovis stared at his ally a moment, then, drawing the old, long-barreled gun from his belt, crossed the room quickly, ignoring A'Gaeris and vanishing through the far door, heading for the far room and the corridor beyond.

Anna slammed the door behind her then reached up and slipped the bolt into place. Hurrying over to the bench, she took the stoppers from bottles and jars then began to pour things into various containers.

She could hear A'Gaeris's screams, even where she was,

through the thickness of stone and wood, and knew that Veovis would be coming after her.

Taking her concoction, Anna poured some of the clear, thick liquid over the door, soaking the wood with it, then laid a trail of it across to the far side of the room, where the Linking Books were piled up. That done, she put the bowl aside and went back to the door, sliding the bolt back once again and pulling the door slightly ajar.

She could hear footsteps now, hurrying up the twist of steps.

Anna scrambled back across the room, setting the Linking Book she was to use to return to D'ni down on the desk to one side, open to the descriptive panel. Then, taking the length of wick, she lit it from the tinder, blowing on the smoldering end of it until it glowed.

The footsteps came to the head of the steps and stopped. There was a moment's hesitation and then the door on the far side of the room was kicked open. Veovis stepped inside, the cocked gun raised, its dark mouth pointed directly at her.

Seeing her, Veovis gave a surprised laugh. "Ti'ana! You were the last person I expected."

Anna stared back at him defiantly, her left hand hovering over the glowing panel, her right holding the smoldering wick.

Noticing the Books, he blinked, reassessing the situation. "What are you doing?"

"I am putting a stop to this. Before things get out of hand."

His face grew hard. "Give me the book, Ti'ana. Give it to

413

me and I shall spare you. You and your son both. The rest will die. They have to. But you and Gehn can live . . . *if* you give me the Book."

Anna smiled and dropped the wick onto the pile of Linking Books, igniting it, at the same moment placing her other hand against the linking panel.

As the Books went up in a great rush of flame, Veovis roared and pulled the trigger. The sound of the detonation filled the room as the bullet hurtled toward her disappearing shape. At the same moment, the trail of liquid chemicals flared, the flame running along it like a trail of magma searing through the rock.

There was a great hiss and then the door behind Veovis exploded into flame, throwing him forward, his hair and cloak on fire.

But Anna did not see it. Anna had already gone.

The great chamber was almost dark. Only at its very center, where the five great thrones were, was there a small pool of light, where a single flame flickered between the pillars. Beneath its scant illumination the five great Lords of D'ni sat, their ancient faces etched with deep concern.

"We must search the city from end to end," R'hira said, echoing what Master Jadaris had said to him not an hour before. "Every room, and every drawer of every desk. We must find these Linking Books and destroy them, else no one here is safe."

"Is it possible?" another of them asked. "Have we the time or the numbers to make such a search?"

"No," R'hira admitted, "yet we must make the attempt. Unless we do . . . "

He stopped dead, staring in astonishment as a figure materialized in the space before the thrones.

"What in the Maker's name . . . "

"Ti'ana!" R'hira cried, standing and stepping down from his throne.

Anna looked up, her face pale, then slumped down onto the floor. Blood poured from a wound in her shoulder.

"Bring help!" R'hira cried, speaking to one of the guards who stood in the shadow surrounding them. "Quick now, Guildsman! Ti'ana is badly hurt!"

Yet even as he stooped to try to help her, another figure shimmered into being right beside her.

The man's face was blackened. His hair was aflame. Smoke curled up from his burning clothes. He was doubled up, almost choking for breath, but even in that state R'hira recognized him at once.

"Veovis!"

PART SEVEN: LAST DAYS

IT WAS OVER. THE EVIDENCE HAD BEEN HEARD, THE verdict of the Council unanimously given. It remained now only for the Five Lords to announce the sentence.

The great chamber was hushed as Lord R'hira got to his feet and, stepping from his throne, stood over the kneeling Veovis.

Veovis was chained at hand and foot. His head had been shaved and he wore a simple prison gown of rust red, which showed his bare arms and calves. Seated just behind the kneeling prisoner, looking on attentively, were Aitrus and his wife, Ti'ana, who, because of her part in things, had been allowed to attend this final ceremony.

It was only two weeks since that moment when, to the astonishment of the five great Lords, both Ti'ana and Veovis had linked through into this self-same chamber. Both Aitrus and his wife were now much improved from their wounds. Aitrus sat there with his head bound, Ti'ana with a bandage about her wounded shoulder.

There was a silent tension in the chamber as R'hira looked about him at the seated ranks of guildsmen.

"Veovis," R'hira said quietly. "You have betrayed the trust of this Council. You have deceived us and stolen from us, destroyed our property, and . . . yes, *murdered* our fellow guildsmen. Such behavior is without parallel in all our long history, and it is felt that our sentence ought to reflect that. I therefore declare that you, Veovis, son of Rakeri, Lord of D'ni, shall be taken from here to the steps of the Library and there, at the seventeenth hour, before witnesses, be beheaded for your treachery."

There was a sharp intake of breath. Beheaded! It was unheard of. But Lord R'hira seemed as hard as granite as he looked about him.

"Such is the decision of the Five Lords. Will anybody speak for the accused?"

It was a traditional request at such moments, when a prisoner had been sentenced, and though this sentence was without recent parallel, it was clear that none among the Five expected anyone to speak.

Anna stood.

"Forgive me, Lord R'hira. I know I am here as a guest of the Council and as such have no right to voice my feelings; even so, I *would* like to speak in favor of the prisoner."

R'hira turned, looking to his fellows. There was a moment of eye contact among the ancients and then R'hira turned back.

"If anyone deserves the chance to speak, it is you, Ti'ana, though why you should wish to utter a word in favor of this miscreant is quite beyond my imagining. Step forward."

At that moment Veovis screamed, "That barbaric animal is going to speak on my behalf?! Never! I won't allow it!"

"Silence," R'hira shouted with the pounding of his hand.

Veovis continued in his rage. "She's a traitor, not one of us! She has breached the sanctity of the D'ni blood! Don't you see!?"

"Guards, remove him!" R'hira shouted. "Now!"

They dragged the screaming man from the room. Calm returned to the chamber.

Anna stepped out. She bowed to each of the Five in turn, then turned about, facing the ranks of guildsmen.

"My Lords . . . Guildsmen. I do not wish to play down the severity of what your once-fellow Veovis has been found guilty of. Nor have I reason to feel anything but hatred for the man who tried to kill my husband and, but for a poorly aimed shot, would undoubtedly have killed me. Yet as an outsider, a newcomer to the great empire of D'ni, let me make an observation.

"This great cavern is an island of reason, of rational, considered behavior. You D'ni have developed codes of behavior, ways of dealing with situations, that are the result of thousands of years of experience. The most important of those codes, and the wisest of all, perhaps, is that which deals with those who transgress and step outside the codes. Until now, the D'ni have only rarely taken a life for a life. Until now, you have chosen the path of segregation, of cutting out the bad from your midst and isolating it, as a surgeon might isolate a virus. That, I would argue, is the path of sanity, whereas this . . ."

Anna paused, as if she could read the objection that was in most of their minds.

"I know what you are thinking. He escaped once. He might well escape again. And the so-called Philosopher, A'Gaeris, is still at large. Such factors must, I agree, come into your thinking. But there is one important factor that has not been considered, and that is precisely why Veovis behaved as he did."

Anna took something from her pocket and held it up. It was a notebook of some kind.

"I have here a journal—A'Gaeris's private journal—which I took from his room in the Age from which they launched their attacks on D'ni. Had I not been ill these past few weeks, I might have read it sooner—and then could have laid this before the Council as evidence in Lord Veovis's favor, for its contents are most revelatory. As it is, I offer it to you now as a plea for clemency."

Lord R'hira, who had been listening in silence until this moment, now spoke up.

"Forgive me, Ti'ana, but what might that villain A'Gaeris possibly have to say that would excuse the prisoner's behavior?"

Anna turned, facing him. "It is all here, my Lord, every last part of it, fully documented in A'Gaeris's own hand. How he planned things; how he forged papers; how he worked through Guildsman Suahrnir to ensnare Lord Veovis into his perverse schemes; even how he manipulated my husband into going to Master Jadaris with what he 'knew.'

"Whatever he has done since, that first great wrong cannot be denied. Veovis was an innocent man. Think, then, of the bitterness he must have felt in being stripped of all title and incarcerated upon that prison rock. Oh, it is no excuse for what he subsequently did, yet I offer it as explanation."

Lord R'hira took the book from Anna and read a page or two, blinking from time to time. Then he looked up.

"We must have time to study this, Ti'ana."

"Of course," she said, giving him a grateful bow. "But as you study it, my Lord, consider the balance of good and ill that exists in all men, and try to imagine in what circumstances that balance could be tilted either way—toward great good, or toward the kind of behavior Veovis displayed toward the society that spurned him."

R'hira gave a tiny nod, his eyes smiling at Anna, then he turned, his eyes quickly gauging the response of his fellow Lords. There were nods.

"Very well," he said, turning back. "The sentence of this Council is set in abeyance until this matter can be fully considered. Until then the prisoner will be placed under constant guard."

As the meeting broke up and guildsmen began to drift out of the chamber and into the nearby rooms, R'hira came over to Anna.

"I am grateful for your intercession, Ti'ana, yet one thing bothers me. You may be right. Veovis may once have been innocent. Yet that is in the past. If we do not end his life for what he subsequently did, then we have but a single course before us, and that is to incarcerate him for the rest of his natural life. Such a course we tried before . . . and failed with. What if we fail a second time?"

"Then make sure you do not, Lord R'hira. Make a new and special Age for him, then, once he is safe within that place, burn the book so that no one can help him escape. Vigilance, not vengeance should be your byword."

R'hira bowed his head, impressed by her words. "Well spoken, Ti'ana."

She gave a little bow.

"Oh, and Ti'ana . . . do not worry. Whatever we decide, Veovis will *never* be allowed his freedom."

A'Gaeris sat at his desk, studying the notebook. The wooden door of the hut was closed, the blinds drawn against the sunlight. From outside came the busy sound of sawing and hammering.

He closed the book then nodded to himself. Standing, he yawned and stretched. He was wearing a simple rust-red gown that fitted tightly at the waist. A pair of D'ni glasses rested atop his freshly shaven head. Walking over to the door, he pulled them down over his eyes, then stepped outside.

Just below the hillock on which the hut stood, in a clearing between the trees, his slaves were hard at work. Already the basic frame of the room had been constructed. Now they were building the seats and shelves and, at the center of it all, the podium.

He walked down, stopping at the edge of the clearing to take out the notebook once again, turning to the page he had been looking at a moment earlier. For a moment he compared Suahrnir's sketches to the room that was being constructed in the clearing, then he slipped the book away once more. There was no doubting it, Suahrnir had had a good eye. No detail had evaded him. Everything he needed was here. Every measurement.

He began to laugh; a deep, hearty laughter that rolled from his corpulent frame, making the natives glance up at him fearfully before returning to their work.

"But we shall change all that," he said, as his laughter subsided. "No rules. No guidelines. Nothing but what I want."

The thought of it sent a tiny shiver up his spine. "Nothing . . . but what *I* want."

The preparations were meticulous.

Four of the guild's finest Writers were assigned the task of making the new Age; each of them allocated one specific strand of the whole. Working to Lord R'hira's brief, in copy books that had no power to link, they patiently produced their words, passing on their finished creations to the Grand Master of their Guild, Ja'ir, who, in coordination with Grand Master Jadaris of the Maintainers, compared the texts and made his subtle corrections, ensuring that the resultant Age was consistent and thus stable.

In all a hundred days passed in this fashion. But then it was finally done and, after consultation with Lord R'hira, a blank Book—a Kortee'nea—was taken from the Guild's Book Room and placed on a desk in a cell at the center of the Hall of the Maintainers. There it was guarded day and night, its pages never out of sight for a single instant as, one by one, the four Writers returned to copy their work into the Book.

By this means the privacy of the Book was maintained, for none of the four had any knowledge of what the other three had written. Only Jadaris and Ja'ir and R'hira, three of the most trustworthy men in the entire empire, knew that.

Meanwhile, in a cell just down the passageway, they placed Veovis, shackled hand and foot, two members of the City

Guard with him every moment of the day and night, linked to him by chains of nara, waking and sleeping.

And so the days passed, until the Prison Book was done.

At the seventeenth hour on the day of judgment the great bronze bell rang out from the tower above the Hall of the Guild of Maintainers. Far below, in the lowest level of that great labyrinthine building, in the deep shadows of the Room of Punishment, the Great Lords and Grand Masters of D'ni looked on as Veovis, his head unbowed, the cords that had bound his hands and feet cut, stepped over to the podium and faced the open Book.

As the bell rang, Veovis looked about him, no flicker of fear in those pale, intelligent eyes, only, at this final moment, a sense of great dignity. Then, as the final stroke rang out, he placed his hand upon the glowing panel and linked.

As he vanished, a sighing breath seemed to pass through the watching guildsmen. Heads turned, looking to Lord R'hira.

"It is done," he said quietly. "Master Jadaris . . . take the Book away and burn it."

Yet even as he spoke the words there was a faint disturbance of the air before the Book, the faintest blur. For the briefest instant, R'hira thought he glimpsed a figure in a rust-red prison gown, his head shaved bare.

R'hira looked about him, surprised. Was he the only one to have seen it? And what precisely had he seen? An afterimage?

Or was this some flaw in the Book itself? After all, it was rare for a Book to be made by four separate writers, and it was possible that some minor errors had crept into the text.

He frowned, then set the matter from his mind. It was of no importance. All that mattered was that they burned the Book. Then D'ni would be safe.

Master Jadaris stepped up to the podium and, closing the Book, lifted it ceremonially in both hands, then carried it from the room.

They followed, along a passageway and through into the furnace room. Here, since time immemorial, they had burned faulty Books, destroying their failed experiments and shoddy work.

But this was different. This was a world that functioned perfectly.

And so we break our own rules, R'hira thought. And even if it were for a good cause, he still felt the breach as a kind of failure.

This is not the D'ni way. We do not destroy what is healthy.

Yet Ti'ana was right. It was either this or put Veovis to death. And there was no doubt about it now: Veovis had been an innocent man when first they found him guilty and incarcerated him.

R'hira watched as the great oven door was opened and the Book slid in. There was a transparent panel in the door. Through it he could see the gray-blue cover of the Prison Book clearly. R'hira bent slightly, looking on as the oven fired and the flames began to lick the cover of the Book.

The months passed swiftly. Things quickly returned to normal. For young Gehn these were strangely happy times— strange, because he had never dared hope to thrive away from his mother's side.

In his eighth year, on the last day of his first term at the Guild College, his father and mother visited him. It was an Open Day, and most of the students' parents were to be there, but for Gehn it was a very special occasion, for he had been chosen to represent the College and read out a passage from the great history of his guild that spoke of the long tradition of the Guild of Books.

The days of illness, of bullying in the night, and tearful homesickness were long behind Gehn. He had become a strong child, surprisingly tall for his age, and confident in all he did, if never outspoken. Yet he was strangely distant with his mother, as if some part of him had never quite forgiven her for sending him away. It was thus that he greeted her on this special day, with a respectful distance that might have been expected from any other student meeting the great Ti'ana, but not, perhaps, from her only son.

He bowed formally. "Mother. I am glad you came."

Anna smiled and briefly held him, but she, too, sensed how things were between them. As she stepped back, Aitrus embraced Gehn.

"Well done, Gehn!" he said, grinning down at his son. "I hear nothing but good from your Guild Masters! I am very proud of you boy. We both are!"

Gehn glanced at his mother. He could see that she was indeed proud of him, yet strangely that mattered very little beside the praise of his father. After all, his father was D'ni—

of the blood—and a Council member, too. To have *his* praise was something. Yet he did not say this openly.

"I try to do my best," he said, lowering his head with the modesty that was drilled into all students.

"Guild Master Rijahna says you have a promising future, Gehn," Anna said, her smile more guarded than his father's. "Indeed, he has talked to your father of private tuition."

This was the first Gehn had heard of this. He looked to his father wide-eyed.

"Is that true?"

Aitrus nodded. "If you want it."

Gehn beamed. "Of course I want it! Who would not? Oh, I ache to be like them, Father! Like the Masters, I mean. To know what they know. To be as they are!"

Aitrus laughed. "I understand that feeling, Gehn, but you must be patient, too."

Gehn lowered his head again. "Of course." He calmed, matching his demeanor to a more somber mood. "Thank you. Thank you both. I shall make you proud of me."

Anna smiled and reached out, ruffling his hair. "We are already proud of you, Gehn. More proud than you could ever imagine."

As Gehn finished the oration, Anna felt the tightness in her stomach vanish, her anxiety replaced by a great uprush of pride. To think he had nearly died—and not once but several times! And now here he was, standing confidently before his peers and

Masters—yes, and before a great hall full of parents, too—speaking with real feeling and pride of the great tradition into which he had been born.

She glanced at Aitrus and saw the great beam of a smile on her husband's face and knew he shared all she felt.

My son.

Oh, it was difficult sometimes. Gehn could be cold and distant, but she put that down to his age, yes, and to other things. It had not been easy for him being of mixed blood. Yet he had come through it all triumphantly.

As Guild Master Rijahna stepped up to the podium, he gave a little bow to Gehn. There was the faintest trace of a smile on his lips, a trace that vanished as he turned to face the audience.

"And now, guildsmen, ladies, if you would like to come through to the refectory . . . "

But Master Rijahna had barely formed the word when the whole building shook. He looked up, surprised, as if he had imagined it, but from the murmur in the audience, from the way a number of the guildsmen and their ladies had risen to their feet, he was not alone in experiencing that tremor.

It came again, stronger this time, and with it a low rumbling noise. Dust fell from overhead.

Outside, the great bell of D'ni was sounding.

And there were only two reasons for that bell to sound: the death of one of the Five, or a threat to D'ni itself.

Rijahna swallowed back his momentary fear and leaned upon the podium.

"Ladies, guildsmen. Please remain calm."

He turned, looking to his fellow Masters and to the

young pupils, who stared back at him, silent yet clearly afraid.

"It will be all right," he said quietly, his voice offering them a reassurance he did not feel. "Be calm and follow me outside and all will be well, I promise you. All will be well . . ."

Anna saw it at once as she emerged from the Guild Hall, there on the far side of the great cavern. A great crack had opened in the wall of the cave, and from it spewed a dark cloud of gas.

She looked to Aitrus, as if he might explain it, but from the expression on his face he seemed as dumbfounded as anyone.

"What is it?" she asked, trying not to succumb to the panic that seemed to be spreading among the people all about her. At the sight of the dark cloud some of the women had started screaming and wailing.

"I do not know," he said, unable to tear his eyes from it, "but it might be best to link away from here, until more is known."

"But you will be needed, Aitrus . . ."

He looked to her. "I did not mean myself. You and Gehn. You should take him home, to the mansion, then go to Gemedet. At once. There are provisions there."

"And you?" she asked, fearing for him suddenly.

He smiled, then kissed her. "I shall come when I can, Ti'ana. But take Gehn straightaway. And look after him."

"All right. But take care, my love. And come when you can."

431

"I shall," he said, then, turning, he hastened away, heading for the Guild House.

Anna hesitated a moment, watching Aitrus go, an awful feeling filling her at the sight of him making his way through the crowd; then, determined to do as he had asked, she turned, beginning to make her way back up the steps, anxious to find Gehn.

Slowly the dark cloud spread, like a mighty veil being drawn across the far side of the cavern. Inch by inch it crept across the lake, edging toward D'ni, and where it touched the surface of the lake, the light from the lake was extinguished.

The light-giving algae were dying, by the look of it; poisoned by the noxious fumes of the cloud.

And if that cloud were to reach out its fingers to D'ni city?

Then they would also die.

The city below was in turmoil. The shrieks of terror and wailing of the desperate were dreadful to hear. There were great queues now at all of the Common Libraries, as people made their way to the safety of the common Ages.

Anna stared across the cavern for a moment longer, horrified, then hurried on, taking Gehn's hand and pulling him along behind her. There was not far to go now and she was beginning to think about what she would need to pack—journals and books and the like—when the third tremor struck.

It was by far the largest of the three tremors and threw

them both from their feet, showering them with dust and debris.

Walls were crumbling now. Buildings were crashing to the ground. Just up ahead of them, the front of one of their neighbors' mansions tumbled into the alleyway, throwing up a great cloud of dust.

As the tremor faded, Anna lifted herself onto her hands and knees and turned anxiously. But Gehn was fine: he had a small cut on his brow, but it was almost nothing.

"Come on," she said, getting to her feet then taking his hand again, "before the next one hits."

But they had barely gone a dozen paces when the whole cavern seemed to resound like a struck gong.

They clung to each other, waiting for the great ceiling to come down on them or the earth to open up beneath them, but despite the mighty roar of falling masonry and cracking walls, they came through untouched.

Indoors, Tasera was waiting for them anxiously.

"Thank the Maker you are here," she said, relieved to see at least two of her family home safe. "But where is Aitrus?"

"He has gone to the Guild House," Anna said, more calmly than she felt. "He will come when he can."

Tasera gave a nod of resignation. "Kahlis went, too, as soon as the first tremor struck. No doubt they will return together."

Anna nodded, then said, "I need to get one or two things from the study. Take Gehn and link through. I will follow you just as soon as I can. Aitrus said we were to link to Gemedet."

"Gemedet? But surely Ko'ah would be safer?"

"It is what he said."

Tasera bowed her head, for once giving in to her daughter-in-law. "Then go quickly, Ti'ana. I shall see you in Gemedet."

Anna slipped the knapsack onto her back, then went out into the corridor. Time was pressing now, but she could not go until she had taken one final look at things. Climbing the stairs, she emerged onto the balcony then hurried over to the rail.

The great city was stretched out below where she stood, layer after layer of ancient stone streets and houses, reaching down to the great circle of the harbor and Kerath's massive arch. Though it was day, lights burned in most of the houses, for a strange twilight was falling over D'ni as the great cloud spread, its poisonous fumes dousing the lake's soft glow.

The dark cloud now filled almost half of the cavern, its color now discernible as a filthy brown. The edges of it drifted slowly, in a dreamlike fashion, more like a sluggish liquid than a gas. Even as she watched, wispy brown tendrils of the gas extended about Kerath's Arch and slowly curled across the surface of the harbor.

And where the gas touched, the algae faded, the bright glow dying like sputtering embers.

The sight of it chilled her.

Where are you, Aitrus? she wondered, looking across to the left, where the Guild House stood, its massive, tiered roof dominating the surrounding Halls. *Are you safe, my love?*

As if voicing the fear she felt at that moment, a great noise of wailing drifted up from the lower city. Many were safe now, but there were still some—hundreds, maybe more—who had not made it to the Common Libraries and the safety of the Ages. It was they who now faced the coming of the great cloud as it slowly filled the harbor with its rolling darkness, then spilled into the narrow lanes and alleyways that led up from the waterfront.

The Maker help them . . .

Yet even as she thought it, she caught a glimpse of a guildsman hurriedly ascending the main street that led between the gates, his cloak streaming behind him as he ran. He was carrying something odd, some kind of cylinder, yet she knew at once who it was.

"Aitrus!" she yelled, waving frantically at him.

He slowed, his head turning, and then he waved back at her, hurrying on again, disappearing briefly behind a row of houses, while far below him, like the breath of fate itself, the dark gas slowly climbed the levels, destroying any living thing it touched.

It was raining in Gemedet, a fresh, pure rain that, after the nightmare of the cavern, seemed to wash all stain of it from them as they walked down the slope toward the encampment.

Seeing them step out from among the trees, Gehn stood then ran toward them, hugging his father fiercely. The boy's hair was slicked back, his clothes soaked, but he seemed not to mind.

Picking him up, Aitrus carried Gehn down the rest of the slope and into the shelter of the cabin. Tasera looked up as they entered, a great beam of a smile lighting her face at the sight of Aitrus. Then, seeing only Anna enter behind him, she frowned.

"Where is your father, Aitrus?"

"In D'ni," Aitrus answered somberly, slipping the cylinder from his back and balancing it in the corner.

"He stayed?"

"He agreed to. Along with the Five and all the other Grand Masters. It was their plan to go to one of the Guild worlds and there to debate things further."

"Then he is safe," she said, relieved.

"For a time," Aitrus answered, taking the mask from his cloak pocket and placing it on top of the cylinder, the end of it dangling from the great silver nozzle.

"What do you mean?"

Aitrus shrugged. "I mean only that none of us knows yet what has really happened or where the gas is coming from. As for the tremors, there were no early signs in the rock, nor is there any history of such local disturbances."

"So what are we to do? Stay here?"

"For a time, yes. Until things blow over. I have been ordered to remain here for ten days. At the end of that I am to return to D'ni, wearing the mask and cylinder. Others will return at the same time. If all is well, we shall bring the people back to D'ni."

"And if it is not?" Tasera asked, her face gaunt.

Aitrus sighed. "Then we stay here . . . for a time. Until we can *make* things well again in D'ni."

The air was a horrible, sickly yellow-brown, choking the ancient streets and alleyways, as though a wintry fog had descended upon the great tiered city in the cave. Silent it was, and dark, though not as dark now as at first.

Here and there, at crossroads and at gates, lamps had been set on the top of poles. Huge fire-marbles the size of fists glowed red, or blue, or green behind the thick glass panes of the lamps; yet their lights burned dimly, as though through depths of dark and murky water.

Silent it was, yet in that silence the creaking of a cart could now be heard, along with the shuffle of two men, making their slow way through that subterranean place.

As they came into a pool of dark red light, one could see the airtight masks that encased their heads, linked by strong hoses to the air tanks on their backs. They wore long leather boots and thick gloves that reached to their elbows.

Their cart was loaded high, pale hands and feet jutting lifelessly from the midst of that macabre bundle of rags and bones. Leaning forward, they pushed in silence, sharing the weight without complaint. Ahead, just beyond the lamp, was their destination.

Coming to the foot of the steps, they set the handles of the cart down, then began to unload, taking each body by its wrists and ankles and carrying it up into the semi-darkness of the entrance hall.

Here, too, they had placed lamps, lighting the way into the great Book Room.

It was not their first journey, nor would it be their last. For a full week now they had gone about their task, patiently, unendingly, collecting in the harvest of their sowing.

So many bodies, there were. So much illness and death. It was hard to credit that the gas had undone so many. And then the quakes.

While one held the body propped against the podium, the other took its hand and placed it over the glowing panel of the Book, moving his own hand back as the link was made.

The body shimmered for an instant and was gone.

And so on, endlessly, it seemed. A thousand corpses, maybe more: their dead hands, filled yet with living cells, linking into the Ages; their bodies wracked with illness; rife with the contagion that had swept these mortuary streets.

Looking through their masks at one another, the two men smiled grimly.

"Another, Philosopher?"

"Oh, another, my Lord. Most certainly another."

The two men laughed; a dark and bitter laughter. And then they returned, to bring another body from the cart. To send another of their dark seeds through into the Ages. Destroying the sanctuaries one at a time: finishing the work they had begun.

It was the evening of the ninth day. Tomorrow Aitrus would return to D'ni. As the day ended, they sat on a platform of rock just above the falls, just Anna and Aitrus, looking out over the little world they had made.

The sun, behind them, cast their shadows long across the lush greens of the valley. For a long time they were silent, then Anna spoke.

"What do you think you will find?"

Aitrus plucked a stem of grass and put it to his mouth. Now that it was evening, he had pushed his glasses up onto his brow, but where they had sat about his eyes, his pale flesh was marked with thin red furrows. He shrugged. "Who knows? Yet I fear the worst. I had hoped some message would have come through earlier than this. Or my father . . . "

Anna reached out, laying her hand softly against his neck. He feared for his father, more than for himself. So it was with Aitrus. It was always others before himself. And that was why, ultimately, she loved him: for that selflessness in him.

"How long will you be?"

Aitrus turned slightly, looking at her. "As long as I am needed."

"And if you do not return?"

"Then you will stay here."

She began to shake her head, but he was insistent. "No, Ti'ana. You *must* do this for me. For me, and for Gehn."

The mention of Gehn stilled her objections. Aitrus was right. Gehn was still only eight. Losing one parent would be bad enough, but to lose both could prove devastating, even though Tasera would still be here.

She gave the barest nod.

"Good," Aitrus said, "then let us go back to the encampment. I have much to prepare before I leave."

It was early when Aitrus set off. All farewells had been said; now, as Anna looked on, Gehn cuddled against her, Aitrus pulled on the cylinder, checked it was working properly, then slipped the airtight mask down over his head.

Seeing him thus, Anna felt her stomach tighten with anxiety.

Aitrus turned, waved to them, then turned back, placing his hand against the open Linking Book.

The air about his figure swirled as if it had been transformed into some other substance, then cleared. Aitrus was gone.

Anna shivered. Words could not say the fear she felt at that moment: a dark, instinctive fear for him.

"Be brave, my darling," she said, looking down at Gehn. "Your father will come back. I promise he will."

Aitrus could hear his own breathing loud within the mask as he linked into the study. He took out the lamp he had brought and, striking the fire-marble, lit it and held it up, looking about him.

Nothing had been disturbed, yet all had been transformed. The gas had gone, but where it had been it had left its residue, coating everything with a thin layer of yellow-brown paste.

The sight of it sickened him to his stomach. Was it all like this, everywhere in D'ni? Had nothing survived untouched?

Outside in the corridor it was all the same, as though some host of demons had repainted everything the same hellish shade. Where his booted feet trod he left long smearing marks upon the floor.

Aitrus swallowed. The air he breathed was clean and pure, yet it seemed tainted somehow by what he saw.

He went down the stairs, into the lower level of the house. Here some of the gas remained, pooled in the corners of rooms. Faint wisps of it drifted slowly through open doorways.

Aitrus watched it a moment. It seemed alive, almost; hideously, maliciously alive.

No sooner had he had the thought, than a second followed. This was no simple chemical mix. He should have known that by the way it had reacted with the algae in the lake. This was biological. It *was* alive.

He went out again, heading for the front door, then stopped, deciding to douse the lantern, just in case. He did so, letting the darkness embrace him, then he stepped up to the door, finding his way blindly.

Outside it was somewhat lighter, but only comparatively so. Most of the cavern was dark—darker than Aitrus had ever imagined possible—but there *were* lights, down below him and to his left, not far off if he estimated correctly; approximately where the great Halls of the guilds had once stood.

Had stood. For even in the darkness he could see evidence of the great ruin that had fallen upon D'ni. Between him and the lights, silhouetted against them, was a landscape of fallen houses and toppled walls, as if a giant had trampled his way carelessly across the rooftops.

Aitrus sighed, then began to make his way toward those lights. There would be guildsmen there, he was certain of it. Maybe even his father, Kahlis. They would have news, yes, and schemes to set things right again.

The thought of that cheered him. He *was* D'ni, after all!

Aitrus stopped and, taking out the lantern, lit it again. Then, holding it up before him, he began to make his way through the ruin of the streets and lanes, heading for the Guild House.

The Guild House was empty, its great doors, which had once been proudly guarded, were now wide open. It had been built well and had withstood the ravages of the great quakes that had struck the city, yet all about it was a scene of devastation that had taken Aitrus's breath. There was barely a building that had not been damaged.

And everywhere the sickly yellow-brown residue of the gas.

Aitrus stood in the great Council chamber, facing the five thrones, his lantern held up before him. It was here that he had left his father. Here that he had made his promise to return on the tenth day. So where were they all? Had they been and gone? Or had they never come?

There was one sure and certain way to find out.

He walked through, into one of the tiny rooms that lay behind the great chamber. There, open on the desk, was a Linking Book. As all else, it was covered with the pastelike residue, yet the glow of the linking panel could be glimpsed. Though a thin layer of the paste covered the glowing rectangle, a hand print could be clearly seen upon it.

Someone had linked *after* the gas had settled.

Aitrus went across and, using the sleeve of his cloak, wiped the right-hand page clean. At once the glow came clear. If the Five Lords and his father were anywhere, they were there, in that Age.

He doused the lantern and stowed it, then placed his hand upon the panel. He linked.

At once Aitrus found himself in a low cave. Sunlight filtered in from an entrance just above him. He could hear birdsong and the lulling noise of the sea washing against the shoreline.

He sighed, relieved. All was well.

Releasing the clamp at the side of his mask, he eased it up, taking a deep gulp of the refreshing air, then, reaching behind him, switched off the air supply. He would need it when he returned to D'ni.

Quickly he climbed the twist of steps that had been cut into the side of the cave wall, pausing only to take out his glasses and slip them on. Then, his spirits raised, he stepped out, into the sunlight.

The buildings were just below him, at the end of a long grassy slope. They blazed white in the sunlight, their perfect domes and arches blending with the green of the surrounding wood, the deep blue of the shimmering sea that surrounded the island.

They would be inside the Great Library, of course, debating what to do. That was why they were delayed, why they had not come. Even so, Aitrus was surprised that they had not set a guard by the Linking Book.

He stopped dead, blinking, taking that in.

There *would* have been a guard. There always *was* a guard. In fact, he had never come here, before now, without there being a guard in the cave.

Something was wrong.

Aitrus drew his dagger then walked on, listening for any sound. Coming around the side of the library, he slowed. The silence was strange, unnatural. The great wooden door was open. Inside the room was shadowy dark.

The elders of D'ni sat in their seats about the chamber, thirty, maybe forty in all. In the darkness they seemed to be resting, yet their stillness was not the stillness of sleep.

Slipping his dagger back into its sheath, Aitrus took out his lamp and lit it, then stepped into the chamber.

In the glow of the lantern he could see the dreadful truth of things. They were dead, every last one of them, dead, their faces pulled back, the chins slightly raised, as if in some final exhalation.

Aitrus shuddered, then turned.

"Father . . . "

Kahlis sat in a chair close by the door, his back to the sunlight spilling in from outside. His hands rested on the arms of the chair, almost casually it seemed, yet the fingers gripped the wood tightly and the face had that same stiffness in it that all the other faces had, as if they had been caught suddenly and unawares by some invisible enemy.

Aitrus groaned and sank down to his knees, his head

lowered before his father. For a long while he remained so. Then, slowly, he raised his head again.

"What in the Maker's name has happened here?"

Aitrus turned, looking up into the masked face of the new-comer. The man was standing in the doorway, the sunlight behind him. He was wearing the purple cloak of the Guild of Ink-Makers, but Aitrus could not make out his features clearly in the gloom.

"It's some kind of virus," he began, then, seeing that the other made to unmask himself, shook his head. "No! Keep that on!"

The guildsman let his hand fall away from the strap, then looked about him. "Are they all dead?" he asked, a note of hopelessness entering his voice.

"Yes," Aitrus answered bleakly. "Or so it seems."

The grave was new, the earth freshly turned. Nearby, as if surprised, a guard lay on his back, dead, his hands gripping each other as if they fought, his jaws tightly clenched.

Aitrus stared at the guard a moment, then, looking to his fellow guildsman, Jiladis, he picked up the spade once more and began to dig, shoveling the last of the dark earth back into the hole. They really were all dead—guildsmen and guards, servants and natives. Not one had survived the plague, if plague it was.

And himself? Was *he* now infected with it?

The last book of commentary told the tale. They had found it open on a desk in one of the other buildings, its scribe, an ancient of two hundred years or more, slumped over it. The body had come through a week ago, only two days after the evacuation of D'ni. They had burned it, naturally, but the damage had been done.

"What will you do?" Jiladis asked, his voice muted through the mask he still wore.

"I suppose I will go back," Aitrus answered. "To D'ni, anyway."

And there was the problem. If he *was* infected, he could not go back to Gemedet, for he could not risk infecting Gehn and Anna and his mother. Yet was it fair not to let them know what had happened here?

Besides which, he needed to get back, now that he knew what was happening, for he had to return to the mansion and get the Linking Book. Gemedet at least would then be safe.

If he was not already too late.

"I shall come with you," Jiladis said finally. "There's nothing here."

Aitrus nodded, then looked up at the open sky and at the sun winking fiercely down at him.

The surface. He could always make his way to the surface.

Yes. But what about any others who had survived? Could he persuade Jiladis, for instance, that his future lay on the surface?

Aitrus set the spade aside, then knelt, murmuring the D'ni words of parting over the grave. Then, standing again, he made his own, more informal farewell.

"Goodbye, my father. May you find peace in the next Age, and may Yavo, the Maker, receive your soul."

Aitrus lingered awhile, his eyes closed as he remembered the best of his father. Then he turned and slowly walked away, making his way back to the linking cave, Jiladis following slowly after.

The door to the family Book Room had been smashed open, the shelves of the room ransacked. On the podium the Book of Ko'ah lay open, its pages smeared, a clear handprint over the panel.

Aitrus stared at it in shock.

Signs of desecration were everywhere—smeared footprints in the hallways and in almost every room—but had they gone upstairs.

His heart almost in his mouth, Aitrus slipped and skidded up the stairs in his haste.

His workroom was at the far end of the corridor. Footsteps led along the corridor toward it. Aitrus stopped dead, staring at them in horror.

So they had been here, too.

In the doorway he paused, looking about him. A circle of footprints went halfway into the room then came away.

He frowned, not understanding, then rushed across the room. The Book of Gemedet was where he had left it on the desk. The open pages were undisturbed, the thin layer of pasty residue untouched.

Aitrus sighed with relief. Taking a clean cloth from a

drawer, he cleaned the cover carefully, then tucked it into the knapsack beside the other things he had packed for the journey.

He had taken extra cylinders from the Hall of the Guild of Miners and food from the sealed vaults in the Hall of the Caterers—enough for an eight-day journey.

If he had eight days.

And Anna? Would she keep her word? Would she stay in Gemedet and not try to come after him? He hoped so. For if she linked here, there would be no linking back for her. Not to Gemedet, anyway, for the book would be with him, and he was going to the surface.

Aitrus went to the front door and looked out across the darkness of the cavern.

He had seen them, yesterday, on his return, or thought he did: the ghostly figures of A'Gaeris and Veovis, pushing their cart of death. And, seeing them, he had known that nowhere was safe from them: not in D'ni, anyway, nor in any of the linked Ages.

If he and Anna and the boy were to have any kind of life, it would have to be up there, on the surface. But were the tunnels still open? Or had the great quakes that had flattened so much in D'ni destroyed them also?

He would have to go and see for himself. If he lived that long. If sickness did not take him on the journey.

It was the evening of the sixteenth day, and Anna sat at Gehn's bedside, listening to his gentle snores in the shadows of the room. A book of D'ni tales lay beside her, facedown where she had put it. Worn out by a day of playing in the woods, Gehn had fallen asleep even as she read to him. Not that she minded. Anything that took his mind off his father's prolonged absence was welcome, and it was good to see him sleep so deeply and peacefully.

Leaning across, she kissed his brow, then stood and went outside. The stars were out now, bright against the sable backdrop of the sky. Anna yawned and stretched. She had barely slept this past week. Each day she expected him back, and each day, when he did not come, she feared the very worst.

Tasera, she knew, felt it almost as keenly as she did; maybe more so, for she, after all, had both a husband and a son who were missing; yet Tasera found it much easier to cope with than she did, for she was D'ni and had that rocklike D'ni stoicism. Had it been a thousand days, Tasera would have waited still, patient to the last.

Am I so impatient, then? Anna asked herself, walking over to the rock at the head of the valley.

She smiled, knowing what Aitrus would have said. It was the difference in their life expectancy, or so he argued. She was a short fuse and burned fast, while he . . .

Come back, she pleaded silently, looking out into the star-filled night. *Wherever you are—whenever you are—come back to me, Aitrus.*

If they had to spend the rest of their years on Gemedet, she would be content, if only she could be with him.

And if that is not your fate?

It was her father's voice. It was a long time since she had

heard that voice—a long, long time since she had needed the comfort of it.

He has been a good man to you, Anna.

"Yes," she said quietly, speaking to the air. "I could not have wished for a better partner."

But now you must learn to be alone.

She blinked. There was such certainty in that voice. "No," she said, after a moment. "He will come back. He promised, and he always keeps his promises."

The voice was silent.

"Ti'ana?"

Anna started, then turned. Tasera was standing not ten paces from her, just below her on the slope. She must have been walking down by the stream. Coming closer, Tasera looked at her and frowned.

"Who were you talking to?"

Anna looked aside, then answered her honestly. "I was speaking to my father."

"Ah . . ." Tasera stepped closer, so that Anna could see her eyes clearly in the half-light. "And what did he say?"

"He said I must learn to be alone."

Tasera watched her a moment, then nodded. "I fear it might be so."

"But I thought . . ."

"Kahlis is not there. I cannot feel him anymore. No matter where he was, no matter *when,* he was always there, with me. So it is when you have lived with a man a century and more. But suddenly there is a gap—an absence, if you like. He is not there anymore. Something has happened to him."

Tasera fell silent.

"I did not know. I thought . . . " Anna frowned. What *had* she thought? That only *she* felt like that? That only she and he were related to each other in that strange, nonphysical manner? No. For how could that possibly be? Even so, sometimes it felt as if they were the books of each other—to which each one linked. And when one of those books was destroyed, what then? Would there no longer be a connection? Would there only be a gap, an awful, yawning abyss?

The thought of it terrified her. To be *that* alone.

"I am sorry, Tasera," Anna said finally. "I do hope you are wrong."

"And I," Tasera said, reaching out to take her hands. "And I."

Aitrus woke. The darkness in his head was matched by the darkness in which he lay. It was damp and cold and his whole body ached, yet the air was fresher than he remembered it.

He put his hand up to his face, surprised. The mask . . .

And then he remembered. The air had given out. He had had to take off the mask or suffocate. And that was when he had linked—linked back to Gemedet.

Aitrus lay there a while, letting his eyes grow accustomed to the darkness of the cave. It had to be night outside, for not a trace of sunlight filtered down from above. He listened, straining to hear some sound, but it was hard to know whether he was imagining it or not. For eight days now he had known nothing but silence. The awful, echoing silence of the rock.

All of his life, he realized now, there had been noises all

about him—the faint murmur of the great fans that brought the air into the caverns, or the dull concussion from a mining rig, busy excavating in the deep; the noises of the city itself, or of boats out on the lake; the bells that sounded out each hour of every day, and the normal noises of the household all about him. Such sounds had formed the continuum of his existence, ceaseless and unnoticed. Until now.

Now death had come to D'ni. Yes, and to every part of its once great empire. Even in the tunnels he had found the dead—Miners at their work, or Maintainers, whose job it was to patrol the great perimeter.

Yes, and he had even found the source of death: the great machine that had proved D'ni's bane. In one of the lower caverns he had come upon it, its huge canisters empty now. They had used such machines in the Guild of Surveyors, to provide air for tricky excavations, or before a regular supply could be pumped up from D'ni itself. But Veovis had used it to pump poisons back into D'ni, letting D'ni's own circulatory system distribute it to every tiny niche.

Even had they switched the great fans down, which eventually they did, it would have proved a bleak choice: to suffocate from lack of air, or die of the poisonous bacteria that that same air carried.

It was not until he saw the machine that he knew for sure; not until then that he knew Anna had been wrong to intercede.

It is not her fault, he kept telling himself; *she was not to know.* Yet it was hard to see it otherwise. All of this death, all of this vast suffering and misery, was down to a single man, Veovis. For all that A'Gaeris had been a willing partner, it was Veovis's bitterness, his anger and desire for revenge, that had been behind this final, futile act. And if he had been dead?

Then my father would yet be alive. And Lord R'hira. And Master Jadaris. And Jerahl . . .

Aitrus sat up, shaking his head, but the darkness kept coming back. *Ti'ana is to blame. My darling wife, Ti'ana.*

"No!"

Outside a bird flapped away between the trees.

It was the first natural sound he had heard in days.

Aitrus sniffed the air. It smelled sweet. He could still smell the rubber of the mask upon his face, but this air was different. It lacked the strange metallic taste of the air he had grown accustomed to.

Slowly, almost stumblingly, he climbed up, until he stood at the mouth of the cave, looking down through the trees toward the encampment. It seemed empty, deserted, but then it was late.

He sighed. *I ought to wash,* he thought. *More than that, I ought to burn these clothes, or bury them. Just in case . . .*

In truth, he ought not to have come. Indeed, he would not have come but for the fact that lack of air had addled his brain. But now that he was back he would make the best of things.

At least the Linking Book was relatively safe; though who knew how thorough Veovis would be? If he chose to search the tunnels, then he might come upon it, lying there, and then even Gemedet would not be safe.

The thought of it petrified him.

He had the urge to cough. Stifling it, he turned, looking up beyond the cave. If he remembered correctly, there was a path that led up and to the left, curving across to the head of the falls. He would find a place up there and bury the suit, then wash himself.

And then he would come back here, naked, the bearer of ill news, to face his mother and his wife.

They had found Aitrus up by the pool, beside the waterfall, his body bathed in sweat, his eyes staring. Getting two servants to carry him, they had brought him back to the encampment and laid him on the bed. Then, for the next three days, Tasera and Anna took turns tending him, bathing his brow, and holding his hand while the fever raged on.

On the morning of the fourth day he finally woke. Anna had been sleeping in the tent nearby when Gehn came and shook her.

"Mother! Mother! Father is awake!"

She hurried across to the cabin to find Aitrus awake, his eyes clear and lucid. Tasera sat beside him, smiling and holding his hand. He looked weak, but he was alive, and seeing Anna, a faint smile came to his lips.

"Ti'ana . . ."

His voice was little more than a breath.

"Do not talk," she said, going over to kneel beside the bed and take his hand.

"I must," he said, the words the faintest whisper.

"No," she said. "You must rest. You must get back your strength."

But Aitrus shook his head. "I am dying, Ti'ana. I know it.

But I have been given this moment and I must use it."

He paused, coughing a little, then continued, his voice wavering a little.

"They are dead. Everyone . . . dead. My father . . . I buried him. And D'ni . . . D'ni is ended. But there is a way out. Through the tunnels. I mapped it. My notebook . . . "

"Yes, yes," Anna said, impatiently. "But you must rest now, Aitrus, *please*."

For a moment his eyes blinked closed. With an effort he opened them again, his eyes looking to Anna pleadingly. "You must go, Ti'ana. Please. Promise me you will go. You are not safe here . . . "

"Why? Why aren't we safe here?"

But Aitrus had drifted into sleep again. His head had fallen back and his breathing was shallow.

"Let him sleep," Tasera said, looking to Anna, as if concern for her boy was the only thing in the universe; yet Anna could see that Aitrus's news had shocked her. Indeed, it had shocked them both. Then, suddenly, she remembered Gehn.

She whirled about. Gehn was standing in the doorway, staring, his face aghast.

"It isn't true," he said, his voice tiny. "Tell me it isn't true!"

But she could not lie, and as he saw it in her face, so that look returned: a look of purest horror. Turning, he fled.

"Gehn!" she cried, going to the doorway. "Gehn! Come back!"

But Gehn was already at the edge of the wood. With the barest glance back, he disappeared among the trees.

Anna turned back, looking to Tasera, but Tasera was not there. Her eyes seemed distant and hollow now and her shoulders sagged, as if her son's soft words—so quiet, so insubstantial—had broken her. Even as Anna looked, a tear trickled down Tasera's cheek and fell.

Gone. All of it gone. But how was that possible? Surely some had survived?

She stared at Aitrus, wondering what else he had not told her. Why was this Age not safe? Why?

"Tell me, Aitrus," she said quietly. "*Please* tell me."

But Aitrus did not answer her.

That afternoon Tasera took to her bed, complaining of a migraine. Anna, thinking it had to do with Kahlis's death, decided it was best to leave her be to grieve. Having made certain Tasera was comfortable, she went to see if she could find where Gehn had got to. There was no sign of him. But when she returned two hours later it was to find that Tasera had worsened considerably.

Not only that, but the two servants who had helped carry Aitrus down from the pool were now displaying the exact same symptoms he had shown. They had been suffering from minor stomach pains for days, but now both of them had gone down with a full-blown fever.

As the afternoon became evening, Anna began to grow worried. Aitrus still showed no sign of waking, yet it was for Tasera she was most concerned, for she had slipped into a fretful, fevered sleep. Then, just after sundown, Anna went to check on the two servants, whom she had placed nearby in the storage tent, and found that one of them had died.

She was standing there, outside the tent, when Gehn wandered back into the camp.

"Gehn?"

Gehn did not even glance at her, but walked on past her, going inside the cabin.

Anna walked across. Gehn was sitting in a corner, in the darkness, staring at his father's reclining form. She watched him a moment, her heart going out to him. Then, taking the lantern from the side, she struck the fire-marble, closed the plate, and hung it on the hook overhead.

In its sudden glow she could see that Gehn had been crying.

"Gehn? Are you all right?"

He turned his head and looked at her, coldly, sullenly, then looked away.

"Two of the servants are ill," she said quietly.

Gehn made no gesture, no response. He simply stared at his father.

"Gehn . . . we must think of leaving here."

But Gehn was like a statue, his child's face hard and cold as it stared at his dying father.

That night the rest of the servants ran away. While Gehn slept, Anna sat beside Tasera, bathing her face and holding her hand. Yet in the early hours of morning, Aitrus's mother convulsed and died.

Anna sat there for a long time afterward, staring into space. Gehn was asleep in the corner. Aitrus lay nearby, his shallow breathing barely audible. In this one room was her whole world—all that mattered to her, anyway—and it was slowly falling apart about her.

Just as before, she thought, real despair touching her for the first time.

She stood up abruptly then crossed the room, picking up the bag Aitrus had brought back with him from D'ni. She had been busy until now even to remember it, but now she sat down and rummaged through it.

Here was his journal, that he kept with him at all times.

Lighting a lamp, she opened the notebook and began to leaf through it, stopping finally at a series of maps and diagrams Aitrus had made. The first were of the tunnels leading to the cavern where the machines were and, beyond it, several miles distant, the Lodge. Aitrus had added to this map, drawing thick dark lines across a number of the tunnels. It was clear that they were blocked. Indeed, looking at the map, she saw that there was no access to the surface by this route. On the next page was another map, but this one ended in dead-ends and white, unfilled space.

Anna looked up, understanding. Aitrus had spent the last week or so tramping through the tunnels, trying to find a route for their escape, spending his precious energies so that they might find a safe way to the surface.

Aitrus was dying, she knew that now for certain. Yet even at the end he had been true. Even at the end he had thought of others before himself. Of her, and Gehn.

She looked back at the journal. The next map was

different—much more complex than the others. It extended over several pages.

Anna smiled, appreciating what he had done here. Elevations, rock-types, physical details—all were noted down. It was a real labyrinth, but Aitrus had done his best to make each twist and turn as clear as he could. She traced the zigzag line of it with her finger over several pages, then looked up, laughing softly.

The volcano! It came out at the old dormant volcano where her father and she had used to stop on their way to Tadjinar.

She smiled and spoke softly to the air. "You did well, my love."

"Did I?"

His voice, so unexpected, startled her. She turned to find him sitting up, watching her.

"Aitrus?"

"We have to go."

Anna blinked. *You are dying,* she thought. *You are not going anywhere.* But he was insistent.

"You must pack, Ti'ana. Now, while there is still time."

"Time for what?"

"I am coming with you," he said, then coughed. "Back to D'ni. I will help you find the way."

"But you are ill, Aitrus."

In answer he threw back the sheet and, steadying himself against the wall with one hand, slowly stood. His eyes looked to her imploringly. "I must do this, Ti'ana. Do you understand that?"

She stared at him, her fear and love for him mixed

violently at that moment, and then she nodded. "I understand."

Packing the last few things into the bag, she slipped it onto her back and went outside, into the sunlight. Gehn was just below her, standing beside his father, supporting him, as they looked down at Tasera's grave.

Anna sighed, then walked across. Gehn was wearing the suit she had made for him and the mask lay loose about his neck. His own knapsack was on his back.

"Are you ready?"

Both Gehn and Aitrus looked to her and nodded. Then, on impulse, Gehn ran down the slope and, bending, leaned out over the edge.

Anna looked to Aitrus and frowned, wondering what he was doing, but in a moment Gehn was back, holding out a tiny sheath of white flowers for her to take. Two other bunches were in his other hand.

She took them from him, then, knowing what he intended, cast the flowers onto Tasera's grave and stepped back, allowing Gehn and Aitrus to do the same.

"Farewell, dear Mother," Aitrus said, looking out past the mound at the beauty of the valley. "You will be with me always."

Gehn stood there a moment, then, bowing his head, scattered the flowers and said his own farewell: "Goodbye, Grandmother. May we meet again in the next Age."

Anna blinked, surprised. He seemed to have grown up so much these past few weeks. She put out her hand to him.

"Come, Gehn. We must go now."

Gehn hesitated a moment, then, with a glance at his father, reached out and took her hand. Anna gave it a little squeeze, then, turning from the grave, began to climb the slope, heading for the linking cave, Aitrus following behind.

It was the twenty-second day after the fall.

Anna stood beside Aitrus on the balcony of the mansion, Gehn in front of her, her arms about his shoulders as they looked out over the ruins of D'ni. To her surprise the air had proved clean, and after several tests in the workroom, they had decided to remove their masks. There was no trace now of the gas that had wreaked such havoc, though its residue remained, like a dried crust over everything. Moreover, someone had reactivated the great fans that brought the air into the cavern, and the algae of the lake had recovered enough to give off a faint, almost twilight glow. In that faint illumination they could see the extent of the devastation.

The sight was desolate beyond all words. What had once been the most magnificent of cities was now a mausoleum, an empty, echoing shell of its former glory.

She could feel Gehn trembling and knew that he was close to tears. All that he had ever known lay within the compass of his sight. His shattered hopes and dreams were here displayed, naked to the eye. Why, even the great rock that stood in the very midst of the lake had split, like wood before the axe.

"Come," she said gently, meeting Aitrus's eyes. "Let us go from here."

Walking down through the dead streets, their sense of desolation grew. Barely a house stood without great cracks in its walls; barely a wall or gate remained undamaged. From time to time the rubble of a house would block their way and they were forced to backtrack, but eventually they came out by the harbor's edge.

The great statues that had once lined the harbor wall were cracked or fallen. The great merchant fleet that once had anchored here now rested on the harbor's floor. They could see their long shadows thirty, forty feet below the surface.

Anna turned, looking about her. There was no sign anywhere of a boat, and they needed a boat. Without one there was no chance of getting across the lake.

"There are boathouses to the east of the harbor," Aitrus said, "down by the lake's edge. There will be barges there."

But the boathouses were burned, the barges smashed. Someone had made sure they could not get across. Aitrus sighed and sat, his remaining strength almost spent.

"I'll go and look," Anna said, gesturing to Gehn that he should sit with his father and take care of him. "There must be something."

In a moment she was back, her eyes shining. "There is!" she said. "One boat. A small thing, but big enough for us three."

Aitrus's eyes came up, suspicion in them. "Was it tied up?"

She nodded, then frowned. "What is it?"

But Aitrus merely shook his head. "Nothing. Let us go at once."

Gehn helped his father stand, then supported him as they made their way toward where the boat was moored. They were not halfway across when a fearful cry rang out from the lower city at their backs.

All three of them turned, shocked by the sudden sound.

It came again.

Aitrus looked to his wife. "Go to the boat, Ti'ana. Take Gehn and wait there for me. It might be Jiladis."

"But Aitrus . . ."

"Go to the boat. I'll join you in a while."

Anna hesitated, reluctant to let him go, yet she knew that this, too, was his duty—to help his fellow guildsmen if in need. Taking Gehn's hand she led him away, but all the while she kept glancing back at Aitrus, watching as he slowly crossed the open harbor front, then disappeared into one of the narrow alleyways.

"Come, Gehn," she said. "Let us secure the boat for when your father returns."

Aitrus leaned against the wall, doubled up, getting his breath. The pain in his limbs and in his stomach was growing worse and he felt close now to exhaustion. Moreover, he was lost. Or, at least, he had no idea just where the sounds had come from. He had thought it was from somewhere in this locality, but now that he was here there was nothing. The deserted streets were silent.

Across from him a sign hung over the shadowed door of

a tavern. There were no words, but the picture could be glimpsed, even through the layer of gray-brown residue. It showed a white, segmented worm, burrowing blindly through the rock. The sight of it made him frown, as if at some vague, vestigial memory. The Blind Worm. Where had he heard mention of that before?

Aitrus straightened, looking up. The windows of the upper story were open, the shutters thrown back.

Even as he looked, there came a loud, distinctive groan.

So he had not been wrong. Whoever it was, they were up there, in that second-floor room.

Aitrus crossed the street then slowly pushed the door open, listening. The groan came again. A set of narrow stairs led up to his right. They were smeared, as if many feet had used them. Cautiously, looking about him all the while, he slipped inside and began to climb them, careful to make no noise.

He was almost at the top when, from the room above came a grunt and then another pained groan. Something creaked.

Aitrus stopped then turned his head, looking up into the open doorway just behind him, beyond the turn in the stairs.

A soft, scraping noise came from the room, and then a tiny gasp of pain. That sound released Aitrus. Finding new reserves of energy, he hurried up the final steps.

Standing in the doorway, he gasped, astonished by the sight that met his eyes.

It was a long, low-ceilinged room, with windows overlooking the harbor. In the center of the room a table was overturned and all three chairs. Blood smeared the floor surrounding them, trailing away across the room. And at the end of that trail of blood, attempting to pull himself up onto the window ledge, was Veovis, the broad blade of a butcher's cleaver buried deep in his upper back.

"Veovis!"

But Veovis seemed unaware of his presence. His fingers clutched at the stone ledge as his feet tried to push himself up, his face set in an expression of grim determination.

Horrified, Aitrus rushed halfway across the room, yet even as he did, Veovis collapsed and fell back, groaning.

Aitrus knelt over him.

"Veovis . . . Veovis, it is Aitrus. What happened here?"

There was a movement in Veovis's face. His eyes blinked and then he seemed to focus on Aitrus's face. And with that came recognition.

"What happened?"

Veovis laughed, then coughed. Blood was on his lips. His voice, when he spoke, came raggedly, between pained breaths.

"My colleague and I . . . we had a little . . . *disagreement.*"

The ironic smile was pained.

"A'Gaeris?"

Veovis closed his eyes then gave the faintest nod.

"And you fought?"

Veovis's eyes flickered open. "It was no fight . . . He . . ." Veovis swallowed painfully. "He stabbed me . . . when my back was turned."

Veovis grimaced, fighting for his breath. Aitrus thought he was going to die, right there and then, but slowly Veovis's breathing normalized again and his eyes focused on Aitrus once more.

"I would not do it."

"What? What wouldn't you do?"

"The Age he wanted . . . I would not write it." A tiny spasm ran through Veovis. Aitrus gripped him.

"Tell me," he said. "I need to know."

Veovis almost smiled. "And I need to tell you."

He swallowed again, then, "He wanted a special place . . . a place where we could be gods."

"Gods?"

Veovis nodded.

It was the ultimate heresy, the ultimate misuse of the great Art: to mistake Writing, the ability to link with preexistent worlds, with true creation. And at the end, Veovis, it seemed, had refused to step over that final line. He looked up at Aitrus now.

Aitrus blinked. Suddenly, the image of his workroom had come to his mind—the trail of footprints leading halfway to the Book but no farther.

"Was that you?" he asked softly. "In my workroom, I mean."

Veovis took two long breaths, then nodded.

"But why? After all you did, why let *us* live?"

"Because she spoke out for me. Because . . . she said there was good in me . . . And she was right . . . even at the end."

Veovis closed his eyes momentarily, the pain overwhelming him, then he continued, struggling now to get the words out before there were no more words.

"It was as if there was a dark cloud in my head, poisoning my thoughts. I felt . . . " Veovis groaned, "nothing. Nothing but hatred, anyway. Blind hatred. Of everything and everyone."

There was a shout, from outside. Carefully laying Veovis

down, he went to the window and looked out, what he saw filling him with dismay.

"What is it?" Veovis asked from below him.

Out on the lake a single boat was heading out toward the distant islands. Standing at its stern, steering it, was the distinctive figure of A'Gaeris. And before him in the boat, laying on the bare planks, their hands and feet bound, were Anna and Gehn.

"It's A'Gaeris," he said quietly. "He has Ti'ana and my son."

"Then you must save her, Aitrus."

Aitrus gave a bleak cry. "How? A'Gaeris has the only boat, and I am too weak to swim."

"Then *link* there."

Aitrus turned and looked down at the dying man. "Where is he taking them?"

Veovis looked up at him, his eyes clear now, as if he had passed beyond all pain. "To K'veer. That's where we are based. That's where all the Books are now. We've been collecting them. Hundreds of them. Some are in the Book Room, but most are on the Age I made for him. They are in the cabin on the south island. That's where you link to. The Book of that Age is in my study."

Aitrus knelt over Veovis again. "I understand. But how does that help me? That's in K'veer. How do I get *there?*"

In answer, Veovis gestured toward his left breast. There was a deep pocket there, and something in it. Aitrus reached inside and took out a slender book.

"He did not know I had this," Veovis said, smiling now. "It links to Nidur Gemat. There is a Book there that links directly to my study on K'veer. You can use them to get to the island before he does."

Aitrus stared at the Book a moment, then looked back at Veovis.

Veovis met his eyes. "Do you *still* not trust me, Aitrus! Then listen. The Book I mentioned. It has a green cover. It is there that A'Gaeris plans to go. It is there that you might trap him. You understand?"

Aitrus hesitated a moment, then, "I will trust you, for I have no choice, and perhaps there *is* some good in you at the last."

The city was receding now. In an hour he would be back in K'veer. A'Gaeris turned from the sight and looked back at his captives where they lay at the bottom of the boat.

He would have killed them there and then, at the harbor's edge, and thought nothing of it, but the woman had betrayed the fact that her husband was still abroad.

And so, he would use them as his bait. And once he had Aitrus, he would destroy all three of them, for he had not the sentimental streak that had ruined his once-companion, Veovis.

"He will not come for us, you know."

A'Gaeris looked down at the woman disdainfully. "Of course he'll come. The man's a sentimental fool. He came before, didn't he?"

"But not this time. He'll wait for you. In D'ni."

"While you and your son are my captives?" A'Gaeris

laughed. "Why, he will be out of his mind with worry, don't you think?"

He saw how that silenced her. Yes, with the two of them safe in a cell on K'veer he could go back and settle things with Guildsman Aitrus once and for all.

For there was only one boat in all of D'ni now, and he had it.

"No," he said finally. "He'll wait there at the harbor until I bring the boat back. And then I'll have him. Oh yes, Ti'ana. You can be certain of it!"

The first book had linked him to a room in the great house on Nidur Gemat, filled with Veovis's things. There, after a brief search, he found the second Book that linked to this, more familiar room on the island of K'veer, a place he had often come in better times.

Aitrus stood there a moment, leaning heavily against the desk, a bone-deep weariness making his head spin. Then, knowing he had less than an hour to make his preparations, he looked about him.

The Book with the emerald green cover was on a table in the far corner of the room, beside a stack of other, older Books. Going across to them, Aitrus felt a sudden despair, thinking of what had been done here. So much endeavor had come to naught, here in this room. And for what reason? Envy? Revenge? Or was it simple malice?

Was A'Gaeris mad?

Aitrus groaned, thinking of the end to which Veovis had

come. Then, determined to make one final, meaningful effort, he lifted the Book and carried it back over to the desk.

There he sat, opening the Book and reading through the first few pages. After a while he lifted his head, nodding to himself. Here it was, nakedly displayed: what Veovis might, in time, have become; a great Master among Masters, as great, perhaps, as the legendary Ri'Neref.

He began to cough, a hacking, debilitating cough, then put his fingers to his lips. There was blood there now. He, too, was dying.

Taking a cloth from his pocket, Aitrus wiped his mouth and then began, dipping the pen and scoring out essential phrases and adding in others at the end of the book. Trimming and pruning this most perfect of Ages. *Preparing* it.

And all the while he thought of Anna and of Gehn, and prayed silently that they would be all right.

A'Gaeris climbed the steps of the harbor at K'veer, Anna and the boy just in front of him, goaded on by the point of his knife.

At the top he paused and, grasping the loose ends of the ropes by which their hands were bound, wrapped them tightly about his left hand. Then, leading the two behind him like a pair of hounds, he went inside the mansion.

K'veer had not been untouched by the tremors, and parts of its impressive architecture had cracked and fallen away into the surrounding lake, yet enough of it remained for it to be recognizable. Anna, who had wondered where they were going, now felt a sense of resignation descend on her.

If Veovis was here then there was nothing Aitrus could do.

Anna glanced at her son. Gehn's face was closed, his eyes sullen, as if this latest twist were no more than could be expected. Yet he was bearing up, for all his trials, and she felt a strange twinge of pride in him for that.

She was about to speak, when she caught the scent of burning. A'Gaeris, too, must have noticed it at the same moment, for he stopped suddenly and frowned.

For a moment he sniffed the air, as if he had been mistaken, then, with a bellow, he began to hurriedly climb the stairs, dragging them along after him.

As they approached the Book Room the smell of burning grew and grew until, at a turn in the stairs, they could see the flickering glow of a fire up ahead of them.

A'Gaeris roared. "My Books!"

For a moment, as he tugged at the rope, Anna almost fell, but she kept her footing. Gehn did, however. She heard his cry and saw that A'Gaeris had let go of the rope that held him. But there was no time to see if he was all right. The next instant she found herself behind A'Gaeris in the doorway to the Book Room. Beyond him the room was brilliantly lit. Smoke bellowed from a stack of burning Books. And just to one side of the flaming pile—a Book in one hand, a flaming torch in the other—stood Aitrus.

A'Gaeris slammed the great door shut behind him, then took a step toward Aitrus, yet even as he did, Aitrus raised the torch and called to him:

"Come any closer and I'll burn the rest of your Books, A'Gaeris! I know where they are. I've *seen* them. In the cabin on the south island. I linked there. I can link there now, unless . . . "

Anna felt A'Gaeris's hand reach out and grasp her roughly, and then his arm was about her neck, the dagger raised, its point beneath her neck.

"I have your wife, Aitrus. Go near those Books and I shall kill her."

"Kill her and I shall destroy your Books. I'll link through and put them to the torch. And what will you have then, *Master* Philosopher? Nothing. Not now that you've killed Veovis."

Anna could feel A'Gaeris trembling with anger. Any false move and she would be dead.

"Give me that Book," he said once more in a low growl. "Give it to me, or Ti'ana dies."

Aitrus was smiling now. He lifted the Book slightly. "This is a masterful work. I know Veovis was proud of it."

A'Gaeris stared at Aitrus. "It was called Ederat."

"No," Aitrus said, his eyes meeting Anna's. "Veovis had another name for it. He called it Be-el-ze-bub."

Anna caught her breath. She stared at him, loving him more in that instant than she had ever loved him.

I love you, she mouthed.

Aitrus answered her with his eyes.

"Well?" he asked, returning his attention to A'Gaeris. "Do we have a deal? The Book—and all those Books within—for my wife?"

But A'Gaeris simply laughed.

Aitrus lowered the torch. His eyes went to the cover of the Book, then, with a final loving look at Anna, he placed the hand that held the burning torch upon the glowing panel.

A'Gaeris howled. Thrusting Anna away from him he ran across the room.

"Aitrus!" she yelled as his figure shimmered and vanished. "Aitrus!"

But he was gone. The great Book fell with a thud to the floor beside the burning stack.

A'Gaeris threw himself at it in unseemly haste and almost wrenched the cover from the spine forcing it open.

Anna watched, her heart in her throat as, his chest heaving, A'Gaeris looked across at her and, with a smile that was half snarl, placed his hand against the descriptive panel and linked.

Even as he linked into the cave, A'Gaeris stumbled, doubling up in pain. The air was burning, the reek of sulphur choking. The first breath seared his lungs. Putting out an arm, A'Gaeris staggered forward, howling, looking about him desperately for the Linking Book back to D'ni. Yet even as he did, a great crack appeared in the floor of the cavern. The heat intensified. There was a glimpse of brilliant orange-redness, one stark moment of realization, and then the rock slab on which he stood tilted forward, A'Gaeris's shrill cry of surprise cut off as he tumbled into the molten flow.

And then silence. The primal, unheard silence of the great cauldron of creation.

Anna cried quietly, crouching over the green-covered Book and studying the glowing image there.

For a moment or two there was the temptation to follow him: to end it all, just as Aitrus had. Then someone hammered on the Book Room door.

It brought her back to herself. *Gehn*.

Anna turned to face the smoldering pile of ashes that had once been D'ni Books, then dropped the green-covered Book upon the rest. Sparks scattered. A cloud of smoke wafted up toward the high ceiling of the room. A moment later, flames began to lick the burnished leather of the cover.

For a moment she simply stared, feeling the gap there now where the other book of her life had been, just as Tasera had described it. Then, getting to her feet again, she turned, even as the knocking came again, more urgently this time, and began to walk across.

EPILOGUE

THE SUN WAS EDGING ABOVE THE MOUNTAINS FAR TO the east as the figure of a woman emerged from the lip of the volcano, cradling a sleeping child. The desert floor was still in deep shadow. It lay like a dark sea about the bright, black-mouthed circle of the caldera. The woman paused, lifting her chin, slowly scanning the surrounding desert, then began to descend the rock-littered slope, her shadow stretched out long and thin behind her, black against the dawn's red.

As she came closer to the cleft, a light wind began to blow, lifting the dark strands of her hair behind her. Sand danced across the rock then settled. The woman seemed gaunt and wraithlike, and the child in her arms was but skin and bone, yet there was a light in her eyes, a vitality, that was like the fire from the deep earth.

Seeing the cleft, she slowed, looking about her once more, then went across and knelt, laying the child down gently on a narrow ledge of rock. Taking the two packs from her shoulders, she set them down. Then, using her hands and feet to find her way, she ducked down into the dark gash of the cleft.

There was a pool down there at the foot of the cleft. In the predawn darkness it was filled with stars, reflected from the sky far overhead. Like a shadow, she knelt beside it, scooping up a handful of the pure, cool water, and drank. Refreshed, she turned, still kneeling, and looked about her. It was cool down here, and there was water. With a little work it could be more.

Anna nodded, then stood, wiping her hands against her shirt. "Here," she said. "We'll begin again here."

A SELECTED LIST OF FANTASY TITLES
AVAILABLE FROM CORGI BOOKS

14509 2	THE GREAT GAME 1: PAST IMPERATIVE	*Dave Duncan*	£5.99
14500 9	THE GREAT GAME 2: PRESENT TENSE	*Dave Duncan*	£5.99
13017 6	MALLOREON 1: GUARDIANS OF THE WEST	*David Eddings*	£5.99
13018 4	MALLOREON 2: KING OF THE MURGOS	*David Eddings*	£5.99
12284 X	BELGARIAD 1: PAWN OF PROPHECY	*David Eddings*	£5.99
12348 X	BELGARIAD 2: QUEEN OF SORCERY	*David Eddings*	£5.99
14490 8	THE DIG	*Alan Dean Foster*	£4.99
14252 2	THE LEGEND OF DEATHWALKER	*David Gemmell*	£5.99
14253 0	DARK MOON	*David Gemmell*	£5.99
14254 9	WINTER WARRIORS	*David Gemmell*	£5.99
14111 9	HOUSE OF TRIBES	*Garry Kilworth*	£4.99
14464 9	A MIDSUMMER'S NIGHTMARE	*Garry Kilworth*	£5.99
08453 0	DRAGONFLIGHT	*Anne McCaffrey*	£5.99
14180 1	TO RIDE PEGASUS	*Anne McCaffrey*	£3.99
14098 8	POWERS THAT BE	*Anne McCaffrey & Elizabeth Ann Scarborough*	£4.99
14271 9	FREEDOM'S LANDING	*Anne McCaffrey*	£5.99
14386 3	MYST	*Rand & Robyn Miller with David Wingrove*	£4.99
14478 9	AUTOMATED ALICE	*Jeff Noon*	£5.99
14235 2	INTERESTING TIMES	*Terry Pratchett*	£5.99
14236 0	MASKERADE	*Terry Pratchett*	£5.99
14237 9	FEET OF CLAY	*Terry Pratchett*	£5.99
13703 0	GOOD OMENS	*Terry Pratchett & Neil Gaiman*	£5.99
13681 6	ARMAGEDDON THE MUSICAL	*Robert Rankin*	£4.99
13841 X	THE ANTIPOPE	*Robert Rankin*	£4.99
14213 1	A DOG CALLED DEMOLITION	*Robert Rankin*	£4.99
14355 3	NOSTRADAMUS ATE MY HAMSTER	*Robert Rankin*	£5.99
14112 7	EMPIRE OF THE ANTS	*Bernard Werber*	£5.99

Tie break question: What is the relationship between Catherine and Atrus?.....................
....

I would like to win a copy of :
❑ Myst® ❑ Riven™:The sequel to Myst®
Please state format:
❑ MPC CD-ROM ❑ MAC CD-ROM

Name ....
Address...
Town ....
County ....
Country ....
Postcode..
Telephone No. ....
❑ Female ❑ Male
Age ....

Do you own a computer? ❑ Yes ❑ No
What kind of computer do you own
❑ IBM compatible ❑ Mac
If you have an IBM compatible, what kind
of system do you use?
❑ 386 ❑ 486 ❑ Pentium
How much memory does it have?
❑ 8MB ❑ 16MB ❑ 32MB

What is the main use for your home computer system?
❑ Taking work home ❑ Word processing ...
❑ Games ❑ Education for your child
❑ Productivity - home finance or graphics
❑ Education for yourself

What types of software are you interested
in? ❑ Children's entertainment ❑ Games
❑ Education ❑ Reference

What other CD-ROM titles do you have?
....
....

What types of games computer games do
you like? ❑ Flight simulators ❑ Action
❑ Adventure ❑ Sport simulators
❑ Strategy ❑ Role Playing

Would you like to receive further information on Brøderbund's products?
❑ Yes ❑ No

Competition

Now you have the chance to explore the wonderful worlds created by Rand and Robyn Miller

Win your very own copy of the CD-ROM computer game Riven™: The Sequel to Myst® or Myst®, the graphic adventure that has become the world of over 3 million people!

There are 25 copies of the PC CD-ROM games to be won! - over one thousand pounds worth of software!

Simply answer the questionaire attatched and the tie breaker question then send your entry to: Brøderbund Software Europe, Ti'Ana Competition, C/O Starpak International, P.O. Box 63, Hartlepool, Cleveland TS25 2YP United Kingdom.

All entries received before 20th May 1998 will be entered into the grand draw. The draw will take place on 1st June 1998 and the 25 winners will be notified by post, no later than 15th June 1998. All competition winners will receive their prize by 30th June 1998. No purchase necessary to enter the draw.

LET'S TALK
Romance

For exclusive extracts, competitions
and special offers, find us online:

f facebook.com/millsandboon

⊙ @millsandboonuk

𝕏 @millsandboon

Or get in touch on 0844 844 1351*

For all the latest titles coming soon, visit
millsandboon.co.uk/nextmonth

CHAPTER ONE

'COME ON,' ZAC DA ROCHA chided his brother. 'There's got to be some room for manoeuvre here, something that you want more than that car. Sell it to me and I'll buy you anything you want.'

Fierce hostility roared through Prince Vitale Castiglione because his Brazilian half-brother irritated the hell out of him. The fact that they were both luxury-car collectors had to be the only thing they had in common. But no didn't ever mean no to Zac; no only made Zac raise the price. He couldn't seem to grasp the reality that Vitale couldn't be bribed. But then, Zacarias Da Rocha, heir to the fabled Quintel Da Rocha diamond mines and fabulously wealthy even by his brothers' standards, was unaccustomed to refusal or disappointment and constitutionally incapable of respecting polite boundaries. His lean, strong face grim, Vitale shot a glance at the younger man, his brilliant dark eyes impassive with years of hard self-discipline.

'No,' Vitale repeated quietly, wishing his older brother, Angel Valtinos, would return and shut Zac up because being rude didn't come naturally to Vitale, who had been raised in the stifling traditions and formality of a European royal family. A lifetime of rigid condi-

tioning invariably stepped in to prevent Vitale from losing his temper and revealing his true feelings.

Of course, it had already been a most unsettling morning. Vitale had been disconcerted when his father, Charles Russell, had asked both him and his two brothers to meet him at his office. It had been an unusual request because Charles usually made the effort to meet his sons separately and Vitale had wondered if some sort of family emergency had occurred until Charles had appeared and swept his eldest son, Angel, off into his office alone, leaving Vitale with only Zac for company. Not a fun development that, Vitale reflected before studiously telling himself off for that negative outlook.

After all, it wasn't Zac's fault that he had only met his father the year before and was still very much a stranger to his half-brothers, who, in spite of their respective parents' divorces, had known each other since early childhood. Unhappily, Zac with his untamed black hair, tattoos and aggressive attitude simply didn't fit in. He was too unconventional, too competitive, too *much* in every way. Nor did it help that he was only a couple of months younger than Vitale, which underlined the reality that Zac had been conceived while Charles Russell had still been married to Vitale's mother. Yet Vitale could understand how that adulterous affair had come about. His mother was cold while his father was emotional and caring. He suspected that while caught up in the divorce that had devastated him Charles had sought comfort from a warmer woman.

'Then let's make a bet,' Zac suggested irrepressibly.

Vitale was tempted to roll his eyes in comic disbelief but he said nothing.

'I heard you and Angel talking earlier about the big palace ball being held in Lerovia at the end of next month,' Zac admitted softly. 'I understand that it's a very formal, upmarket occasion and that your mother is expecting you to pick a wife from her selection of carefully handpicked female guests…'

Faint colour illuminated Vitale's rigid high cheekbones and he ground his even white teeth. 'Queen Sofia enjoys trying to organise my life but I have no current plans to marry.'

'But it would be a hell of a lot easier to keep all those women at bay if you turned up with a partner of your own,' Zac pointed out without skipping a beat, as if he knew by some mysterious osmosis how much pressure Vitale's royal parent invariably put on her only child's shoulders. 'So, this is the bet… I bet you that you couldn't transform an ordinary woman into a convincing socialite for the evening and pass her off as the real thing. If you manage that feat, I'll give you my rarest vehicle but naturally I'll expect an invitation to the ball. If your lady fails the test, you hand over your most precious car.'

Vitale almost rolled his eyes at that outrageously juvenile challenge. Obviously he didn't do bets. He raked his black glossy hair back from his brow in a gesture of impatience. 'I'm not Pygmalion and I don't know any *ordinary* women,' he admitted truthfully.

'Who's Pygmalion?' Zac asked with a genuine frown. 'And how can you not know any ordinary women? You live in the same world I do.'

'Not quite.' Vitale's affairs were always very discreet and he avoided the sort of tacky, celebrity-chasing women likely to boast of him as a conquest, while Zac

seemed to view any attractive woman as fair game. Vitale, however, didn't want to run the risk of any tabloid exposés containing the kind of sexual revelations that would dishonour the Lerovian throne.

In addition, he was an investment banker and CEO of the very conservative and respectable Bank of Lerovia, thus expected to live a very staid life: bankers who led rackety lives made investors unprofitably nervous. Lerovia was, after all, a tax shelter of international repute. It was a small country, hemmed in by much larger, more powerful countries, and Vitale's grandfather had built Lerovia's wealth and stability on a secure financial base. Vitale had had few career options open to him. His mother had wanted him to simply be the Crown Prince, her heir in waiting, but Vitale had needed a greater purpose, not to mention the freedom to become a man in his own right, something his autocratic mother would never have willingly given him.

He had fought for his right to have a career just as he now fought for his continuing freedom of choice as a single man. At only twenty-eight, he wasn't ready for the responsibility of a wife or, even more depressingly, the demands of a baby. His stomach sank at the prospect of a crying, clinging child looking to him for support. He also knew better than anyone how difficult it would be for any woman to enter the Lerovian royal family and be forced to deal with his domineering mother, the current Queen. His unfortunate bride would need balls of steel to hold her own.

At that point in Vitale's brooding reflections, Angel reappeared, looking abnormally subdued, and Vitale sprang upright with a question in his eyes.

'Your turn,' his older brother told him very drily

without making any attempt to respond to Vitale's unspoken question for greater clarification.

Angel was visibly on edge, Vitale acknowledged in
surprise, wondering what sensitive subject Charles Russell had broached with his eldest son. And then Vitale
made a very good guess and he winced for his brother,
because possibly their father had discovered that Angel
had an illegitimate daughter he had yet to meet. That
was Angel's biggest darkest secret, one he had shared
only with Vitale, and it was likely to be an inflamma-
tory topic for a man as family-orientated as their parent. It wasn't, however, a mistake that Vitale would
ever make, Vitale thought with blazing confidence, because he never ever took risks in the birth-control department. He knew too well how narrow his options
would be in that scenario if anything went wrong. Either he would have to face up to a colossal scandal or
he would have to marry the woman concerned. Since
the prospect of either option chilled him to the bone,
he always played safe.

A still-handsome middle-aged man with greying
hair, Charles Russell strode forward to give his taller
son an enthusiastic hug. 'Sorry to have kept you waiting so long.'

'Not a problem,' Vitale said smoothly, refusing to
admit that he had enraged his mother with his insis-
tence on travelling to London rather than attending yet
another court ceremonial function. Even so, his lean
muscular length still stiffened in the circle of the older
man's arms because while he was warmed by that open
affection he was challenged to respond to it. Deep down
somewhere inside him he was still the shrinking little
boy whose mother had pushed him away with distaste

at the age of two, telling him firmly that it was baby-ish and bad to still seek such attention.

'I need a favour and I thought you could deal with this thorny issue better than I could,' Charles admitted stiffly. 'Do you remember the housekeeper I employed at Chimneys?'

Vitale's eloquent dark eyes widened a little in dis-concertion, lush black gold-tipped lashes framing his shrewd questioning gaze. He and Angel had spent countless school vacations at their father's country house on the Welsh border and Vitale had cherished every one of those holidays liberated from the stuffy traditions and formality of the Lerovian court. At Chim-neys, an Elizabethan manor house, Vitale had been free as a bird, free to be a grubby little boy, a moody dif-ficult adolescent, free to be whatever he wanted to be without the stress of constantly striving to meet arbi-trary expectations.

'Not particularly. I don't really remember the staff.'

His father frowned, seemingly disappointed by that response. 'Her name was Peggy. She worked for me for years. She was married to the gardener, Robert Dickens.'

A sliver of recollection pierced Vitale's bemused gaze, a bubble of memory about an old scandal finally rising to the surface. 'Red-haired woman, ran off with a toy boy,' he slotted in sardonically.

His tone made his father frown. 'Yes, that's the one. He was one of the trainee gardeners, shifty sort with a silver tongue,' he supplied. 'I always felt responsible for that mess.'

Vitale, who could not imagine getting involved or even being interested in an employee's private life, looked at the older man in frank astonishment. 'Why?'

'I saw bruises on Peggy on several occasions,' Charles admitted uncomfortably. 'I suspected Dickens of domestic abuse but I did nothing. I asked her several times if she was all right and she always assured me that she was. I should've done more.'

'I don't see what you could have done if she wasn't willing to make a complaint on her own behalf,' Vitale said dismissively, wondering where on earth this strange conversation could be leading while marvelling that his father could show visible distress when discussing the past life of a former servant. 'You weren't responsible.'

'Right and wrong isn't always that black and white,' Charles Russell replied grimly. 'If I'd been more supportive, more encouraging, possibly she might have given me her trust and told me the truth and I could have got her the help she and her daughter needed. Instead I was polite and distant and then she ran off with that smarmy little bastard.'

'I don't see what else you could have done. One should respect boundaries, particularly with staff,' Vitale declared, stiffening at the reference to Peggy's daughter but striving to conceal that reality. He had only the dimmest memory of Peggy Dickens but he remembered her daughter, Jazmine, well but probably only because Jazz figured in one of his own most embarrassing youthful recollections. He had little taste for looking back to the days before he had learned tact and discretion.

'No, you have to take a more human approach, Vitale. Staff are people too and sometimes they need help and understanding,' Charles argued.

Vitale didn't want to help or understand what motivated his staff at the bank or the palace; he simply

wanted them to do their jobs to the best of their ability. He didn't get involved with employees on a personal level but, out of respect for his father, he resisted the urge to put his own point of view and instead tried to put the dialogue back on track. 'You said you needed a favour,' he reminded the older man.

Charles studied his son's lean, forbidding face in frustration, hating the fact that he recognised shades of his ex-wife's icy reserve and heartless detachment in Vitale. If there was one person Charles could be said to hate it would have to be the Queen of Lerovia, Sofia Castiglione. Yet he had loved her once, loved her to the edge of madness until he'd discovered that he was merely her dupe, her sperm donor for the heir she had needed for the Lerovian throne. Sofia's true love had been another woman, her closest friend, Cinzia, and from the moment Sofia had successfully conceived, Charles and their marriage as such had been very much surplus to requirements. But that was a secret the older man had promised to take to the grave with him. In the divorce settlement he had agreed to keep quiet in return for liberal access arrangements to his son and he had only ever regretted that silence afterwards when he had been forced to watch his ex-wife trying to suck the life out of Vitale with her constant carping and interference.

'Yes…the favour,' Charles recalled, forced back into the present. 'I've received a letter from Peggy's daughter, Jazmine, asking for my help. I want you to assess the situation and deal with it. I would do it myself but I'm going to be working abroad for the next few months and I don't have the time. I also thought you would handle it better because you knew each other well as children.'

Vitale's lean, strong, darkly good-looking face had tensed. In truth he had frozen where he stood at the threat of being forced to meet Jazz again. 'The situation?' he queried, playing for time.

The older man lifted a letter off the desk and passed it to him. 'The toy boy ripped Peggy off, forged her name on a stack of loans, plunged them into debt and *ruined* their financial standing!' he emphasised in ringing disgust. 'Now they're poor and struggling to survive. They've tried legal channels and got nowhere. Peggy's ill now and no longer able to work.'

Vitale's brow furrowed and he raised a silencing hand. 'But how is this trail of misfortune your business?' he asked without hesitation.

'Peggy Dickens has been on my conscience for years,' Charles confided grudgingly. 'I could have done something to help but I was too wary of causing offence so... I did nothing. All of this mess is on me and I don't want that poor woman suffering any more because I failed to act.'

'So, send her a cheque,' Vitale suggested, reeling from the display of guilt his father was revealing while he himself was struggling to see any connection or indeed any debt owed.

'Read the letter,' his father advised. 'Jazmine is asking for a job, somewhere to live and a loan, not a cheque. She's proud. She's not asking for a free handout but she's willing to do anything she can to help her mother.'

Vitale studied the envelope of what was obviously a begging letter with unconcealed distaste. More than ever he wanted to argue with his father's attitude. In Vitale's opinion, Charles owed his former employee

and her daughter absolutely nothing. By the sound of it, Peggy Dickens had screwed up her life; however that was scarcely his father's fault.

'What do *you* want me to do?' Vitale asked finally, recognising that how he felt about the situation meant nothing in the face of his father's feelings.

Yet it amazed Vitale that his father could still be so incredibly emotional and sentimental and he often marvelled that two people as ridiculously dissimilar in character as his parents could ever have married.

'I want you to be compassionate and kind, *not* judge-mental, *not* cynical, *not* cold,' Charles framed with anxious warning emphasis. 'And I know that will be a huge challenge for you but I also know that acknowledging that side of your nature will make you a better and stronger man in the process. Don't let your mother re-make you in her image—never forget that you are *my* son too.'

Vitale almost flinched from the idea of being compassionate and kind. He didn't do stuff like that. He supported leading charities and always contributed to good causes but he had never done anything hands-on in that area, nor had he ever felt the need to do so. He was what he was: a bred-in-the-bone royal, cocooned from the real world by incredible privilege, an exclusive education and great wealth.

'I don't care what it costs to buy Peggy and her daughter out of trouble either,' his father added expansively. 'With you in charge of my investments, I can well afford the gesture. You don't need to save me money.'

'I'm a banker. Saving money and making a profit comes naturally,' Vitale said drily. 'And by the way, my mother is *not* remaking me in her image.'

Charles vented a roughened laugh. 'It may be grave-yard humour but I wouldn't be a bit surprised if you find yourself engaged by the end of that ball next month! Sofia is a hell of a wheeler dealer. You should've refused to attend.'

'I may still do that. I'm no pushover,' his son stated coldly. 'So you want me to stage a rescue mission in your name?'

'With tact and generosity,' the older man added.

Exasperation leapt through Vitale, who used tact every day of his life because he could never be less than courteous in the face of the royal demands made of him. But no matter how onerous the demand Charles had made struck him, there was, nevertheless, a certain pride and satisfaction to the awareness that his father was *trusting* him to deal with a sensitive situation. He realised that he was also surprisingly eager to read Jazz's letter.

Jazz, a skinny-as-a-rail redhead, who had developed a massive crush on him when she was fourteen and he was eighteen. He had been wildly disconcerted that he rather than the friendlier, flirtier Angel had become the object of her admiration and he had screwed up badly, he acknowledged reluctantly, cracking a wounding joke about her that she had sadly overheard. But then Vitale had never been the sensitive sort and back then he had also essentially known very little about women because he had stayed a virgin for many years longer than Angel. But, not surprisingly, Jazz had hated him after that episode and in many ways it had been a relief to no longer be the centre of her attention and the awful tongue-tied silences that had afflicted her in his presence. In the space of one

awkward summer, the three of them had travelled from casual pseudo friendship to stroppy, strained discomfiture and then she and her mother had mercifully disappeared out of their lives.

Compassionate... Kind, Vitale reminded himself as he stood outside his father's office reading Jazz's letter, automatically rating it for use of English, spelling and conciseness. Of course it had been written on the computer because Jazz was severely dyslexic. Dyslexic and clumsy, he recalled helplessly, always tripping and bumping into things. The letter told a tale of woe that could have featured as a Greek tragedy and his sculpted mouth tightened, his momentary amusement dying away. She wanted help for her mother but only on her own terms. She wanted a job but only had experience of working as a checkout operator and a cleaner.

Per carita…for pity's sake, what did she think his father was going to find for her to do on the back of such slender talents? Even so, the letter was pure Jazz, feisty and gauche and crackling with brick-wall obstinacy. An ordinary woman, he thought abstractedly, an ordinary woman with extraordinarily beautiful green eyes. Her eyes wouldn't have changed, he reasoned. And you couldn't get more ordinary than Jazz, who thought a soup spoon or a fish fork or a napkin was pure unnecessary aristocratic affectation. And she *was*, evidently, badly in need of money…

A faint smile tilted Vitale's often grim mouth. He didn't need a stunning beauty to act as his partner at the palace ball and he was quite sure that if he hired the right experts Jazz could be transformed into something reasonably presentable. Having a partner for the ball to

fend off other women would make sense, he acknowledged reluctantly. But shooting Zac down in flames
would undeniably be the most satisfying aspect of the
whole affair. Jazz might be ordinary and dyslexic but
she was also clever and a quick study.

Vitale strolled back to his younger brother's side
with a rare smile on his wide sensual mouth. 'You're
up next but before you go…the bet,' he specified in an
undertone. 'Remember that blonde waitress who wanted
nothing to do with you last week and accused you of
harassment?'

Zac frowned, disconcerted colour highlighting his
high cheekbones at that reminder of his rare failure to
impress a woman.

'Bring her to the ball acting all lovelorn and clingy
and suitably polished up and you have a deal on the
bet,' Vitale completed, throwing down the gauntlet of
challenge with pleasure while recalling the very real
hatred he had seen in that woman's eyes. For once,
Zac, the smooth-talking seducer, would have his work
cut out for him…

Jazz straightened her aching back at the checkout because she had worked a very long day. Her schedule had
kicked off at dawn with a cleaning shift at a nearby hotel
and then she had got a call to step in for a sick work-
mate at the till in the supermarket where she earned
extra cash on a casual basis. Both her jobs were casual,
poorly paid and unreliable. But some work was better
than no work, she reminded herself doggedly, better
than living on welfare, which would have distressed her
mother more even though that choice would have left
mother and daughter somewhat better off.

But while Peggy Dickens had raised her daughter to be a worker rather than a whinger or a freeloader, Jazz still occasionally let her thoughts drift into a dream world where she had got to complete the education that would have equipped her with a degree that enabled her to chase better-paid jobs and climb an actual career ladder. Unfortunately, the chaos of her private life had prevented her from, what was that phrase…achieving her full potential? Her full pink mouth curled at the corners with easy amusement for who was to say that she was worth any more than the work she was currently doing? No point getting too big for her boots and imagining she might have been more, not when she came from such humble roots.

Her mother had been a housekeeper, who married a gardener and lived in accommodation provided by their employer. Nobody in Jazz's family tree had ever owned a house or earned a university degree and Peggy had been bemused when her daughter had chosen to continue her education and aim so much higher than any of her ancestors, but her mother had been proud as well.

And then their lives had gone down the tubes again and Jazz had had to put practicality first yet again. Unfortunately, it was virtually impossible to regain lost ground. Jazz had almost had a nervous breakdown studying to overcome the drawbacks of changing schools three times over during her teen years. She had not wept when her parents' unhappy marriage had finally broken down because her father had often beaten up her mother and had hurt Jazz as well when she had been foolish enough to try and intervene. She had grieved, though, when her father had died unexpectedly only a couple of years afterwards without hav-

ing once tried to see her again. Evidently her father had never much cared for his only child and that knowledge had hurt. She had been sincerely aghast, however, when her mother, Peggy fell in love with Jeff Starling, a much younger man.

Love could be the biggest risk out there for a woman, Jazz reflected with an inner shiver of repulsion, most especially the kind of love that could persuade an otherwise sensible woman into jumping straight out of the frying pan into the fire.

But there were other kinds of love as well, she reminded herself comfortingly, life-enriching family connections that soothed and warmed, no matter how bad life got. When Jeff's bad debts had ensured that Peggy and her daughter couldn't even get a lease on a rental property, Peggy's kid sister, Clodagh, had given them a home in her tiny apartment. When Peggy had been diagnosed with breast cancer, Clodagh had stepped back from her little jewellery business to shepherd her sister to her appointments and treatments and nurse her tenderly while Jazz tried to keep on earning what little money she could.

Bolstered by those more positive thoughts, Jazz finished her shift and walked home in the dusk. Her phone pinged and she dug it out, green eyes widening when she read the text with difficulty. It was short and sweet, beginning, *re: letter to Charles Russell*.

Holy Moses, she thought in shock, Charles Russell was actually willing to meet her to discuss her mother's plight! Ten o'clock tomorrow morning, not much notice, she conceded ruefully, but beggars couldn't be choosers, could they?

In desperation, she had written to her mother's for-

mer employer pleading for help. Charles was a kind
man and generous to a fault but almost ten years down
the road from Peggy's employment, Jazz had not even
expected to receive a reply. That letter had been a long
shot, the product of a particularly sleepless night when
she was stressing about how she could best help her
mother with the stable, stress-free existence she needed
to recover from what had proved to be a gruelling treatment schedule. After all, they couldn't live with Clodagh for ever. Clodagh had sacrificed a lot to take them
in off the street, not least a boyfriend, who had vanished
once the realities of Clodagh's new caring role had sunk
in. Ironically, Jazz had not thought that there was the
remotest possibility that her letter to Charles Russell
would even be acknowledged...

A hot feeling of shame crept up inside her, burning
her pale porcelain skin with mortified heat because the
instant she had posted that letter, she had squirmed with
regret over the sacrifice of her pride. Hadn't she been
raised to stand on her own feet? Yet sometimes, no matter what you did and no matter how hard you worked,
you needed a helping hand to climb up out of a ditch.
And evidently, Charles Russell had taken pity on their
plight and maybe, just maybe, he had recognised that he
could offer his assistance in some way. With somewhere
to live? With employment? Hope sprang high, dousing
the shame of having written and posted a begging letter. Any help, no matter how small or seemingly insignificant, would be welcome, she told herself sternly.

Stuffing her phone back in her pocket, Jazz unlocked
the door of the apartment, suppressing a sigh when she
saw the mess in the living and kitchen area. Clodagh
wasn't tidy and she wasn't much for cleaning or doing

dishes or laundry but Jazz did what she could to pick up
the slack, always conscious that she lived in Clodagh's
home while remaining equally aware that her neat freak
of a mother found it depressing to live in such messy
surroundings. But there wasn't much that could be done
to make a one-bedroom apartment stretch to the occupation of three adults, one of whom was still struggling to regain her strength. The treatments might have
concluded but Peggy was still in the recovery phase.
Clodagh shared the bedroom with her sister but when
Peggy had a restless night, Clodagh took the couch and
Jazz slept in a sleeping bag on the floor.

'I had a good day,' Peggy announced chirpily from
in front of the television, a thin-faced, pale and still-
frail-looking woman in her forties. 'I went for a walk
in the park after mass.'

'That's brilliant,' Jazz said, bending down to kiss the
older woman's cheek, the baby fine fuzz of her mother's
regrown hair brushing her brow and bringing tears to
her tired eyes. The hair had grown again in white, rather
then red, and Peggy had refused to consider dying it as
Clodagh had suggested, confessing that as far as she
was concerned any hair was better than no hair.

Jazz was intensely relieved that her mother was re-
gaining her energy and had an excellent prognosis. Having initially faced the terrifying prospect that she might
lose her mother, she was merely grateful to still have
her and was keen to improve the older woman's life as
much as possible.

'Hungry?' Jazz prompted.

'Not really,' Peggy confessed guiltily.

'I'll make a lovely salad and you can do your best
with it,' Jazz declared, knowing it was imperative to

encourage her mother to regain some of the weight she had lost.

'Clodagh's visiting her friend, Rose,' Peggy told her. 'She asked me to join them but I was too tired and I like to see you when you come in from work.'

Suppressing her exhaustion, Jazz began to clean up the kitchen, neatly stowing away her aunt's jewellery-making supplies in their designated clear boxes and then embarking on the dishes before preparing the salad that was presently the only option that awakened her mother's appetite. While she worked, she chattered, sharing a little gossip about co-workers, bringing her working day home with her to brighten her mother's more restricted lifestyle and enjoy the sound of her occasional chuckle.

They sat down at the table to eat. Jazz was mentally running through her tiny wardrobe to select a suitable outfit for her morning appointment with Charles Russell. Giving up the luxury of their own home had entailed selling off almost all their belongings because there had been no money to spare to rent a storage facility and little room for anything extra in Clodagh's home. Jazz had a worn black pencil skirt and jeans and shorts and a few tops and that was literally all. She had learned to be grateful for the uniform she wore at both her jobs because it meant that she could get by with very few garments. Formality insisted on her wearing the skirt, she conceded ruefully, and her only pair of high heels.

She had not mentioned her letter to either her mother or her aunt because she hadn't expected anything to come of it and, in the same way, she could not quite accept that she had been given an appointment. Indeed, several times before she finally dropped off to sleep on

the couch that evening, she had to dig out her phone and anxiously reread that text to persuade herself that it wasn't a figment of her imagination.

Early the next morning, fearful of arriving late, Jazz crossed London by public transport and finally arrived outside a tall town house. She had been surprised not to be invited to the older man's office where she had sent the letter, but perhaps he preferred a less formal and more discreet setting for their meeting. She was even more surprised by the size and exclusive location of the house. Charles Russell had once been married to a reigning queen, she reminded herself wryly. A queen who, on her only fleeting visit to her former husband's country home, had treated Jazz's mother like the dirt beneath her expensively shod feet.

But Charles had been infinitely kinder and more gracious with his staff, she recalled fondly, remembering the older man's warm smiles and easy conversation with her even though she was only his housekeeper's daughter. Unlike his royal ex-wife and second son, he was not a snob and had never rated people in importance solely according to their social or financial status. A *kind* man, she repeated doggedly to herself to quell her leaping nervous tension as she rang the doorbell.

A woman who spoke little English, and what she did speak was with an impenetrable accent, ushered her into an imposing hall furnished with gleaming antiques and mirrors. Scanning her intimidating surroundings and feeling very much like an interloper, Jazz began to revise up her estimate of Charles Russell's wealth.

Another door was cast open into what looked like a home office and a man sprang up from behind the solid wooden desk.

Jazz was so aghast by the recognition that roared through her slender frame that she froze on the threshold of the room and stared in dismay, all her natural buoyance draining away as though someone very cruel had stabbed a pin into her tender flesh and deflated her like a balloon. It was Vitale, not his father, and that had to be… Her. Worst. Nightmare. *Ever…*

CHAPTER TWO

VITALE STARED, TAKEN aback by the woman in the door-way because she was a knockout, the kind of vibrant beauty who turned male heads in the street with her streaming red-gold curls and slender, supple body. About the only things that hadn't changed about Jazz were her eyes, green as jade set in a triangular face, skin as trans-lucent as the finest pale porcelain and a surprisingly full pink mouth, little white teeth currently plucking at her lower lip as she gazed at him in almost comical horror.

'Come in and close the door,' Vitale urged smoothly, wondering how on earth he was going to teach her to stop wearing her every thought on her face while also wondering why he found that candidness attractive.

Jazz made a valiant attempt to stage a recovery even though every ounce of her hard-won confidence had been blown out of the water. Shock waves were trav-elling through her slight body. One glimpse of Vitale and her brain was mush at best and at worst sending her back in time to a very vulnerable period she did not want to remember. But there Vitale was, as sleek and drop-dead gorgeous as he had ever been and so com-pelling in his undeniable masculine beauty that it took terrible effort to even look away from him.

What was it about Vitale, what crazy weakness in her made him seem so appealing? His brother, Angel Valtinos, had been too pretty and vain to draw her and she had never once looked at Angel in *that* way. But then, Vitale was a much more complex and fascinating creature, all simmering, smouldering intensity and conflicts below the smooth, sophisticated surface he wore for the world. Those perfect manners and that cool reserve of his couldn't mask the intense emotion he held in restraint behind those stunning dark golden eyes. And he was *so* sexy. Every sinuous movement of his lean, muscular body, every downward dip of his gold-tipped, outrageously thick black lashes, and every quirk of his beautifully shaped sensual mouth contributed to his ferocious sex appeal. It was little wonder that when she had finally been of an age to crush on a man, her attention had immediately locked onto Vitale, even though Vitale had found it quite impossible to treat her like a friend.

Jazz closed the door in a harried movement and walked towards the chair set in front of the desk. You're a grown-up now. The embarrassing stuff you did as a kid no longer matters, her defences were instructing her at a frantic pitch, and so intent was she on listening to that face-saving voice that she didn't notice the edge of the rug in front of her. Her spiky heel caught on the fringe and she pitched forward with a startled cry.

And Vitale was there at supersonic speed, catching her before she could fall and steadying her with a strong arm to her spine. The heat of his hand at her waist startled her almost as much as his sudden proximity. She jerked skittishly away from him to settle

down heavily into the chair but her nostrils flared appreciatively. The dark sensual scent of his spicy cologne overlying warm earthy male plunged her senses into overdrive.

Vitale had finally touched her, Vitale, who avoided human contact as much as possible, she recalled abstractedly, striving not to look directly at him until she had got her stupid brain back on line. He would be smiling: she *knew* that. Her clumsiness had always amused him because he was as lithe and sure-footed as a cat. Now he unnerved her more by not returning to the other side of the desk and instead lounging back against it with unusual casualness, staying far too close for comfort, a long, muscular, powerful thigh within view that did nothing to restore her composure.

Her fingertips dug into her palms as she fought for calm. 'I was expecting to meet with your father,' she admitted thinly.

'Charles asked me to handle this,' Vitale confided, barely resisting the urge to touch the wild corkscrew mane of flaming ringlets tumbling across her shoulders with gleaming electric vigour. So, he liked the hair and the eyes, he reasoned, wondering why he had abandoned his usual formality to sit so close to her, wondering why the simple smell of soap that she emanated was so surpassingly sexy, wondering why that slender body with its delicate curves, tiny waist and shapely legs should suddenly seem so very tempting a package. Because she wasn't his type, not even remotely his type, he told himself sternly. He had always gone for tall, curvy blondes, redheads being too bright and brash for his tastes.

On the other hand he had never wanted so badly to

touch a woman's hair and that weird prompting unnerved him into springing upright again and striding across the room. The dulled throb of awakening desire at his groin inspired him with another stab of incredulity because since adulthood he had always been fully in control of that particular bodily affliction.

'I can't think why,' Jazz said, dry-mouthed, unbearably conscious of him looming over her for that split second before he moved away because he stood well over six feet tall and she barely made a couple of inches over five foot.

'I assure you that the exchange will work out very much to your advantage,' Vitale husked, deciding that his uncharacteristic interest had simply been stimulated by the challenge that he now saw lay ahead of him: the transformation of Jazz. Number one on the agenda would be persuading her to stop biting her nails. Number two would be ditching the giant fake gold hoop earrings. Number three would be avoiding any shoe that looked as if a stripper might wear it.

Jazz let slip a very rude startled word in response to that unlikely statement.

And number four would be cleaning up her vocabulary, Vitale reflected, glad to so clearly see her flaws so that he could concentrate on the practicalities of his challenge, rather than dwell on any aspect that could be deemed personal.

'Don't swear,' Vitale told her.

Jazz reddened as high as her hairline because she could remember him saying the same thing to her when she was about twelve years old while warning her that once she became accustomed to using such words, using them would become an embarrassing habit. And being

Vitale, he had been infuriatingly bang on target with that advice. Using curse words had made her seem a little cooler at school back then…well, as cool as you could be with bright red hair and a flat chest, puberty having passed her by for far longer than she cared to recall, making her an anomaly amongst her peers.

'You need financial help,' Vitale pointed out with undiplomatic bluntness, keen to get right to the heart of the matter and remind her of her situation. If he neglected to remind her of her boundaries, Jazz would be a stubborn, defiant baggage and hard to handle.

Living up to that assessment, Jazz flew upright, earrings swinging wildly in the torrent of her burnished hair, colour marking her cheekbones, highlighting eyes bright with angry defensiveness. 'I did *not* ask for money from your father!' she snapped back at him.

'Employment, a home, the settlement of outstanding loans?' Vitale reminded her with cruel precision. 'How could any of those aspirations be achieved without someone laying out a considerable amount of money on your behalf?'

The angry colour drained from her disconcerted face, perspiration breaking out on her short upper lip as he threw her crash-bang up against hard reality, refusing to allow her to deny the obvious. She stared back at him, trapped like a rabbit in headlights and hating him for it. Mortification claimed her along with a healthy dose of shame that she should have put herself in such a position and with Vitale of all people. Vitale, who had never treated her like an equal as Angel had done, Vitale who had never for one moment forgotten that she was essentially a servant's child, thrown into the brothers' company only by proximity.

Vitale watched Jazz crash down from fury to bitter, embarrassed acceptance. *Sì*...yes, he told himself with satisfaction, that had been the right note to sound. She dropped back into the chair, sunset heat warming her cheeks and bowing her head on her slender neck.

'And the good news is that I'm willing to provide that money *if*...in return, you are willing to do something for me.'

'I can't imagine anything that I could do for you,' Jazz told him truthfully.

'Then listen and learn,' Vitale advised, poised by the window with the light glimmering over his luxuriant blue-black hair, the suave olive planes of his cheekbones taut. 'At the end of next month my mother is throwing a ball at the palace. Her objective is to match me up with a future bride and the guest list will be awash with young women who have what the Queen deems to be the right pedigree and background.'

Jazz was staring at him now in wide-eyed wonderment. 'Are you kidding me?'

His sculpted mouth quirked. 'I wish I was.'

Her smooth brow furrowed as she collided with hot dark golden eyes and suddenly found it fatally difficult to breathe. 'You're angry about it.'

'*Oviamente*...of course I am. I'm nowhere near the stage in life where I want to get married and settle down. But having considered the situation, it has occurred to me,' Vitale murmured quietly, 'that arriving at the ball with what appears to be a partner, whom I'm seriously involved with, would be my best defence. I want you to be that partner.'

'*Me?*' Jazz gaped at him in disbelief, green eyes a pool of verdant jade bemusement as she gazed up at

him, soft full pink lips slightly parted. 'How could *I* be your partner? I couldn't go to a royal ball!'

'Suitably gowned and refined, you could,' Vitale disagreed, choosing his words with care because the throb below his belt went up tempo when he focused on that soft, oh, so inviting full lower lip of hers. 'But you would have to be willing to work at the presentation required because you would have to both *look* like and *act* like the sort of woman I would bring to a royal ball.'

'Impossible,' Jazz told him. 'It would take more than a fancy dress and not swearing.'

'It would but, given that we have several weeks at our disposal in which to prepare, I think you could easily do it,' Vitale declared, shocking her even more with that vote of apparent confidence. 'And whether you successfully contrive the pretence or fail it, I will still pay you well for trying to make the grade.'

'But why me?' Jazz spluttered in a rush. 'Why someone like me? Surely you have a friend who could pretend to be something more for the evening?'

'Why you? Because someone bet me that I couldn't pass off an ordinary woman as a socialite at a royal ball,' Vitale delivered, opting for the truth. 'You fit the bill and I prefer to *pay* for the pretence rather than ask anyone to do me a favour. In addition, as it will be in your best interests to succeed, you will make more effort to meet the standard required.'

Jazz was transfixed by his admission. 'A bet,' she echoed weakly. 'To go to all that effort and put out money simply to win a bet…it would be absurd.'

Vitale shrugged a wide shoulder, sheathed in the finest silk and wool blend, the jacket of his exquisitely

well-tailored suit sliding open to reveal his torso, lean, strong muscles flexing below the thin cotton shirt. Her mouth ran dry because he was a work of art on a physical level, every silken, honed line of his lean, powerful physique hard and muscular and fit. 'Does the absurdity of it have to concern you?'

'I guess not…' she said uncertainly, knowing that what was what he wanted her to say, playing it sensibly by ear and reluctant to argue while momentarily lost in the dark, exciting challenge of his hard, assessing gaze.

She had almost forgotten what that excitement felt like, had never felt it since in a man's radius and had been much too young and naïve to feel its mortifying bite at the age of fourteen. She had experienced what felt like all the sensations of a grown woman while still trapped in the body of an undeveloped child. Unsurprisingly, struggling to deal with that adolescent flood of sexual awakening had made her so silent, so awkward and so wretched around Vitale that she had been filled with self-loathing and shame.

Now that same excitement was curling up hot in the pit of her stomach and spreading dangerous tendrils of awareness to more sensitive places. She felt her nipples pinch tight below her tee shirt and her small breasts swell with the shaken breath she snatched in as she willed the torture to stop. But her body's reaction to Vitale had never been something she could control and the inexorable pulse of that heat between her thighs made her feel murderously uncomfortable and foolish.

A bet, she was still thinking with even greater incredulity, desperate to stop thinking about her physi-

cal reaction to him. Vitale was willing to invest good money in an attempt to win a bet. That was beyond her capacity to imagine and she thought it was very wrong. In her experience money was precious and should be reserved to cover the necessities of life: rent, heat and food. She had never lived in a world where money was easily obtained or where there was ever enough of it. Even when her parents had still been together, having sufficient money simply to live had been a constant source of concern, thanks to her father's addiction to online betting.

But Vitale lived at a very different level, she reminded herself ruefully. He took money for granted, had never gone without and could probably never understand how bone-deep appalled she was by his lighthearted attitude and how even more hostile she was to any form of gambling.

'I don't approve of gambling,' she admitted tightly, thinking of the families destroyed by the debts accrued and the addicts who could not break free of their dream of a big win.

'It's *not*—'

'It *is* gambling,' Jazz cut in with assurance. 'You're betting on the outcome of something that can't be predicted and you may make a loss.'

'That's my problem, not yours,' Vitale delivered without hesitation. 'You need to think about how this arrangement would benefit you. I would settle those loans and find a place of your choosing for you and your mother to live. I don't know what I could offer on the employment front but I'm sure I could provide some help. The decision is yours. I'll give you twenty-four hours to think it over.'

Her green eyes flared in anger again. 'You haven't even told me what would be involved if I accepted!'

'Obviously you'd have to have a makeover and a certain amount of coaching before you could meet the demands of the role,' Vitale imparted, marvelling that she hadn't eagerly snatched at his offer straight away. 'Right now you're drowning in debt and you have no options. I can *give* you options.'

It was the bald truth and she hated him for spelling it out. If wishes were horses, then beggars would ride, she chanted inside her head. Being badly in debt meant that she and her mother had virtually no choices and little chance of improving their lot in life. She swallowed hard on that humiliating reality that put Vitale squarely in the driver's seat. A makeover, *coaching*? Inwardly she cringed but it was no surprise to her that she would not do as she was. She would never be good enough for Vitale on any level. She didn't have the right breeding or background and found it hard to credit that even a makeover would raise her to the standard required by a highly sophisticated royal prince, who couldn't even drink beer out of a bottle without looking uncomfortable.

'Yes, if I can trust you, you could give us options,' she conceded flatly. 'But how do I know that you will keep your promises if this doesn't work?'

Vitale stiffened as though she had slapped him. 'I give you my word,' he bit out witheringly. 'Surely that should be sufficient?'

'There are very few people in this world that I trust,' Jazz admitted apologetically.

'I will have a legal agreement drawn up, then,' Vitale breathed with icy cool. 'Will that satisfy you?'

Jazz lifted her head high, barely able to credit that she was bargaining with Vitale. 'We don't need a legal agreement for something this crazy. You get rid of the loans first as a show of faith,' she dared. 'I'm fed up trying to protect my mother from debt collectors.'

'I don't understand why you're even trying to repay loans that were fraudulently taken out in your mother's name.'

'It's incredibly difficult to prove that it *was* fraud. Jeff died in an accident last year and he wasn't prosecuted. A solicitor tried to sort it out for Mum but we didn't have enough proof to clear her name and she won't declare herself bankrupt because she sees that as the ultimate humiliation,' she explained, wanting him to know that they had explored every possible avenue. 'She was ill and going through chemo at the time and I didn't want to put any more pressure on her.'

'You give me all the paperwork for the loans and I will have them dealt with,' Vitale asserted. 'But if I do so, I will own you body and soul until the end of next month.'

'Nobody will *ever* own me body and soul.'

'Apart from me for the next couple of months,' Vitale contradicted with lethal cool. 'If I pay upfront, I call the shots and you do as you're told, whether you like it or not.'

Jazz blinked in bewilderment, wondering how she had got herself into the situation she was in. He thought he had her agreement and why wouldn't he when she had bargained the terms with him? Even the prospect of those dreadful loans being settled knocked her for six. A visit or a phone call from a debt collector upset her mother for days afterwards, depriving her of the peace

of mind she needed to rebuild her life and her health. How could Jazz possibly turn her back on an offer like Vitale's? Nobody else was going to give them the opportunity to make a fresh start.

'You haven't given me a chance to think this through,' she argued shakily.

'You were keen enough to set out your conditions,' Vitale reminded her drily.

And her face flamed because she was in no position to protest that assumption. The offer of money had cut right through her fine principles and her aversion to gambling. The very idea that she could sort out her mother's problems and give her a happier and more secure future had thoroughly seduced her.

'You'll move in here as soon as possible,' Vitale decreed.

Her head flew up, corkscrew curls tumbling across her shoulders, green eyes huge. 'Move in here? With *you*?'

'How else can we achieve this? You must be readily available. How else can I supervise? And if I take you to the ball it will be assumed we are lovers, and should anyone do a check, it will be clear that you were already living here in my house,' Vitale pointed out. 'If we are to succeed, you have to consider little supporting details of that nature.'

Jazz studied him, aghast. 'I can't move in with you!' she gasped. 'What am I supposed to tell my mother?'

Vitale shrugged with magnificent lack of interest. 'Whatever suits. That I've given you a job? That we're having an affair? I don't care.'

Her feathery lashes fluttered rapidly, her animated face troubled as she pondered that problem. 'Yes, I

could admit I sent the letter to your father and say I've been offered a live-in job and my aunt would look after Mum, so I wouldn't need to worry about her,' she reasoned out loud. 'Would I still be able to work? I have two part-time jobs.'

'No. You won't have the time. I'll pay you a salary for the duration of your stay here,' Vitale added, reading her expression to register the dismay etched there at the news that she would not be able to continue in paid employment.

'This is beginning to sound like a very expensive undertaking for you,' Jazz remarked uncomfortably, her face more flushed than ever.

'My choice,' Vitale parried dismissively while he wondered how far that flush extended beneath her clothing and whether that scattering of freckles across the bridge of her nose was repeated anywhere else on her delicate body. He wondered dimly why such an imperfection should seem even marginally appealing and why he should suddenly be picturing her naked with all the eagerness of a sex-starved teenage boy. He tensed, thoroughly unsettled by his complete loss of concentration and detachment.

'I'll say you've offered me a job,' Jazz said abruptly, her thoughts leaping ahead of her. 'Are there many art works in this house?'

Vitale frowned and stared enquiringly at her. 'Yes, but—'

'Then I could say that I was cataloguing them or researching them for you,' Jazz announced with satisfaction. 'I was only six months off completing a BA in History of Art when Mum's life fell apart and I had to drop out. I may not have attained my degree but I have

done placements in museums and galleries, so I do have good working experience.'

'If what you're telling me is true, why are you working in a shop and as a cleaner?'

'Because without that degree certificate, I can't work in my field. I'll finish my studies once life has settled down again,' she said with wry acceptance.

Vitale struggled to imagine the added stress of studying at degree level in spite of her dyslexia and all its attendant difficulties and a grudging respect flared in him because she had fought her disability and refused to allow it to hold her back. 'Why did you drop out?'

'Mum's second husband, Jeff, died suddenly and she was inconsolable.' Jazz grimaced. 'That was long before the debt collectors began calling and we found out about the loans Jeff had taken out and forged her name on. I took time out from university but things went downhill very quickly from that point and I couldn't leave Mum alone. We were officially homeless and living in a boarding house when she was diagnosed with cancer and that was when my aunt asked us to move in with her. It's been a rough couple of years.'

Vitale made no comment, backing away from the personal aspects of the information she was giving him, deeming them not his business, not his concern. He needed to concentrate on the end game alone and that was preparing her for the night of the ball.

'How soon can you move in?' he prompted impatiently.

Jazz stiffened at that blunt question. 'This week sometime?' she suggested.

'I'll send a car to collect you tomorrow at nine and

pack for a long stay. We don't have time to waste,' Vitale pronounced as she slid out of the seat and straightened, the pert swell of her small breasts prominent in a tee shirt that was a little too tight, the skirt clinging to her slim thighs and the curve of her bottom, the fabric shiny with age. Her ankles looked ridiculously narrow and delicate above those clodhopper sandals with their towering heels. The pulse at his groin that nagged at his usually well-disciplined body went crazy.

'Tomorrow's a little soon, surely?' Jazz queried in dismay.

Vitale compressed his lips, exasperated by his physical reaction to her. 'We have a great deal to accomplish.'

'Am I really that unpresentable?' Jazz heard herself ask sharply.

'Cinderella *shall* go to the ball,' Vitale retorted with diplomatic conviction, ducking an answer that was obvious to him even if it was not to her. 'When I put my mind to anything, I make it work.'

In something of a daze, Jazz refused the offer of a car to take her home and muttered the fiction that she had some shopping to do. In truth she only ever shopped at the supermarket, not having the money to spare for treats. But she knew she needed time to get her head clear and work out what she was going to say before she went home again, and that was how she ended up sitting in a park in the spring sunshine, feeling much as though she had had a run-in with a truck that had squashed her flat.

'She's as flat as an ironing board, not to mention the hideous rag-doll hair but, worst of all, she's a *child*, Angel…'

Vitale's well-bred voice filtered down through the

years to sound afresh inside her head. Angel spoke Greek and Vitale spoke Italian, so the brothers had always communicated in English. Angel had been teasing Vitale about her crush and of course Jazz had been so innocent at fourteen that it had not even occurred to her that the boys had noticed her infatuation, and that unwelcome discovery as much as Vitale's withering description of her lack of attractiveness had savaged Jazz. She had known she wasn't much to look at, but knowing and having it said out loud by the object of her misplaced affections had cut her deep. Furthermore, being deemed to be still a child, even though in hindsight she now agreed with that conviction, had hurt even more at the time and she had hated him for it. She still remembered the dreadful moment when the boys had appeared out of the summerhouse and had seen her standing there, white as a sheet on the path, realising that they had been overheard.

Angel had grimaced but Vitale had looked genuinely appalled. At eighteen, Vitale hadn't had the ability to hide his feelings that he did as an adult, and at that moment Vitale had recognised how upset she was and had deeply regretted his words, his troubled dark golden eyes telegraphing that truth. Not that he would have admitted it or said anything, though, or even apologised, she conceded wryly, because royalty did not admit fault or indeed do anything that lowered the dignified cool front of polished perfection.

"Cinderella shall go to the ball," he had said as if he were conferring some enormous honour on her. As if she cared about his stupid fancy ball, or his even more stupid bet! But she *did* care about her mother, she reminded herself ruefully, and if Vitale was willing to

help her family, she was willing to eat dirt, strain every
sinew to please and play Cinderella…even if the process
did sting her pride and humiliate her and there would
be no glass slipper waiting for her!

CHAPTER THREE

'I'M ONLY WORRIED because you had such a thing for him when you were young.' Peggy Starling rested anxious green eyes on her daughter's pink cheeks. 'Living in the same house with him now, working for him.'

'He's a prince, Mum,' Jazz pointed out, wishing her colour didn't change so revealingly, wishing she could honestly swear that she now found Vitale totally unattractive. 'I'm not an idiot.'

'But you were never really aware of him being a royal at Chimneys because Mr Russell wanted him treated like any other boy while he was staying there and his title was never used,' her mother reasoned uncomfortably. 'I just don't want you getting hurt again.'

'Oh, for goodness' sake, Peggy, stop fussing!' Clodagh interrupted impatiently, a small woman in her late thirties with the trademark family red hair cut short. 'Jazz is a grown woman now and she's been offered a decent job and a nice place to live for a couple of months. Don't spoil it for her!'

Jazz gave her aunt a grateful glance. 'The extra money will come in useful and I'll visit regularly,' she promised.

Her possessions in a bag, Jazz hugged her mother and

her aunt and took her leave, walking downstairs, because the lift was always broken, and out to the shabby street where a completely out-of-place long black shiny limousine awaited her. Amusement filtered through her nerves when she saw that the muscular driver was out patrolling round the car, keen to protect his pride and joy from a hovering cluster of jeering kids.

Vitale strode out of his office when he heard the slam of the front door of the town house because somewhere in the back of his mind he couldn't quite credit that he was doing what he was doing and that Jazz would actually turn up. More fool him, he thought sardonically, reckoning that the financial help he was offering would be more than sufficient as a bait on the hook of her commitment.

He scanned her slim silhouette in jeans and a sweater, wondering if he ought to be planning to take before and after photos for some silly scrapbook while acknowledging that her hair, her skin, her eyes, her truly perfect little face required no improvement whatsoever. His attention fell in surprise to the bulging carrier bag she carried.

'I told you to pack for a long stay,' he reminded her with a frown. 'I meant bring everything you require to be comfortable.'

Jazz shrugged. 'This *is* everything I own,' she said tightly.

'It can't be,' Vitale pronounced in disbelief, accustomed to women who travelled with suitcases that ran into double figures.

'Being homeless strips you of your possessions pretty efficiently,' Jazz told him drily. 'I only kept *one* snow globe, my first one...'

And a faint shard of memory pierced Vitale's brain. He recalled her dragging him and Angel into her bedroom to show off her snow globe collection when they must all have been very young. She had had three of those ugly plastic domes and the first one had had an evil little Santa Claus figure inside it. He and Angel had surveyed the girlie display, unimpressed. 'They're beautiful,' Vitale had finally squeezed out, trying to be kind under the onslaught of her expectant green eyes, and knowing that a lie was necessary because she was tiny, and he still remembered the huge smile she had given him, which had assured him that he had said the right thing.

'The Santa one?' he queried.

Disconcerted, Jazz stared back at him in astonishment. 'You remember that?'

'It stayed with me. I've never seen a snow globe since,' Vitale told her truthfully, relieved to be off the difficult subject of her having been homeless at one stage, while censuring himself for not having registered the practical consequences of such an upsetting experience.

'So, when do the lessons start?' Jazz prompted.

'Come into my office. The housekeeper will show you to your room later.'

Jazz straightened her slender spine and tried hard not to stare at Vitale, which was an enormous challenge when he looked so striking in an exquisitely tailored dark grey suit that outlined his lean, powerful physique to perfection, a white shirt and dark silk tie crisp at his brown throat. So, he's gorgeous, *get over it*, she railed inwardly at herself until the full onslaught of spectac-

ular dark golden eyes heavily fringed by black lashes
drove even that sensible thought from her mind.

'First you get measured up for a new wardrobe. Next
you get elocution.'

'Elocution?' Jazz gasped.

For all the world as though he had suggested keelhaul-
ing her under Angel's yacht, Vitale thought helplessly.

'You can't do this with a noticeable regional accent,'
Vitale sliced in. 'Stop reacting to everything I say as
though it's personal.'

'It *is* freaking personal when someone says you don't
talk properly!' Jazz slashed back at him furiously, her
colour heightened.

'And the language,' Vitale reminded her without
skipping a beat, refusing to be sidetracked from his
ultimate goal. 'I'm not insulting you. Stop personal-
ising this arrangement. You are being prepared for an
acting role.'

The reminder was a timely one, but it still struck
Jazz as very personal when a man looked at her and
decided he had to change virtually everything about
her. She compressed her lips and said instead, *'Freaking* is not a bad word.'

Vitale released a groan, gold-tipped lashes flying
high while he noticed the fullness of her soft pink lips
even when she was trying to fold them flat, and his
body succumbed to an involuntary stirring he fiercely
resented. 'Are you going to argue about everything?'

Common sense assailed Jazz and she bent down to
rummage industriously in her carrier bag. 'Not if you
settle these loans,' she muttered in as apologetic a tone
as she could manage while still hating him for picking
out her every flaw.

Vitale watched her settle a small heap of crumpled papers on his desk while striving to halter her temper, a battle he could read on her eloquent face. He supposed he could live with 'freaking' if he had to. For that matter he knew several socialites who swore like troopers and he wondered if he was setting his expectations rather too high, well aware that if he had a flaw, and he wasn't willing to acknowledge that he *did*, it was a desire for perfection.

'After elocution comes lessons in etiquette,' he informed her doggedly, suppressing that rare instant of self-doubt. 'You have to know how to address the other guests, many of whom will have titles.'

'It sounds like a *really* fun-packed morning,' Jazz pronounced acidly.

Amusement flashed through Vitale but he crushed it at source, reluctant to encourage her irreverence. Of course, he wasn't used to any woman behaving around him the way Jazz did. Jazz had smoothly shifted straight back into treating him the same way she had treated him when they were teenagers and it was a disorientating experience, but not actively unpleasant, he registered in surprise. There was no awe or flattery, no ego-boosting jokes or flirtatious smiles or carefully choreographed speeches. In the strangest way he found her attitude, her very refusal to be impressed by his status, refreshing.

Later that same day, Jazz got a break at lunchtime. She heaved a sigh over the morning she had endured; lessons had never before made her feel so bored and fed up because all the subject matter was dry as dust. For the first time, however, she was becoming fully aware that Vitale occupied a very different world from her own

and the prospect of having to face weeks of such coaching sessions made her wince. But if that was what rescuing her mother demanded from her, she would knuckle down and learn what she had to learn, she conceded reluctantly. A sheaf of supporting notes in front of her, she stroked coloured felt-tipped pens through salient points to highlight them, a practice she had used at university to make reading less of a challenge for her dyslexia. It would be easier for her to ask for spoken notes that she could listen to but she absolutely hated asking for special treatment that drew attention to her learning disability, particularly when it would only remind Vitale of yet another one of her flaws.

Her room, however, was beautiful, she allowed with a rueful smile that took in her silk-clad bed, the polished furniture and the door into the en-suite bathroom. She might as well have been staying in a top-flight exclusive hotel because her surroundings were impossibly luxurious and decidedly in the category of a major treat. The lunch, served in a fancy dining room, had been excellent as well, she was thinking as she sped downstairs for the afternoon session of coaching, wondering what was next on the agenda.

'*Jazz?*' a voice said in disbelief.

Jazz stopped dead mid-flight and stared down at the tall dark man staring up at her from the foyer, swiftly recognising him from his high public profile in the media. 'Angel?' she queried in shock.

'What the hell are you doing in my brother's house?' Angel demanded bluntly, scanning her casual jeans-clad appearance with frowning attention.

Trying to think fast, Jazz descended the stairs, wondering what she was supposed to say to Vitale's half-

brother. Were the two men still as close as they had been as kids?

'I think that's a secret so I'd rather not go into detail,' she parried awkwardly. 'How are you?'

'That's OK, Jenkins,' Angel addressed the older man still standing at the front door as if in readiness for the Greek billionaire's departure. 'You can serve coffee in the drawing room for Jazz and I.'

'Where's Vitale?' Jazz enquired nervously.

'Out but we *must* catch up,' Angel said with innate assurance while the older man spread wide the door of what she assumed to be the drawing room.

'Who's Jenkins?' she asked to forestall further questions when the door was closed again.

'Vitale's butler. This is a pretty old-fashioned household,' Angel told her cheerfully. 'Now tell me about the secret because I know my brother better than anyone and Vitale does not *have* secrets.'

'I can't… Don't push me,' Jazz protested in desperation. 'My mother and I are in a bit of a pickle and Vitale is helping us out.'

'Charitable Vitale?' Angel inclined his head thoughtfully. 'Sorry, that doesn't wash.'

'I contacted your father first,' Jazz admitted, hoping that fact would distract him, because Angel was displaying all the characteristics of a terrier on the scent of a juicy bone.

'Tell me about your mother,' Angel invited smoothly.

Jazz gave him a brief résumé of their plight and confided that she had told her family that she was working for Vitale even though she strictly wasn't. 'But if it hadn't been for the *b-bet*—' she stumbled helplessly at

letting that word escape '—Vitale wouldn't have needed me in the first place.'

'Bet,' Angel repeated with a sudden flashing smile of triumph. 'Zac, our kid brother, I surmise. And what *is* the bet? Vitale tells me everything.'

And since she had already given away half the story she gave him the whole. Angel gave her a shattered appraisal before he dropped down beside her on the sofa and burst out laughing, so genuinely amused at the prospect of her being coached for a public appearance at a royal ball that she ended up laughing too. Angel had always been so much more down-to-earth than his brother.

That was the point when Vitale entered the room, seeing his brother and Jazz seated close and laughing in a scene of considerable intimacy. That unanticipated sight sent a current of deep-seated rage roaring through Vitale like a hurricane.

'Jazz…you're supposed to be with Jenkins right now, not entertaining my brother!' he bit out rawly, dark golden eyes scorching hot with angry condemnation on her flushed face.

'Jenkins?' she queried, rising upright.

'Table manners,' he extended crushingly, sending a tide of red rushing across her stricken face and not feeling the slightest bit guilty about it.

Jazz fled, mortified that he would say that to her in front of Angel as if she were a half-bred savage, who didn't know how to eat in polite company. Was she? Ridiculous tears prickled at the backs of her eyes and stung. Did Vitale remember her as having had dreadful table manners when she was younger? It was a deeply embarrassing suspicion.

'Well, wasn't that unroyal eruption educational?' Angel quipped as he sprang upright and studied Vitale with a measuring scrutiny. 'Yes, she's turned out quite a looker, our childhood playmate.'

Jazz was only a little soothed to learn that Vitale's butler had been co-opted into teaching her about the right cutlery to use, rather than her manners. Furthermore, for once, she was receiving a lesson she needed, she acknowledged grudgingly, when she was presented with a formal table setting in the dining room that contained a remarkably bewildering choice of knives, forks and spoons. When that was done, she returned to her room and was seated against the headboard, reading a book she had got in a charity shop, when the door opened with an abrupt lack of warning.

It was Vitale and he was furious, as she had never seen him before. A dark flush lay along his high cheekbones, only contriving to accentuate the flaming gold of his spectacular eyes. 'You spilled it all like an oil gusher!' he condemned wrathfully. 'Don't you have any discretion?'

Stiff with discomfiture, Jazz scrambled off the bed in haste. 'I let one word slip and then there didn't seem much point in holding back,' she admitted ruefully. 'I'm sorry if you didn't want him to know.'

'You were too busy flirting with my brother to worry about what you told him!' Vitale accused fiercely.

Jazz was stunned by that interpretation, particularly when her response to Angel had always been more like a sister with a big brother than anything else. She had never felt the smallest spark in Angel's radius, while Vitale could set her on fire with a careless glance. 'I

wasn't *flirting* with him!' she replied forcefully. 'That's nonsense.'

'I know what I saw,' Vitale sliced in with contempt. 'You were all over him like a rash!'

Anger began to stir within Jazz as she stared up at Vitale, who was towering over her like a particularly menacing stone wall. 'I didn't even touch him, for goodness' sake! What the hell are you trying to imply?' she demanded.

Already struggling to master a fury unlike any he had ever experienced, Vitale stared down at her, his lean brown hands clenched into fists because he felt incredibly violent. Angel was an incorrigible flirt and women went mad for him. Vitale had never had that freedom, that ready repartee or level of experience, and suddenly that lowering awareness infuriated him. His attention zeroed in on Jazz's luscious pink mouth and suddenly he wanted to taste that mouth so badly it hurt, his body surging in a volatile wave straight from rage to sexual hunger. His brain had nothing to do with that unnerving switch.

Vitale snatched her up off her feet and kissed her in a move that so disconcerted her she didn't fight, she only gasped. A split second on, the punishing, passionate force of his hard mouth was smashing down on hers, driving her lips apart, his tongue penetrating that moist and sensitive internal space. She shuddered with reaction, her arms balancing on his shoulders, her hands splaying round the back of his neck, fingers delving into the luxuriant depths of his black hair. A tsunami of excitement quivered through Jazz with every deeply sensual plunge of his tongue. It was like nothing she had ever felt in a man's arms before and the

very intensity of it was mind-blowing because it was everything she had ever dreamt of and nothing she had ever thought she could feel. He could certainly kiss, she thought helplessly, awash with the stimulation spreading through her heated body.

Without warning, it was over and Vitale was setting her back down on the floor, swinging on his heel and walking out again without a word, even closing the door behind him. Jazz almost laughed, her fingers rising to touch her tingling mouth, wild butterflies unleashed in her tummy. Vitale hadn't said a word, which was *so* typical of him. He would walk away and refuse to think about it or talk about it, as if talking about it would make it more damaging.

But Vitale was genuinely in shock, throbbing with such raw sexual arousal he was in pain, dark golden eyes burning with the self-discipline it had taken to tear himself away. She tasted like strawberries and coffee but she had engulfed him like too much alcohol in his veins. He felt strangely disconnected from himself because his reactions, his very behaviour, were unacceptable and abnormal. He could barely credit that he had been so angry that he had wanted to smash his brother through the wall, couldn't begin to explain what had awakened that anger. He loathed every one of those weird feelings and fought to suppress them and bury them deep. He stripped where he stood in his bedroom before heading for the shower.

In comparison, Jazz lay on top of her very comfortable bed and thought about that kiss, the ultimate kiss, which had shot her full of adrenalin, excitement and longing. She felt as if she had been waiting half her life to discover that a kiss could make her feel like that, but

it was a terrible disappointment that Vitale had achieved that feat because there would be no interesting future developments happening in that quarter, she reflected wryly. It was just sex, stupid, confusing sexual urges that had neither sense nor staying power, and she should write it off to a silly impulse and a moment of forgetfulness. He wasn't even the sort of guy she wanted in her life and he never would be. He was too arrogant, too reserved, too quick to judge…but, my goodness, he knew how to kiss…

Fate had short-changed her, she thought resentfully. She was still a virgin because she had always been waiting to meet a man, who would make her crave more of his touch. She had wanted her first lover to be someone whom she desired and cared about. Unfortunately, desire had evaded her in the invasive groping sessions that had been her sad experience as a student. Even worse, she still remembered the emotional hurt inflicted by her father's abuse. How could she trust any man when her own father had attacked her? Jazz had been wary of the opposite sex ever since, even though she was now wishing she had a little more sexual experience because then she would have had a better idea of how to read Vitale and deal with him.

Had her crush on Vitale at fourteen made her more vulnerable? Jazz cringed at the suspicion and dismissed it because she hadn't actively thought about Vitale in years and years. He had only come to mind when she'd seen him in some glossy magazine, squiring some equally superior beauty at some sparkling celebrity event and, like Cinderella in real life, she thought sadly, she had known how impossible her dream had been at fourteen. He was what he was: a prince, born

and bred to a life so different from hers that he might as well have been an alien from another planet. He wasn't a *happy* prince either, she thought with unwilling compassion. Even as an adolescent she had recognised that Vitale didn't really know what being happy was.

When she was informed that she had another coaching session late that afternoon, she was incensed to learn that it was in deportment. She put in the time with the instructor and then knocked on Vitale's office door.

'Yes?' Vitale looked up from his laptop and then sprang upright with the perfect courtesy that was engrained in him. Woman enters room: *stand*, she reflected ruefully, and it took just a little bit of the edge off her temper and the faint unease she had felt at seeing him again so soon after that kiss. It definitely didn't help, though, that he still looked gorgeous to her from the head of his slightly ruffled black hair down to his wonderful dark deep-set eyes that even now were clearly registering wariness. She knew exactly what he was thinking and almost grinned. He was still waiting to be attacked over the kiss.

'Deportment?' she queried drily instead. 'Don't you think that's overkill? I don't slouch and I can walk in a straight line in heels. What more do you want?'

His dark eyes flared gold and he tensed, reining back all that leaping energy of his. 'I thought it might be necessary but if it's not—'

'It's not,' Jazz cut in combatively.

'Then we can wave goodbye to that session,' Vitale conceded mildly, watching her walk across his office to look out of the window. She was wearing that damnably ugly skirt and heels again, but had he been of a literary bent he could have written a poem along the lines

of what that cheap fabric did to the curve of her little rounded bottom where he had had both hands clasped only hours earlier. It had felt every bit as good and femininely lush as it looked, he acknowledged, thoroughly unsettled by that thought and the pulse at his groin. The effect she had on his body was like a kind of madness, he decided then in consternation.

'I have some questions about this bet and you may not think I'm entitled to answers,' Jazz remarked stiffly. 'Who are you planning to say I am at the ball?'

His winged ebony brows drew together in bewilderment. 'What do you mean?'

Jazz threw her shoulders back. 'Well, I assumed you'd be giving me a fake name.'

Vitale frowned, currently engaged in noticing how red and full her lips seemed, wondering if he had been rough because he had *felt* rough, drunk on lust and need, out of control. 'Why would I give you a fake name?'

'Because if I'm pictured with you anywhere the press might go digging and wouldn't they just love pointing out that the Prince has a housekeeper's daughter on his arm?' Jazz extended stiffly, gooseflesh rising in the claustrophobic atmosphere and the intensity of his gaze.

'*So?*' Vitale prompted thickly, acknowledging that kissing her had been one of the most exhilarating encounters he had ever had and cringing at the awareness. He was an adult man with a great sex life, he reminded himself doggedly. As Angel would say, he really needed to get out more.

'Doesn't that bother you?' Jazz asked in surprise.

'No. Why would it? I'm not foisting a fake personality or some sort of scam on the public. This bet is for

private consumption only,' Vitale explained. 'There's nothing wrong with being a housekeeper's daughter.'

'No, there's not,' Jazz agreed with the glimmerings of her first real smile in his presence and the startling realisation that Vitale was not quite the snob she had believed he was. It was as if a giant defensive barrier inside her dropped and, disturbed by the discovery, she quickly turned to leave him alone again.

'Jazz…once you get clothes delivered tomorrow we'll be going out to dinner in the evening,' Vitale informed her, startling her even more. 'Your first public appearance.'

Dining out with Vitale, Jazz ruminated in wonder as she returned to her room, planning an evening composed of a long luxurious bath, washing her hair and watching something on TV.

CHAPTER FOUR

JAZZ COULDN'T SLEEP. Accustomed to a much more physically active existence, she wasn't tired and at two in the morning she put the light back on and tried to read until hunger took over and consumed her. She knew she shouldn't but she loved a slice of toast and a hot drink before bed and the longer she lay awake, the more all-consuming the craving became. Inevitably she got up, raising her brows at her appearance in the faded long tee shirt she wore to bed. No dressing gown, no slippers in her wardrobe but so what? If she was quiet she doubted if she would wake up the very correct Jenkins.

The stairs creaked and she didn't like moving round in total darkness but a light could rouse someone likely to investigate. By touch she located the door at the back of the hall and through that a flight of stairs, which ran down into the basement area where she assumed the kitchen lay. Safely through that door, she put on lights and relaxed. The kitchen was as massive as a hotel kitchen and she padded about on the cold tiles, trying not to shiver. She located bread and the toaster and milk and then, wonder of wonders, some hot-chocolate powder to make her favourite night-time drink. Jazz was grateful she wasn't like her aunt, who

joked that she only had to look at a bar of chocolate to gain an inch on her hips.

Her toast ready, she sat down at the table to eat with appetite, eyes closing blissfully as she munched hot butter-laden toast, which was the first glimpse Vitale had of her as he strode barefoot through the door.

'You can't wander round here in the middle of the night!' he began impatiently. 'My security team wakened me.'

'Your security... *What?*' Jazz gasped, startled out of her life by the interruption and even more startled by the vision Vitale made bare-chested and barefoot, clad only in a pair of tight jeans. He was completely transformed by casual clothing, she conceded in awe.

Vitale groaned out loud. 'The whole house is wired with very sensitive security equipment and I have a full team of bodyguards who monitor it.'

'But I didn't see anything and no alarm went off.'

'It's composed of invisible beams and it's silent. As soon as the team established that it wasn't an intrusion but a member of the household they contacted me, not wishing to frighten you.'

'Well, I'm not frightened of you,' she mumbled round a mouthful of toast that she was trying to masticate enough not to choke when she swallowed because, in reality, Vitale was delicious shorn of his shirt and her mouth had gone all dry.

He was a classic shape, all broad shoulders, rippling muscular torso sprinkled with dark curls of hair leading down into a vee at his hips and a flat, taut stomach. Clothed she could just about contrive to resist him, half-naked he was an intolerable lure to her eyes.

'They saw you on camera, realised that you weren't

fully dressed and surmised that the sudden intrusion of a strange man could scare you.'

'On *camera*?' she repeated in horror, striving to recall if she had scratched or done anything inappropriate while she was in the kitchen, bracing her hands on the table top to rise to her feet and move away from it.

Vitale shifted lean dark hands upward in a soothing motion. 'Relax, they've all been switched off. We're not being monitored right now.'

'Thank goodness for that,' she framed tremulously, the perky tips of her nipples pushing against the tee shirt below Vitale's riveted gaze. 'I only got up to get something to eat.'

'That's perfectly all right,' Vitale assured her thickly, inwardly speculating on whether she was wearing anything at all below the nightshirt or whatever it was. 'But for the future, I'll show you a button you can press just to let security know someone's wandering around the house and this won't happen again.'

'OK,' Jazz muttered, still shaken up at the idea that she had been watched without her knowledge by strange men.

Vitale ran a surprisingly gentle hand down the side of her downturned face. 'It's not a problem. You haven't done anything wrong,' he murmured sibilantly, his accent catching along the edges of his dark, deep, masculine voice.

A shocking flare of heat rose up from the heart of her as he touched her face and Jazz threw her head back in mortification, her green eyes wide with diluted pupils.

'Don't look at me like that,' Vitale framed hoarsely. 'You have the most beautiful eyes... You always did.

And I didn't intend to say that, don't know which random brain cell it came from.'

An overpowering need to smile tilted Jazz's tense lips because he sounded so stressed and so confounded by his own words. Beautiful eyes, well, that was something, her first and probably only ever compliment from Vitale, who worked so hard at keeping his distance. But he had touched her first, she reminded herself with faint pride in what felt vaguely like an achievement. Her body was taut as a bowstring and breathing was a major challenge as she looked up into dark, smouldering golden intensity. Ditto, beautiful eyes, she labelled, but she didn't really think women were supposed to say things like that to men so she kept quiet out of fear that he would laugh.

'*Troppa fantasia*... I have too much imagination,' Vitale breathed, being steadily ripped in two by the conflicting impulses yanking at him. He knew he should let her go and return to bed but he didn't want to. He was ridiculously fascinated that, even in the middle of the night and fresh from her bed with tousled hair, she looked fantastic. And so very different from the women he was used to, women who went to bed in make-up and rose before him to put on another face to greet the dawn, and his awakening, plastic perfect, contrived, artificial, everything that Jazz was not. Jazz was *real* right down to her little naturally pink toenails and that trait was incredibly attractive to him. With Jazz what you saw was literally what you got and there were no pitfalls of strategy or seduction lined up to trip him.

'I would never have thought it,' Jazz almost whispered, so painfully conscious of his proximity that the

little hairs were rising on the back of her neck. 'You're a banker.'

'And I can't have an imagination too?' Vitale inserted with a sudden flashing smile of amusement that would have knocked for six the senses of a stronger woman than Jazz.

'It's unexpected,' she mumbled uncertainly, all of a quiver in receipt of that mesmerising, almost boyish grin. 'You always seem so serious.'

'I don't feel serious around you,' Vitale admitted, tiring of looking down at her and getting a crick in his neck. In a sudden movement that took her very much by surprise, he bent, closed his hands to her tiny waist and lifted her up. He settled her down on the end of the table. He was incredibly, ferociously aroused but Jazz seemed curiously unaware of the chemistry between them, almost innocent. No way could she be *that* innocent, he told himself urgently, because he would never touch an innocent woman and he desperately needed to touch her. His lovers were always experienced women, who knew the score.

'But then you never know what you're feeling,' Jazz quipped. 'You're not into self-analysis.'

'How do you know that?' Vitale demanded with a frown.

'I see it in you,' Jazz told him casually.

Vitale didn't like the conversation, didn't want to talk either. He spread his hands to either side of her triangular face and he tasted that alluring pink mouth with unashamed passion.

Jazz was afraid her heart was about to leap right out of her chest, her breathlessness as physical as her inability to think that close to him. She felt nebulously

guilty, as if on some level her brain was striving to warn her that she was doing something wrong, but she absolutely refused to listen to that message when excitement was rushing like fire through her nerve endings. Her nipples tightened, her slender thighs pushing firmly together on the embarrassing dampness gathering at the apex of her legs.

'Per l'amor di Dio...' Vitale swore, fighting for control because he was already aching. 'What do you do to me?'

'What *do* I do to you?' Jazz whispered, full of curiosity.

She excited the hell out of him but he was too experienced to let that salient fact drop from his lips. 'You tempt me beyond my control,' Vitale heard himself admit regardless and was shocked by the reality.

'That's all right,' Jazz breezed, one hand smoothing up over a high cheekbone, the roughness of his stubbled jaw lending a brooding darkness to his lean, strong face in the dimly lit kitchen, her other hand tracing an exploring path up over the sweep of his long, smooth back. 'Are you sure those cameras are all off?' she framed, peering anxiously round the brightly lit kitchen.

'*All* of them,' Vitale stressed, but he strode back to the door to douse the strong overhead illumination, plunging them into a much more welcoming and more intimate space only softly lit by the lights below the cupboards.

Her hand slid back to his spine. His skin was hot, faintly damp but it was his eyes she was watching and thinking about, those beautiful black-fringed eyes singing a clear song of stress and bewilderment and the glorious liberating message that he wasn't any more

in charge of what was happening between them than she was.

'I want you, *bellezza mia*,' he growled all soft and rough, sending shimmying awareness right down her taut spine just as he reached down and lifted her tee shirt and whipped it off over her head.

Jazz loosed a startled yelp and almost whipped her hands up to cover her naked body, but in that same split second of dismay she asked herself if she wanted to be a virgin for ever and if she would ever have the chance to have such a skilled lover, as Vitale was almost certain to be, again. And the answer to both questions was no. He wasn't going to want a shy woman, was he? And he had to know all the right moves to ensure the experience was good for her, hadn't he?

'You are *so* beautiful,' Vitale almost crooned, his hands rising to cup her delicate little breasts, which were topped with taut rosy tips that he stroked appreciatively with his thumb.

And that fast, Jazz had no desire to either cover up or breathe because the fabulous joy and satisfaction of being deemed beautiful by Vitale overwhelmed her. In gratitude, she stretched up to find his mouth again for herself, nibbling at his lower lip, circling slowly with newly discovered sensuality while all the time he was stroking and rolling and squeezing the peaks of her breasts that she had never known could be so responsive to a man's touch. Little fiery arrows were travelling down to the heart of her, making her hips shift and squirm on the table as the heat and tightness increased there. And then, with what felt like very little warning to her, a climax shot through her like an electric charge, making her cry out in surprise and pleasure.

'And as responsive as my most erotic dream,' Vitale husked, wrenching at the zip of his jeans.

A lean brown hand pried her legs apart while she was still in a sort of blissful cocoon of reaction. Vitale pulled her closer and tipped her back to facilitate his intentions. A long finger traced her entrance and eased inside. He uttered a hungry groan of appreciation because she was very wet and tight and then he froze. 'I'll have to take you upstairs to get a condom,' he bit out in frustration.

'I'm on birth control,' Jazz muttered helpfully. 'But are you...safe?'

'Yes because I've never had sex without a condom,' Vitale confided, but the temptation to try it without that barrier was huge. He tried to argue with himself but, poised between her legs, craving the welcome her slender, lithe body offered his raging arousal, he realised it was a lost battle for him before it even started.

With strong hands he eased her closer still and she felt him, hard and demanding against her most tender flesh, and both nerves and eagerness assailed her. Her whole body came alive with electrified longing as if that first redemptive taste of pleasure had ignited an unquenchable fire of need inside her. He sank into her by easy degrees, groaning something out loud in Italian as she buried her face against a satin-smooth brown shoulder, barely crediting she was making love with Vitale, every sense she possessed rioting with sensation, the very smell and taste of his skin thrilling her.

And then he slammed right to the heart of her and a stinging pain made her grit her teeth and jerk in reaction. Withdrawing a little, Vitale paused for an instant, pushing up her face and looking down at her with what

appeared to be brazen incredulity, and she knew then that at the very least he suspected he had been her first lover and he wasn't pleased. But she ignored that unwelcome suspicion and wriggled her hips with feminine encouragement, watching him react and groan with a newly learned sense of empowerment.

'Don't stop,' she told him.

And for the very first time ever, Vitale did exactly as she told him. He sank deeper again, stretching the tender walls of her heated core with hungry thoroughness and, that instant of pain forgotten, Jazz craved his contact. He gave her more, picking up speed, hard and fast until he was pounding into her and her excitement climbed with his every fluid, forceful thrust. It was much wilder and infinitely more uninhibited than she had dimly expected from a man as reserved as Vitale; indeed it was passionately explosive. She reached another climax and her body convulsed around his, the whole world, it seemed, erupting around her as he shot her into a deeply erotic and exhilarating release. A faint ache pulled at her as he withdrew and zipped his jeans.

'*Diavolo!*' Vitale exclaimed, stepping back from her while she fumbled for her tee shirt and hurriedly pulled it on over her head with hands that felt clumsy and unable to do her bidding. 'Why the hell didn't you tell me you were a virgin?'

Fixing her face to a determined blank, Jazz slid off the table, only just resisting a revealing moan as discomfort travelled through her lower body. 'We're not having a post-mortem,' she parried sharply, mortification engulfing her in an unanticipated tide that threatened to drown her. 'You're not entitled to ask nosy questions.'

She had had sex on a kitchen table with Vitale and she couldn't quite believe it but she certainly knew she didn't intend to linger to discuss it!

For a split second of frustration, Vitale wanted to strangle her. Her hectically flushed face was mutinous and furious and she was pointedly avoiding looking at him, which annoyed the hell out of him even though he didn't understand why. After all, he didn't want a post-mortem either, didn't have a clue why or how what they had just done had happened and could think of at least ten good reasons why it *shouldn't* have happened.

He watched her limp across the tiled floor as if she had had a run-in with a bus instead of her first experience of sex and he felt hellishly guilty and responsible. He experienced a sudden, even more startling desire to scoop her up and sink her into a warm reviving bath... and then have sex with her again? As if that were likely to improve anything, he reflected sardonically, raking unsteady fingers through his tousled black hair. What the hell was wrong with him? His brain was all over the place and he couldn't think straight but he knew he had just enjoyed the best sex of his life and that was downright terrifying...

Jazz had informed Vitale that there would be no post-mortem but, seated in a bath at three in the morning, Jazz was unhappily engaged in staging her own. Had she actually thought of what they had done as 'making love'? Yes, she had and she was so ashamed of herself for that fanciful label because she really wasn't *that* naïve. It had been sex, pure and simple, and she knew the difference because she wasn't a dreamy teenager any longer, she was an adult. Or *supposed* to be, she

thought with tears stinging the backs of her eyes and regret digging wires of steel through her shrinking body.

Of course, they would both pretend it hadn't happened…a moment of madness, the mistake swiftly buried and forgotten. After all, this was Vitale she was
dealing with and he wasn't going to want to talk about
it either. On that front, therefore, she was safe, she assured herself soothingly. It was his fault in any case—
he had had no business parading around half-naked in
jeans and tempting her into that insanity. She hugged
her knees in the warm water and sighed. She had done
a stupid, stupid thing and now she had to live with it
and with Vitale for weeks and weeks, being all polite
and standoffish, lest he think she was up for a repeat
encounter. Running away or hiding wasn't an option.

A knock sounded lightly on the door and she almost
reared out of the bath in her horror because she abruptly
appreciated that Vitale was *not* running true to form.
In a blind panic she snatched at a towel and wrapped
it round her, opening the door the merest chink to say
discouragingly, 'Yes?'

Vitale discovered that he was immediately possessed by an impossibly strong urge to smash the door
down and he gritted his teeth on yet another unfamiliar prompting to act unreasonably and violently. 'Will
you please come out? You have been in there for ages.'

From that point he wasn't the only individual val-
iantly gritting teeth. Her flushed face frozen as he had
never seen it before, Jazz emerged from the bathroom,
noting that he had put on a black shirt. 'I didn't know
you were waiting,' she said dulcetly, leaning heavily on
her one and only elocution lesson.

'Look, don't go all girlie on me. I don't expect that

from you,' Vitale countered crushingly. 'I only want the answer to one question.'

Jazz tried to unfreeze a little and look normal, or as normal as she could feel being confronted by Vitale when she was wearing only a towel. 'OK.'

'Why is a virgin on birth control?' he asked gravely.

'I don't really think that's any of your business. It was for…well, medical reasons,' she told him obliquely, unwilling to discuss her menstrual cycle with him, her colour heightening until she felt like a beetroot being roasted and wanted to slap him for it.

'It will be very much my business if you get pregnant,' Vitale breathed witheringly.

'It's so like you to look on the dark side and expect the very worst,' Jazz replied equally witheringly. 'It's not going to happen, Vitale. Relax and go back to bed and please forget this ever happened for both our sakes.'

'Is that what you want?' Vitale wanted to rip off the towel and continue even though he knew she was in no condition to satisfy him again. It had nothing whatsoever to do with his brain. It was pretty much as if his body had developed an agenda all of its own and he couldn't control it.

'We just had a sleazy encounter on a kitchen table in the middle of the night. What do you think?' Jazz enquired saccharine sweet.

Vitale was receiving a strong impression that anything he said would be taken down and held against him. *Sleazy?* That single descriptive word outraged him. He swung on his heel, his lean, powerful body taut, and left the room and just as quickly Jazz wanted to kick him for giving up on her so easily. Her thoughts were a turbulent sea of conflict and confusion and self-loath-

ing, sending her seesawing from one extreme to the other. No sooner was he gone than she wanted him back and she flung off the towel and climbed into bed, hating herself. It was so typical of Vitale to worry about the fact that he hadn't used contraception. Now he would be waiting on that axe to fall and that was a humiliating prospect, even though it also reminded her that she hadn't yet taken her daily pill. She dug into her bag and took it before switching off the light.

What was done was done and it had been amazing, she thought ruefully, but it was better not to think about that imprudent sudden intimacy that had changed everything between them. Now she was no longer thinking about Vitale as the boy he had once been, but Vitale, very much a man in the present and that switch in outlook disturbed her, made her fear that somewhere deep down inside her there was still a tiny kernel of the fourteen-year-old who had believed the sun rose and set on Prince Vitale Castiglione...

CHAPTER FIVE

'WOMEN MY AGE don't wear clothes like this,' Jazz was saying by late morning the next day, appalled by the vast collection of garments, all distinguished solely by their lack of personality. 'I'm not your future wife or one of your relatives. I'm supposed to be only a girl-friend. Why would I be dressed like an older woman?'

'I want you to be elegant,' Vitale responded, unim-pressed by her reasoning. He wanted every bit of her covered up. He didn't want her showing off her shapely legs or her fabulous figure for other men to drool over. Recognising Angel's appreciation of the beauty Jazz had become had been quite sufficient warning on that score. 'I imagine you would prefer to show more flesh.'

That was the last straw for Jazz after a trying few hours of striving to behave normally when she did see Vitale between coaching sessions. Temper pushed up through her like lava seeking a crack to escape. 'Where do you get all these prejudices about me from?' she demanded hotly. 'I don't wear revealing clothes. I never have. And as you know I haven't got much to reveal!'

'You have more than enough for me, *bellezza mia*,' Vitale breathed half under his breath, heat stirring at

his groin as he thought about the delectable little swells he had explored the night before.

Jazz flinched and acted studiously deaf in receipt of that tactless reminder. He was no good at pretending, she recognised ruefully. 'This stuff is all so bland,' she complained instead, fingering a pair of tailored beige trousers with a curled lip. There was a lot of beige, a lot of navy and a lot of brown. He was even biased against bright colour. 'If this is your taste, you certainly didn't miss out on a chance of fame in the fashion industry.'

Vitale reached a decision and signalled the stylist waiting at the far end of the very large room. 'Miss Dickens is in charge of the selections. By the sound of it, she will be ordering a more adventurous wardrobe,' he declared, watching the slow smile that lit up Jazz's piquant little face while smoothly congratulating himself on knowing when to ease up on exerting control. 'But pick out something here to wear tonight.'

Jazz chose a fitted navy dress and shoes and lingerie as well as a bag.

'Thanks!' she called in Vitale's wake as he left her alone with the stylist to share her own likes and dislikes.

His arrogant dark head turned in acknowledgement, brilliant dark-fringed eyes a fiery gold enticement, and desire punched her so hard in the chest that she paled, stricken that she could have made herself so vulnerable. Putting such pointless thoughts from her mind, she concentrated on choosing clothes and particularly on the necessary selection of a spectacular gown for the royal ball.

After asking for lunch to be served in her room she was free to go home and visit her family for a few hours, and it was a welcome break from the hothouse atmo-

sphere of Vitale's imposing London home. Her mother
and her aunt were baking and Jazz sat down with a cup
of tea and tried to feel normal again.

But she didn't feel normal after she had put on the
navy dress over the silk lingerie, her feet shod in hand-
stitched leather sandals with smart heels. Although she
had never bothered much with make-up she made a special effort with mascara and lipstick, knowing that that
was one thing she did need that Vitale probably hadn't
thought about: make-up lessons.

'No, I like you the way you are,' Vitale asserted, startling her in the limo on the way out to dinner. 'Natural, healthy. You have beautiful skin… Why cover it?'

Jazz shifted an uncertain shoulder. 'Because it's what
women do… They make the most of themselves.'

Vitale studied her from his corner of the limo. She
looked stunning, the dark dress throwing her amazing hair into prominence and emphasising her delicate
figure and long slender legs. He willed his arousal to
subside because he had made decisions earlier that day.
He was going to step back, play safe, ensure that there
was no more sex, no more blurring of the lines between
them, but he only had to look at her to find his resolution wavering.

That had never happened to Vitale before with a
woman. He had never succumbed to an infatuation,
had always assumed that he simply wasn't the emotional type. His affairs were always cool and sexual,
nothing extra required or needed on either side. Naturally he had been warned since he was a teenager that
he would, in all likelihood, have to marry for dynastic reasons rather than love and he had always guarded
himself on the emotional front. What he felt for Jazz

was desire, irresistible burning desire, and there was no great mystery about that when it was simply hormones, he told himself soothingly.

A current of discreetly turned heads and a low buzz of comment surrounded their passage to their table in the wildly exclusive restaurant where they were to dine. Vitale's gaze glittered like black diamonds when he saw other men directing lustful looks at Jazz. For the moment, Jazz was *his*, absolutely his, whether he was having sex with her or otherwise, he reasoned stubbornly.

Jazz sat down, surveying the table to become belatedly grateful for Jenkins's lesson in cutlery clarification. 'So, tell me what you've been doing since you left school?' she invited him cheerfully. 'Apart from being a prince and all that.'

They talked about being students. Vitale admitted that banking had been the only viable option for him. He also told her that he had a house in Italy where he planned to take her before the ball.

'For how long?' she asked, her lovely face pensive in the candlelight, which picked up every fiery hue in her multi-shaded red mane of hair for his appreciation. 'I like to see my mother regularly.'

'A couple of weeks, no more. When this is over, *after* the ball—' Vitale shifted a fluid, lean brown hand in emphasis '—I will pay for you to finish your degree so that you can work in your chosen field.'

'That's a very generous offer but you're already covering quite enough in the financial line,' she began in surprise and some embarrassment.

'No. I tricked you,' Vitale divulged, disconcerting her even more with that abrupt confession of wrong-

doing. 'My father is settling your mother's loans. He wanted to. It makes him feel that he has helped her.'

'You...*tricked*...me?' Jazz gasped in disbelief that he could quietly admit that.

'Being a bastard comes naturally. I needed you to accept the bet and I used *your* need for money to win your agreement,' Vitale pointed out levelly. 'I feel that I owe you that amount of honesty because you have been honest with me.'

'So, you're saying your father would *always* have helped?' Jazz prodded in even greater surprise because she wasn't, once she thought about it, that shocked to discover that Vitale could be extremely calculating and shrewd. She didn't, however, feel that she was in a position to complain or protest because if he had used her to suit his own purposes, she was also most assuredly using *him*. Having already received a discreet cheque in payment for her supposed salary, she had given it in its entirety to her mother. No, she wasn't proud that she had accepted money from a man she had also slept with, but she really could not bear to watch her mother scrimp and struggle. Being seriously poor had taught Jazz a lot of tough life lessons.

'Papa feels very guilty about your mother. He was concerned that there was a possibility of domestic abuse in your parents' marriage...' Vitale volunteered very quietly after their plates had been cleared away.

Jazz turned sheet white and her fingers curled into the tablecloth, scrunching it. 'There was,' she conceded, thrown back in time to a period she rarely revisited. 'My father was violent when life didn't go his way and he took it out on us.'

Vitale was appalled and then shocked that he was

appalled because he had heard of such situations, but then he had never personally known anyone who confessed to being a victim of domestic abuse. 'You…as well as your mother?'

'On several occasions when I tried to protect Mum. Poor Mum got the worst of it,' Jazz conceded heavily. 'Dad was hooked on online gambling and when he lost money he took it out on his family with his fists.'

A very real stab of anger coursed through Vitale at that news. He was remembering Jazz as a tiny child and a skinny teen and realising that she knew what it was to live in fear within a violent home where she should have been safe. His strong jawline was rigid. 'I'm sorry you had to go through that experience.'

Jazz pursed her lips and sighed. 'I think that was why Mum ran off with her second husband, Jeff. He was supposed to be her escape but he was more of a dead end. He wasn't violent, just dishonest. But you know, the older I get, the more I realise that many people have had bad experiences when they were young,' she told him in an upbeat tone. 'It doesn't have to define you and it doesn't have to hold you back and make you distrust everyone you meet. You can move beyond it. I know I have.'

Vitale stretched out a hand and squeezed hers to make her release the tablecloth and she laughed and let go of it when she appreciated what she had been doing, her lack of self-pity and her strength delighting him.

'I have the mother from hell,' he confessed unexpectedly. 'Controlling, domineering, very nasty. If she has a heart, I've never seen it. All she cares about is the Lerovian throne and all the pomp and ceremony that go with it.'

Jazz smiled, pleased that he trusted her enough to

admit that. 'You're very lucky to have such a pleasant father, then,' she pointed out.

'*Sì*...' Vitale confirmed, startled that he had spoken ill of his mother for the first time ever and quite unable to explain where those disloyal words had come from. There was something odd about Jazz that provoked him into acting against his own nature, he decided darkly. Maybe it was simply the fact that she was so relaxed in his company that she broke through his reserve. Was that why he was acting out of character?

As for the problem that was his mother, he had only told the truth, he reasoned ruefully. Sofia Castiglione was feared even by the royal household. It was not disloyalty to tell the truth, he acknowledged then, while marvelling that in admitting that salient fact to Jazz he felt some of his tension drop away.

Outside the restaurant, the limousine awaited them, two security guards forcing a man with a camera to back off. The flash of a photo being taken momentarily blinded her as Vitale guided her at speed back into the limo.

'Who is she?' another voice shouted.

'Who am I?' she teased Vitale with amusement as she settled back into her seat.

'A mystery redhead. I will not give out your name. I have no intention of doing the work of the paparazzi for them,' Vitale supplied, his attention locked to her small, vivid face, so pale against the backdrop of that mass of vibrant hair, fine freckles scattered across her diminutive nose. Hands off, he reminded himself doggedly even as he ached.

'Do you want a drink?' he enquired as they entered the house.

'No, thanks. I'm sort of tired,' she admitted, because she had had little sleep the night before, but she was not about to allude to that reality when Vitale was behaving like a perfect gentleman who had never once touched her. 'Goodnight.'

She kicked off her shoes inside her room, feeling oddly lonely, and wriggled down the zip on her dress to peel it off and hang it up with the care demanded by a superior garment. She stripped and freshened up before reaching for the silky robe she had taken from the clothes selection earlier that day and that was when someone rapped on the door and it opened almost simultaneously.

Vitale strode in, leant back against the door to close it again and said thickly, 'I don't want to say goodnight…'

Surprised in the act of frantically tying the sash on her robe closed, Jazz literally stopped breathing. Smouldering dark golden eyes assailed hers in an almost physical assault and her heart started banging inside her chest like a drum. 'But we—'

'We are both single, free to do whatever we like,' Vitale incised, suppressing every thought he had had, every decision he had made only hours earlier in favour of surrendering to the hunger that had flamed up inside him the instant she'd tried to walk away from him.

Air bubbled back into her lungs and she snatched in a sudden deep breath. *'But,'* she started afresh, inexplicably feeling that *she* had to be the voice of reason.

Vitale prowled forward with the grace of a jungle cat. 'Is there anyone else in your life?'

'Of course not. If there had been, last night wouldn't have happened,' she protested.

'Then I don't see a problem, *bellezza mia,*' Vitale pro-

claimed in a roughened undertone as he teased loose the knot in the sash in a very slow way. 'Let's keep it simple.'

Simple? But it *wasn't* simple, she wanted to scream while knowing that he was taking his time with the sash to give her the opportunity to say no if she wanted to. But she didn't want to say no, didn't want him to leave her again and that disturbing awareness shook her up. Her heart was thumping so hard she could've been in the last stage of running a marathon and all she could see was Vitale ahead of her, those scorching dark golden eyes with a black fringe of gold-tipped lush lashes that a supermodel would have envied. Somehow, *he* was her finishing line and she couldn't fight that, didn't have that amount of resistance when he was right there in front of her, wanting her, *needing* her, Jazmine Dickens, against all the odds...

He eased the robe off her slight shoulders and let it drop and when her hands whipped up to cover herself, he groaned and forestalled her, trapping her small hands in his. 'I want to see you, *all* of you.'

Her hands fell away, green eyes wide with uncertainty, and he lifted her up, threw back the covers on the bed and laid her down.

'You're wearing too many clothes,' she told him shakily.

Vitale dealt her a slanting grin that lit up his lean, darkly handsome features like the sunrise. He undressed with almost military precision, stowing cuff links by the bed, stacking his suit on a chair, peeling off snug black briefs that could barely contain his urgent arousal. A slow burn ignited in her pelvis, her nipples tinging into tight buds, a melting sensation warming between her thighs.

It was only sex, she bargained fiercely with the troubled thoughts she was refusing to acknowledge, only sex and lots of people had sex simply for fun. She could be the same, she swore to herself, she would *not* make the mistake of believing that what they had was anything more serious than a casual affair. That was what Vitale had meant when he said, 'Let's keep it simple…'

He joined her on the bed, all hair-roughened brown skin and rippling muscle, so wonderfully, fundamentally different from hers, the sexual allure of his body calling to her as much as her body seemed to call to him. He kissed her and the fireworks started inside her, heat and longing rising exponentially with every searing dip of his tongue inside the moist interior of her mouth.

Her entire body felt sensitised, on an edge of unbearable anticipation.

'I want to show you the way it should have been last night,' Vitale husked. 'Last night was rough and ready.'

'But it worked,' she mumbled unevenly, running a forefinger along the wide sensual line of his lips, revelling in the freedom to do so.

'You deserve more,' Vitale insisted, bending his arrogant dark head to catch a swollen pink nipple in his mouth and tease it. 'Much more…'

And much more was very much what she got as Vitale worked a purposeful passage down over her slender length, pausing in places she hadn't even known had nerve endings and dallying there until she was writhing in abandonment, before finally settling between her spread thighs and addressing his attention to the most sensitive place of all.

Self-consciousness was drowned by excitement, sheer physical excitement that she could not restrain. He

used his mouth on her, circling, flicking, working her body as though it were an instrument and her pleasure grew by tormentingly sweet degrees until the tightness banding her pelvis became a formless, overwhelming need she could no longer withstand. When he traced the entrance to her lush opening, her spine arched and she cried out as a drowning flood of pleasure surged through her slight body and left her limp.

'Much better,' Vitale pronounced hoarsely, staring down at her enraptured expression with satisfaction. 'That's how it should have been the first time and if you'd warned me—'

'You probably wouldn't have continued,' Jazz interrupted, tying him back down to earth again with that frank assessment.

'You don't know that,' Vitale argued fierily, pushing back her slim thighs and sliding between them, the urgency in his lean, strong body unashamed.

Jazz looked up at him, wondering how she knew it, but know it she did even though it wasn't very diplomatic to drop it on him like that when he was so hopeless at grasping the way his own mind worked. 'I suspected it,' she admitted.

'Nothing short of an earthquake would have stopped me last night!' Vitale swore vehemently, finally surging into her moist, tender sheath with a bone-deep groan of appreciation. 'You feel glorious, *bellezza mia…*'

And the powerful surge of his thick, rigid length into her sensitive core felt equally glorious to Jazz, stretching the inner walls, filling her tight. Her eyes closed and her head rolled back on the pillow as she let the pulsing pleasure consume her. Ripples of delight quivered through her and she arched up her hips, helpless

in the grip of her need. Nothing had ever felt so right or so necessary to her. He ground his body into hers and she saw stars behind her lowered eyelids. She began to move against him, hot and frenzied as he slammed into her, primal excitement seizing her with his heart thundering over hers. And then she reached a ravishing peak and rhythmic convulsions clenched her womb as he shuddered over her with an uninhibited shout of satisfaction. A rush of sensation washed her away in the aftermath of lingering pleasure.

'It's amazing with you,' Vitale gritted breathlessly, releasing her from his weight.

Jazz stretched out her arms and tried to snatch him back. 'Don't move away.'

'I'm not into hugging.'

'Tough,' Jazz told him, snuggling up to him regardless. 'I need hugs.'

Vitale's big body literally froze, tested out of his comfort zone.

'It's called compromise and we are all capable of it,' Jazz muttered drowsily against his chest, one arm anchoring round him like an imprisoning chain. 'I'm not telling you I love you because I *don't*. I'm just fond of you, so don't make a fuss about nothing.'

In a quandary, Vitale, who had been planning to return to his own room, lay staring up at the ceiling. He had to stretch away from her to switch off the light, but she hooked him back with the efficiency of a retriever picking up game even though from the sound of her even breathing he knew she was definitely asleep.

She was so blunt, he reflected helplessly, wondering if he should simply push her away to make it back to his own bed. He was relieved that she had no evi-

dent illusions about their relationship and wasn't thinking along the lines of love because he didn't want to hurt her. Seducing a virgin was a dangerous game, he acknowledged, wondering why she had still been untouched, wondering why he was even interested because his interest in his lovers was usually very superficial. He didn't quite know how he had ended up having sex with her again and wondered if it mattered. He decided it didn't and if he slept with her, he could have her again in the morning, so staying put made very good sense...

'Could we just rough it for a night?' Jazz asked hopefully a week later.

Vitale frowned. 'Rough it?'

'Instead of going to some very fancy restaurant, we could go to a supper club I know that does ethnic dishes. It's cheap but the food's great.' Studying his unenthusiastic expression, Jazz grimaced. 'Vitale, just for once can we go off the official map?'

'I don't follow an official map,' Vitale argued, meeting hopeful eyes and simply wanting to see the liveliness return to her lovely face, which was telegraphing her conviction that he would refuse her suggestion. 'All right, just this once but if either of us get food poisoning, you're dead!'

'We're not going to get food poisoning,' she assured him with a confident grin.

They ate a delicious and surprisingly elaborate five-course meal in a private city garden and Vitale drank out of a bottle without complaint and watched Jazz sparkle across the table. He was more relaxed than he could ever remember being with a woman. She had so much verve and personality he couldn't take his eyes off her

and the awareness that he was taking her home to bed gave him a supreme high of satisfaction.

A week later she dragged him out to the flower market on Columbia Road and he took a photograph of her, her slender figure almost lost in the giant armful of flowers he had bought her. They walked along the South Bank and he watched street performers entertain for the first time ever, laughing when she called him a stuffed shirt for admitting that.

'You can't always have been so sensible, so careful about everything you do and say,' she remarked with a frown.

'I learned to consider everything I did and said when I was very young,' Vitale confided. 'As a child, I was always trying to please my mother but eventually I gave up. I don't think she much likes children…or maybe it was only me.'

Jazz was shocked. 'You don't think she liked you even as a child?'

Vitale frowned. 'If being a queen hadn't demanded that she produce an heir I don't think she would ever have had children. I was a typical little boy—noisy, dirty and always asking inconvenient questions. She often cut short the time she was supposed to spend with me because I irritated her.'

'But you were only being a normal kid,' Jazz contended feelingly, catching his taut fingers in hers to squeeze them and gazing up at his shadowed features. 'That wasn't about you, it was about her and her flaws, not yours. Obviously she didn't enjoy being a mother but that wasn't your problem and you shouldn't let it make you feel guilty or responsible. You're an adult now and you don't need her the same way.'

That was certainly true, Vitale conceded, thinking back to his cold, distant relationship with his mother and his once childish efforts to improve it and win her approval. But as an adult he *knew* Sofia Castiglione now and he no longer expected her to change or tried to please her. Maturity had taught him that he was tough enough to get by on his own.

'I don't feel guilty,' he told Jazz, 'but I do get embarrassed when she treats people badly. When you're born into a privileged life like ours, you can't take it for granted and you can't afford to forget that you rule, not just by right of birth but only with the agreement and the support of the people.'

He was a deeper thinker than she had ever acknowledged and she was impressed by that distinction that he made. By the sound of it, his mother was a right old horror, she thought ruefully, annoyed that Vitale had clearly been so damaged by the wretched woman's inability to love her son. That night she lay awake for a long time, secure in the circle of Vitale's arms, thinking with warm appreciation of how tender he could be with her even though he had evidently had very little tenderness shown to him. He was so much more than he seemed on the outside…

'But I can't be… I'm flying to Italy tomorrow,' Jazz framed without comprehension because what she had been told had come as such a gigantic shock that every scrap of natural colour had drained from her rigid face.

'You're pregnant, around six weeks along,' the brisk female doctor repeated quietly.

'But I'm on the pill!' Jazz exclaimed shakily. 'How can I be pregnant?'

The doctor consulted her computer screen. 'I see you've been taking the mini pill for menstrual irregularity. Have you been careful to take it at the same time every day? It can be a little less effective as birth control than other methods. For contraceptive purposes, I would have recommended an implant.'

'The *same* time every day?' Jazz gasped in dismay.

'That information would've been in the instruction leaflet with the tablets.'

Jazz winced, acknowledging an own goal. 'I didn't read it.'

The doctor gave her a résumé of the various conditions that could make the birth-control pill less reliable and then added that nothing was one hundred per cent guaranteed to prevent pregnancy and that there was always a tiny proportion of women who still conceived regardless.

Jazz was in so much shock that she collided with someone as she left the surgery and spluttered an apology before she wandered aimlessly down the street into a café to sit with a cup of tea and contemplate her predicament. Vitale would go spare, that was all she could initially think. He might even think she had done it deliberately and had lied about being on the pill. Vitale was a naturally suspicious man when it came to women.

Other thoughts began to intrude. She was pregnant. She hadn't thought she could be when the nurse had asked for samples on her first visit to the surgery. No chance, she had cheerfully told the nurse, secure in her conviction that she could not conceive. But she had gone to the surgery in the first place because she was having troublesome symptoms. Very tender breasts, heartburn,

occasional bouts of dizziness, increasing nausea and a sensitivity towards certain smells. Ironically she had suspected the pill, the only medication she took, might be causing those effects and had thought she might be offered another brand to try. Oh, dear heaven, what was she going to tell her mother? Her mother would be so disappointed in her daughter when she became a single parent…

Jazz heaved a distraught sigh, her eyes stinging madly. Peggy Dickens had always been very frank about the reality that *she* had had to get married back in the days in Ireland when a man was still expected to marry a pregnant girlfriend. She had admitted that she would never have married her daughter's father otherwise because she had already seen worrying evidence of his violent temper. Well, there would be no question of marriage to worry anyone, Jazz reflected limply. Vitale was highly unlikely to propose to a housekeeper's daughter, whom he had hired to fulfil a bet.

But Jazz also knew that she wanted her baby. Her baby, part of her *and* Vitale, which was an unexpectedly precious thought, she acknowledged. And it would be a royal baby too, she reflected, because Vitale *was* a prince. Although maybe her baby wouldn't be royal, she reasoned hesitantly, because their child would be born illegitimate. They were only involved in a casual sexual affair, she reminded herself with painful honesty, because on some level that truth made her feel ashamed, as though she secretly thought she had traded herself too cheaply. There was, after all, nothing solid or secure about their current intimacy. For the sake of the bet, Vitale had trotted her out to dinner several times

and once to a West End showing of a new film. Only it still wasn't a *real* relationship, was it?

For six weeks, she had suppressed the wounding fear that she was merely a convenient sexual outlet for Vitale because she was living in the same house. The only time he didn't share her bed was when he was travelling on business or returning to Lerovia to appear at some royal function. Should she have kicked him out of bed?

A rueful smile tilted Jazz's generous mouth. Pride said one thing, her heart said another. She loved having Vitale in her bed and his uninhibited hunger for her delighted her. Was that why she had never once said no? He behaved as though he needed her and that made her feel special and important. Perhaps that fiery sexual intimacy wasn't very much to celebrate but it was certainly more than she had ever hoped to have with Vitale and it made her happy.

Now it seemed that she was paying the price for that freewheeling happiness. She must have conceived right at the beginning of their relationship, she reckoned heavily, to be already six whole weeks along. What was she going to do if he asked her to have a termination? She would simply have to tell him that she was very sorry but, while her pregnancy might be unplanned and inconvenient, she still wanted her child. *His* child too, she conceded wretchedly, digging out her phone to text him.

We need to talk when you get back tonight.

Problem?

Don't try to second-guess me.

She knew that if she wasn't careful he would dig and dig by text until he got it out of her, and it really wasn't something she was prepared to divulge remotely.

The phone pinged and kept on pinging with more texts. More questions for clarification, Vitale getting increasingly impatient and annoyed with her for her lack of response. Maybe she shouldn't have said anything at all, maybe that would have been more sensible. But Jazz had always suffered from the kind of almost painful honest streak that made immediate confession a necessity. She ignored her phone and stared down into her tea, feeling as if the world had crashed down on her shoulders because her discovery meant that she and Vitale were already over and done.

The end, she thought melodramatically because what little they had would not survive the fallout from a pregnancy that she already knew he didn't want.

'Leave your phone alone!' Sofia Castiglione, the Queen of Lerovia, snapped furiously at her son in the office of the royal palace. 'I want you to look at these profiles.'

Vitale resisted even glancing fleetingly down at the women's photographs lined up on his mother's glass desk and the neatly typed background info set beside each. Even a glance would encourage his mother's delusions and he refused to be bullied by her. 'I've already made it clear that I have no intention of getting married *any* time in the near future. It's pointless to play this game with me. It's not as though you want to step down from the throne. It's not as though we are in need of another generation in waiting,' he intoned drily.

'You are almost thirty years old!' his mother practically spat at him. 'I married in my twenties.'

'And think of how well that turned out,' her son advised sardonically, recognising that his mother appeared to dislike him even more now than she had disliked him when he was a child and wondering if that was his fault.

As a little boy he had found her scorn and constant criticism profoundly distressing. He had soon discovered that even when he excelled at something he did not receive praise. For a long time he had struggled to understand what it was about him that evidently made him so deeply unlovable. Did he remind her of his father? Or was it simply that she would have resented any son or daughter waiting in the royal wings to become her heir? Or was Jazz right and was it simply that his mother disliked children?

'Don't you *dare* say that to me!' the older woman launched in a tone of pure venom, her heavily Botoxed and still-beautiful face straining with rage. 'I did my duty and produced an heir and I expect *you* to do your duty now as well!'

'No, possibly in another ten years, *not now*,' Vitale spelt out with emphatic finality and strode out of the room to continue texting Jazz, whose refusal to reply was seriously taxing his already shredded temper.

CHAPTER SIX

'I SAW IT at the airport,' Vitale lied, because for some reason Jazz was staring at the very expensive snow globe he had bought her as though it had risen up out of hell accompanied by the devil waving a pitchfork.

Jazz could feel silly tears flooding her eyes, knew it was probably another side effect of pregnancy and inwardly cringed. Why now? Why now, this evening of all evenings, did he have to do something really thoughtful and generous? It was the snow globe to top all other snow globes too, she acknowledged numbly, large, gilded and magnificent, full of little flying cupids, whose wings looked suspiciously diamond-studded and, when you shook it, it rained golden snow rather than white. It put her Santa globe to shame, lowering it to plastic bargain-basement level.

'It's really, really beautiful,' she told him chokily because it was, it was divine, but even if it had been hideous she would have said the same because she was so touched that he had bought her a personal gift. The globe, unlike the new wardrobe and the jewellery he had purchased and insisted she wear, had not been given to facilitate her leading role in a bet to be staged at a royal ball. All of that was fake, like the fake accent

she had picked up from the elocution and the knowledge of how to curtsy to royalty that she had learned. She was to pretend to be something she was not for Vitale's benefit.

'What's the matter with you?' Vitale demanded with a raw edge to his dark, deep voice. 'And why did you send me that weird text?'

Jazz's legs turned all weak and she dropped down abruptly on the edge of a sofa in the big imposing drawing room where she never ever felt comfortable because it was stuffed with exceedingly grand furniture and seats as hard as nails. 'Something's happened, well, actually it happened weeks ago although I didn't know it then,' she muttered in a rush. 'You should sit down and take a very deep breath because you're going to be furious.'

'Only my mother makes me furious,' Vitale contended impatiently, studying her with keen assessing eyes, picking up on her pallor and the faint bluish shadows below her eyes. 'Are you ill?'

Jazz focused on him, poised there so straight and tall and gorgeous with his blue-black hair, arresting features and wonderful eyes, and she snatched in a very deep breath. 'Not ill...*pregnant*,' she told him with pained reluctance.

Vitale froze, engulfed in a sudden ice storm. He stared back at her, his eyes hardening and narrowing, and she watched him swallow back hasty words and seal his mouth firmly shut again.

'No, you can say what you like,' Jazz promised him ruefully. 'No offence will be taken. Neither of us were expecting this development and I know it's bad news as far as you're concerned.'

'*Very* bad news,' Vitale admitted in shock, paler than she had ever seen him below his naturally bronzed complexion. 'You said you were on birth control. Was that a lie?'

'No, it wasn't,' Jazz assured him. 'But for whatever reason, although I didn't miss taking a single pill, I've conceived and I'm about six weeks in.'

'And we've only been together around seven weeks!' Vitale thundered, cursing in Italian only half under his breath, his lean hands coiling with tension. 'Right, the first thing we will do is check this out in case it's a false alarm.'

'It's *not* a false alarm,' Jazz argued but Vitale had already stalked angrily to the far end of the room to use his phone, where she listened to him talking to someone in fast and fluent Italian.

All of a sudden even the sound of his voice was grating on her because, within the space of a second, everything had changed in his attitude to her. His voice was now ice-cool and his gaze had blanked her because he was determined to reveal no normal human reaction beyond that '*very* bad news', which really, when she thought about it, said all that she needed to hear and know. He had seemed so relaxed with her before and now that was gone, probably never to return.

Vitale studied Jazz while he spoke to his friend and discomfiture lanced through him. No, it wasn't a deliberate conception, and he knew that because he trusted her, and there she sat as if the roof had fallen in on top of her and she wasn't a skilled enough actress to look like that if that wasn't how she truly felt. Pregnant? *A baby?* Vitale was shattered but, unlike his brother Angel, he wouldn't make the mistake of running away

from his responsibilities. He also knew that Jazz was a devout churchgoer from a rural Irish Catholic background and that a termination was a choice she was unlikely to make. He would be a father whether he liked it or not. But, before he agonised over that truth and its consequences, he was determined to take her to see a gynaecologist, who was a close friend and could be trusted to be discreet.

'Giulio Verratti is a close friend, whom I've known since my teens,' he volunteered stiffly. 'He also has a private practice as a consultant gynaecologist here in London.'

In silence, Jazz nodded, resigned to his need for a second opinion.

'I'll feel happier if he confirms it,' Vitale completed grimly.

Jazz thought that that was the wrong choice of words because the taut, forbidding lines of Vitale's lean, strong face suggested he might never be happy again. Regret filled her to overflowing. Her announcement had destroyed their affair. It would have ended anyway after the royal ball, she reminded herself ruefully. There had always been a clock ticking on their relationship and the ball was now only a week away.

'Let's talk about something else,' Vitale suggested as he steered her out to the waiting limo.

'How can we?' Jazz exclaimed.

'How do you feel about this situation?' he shot at her without warning.

'I was devastated at first,' Jazz confided. 'But now I can't help being a little bit excited too... Sorry.'

'You don't need to apologise,' Vitale intoned. 'Obviously you like children.'

'Don't you?'

'It's not something I've thought about. It's something I assumed was light years away in the future,' he breathed tautly.

He had defrosted a tad and she wanted to reach for his hand but resisted the temptation, recognising that it was not a good moment. Only two nights back, he had slept with her in his arms all night, but those days were over, she thought sadly. In a casual affair, a pregnancy was divisive, a source of concern rather than celebration. He would want their child to remain a secret as well, she mused unhappily. He wouldn't want the existence of an illegitimate kid splashed all over the media. Would he want to be involved in their child's life in any way? Or would he hope that giving her money would keep her quiet and persuade her to accept that he could not play *any* sort of active paternal role?

Giulio Verratti was a suave Italian in his thirties with prematurely greying hair. They didn't even have to sit down in the waiting room before a nurse swept them into the consulting room and the gynaecologist explained the tests that could be done on the spot. The nurse shepherded Jazz off to perform the tests before Jazz returned to the plush consulting room where the results were passed to Giulio.

'You're definitely pregnant,' he announced.

Vitale's shuttered expression betrayed nothing to her anxious glance.

'I'm a little concerned by a rather high reading in your hCG,' he confided and he went on to offer her a transvaginal ultrasound, which could be more accurate at an earlier stage than a normal scan.

Vitale flinched. 'No. We won't put her through that unless it is strictly necessary for her health.'

'Are there any twins in your family?' Mr Verratti asked smoothly.

'Several,' Jazz volunteered. 'My grandmother and some cousins.'

'There's a strong possibility that this could be a multiple pregnancy and I'll do an ordinary ultrasound now to see if I can pick up the heartbeat or heartbeats yet,' the older man informed them calmly and he called the nurse to help Jazz prepare for the scan.

Gel was rubbed on her abdomen and a hand-held scanner was run over her. Eyes wide, she stared at the monitor and then she heard the very fast sound of the foetal heartbeat and Mr Verratti laughed with satisfaction. He pointed at the monitor to indicate two blurred areas that he said were her babies. 'You do indeed carry twins,' he assured her.

Twins? Vitale had never worked so hard at controlling his expression. *More* than one child? The bad news just got worse and worse, he conceded helplessly. But every cloud had a silver lining, he instructed himself grimly. There had to be a plus side to even this disaster, although he had yet to see it. He would gain the heir his mother was so keen for him to produce but to achieve that he would have to marry Jazz, an alliance that Queen Sofia, the supreme elitist, would never agree to. But then he was fortunate that he did not actually require his mother's consent to marry. She had always assumed that, somewhere in the Lerovian tomes of royal dynastic law, such a prohibition existed but Vitale knew for a fact that it didn't. He was free to marry whomever he liked even if, at that precise moment, he

hadn't the slightest desire to get married to Jazz or any other woman.

And he blamed himself entirely for taking on that crazy competitive bet with his younger brother, Zac. What insanity had possessed him? Of all three of the brothers, Vitale was indisputably the sensible, steady one and yet look at the mess he was in now! Somehow, he had contrived to choreograph his own downfall by moving a young woman into his home, whom he couldn't keep his hands off, he thought with raw self-loathing and distaste. He had known from the outset that Jazz attracted him and he had still gone ahead, believing that he had vast self-discipline and learning differently very, very quickly.

And it was hardly surprising that it threatened to be a multiple pregnancy, he conceded even more grimly, considering that they had been having sex every night for weeks on end. Not once had he used a condom as an extra safeguard. His *own* mistakes, his own indefensible errors of judgement, piled up on top of Vitale like a multiple road crash and plunged him into brooding silence.

Jazz lay awake alone most of that night. Vitale had barely spoken after leaving Mr Verratti's surgery. He hadn't even come to say goodnight to her, indeed had been noticeably careful not to touch her again in any way. It was as if she now had a giant defensive forcefield wrapped round her. Or as if her sudden overwhelming attraction had just died the very instant he'd realised she was pregnant with twins. The truth of their predicament was finally settling in on him and of course, he was upset. But she had kind of—secretly—hoped he would come to her if he was upset, as he had one other

night after a more than usually distressing argument on the phone with his shrewish mother. He had shared that with her and she had felt important to him in a different way for the first time.

A little less fanciful now, she sat up in bed and put on the light to study her gilded and very ornate snow globe and her eyes simply overflowed again, tears trickling down her cheeks while she sniffed and dashed them away and generally hated herself for being such a drip. She had got attached to him, hadn't she? She was *more than fond* of Vitale after so many weeks of living with him.

How had she felt as though they were tailor-made for each other when that was so patently untrue? She, a housekeeper's daughter, he, a royal prince? Would he even continue with the bet now? He wouldn't want her in the public eye again, she reckoned, wouldn't wish to be associated with a woman who would be looking very pregnant in a few months' time. When Mr Verratti had mentioned that provocative word, 'twins', Vitale had looked as though he had been hand sculpted out of granite. She had practically heard Vitale thinking that *one* child would have been quite enough to contend with. She recognised that she was getting all het up with no prospect of calming herself down again. Eventually sheer exhaustion made her sleep.

First thing the next morning, she found herself in the bathroom being horribly sick and that shift from nausea to actual illness felt like the last straw. Washing away the evidence, she examined her wan reflection in the mirror and decided she had a slight greenish cast that was not the tiniest bit attractive. The sore boobs squashed into a bra that had become too small didn't

help either, she thought miserably as she got dressed, selecting jeans and a colourful top in the hope of looking brighter and less emotionally sensitive than she actually felt.

She walked slowly downstairs. Vitale appeared in the dining-room doorway.

'Breakfast… Join me,' he suggested in that same hatefully distant tone.

'I didn't want this development either,' she said in her own defence as she moved past him, avoiding looking at him quite deliberately.

'I think I know that,' he conceded curtly.

Her bright head flew up and she looked at him. *'Do you?'*

Exasperation flared in his forbidding gaze. 'Yes, but it doesn't change the situation.'

She supposed it didn't. He accepted that she wasn't guilty of intent but somehow she still felt that she was being held to blame. And possibly she *was* to blame, thinking about the instructions she had failed to read because at the time contraception had not been an issue she'd cared about or needed. She had assumed she was safe from conception when she wasn't but he had made the same assumption. What did it matter now anyway? He was right. A lack of intent didn't change anything.

She lifted a plate and helped herself to toast and butter, her unsettled stomach cringing at the prospect of anything more solid.

'Shouldn't you be having something more to eat?'

'I'm nauseous. That's why I went to the doctor in the first place,' she admitted stiltedly as Jenkins poured tea and coffee while Vitale simply ignored the older man's presence.

When the butler had closed the door on his exit, Vitale studied her and said flatly, 'We have to get married and quickly.'

Jazz stared back at him wide-eyed and stunned by incredulity at that declaration. 'That's ludicrous!' she gulped.

'No, it isn't. There is another dimension to this issue which you are ignoring but which I cannot ignore,' Vitale imparted coolly. 'The children you carry will be heirs to the throne of Lerovia with the firstborn taking precedence. If they are born illegitimate they *cannot* be heirs and I know that I don't want a child of mine in this world that feels cheated of their birthright because I failed to marry you.'

He was quite correct. Jazz had not considered that issue in any depth or how any such child would feel as he or she grew up and realised the future they had been denied by an accident of birth. She swallowed hard but still said, 'Be sensible, Vitale. You can't marry someone like me. You're a prince.'

'I don't think we have a choice. We'll get married very discreetly and quietly in a civil ceremony and keep the news to ourselves until after the ball,' Vitale informed her.

'You're still taking me to the ball?' she murmured in surprise.

'If you're going to be my wife, why wouldn't I take you?'

'But you don't *want* to marry me,' she pointed out shakily. 'And feeling like that it would be all wrong for both of us.'

Vitale dealt her a cool sardonic appraisal. 'We don't have to stay married for ever, Jazz. Only long enough to legitimise our children's birth.'

'Oh…' Jazz reddened fiercely, feeling foolish for not having recognised the obvious escape clause in his startling announcement that they should marry. He wasn't talking about a normal marriage, of course he wasn't. He was suggesting a temporary marriage for their children's sake followed by divorce, a relationship that would be, in its own way, as false as the role he had already prepared her to play at the ball as his partner.

'And there *is* a plus side for me,' Vitale continued smoothly. 'I get the heir my mother so badly wants me to have and there will be no pressure on me to marry a second time.'

Jazz had lost colour as the true ramifications of what he was proposing slowly sank in, but pride made her contrive an approximation of a smile. 'So, everybody gets what they want,' she completed tightly.

Everybody but me, she conceded painfully, forced to listen to how he wanted to marry her and then get rid of her again after profiting from her unintentional fertility. She was seeing the side of Vitale that she hated, that sharp-as-knives, cold, calculating streak that could power him in moments of crisis. And it chilled Jazz right down to the marrow bone.

Inside her chest her heart felt as though he had stuck an actual knife in it. Over the past weeks, she had become attached but *he had not*. For Vitale, she had been a means to an end, a convenient lover, not someone he valued in any more lasting way. Now he planned to make the best of a bad situation and marry her to legitimise the children she carried. That would benefit him and it would benefit their children as well. But there would be no benefit for Jazz in becoming Vitale's temporary wife. Continued exposure to Vi-

tale's callous indifference would only open her up to a world of hurt. And what on earth would it be like for her to become a member of a *royal* family? Ordinary women like her didn't marry princes, she reflected with a sinking stomach. How the heck could she rise to the level of a royal?

But, seriously, what choice did she have? She didn't have the luxury of saying no to what was surely the most unromantic proposal of marriage that had ever been voiced by a man. How could she deny her unborn twins the right to become accepted members of the Lerovian royal family? That would be a very selfish thing to do, to protect herself instead of securing her children's future. And she could see that Vitale had not a doubt that she would accept his proposal, which made her want to throw a plate of really messy jelly at him. All those years being chased by princess-title-hunters hadn't done him any favours in the ego department. Evidently, he believed he was a hell of a catch, even on a temporary basis. Below her lowered lashes, her green eyes flared with slow-burning anger. He was rich and handsome and titled. He put in a terrific performance in bed and bought a good snow globe. But really, what else did he have to offer? Certainly not sensitivity, anyhow.

'We'll be married within a few days.'

Vitale dealt her an expectant appraisal as if he was hoping she would jump about with excitement or, at the very least, loose an unseemly whoop of appreciation. Cinderella got her Prince Charming—*not*, she recognised angrily. He hadn't even asked her if she wanted to marry him because he took assent for granted. And why not? The marriage wouldn't last any longer than possi-

bly eighteen months and then he would be free again, free of the housekeeper's daughter and her baggage.

'My babies live with me,' Jazz declared combatively, lest he be cherishing any other sort of plan for their children. 'I raise my children.'

Vitale lifted and dropped a broad shoulder, the very picture of nonchalance. 'Of course. I believe you have an elocution lesson now.'

Jazz flushed in surprise. 'I'm to continue with those lessons?'

'Naturally. For a while at least you'll have public appearances to make in your role as my wife. Your pregnancy, though, will eventually make it easier to excuse you from such events,' he pointed out calmly.

'You really do have it *all* worked out.' Jazz rose stiffly from her seat and walked out of the room without a backward glance.

Vitale gritted his even white teeth in frustration. He would never understand women if he lived to be a thousand! What was wrong with her now? Why was she sulking? Jazz didn't sulk. She was never moody. He liked that about her. So, what was the problem?

During a long, sleepless night he had contrived to find the silver lining in their predicament and he had been satisfied with the solution he had chosen. Why wasn't *she* delighted? He was willing to marry her, jump through all the hoops he had always avoided, just for her benefit and the twins'. OK, his wide sensual mouth curled, he wasn't saying that there wasn't *anything* in the arrangement for him. Jazz officially in his bed would be a personal gain, a sort of compensation for the pain and sacrifice of getting shackled at a mere twenty-eight years old to a woman his mother would

despise and attack for her commonplace background. Anger flooded him. What more could he do in the circumstances?

On the morning of Jazz's wedding day, three days later, sunshine flooded into the apartment living area but she still didn't feel the slightest bit bridal. Sworn to secrecy, her mother and her aunt were attending the ceremony, but the very fact that Vitale had not asked to meet her family beforehand only emphasised to Jazz how fake their wedding would be. Angel and his wife, Merry, were to attend as witnesses.

In the preceding three days, Jazz had gone shopping for the first time armed with a credit card given to her by Vitale. She had got fitted for new bras and had picked an off-white dress and matching jacket to wear. But it had not been a happy time for Jazz. Her mother, Peggy, had been distraught when Jazz had announced that she had fallen pregnant by Vitale. It had taken her daughter and her sister's combined efforts to persuade the older woman that Jazz's pregnancy did not have to be viewed as a catastrophe when Vitale was about to marry her. Naturally Jazz had not even hinted to either woman that Vitale was not planning on a 'for ever' marriage.

That, for the moment, was her secret, her private business, she thought ruefully, but pretending for the sake of her mother and her family that Vitale genuinely cared enough about her to *want* to marry her cost her sleep. Her bouts of sickness had become worse and when, the second evening, Vitale had walked into her bedroom and found her being horribly ill in the bathroom he had insisted on asking his friend, Giulio, to make a house call. Mr Verratti had told her that the

excessive sickness was probably the result of her twin pregnancy, warned her about the danger of dehydration and given her medication that would hopefully reduce the nausea. None of those experiences had lifted Jazz's low spirits or the horrible feeling of being trapped in a bad and challenging situation over which she had no control.

'How do you feel?' was Vitale's first question when they met at the register office, because Peggy Dickens had begged her daughter to spend that last night at home in her aunt's apartment, which had meant, traditional or otherwise, that Jazz had had very little sleep resting on a lumpy couch after having enjoyed the luxury of a bed of her own for weeks.

'I'm fine,' she lied politely, turning to greet Angel, who was smiling, and then be introduced to his glowing dark-haired wife, who was wonderfully warm and friendly. But Jazz went red, just knowing by the lingering look Angel gave her that he knew she was pregnant as well and she felt humiliated and exposed while wondering if Angel's wife was being so nice because she pitied her.

'I should have said that you look amazing in cream,' Vitale said hastily, as if belatedly grasping that that was more what people expected from a bridegroom than an enquiry about her health.

Not so amazing that he had felt any desire to so much as kiss her since her pregnancy announcement, Jazz reflected bitterly. But then Vitale, trained from childhood to say the right thing at the right time, couldn't always shake off his conditioning. In the future, she expected him to treat her with excessive politeness and distance, much as he had been treating her since she had told

him she had conceived. And it hurt Jazz, it hurt much more even than she had thought it would to live with that forbidding new chill in his attitude towards her. It was as if Vitale were flying on automatic pilot and she was now a stranger because all intimacy between them had vanished.

If only she could so easily banish her responses, she thought unhappily, studying Vitale where he stood chatting with his brother and his wife. Vitale was a devastatingly handsome male distinguished by dark golden black-fringed eyes that sent heat spiralling through her pelvis, which made her avert her eyes from him uneasily. Her body still sang and tingled in his presence, all prickling awareness and sensual enthusiasm, and it mortified her, forced her to crave the indifference he seemed to have embraced with ease.

The wedding ceremony was short and not particularly sweet. For the sake of their audience, Jazz kept a determined smile on her lips and studied the plain platinum ring she had been fitted for only the morning before. She was also thinking about the very comprehensive prenup she had signed an hour after that ring fitting and her heart was still sinking on that score. That document had even contained access arrangements for their unborn children and a divorce settlement. Reading that through to the end had been an even more sobering experience. Vitale had thought of everything going into their temporary marriage and he had taken every possible precaution, so it was hardly surprising that any sense of being a bride escaped her.

'Give him time,' Angel urged her in an incomprehensible whispered aside before he departed with his wife,

after a brief and extremely formal lunch at an exclusive hotel with her family. 'He's emotionally stunted.'

Vitale joined his bride in the limo that was taking them to the airport and their flight to Italy for a long weekend preceding the ball and said, 'It's completely weird seeing Angel like that with a woman.'

'Like what?' Jazz prompted.

'Besotted,' Vitale labelled with a grimace. 'Didn't you notice the way he kept on touching her and looking at her?'

'I noticed that they seemed very happy together.'

'They started out like us. Merry had Angel's daughter last year and at first Angel didn't want anything to do with either of them and now look at them,' Vitale invited in apparent disbelief. 'Already hoping for another child some day, he told me…'

Jazz perked up… Well, it was an encouraging story. 'Fancy that,' she remarked lightly.

'I wouldn't ever want to feel that way,' Vitale admitted.

'Why not?' she asked boldly.

The silence dragged and she thought she had got too personal and that he wasn't going to answer her.

But Vitale was grimacing. 'I saw my father crying once. I was very young but it made a big impression on me. He explained that he wouldn't be living with my mother and I any longer. They were splitting up. At the time, I didn't really understand that but later, when I looked back, I understood. I don't know why they divorced but I don't think it was related to anything Papa did. He was heartbroken.'

Jazz winced but persisted. 'Didn't you ask him why they broke up?'

'I never liked to. I was afraid of upsetting him. He's a very emotional man.'

But Jazz was thinking of Vitale as a little boy seeing his father distraught over the loss of a woman. Had that disturbing glimpse put Vitale off falling in love? After all, he already had a mother in his life who must surely have damaged his ability to trust women. Exposed to Charles's heartbreak, Vitale must always have tried to protect himself from getting too attached to a woman. After all, the very first woman he had been attached to, *his mother*, had rejected him.

'I should have invited Papa today and he'll be hurt that I left him out but I didn't want to get him involved in our predicament,' Vitale continued.

And that's the reward you get for digging where you shouldn't, Jazz told herself unhappily. Vitale knew their marriage would be a short-lived thing and that was why he had left his father out. 'Did you tell Angel the truth?' she asked, even though she felt that she already knew the answer to that question.

'*Sì...*' Vitale confirmed quietly. 'I have no secrets from Angel.'

'Apart from the bet,' she reminded him.

And disconcertingly, Vitale laughed at that reminder with genuine appreciation. 'I felt it was so juvenile to try and one up Zac that I was embarrassed. I don't know what got into me that day at my father's office. Or that day when you told Angel about the bet. I was in a very bad mood.'

In the days that followed that meeting with Angel at Vitale's house Jazz had come to suspect that Vitale had been angry because he had misinterpreted her friendly ease with his older brother as flirtation, forgetting that

when they were kids Angel had been as much her playmate as he had been. She had thought, even *hoped* that Vitale was possessive of her attention and jealous. Now she knew better, she thought wryly.

Feeling like a wet weekend, she stepped onto her first private jet, stunned by the opulent interior and the spaciousness of the cabin.

'There's a bedroom you can rest in at the far end,' Vitale told her helpfully as he opened up his laptop, evidently intending to work.

'I might just do that,' she said tartly since it seemed to her that he was hoping to be left in peace.

She kicked off her shoes, and removed her jacket and lay down on the comfortable bed and slept like a log. Vitale remembered it was his wedding day when he was warned that the flight was about to land and he strode into the sleeping compartment to wake Jazz.

She looked so small and fragile lying there that he was taken aback because Jazz always seemed larger than life inside his head. Not since she got pregnant though, he reflected grimly. That had changed everything for them both as well as adversely affecting her health. Giulio had advised him to be very careful because a multiple pregnancy was both more dangerous and more likely to result in a miscarriage and one could not be too careful either with one's wife or with children, one of whom would be the next heir to a throne. Blasted pregnancy, Vitale thought bitterly, because he could see how wan and thin she was already. Her appetite was affected…her mood was affected. Nothing was the same any more and he missed her vivacity and spontaneity.

Jazz wakened with a start to find Vitale bent over

her, his stunning dark golden eyes grim as tombstones. In haste, she edged back from him and sat up.

'We're about to land. You'll have to come back out,' he warned her.

'I must've been more tired than I appreciated,' she muttered apologetically while wondering if her absence had even registered with him.

CHAPTER SEVEN

ONE OF VITALE'S security team drove the four-wheel-drive up what Vitale assured her was the very last twisting, turning road because Jazz was carsick and they had to keep on stopping lest she throw up. It made her feel like an irritating young child and the politer Vitale was about the necessity, the more exasperated she suspected he was. So much for the honeymoon she had assured her family he was taking her on, even if events had conspired to ensure they only got to take a long weekend in Italy before the royal ball in Lerovia. It would be the honeymoon from hell, she decided wretchedly.

And then the car turned down a leaf-lined lane and way at the top of that lane lay the most beautiful house she had ever seen. Not as big as she had expected, not extravagant either. It was a sprawling two-storey farmhouse built in glorious ochre-coloured stone that was colouring into a deeper shade below the spectacular setting sun above. It was surrounded, not by a conventional garden, but by what looked very like a wildflower meadow and the odd copse of leafy trees.

'It's gorgeous,' she said, speaking for almost the first time since she had left the plane about something other

than an apologetic reference to the reality that she felt ill again.

Vitale sprang out of the car and opened the passenger door with a flashing smile that disconcerted her, his lean, darkly handsome features appreciative. 'I thought you mightn't like it,' he admitted. 'It's not luxurious like the town house or the palace. It's more of a getaway house.'

'It'll probably still be fancier than I'm used to,' Jazz pointed out, simply relieved that he was acting human again instead of frozen.

A light hand resting at her spine, Vitale walked her down the path and into a hall with a polished terracotta tiled floor. Jazz shifted away from him again to peer through open doors, registering that the furnishings were simple and plain, not a swag nor any gilding in sight, and she relaxed even more, smiling when Vitale called her back to introduce her to the little woman he called Agnella, who looked after the house. Jazz froze to the floor when Agnella curtsied to her as if she were royalty.

'Why did she do that?' she asked Vitale as they followed their driver and their luggage up the oak staircase.

'Because you're my wife and a princess even though I don't think you quite feel like one yet,' Vitale suggested. 'I'm afraid you'll have to curtsy to my mother every time you see her because she's a stickler for formal court etiquette. When I'm King, which is a very long way away in my future,' he admitted wryly, 'I will modernise and there will be a lot less bowing and scraping. Unfortunately, the Queen enjoys it too much.'

'Is that so?' Jazz encouraged, stunned by his sudden chattiness.

'Yes, the monarchy in Lerovia would never be described as one of the more casual bicycling royal families,' Vitale admitted with regret. 'Life at the palace is pretty much the same as it must have been a couple of hundred years ago.'

Jazz pulled a face. 'Can't say I'm looking forward to that. How on earth is your mother going to react to me?' she prompted anxiously.

'Very badly,' Vitale told her bluntly. 'I intend to break that news by degrees for your benefit. You'll be attending the ball as my fiancée.'

'Fiancée?' Jazz repeated in surprise. 'How... For *my* benefit?'

'My mother is likely to go off in an hysterical rant and she can be very abusive. I don't want to risk her throwing a major scene at the ball and I'm determined to protect you from embarrassment. I'll tell her after the ball that we are already married but not with you present. Be assured that, whatever happens, *I* will deal with the Queen.'

Merely inclining her head at that unsettling information about the kind of welcome she could expect from his royal mother, Jazz walked into a beautiful big bedroom with rafters high above, a stripped wooden floor and an ancient fireplace at the far end. In the centre a bed festooned in fresh white linen sat up against an exposed stone wall while a windowsill sported a glorious arrangement of white lilac blossoms. 'I really love this house. Can't you just imagine that fire lit in winter? You could add a couple of easy chairs there and use that chest by the wall as a coffee table.'

Vitale blinked in bewilderment, stealing a startled glance at her newly animated face. 'What a great idea,' he intoned, although he had never in all his life before thought about interior décor or furniture. 'We could go shopping for chairs.'

'Could we?' A little of her animation dwindling, Jazz wondered why she was rabbiting on as if he were truly her husband and the farmhouse their home and her colour heightened with embarrassment. 'I was just being silly and imaginative,' she completed, kicking off her shoes and settling down on the side of the low bed because she was tired, worn down by her stress and her worries.

'We'll look for chairs. I hired a designer to do the basics here and never added anything else,' Vitale repeated a shade desperately, keen to keep the conversation afloat even if he had to talk about furniture to do it. He could not stand to see Jazz look so sad and her interest in the farmhouse had noticeably lifted her mood for the first time that day. Considering that it had been their wedding day, Vitale felt very much to blame. 'I didn't really have the time to think about finishing touches but I'm grateful for any advice.'

'I'm sure you could hire another interior designer,' Jazz told him quellingly, recalling the wealth of the male she was addressing and feeling even more foolish.

'I'd prefer you to do it,' Vitale asserted in growing frustration, having watched her face dim again as though a light had been switched out. 'You won't make it too grand.'

'Well, no,' Jazz agreed dulcetly. 'I have no experience of grand, so I could hardly make it that way.'

He watched her slight shoulders slump again and

strode forward. 'Would you like to wear your engagement ring?' he asked with staggering abruptness.

'My…*what*?'

Eager to employ any distraction available to him, Vitale dug a ring box out of his pocket and flipped it open, it being his experience that women loved jewellery. Although, as he extended the opulent emerald and diamond ring, he was belatedly recalling that Jazz had been annoyingly reluctant even to accept the basics like a gold watch and plain gold stud earrings from him.

'Lovely,' Jazz said woodenly, making no move to claim the ring.

Vitale's strong jawline squared with stubborn determination. He lifted her limp hand and threaded the diamond ring onto her finger until it rested up against her wedding ring. 'What do you think?' he was forced to prompt when the silence stretched on even after she had snatched her hand back.

'Stunning,' Jazz said obediently since she could see it was expected of her.

'It is yours. I'm not going to ask for it back!' Vitale launched down at her with sudden impatience, wondering if that was the problem. 'When we split up, everything I have given you is yours!'

Instead of being reassured, Jazz flinched and rose upright in a sudden movement, colour sparking over her cheekbones. 'And isn't that a lovely thing to say to me on our wedding day?' she condemned sharply. 'Of course, it wasn't a *real* wedding day, was it?'

Thoroughly taken aback by her angry, aggressive stance, Vitale stared at her with bemused dark eyes. 'It felt real enough to me.'

'But it *wasn't* real! Did you think I was in any dan-

ger of forgetting that for a moment? Well, don't worry yourself! I wasn't in danger of forgetting for a *single* moment. I had no wedding dress. You haven't touched me since I told you I was pregnant, not even to kiss the bride! I know it's all fake, like the stupid wedding ring and the ceremony and now an even stupider engagement ring. You don't *want* to be engaged or married to me. Did you think that little piece of reality could possibly have escaped my notice?' she demanded wrathfully at the top of her voice, which echoed loudly up into the rafters.

'I didn't want to be engaged or married to anyone,' Vitale confessed in a driven undertone while he tried to work out what they were arguing about. 'But if I have to be, you would definitely be my first choice.'

'Oh, that makes me feel *so* much better!' Jazz flung so sarcastically that even Vitale picked up on it.

Instantly Vitale regretted admitting that he hadn't wanted to be engaged or married to anyone. Was that quite true though? He had looked at Jazz throughout the day and had felt amazingly relaxed about their new relationship. But obviously, not kissing his bride had gone down as a big fail, but then Vitale had never liked doing anything of that nature in front of other people.

'I was trying to compliment you.'

'News flash…it didn't work!' Grabbing up a case from her collection of brand-new matching designer luggage, Jazz plonked it down on the bed.

'You're pregnant and you're not supposed to lift heavy things!' Vitale raked censoriously at her.

Jazz ignored him, ripping into the case, carelessly tossing out half the contents and finally extracting a robe. 'There'd better be a bath in there for me to soak

in,' she muttered, stalking across the floor to the ajar door of the en suite, checking that there was and then recalling that she didn't have her toiletries.

In a furious temper she went back to check the luggage and, still finding the all-important bag missing, left the bedroom to go back downstairs and see if it had been left in the car.

Vitale released his breath in an explosive surge, genuinely at a loss. Somehow everything was going wrong. He had been too honest with her. He should never have mentioned splitting up or her keeping the jewellery. Angel had said women were sentimental and sensitive and all of a sudden that prenuptial agreement he had settled in front of her loomed like a major misjudgement. He had to turn things around but he hadn't a clue how and he sprang up again, concentrating on the overwhelming challenge of needing to please a woman for the first time in his life.

The bath, he thought, and then he had it, the awareness of her love of baths prompting him. He grabbed the flowers on the window sill up and strode into the bathroom like a man on a mission.

Hot, perspiring and cross as tacks after having to locate their driver and interrupt him at his evening meal to gain access to the bag that had been left in the car, Jazz made it back into the bedroom, which was comfortingly empty because she had had enough of Vitale for one day. She got to keep the jewellery, yippee, big wow there if she was a gold-digger but, sadly, she wasn't. She had wanted to keep *him*, not the jewellery, which was the sort of thought that tore Jazz apart inside and made her feel humiliated because Vitale had

made it very clear that *he* did not want to keep *her*. She undressed and slid on the robe.

Entering the bathroom, Jazz was sharply disconcerted to find it transformed. The bath had already been run for her and candles had been lit round the bath, turning it into a soothing space while the lilac blossoms exuded a pale luminous glow in one corner. Rose petals floated on the surface of the water and she blinked in disconcertion at the inviting vision. Vitale? No, she decided. He wasn't capable of making that kind of romantic effort. She tested the water, found it warm and, with a shrug, she dropped the robe and climbed in.

Vitale pushed open the door, relieved she hadn't locked it, and extended a wine glass to her.

At the intrusion, Jazz jerked in surprise, water sloshing noisily around her slight body as she raised her knees automatically to conceal herself in a defensive pose. 'What are you doing?' she exclaimed, her voice sharp, accusing.

'Trying,' Vitale retorted curtly. 'Maybe I'm not very good at this.'

'*You* ran my bath, lit the candles?' Jazz gasped, wide-eyed with astonishment.

Vitale crouched down by the side of the bath, far too close for comfort, dark golden eyes enhanced by curling gold-tipped lashes stunningly intent on her flushed face. 'You're my wife. This is our wedding day. You're sick and you're unhappy. Isn't it believable that I would try to turn that around?'

Her soft pink mouth opened uncertainly and then closed again, her lashes fluttering up on disconcerted green eyes. 'You don't usually make any effort,' she pointed out somewhat ungraciously.

'Situations change,' Vitale reasoned, speaking as though every word he spoke might have a punitive tax imposed on it and he were being forced to keep speech to the absolute minimum.

'I suppose they do,' Jazz muttered, accepting the glass. 'You know I can't drink this?'

'It's non-alcoholic,' he informed her.

Jazz sipped the delicious ice-cool drink and suddenly laughed with real amusement, startling herself almost as much as him. 'It's homemade lemonade!'

'My cousins visit me here occasionally. They have children and Agnella always likes to be prepared. She was my nurse when I was a child,' he confided. 'My mother sacked her when she reached a certain age because she prefers a youthful staff but Agnella wasn't ready to be put out to grass. She and her husband look after this place for me.'

'You're making your mother sound more and more like an evil villain,' Jazz whispered, for the bathroom with little flames sending shadows flickering on the stone walls was as disturbingly intimate as Vitale's proximity.

Vitale lifted and dropped a wide shoulder in silent dismissal. His jacket and tie had vanished but he hadn't unbuttoned his collar and, without even thinking about it, Jazz stretched out her hand and loosened the button, spreading the edges apart to show off his strong brown throat. 'There, now you look more relaxed,' she proclaimed, colouring a little at what she had done. 'Everything's changed, Vitale.'

'Sì…but we're in this *together*,' Vitale reminded her with gruff emphasis.

'Obviously,' she conceded. 'But I don't know where we go from here.'

'*We* don't have to change,' he argued with a sudden vehemence that disconcerted her. 'We can go on exactly the way we were in London.'

'I don't think so,' Jazz declared, her heart quickening its beat with a kind of panic at how vulnerable that would make her, to continue as though she didn't know her happiness was on a strict timeline with a definite ending. She had to protect herself, be sensible and look to the future. Continuing what they had shared before now looked far too dangerous. 'I mean, since the moment I announced that I was pregnant, you backed off like I'd developed the bubonic plague.'

'Giulio warned to be careful with you.'

'Giulio? Mr Verratti?' she queried. 'He *told* you not to touch me? That we couldn't have sex?'

Vitale frowned. 'No, only to be *careful* and you were so obviously tired and unwell I respected the warning. Naturally, I left you alone,' he confided grittily. 'I didn't want to be selfish and I am naturally selfish and thoughtless. I was raised to always put myself first in relationships, so I have to look out more than most to avoid that kind of behaviour.'

He was so serious in the way in which he told her that that it touched Jazz. He knew his flaws, strove to keep them under control, didn't trust in his senses to read situations, never thought of explaining himself, simply strove to avoid the consequences of doing something wrong. It was a very rudimentary approach to a relationship and almost certain to result in misunderstandings. Jazz studied the disturbingly grave set of his lean, darkly handsome features and stroked her fingers down the side of his sombre face, fingertips brushing through a dark shadow of prickly black stubble.

'If you're coming to bed with me, you need a shave,' she told him softly, knowing she couldn't fight the way she felt at that moment, the yearning that was welling up from deep inside her to be with him again.

Right at this moment, Vitale was hers, and maybe she would never have more than a few fleeting moments feeling like that but did that mean she shouldn't have him at all? Yes, it would hurt when it ended but why shouldn't she be happy while she still could be? Wasn't trying to prepare for the end of their relationship now simply borrowing trouble?

Stark disconcertion had widened Vitale's dark gaze, letting her know that sex had not actually been his goal for once and Jazz smiled sunnily, replete with the feminine power of having surprised him.

'OK, *bellezza mia*…' His dark deep masculine drawl was slightly fractured and he vaulted back upright, sending her a flashing brilliant smile that made her tummy perform a somersault. 'I'll shave.'

And away he went to do it, where she had no idea, as she lay back in her candlelit bath, full of warm fuzzy feelings powered only by lemonade and candlelight. He had surprised her too and she was genuinely amazed by that reality. Vitale could be so very conservative and polite that it was often hard to catch a glimpse of what lay beneath. A man who was worried and concerned enough about their troubled relationship to run her a bath and put candles and flowers around it. Only a little thing though, much like her snow globe but it showed her the other side of Vitale, the side he worked so hard to hide and suppress, the sensitive, caring side. That could be enough for her, she told herself firmly, that could be enough to make the risk of loving him

worthwhile even if it couldn't last for ever. Not everyone got a happy-ever-after.

He had said he was 'trying'. Well, she could try too, no shame in that, she told herself urgently, blowing out the candles and drying her overheated skin with a fleecy towel before walking naked into the empty bedroom to climb into the bed and rejoice in the cool linen embrace of the sheets.

Vitale reappeared, closed the door and surveyed her where she lay, Titian ringlets spilling across the white pillows like a vibrant banner. Hunger leapt through him with a ferocity that still disturbed him. His motto was moderation in all things but there was nothing moderate or practical about his desire for Jazz. It was a need that took hold of him at odd times of the day even when she wasn't in front of him, a kind of craving that had creeped him out when he'd first learned that she was pregnant because what had been going on inside his head should, in his estimation, have killed all desire for her, not fuelled it. But now he didn't even have to think about that anomaly, he told himself with fierce satisfaction. They had reached an accord, he didn't know how and he didn't *need* to know, did he? How wasn't important; that the accord existed was enough for him.

'Jazz…' he breathed hoarsely, standing beside the side of the bed, wrenching at his shirt.

Jazz sat up abruptly. 'Come here,' she told him with a sigh. 'You just ripped a button off your shirt.'

And he dropped down on the edge of the bed and she unbuttoned the shirt, full pert little rose-tipped breasts shifting beneath his mesmerised gaze with every movement. He tossed the shirt, stood up, unzipped his pants, thrust it all down, ran irritably into shoes and socks

while wondering how any male could be so impatient for one woman that he forgot how to undress.

Jazz spread herself back luxuriantly against the pillows.

'What are you smiling at?' Vitale enquired almost curtly, feverish colour scoring his high cheekbones.

'You look gorgeous,' she told him truthfully, admiring every long, lean, powerfully muscular line of his big body and most particularly the potent proof of his hunger for her.

Vitale could feel his face burn because no woman had ever said that to him before. He had never encouraged that kind of familiarity in the bedroom but that would not inhibit Jazz, who would say exactly what she felt like saying. There was something wonderfully liberating about that knowledge. He didn't know what it was, but it put to flight the stress of the long day and the very uncomfortable phone call he had just shared with his father.

'You *married* Jazz?' he had said. 'Your mother will throw a fit.'

But Vitale could not have cared less at that moment as he hauled Jazz up to meet his mouth, all dominant male powered by seething hormones. His hunger currented through her like a wake-up call, setting every skin cell alight with his passion. And Jazz revelled in that awareness of his desire for her. It acted as a soother for other slights and insecurities. Nobody had ever wanted her the way Vitale seemed to want her. True, she hadn't given any other man the chance, she conceded, but Vitale's passion made her feel ridiculously irresistible. His sensual mouth greedily ravished hers, a knot of warmth already curling at the heart of her in welcome.

And then his hands roved over her, those sure skilled hands, fingertips plucking gently at her swollen nipples, stirring an ache between her slender thighs that dragged a moan from her because her whole body felt amazingly sensitised, amazingly eager, over-the-top eager, she adjusted in shame, squirming below his caresses, back arching as he began to employ his carnal mouth in a sweet tormenting trail down over her twisting length.

'Don't stop...' she exclaimed helplessly, her narrow hips writhing and rising until he caught them in firm hands and stilled her to withstand the onslaught of his sensual attention.

'Per l'amor di Dio,' Vitale groaned against her where she ached unbearably. 'If I had known I was this welcome, I'd never have kept my distance—'

'Pregnancy hormones,' Jazz cut in shakily. 'That's all it is.'

'Possibly multiple pregnancy hormones,' Vitale teased with unholy amusement dancing in his stunning eyes. 'Bring it on, bellezza mia. That aspect went unmentioned on the website I read.'

'Maybe it's just me,' she mumbled uncomfortably, her face hot as fire.

'No, it's intriguing to know a piece of me is in there,' Vitale growled, splaying his fingers across her stomach. 'It makes me feel like you really belong to me...weird,' he added for himself.

'All of it feels weird because it's wonderfully new to us,' Jazz reasoned, her fingers delving through his luxuriant black hair. 'I still can't quite believe it.'

Vitale let a fingertip trace lower and her head fell back, the power of speech stolen by an unexpectedly powerful flood of sensation that made her legs tremble.

He bent his head and employed the tip of his tongue and her entire body jerked and shifted, little sounds of delight breaking from her throat that she couldn't hold back. And then there was no more talking because she was trapped in the relentless need for fulfilment, need controlling her, hunger roaring through her like a greedy tempest, craving more and crying out in wonder as he gave her more and the all-consuming clenching of her body powered her into an unstoppable climax.

'In bed, you're my every dream come true,' she whispered shakily, still rocked by the final waves of pleasure.

'It's the same for me,' Vitale admitted raggedly as he rose over her, forging a strong path into the tender flesh he had prepared to take him. 'It's never been this good for me.'

He plunged into her and withdrew in a timeless rhythm as old as the waves in the sea. Erotic excitement gripped her as she gripped him, little gasps racking her, tiny muscles convulsing around him. She quivered with sheer anticipation as his pace quickened, stirring every atom of her being, driving her back up to the heights with every thrust until the bands low in her body began to tighten and she strained until he drove her over the edge again into glorious release. She watched him reach the same satisfaction as he shuddered over her, his lean, muscular body taut and damp and beautifully virile as he lifted himself at the last possible moment, striving not to crush her with his weight.

'I feel good now,' Vitale husked, sliding off her and pausing to drop a kiss on her brow before moving away.

'I'm so pleased about that,' Jazz said laughingly.

'You can hug me if you want. I've got used to it,' Vitale assured her arrogantly.

Jazz rolled her eyes at the ceiling. There he was making allowances for her again but not actively joining in. She had taught him to tolerate being hugged but it wasn't enough for her. She needed *him* to grab *her* and hold her close and he wasn't going to do that. But at the same time she couldn't be a gift that kept on giving for ever. Shows of such affection from her would be thin on the ground from here on in, she told herself firmly.

'Are you in a mood?' Vitale asked quietly, leaning over her and gazing down at her with a very wary cast to his lean dark features.

'No.' Jazz stretched slowly and smiled. 'I'm hungry.'

'Agnella is holding dinner for us,' he volunteered.

'Holding it? You mean it's ready?' Jazz exclaimed in dismay. 'Why didn't you tell me?'

'It's fine. I told her you were in the bath,' Vitale explained with the carelessness of a male accustomed to staff who worked to his timetable rather than theirs,

'And how long ago was that?' Jazz groaned, sliding hurriedly out of bed to head for the bathroom at speed. 'We should be more considerate, Vitale.'

'It's our wedding night,' Vitale reminded her, stepping into the spacious shower with her. 'That's different.'

'Don't you dare get my hair wet,' Jazz warned him as he angled the rainforest spout. 'It takes for ever to dry.'

Vitale laughed out loud and watched her wash at speed and step back out again.

'You know there are other pastimes you can enjoy in the shower,' he husked, humour sparkling in his dark eyes.

'We're going downstairs for dinner,' Jazz told him squarely, leaving the bathroom to root through the tan-

gle of garments she had tossed out of her case earlier and find fresh comfortable clothing.

Their evening meal was served on an outside terrace shaded by vine-covered metal arches. A silver candelabra illuminated the exquisitely set table in a soft glow of light.

The first course arrived and Jazz tucked in with appetite, conscious of Vitale's scrutiny. 'What?' she finally queried in irritation.

'I like the fact that you enjoy food. So many women don't.'

'No, I think there's a certain belief out there that a healthy appetite in a woman is a sin and that it's somehow more feminine to pick daintily at food,' she told him, watching and copying what he did with his bread roll, still learning the little things she knew she needed to learn before she appeared at the fancy dinner that would precede the ball. Without warning, the concept of doing anything that could embarrass Vitale in public made Jazz cringe.

'You must have been appalled by my table manners when we were children,' she remarked uncomfortably.

'No. You were always dainty in your habits. But I will admit that I envied your freedom. You did as you liked and you said what you liked, just like Angel,' Vitale pointed out ruefully. 'I only ever had that luxury during those holidays. My childhood was in no way normal at the palace. My mother expected me to have the manners and outlook of an adult at a very early age.'

'I don't want our children growing up like that,' Jazz told him bluntly.

Vitale lounged back in his chair, all sleek, sophisticated male in the candlelight and devastatingly hand-

some. 'In that aim, we are in complete agreement,' he admitted. 'I want them to enjoy a normal happy childhood, free of the fear that they have to be perfect to be loved.'

'Does it matter to you whether they are boys or girls or even one of each?' she asked curiously.

'No. I have no preference. I will be very honest...' Vitale regarded Jazz with cautious dark golden eyes surrounded by gold-tipped lush black lashes. 'I have never wanted children but I have always accepted that I would have to have at least one for the sake of the throne. You have already achieved that requirement for me and to some extent, I can now relax, duty done...'

So, now I'm rent-a-womb, Jazz reflected, struggling not to react in too personal a way. He had told her the truth and she should respect that. *Duty done?* But he had *never* wanted children? That really worried her. His tender preparation of her bath had touched her heart and revitalised her but that blunt admission about never having wanted a child simply upset her again. All right, he was making the best of a bad job, as the saying went, but, as the woman playing a starring role and being made the best of, she felt humiliated and utterly insignificant in the grand scheme of Prince Vitale Castiglione's life...

CHAPTER EIGHT

JAZZ WAS UNPREPARED for the barrage of journalists and photographers who awaited their arrival at the airport in the capital city of Lerovia, Leburg. The amount of interest taken in her arrival with Vitale was phenomenal and she was no longer surprised by his request that she remove her wedding ring before their flight landed. Amidst the shouted madness of questions, flash photography and outright staring, Jazz felt as though she had briefly strayed into some mirror world, terrifyingly different from her own.

'The press know about the ball and my mother is too outspoken for there to be much doubt about its purpose, which was to find me a wife,' Vitale told her very drily when they had finally escaped into the peace of a limousine with tinted windows and a little Lerovian flag on the bonnet. 'So, obviously my arrival in Leburg with a woman is a source of great speculation.'

'But surely you've brought other women here?' Jazz exclaimed, still a little shaken up by her first encounter with the press en masse.

'You're the first. My affairs have always been kept off the radar and discreet,' Vitale explained reluctantly. 'Unlike Angel, I was never an international playboy and

until today I have not been much troubled by the attentions of the paparazzi.'

'Did I hear someone shout a question about the engagement ring?'

'There were several, some in Italian and German,' Vitale advanced. 'That's why I gave it to you.'

'No, you gave it to me when you did because I was in a funk and you were trying to distract me,' Jazz told him wryly. 'Although I've no doubt you planned for me to arrive here flashing it.'

She liked the last word. His mother did as well. But somehow when Jazz cut in with one of her cute little last words, it didn't annoy him to the same degree, although her ability to read his motives unsettled him and made him feel tense. His lean, strong face clenched hard because he had already been tense. He hated conflict with Queen Sofia because it was a challenge to fight back when he was forced to give his aggressor the respect and obligation due to his monarch. It could never be a fair battle.

Jazz was merely relieved that she had put on an elegant dress and jacket for her arrival in Lerovia and had braided her hair, which left loose could look untidy. It had not escaped her attention that Vitale had grown steadily grimmer the closer they got to the country of his birth. Did he hate living in Lerovia, she wondered, or was it simply the problems he had dealing with his mother, the Queen?

She peered out at the city of Leburg, which appeared to have a skyline that could have rivalled Dubai's. It was an ultramodern, fully developed European city and a tax haven with very rich inhabitants, which she had learned from her own research on the internet. Fur-

thermore, the man she had married, the father of her unborn twins, might be the heir to the Lerovian throne but he was also the CEO of the Bank of Lerovia. He hadn't told her any of that but then Vitale had never been much of a talker when it came to himself, so she wasn't the least offended by his omissions. In any case, she was perfectly capable of doing her own homework concerning the country where she was to live for the foreseeable future. Italian, German and English were widely spoken in Lerovia and many residents were from other countries.

The royal family had ruled Lerovia since the thirteenth century, which had disconcerted Jazz because for some reason she had always assumed that the Castiglione family were more recent arrivals. The ruling family, numbering only mother and son, lived in Ilrovia Castle, a white, much turreted and very picturesque building in the hills just outside the city.

Stealing a glance at Vitale's taut bronzed profile, she suddenly found herself reaching for his hand. 'You're not on your own in this,' she reminded him quietly. 'We got married for the sake of the children. I'm as much involved as you are.'

'No, you won't be. I won't put you in the path of my mother's spite. The Queen is my cross to bear,' he said very drily, quietly easing his fingers free. 'In any case, you're pregnant and you shouldn't be upset in *any* way.'

'Nonsense!' Jazz parried roundly, her backbone of steel stiffening but her pride and her heart hurt by the way he had instantly freed her hand. She gritted her teeth, inwardly urging herself to be patient and not to expect change overnight.

But even so, Vitale had been very different over their Italian weekend. He had been relaxed, not once retreating into the reserved and rather chilly impersonal approach that she was beginning to appreciate was the norm for him in public places or with strangers. Change had loomed only when they had landed in Lerovia, which really said it all, she thought ruefully. In her very bones, she was aware that she was soon to meet the mother-in-law from hell and that she had absolutely no defensive armour with which to fight back.

After all, she *was* the daughter of a humble housekeeper with no impressive ancestors, a little better educated than those ancestors but still without the official sanction of a degree even if she had almost completed one. And she was pregnant into the bargain, she conceded ruefully. She didn't qualify as an equal in Vitale's world. To put it bluntly, and Clodagh had, Jazz had married *up* in her aunt's parlance and Vitale had married *down*. Well, she was what she was and perfectly happy on her own account but it seemed only reasonable to expect the Queen of Lerovia to be severely disappointed in her son's choice of bride.

The car purred through a medieval stone archway guarded by soldiers, who presented arms in acknowledgement of Vitale's arrival. Jazz struggled not to feel intimidated as they entered a giant, splendidly furnished hall awash with gleaming crystal chandeliers and grand gilded furniture. Vitale immediately turned left to head up a staircase to one side.

'I have my private quarters in the castle. The Queen lives in the other wing and the ground houses the royal ceremonial apartments where official events are held and where we entertain,' Vitale told her on the stairs.

'You do realise that that is the only information you have ever given me about Lerovia?' Jazz remarked drily.

Vitale paused on the landing, dark golden eyes visibly disturbed by that observation.

'Oh, don't worry. The internet made up for your omission,' Jazz assured him ruefully. 'I've picked up the basics. It was interesting. I had no idea your family had been ruling here for so many generations or that gay people still live a restricted life here.'

He clenched his jaw. 'The Queen will countenance nothing that goes against church teaching. Unfortunately, the monarch in Lerovia also still has the right to veto laws proposed by parliament,' he admitted. 'I wasn't joking when I warned you that we lived in the past here.'

'Some day you'll be able to shake it up a little,' Jazz pointed out as he guided her through a door into a hallway that was surprisingly contemporary in contrast to the rather theatrical ground-floor décor.

'That day is a long way off,' Vitale intoned with firm conviction. 'The Queen will never voluntarily give up power.'

Jazz wandered round her new home, followed by two members of Vitale's domestic staff, Adelheid the housekeeper and Olivero, the butler. Both spoke excellent English and she learned that Vitale's wing had originally been the nursery wing devoted to his upbringing and in complete isolation from his mother's living accommodation. Obviously, the Queen was not the maternal type, Jazz acknowledged, knowing that she would never accept her children being housed at such a distance from her and solely tended to by staff. The more little glimpses she gained of Vitale's far from sunny childhood, the better she understood him.

Their spacious home stretched to three floors and steps led down from the big airy drawing room to the gardens. Jazz was smothering yawns by the time the official tour reached the master bedroom, which was decorated in subtle shades of green and grey. She was introduced to *her* maid, Carmela, who was already unpacking her luggage to fill the large, well-appointed dressing room off the bedroom. A maid, her own *maid*, she thought in awed disbelief.

Vitale entered after the maid had gone and found Jazz lying down on the bed with her shoes and jacket removed.

'I thought I'd go for a nap before I start getting ready for the ball. I'm really quite sleepy,' she confided, pushing herself up on her elbows, the braid she had undone to lie down now a tumbling mass of vibrant tresses falling over one shoulder, the arch of her spine pushing her breasts taut up against the fine silk bodice of her dress.

Vitale studied her with brutally male appreciation and a heat she was instantly aware of, his dark eyes scorching hot with the thought of possibilities, and something clenched low in her body, the stirring primal impulses of the same hunger.

'I'll leave you in peace,' he began.

'No,' Jazz countered, reaching out her hand to close into his sleeve. 'I'm not *that* tired.'

Vitale dealt her a sizzling smile that sent butterflies tumbling in her tummy and bent his head to kiss her, both his hands sinking into the torrent of her hair. Excitement leapt into her slender body like a lightning bolt and then just as suddenly the bedroom door burst noisily open. Vitale released her instantaneously and Jazz thrust herself up on her hands, her face flushed

with annoyance and embarrassment as she focused on the woman who had stalked into their bedroom without so much as a warning knock. Even worse, a gaggle of goggle-eyed people were peering in from the corridor outside.

'Close the door, Vitale,' Jazz murmured flatly, staring at the enraged blonde, garbed in a stylish blue suit and pearls, standing mere feet away. 'We don't need an audience for this—'

'Oh, I think we do, leave the door wide, Vitale,' Queen Sofia cut in imperiously. 'I'd like an audience to see your red-headed whore being thrown out of the palace.'

Vitale closed the door and swung round. 'I will not tolerate so rude an intrusion, nor will I tolerate such abuse.'

'You will tolerate whatever I ask you to tolerate because I am your *Queen*!' the blonde proclaimed with freezing emphasis. 'I want this creature gone. I don't care how you do it but it *must* be done before the ball this evening.'

'If my fiancée leaves, I will accompany her,' Vitale parried.

'You wouldn't *dare*!' his mother screeched at him, transforming from ice to instant fiery fury.

A woman with no volume control, Jazz registered, only just resisting the urge to physically cover her ears. The Queen shot something at Vitale in outraged Italian and the battle commenced, only, frustratingly, Jazz had no idea what was being said. Vitale's mother seemed to be concentrating on trying to shout him down while Vitale himself spoke in a cool, clipped voice Jazz had never heard him employ before, his control absolute.

'Jazz will be my partner at the ball this evening,' Vitale declared in clarifying English. 'Nothing you can say or do will change that.'

'She's a servant's daughter... Oh, yes, I've found out all about you!' Queen Sofia shot triumphantly at Jazz, her piercing pale blue eyes venomous.

Jazz slid off the bed and stood up, instantly feeling stronger.

'You're a nothing, a nobody, and I don't know what my son's doing with you because he *should* know his duty better than anyone.'

'As you have often reminded me, my duty is to marry and produce a child,' Vitale interposed curtly. 'Jazz is the woman I have chosen.'

'I will not accept her and therefore she has to go!' The older woman cast the file she had tightly gripped in one hand down on the bed beside Jazz. 'Have a look at the candidates I selected. You couldn't compete with a single one of those women! You have no breeding and no education, none of the very special qualities required to match my son's status.'

'Get out,' Vitale breathed with chilling bite, closing a firm hand to the older woman's arm to lead her back to the door. 'You have said what you came to say and I will not allow you to abuse Jazz.'

'If you bring her to the ball, I will not acknowledge her!' Queen Sofia threatened. 'And I will make your lives hell!'

'I imagine Vitale is quite used to you making his life hell,' Jazz opined dulcetly, her head held high as the older woman stared at her in disbelief, much as though a piece of furniture had moved forward and dared to

address her. 'And as long as I have Vitale by my side, you will not intimidate me with your threats either.'

'Are you going to let this interloper speak to your Queen like that?' his mother raged.

In answer, Vitale strode forward and addressed his mother in an angry flood of English, a dark line of colour edging his hard cheekbones. The older woman tried to shout him down but Vitale slashed an authoritative silencing hand through the air and continued in the same splintering tone, 'You will not call my fiancée vile names *ever* again. You will not force your way into my private quarters again either. I am an adult, not a child you can bully and disrespect. Other people may tolerate such behaviour from you but I no longer will. Be careful, Mother, *very* careful because your future plans could easily fall apart. Your insolence is intolerable and if it continues I will leave the palace and I will leave Lerovia,' he completed harshly. 'I will not live anywhere where my fiancée is viciously abused.'

The Queen was pale and seemed to have shrunk in size. She opened her mouth but then just as suddenly closed it again, visibly shattered by his threat to leave the country. As she left, Vitale shut the door firmly again.

For an instant there was complete silence. Jazz was shaken by his vigorous defence but still unconvinced by his decision not to tell the whole truth immediately.

'You should have told your mother that the deed was already done and that you are married,' Jazz told him unhappily. 'Why wait to break that final bit of news when she's already in such a snit?'

'I have my own ways of dealing with my mother,' Vitale countered curtly. 'Don't interfere and give her another excuse to attack you.'

'There's more than one way of skinning a rabbit!' Jazz tossed back at him, determined to fight her corner as best she could. 'Could you have my cases brought back in?'

Vitale froze, a winged ebony brow lifting. 'Why would you want your cases?'

'Because if your mother is free to walk into our bedroom any time she likes, I'm not staying,' Jazz told him bluntly.

'Dannazione...' Vitale swore with clenched fists of frustration. 'You heard what I told her.'

'I just witnessed a grown woman throwing a tantrum and hurling outrageous insults with apparent impunity. Being royal, being a queen, does not excuse that kind of behaviour.'

Vitale ground his teeth together and raked long brown fingers through his cropped blue-black hair. 'I agree,' he conceded. 'But I threatened to leave this country if she interferes again and that shocked her.'

'Ask for my cases, Vitale,' Jazz urged, refusing to listen. 'We could have been *in* bed when your mother walked in and she wouldn't have cared.'

In a provocative move, Vitale settled his broad shoulders back against the door and braced his long powerful legs. 'You can't leave. I won't let you,' he told her lethally.

'If you can't protect me in your own home, I'm leaving.'

'Over my dead body,' Vitale murmured, dark eyes glittering with challenge even as he stood his ground. 'You *will* be protected. I will accept nothing less.'

In reality Jazz was more incensed by his stubborn refusal to take her advice. 'I still think you need to tell the Queen now that we are married, I'm pregnant and

that the marriage is only a temporary measure,' she
countered between stiff lips.

'You don't know what you're talking about!' Vitale
could feel his temper suddenly taking a dangerous and
inexplicable leap forward again.

Jazz angled her head back, aware of the flare of
angry gold brightening his forceful gaze but quite unafraid of it. 'Well, of course I don't… You don't tell
me anything. It's all too personal and private for you
to share, so you hoard all your secrets up like a miser
with treasure!' she condemned resentfully.

'Don't be ridiculous!' Vitale shot back at her quellingly.

But Jazz was in no mood to be quelled. 'You had
no problems telling *me* that I would only be your wife
until the twins are born, so I can't understand why you
would be so obstinate about sharing that same information with your mother! After all, she'll undoubtedly be
delighted to hear that I'm not here to stay.'

At that unsought reminder of the terms he himself
had laid down, Vitale's lean, strong features set like a
granite rock and the rage he was struggling to control
surged even higher. 'Now you are making a most inappropriate joke of our situation, which I intensely dislike.'

Jazz's green eyes took on an emerald glow of rage
at that icily angry assurance because if there was one
thing that drove her mad, it was Vitale aiming that icy
chill at her. She had been proud of him when he'd targeted his mother with that chill though. 'Oh, do you indeed? I intensely dislike a stranger blundering into what
is supposed to be the marital bedroom when we're on
the bed! She's the kind of royal who gives me Repub-
lican sympathies! I will never *ever* forget that woman

calling me a whore and I won't forgive her for it either, no, not even if she apologises for it.'

'The Queen does not do apologies. You are safe from that possibility,' Vitale derided. 'Now, you will calm down and have lunch, which is being prepared.'

'You will not tell me to calm down!' Jazz raged back at him. 'I will shout if I feel like it.'

'You're pregnant. You need to keep calm,' Vitale proclaimed.

'That is not an excuse to shut me up!' Jazz hissed back at him.

Vitale startled her by striding forward without warning and lifting her off her feet to settle her down squarely on the bed she had only recently vacated. 'It is the only excuse I need. Lunch will wait until you have rested.'

'Do I look like I'm in the mood to rest?' Jazz argued fierily.

'No, but you know it's the sensible option and you have to think about *them*.' Vitale unsettled her even more by resting his hand with splayed fingers across her stomach. 'Neither of us want you to run the risk of a miscarriage by getting overexcited and pushing yourself too hard when you're already exhausted and stressed. The ball tonight will tire you even more,' he reminded her grimly.

Jazz had paled and she closed her eyes, striving for self-control, but she was still so mad at him and frustrated that it was an appalling struggle to hold back the vindictive words bubbling on her tongue. And then her green eyes flew wide again, crackling with angry defiance. 'Surely a miscarriage would *suit*—'

Vitale froze, wide sensual mouth setting hard, dark golden eyes flashing censorious reproach. 'Don't you

dare say that to me!' he breathed in a raw undertone. 'They are my children too and I want them, no matter how inconvenient their timing may be! No matter how much trouble their conception may have caused us!'

Jazz had stilled, her anger snuffed out at source by the wrathful sincerity she saw in his gaze and heard in his voice. 'I thought you didn't want children,' she reminded him.

'I thought so too but for some reason I'm getting excited by the idea of them now,' Vitale admitted reluctantly.

Surprisingly, a kind of peace filtered in to drain away her anger. She was ashamed of what anger had provoked her into saying to him but soothed too by her first real proof that Vitale truly *did* want their unborn children, regardless of their situation. Given sufficient time, he too had adjusted his attitude and his outlook had softened, readying him for change. She closed her eyes again, drained by the early morning start to the day, the travel and all that had followed their arrival at the palace. Fit and healthy though she was, the exhaustion of early pregnancy was pushing her to her limits and the imminent prospect of the ball simply made her suppress a groan.

Vitale glowered down at her prone figure. She had lost her temper, lost control, he reasoned grimly, had barely known what she was saying. Wasn't that why he guarded his own temper? But during that scene with his mother one unmistakable reality had powered Vitale. His wife and his children *had* to come first because they depended on him. His mother, in comparison, was surrounded by supporters comprised of flattering subordinates and socially ambitious hangers-on, not to mention

her chief lady-in-waiting, the Contessa Cinzia, who had
never been known to contradict her royal mistress.

Jazz only stirred when a maid entered the room
bringing a tray and she sat up with a start, blinking
rapidly while wondering what was crackling beneath
her hips. Her seeking hand drew out a file and a dim
memory of the Queen tossing it there surfaced.

'Thank you,' she told the maid. 'I'll eat at the table.'

She settled the file down on the table by the window.
Carmela informed her that her hair and make-up stylist
would be arriving in half an hour and, killing the urge
to roll her eyes at that information, Jazz lifted her knife
and fork and then paused to open the file…

CHAPTER NINE

'BUT IF THIS belonged to your grandmother that means it's royal, so how can I wear it?' Jazz protested as she held the delicate diamond tiara that shone like a circlet of stars between her reverent fingers.

'You're my wife and my grandmother bestowed her jewellery on me in her will for my wife's use,' Vitale explained. 'And if that is still not sufficient reason for you, think of how it will enrage my mother to see you draped in her mother's fabulous diamond suite.'

Her green eyes glinted with amused appreciation of that sally and she sat down by the dressing table to allow Vitale to anchor the tiara in her thick hair. With careful hands, she donned the earrings and the necklace from the same box and forced a smile, refusing, absolutely refusing to think about what she had read in that ghastly file that very afternoon. She needed to be confident for the ball, was determined to look as though she belonged at such a glittering event purely for Vitale's sake. The prospect of doing anything socially wrong in his mother's radius literally made her stomach clench with sick horror.

'You look wonderful,' Vitale husked as she rose again, a slim silhouette sheathed in a green gown that

glistened with thousands of beads. Cut high at the front, it bared her slender back, skimming down over her narrow hips to froth out in sparkling volume round her stiletto-clad feet.

'Wonderful enough to win your bet?'

Vitale, designer chic in a beautifully tailored evening jacket and narrow black trousers, groaned out loud. 'I couldn't care less about that bet now and you know it. Accepting that bet was a foolish impulse I now regret.'

Jazz smiled, the generous curve of her lush mouth enhanced by soft pink, and Vitale shifted forward, dark golden eyes flaring. 'No,' she said succinctly. 'If you knew how long it took the stylist to do my make-up, you wouldn't dare even *think* of kissing me.'

Vitale laughed, startling himself, it seemed, almost as much as he startled her, amusement lightening the forbidding tension that had still tautened his strong features. 'You're good for me,' he quipped.

But nowhere near as good in the royal wife stakes as Carlotta, Elena or Luciana or their equivalents would have been, a rebellious little voice remarked somewhere down deep inside her where the file had done the most damage by lowering her self-esteem and making her feel almost ashamed of her humble background. Shutting off that humiliating inner voice, Jazz drank in a deep steadying breath and informed him that she was ready to leave.

The female staff had assembled to see her ball gown and Jazz smiled, pleased by their approbation, secure in her belief that she had chosen well when she'd decided not to pick the plain and boring black dress that Vitale would have selected. With diamonds sparkling at her

every step, she caught a glimpse of her reflection in a tall hall mirror and barely recognised that glitzy figure.

Vitale's arm at her back, they entered a vast reception room on the ground floor where pre-dinner drinks were being served. Glorious landscape paintings of Lerovia lined the walls. Waiters in white jackets served drinks below the diamond-bright light of the gleaming crystal chandeliers twinkling above them. Angel and Merry headed straight for them and relief washed through Jazz the minute she saw their familiar faces.

'Super, *super* dress,' Merry whispered warmly.

'And yours,' Jazz responded, admiring the elaborate embroidery that covered her sister-in-law's pale gown. 'Vitale didn't tell me you'd both be here.'

'Vitale's on another planet when the Queen Bee is around,' Angel remarked very drily. 'One thing you will learn about Charles's sons, Jazz. He didn't pick our mothers very well.'

'But Charles is so lovely that he makes up for that,' Merry chipped in soothingly into the rather awkward silence that had fallen, because Jazz would not risk uttering a single critical word about the Queen, lest she be overheard and embarrass Vitale.

'Yes,' Jazz agreed as Angel roamed off to speak to his brother.

Place cards were carelessly swapped at the dining table to ensure that they sat with Angel and Merry and Jazz tucked into the first course with appetite, striving not to look in the direction of the Queen at the top of the exceedingly long table.

'Why's Zac not here?' Jazz asked curiously. 'I was hoping to meet him.'

'He'll be at the ball. He's not a fan of formal dinners,' Angel explained. 'He hates restrictions of any kind.'

'Very different from Vitale then… Interesting,' Jazz mused, incredibly curious about the third brother and already conscious that although Vitale hadn't actually admitted it, he didn't seem to like his Brazilian sibling much.

An hour later, Jazz was busily identifying the women in the ball room from their photographs in Queen Sofia's file, the 'suitable wives' file as she thought of it. And not a plain face or a redhead amongst the six candidates, all of them terrifyingly well-born, several titled, all possessed of the ability to speak more than one language, a high-flying education and a solid background of charitable good works. None of them would have required lessons on how to use cutlery or how to address an ambassador or curtsy to a reigning monarch. By the time she had finished perusing that damning file Jazz had felt horrendously inadequate. She had also felt ashamed that she had instinctively resented Vitale's certainty that theirs could only be a temporary marriage.

Of course, he didn't want to keep her when she was so ill-qualified for the position of a royal wife. Obviously, he would want a bride with all the accomplishments that he himself took for granted. Like with like worked best even in nature. It didn't mean that she was something lesser than the male she had married, she reasoned painfully, it only meant that they were too different.

'Zac's around here somewhere but I keep on missing him,' Vitale breathed impatiently, a lean bronzed hand settling to her slender spine as he walked out to

the grand foyer where guests stood in clusters served by another army of waiters bearing drinks trays.

An older man intercepted them and urged Vitale to introduce him to his fiancée. 'Jazz.'

'Short for?'

'Jazmine,' she slotted in with a smile, because it was the first time she had been asked. 'My father registered my birth and he spelt it with a *z* rather than an *s*, which is how I became Jazz.'

'And a very good friend in the media told me that you've known each other since you were children,' the older man filled in with amusement. 'That's one in the eye for your mother,' he pronounced with satisfaction before passing on.

'Who was that?'

'My mother's younger half-brother, Prince Eduardo.'

'Your *uncle*?' Jazz repeated in surprise.

'My mother wouldn't even let him live here after she was crowned. She has always behaved as though she were an only child refusing to share the limelight...'

Jazz's attention had strayed to the male exiting from a room further down the hall, smoothing down his jacket, running careless fingers through his long black hair, his light eyes bright beneath the lights. 'Is that Zac?' she asked abruptly, recognising the resemblance.

Two giggling women, one blonde, one brunette in rather creased ball gowns emerged from the same room only one telling step in the man's wake.

'*Sì*...that's Zac,' Vitale confirmed with audible distaste. 'I wonder what he did with his partner while he was in there.'

A moment later, Zac answered that question for himself. 'Well, obviously you win. Jazz is amazing and I

came alone,' he spelt out with a surprisingly charismatic grin of acknowledgement. 'My car is already in transit.'

While the brothers chatted, Jazz wandered off. Her mother-in-law was talking to a bunch of people at the far end of the hall and Jazz tactfully avoided that area.

Vitale rejoined her by sliding his arm round her back and she smiled. 'So, you won,' she commented.

'I set Zac up to fail. I feel a little guilty about doing that now,' Vitale confided in an undertone. 'But even so, this evening you have been a triumph of cool and control and I'm proud to be with you.'

Jazz gazed up at him in shock.

Vitale sighed. 'It needed to be said and I'm sorry that it took my kid brother to say it first,' he admitted.

'Who were those women Zac was with?'

'Willing ladies?' Vitale suggested.

'Don't be so judgemental!' Jazz urged. 'Nothing may have happened between them and Zac.'

'They're both on my mother's staff. I'm not in a charitable mood,' he admitted wryly. 'In any case, Zac is a player with the morals of an alley cat.'

Recognising that Vitale's judgemental streak ran to both sexes, Jazz almost laughed. She wondered if he had ever resented his inability to behave the same way. Of course, he had, she decided, of course he must have envied his brothers' freedom. Zac and Angel had freely chosen their lifestyles but birth had forced a rigid framework of dos and don'ts on Vitale and choice had had nothing to do with it.

'Did you ever just want to walk away from being royal?' Jazz asked him as he whirled her onto the dance floor for the opening dance beneath his mother's freezing gimlet gaze. But the ballroom was so colourful that

Jazz was entranced as more and more couples joined them on the floor, the ladies clad in every colour of the rainbow, their dresses swirling gracefully around them, the men elegant in black or white dinner jackets.

'Frequently when I was a child, more often as an adult,' Vitale confided, surprising her with that frankness. 'But a sense of duty to our name must be stamped into my DNA. Although I consider the idea, I know I won't actually *do* it.'

And it finally dawned on her that the unhappiness she had sensed in Vitale even as a child had been genuine and that acknowledgement saddened her. Shortly after midnight, soon after the Queen's regal exit from the ball, Vitale accompanied her up to the door of their apartment and she knew he intended to go and tell the older woman that he was a married man.

'If you're going to confront your mother,' she had argued all the way up the winding staircase. 'I should come with you.'

'There's no reason for you to be subjected to hours of her ranting and raving. For a start, she will initially insist that my having married without her permission makes the ceremony illegal,' Vitale retorted crisply. 'I'm used to her hysterics and she won't even listen until she calms down. Don't wait up for me.'

Thinking about Vitale poised like a soldier, icily controlled in the face of his Queen's wrath, made Jazz's hands clench into angry fists of frustration. She had arrived in Lerovia with an open mind concerning Queen Sofia but that single scene in their bedroom had convinced her that Vitale's mother was a despotic monster. And she cared, of course she *cared*, she reflected as she got ready for bed and finally climbed into that bed alone.

She loved Vitale. Oh, she hadn't matched the word to the feelings before in an effort to protect herself from hurt, but the hurt would come whether she labelled her emotions or not. She loved the male who had lit her candles round her bath, who had held her close all night before they travelled to Lerovia. He was amazingly affectionate when he thought she was safely asleep, she conceded with tender amusement, but wary of demonstrating anything softer during the hours of daylight.

Angel had deemed his younger brother 'emotionally stunted', but he had been wrong in that assessment. Vitale bore all the hallmarks of someone damaged in childhood. He had taught himself to hide his emotions, had learned to suppress his pain and his anger to the extent that he barely knew what he felt any more. Yet he was working so hard at protecting her from his horrible mother, she thought fondly before she drifted off to sleep.

Breakfast was served to her in bed late the next morning and her phone already carried a text from Vitale, letting her know that he was attending a board meeting at the bank and would be out most of the day. She ate sparsely, awaiting the nausea that often took hold of her but evidently it was to be one of her good days and she could go for a shower and dress, feeling healthy and normal for once instead of simply pregnant.

Clad in an unpretentious white sundress, she went down the stone steps into the gardens to explore and enjoy the early summer sunshine. She was slightly unnerved to be closely followed by the housekeeper, Adelheid, and introduced to the very large plain-clothed man with her as her bodyguard. Striving to forget that she had company, Jazz went for a walk and then phoned her

mum to catch up. She was sitting on a bench beside an ornamental stone fountain when a young woman approached her with a folded note on a silver salver.

'It is an invitation to lunch from the Queen, Your Highness,' the woman informed her with a bright smile.

Shock both at the form of address and the explanation of the note engulfed Jazz. Obviously, Vitale had spoken to his mother after the ball and the royal household were now aware that she was a wife rather than a fiancée. Even so, Jazz had expected the Queen to react with rage to the news that her son was married to his red-headed whore rather than a luncheon invite, and she was perplexed, lifting the note from the ludicrous salver and opening it while struggling to control her face.

Yes, she had also noted that the young woman delivering the note had been one of the women who had been in that room the night before with her brother-in-law, Zac. She concentrated, however, on the single sheet of notepaper and its gracious copperplate written summons and gave her consent to lunching with Vitale's mother even though she would much have preferred to say no. Vitale would probably want her to say no, but then Jazz was made of much tougher stuff than the man she had married seemed willing to appreciate. Sticks and stones would not break her bones, indeed they only made her stronger. In fact, if *she* could for once take a little heat off Vitale, Jazz was delighted to take the opportunity.

'My dear,' Queen Sofia purred, rising to greet Jazz as if she were a well-loved friend as soon as she entered the imposing dining room with a gleaming table that rejoiced in only two place settings set directly opposite each other. 'Vitale shared your *wonderful* news with me.'

And the wonderful news, Jazz learned in disbelief, was that she was pregnant with twins. The Queen also trotted out that old chestnut about the heir and a spare with a straight face. In fact, she seemed to be, at that point, an entirely different woman from the one Jazz had met so unforgettably the day before. Sadly, though, that impression was to be a transitory one.

'Of course, Vitale has left me to organise the royal wedding,' the older woman continued smoothly.

'Wedding?' Jazz echoed in astonishment.

'You may legally be married now but for the benefit of our country and the dignity of the family there must be a religious ceremony in which you are *seen* to get married,' Queen Sofia clarified. 'Didn't my son explain that to you?'

'No,' Jazz admitted, thoroughly intimidated by the prospect of a royal wedding.

'Of course, you probably think it is a great deal of fuss over nothing when you and Vitale will not be together very long,' the older woman continued in a measured tone of false regret that told Jazz all she needed to know about why she was currently receiving a welcome. 'But our people expect a wedding and a public holiday in which to celebrate the longevity of the Castiglione family's rule.'

Jazz was holding her breath after that stabbing little reminder that as a wife she would not be enjoying family longevity. 'Of course,' she said flatly, because clearly her private wants and wishes were not to be considered in the balance of royal necessities.

'We are so fortunate that Vitale married you quickly and that your condition is not obvious yet,' the Queen carolled in cheerful addition.

My goodness, the prospect of a couple of babies truly transformed Vitale's mother, Jazz thought limply.

'Obviously we will announce that a civil ceremony took place in London some weeks ago,' the older woman assured her. 'Not that I think these days people will be counting the months of your pregnancy, but it will add to what my PR team regard as the romantic nature of this whole affair.'

'*Romantic?*' Jazz exclaimed, wondering if she would ever work up the nerve to say more than one word back to the Queen.

The Queen waved a dismissive hand. 'Your low birth. Your having known my son from childhood. His apparent decision to marry out of his class,' she pronounced with unconcealed distaste. 'We know that is not the true story. *We* know he *had* to marry you but our people will prefer the romantic version—the totally ridiculous idea that he could have fallen madly in love with you!'

Jazz was now pale as death with perspiration beading her short upper lip. She could no more have touched the plate of food in front of her than she could have spread wings and flown out of the window to escape the spite of the woman opposite her. She swallowed hard on her rising nausea, determined not to show weakness or vulnerability. She pushed her food around the plate while the Queen chattered about how very quickly the wedding could be staged and about how she would have Jazz's measurements taken immediately for her dress. After the meal, she was shown into another room where a dressmaker did exactly that and then she escaped back up to the apartment feeling as battered and bruised as though she had gone ten rounds with a champion boxer.

Jazz now understood exactly why the Queen of Lerovia was willing to make her the reluctant star of a royal wedding. The twins would be Vitale's heirs and that was seemingly important enough to the Castiglione dynasty to counteract his bride's notoriously humble beginnings. Jazz tried to comprehend her mother-in-law's unreservedly *practical* viewpoint. Vitale could have married a woman who did not conceive or a woman who had other difficulties in that field. Instead his heir and a spare were already on the way. The Queen despised her lowborn daughter-in-law but would tolerate her because Jazz was not in Lerovia to stay. Evidently, Vitale had told his mother the whole truth about his marriage and Jazz could not work out why she felt so wounded and betrayed by that reality when she had urged him to do exactly that.

There were no more secrets now and it was better that way, she told herself over a lonely dinner. The Queen would throw no more tantrums and would play along for the sake of appearances until Vitale and Jazz broke up. Everyone could now relax—everyone could be happy.

'You're having a bad dream… Wake up!' Vitale shook her shoulder.

In the darkness, Jazz blinked rapidly, extracted from a nightmare in which she was fleeing from some menace in a haunted castle remarkably similar to Vitale's home. 'I'm fine,' she whispered shakily. 'When did you get back?'

'Midnight.' His lean, powerful body perfectly aligned to hers. 'I let you down by not being here. I didn't expect my mother to invite you for lunch. I *told* her to stay out

of my life. What the hell is she playing at?' he demanded in furious frustration.

'She's crowing about the twins.' Jazz sighed, drowsily stretching back into the reassuring heat of him. 'And organising a royal wedding.'

'You should never have joined her for lunch,' Vitale declared rawly. 'You should've said you were ill and left me to deal with her.'

'I managed. It was OK,' Jazz lied.

'I don't believe you,' Vitale admitted, flipping her over onto her back and leaning over her, his lean, darkly beautiful face shadowed by moonlight into intriguing hard edges and hollows. 'She would've been poisonous. Don't treat me like I'm stupid!'

'For goodness' sake…' Jazz faltered as he stretched over and switched on the light to stare down at her accusingly. 'She was a bit bitchy, little jibes…you know…'

'Of course I know,' Vitale asserted grimly, his strong jaw clenching hard. 'I've seen her in action many times when she wants to punish those who have crossed her. What did she say to you?'

'Nothing that wasn't the truth,' Jazz dismissed. 'That you *had* to marry me. Well, can't argue with that.'

Vitale swore long and low in Italian. 'Don't you understand that that is why I want you to stay away from her at all costs? I refuse to have you exposed to her malice.'

'It really doesn't matter to me,' Jazz fibbed with pride. 'It's not as if I'm going to be living here under her roof for ever, so I don't care what she thinks of me or what she says to me.'

'I care,' Vitale ground out fiercely, thinking of what he had learned about himself after he had forced out the

admission to his mother that his marriage was not to be of the permanent variety. 'I care a great deal.'

'Why are you in such a mood?' Jazz asked, running a teasing pale hand down over his bare bronzed chest, feeling him tense against her, watching his eyes flare with luminous revealing gold.

'I'm convinced you're a witch, *moglie mia*,' Vitale growled, his passionate mouth crashing down hungrily on hers.

Smiling inside herself, Jazz slid like a temptress along the long, taut and fully aroused length of him and, returning that kiss with equal heat, concluded the awkward conversation.

Three weeks later, Queen Sofia had the last laugh, after all, Jazz conceded as she watched her six bridesmaids fuss over her train and her veil, both of which demanded considerable attention due to their length and ornate decoration. Less was not more in the Queen's parlance, but Jazz had picked her favourite of the options presented to her. The pressure of starring as the leading light in a royal wedding sat heavily on her shoulders and it was several days since she had enjoyed a decent night of sleep.

It was a fairy-tale wedding gown and very sophisticated. It was composed of tulle and glitter net with a strapless dropped-waist bodice adorned with metallic embroidered lace. The neckline and waistline were richly beaded with pearls, crystals and rhinestones. Exquisite and stylish, the draped full skirt glittered with delicately beaded lace appliques. The veil was full length and fashioned of intricate handmade lace.

The bridesmaids, however, were a cruel plunge of a

knife into Jazz's still beating heart. The file of bridal candidates she had hidden in the bottom of her lingerie drawer were all fully present and correct in the bridesmaids. So, naturally, Jazz was studying them, listening to their chatter, struggling to work out which one Vitale would eventually marry for *real*. Would it be Elena, who never ever shut up? Carlotta, who out of envy could barely bring herself to look at Jazz? Or Luciana, who either didn't speak any English or who didn't want to be forced to speak to the bride? Or one of the other three young women, all bright and beautiful and perfect?

The organ music in the cathedral swelled and Jazz walked down the aisle on the arm of Vitale's uncle, Prince Eduardo. Her family were present but her mother had shrunk from such public exposure when her daughter had asked her to walk her down the aisle, so the Queen had, once again, got her wish and had co-opted her brother into the role of giving away the bride.

Jazz was troubled by having to go through a religious service when her marriage was already destined to end in divorce but nobody had asked Jazz how she felt about taking such vows in church and she suspected that nobody would be the least interested in her moral objections. There was no fakery in *her* heart, nothing false about *her* feelings, she reminded herself resolutely as she knelt down before the Cardinal in his imposing scarlet robes.

Disconcertingly, Vitale chose that same moment to cover her hand with his and she turned her head to look at his lean, darkly handsome face, her heart jumping behind her breastbone, her tummy fluttering with butterflies while she marvelled at the compelling power of

that sidewise glance of his and the curling lashes darker and more lush than her own false ones. His wide sensual mouth curled into a faint smile and she thought, Why is he smiling? and only then did she remember that there were cameras on them both and quite deliberately Jazz beamed back at him, doing what was expected of her, fearful of the misery inside her showing on the outside and equally fearful of doing the wrong thing.

Once again a wedding ring slid onto her finger and once again there was no kissing of the bride, Vitale being no fan of public demonstrations of affection. They left the cathedral to a barrage of whirring, clicking cameras and the roar of the irritatingly happy crowds assembled behind the crash barriers in the square beyond. It was lovely that people were happy for them, Jazz reflected, trying to find something positive in the event, but sad that those same people would be disappointed when their marriage ended again.

She would not miss being royal, she told herself as they stepped into the waiting horse-drawn carriage and Vitale complained bitterly about how rocky and uncomfortable it was to travel in such a way. Then without any warning whatsoever he gripped her hand, almost crushing her poor fingers, and shot something at her in driven Italian. '*Cosa c'e di sbagliato?* What's wrong?'

'Nothing's wrong!' she snapped, trailing her hand back in a trice.

'That is so patently a lie that my teeth are gritting,' Vitale told her roundly.

Well, that was tough but he would just have to live with it. She had been forced into a second very public wedding with the future replacement-wife candidates trailing her down the aisle as bridesmaids. Hadn't

he even recognised them? Of course, he would have looked at the ladies in that file at some stage because his mother was too pushy to have let him sidestep it. Jazz felt very married and very cross with her two wedding rings and her husband who didn't love her. Not that that meant that he kept his hands off her though, she reflected hotly. Of course, she was in a bad mood. Yes, she was doing this for her children, but deciding to do it had been considerably easier than actually living the experience.

Vitale flipped mentally through every possible sin or omission he could have committed and acknowledged that he had made more mistakes than he could count. It made him uncomfortable when Jazz went quiet because she was never naturally quiet. 'Did the doctor say something that worried you?' he asked.

'Will you stop *reminding* me that I'm pregnant?' Jazz launched at him. 'Can't I just forget about being an incubator in a wedding gown for five minutes?'

Vitale clamped his mouth firmly shut because even he could take a hint that landed with the crushing weight of a boot. Maybe it was hormones, something like that, he reasoned uneasily. Or maybe she was feeling sick again. He parted his lips to enquire and then breathed in deep to restrain the urge, relieved that the palace was already in view. *An incubator in a wedding gown?* Where had that bizarre image come from? He would have a word with his father at the reception. Charles Russell had impregnated three women. He had to know something about pregnancy. Jazz sounded really upset and she didn't get upset, at least not in his experience. He stole a covert glance at her rigid profile and watched in absolute horror as a tear slid down her cheek.

'Jazz…?' Vitale stroked a soothing forefinger down over her tightly clenched hands. 'What can I do?'

'I just wish…' she began in a wobbly voice, 'that we were already divorced. Then it would all be done and dusted and in the past and I could get *my* life back.'

Vitale froze, his shrewd banker's mind going utterly blank at that aspiration. 'I don't want to discuss that,' he finally replied flatly. 'I don't want to discuss that at all.'

'Tough,' Jazz pronounced grittily.

Vitale decided at that point that talking was sometimes a vastly overrated pursuit, particularly when it was heading towards what promised to be a multiple-car crash of a conclusion. It was definitely the wrong moment. In a few minutes, they would be the centre of attention again at a reception attended by the crowned heads of Europe. What he said to Jazz needed to be said in private. It would have to be measured, calm and sincere even though it wouldn't be what she wanted to hear, even though he would be breaking his word. That acknowledgement silenced Vitale because he was appalled at that truth.

The reception was endless. Jazz shook hands and smiled and posed for photos, feeling like a professional greeter at a very upmarket restaurant. Charles Russell warmed her by giving her a hug and saying, 'Well, when I sent Vitale in your direction I wasn't expecting a wedding but I'm delighted for you both, Jazz.'

The older man greeted her mother with equal friendliness while Vitale bored the hind legs off her aunt by telling her all about Lerovia. At least he was *trying*, she conceded, striving to be more generous in her outlook. But that she was in a bad mood was really all his fault. They had supposedly only married to give the twins

legitimacy, so why was he still sharing a bed with her? Why was he draping her in his grandmother's fabulous jewellery? She had more diamonds than she knew what to do with and he kept on buying gifts for her as well.

She thought about the tiger pendant with the emerald eyes that she cherished. She thought about the ever-expanding snow globe collection she now possessed. Vitale had given her the wrong signals from the outset and it was hardly surprising that she had fallen for him hard or that she had foolishly continued having sex with him, hoping to ignite emotions that he wasn't capable of feeling. He had as much emotion as a granite pillar! Didn't she have any pride or sense of self-preservation? Lashing herself with such thoughts, Jazz held her head high and continued to smile while deciding that things were about to change…

CHAPTER TEN

'THE STORY'S ALL over the internet...' a vaguely familiar voice was saying urgently. 'And apparently the *Her-
ald* is publishing the article tomorrow, complete with
revealing photos. Your mother's request that they pull
the article was refused. The whole household is in uproar and Sofia's planning to flee to her Alpine chalet.
Nobody knows how to handle this.'

'Yet you *knew* and you didn't warn me,' Vitale
framed with raw-edged bitterness as Jazz peered drowsily at the clock by the bed and noted that it was three
in the morning.

'It wasn't any of my business. She threw me out of the
palace the day before her coronation. Saw her kid brother
as competition, you see, refused to accept me as family.'

'*Sì*, Eduardo,' Vitale agreed flatly. 'I'll get dressed
and see what I can do.'

'There's nothing anyone can do!' Vitale's uncle proclaimed on a telling note of barely concealed satisfaction. 'Too late for any emergency cover-ups now!'

As the bedroom door closed Jazz sat up and stared in
the dim light of the lamp by the door at Vitale, naked but
for a pair of black boxers. He looked shattered. 'What's
happened?' she asked straight away.

'Apparently my mother's been involved in an affair with her best friend, Countess Cinzia, for over thirty years and it's about to be exposed in the press. The scandal's already online,' he revealed with harsh clarity.

'A gay affair?' Jazz questioned in astonishment.

'How did I *not* know?' Vitale groaned. 'That's why my parents divorced. Apparently, my father once found my mother and Cinzia together. After I was wakened and told, I phoned Papa at his hotel because, at first… I couldn't believe it. But he confirmed that it was the truth. Yet I *still* can't believe it,' he admitted with growing anger. 'I've lost good friends, friends who left this country because of the restrictive laws that the Queen actively promoted. How could my mother oppose gay liberation when she's gay herself? What kind of hypocrite behaves like that?'

'I don't know…' It was completely inadequate but Jazz could think of nothing to say because she was equally stunned by what he was telling her.

'I'll deal with it as best I can,' Vitale said angrily. 'But we won't be helped by the number of enemies the Queen's made of influential people.'

'Is there anything I can do to help?' Jazz enquired weakly.

'Go back to sleep,' Vitale advised succinctly. 'My mother will step down from the throne. She's too proud to face this out.'

'But *that* means…' Jazz gasped and then dismay sentenced her to a silent stare of consternation at the lean, powerful male poised at the foot of the bed.

'*Sì*. Let's hope you take to being a queen better than you took to being a bride a second time,' Vitale pronounced with lashings of sarcasm while secretly won-

dering how he would take to the transformation of his own life. He could barely imagine a future empty of his mother's constant demands and complaints, but the prospect loomed ahead of him with a sudden brightness that disconcerted him, like the light at the end of a dark tunnel.

Jazz hunched back under the covers, too exhausted to snark back at him. She had collapsed into bed late the previous evening so exhausted that she had had all the animation of a corpse and had immediately fallen asleep. Certainly, it could not have been the second wedding night of any bridegroom's dreams. She had, however, been looking forward to escaping the palace in the morning and relaxing on the yacht Angel was loaning them for a Mediterranean cruise. Now she reckoned that any chance of a honeymoon was gone because, whatever Sofia Castiglione chose to do next, Vitale would be heavily involved in the clean-up operation and far too busy to leave the palace.

Vitale reappeared while she was having breakfast out on the terrace that overlooked the gardens. He told her that people were marching with placards outside the palace and that she was fortunate to be at the back of the building.

'How's your mother?' she asked awkwardly.

'She's already gone,' he breathed almost dazedly, as if he could not quite accept that astonishing reality. 'Cinzia and her together. She wasn't willing to talk to me and she released a statement declaring that her private life was exactly that, so no apologies either for a lifelong deception.'

'Did you really expect any?' She studied him worriedly, recognising the lines of strain and fatigue etched

in his lean, strong face, and he shook his head in grim acknowledgement of that point.

The silence stretched while a member of staff brought fresh coffee to the table. Even the staff were creeping about very quietly as though there had been a bereavement rather than a massive scandal that had blown the Lerovian royal family wide open to the kind of international speculation it had never had to endure before. Jazz poured coffee for Vitale and urged him to eat. After his mother's hasty departure, he was heading straight into a meeting with government representatives.

'The Prime Minister persuaded her to abdicate,' Vitale groaned. 'Nothing to do with her being gay. Ironically, she could have come out of the closet years ago had she been willing, but she wasn't. It was her hypocrisy in opposing equality laws that are normal in the rest of Europe that brought her down. Her behaviour was indefensible.'

'Just move on from it,' Jazz muttered, feeling useless and helpless when she wanted to be the exact opposite for his sake.

'We all will,' Vitale declared more smoothly. 'But, more importantly, I've made arrangements for you, your mother and aunt to fly out to Angel's yacht this morning.'

'I can't leave you here alone!' Jazz exclaimed.

'There's nothing you can do here,' Vitale pointed out with inescapable practicality. 'We have protestors outside the palace and in the city. Lerovia is in uproar. I cannot leave right now but you and your family can.'

'But—'

'It *would* be a comfort to me to know that you are safe on Angel's yacht and protected from anything that

could distress you,' Vitale incised in his chilly take-no-prisoners command voice that always made her tummy sink like a stone.

Jazz's protests died there. He didn't want her to stay. He was sending her away. It was clear that her presence was neither a consolation, nor a necessity. It was a lesson, she conceded painfully, a rather hard lesson and overdue. Vitale didn't *need* her. She might feel a need for him pretty much round the clock but that bond did not stretch both ways. She sucked in a steadying breath and contrived a smile when she felt more like crying, a reaction he certainly did not deserve. 'OK. What time do I leave?' she asked quietly without a flicker of reaction.

Relief at her assent showed openly in Vitale's stunning dark golden eyes and her heart clenched that her leaving could so obviously be a source of respite for him. Of course, he wasn't in love with her and he didn't depend on her, so she was, very probably, just one more person in his already very crowded life to worry about.

It was way past time she began accepting the limits of their relationship, she reflected unhappily, because here she was even now, always looking for more from Vitale, asking for more, *hoping* for more. And those fond wishes were unlikely to be granted. Nor, to be fair to him, had he ever suggested that there would be more between them than he had originally offered.

Carmela had already packed for the proposed cruise round the Mediterranean and Jazz chatted on the phone to her mother and her aunt, who were all agog and fascinated by the newspaper revelations but wildly overexcited at the prospect of staying on a billionaire's yacht for at least a week.

Back to basics, Jazz told herself firmly as she climbed into the helicopter that had landed in the castle grounds with her mother and her aunt already on board. And the basic bottom line on her marriage with Vitale was that they had married solely to legitimise their unborn children. It shocked Jazz to force herself to remember that modest truth. When had she begun moving so dangerously far from that original agreement? Hadn't she known in her heart even at the beginning that she felt far more for Vitale than she should? In other words, she was suffering from a self-inflicted injury. He had not asked her to love him, had never sought that deeper bond or hinted at more lasting ties. In fact, Vitale had married her while openly talking about divorcing her, so she couldn't blame him for misleading her or lying in any way. No, she could only blame herself for not keeping better control of her emotions.

Angel's yacht, *Siren*, rejoiced in such size and splendour that Jazz's mother and aunt were completely overpowered by the luxury and quite failed to notice Jazz's unusual quietness. Separated from Vitale, she felt horribly alone and empty.

Over the next few days while the trio of women sunbathed, swam and shopped in the island towns the yacht visited, Jazz continued to avidly read online reports of the latest developments in Lerovia. Vitale had been declared King and the popular unrest had subsided almost immediately because he was expected to be a modern rather than traditional monarch as his mother had been described. He phoned Jazz every evening, polite strained calls that did nothing to raise her spirits. The coronation had been scheduled for the following month.

Vitale was free now, Jazz thought unhappily, free for the first time in his life from his mother's demands and interference. But he wasn't free in his marriage, Jazz acknowledged wretchedly, feeling like the final obstacle in his path to full liberation. After all, if she hadn't fallen pregnant he wouldn't have been married to a woman unqualified to become his Queen. But what could he possibly do about it now? He could hardly divorce her while she was still pregnant, so he was stuck with making the best of things until he was free to make a better choice.

Thinking such downbeat thoughts, Jazz studied her changing body shape in the bedroom mirror. Her stomach was developing a rounded curve while her waist was losing definition and her breasts were now overflowing her *new* bras. Shopping for maternity clothing could not be put off much longer but the very idea of such a trip made her feel unattractive.

'I've decided to go home to London with Mum and Clodagh tomorrow,' Jazz informed Vitale when he phoned that evening. 'It would get me out of your hair.'

An abrupt little silence fell on the line.

'What if I don't want you out of my hair?' Vitale demanded with sudden harshness.

'Well, you did say that you were comforted by the idea of me being away from you on this yacht, so I thought that possibly me being in London would have the same effect.'

'It *wouldn't*.' Vitale's voice was cold and clipped and very emphatic in tone.

'Oh… I expect I'm needed for things at the palace,' she muttered ruefully.

'You are,' Vitale confirmed without skipping a beat,

wondering what on earth had got into her, and from where she had picked up such strange ideas.

Only slowly and with effort did he register that avoiding talking about the kind of stuff he had always avoided talking about could be the single biggest mistake he had ever made. Silence didn't work on Jazz as it had on his mother. Jazz wasn't content to fill the silence with the sound of her own voice. She would be too busy judging everything he said and did as though it were a crime scene and reaching her own dangerous conclusions.

Vitale got off the phone very quickly after that exchange and it unnerved Jazz, who had assumed that he would encourage her to go to London. She wondered if she would ever understand the conflicting signals he gave her. First, he wanted her, next he didn't want her, then he wanted her again. She supposed the crisis was over now and possibly that was the cause of his change of attitude. Weary of speculating about a man who had always confounded her expectations but whom she would have walked over fire to protect, Jazz dined with her family and then went for a shower.

When the helicopter came in to land, she was wrapped in a towel and seated out on the private terrace off the master suite watching the sun go down in flaming splendour. Having assumed that the craft was merely delivering supplies, she sped indoors again to escape the noise and was completely taken aback when Vitale strode in only minutes later.

'What are you doing here?' Jazz gasped in disconcertion while her eyes travelled with guilt-ridden enthusiasm over his lean, powerful figure, admiring the fit of his jeans over his long, hard thighs and the breadth of his chest below his black shirt. He returned her scrutiny,

attention lodging on the edge of the towel biting into the exuberant fullness of her breasts, and she reddened, horribly self-conscious at being caught undressed and without a lick of make-up on.

'I… I missed you,' Vitale declared with unexpected abruptness.

Her green eyes widened. 'You…*did*?'

'Of course, I did. I only sent you away for your benefit and I assumed you'd appreciate a private break with your family,' Vitale asserted almost accusingly. 'I had too much official business to take of at the palace and very little time to spare for you.'

Jazz stiffened at the reminder. 'I understood that.'

'No, you seem to think I wanted to get rid of you and that is not true at all. In fact it is *so* untrue, it's ridiculous!' Vitale informed her on a rising note of unconcealed annoyance. 'If you'd stayed on at the palace you wouldn't have been able to go out those first few days and I was in back-to-back meetings. It would have been selfish to keep you cooped up just for my own pleasure.'

Jazz froze. 'When you sent me away I felt like I was an annoying distraction to you, just one more burden.'

Vitale stilled by the door that led out to the terrace, his lean, darkly handsome features rigid. 'You are not and have never been a burden. In fact you are the only thing in my life that has ever given me pure pleasure…'

Jazz loved to hear nice things about herself but that was too over-the-top and from Vitale, of all people, to convince her. 'I can't believe that.'

Vitale's hands knotted into fists of frustration and he made a gesture with both arms that telegraphed his inability to explain what he had meant with that statement.

'I'm being snappy because I was hurt when you sent

me away,' Jazz admitted guiltily, badly wanting to put her arms round him and only just resisting the temptation by filling the uneasy silence for him.

'Do you think it didn't hurt me to be without you every day?' Vitale shot back at her at startling speed. 'Not even to have a few minutes I could call my own with you? But I was trying to do the right thing, only somehow it seems to have been the wrong thing...the story of my *every* dealing with you!' he completed bitterly.

'Would you like a drink?' she asked uncomfortably.

'No, thanks. I had a couple of drinks after you announced your intention of returning to London and it didn't noticeably improve my mood,' he admitted wearily.

'I thought you might welcome my departure. Clearly I misunderstood,' Jazz said for him, reading between the lines, reckoning that he had flown out to the yacht because he was panicking at the idea that she might run out on their marriage even before the coronation and cause yet another scandal. 'I wasn't threatening to leave you, Vitale.'

'*Per meraviglia*...you *weren't*?' Vitale froze to prompt in open bewilderment and disbelief.

'No, I wouldn't let you down like that. I wouldn't do that to you. As you said, we're in this together. Whatever happens, I'll stick things out at the palace until you think it's the right time for us to separate and go for a divorce,' Jazz promised him earnestly.

Vitale paled below his bronzed complexion, stunning dark golden eyes narrowing as if he was pained by that speech. 'I don't want a divorce any more. I want to stay married to you until the day I die, *amata mia*. I

know we didn't start out with that understanding and that I'm ignoring the terms we agreed on but... I've changed.'

'Have you?' Jazz said doubtfully. 'Or is it that you feel us divorcing so soon after your mother's abdication will look bad?'

'You are a very difficult woman to reason with,' Vitale groaned, raking long brown fingers through his already-tousled black hair. 'When I said I changed, I meant *I* changed, nothing to do with the crown or my mother or anyone else. You and I are the only two people in this marriage and I really don't want to lose you. That's why I'm here. I also had to resign from the bank.'

'You've resigned?' Jazz was taken aback.

'Naturally. I can't be a king and a banker as well. I also need time to be a husband and father. Something had to go to give us enough space for a family life,' he pointed out. 'But if you still want a divorce, of course—'

'I didn't say that!' Jazz interrupted in haste.

'Everything you've said and done implies that, though,' Vitale condemned with curt finality, squaring his broad shoulders as if awaiting a physical blow.

'You take the worst possible meaning out of everything I say,' Jazz scolded without meaning to. 'I'm waiting for you to tell me why you decided you wanted to stay married to me...'

'I answered that,' Vitale contradicted squarely. 'You make me happy...and,' he hesitated before adding with visible discomfiture, 'I love you.'

He said it so quietly and so quickly that she wasn't quite sure she had heard him correctly.

'I mean,' Vitale began afresh with a faint air of desperation, 'I *suppose* it's love. I *hate* it when you're away

from me. I miss you so much. I can't imagine being with any other woman. You're different somehow—*special*—and you know how I think—which I didn't like at first—but I'm beginning to believe I should be grateful for that. I know you're not happy at the idea of me becoming King… I *did* see your face when that reality dawned on you but I really don't think I can do it without you,' he told her awkwardly. 'If it came to a choice between the throne and you, I would choose you…'

Jazz's heart expanded like a giant warm globe inside her ribcage as she appreciated that she was listening to a genuine but rather clumsy declaration of love and in a sudden movement she moved closer and wrapped both arms round him. 'I'd never ask you to make a choice like that. I'm not thrilled at the idea of being a queen or being on show all the time, but if I have you with me I'll survive it,' she declared breathlessly, her hands sliding up over his torso and round his neck. 'Why? Because I love you too, you crazy man. How could you miss the fact that I love you?'

Vitale released his pent-up breath in an audible surge and closed both arms tightly round her, a slight shudder of reaction rocking his lean body against her. 'You do?' he pressed uncertainly. 'But why? I'm kind of boring compared to you.'

'No, you're not!' she argued feelingly, hurt that he could think that of himself.

'You're chatty and funny and lively, everything I'm not,' Vitale persisted argumentatively. 'It's like you're a magnet. You pulled me in even though I tried very hard to resist you.'

'You didn't resist for very long,' Jazz commented,

thinking about their encounter in the kitchen on the first night of her stay at his town house.

'You were more temptation than I could resist. Everything about you attracted me.'

'No, you tried to change everything about me to make me presentable,' she reminded him. 'All those lessons.'

'That was educational stuff to ensure that you could hold your own in any company. I live in a different world and I wanted you to feel as comfortable and confident in it as I do. That's past. We've moved way beyond that level now,' he pointed out.

'Yes.' Momentarily, Jazz simply rested her brow against a warm shoulder sheathed in fresh scented cotton and drank in the familiar smell of him. A silly, happy sense of peace was flooding her because Vitale was finally hers, absolutely, irretrievably hers. He had learned to love her in spite of their many differences and perhaps the most wonderful discovery of all was that, mismatched or not, together they made a very comfortable and secure whole.

'But you kept on reminding me that we were supposed to be getting a divorce,' he muttered grimly.

'Well, that is how you set up our marriage,' Jazz reminded him helplessly.

'I know,' Vitale groaned out loud. 'But every time you threw that at me, panic gripped me. I'd dug myself into this ridiculous deep dark hole and I didn't know how to get out of it again. I didn't want to let you go but I'd *promised* you that I would and I always keep my promises. I made such a mess out of everything between us. I should've told you sooner that I no longer wanted a divorce but I was afraid you'd tell me that you still

wanted your freedom back and I couldn't face that. In fact I thought it was wiser to keep quiet about my plans.'

'Honesty works best with me…even if I don't want to hear it, and what you *didn't* say,' she told him for future reference, 'was what I most wanted to hear these past few weeks.'

'Why did our royal wedding upset you so much?'

Jazz withdrew her arms and stepped back from him to look at him. '*Seriously?* You're asking me that when *six* suitable wife candidates followed me down the aisle?'

His brow furrowed in bewilderment. 'Suitable wife candidates?'

'From that file of your mother's. Didn't you recognise them? I mean, you must have met at least a couple of them prior to our big day,' she reasoned.

'The bridesmaids were the women in that file?' Vitale demanded, dark colour edging his hard cheekbones as comprehension sank in and he muttered something unrepeatable in Italian. '*Madonna diavolo…* I never looked at those photographs or that file. It's called passive resistance and I refused to encourage my mother's delusions by playing along with them.'

'You never even looked?' Jazz repeated in astonishment.

'No, I refused. Even when she spread the photos on her desk in front of me, I refused to look. But that she asked them to act as your bridesmaids sickens me,' Vitale admitted with a furious shake of his proud dark head. 'It's hard to credit that even she could be that vindictive. You should've told me.'

'I assumed that you would recognise them. Anyway,' Jazz framed uncomfortably, 'reading that file was bad

for my confidence. I started making these awful comparisons between me and those women and my self-esteem sank very low and that made me very touchy and more inclined to misinterpret everything you did.'

'Even though you are head and shoulders above the women in that pointless pretentious file?' Vitale demanded. 'Because you are the woman I love and the *only* woman I want as a wife!'

And he *meant* every word of that declaration, Jazz recognised with her self-esteem taking a resulting leap as she accepted that wonderful truth. He thought more of her than she thought of herself, she registered in awe.

'Even though you once said I was as flat as an ironing board?' she began teasingly.

'Not a problem we have now,' Vitale told her with a flashing smile as he unwound the towel and backed her purposefully towards the bed. 'As for the hair—I love your hair and you know I do. I've told you often enough.'

And he was always playing with her hair, she conceded thoughtfully while she allowed herself to be rearranged on the bed, a little tremor of awareness and hunger sliding through her as Vitale lowered his long, lean, powerful body down over hers. 'I love you,' he said again. 'And I haven't slept a night through since you left me. I miss the hugs.'

'Well, you have to start hugging back to get them,' Jazz informed him with dancing eyes of challenge.

And he hugged her and she giggled like a drain. 'Again!' she demanded like a child.

The happiness Jazz had brought into his life far outweighed every other concern, Vitale appreciated, and his answering smile was brilliant.

'Oh, I do love you, Vitale,' she whispered when she could breathe again, because he was a little too enthusiastic with his hugs. 'When did you realise how you felt about me?'

'I should've realised the day I almost punched Angel for flirting with you because I was jealous.'

'You *were*.' Jazz savoured that belated admission with unhidden satisfaction.

'But it took me a lot longer to realise what you'd done to me.'

'What I'd done to you?' Jazz queried.

'*Sì*...turned me upside down, inside out and head over heels and all without me having a clue about what was happening,' Vitale confided ruefully. 'And then you never missed a chance to remind me about the divorce plan. That was a real own goal on my part.'

Jazz smiled. 'Glad you recognise that.'

Vitale rubbed his jawline gently over her smooth cheek. 'I shaved... Do I have to keep on talking all night?'

Jazz laughed, feeling amazingly cheerful. 'No, you don't have to talk any more.'

'*Grazie a Dio*,' Vitale's sigh of relief was heartfelt. He realised that he was much more like his emotional father than he had ever appreciated, although he still lacked his father's ability to easily discuss his feelings. But the key to his happiness was Jazz, he acknowledged. Jazz, who had taught him how to enjoy life again. He could cope with anything as long as she was by his side.

And Jazz looked up at him with eyes that shone with love and appreciation and, eagerly drinking in that appraisal, Vitale kissed her with all the passion she in-

spired in him. They made love and the rest of the world was forgotten. Later, much, much later, she twitted him about the prenup agreement that had so depressed her and he kissed her again, contriving to avoid talking once more with remarkable efficiency, but then when Vitale learned anything to his advantage he was always quick to use it.

EPILOGUE

FIVE YEARS LATER Jazz lay back on her sun lounger in the shade and watched the children play in the new swimming pool. Angel was on duty as a lifeguard and, considering that a good half of the overexcited children belonged to him and Merry, that was only fair. Jazz had had to nag at Vitale to get him to agree to a pool at the Italian farmhouse because he liked their lifestyle there to be simpler and less luxurious than life in Lerovia.

'Enrico!' her husband suddenly yelled full throttle at the four-year-old trying to push his twin brother into the pool. 'Stop it!'

Enrico grinned, mischief dancing in his dark eyes, and while he wasn't looking his twin, Donato, gave him a crafty shove into the water.

'That was dangerous!' Vitale thundered.

'The men get so het up when the kids are only doing what comes naturally,' Merry marvelled from her seat beside Jazz while her own little tribe frolicked in the water, noisily jumping up and down and splashing each other.

'But then they're not as accustomed as we are to the daily shenanigans.' Jazz sighed, smoothing her light dress down over the prominent swell of her abdomen.

'Are you hoping for a girl this time around?' Merry asked with the casual curiosity of a close friend.

'I think Vitale is but I don't care as long as the baby's healthy,' Jazz confided, thinking how worried and stressed she had been when her newly born twins had had to go straight into incubators after their premature birth.

Enrico and Donato had thrived from that point on and had soon gained sufficient strength to take up residence in the colourful nursery their parents had created for them at the palace. But, still, Jazz would not have liked to go through the experience of having to leave her babies in hospital again while she went home alone. Her current pregnancy, however, had been much easier than the first. She had been less sick and she felt much more relaxed about her condition, although, if anything, Vitale fussed even more than he had the first time around.

Their lives in Lerovia had gone through a dizzying cycle of change in every sphere. First of all, they had had to move into what had previously been Vitale's mother's wing of the palace. A full-scale redecoration had been required and Jazz still sometimes suspected that she could smell wet paint. Vitale had opened up the ceremonial rooms of the palace to the public for the first time and now Jazz's mother was happily engaged in running the palace gift shop and café opened in a rear courtyard.

Peggy Dickens had made a new life in Lerovia. She had wanted to be close to her grandchildren and she now occupied a small palace apartment where her sister, Clodagh, was a regular guest. Jazz had been relieved when her mother had passed her most recent health check with flying colours and she was delighted

to have her only parent living within easy reach. Vitale had been very generous agreeing to that development, she thought fondly. Not every man would have wanted his mother-in-law living on his doorstep. He had been equally generous when Peggy had told him that she wanted to get involved with the huge challenge of opening part of the palace to the public. Able to engage in meaningful work again, Peggy had gone from strength to strength and had rediscovered her vitality and interest in life.

When the twins were a few months old, Jazz had completed her degree in the History of Art at the University of Leburg and had graduated with honours. Now she was one of the directors of the Leburg Art museum and all the paintings in the palace had finally been exhaustively catalogued, which had led to the exciting discovery of an Old Master of one of Vitale's ancestors. Her life was incredibly busy but she loved it.

The tiny country of Lerovia had become her home and she was a very popular working royal. Prince Eduardo now regularly conducted public engagements on his nephew's behalf and was fully restored to the status his sister had once taken from him. Jazz had been shocked when Vitale had informed her that it had been Eduardo who had choreographed Queen Sofia's downfall by tipping off a friend in the media about her affair.

'It was payback for a lifetime of slights. Mean and cruel of him,' Vitale had conceded of his uncle's behaviour. 'But who am I to criticise? Eduardo was once a very popular member of the family and my mother cut him out of our lives and kept him criminally short of money. He didn't deserve that and her mistreatment of her brother came back to haunt her.'

Sofia Castiglione, now known as Princess Sofia, was still living in her opulent Alpine chalet with Cinzia. She phoned Vitale from time to time to reprimand him about changes she had heard he was instigating and she warned him that he would lose the respect of the people if he lessened the mystique of the monarchy by embracing a less luxurious lifestyle. She had flatly refused to ever set foot in Lerovia again, confessing that she had never liked the Lerovians, and Vitale had laughed heartily when he'd shared that particular gem with Jazz. He had visited his mother on several occasions but he did it out of duty, rather than affection. His failure to divorce Jazz had infuriated his mother and Jazz was still waiting, but not with bated breath, for an invitation to the Alpine chalet.

Charles Russell, on the other hand, was a regular visitor, particularly when the family were vacationing at the farmhouse where he too enjoyed relaxing. He was a great grandparent, always ready to put his book down to enter the world of small children and entertain them.

After dinner that evening, Jazz stepped gratefully into the candlelit bath awaiting her and smiled widely when Vitale brought her lemonade in a wine glass.

'You're not supposed to climb in until I'm here in case you fall,' Vitale censured, his lean, darkly handsome face full of concern.

'I'm not as big as I was with the twins,' Jazz murmured softly. 'I'm not going to fall.'

Vitale smoothed a coiling ringlet back from her damp brow. 'Naked in candlelight you look incredibly sexy, *bellezza mia*…'

'Don't call me beautiful like this,' Jazz scolded with

a slight grimace down at the swell of her stomach. 'Or sexy.'

'But it's the truth.' Vitale levelled stunning dark golden eyes on her and smiled again. 'You want me to lie?'

'Oh, for goodness' sake,' she muttered, passing him her empty glass and rising to leave the bath.

Vitale wrapped her in a fleecy towel and scooped her out.

'You're getting wet!' she cried crossly.

Vitale grinned wickedly down at her. 'I won't be keeping my wet clothes on for long.'

Jazz rolled her beautiful green eyes. 'Now there's confidence for you,' she teased as he carried her back into their bedroom, a big airy space with a cosy corner by the fire for their winter visits.

'Am I wrong?' Vitale husked, pressing a kiss to the pulse point at her throat, sending her body haywire with response.

'Sadly, no. I'm always a pushover,' she sighed, finding his beautiful mouth again for herself and exulting in the love he gave her so freely and the happiness they had found together against all the odds.

* * * * *

BLACKMAILED INTO THE MARRIAGE BED

MELANIE MILBURNE

To Franca Poli, thank you for being such a loyal fan.

This Italian hero is for you,
even though I know you already have one. Xxxx

CHAPTER ONE

Aᴵʟꜱᴀ ᴅᴇᴄɪᴅᴇᴅ ᴛʜᴇʀᴇ was only one thing worse than having to see Vinn Gagliardi after almost two years of separation, and that was being made to wait to see him.

And wait.

And wait.

And wait.

Not a couple of minutes. Not ten or fifteen or even twenty, but a whole stomach-knotting, nerve-jangling hour that crawled by like a wet century.

Ailsa pretended to read every glossy magazine Vinn's young and impossibly glamorous receptionist had artfully fanned on the handcrafted coffee table in front of her. She drank the perfectly brewed coffee and then the sparkling lemon-infused mineral water. She ignored the bowl of breath mints and chewed her nails instead. Right down to her elbow, and if Vinn didn't open his office door soon her shoulder would be next.

Of course he was doing it deliberately. She could picture him sitting behind his acre of French polished desk, idly passing the time sketching new furniture designs, a lazy smile tilting his mouth as he enjoyed every ex-

cruciating minute of the torture she was enduring out here at the prospect of seeing him again.

Ailsa squeezed her eyes shut, trying to rid her mind of the image of his smiling mouth. *Oh, dear God, his mouth.* The things his mouth had made her feel. The places on her body his mouth had kissed and caressed and left tingling for hours after.

No. No. No. Must not think about his mouth. She repeated the mantra she had been saying for the last twenty-two months. She was over him. Over. Him. There was a thick black line through her relationship with Vinn Gagliardi, and she had been the one to put it there.

'Mr Gagliardi will see you now.' The receptionist's voice made Ailsa's eyes spring open and her heart stutter like a lawnmower running over rocks. She shouldn't be feeling so…so nervous. What did she have to be nervous about? She had a perfect right to demand an audience with him, especially when it involved her younger brother.

Although…maybe she shouldn't have flown to Milan without making an appointment first, but she'd been in Florence for an appointment with some new clients when she got the call from her brother Isaac, informing her Vinn was going to sponsor his professional sporting career. She wasn't going to leave the country without confronting Vinn about his motive in investing in her brother's dream of becoming a pro golfer. She'd made up her mind if Vinn wouldn't see her today then she would damn well camp in his office building until he did. She had her overnight bag with her from her short

trip to Florence so at least she had a change of clothes if it came to that.

Ailsa rose from the butter-soft leather sofa, but she'd been sitting for so long her legs gave a credible impression of belonging to a newborn foal. A premature newborn foal. She smoothed her damp hands down the front of her skirt, hitched her tote bag more securely over her shoulder and wheeled her overnight bag with the other hand, approaching the still closed office door with resentment bubbling like a boiling pot in her belly. Why didn't Vinn come and greet her out here in Reception? Why make her walk all the way to his door and knock on it like she was some servile little nobody? Damn it. She'd been his wife. Slept in his bed. Shared everything with him.

Not quite everything…

Ailsa ignored the prod of her conscience. Who said husbands and wives had to share every single detail of their background? Especially with the sort of marriage she'd had with Vinn. It had been a lust match, not a love match. She'd married him knowing he didn't love her, but she'd convinced herself his desire for her more than made up for that. She'd convinced herself it would be enough. That *she* would be enough. But he'd wanted more than a trophy wife. Much more. More than she was prepared to give.

Ailsa was pretty sure Vinn hadn't told her everything about his background. He'd always been reluctant to talk about the time his father went to jail for fraud and how it impacted on his family's business. She'd soon got tired of pushing him to talk to her about it and let

it slide, figuring she would hate it if he, or anyone for that matter, kept on at her to slide back the doors on her family's closet. She didn't have too many skeletons in there, just one big, stinking rotten carcass.

Ailsa stood in front of his office door and aligned her shoulders as if she were preparing for battle. No way was she going to knock on his door and wait for his permission to enter.

No flipping way.

She switched her tote bag to the other shoulder and, grasping her overnight bag with her other clammy hand, took a deep breath and turned the knob and stepped over the threshold to find him standing with his back to her at the window overlooking the bustling streets of Milan. If that wasn't insult enough, he was seemingly engrossed in a conversation on his phone. He barely gave her a glance over his shoulder, just cursorily waved his hand towards one of the chairs opposite his desk and turned back to the view and continued his conversation as if she were some anonymous blow-in whom he had graciously shoehorned into his incredibly busy day.

A sharp pain seized her in the chest, his casual dismissal piercing the protective *I'm over him* membrane around her heart like a carelessly flung dart. How could he ignore her after not seeing her for so long? Hadn't she meant anything to him?

Anything at all?

The conversation was in Italian and Ailsa tried not to listen because listening to Vinn speak in his mother tongue always did strange things to her. Even when he talked in English it did strange things to her. She sus-

pected even if he talked gibberish her spine would still go all mushy and every inch of her skin would tighten and tingle.

While he was talking she took a moment to surreptitiously study him…or at least she hoped it was surreptitious. Every now and again he would move slightly so she could see a little bit more of his face. It was as if he was rationing her vision of him, which was annoying in itself. She wanted to look him in the eye, to see if he carried any scars from their doomed relationship.

He changed the phone to his other hand and turned to the computer on his desk, his brow frowning in concentration as he clicked on the mouse. Why wasn't he looking at her? Surely he could show a bit more interest? She wasn't vain but she knew she looked good. Damn it, she paid a lot of money to look this good. She'd bought a new designer outfit for her meeting with her clients and had her hair done and had spent extra time on her make-up. Looking good on the outside made up for feeling rubbish and worthless on the inside.

Vinn moved something on the computer screen and then continued with his conversation. Ailsa was starting to wonder if she should have worn something with a little more cleavage to show him what he'd been missing. He was still as jaw-droppingly gorgeous as the last time she'd seen him. And if she hadn't been grinding her teeth to powder her jaw would be embedded in the plush ankle-deep carpet right then and there. His jet-black hair was neither long nor short nor straight nor curly, but somewhere sexily in the middle, reminding

her of all the times she had trailed her fingers through those thick glossy strands, or fisted her hands in them during earth-shattering, planet-dislodging sex. He was clean-shaven but the rich dark stubble surrounding his nose and mouth and along his chiselled jaw was a heady reminder of all the times he'd left stubble rash on her softer skin. It had been like a sexy brand on her face, on her breasts, between her thighs…

Ailsa suppressed a shudder and, ignoring the chair he'd offered, threw him a look that would have frozen lava. In mid-flow. 'I want a word with you. Now.' She leaned on the word 'now' like a schoolmistress dressing down a disrespectful pupil.

The corners of Vinn's mouth flickered as if he were trying to stop a smile…or one of his trademark lip curls. He ended his phone call after another few moments and placed the phone on his desk with unnerving precision. 'If you'd made an appointment like everyone else then I would have plenty of time to talk to you.'

'I'm not everyone else.' Ailsa flashed him another glare. 'I'm your wife.'

A dark light gleamed in his espresso-brown gaze like the flick of a dangerous match. 'Don't you mean soon-to-be ex-wife?'

Did that mean he was finally going to sign off on their divorce? Because they'd married in England they were subject to English divorce law, which stated a couple had to be legally separated for two years. It was strange to think if they had married in Italy they would have been granted a divorce by now because Italian divorce law only required one year of separation.

'This may surprise you, Vinn, but I'm not here about our imminent divorce.'

'Let me guess.' He glanced at the overnight bag by her side and his eyes glinted again. 'You want to come back to me.'

Ailsa curled her hand around the handle of her bag so tightly her bitten-down nail beds stung. 'No. I do not want to come back to you. I'm here about my brother. Isaac told me you're offering to sponsor him for the international golfing circuit next year.'

'That's correct.'

She disguised a swallow. 'But…but why?'

'Why?' One dark eyebrow rose as if he found her question ludicrous and her imbecilic to have asked it. 'He asked me, that's why.'

'He…*asked* you?' Ailsa's mouth dropped open so wide she could have parked one of her brother's golf buggies inside. 'He didn't tell me that…' She took a much-needed breath and, letting go of her bag, gripped the back of the chair opposite his desk instead and swallowed again. 'He said you told him you would sponsor him but there were conditions on the deal. Conditions that involved me.'

Vinn's expression changed from mocking to masked. 'Sit down and we'll discuss them.'

Ailsa sat, not because he told her but because her legs were threatening to go from under her like damp drinking straws. Why had Isaac led her to believe Vinn had approached him over sponsorship? Why had her brother been so…so *insensitive* to invite her soon-to-be ex-husband back into her orbit? Vinn's involvement with

her brother's golfing career would mean she wouldn't be able to avoid him the way she'd been doing for the last two years.

She had to avoid him.

She had to.

She didn't trust herself around him. She turned into someone else when she was with him. Someone who had all the hopes and dreams of a normal person—someone who didn't have a horrible secret in her background. A secret not even her brother knew about.

Her *half*-brother.

Ailsa was fifteen years old when she stumbled upon the truth about her biological father. For all that time she'd believed, along with everyone else, that her stepfather Michael was her dad. For fifteen years that lie had kept her family knitted together…well, knitted together was maybe stretching it a bit, because there were a few dropped stitches here and there. Her parents, while individually decent and respectable people, hadn't been happy in their relationship, but she had always blamed them for not trying hard enough to get on.

She hadn't thought it was *her* fault.

That the lie about her was the thing that made their lives so wretchedly miserable. But after finding out the truth about her biological father and the circumstances surrounding her conception, she could understand why.

Ailsa straightened her skirt over her thighs and took a calming breath, but then her gaze spied a silver photograph frame on Vinn's desk and her heart stumbled like a foot missing a rung on a ladder. Why had he kept that? She had given him that frame after their wed-

ding, with her favourite photo of them smiling at each other with the sun setting in the background. Giving him that photo had been her way of deluding herself she was in a real marriage and not one that was simply convenient for Vinn because he wanted a beautiful and accomplished wife to grace his home. She couldn't see the photo from her side of the desk. Perhaps he had someone else's image in there now. The thought of it churned her belly into a cauldron of caustic jealousy. She knew it was missish of her since she was the one to walk out on their marriage, but it hurt her pride to think he could so easily move on with his life.

And not just her pride was hurt…

Ailsa had always held a thread of hope that Vinn would fall in love with her. What bride didn't want her handsome husband to love her? She had fooled herself it would be enough to be his bride, to be in his bed. To be in his life.

But she had longed to be in his heart. To be the first person he thought of in the morning and the last he thought of at night. To be the person he valued over everyone else or anything else. But Vinn didn't value her. He didn't prioritise her. He didn't love her. Never had. Never would. He was incapable of it.

Vinn leaned back in his chair with one ankle crossed over his muscle-packed thigh, his dark unreadable gaze moving over her body like a minesweeper. 'You're looking good, *cara*.'

Ailsa stiffened. 'Don't call me that.'

His mouth curved upwards as if he found her anger amusing. 'Still the same old bad attitude Ailsa.'

'And why wouldn't I have a bad attitude where you're concerned?' Ailsa said. 'How do I know you didn't plant the idea of sponsorship in Isaac's mind? How often have you been in contact with him since we separated?'

'My relationship with your brother has nothing to do with my relationship with you,' Vinn said. 'That is entirely separate.'

'We don't have a relationship any more, Vinn.'

His eyes became obsidian-hard. 'And whose fault is that, hmm?'

Ailsa was trying to contain her temper but it was like trying to restrain a rabid Rottweiler on a Teacup Chihuahua's leash. 'We didn't have a relationship in the first place. You married me for all the wrong reasons. You wanted a trophy wife. Someone to do little nineteen-fifties wifey things for you while you got on with your business as if my career meant nothing to me.'

A tight line appeared around his mouth as if he too was having trouble reining in his temper. 'I trust your aforementioned career is keeping you warm at night? Or have you found yourself a lover to do that?'

She put up her chin. 'My private life is no longer any of your business.'

He made a sound that was suspiciously like a snort. 'Isaac tells me you haven't even been on a date.'

Ailsa was going to kill her younger brother. She would chain him to the sofa and force him to watch animated Disney classics instead of the sports channel. She would take away his golf clubs and flush all his golf balls down the toilet. She would force-feed him

junk food instead of the healthy organic stuff his sports
dietician recommended.

'Well—' she gave Vinn a deliberately provocative
look '—none that he knows about, that is.'

A muscle in the lower quadrant of his jaw moved in
and out like an erratic pulse. 'Any lovers you've collected will have to move aside for the next three months
as I have other plans for you.'

Plans? What plans? Now it was Ailsa's pulse that
was erratic. So erratic it would have made any decent
cardiologist reach for defibrillator paddles.

'Excuse me?' She injected derision into every word.
'You don't get to make plans for me, Vinn. Not any
more. I'm in the driver's seat of my life and you're not
even in the pit lane.'

He made a steeple with his fingers and rested them
against his mouth, watching her with an unwavering
gaze that made the hairs on the back of her neck prickle
at the roots. But then she noticed the gold band of his
wedding ring on his left hand and something in her
stomach tilted. Why would he still be wearing that?

'Isaac will never make the professional circuit without adequate sponsorship,' he said after a long moment.
'That nightclub incident he was involved in last year has
scared off any potential sponsors. I'm his only chance.
His last chance.'

Ailsa mentally gulped. That nightclub incident could
well have ended not just her brother's career prospects
but his or someone else's life as well. The group of
friends he'd been hanging around with since school attracted trouble and invariably Isaac got caught in the

middle. It wasn't that he was easily led, more that he was a little slow to see the potential for trouble until it was too late to do anything—his approaching Vinn for sponsorship being a case in point. But if he got on the professional circuit he would be away from those troublemaking friends.

'Why are you doing this? Why are you involving me? If you want to sponsor him then do it. Leave me out of it.'

Vinn slowly shook his head. 'Not how it works, *cara*. You're the reason I'm sponsoring him. The only reason.'

Ailsa blinked. Could she have got it wrong about Vinn? Had he married her because he *loved* her, not just because he fancied having a glamorous wife to hang off his arm? Was that why he was still wearing his wedding ring? Had he meant every one of those promises he'd made on their wedding day?

No. Of course he hadn't loved her.

He had never said those three little magical words. But then, nor had she. She had deliberately held back from saying them because she hadn't liked the feeling of being so out of balance in their relationship. The person who loved the most had the least power. She hadn't been prepared to give him even more power over her than he already had. His power over her body was enough. More than enough.

He'd reeled her in with his charm and planted her in his life as his wife, on the surface fine with her decision not to have kids, but then he'd changed his mind a few months into their marriage. Or maybe he hadn't changed his mind at all. He had gambled on his ability to change her mind.

Gambled and lost.

She glanced at the photo frame again. 'Is that what I think it is?'

Vinn turned the frame around so she could see the image of their wedding day. Ailsa hadn't looked at their wedding photos since their separation. She had put the specially monogrammed albums at the back of her wardrobe under some clothes she no longer wore. It had been too embarrassing to look at her smiling face in all of those pictures where she had foolishly agreed to be a trophy wife. She had agreed to become a possession, not a person who had longings and hopes and dreams of her own. Looking at those photos was like looking at all the mistakes she had made. How could she have been so stupid to think an arrangement like that would ever work? That marrying anyone—especially someone like Vinn—would make her feel normal in a way she hadn't felt since she was fifteen? Their marriage hadn't even lasted a year. Eleven months and thirteen days, to be precise.

Vinn had mentioned the B word. A baby—a family to continue the Gagliardi dynasty. She would have ended up a breeding machine, her career left to wither, while his business boomed.

Her interior decorating business was her baby. She had given birth to it, nurtured it and made numerous sacrifices for it. Having a real baby was out of the question. There were too many unknowns about her background.

How could she give birth to a child, not knowing what sort of bad blood flowed in its veins?

Ailsa swallowed against the barbed ball of bitterness in her throat and cast her gaze back to Vinn's onyx one. 'Why do you keep it on your desk?'

He turned the frame back so it was facing him, his expression now as inscrutable as his computer screen in sleep mode. 'One of the best bits of business advice I've ever received is never forget the mistakes of the past. Use them as learning platforms and move on.'

It wasn't the first time Ailsa had thought of herself as a mistake. Ever since she'd found out the circumstances surrounding her conception she had trouble thinking about herself as anything else. Most babies were conceived out of love but she had been conceived by brute force. 'What do your new lovers think when they see that photo on your desk?'

'It hasn't been a problem so far.'

Ailsa wasn't sure if he'd answered the question or not. Was he saying he'd had numerous lovers or that none of them had been inside his office? Or had he taken his new lovers elsewhere, not wanting to remind himself of all the times he had made love to her on that desk? Did he wear his wedding ring when he made love to other women? Or did he take it off when it suited him? She glanced at his face to see if there was any hint of the turmoil she was feeling, but his features were as indifferent as if she were a stranger who had walked in off the street.

'So…the conditions you're proposing…' she began.

'My grandfather is facing a do-or-die liver transplant,' Vinn said. 'The surgeon isn't giving any guarantee he will make it through the operation, but without it he will die within a matter of weeks.'

'I'm sorry to hear he's so unwell,' Ailsa said. 'But I hardly see how this has anything to do with—'

'If he dies, and there's a very big chance he will, then I want him to die at peace.'

Ailsa knew how much respect Vinn had for his grandfather Domenico Gagliardi and how the old man had helped him during the time when Vinn's father was in jail. She had genuinely liked Dom and, although she'd always found him a bit austere and even aloof on occasion, she could well imagine for Vinn the prospect of losing his grandfather was immensely painful. She wouldn't be human if she didn't feel for him during such a sad and difficult time, but she still couldn't see how it had anything to do with her.

'I know how much you care for your grandfather, Vinn. I wish there was something I could do to—'

'There *is* something you can do,' Vinn said. 'I want us to be reconciled until he is safely through the surgery.'

Ailsa looked at him as if he'd told her to jump out of the window, her heart thumping so heavily she could hear it like an echo in her ears. 'What?'

'You heard me.' The set to his mouth was grimly determined, as if he had made up his mind how things would be and nothing and no one was going to talk him out of it. Not even her.

She licked her parchment-dry lips. He wanted her back? Vinn wanted her to come back to him? As his wife? She opened and closed her mouth, trying to locate her voice. 'Are you mad?'

'Not mad. Determined to get my grandfather through this without adding to the stress he's already going

through,' Vinn said. 'He's a family man with strong values. I want those values respected and honoured by resuming our marriage until he is well and truly out of danger. I will allow nothing and no one to compromise his recovery.'

Ailsa got to her feet so abruptly the chair almost toppled over. 'I've never heard anything so outrageous. You can't expect me to come back to you as if the last two years didn't happen. I won't do it. You can't make me.'

He remained seated with his unwavering gaze locked on hers. Something about his stillness made the floor of her belly flutter like a deck of rapidly shuffled cards.

'Isaac is talented but that talent will be wasted without my help and you know it,' he said. 'I will provide him with not one, not two, but three years of full sponsorship if you'll agree to come back to me for three months.'

Ailsa wanted to refuse. She needed to refuse. But if she refused her younger brother might never reach his potential. It was within her power to give Isaac this opportunity of a lifetime. But how could she go back to Vinn? Even for three minutes, let alone three months? She clutched the strap of her bag like it was a lifeline and blindly reached for her overnight bag, her hand curling around the handle for support.

'Aren't you forgetting something? I have a career in London. I can't just pack up everything and relocate here.'

'You could open a temporary branch of your business here in Milan,' he said. 'You could even set up a

franchise arrangement. You already have some wealthy Italian clients, *sì*?'

Ailsa frowned so hard she could almost hear her eyebrows saying *ouch* at the collision. How had he heard about her Italian clients? Had Isaac told him? But she rarely mentioned anything much to her brother about her work. Isaac talked about his stuff not hers: his golfing dreams, his exercise regime, his frustration that their parents didn't understand how important his sport was to him and that, since their divorce, they weren't wealthy enough to help him get where he needed to be, etc. Ailsa hadn't told Isaac this last trip to Florence was to meet with a professional couple who had employed her to decorate their centuries-old villa. They had come to her studio in London and liked her work and engaged her services on the spot.

'How do you *know* that?'

Vinn's mouth curved in a mocking smile. 'I'm Italian. I have Italian friends and associates across the country.'

Suspicion crawled across Ailsa's scalp like a stick insect on stilts. 'So… Do I have *you* to thank for the di Capellis' villa in Florence? And the Ferrantes' in Rome?'

'Why shouldn't I recommend you? Your work is superb.'

Ailsa narrowed her gaze. 'Presumably, you mean as an interior decorator, not as a wife.'

'Maybe you'll be better at it the second time around.'

'There isn't going to be a second time around,' Ailsa said. 'You tricked me into marrying you the first time. Do you really think I'm so stupid I'd fall for it again?'

He leaned back in his leather chair with indolent grace, reminding her of a lion pausing before he pounced on his prey. 'I didn't say it would be a real marriage this time around.'

Ailsa wasn't sure whether to be relieved or insulted. Could he have made it any more obvious he didn't find her attractive any more? Sex was the only thing they were good at in the past. Better than good…brilliant. The chemistry they'd shared had been nothing short of electrifying. From their first kiss her body had sparked with incendiary sexual heat. She had never orgasmed with anyone but him. She hadn't even enjoyed sex before him. And, even more telling, she hadn't had sex *since* him. So why wouldn't he want to cash in on the amazing chemistry they'd shared?

'Not real…as in—?'

'We won't be sleeping together.'

'We…we won't?' She was annoyed her voice sounded so tentative and uncertain. So…crushed.

'We'll be together in public for the sake of appearances. But we'll have separate rooms in private.'

Ailsa couldn't understand why she was feeling so hurt. She didn't want to sleep with him. Well, maybe her traitorous body did, but her mind was dead set against it. Her body would have to get a grip and behave itself because there was no way she was going to dive back into bed with Vinn… She had a sneaking suspicion she might not want to get out of it.

'Look, this is a pointless discussion because I'm not coming back to you in public or private or even in this century. Understood?'

He held her gaze with such quiet, steely intensity a shiver shimmied down her spine like rolling ice cubes. 'Once the three months is up I will grant you a divorce without contest.'

Ailsa swallowed again. This was what she'd wanted— an uncomplicated straightforward divorce. He would give it to her if she agreed to a three month charade. 'But if we're seen to be living together it will cancel out the last two years of separation according to English divorce law.'

'It will delay the divorce for another couple of years, but that would only be a problem if you're intending to marry someone else.' He waited a beat before adding, 'Are you?'

Ailsa forced herself to hold his gaze. 'That depends.'

'On?'

'On whether I find a man who'll treat me as an equal instead of a brood mare.'

He rose from his chair with an expelled breath as if his patience had come to the end of its leash. 'For God's sake, Ailsa. I raised the topic back then as a discussion, not as an imperative. I felt it was something we should at least talk about.'

'But you knew my opinion on having children when you asked me to marry you,' Ailsa said. 'You gave me the impression you were fine with not having a family. I wouldn't have married you if I'd thought you were going to hanker after a bunch of kids before the ink was barely dry on our marriage certificate.'

His expression was storm cloud broody and light-ning flashed in his eyes. 'You have no idea of the word compromise, do you?'

Ailsa gave a mocking laugh. 'That's rich, coming from you. I didn't hear any talk of you offering to stay home and bring up the babies while I worked. You assumed I would gladly kick off my shoes and pad barefoot around your kitchen with my belly protruding, didn't you?'

His expression locked down into his trademark intractable manner. 'I've never understood why someone from such a normal and loving family would be so against having one of her own.'

Normal? There was nothing normal about her background. On the surface, yes, her family life looked normal and loving. Even since their divorce both her mother and stepfather had tried hard to keep things reasonably civil, but it was all smoke and mirrors and closed cupboards because the truth was too awful, too shameful and too horrifying to name.

On one level Ailsa understood her mother and stepfather's decision to keep the information about her mother's rape by a friend of a friend—who'd turned out to be a complete stranger gate-crashing a party—a secret from her. Her mother had been traumatised enough by the event, so traumatised she hadn't reported it to the police, nor had she told her boyfriend—Ailsa's stepfather—until it was too late to do anything about the pregnancy that had resulted. Her stepfather had always been against having a DNA test but her mother had insisted on it, saying she needed to know. When Ailsa was fifteen she had come home earlier than normal from school to overhear her mother and stepfather arguing in their bedroom. She'd overheard

many arguments between her parents before but this one had been different. Overhearing the awful truth about her origin meant that her life and all her dreams and hopes for her own family had died in that stomach-curdling moment.

Ailsa met Vinn's flinty gaze. 'In spite of my refusal to play this game of charades with you, I hope you will still sponsor Isaac. He looks up to you and would be devastated if you—'

'That's not how I do business.'

She raised her chin a little higher. 'And I don't respond to blackmail.'

His gaze warred with hers for endless seconds, like so many of their battles in the past. It was strange, but this was one of the things she'd missed most about him. He was never one to shy away from an argument and nor was she. She had always secretly enjoyed their verbal skirmishes because most, if not all, of their arguments had ended in bed-wrecking make-up sex. She wondered if he was thinking about that now—how passionate and explosive their sex life had been. Did he miss it as much as she did? Did he ever reach for her in the middle of the night and feel a hollow ache deep inside to find the other side of the bed empty?

No, because his bed was probably never empty.

Ailsa was determined not to be the first to look away even though, as every heart-chugging second passed, she could feel her courage failing. His dark brown eyes had a hard glaze of bitterness and two taut lines of grimness bracketed his mouth, as if, these days, he only rarely smiled.

The sound of his phone ringing on the desk broke the deadlock and Vinn turned to pick it up. 'Nonno?' The conversation was brief and in Italian but Ailsa didn't need to be fluent to pick up the gist of it. She could see the host of emotions flickering across Vinn's face and the way the tanned column of his throat moved up and down. He put down the phone and looked at her blankly for a moment as if he'd forgotten she was even there.

'Is everything all right?' Ailsa took a step towards him before she checked herself. 'Is your grandfather—?'

'A donor has become available.' His voice sounded strangely hollow, as if it was coming through a vacuum. 'I thought there would be more time to prepare. A week or two or something but… The surgery will be carried out within a matter of hours.' He reached for his car keys on the desk and scooped up his jacket where it was hanging over the back of his office chair, his manner uncharacteristically flustered, distracted. In his haste to find his keys several papers slipped off the desk to the floor and he didn't even stop to retrieve them. 'I'm sorry to cut this meeting short but I'm going to see him now before—' another convulsive swallow '—it's too late.'

Ailsa had never seen Vinn so out of sorts. Nothing ever seemed to faze him. Even when she'd told him she was leaving two years ago, he'd been as emotionless as a robot. It intrigued her to see him feeling something. Was there actually a heart beating inside that impossibly broad chest? She bent down to pick up the scattered papers and, tidying them into a neat pile, silently

handed them to him. He took them from her and tossed them on the desk, where a couple of pages fluttered back to the floor.

'I can't let him down,' he said in a low mumble, as if talking to himself. 'Not now. Not like this.'

'Would you like me to go with you?' The offer was out before Ailsa could stop it. 'My flight doesn't leave for a few hours so…'

His expression snapped out of its distracted mode and got straight back to cold, hard business. 'If you come with me, you come as my wife. Deal or no deal.'

Ailsa was torn between wanting to tell him where to put his deal and wanting to see more of this vulnerable side of him. She could agree to the charade verbally but he could hardly hold her to anything without having her sign something.

'I'll go with you to the hospital because I've always liked your grandfather. That's if you think he'd like to see me?'

'He would like to see you,' Vinn said and searched through the papers on his desk for something, muttering a curse word in the process.

'Is this what you're looking for?' Ailsa handed him the pages that had fallen the second time.

He took them from her and, reaching for a pen, slid them in front of her on the desk. 'Sign here.'

She ignored the pen and met his steely gaze. 'Do we have to do it now? Your grandfather is—'

'Sign it.'

Ailsa could feel her will preparing for battle. Her spine stiffened to concrete, her jaw set to stone and her

gaze sent a round of fire at his. 'I'm not signing it unless you give me time to read it.'

'Damn it, Ailsa, there isn't time,' Vinn said, slamming his hand down on the desk. 'I need to see my grandfather. Trust me, okay? Just for once in your life trust me. I can't let Nonno down. I can't fail him. He's depending on me to get him through this. Along with Isaac's sponsorship, I'll pay you a lump sum of ten million.'

Ailsa's eyebrows shot up so high she thought they might hit the light fitting above her head. 'Ten...*million*?'

The line of his mouth was white-tight. 'If you don't sign in the next five seconds the deal is off. Permanently.'

Ailsa took the pen from him, his fingers brushing hers in the exchange, sending a riot of fiery sensations from her fingertips to her feminine core. The pen was still warm from where he'd been holding it. She remembered all too well his warmth. The way it lit the wick of her desire like a match on dry tinder. She could feel the smouldering of his touch moving through her body, awakening sensual memories.

Memories she had tried so hard to suppress.

She took a shaky breath and ran her gaze over the document. It was reasonably straightforward: three years of sponsorship for Isaac and giving her a lump sum of ten million on signing. While it annoyed her he'd used money as a lure, she realised it was the primary language he spoke. Money was his mother tongue, not Italian. Well, she could learn to speak Money too. Ten million was a lot of money. She was successful in her

business but with ten million in her bank account she could expand her studio to Europe.

But then she realised how trapped she would be once she signed that agreement. She would have to spend three months with Vinn. She needed time to think about this. She had rushed into marriage with him in the past. How foolish would it be to rush into this without proper and careful consideration? She left the document unsigned and pushed it and the pen back to him. 'I need a couple of days to think about this. It's a lot of money and... I need more time.'

He showed no emotion on his face, which surprised her given how insistent he had been moments earlier. But maybe behind that masked expression he was already planning another tactic to force her to comply with his will. 'We will discuss this further after we've been to the hospital.' He put the paper under a paperweight and, picking up her overnight bag, ushered her out of his office.

He spoke a few quick words to his receptionist Claudia, explaining what was happening, and Claudia expressed her concern and assured him she would take care of everything back here at the office. Ailsa felt a twinge of jealousy at the way the young woman seemed to be such an integral part of the business. She wondered what had happened to the receptionist who had worked for him during their marriage. Vinn liked surrounding himself with beautiful women and they didn't come more beautiful than Claudia, who looked as if she'd just stepped out of a photo shoot.

Ailsa waited until they were in Vinn's car and on

their way to the hospital before she brought up the subject. 'What happened to your other receptionist, Rosa?'

'I fired her.'

She rounded her eyes in surprise. She'd thought his relationship with the middle-aged Rosa had been excellent. She'd often heard him describe Rosa as the backbone of the business and how he would be lost without her. Why on earth would he have fired her? 'Really? Why?'

He worked his way through the gears with an almost savage intensity. 'She overstepped the mark. I fired her. End of story.'

'Overstepped it in what way?'

He sent her a speaking glance. 'Could we leave this until another time?'

Ailsa bit her lip. 'I'm sorry… I know you're feeling stressed and this must be so upsetting for you with your grandfather so desperately ill…'

There was a long silence.

'He's all I have,' Vinn said in the same hollow-sounding voice he'd used back in his office. 'I'm not ready to lose him.'

She wanted to reach for his hand or to put her hand on his thigh the way she used to do, but instead she kept to her side of the car. He probably wouldn't welcome her comfort or he might push her away, which would be even worse. 'You still have your dad, don't you?' she said.

'No.' He made another gear change. 'He died. Car crash. He was driving under the influence and killed himself and his new girlfriend and seriously injured a couple and their two children travelling in the other car.'

'I'm so sorry…' Ailsa said. 'I didn't know that.'

It pained her to think Vinn had gone through such a tragic loss since she'd left and she'd known nothing about it. She hadn't even sent a card or flowers. Had he kept his dad's death out of the press? Not that she went looking for news about Vinn and his family…well, not unless she'd had one too many glasses of wine late at night when she was feeling particularly lonely and miserable.

He shrugged off her sympathy. 'He was on a fast track to disaster from the moment my mother died when I was a child. Without her steadying influence he was a train wreck waiting to happen.'

Ailsa had rarely heard Vinn mention his mother's death. It was something he never spoke of, even in passing. But she knew his relationship with his father had never truly recovered after his father was charged with fraud when Vinn was barely out of his teens. The shame on the family's name and the reputation of the bespoke furniture business had been hard to come back from, but coming back from it had been Vinn's blood, sweat and tears mission and he had done it, building the company into a global success.

'I guess not everyone gets to have a father-of-the-year dad,' she said, sighing as he turned into the entrance of the hospital. 'Both of us lucked out on that one.'

Vinn had pulled into a parking spot and glanced at her again with a frown. 'What do you mean? You've got a great dad. Michael's one of the most decent, hard-working men I've ever met.'

Ailsa wanted to kick herself. She even lifted one

foot to do it, welcoming the stab of pain from her high heel because she was a fool to let her guard slip. A damn fool.

'Yes…yes, I know. He's wonderful…even since the divorce he still makes an effort to—'

'Then why say something like that? He'll always be your dad even though he's divorced from your mother.'

'Forget I said it. I… I wasn't thinking.' Ailsa hated that she sounded so flustered and hoped he'd put it down to the emotion of seeing his grandfather under such tense and potentially tragic circumstances. She had a feeling if he hadn't been in such a rush to see his grandfather before the surgery he might well have pushed her to explain herself a little more. It was a reprieve, but how long before he came back to it with his dog-with-a-bone determination?

It was a timely reminder she would have to be careful around Vinn. He knew her in a way few people did. Her knew her body like a maestro did an instrument. He knew her moods, her likes and dislikes, her tendency to use her sharp tongue as a weapon when she got cornered.

He didn't know her shameful secret, but how soon before he made it his business to find out?

CHAPTER TWO

VINN DIDN'T KNOW what was worse—seeing Ailsa again without a little more notice or walking into the hospital to see his grandfather, possibly for the last time. But, in a way, he'd been expecting to lose his grandfather... eventually. But two years ago when Ailsa called time on their marriage it had not only blindsided him but hit him in the chest like a freight train. Sure, they argued a bit now and again. What newly married couple didn't?

But he'd never thought she'd leave him.

They hadn't even made it to the first anniversary. For some reason that annoyed him more than anything else. He had given her everything money could buy. He had showered her with gifts and jewellery. Surrounded her with luxury and comfort, as was fitting for the wife of a successful man. He might not have loved her the way most wives expected to be loved, but she hadn't married him for love either. Lust was what brought them together and he'd been perfectly fine with that and so had she, or so he'd thought. She had never said the words and he hadn't fished for them. He'd just assumed she would be happy with the arrangement because most

women wanted security over everything else and the one thing he was good at was providing financial security. Financial security was what you could bank on—*pardon the pun*—because emotions were fickle. People were fickle.

But Ailsa had been unwilling to even discuss the subject of having a child. He knew her career was important to her, as was his to him, but surely she could have been mature enough to sit down and discuss it like an adult? He'd told her he wasn't all that interested in having a family when they'd first got together because back then he wasn't. But after a few months of marriage, his grandfather had his first health scare with his liver and had spoken to Vinn privately about his desire for a grandchild to hold in his arms before he died. He had made it sound like Vinn would be letting down the family name by not providing an heir. That it would be a failure on Vinn's part not to secure the family business for future generations.

Letting the family down.
Failure.

With his father already the Gagliardi family's big failure, those words haunted Vinn. They stalked him in quiet moments. It reminded him of how close to losing everything he had been when his father had jeopardised everything with his fraudulent behaviour. Vinn couldn't allow himself to fail at anything. Being an only child had never really bothered him before then, but with his father acting like a born-again teenager at that time and his grandfather rapidly ageing, it had made Vinn think more and more about the future. Who would he leave

his vast wealth to? What was the point of working so hard if you had no one to pass on your legacy to when you left this mortal coil?

But no, practically as soon as he'd brought up the topic, Ailsa had stormed out of his life like a petulant child, refusing to communicate with him except through their respective lawyers. She had dropped another failure on him—their marriage. He would give her the divorce when it suited him and not a moment before. He had far more pressing priorities and top of that list was getting his grandfather through this surgery.

Vinn was banking on Ailsa's love for her younger brother Isaac to get her to agree to his plan for the next three months. But her turning up unannounced at his office was a reminder of how careful he had to be around her.

Careful. Guarded. Controlled.

He'd assumed she would call and make an appointment, but the one thing he knew he should never do with Ailsa was assume anything. She had an unnerving ability to catch him off guard. Like when she'd point blank refused to sign his agreement even though he'd dangled ten million pounds in front of her. He hadn't expected her to ask for time to think about it. He'd expected her to sign it then and there. But with the pressure of getting to the hospital in time to see his grandfather before the surgery, Vinn had allowed her to get away without signing. He had never allowed anyone to do that to him before. Push him around. Manipulate him. He had always put measures in place to avoid being exploited or fooled or thwarted.

All through his life he had aced everything he had ever set out to do, but his marriage to Ailsa was a failure. A big fat failure. How he hated that word—*failure*. Hated. Hated. Hated it. It made him feel out of control, incompetent.

But it wasn't just him who had been affected by Ailsa walking out on him. The breakup of their marriage had shattered his grandfather and it was no surprise the old man's health had gone into a steep decline shortly after Ailsa had left. The death of Vinn's father so soon after her leaving certainly hadn't helped. But in some ways his grandfather had coped better with Vinn's father's death than the breakup of Vinn's marriage. His marriage to Ailsa had been the hope his grandfather had clung to for the future—a future ripe with promise of a new generation, new beginnings and new success. But that hope had been snatched away when Ailsa left.

But just lately, as the two-year mark of the separation crept closer, he'd noticed his grandfather becoming more and more stressed and his health suffering as a result. His grandfather had always been a devoted family man and had stayed faithful and true to Vinn's grandmother, Maria, until her death five years ago. If Vinn could do this one thing—make his grandfather believe he and Ailsa were back together—then at least the old man's recovery wouldn't be compromised by the stress and worry about their imminent divorce.

Besides, this time around, Vinn would be the one in control of their relationship and he would stay in control. He wouldn't allow Ailsa to throw him over again. He had put a time limit on their 'reunion' and he'd

mentioned the no-sex rule just to be on the safe side. When he'd seen her walk into his office unannounced, his loins had pulsed with a drumbeat of primal lust so powerful it nearly knocked him off his feet. And if he hadn't been talking to one of his senior staff on the phone about a tricky problem in one of his workshops, he might well have taken Ailsa into his arms then and there and challenged her to deny the spark that arced between them. The spark that had always arced between them from the first time they'd met at a furniture exhibition in Paris. He was attracted to her natural beauty—her long silky curtain of ash-blonde hair and creamy complexion and coltish model-like figure, and the way her bewitching grey-blue eyes seemed to change with her mood.

The other thing he'd liked about her back then was she hadn't been easy to pick up. With his sort of wealth and profile it had been a new experience meeting a woman who didn't dive head first into bed with him. She had taken playing hard to get to a whole new level. The thrill of the chase had been the biggest turn-on of his adult life. He had seen it as a challenge to get her to finally capitulate and, if he were honest, he would have to admit it was one of the reasons he'd married her instead of offering her an affair like anyone else. Maybe even the major reason. Because nothing shouted *I won* more than getting that wedding ring on her finger.

But that iron-strong determination of hers that had so attracted him in the first place was the same thing that had ultimately destroyed their marriage. She refused to

back down over a position she adopted. It was her way or the highway and to hell with you if you didn't agree.

But Vinn was equally determined, and this next three months would prove it.

Ailsa followed Vinn into the private room where Domenico was being monitored prior to the transplant. Strict sterilisation procedures were being conducted and, according to the nurse, they would be a hundred times more stringent once the surgery was over.

The old man was lying in a bed with medical apparatus tethering him seemingly from every limb. He opened his eyes when Vinn approached the bed and gave a weak smile. 'You made it in time.'

Vinn gently took his grandfather's hand in his and Ailsa was touched to see the warmth and tenderness in Vinn's gaze. Had he ever looked at her like that? As if *she* mattered more than anything at that moment? She felt guilty for thinking such thoughts at such a time with his grandfather so desperately ill, but how could she not wish Vinn had felt something more than just earthy lust for her?

'I made it,' Vinn said. 'And I brought someone with me to see you.'

Domenico looked to where Ailsa was standing and his weary bloodshot eyes lit up like stadium lights. 'Ailsa? Is it really you?'

She stepped forward and put her hand on the old man's forearm, so close to where Vinn's hand was resting she felt a little electric tingle shoot up her arm. 'Hello, Dom.'

Dom's eyes began to water and he blinked a few times as if trying to control his emotions. 'My dear girl… You have no idea how much it thrills me to see you back with Vinn. I've prayed for this day. Prayed and prayed and prayed.'

Back with Vinn.

Those three words sent a wave of heat through her body and two hot pools of it firing in her cheeks. Had Vinn already told his grandfather they were back together? Had he been so arrogantly confident she would sign the agreement? She was glad now she hadn't signed it. Fervently glad. He had given her ten million very good reasons to sign it, but still, it rankled that he thought he could so easily buy her acquiescence by waving indecent amounts of money in front of her.

'But I'm not really—' Ailsa stopped mid-sentence. How could she tell Dom the opposite of what he clearly wanted to hear? She might not have signed Vinn's agreement, but his poor old grandfather was being wheeled into surgery within a matter of minutes for an operation, which he might not survive. What harm would it do to allow Dom this one moment?

She wasn't back with Vinn as in Back With Vinn. She was playing a game of charades to keep an old man happy. Standing here by this old man's bedside with the prospect of his life with a clock ticking on it made her want to do everything in her power to make Dom feel settled and peaceful before his life-saving or, God forbid, life-ending surgery.

'I'm here,' she said and moved her hand so it was on top of Vinn's on Dom's hand. 'We're both here. Together.'

Tears dripped down from Dom's eyes and Ailsa leaned over to pluck a tissue from the box beside the bed and gently mopped them away, her eyes feeling suspiciously moist and her chest so tight it felt like she was having her own medical crisis.

'If I don't make it through this operation then at least I have the assurance you two have patched things up,' Dom said, his voice choked with emotion. 'You're meant to be together. I knew that the first time Vinn introduced me to you. You're a strong woman, Ailsa. And my grandson is a strong man and needs someone with enough backbone to handle him.'

Ailsa was going to handle Vinn all right. She was going to grab him by the front of the shirt and tell him what she thought of him manipulating her into this crazy charade by default. Even though she hadn't committed herself on paper, he must have known she wouldn't be able to help herself once she saw his desperately ill grandfather. No wonder he hadn't made a fuss back in his office when she'd refused to sign the wretched agreement. He had simply bided his time so he could play on her emotions because he knew it was her weak spot. Just like he was using her love and affection for her brother as a bargaining tool, forcing her to bend to his will.

'Time to go to Theatre,' a hospital orderly announced from the door.

Vinn leaned down to kiss his grandfather on both cheeks European style, his voice husky and deep. 'Good luck, Nonno. We'll be waiting for you once you come out of Recovery.'

If you come out of Recovery...

Ailsa could hear the unspoken words like a haunting echo inside her head. Vinn had lost his mother when he was a small child barely old enough to remember her. He had lost his grandmother—who had effectively raised him—five years ago, and lost his father during the last two years. Now he was facing the prospect of losing his grandfather. The grandfather who, in many ways, had been more of a father to him than his own father.

She hadn't expected to feel anything other than hate towards Vinn because of the way he had married her because he wanted a wife and she had somehow measured up to his standards. Little did he know how far below those standards she actually fell. But now she felt an enormous wave of sympathy for what he must be going through. She wasn't supposed to feel anything where Vinn was concerned. She was in the process of divorcing him.

But who wouldn't feel sorry for someone saying goodbye to a grandfather who had been there for them all of their life? Dom and his wife Maria had stepped in when Vinn's mother died when he was so young and again when his father had caused so much financial and emotional mayhem. Dom had been there for Vinn in every way possible and now he was facing the very real prospect of losing him. Not that she had found out any of that information about his grandparents' role in his life from Vinn. She had found out most of it from his previous secretary Rosa, who had filled her in on some of the Gagliardi family dynamics.

Ailsa leaned down to kiss Dom's cheeks and wish him well and, when she straightened, Vinn's arm en-

circled her waist and drew her close to his body. In spite of the layers of her clothes, his touch set off fireworks through her flesh. He was so much taller than she was and even in her high heels she barely came up to his shoulder. She had never been more aware of her femininity than when standing next to him. It was as if his body had secret radar that was finely tuned to hers, signalling to it, making it ping back responses she had little or no control over. She could feel them now. *Ping. Ping. Ping. Tingle. Tingle. Tingle.* The warm press of his hand on her left hip was sending a message straight to her core, like a network of fiery hot wires fizzing and whizzing. Her breasts began to stir, as if remembering the slightly calloused glide of his hands caressing them, his thumbs rolling over her nipples...

Ailsa gave herself a mental slap and eased out of Vinn's hold once Dom had been wheeled away, accompanied by the nurse and three other clinicians. She waited until they were alone before she turned to face Vinn with a skewering glare. 'Did you tell him we were back together before you'd even spoken to me?'

His expression showed faint signs of irritation. 'No. But he must've put two and two together when he saw you come in with me.' He rubbed a hand over his face, the sound of his stubble catching against his skin making something in her belly turn over. 'Thanks, by the way. You've made a frail old man very happy.'

Ailsa shifted her lips from side to side—a habit she'd had since childhood. She did it when she was stressed and she did it when she was thinking. 'But what about when he wakes up? He'll know there's something not

right between us. He might be desperately sick but he's not a fool.'

His dark-as-pitch eyes moved between each of hers in a back and forth motion, as if looking for a gap in her firewall. 'You'll have to work a little harder on convincing him you're in love with me.'

Ailsa gave him an arch look. 'Maybe you could show me how to do it by example.'

His hooded gaze went to her mouth and something dropped off a shelf in her stomach. That was the look that had started their crazy lust-driven relationship. The I-want-to-have-jungle-sex-with-you look. The look that melted her self-control like a scorching flame on sorbet. But then, as if he remembered they were still in a hospital room and likely to be interrupted, he brought his gaze back to hers. 'I'm sure you'll do a great job once you see ten million pounds in your bank account.' He took out his phone and started pressing the keys, adding, 'I'll transfer a quarter of the funds now and the rest on signing.'

Ailsa bristled again at the suggestion she could be bought. 'I don't care if you put twenty million in my account, it won't change the fact that I hate you. And I told you, I'm not signing it until I've had time to think about it.'

He looked up from his phone with an unreadable look. 'Hate me all you like in private, *cara*, but in public—signed agreement or not—you will act like a blissfully happy bride or answer for the consequences.'

She ground her teeth together. 'Don't go all macho man on me, Vinn. It won't work.'

One side of his mouth lifted in an indolent smile

as if he was enjoying her strong will colliding with his. He stepped closer and lifted her chin with the tip of his finger. She knew she should have jerked away from him but for some reason her body was locked in a mesmerised stasis. His eyes were so dark she couldn't make out his pupils and they pulsed with little flashes of heat that could have been anger or red-hot desire or a combination of the two.

'You really are spoiling for a fight, aren't you, *tesoro mio*? But you know where our fights end up, hmm? In bed with you raking your fingernails down my back as I make you come again and again and again.'

Ailsa could feel her cheeks blushing like an industrial furnace. How dare he remind her of how wanton she had been in his arms? He made her turn into an animal in his bed. A wild animal with needs and desires and hungers that had never been awakened, much less satisfied, by anyone but him.

The need to get away from him so she could think straight was suddenly paramount. She didn't care what agreement he wanted her to sign or for how much, but right then and there she had to put some space between them.

'Dream on, Vinn. I need the bathroom. Will you excuse me for a minute?'

'There's a bathroom in here.' He pointed to the signed door in his grandfather's room. 'I'll wait for you.'

Ailsa gave him a tight smile that didn't show her teeth. 'Strange as this may seem given our previous relationship, but I would actually like a little privacy. I'll use the bathroom down the hall.' She moved past him

and mentally steeled herself for him trying to stop her but she managed to escape without him touching her. She glanced back from the doorway but he had already taken out his phone and was tapping again at the screen.

Ailsa walked straight past the bathroom down the corridor and stepped into the first available lift. She would have taken the stairs but she was in too much of a hurry. She had left her overnight bag in Vinn's car but at least she had her passport in her tote bag. But then she began to weigh her options. If she flew back to London he would immediately withdraw his offer of Isaac's sponsorship. She had no reason to think he didn't mean every single word. She had run up against his steely will too many times to count. The only time she had won an argument with him was when she'd walked out on their marriage.

But in a way she hadn't really won.

She had left him almost two years ago but a secret part of her had hoped he would come after her. While on one level she accepted he didn't love her in the traditional sense, on another level she had been so desperate for a sign—any sign—he cared something for her that her walk out had been far more impulsive and dramatic than she'd intended. In hindsight, she realised she had been hormonal and moody and feeling neglected because he'd been working extra long hours. She'd felt like a toy that had been put to one side that no longer held its earlier appeal. When he'd mentioned having kids it had triggered all her fears about their relationship. It had triggered all her fears about herself. What

sort of mother would she be? How could she risk having a child when she didn't know whose DNA she carried?

But Vinn hadn't come after her. He hadn't even called her. It seemed to prove how little he cared about her that he would let her call time on their marriage and not even put up a fight to beg her to stay.

But then, men like Vinn Gagliardi didn't beg. They commanded and people obeyed.

The lift doors opened and Ailsa looked towards the hospital entrance. Could she walk out those doors and hope some decent part of Vinn would make him go ahead with Isaac's sponsorship? But then she noticed a gathering of people outside and her heart began to skip in her chest. Paparazzi. Were they here for a visiting celebrity? It only took her a moment to realise *she* was the celebrity. Why hadn't she realised Vinn would contact the press about their 'reconciliation'? He was always a step or two ahead of her. It was as if he could read her mind as well as her body. She hadn't signed his stupid agreement so he had a Plan B and C and God knew how many others up his designer sleeve.

One of the paparazzo looked Ailsa's way and said something to his colleagues and then they came rushing through the front doors of the hospital.

Ailsa turned and stabbed at the lift button but when she looked up at the numbers she could see it was still on the fourth floor. She went to the next lift and, just as she pressed the button, the doors opened and she came face to face with Vinn.

He took her hand and looped her arm through his. His expression was hard to read but the tensile strength in

his grip was not. She would have to think twice before trying to outwit him. 'Our first press conference is about to begin,' he said. 'Nice that you could join me for it.'

Ailsa had no choice but to paint a plastic smile on her face as he swung her to face the press. The back and forth conversation was mostly in Italian so she could only pick up a few words here and there, but it was clear the press were delighted to hear the runaway wife of high profile billionaire furniture designer Vinn Gagliardi was back.

'Let's have a kiss for the cameras,' one of the journalists said in English.

Ailsa's heart began to race at the thought of Vinn's mouth coming down on hers, but he held up his hand like a stop sign. 'Please respect our privacy. This is a difficult day for both of us with my grandfather undergoing life-saving surgery. *Grazie.*'

The press gang parted like the Red Sea as Vinn led her towards the front doors of the hospital. She understood the gravity of the situation, with his grandfather hovering between life and death upstairs in Theatre, but why hadn't Vinn taken this opportunity to kiss her? Had she misinterpreted the way he'd looked at her mouth earlier? Was he really serious about the no-sex rule? Did it mean he already had someone in his life who serviced those needs for him? A sudden pain gripped her at the thought of him with someone else. For the last twenty-two months she had forced herself not to think about it. He was a man with a healthy sexual appetite. Not just healthy—voracious. He was thirty-five years old—in the prime of his life.

Vinn led her to where he'd parked his car and silently handed her into it. Ailsa knew he was angry. She could feel it simmering in the air like humidity before a storm. He got in behind the driver's wheel and gave her a look that would have blistered paint. 'You might not have signed the agreement yet, but you told my grandfather you're back with me. If you try to run away again I will not only withdraw my offer of sponsorship from Isaac, but I will make sure no one else ever offers to sponsor him. He won't be able to walk onto any golf course in Europe as a spectator, much less play in a tournament. Have I made myself clear?'

Ailsa would have loved to throw his agreement and his ten million back in his face. She would have loved to tear up the money note by note and stuff the pieces down the front of his shirt. But she loved her brother more than she hated Vinn. Much more. Which was kind of scary because she needed to vehemently hate him in order to keep herself safe. But could she ever be safe from Vinn? She raised her chin a fraction, unwilling to let go of her pride. 'You might think you can cleverly blackmail me back into your life for three months but I will always hate you. Ten million, twenty million— even fifty million—won't ever change that.'

'If I thought you were worth fifty million I would pay it.'

His words were as cruel and stinging as a slap and shocked and pained her into silence.

She watched out of the corner of her eye as his hands opened and closed on the steering wheel, his knuckles straining white against the stretched tendons. The air

inside the cocoon of the car felt thick, dense, as if all the oxygen atoms had been sucked out.

Ailsa felt dangerously close to tears, which annoyed her because she wasn't a crier. She was a fighter not a crier. She gave as good as she got and never showed her vulnerability. She didn't like showing her neediness. She fought against her emotional weakness. She'd taught herself from a young age when her mother would turn away from her outstretched arms as if she couldn't bear to be touched, let alone hugged, by her own child.

Ailsa turned her head to stare blindly out of the window, vaguely registering people coming and going from the hospital. People going through the various cycles of life: birth, death, illness and recovery, sadness and happiness and hope and loss and everything in between.

Vinn released a heavy sigh and turned to face her. 'I'm sorry. That was...unkind of me.'

'Unkind?' Ailsa wasn't ready to forgive him. Her hurt was festering, pulsating and throbbing like a re-opened wound. Old hurts and new hurts were twisting around each other like rough ropes tied too tightly against wounded flesh. 'But true in my case. I'm not worth anything to you. In fact, I'm surprised you offered ten million.'

He reached across the space between them and put a gentle hand to the nape of her neck where it seemed every nerve in her body had gathered to welcome his touch. 'I would pay any amount of money to get my grandfather safely through this surgery.' His mouth twisted in a rueful movement that wasn't quite a smile. 'I'm not ready to let him go.'

You were ready to let me go. The words hovered on the tip of her tongue but she didn't say them out loud. 'You really love him, don't you?'

His hand moved closer to the base of her scalp, his fingers moving through her hair sending shivers down her spine. 'He's family. The only family I have left.'

'Don't you have cousins and uncles and aunts and—?'

He made a dismissive sound. 'They ran for cover when my father's shady dealings became public knowledge. I have no time for fair weather family or friends.'

Ailsa hadn't realised until then how isolated he was. She knew there were numerous Gagliardi relatives because she had met a lot of them at their wedding. Some had refused the invitation because of his father's reputation but Vinn had shrugged it off as if it hadn't bothered him one way or the other. But where were they today, the day his grandfather faced the biggest battle of his life? Had anyone reached out to support Vinn? To offer comfort at such a difficult time? Who were his closest friends these days? She had met a few of his business associates in the past but none of them appeared to be close to him or he to them. He had a tendency to hold people at a distance.

And who knew that better than her?

Even though she had shared his body and his home for nearly a year he was as much of an enigma to her as ever.

Ailsa looked into his gaze and felt her resolve melting like an ice cube in a hot tub. She didn't have too many pressing engagements back in London. She had planned to have a week or two out of the studio to work

on some designs for some clients at home. What would it matter if she rescheduled her flight for a day or two? Just until Dom got out of surgery or Recovery. Her assistant, Brooke, could handle anything urgent.

'How soon will you know if your grandfather is going to be out of immediate danger? I could stay in a hotel for a day or two...until I've made up my mind about the agreement.' Would he allow her that much leeway? A day or two wasn't much of a reprieve but she needed to keep as much distance from him as she could—while she still could.

His hand moved further along her scalp, the glide of his fingers sending her senses spinning and her willpower wilting like a daffodil in the desert. 'Is it me you don't trust or is it yourself?' His voice was rich dark honey and gravel swirled together.

Ailsa could feel his body just inches away from hers, his tall frame like a powerful magnet, pulling her body, drawing it inexorably towards his. Her lips were suddenly so dry they felt like cardboard but she daren't moisten them because she knew Vinn would read that as a signal that she wanted him to kiss her.

Damn it. She *did* want him to kiss her. Wanted. Wanted. Wanted. But no way was she going to let him know that. She would get her willpower back into line. Right here. Right now. She glanced at his mouth. *Where the hell was her flipping willpower?* Why did he have to have such a beautiful mouth? Sculptured and firm and yet the lower lip had a sensual fullness to it that her mouth, and other parts of her body, remembered with a frisson of excitement.

Ailsa raised her chin and locked her gaze with his. 'You think I still want you?' She affected a little laugh. 'That ego of yours really is something, isn't it? I feel nothing for you. A big fat nothing.'

His eyes darkened and a knowing smile lifted one corner of his mouth and his fingers shifted back to her nape to toy with the underside of her hair. A sensation shimmied down her spine like a warm flow of melted caramel, gathering in a hot whirlpool between her thighs. His gaze went to her mouth and back to her eyes and back again as if he were in the process of deciding whether to kiss her or not. Every nerve in her lips prepared itself—leaping and dancing and clapping their hands in anticipation. Every cell of her body vibrated with a hum of primal longing as needs she had ignored, suppressed or denied for the last two years came to throbbing life.

But then he suddenly moved away from her and a mask came down over his features like a curtain lowering on a stage. 'Someone's waiting for this car space. We'd better get moving.'

Ailsa had completely forgotten they were still in the hospital car park. But that was typical of being in Vinn's company. She forgot stuff, like how he had only married her so he could tick the job of 'finding a wife' off his to-do list. She was a fool to think he still wanted *her*. Maybe he did physically, but that was a male thing. Men could separate the physical from the emotional far more easily than most women.

Vinn had never been emotionally connected with her. And she had been a fool to accept his proposal on those

terms. He'd offered her marriage but she had a feeling that was only because she had been the first woman to resist him. He'd seen her as a challenge, a conquest, and putting a ring on her finger and having a big flashy society wedding had publicly broadcast his success in claiming her as his prize. Even if he hadn't loved her at the start of their marriage, she had been happy with his desire for her. It had been enough because no one had ever made her feel that way before.

Wanted.

Needed.

As if she was irreplaceable.

But if she had been so irreplaceable, surely he would have fought a little harder to keep her? She'd been let go without a whisper of protest. Sure, he'd been a little difficult over the divorce proceedings, but that was because of the wording of the pre-nuptial agreement. The fact that he'd insisted on a pre-nup was another stark reminder of the sort of marriage they had. She had ignored it at the time, telling herself that of course a man with that sort of hard-earned wealth would want to make sure it was well protected. She had dutifully signed the document, pretending she was happy to do so while a tiny alarm bell tinkled in the back of her mind. She'd slammed the door on it, but now the door was swinging wide open and the alarm bell was clanging with a warning.

Be careful.

CHAPTER THREE

VINN DROVE OUT of the hospital car park with his gut clenched around brutal balls of barbed wire. He would have stayed on the ward until his grandfather was out of surgery but he knew it would be many hours, and then even more, before Nonno was out of Recovery.

If he ever got out of Recovery.

He hated hospitals. Hospitals were places people you cared about went in and never came out. He had been young when his mother had come into hospital for routine surgery—four years old—but he'd been old enough to realise something was horribly wrong when the doctor came out to speak to his father. The look on his father's face was something he would never forget. But his father had lied to him, pretended everything was fine and that *Mamma* was coming home when she got better. It was the first of many lies his father had told him over the next few days, until his grandparents had stepped in and insisted he be told the truth.

Where would Vinn be without his grandfather? Nonno had been there for him through thick and thin and each and every one of his father's sins. He had stal-

wartly stood by Vinn, refusing to allow the shame of his father's behaviour to leave a stain on him.

And then when his father died, two days after Ailsa left, and the distraught family of those poor innocent victims had been baying for blood, Nonno had been steady and supportive, even though his grief at losing his only son must have been devastating. Vinn had mechanically organised his father's funeral and gave a short but respectful eulogy, but he'd done all of it like an automaton. He couldn't remember feeling anything during that time. He'd been blank. Like his motherboard had frozen. People had come up to him at the funeral expressing their condolences and casting their questioning gazes around for Ailsa. He'd made up some excuse for her absence, fully believing at that time she would be back.

But, in a way, his father's death had been a good distraction from Ailsa walking out on him. It meant weeks, almost a month, had passed before he had to face the fact she wasn't coming back. He had assumed she would call him in a couple of days or text him, telling him she didn't mean it, that she was sorry and could they make up. She had often blown off steam like that and, once she got over her little temper tantrum, everything would return to normal.

But it hadn't returned to normal because she hadn't returned.

There had been no phone calls.

No text messages.

Vinn hadn't called her to inform her about his father's death. But then, why would he? She hadn't met

his father and even Vinn rarely had much contact with him during their brief marriage. He'd assumed she'd find out from the press coverage, because there had been plenty of that at the time. Although the London tabloids didn't always carry what the Italian ones carried, which was a good thing as far as Vinn was concerned. The less the rest of the world knew about his father's shady dealings and the misery he'd inflicted on others the better.

But none of that mattered now because Ailsa was back and Vinn was going to make sure that when she left the second time around it would be on his terms not hers. He would get her to sign the agreement if it was the last thing he did.

Ailsa was expecting Vinn to take her to a hotel, but when he took the road that led to his villa in the upmarket district of Magenta she sent him a questioning look, her insides fluttering and flopping with panic... or maybe it wasn't panic. Maybe it was a feeling of excitement, but she refused to acknowledge it. She had no right getting excited around Vinn. That part of their relationship was over. Dead and buried over. 'I said I'll stay in a hotel, not with you.'

'Don't be ridiculous. What will the press make of that if they see you staying at a hotel now our reconciliation has been announced?' he said. 'It might get back to Nonno. You'll stay with me. It's the most sensible thing to do.'

Sensible? Nothing about being in the same country—the same geological era—with Vinn was sensible—never

mind being alone with him in his villa. Not that they would be truly alone since he had a housekeeper and two gardeners. Ailsa had grown up with comfortable wealth—not rich, not poor but somewhere in between. But nothing had prepared her for the wealth Vinn had accumulated.

One of the things she'd enjoyed most about their brief months of marriage was how he'd let her decorate his villa. It had been her project—one of the biggest she'd done—and she'd relished the opportunity to bring the grand old beauty into full glory. Of course, she'd had to deal with the interference of Vinn's grumpy old house-keeper Carlotta, who'd always seemed to take issue with Ailsa over each and every change she'd wanted to bring about. But in the end Ailsa had ignored the old woman's comments and asides and got on with the job. It was her proudest achievement and, while she'd since removed the photos from her website, barely a day went past when she didn't think of the love and hard work she had poured into that beautiful old building.

Had Vinn changed it? Had he stripped every room of her influence? Purged the villa of her? Taken away every trace of her presence in his life? The thought of him undoing all of her work squeezed at her chest like a giant claw.

But then she remembered the one room that had trig-gered the final breakdown of their relationship.

The room that Vinn thought would make a great nursery. At first she'd thought he was joking, but day after day he kept bringing up the subject to the point where she would childishly plug her ears and walk

away. She had planned to decorate the room as a guest-room with en suite bathroom and a lovely reading area near the windows overlooking the garden below. In the end she had left the room untouched.

She had closed the door on it and on their marriage.

'Same old Vinn,' Ailsa said, shooting him a murderous glare. 'Ordering me about as if I'm a child. But aren't you forgetting something? I haven't signed up for this. I'm only here for a day or two, max.'

He released a slow breath as if trying to remain patient. 'Can we just get through the next twenty-four hours without the verbal fisticuffs? I'm not in the mood for it.'

Ailsa remained silent until he pulled up outside the villa. Her chest was tight and her breathing shallow when he helped her out of the car and led her towards the front door. So many memories assailed her. He'd carried her over the threshold the day they returned from their honeymoon. Memories of making love in each room of the house in those first blissfully happy months. Kissing in doorways. Touching, wanting. This house was where they had their first argument…and their last.

Vinn opened the front door and silently gestured for her to enter. Ailsa stepped past him, breathing in the scent of him—the lemon and lime top notes of his aftershave with the base notes of something woodsy, reminding her of a deep, dark secluded forest.

She stepped into the hallway and it was like stepping back in time. Nothing had changed. The colours she had chosen, the furniture and fittings and little touches

she had placed about were still there. Was every room still the same?

Ailsa swung her gaze back to his. 'I thought you would've gutted the place after I left. You know, got rid of my handiwork.'

He shrugged. 'Couldn't be bothered, to be frank.'

'Are all the rooms still the same?'

'Why wouldn't they be?' His expression was hard to read. 'I spent a fortune having it redecorated. I wasn't going to let the walk-out of my wife make me waste even more of my money.'

Ailsa could feel herself bristling like a cornered cat. 'I thought it was *our* money. We were married, for God's sake. Anyway, I spent a lot of my own money on this house because, unlike you, I don't have a problem with sharing.'

His eyes became hard, as if they had been coated with an impermeable sheen. 'I wasn't the one who forgot we were married, Ailsa. That was you.'

She blew out a whooshing breath, anger flooding her like a tide. 'Why is everything always *my* fault? What about your role in this? You shifted the goalposts, just like you did today. You overrode my opinions as if I hadn't spoken. You tried to force me to sign that stupid agreement and then you brought me here even though I expressly told you I wanted to go to a hotel. You don't listen, Vinn. You never have. You just do what you damn well want and to hell with anyone else's wishes. That's not how a marriage is supposed to work.'

His features had a boxed-up look about them, as if he was retreating inside himself. Or maybe it was more

a case of him locking her out. 'I told you my reasons for bringing you here.'

'Yes, but we didn't discuss it first,' Ailsa said. 'You just got behind the wheel of your car and drove here, not once asking if it was okay with me.'

He rolled his eyes in a God-give-me-patience manner. 'Okay. We'll discuss it now.' He folded his arms and planted his feet as if he was settling in for a century or two. 'Talk to me. Tell me why you want to stay in a hotel.'

Because I don't trust myself around you. Because you're still the sexiest man I've ever met and I can barely keep my hands off you. Ailsa kept her expression masked. 'I prefer my own space. I've got used to it after the last twenty-two months.'

His gaze studied hers as if he was seeing through the lie like a detective saw through a false alibi. Then his gaze went to her mouth and something molten-hot spilled in her belly. 'Really.' He didn't say it as a question but in a tone that was faintly mocking.

Ailsa fussed with a loose strand of her hair, securing it back behind her ear for something to do with her hands in case they took it upon themselves to reach for him. A possibility that terrified her as much as it tempted her. Why was she so...so *weak* around him? It was like her body had no connection with her mind. It was running on autopilot and no amount of self-discipline or self-control had any impact.

'Yes. Really,' she said. 'I haven't missed you at all. Not a bit. In fact, on the contrary, I—hey, what are you doing?'

Vinn suddenly placed his hands on her hips, drawing her close enough for their lower bodies to touch pelvis-to-pelvis, heat-to-heat. Male to female. His eyes locked on hers, the slow burn of his gaze unravelling something tightly knotted in her body. 'You've always been a terrible liar.' One of his hands came up to cradle her face, his thumb moving over her cheek in a lazy caress that sent a frisson of electric awareness through her body. If her self-control had been in serious trouble before, now it was on life support. Nothing could have made her move away even though his hold was light.

No one had held her for the last twenty-two months. No one.

Her skin craved human touch. She ached to be crushed to his body, to feel his warm male skin pressed to hers—to feel his mouth come crashing down to hers with its hot erotic promise. She fought the desire to close her eyes and lean into the hard heat of his tempting body. Need pulsed and pounded in each and every cell of her body, making her aware of every inch of her flesh. Flesh he had touched and teased and tantalised with such thrilling expertise in the past.

'I'm n-not lying.' Ailsa was ashamed her voice betrayed her with its wobble and whisper-softness.

Vinn's half smile switched off the ventilator on her self-control. His fingers splayed through her hair and his mouth came down to within a breath of hers, the sexy mingle of their breaths a heart-stopping reminder of other intimacies they'd shared. Intimacies she craved like an addict did a drug they had long been denied. Vinn was exactly like a drug—potent

and powerful and with the unnerving ability to totally consume her.

Ailsa knew she should push him away. Knew it in her mind but her body was offline—it wasn't even in the same Wi-Fi zone. She even got as far as placing her hands on his chest but, instead of pushing, they fisted the front of his shirt until the buttons strained against their buttonholes.

'You think I still *want* you?' she said in a tone that was meant to be scornful but somehow sounded exactly like the cover-up it was.

His gaze flicked to her mouth and back again to her eyes, the pad of his thumb moving against her lower lip in a soft-as-a-puff-of-air motion. 'You want me. I want you. Some things never change.'

Ailsa frowned. 'But you told me before you didn't want to sleep with me. You said our reconciliation would be a hands-off arrangement—or words to that effect.'

He gave a lip shrug as if the prospect of sleeping with her was not much of an issue. Not for him maybe, but for her it was The Issue. 'Why not make the most of what's still between us?'

'There's nothing still between us.' Ailsa tried to pull away but his hold subtly tightened…and a part of her—a part she didn't want to believe existed any more—clapped its hands in glee and cried, *He still wants you!*

Vinn's thumb gently pressed down on the middle of her lower lip—the most sensitive spot where thousands of nerves were already firing off in anticipation for the pressure of his mouth. 'Are you sure about that, *cara*?'

Ailsa knew she had to resist him. She had to stop him kissing her. If he kissed her she was not going to be able to control herself. When had she ever been able to control herself when his mouth connected with hers? But with the tantalising presence of his thumb on her lips, she suddenly found herself parting them and tasting his salty skin with the tip of her tongue as if the connection between her rational brain and her body had been sabotaged. A bomb of lust exploded in his bottomless black gaze. The same explosion went off in her own body, sending flaming-hot darts of longing to sizzle in her core.

One corner of his mouth came up in a sexy slant. 'You really shouldn't have done that.' His deep voice was a silky caress in places that hadn't been caressed in so long Ailsa had almost forgotten what it was to be a woman. Almost.

She knew it was a mistake to moisten her mouth, but there was nothing she could do to stop her tongue sweeping over her lower lip where his thumb had rested. She kept her gaze locked on his. Not that she could have looked away if she'd tried. 'Why not?'

'Because now I have to do this.' And his mouth came down and covered hers.

His mouth was deceptively soft against hers, luring her into a sensual whirlpool in which she knew she could so easily drown. But the feel of his lips moving against hers with such exquisitely gentle pressure left her defenceless, disarmed and desperate for more. She made a sound against his lips—a whimpering, mewl-

ing, approving sound that betrayed her as shockingly as if she had shouted, *I want you*.

His tongue glided through her softly parted lips and rediscovered every corner of her mouth in deliciously arousing detail. The taste of him, the feel of him, the sheer maleness of him excited her senses into a madcap frenzy like someone poking at a hive of bees. Sensations buzzed through her flesh, hot prickles of want and cascading shivers of delight, and sweet little stabs of memory as his lips and tongue danced with hers like two ideally suited dancing partners coming together after a long absence.

Ailsa welcomed each stroke and glide of his tongue, relishing the way his breathing quickened and his hold tightened. At least she wasn't the only one who was affected. But it still worried her that one kiss could do this to her—turn her into a breathless, limbless wanton with zero willpower. She linked her arms around his neck and leaned into him, her breasts tingling at the contact with warm, hard male muscles.

Vinn slid his hands down to her hips, holding her against the potent ridge of his erection, his mouth making teasing little nips and nudges against hers.

'Want to do it here or shall we go upstairs?'

His blunt statement was a shot of adrenalin to her comatose willpower. Ailsa unwound her arms from around his neck and stepped back, throwing him a look that would have curdled milk. Long-life milk.

'Do you really think I would subject myself to more of your...your disgusting pawing?'

He made a soft sound of amusement and his eyes

gleamed. 'You started it, *tesoro*. You know how hot I get for you when you use your tongue on me.'

Ailsa remembered all too well. Over the last two years she'd vainly tried to forget the things she had done with him. Wickedly sexy things she had not done with anyone else, or ever wanted to. It made her hate him all the more for being so damn...*special*.

She straightened her shoulders and looked down her nose at him like a haughty Victorian schoolmistress. 'I merely opened my mouth and your thumb was in the way.'

He gave a deep chuckle that made the floor of her belly shiver like an unset jelly. 'You're unbelievable.'

She forced herself to hold his gaze. 'Right back at you, buddy.'

He closed the distance between them and traced a slow pathway from the front of her left ear and along the line of her jaw, sending every nerve under her skin into raptures. His expression went from amused to serious. 'Thank you.'

It was such an unexpected thing for him to say it shocked her into silence for a moment. She looked at him in confusion. 'For?'

His fingertip traced a lazy circle on her cheek, his eyes holding hers captive. 'For making me forget about Nonno for a while.'

Ailsa was a little shocked that she too had forgotten Dom. But hadn't it always been this way between her and Vinn? It was as if no one else existed when they were in each other's arms. 'Is it too early to call the hospital to see how he is?'

'Way too early.' His hand fell away from her face and went to scrape back his hair from his forehead instead. 'It will be hours and hours before we find out anything…' a worried frown flickered across his forehead '…unless, of course, something goes wrong.'

Ailsa put her hand on his forearm. 'Try not to think like that, Vinn. Your grandfather might be frail but they wouldn't have offered the surgery if they didn't think he had a fair chance.'

'He has no chance without it,' he said, releasing a sigh. 'No chance at all.'

She squeezed her fingers around the muscles of his forearm. 'Is there anything I can do?'

His eyes met hers. 'You're doing it by agreeing to come back to me.'

Ailsa dropped her hand from his arm as if it had been scorched. 'I'll stay one night or two maximum. That's all. Just till he gets out of surgery.' *Or doesn't.* She didn't need to say the words out loud because she knew they were both thinking about the very real possibility that Dom wouldn't make it through the surgery. She crossed her arms over her body and glared at Vinn. 'You can't make me stay any longer than that. I haven't signed the agreement and I have commitments back home and—'

'Cancel them.'

'Oh, like you did during our marriage whenever I needed you?' Ailsa injected a stinging dose of sarcasm in her tone.

A brooding frown formed on his forehead. 'I run a large business that involves a lot of responsibility. I

can't just take a day off to keep my bored wife amused. I have people relying on me for their incomes.'

'And why was I bored? Because you insisted I move to Milan and forget about my job back in London. I wasn't used to having so much spare time on my hands.'

'But you told me you were unhappy in that job,' Vinn said. 'You were working for someone else who was exploiting you.'

'Yeah, funny that,' Ailsa said with a pert tilt of her brow. 'I seem to attract those sort of people, don't I?'

His mouth flattened to a line of white. 'I did not exploit you. I told you what I was prepared to give you and—'

'And then you went and changed the rules,' Ailsa said. 'You thought you'd get me to pop out a baby or two while you go on with your terribly important career that can't be interrupted under any circumstances.'

'You are the most maddening young woman I've ever met,' Vinn said with a thread of anger running through his voice. 'It's impossible to discuss anything with you without it turning into World War Three. I've made it clear how this is going to work. I need you here for this week at the very least. I realise you have responsibilities back in London so I'll allow you to travel back and forth as needs be—'

'You'll *allow* me?' Ailsa could feel her eyes popping in outrage and her pulse thundering.

'I'm prepared to be reasonable.'

She laughed a mirthless laugh. 'Somehow you and the word *reasonable* don't fit too well together. I'll travel to London whenever I want or need to. I will not be ordered about by you, nor can you kidnap me.'

'Don't tempt me.'

Ditto. He was temptation personified. Putting her anger aside, Ailsa didn't know how she was going to keep her distance, and was privately impressed with herself for how she'd got this far without throwing herself upon him and begging him to make love to her. She blew out a breath and picked up her bag from where she'd left it on the floor.

'I need a cup of tea or something. Do you mind if I make myself one?' It seemed strange to be asking permission to do something in the home she used to call her own, but with the surly presence of his housekeeper Carlotta, no doubt still guarding her territory like a junkyard dog, Ailsa was reluctant to breeze in there as she had in the past. She didn't have the same rights and privileges now…but then, maybe she never had, which was something his housekeeper had made clear whenever she'd had an opportunity. Ailsa had tried to strike up a friendship with his housekeeper because she had felt a little daunted by being so far away from everything familiar. She had secretly hoped Carlotta would be a sort of stand-in mother figure for her since her own mother had never been the nurturing type. But Carlotta hadn't been interested in connecting with Ailsa on any level. The older woman had been cold and dismissive towards any attempts on Ailsa's part to offer to help around the villa. Ailsa had felt unwelcome, a hindrance, an inconvenience. A burden to be borne.

Just like she'd felt back at home with her mother.

Vinn waved a hand in the direction of the kitchen. 'Make yourself at home—you know where everything

is. I'm going out for a while. I don't know when I'll be back. But call or text me if you want me.'

That was the whole trouble—Ailsa did want him. She wanted him so badly it was a persistent ache in her flesh. When would she stop wanting him? Would that day ever come? Or had he left his mark on her like a brand? Making her his for ever by the simple fact of making her desire only him and him alone?

'What about Carlotta? Is she going to frogmarch me out of the house as soon as she sees me or have you given her the heads-up?'

His mouth tightened as if he were recalling all the arguments they'd had over his housekeeper's attitude towards her. An attitude he had never witnessed and therefore didn't believe existed. 'She's having the week off.'

'A week off? Wow, wonders will never cease.' Ailsa didn't bother pulling back on the sarcasm. 'I didn't think Carlotta had a life outside this house. She never even had a day off when I was here. Not once.'

He let out a breath that sounded faintly exasperated. 'I hope you're not going to make things difficult for her while you're here.'

'Difficult for *her*?' Ailsa laughed even though she felt like crying at the injustice. 'What about her making things difficult for me? I tried to get close to her and she shut me down like I was a stray dog who'd turned up at the back door looking for scraps.'

'Look, she's an old woman and I don't want—'

'She should've retired by now,' Ailsa said. 'She doesn't even clean the house properly. I was always

going around after her, redoing stuff she'd missed, which I'm sure was another reason why she hated me so much. Why do you still employ her when she's obviously past it?'

He let out an impatient-sounding breath. 'She did not hate you.'

'Not while you were around, no,' Ailsa said. 'She saved it for when you weren't there to witness it. How old is she anyway?'

'Seventy-three.'

Ailsa widened her eyes. 'Seventy-three? That's surely a bit old to be still in full-time employment, isn't it?'

'She's been working for my family for a long time.' He paused for a beat and then continued. 'Since before my mother died. They were…close, or as close as a housekeeper and an employer could be.'

Ailsa tried to read his expression but it was like trying to read invisible ink. 'So you keep her on because of her link to your mother?' He had so rarely mentioned his mother in the past. She had tried to draw him out about what he could remember about his mother but she had got the impression he'd been too young when his mother died to remember much at all.

A shadow passed over his gaze but then his mouth became tightly compressed as if he regretted his uncharacteristic disclosure. 'Please—make yourself at home. I'll let you know if there is any news on Nonno.' And with that he turned and left her in the hallway with just the echo of his footsteps for company.

Ailsa made her way to the kitchen, but instead of making herself a cup of tea, she stood and looked out

of the windows to the courtyard and garden beyond. The two-lane lap pool sparkled in the warm spring sunshine and, even without opening the French doors, she could almost smell the purple wisteria hanging in a scented arras.

How many other women had Vinn made love to in that pool? How many other women had he made love to under the dappled shade of those trees? Her stomach clenched into a fist of anguish.

How many women had he made love to in the bed he had once shared with her?

She turned away from the window and sighed. Why was she even thinking about things like that? She had been the one to leave their marriage. If Vinn had taken up with other women since, surely that was his prerogative? They had been separated almost two years. Longer than they'd been together. Two years was a long time to be celibate for a man who had been having sex since his teens. *Damn it.* It was a long time for her and she'd only been having sex—the sort of sex that was worth mentioning, that was—while she had been married to Vinn.

Ailsa left the kitchen and made her way upstairs to the master bedroom she had once shared with him. Even as she walked towards it, she knew she was inflicting unbearable torture on herself but she felt compelled to revisit that room, to see if anything had been changed. There were numerous other rooms she could have visited first, but no, her legs were carrying her, step by step, to that room.

She pushed open the door and for a moment just stood there, breathing in the faint scent of Vinn's after-

shave that was still lingering in the air. The king-size bed was neatly made and she wondered again who was the last woman to sleep in it with him.

Ailsa swallowed a tight lump as she walked towards the walk-in wardrobe, drawn there like a hapless moth to a deadly flame. *This is going to hurt.* But, even as she mentally said the words, she pulled back the sliding doors...

CHAPTER FOUR

AILSA STOOD AS still as one of the marble statues in the garden below and stared at the rows and rows of her clothes. At first she thought they might have been someone else's but she recognised the fabrics, the styles, the colours. Things Vinn had bought her, expensive things—things she could never have afforded herself.

She'd stormed out in such a hurry that she hadn't bothered packing, mostly because a secret stubborn part of her had always hoped to come back when Vinn pleaded and begged her to, which of course he hadn't done. She hadn't asked him to return anything to her London address because, once it was clear he wasn't going to fight for her, she'd wanted to put her life with him in Milan behind her. She had wanted no reminders, no triggers for memories that could make her regret her impulsive decision to call time on their marriage.

For she could see now, with the benefit of hindsight, how impulsive it had been. How…how immature to storm out like a tantrum-throwing child instead of trying to work at better communication. Why hadn't she

tried harder to understand where Vinn was coming from? If he'd wanted to talk about the possibility of having children then surely she should have been mature enough to have the discussion even if her opinion remained the same. It was becoming apparent to her that his inability to see the flaws in his housekeeper was deeply rooted in his attachment to Carlotta that stretched back to his early childhood. A childhood he had told Ailsa virtually nothing about.

Why hadn't he told her about Carlotta's connection with his mother before?

And why hadn't she made it her business to find out more about his childhood?

Because she hadn't wanted him digging about in her own.

Ailsa trailed her fingers through the silky fabrics on the velvet hangers, releasing a tidal wave of memories as the clothes moved past her fingers. Why hadn't he got rid of them? Why not toss them out in the rubbish or donate them to charity?

Why keep them here, so close to his clothes?

Ailsa slid the doors closed and let out a serrated sigh. How well did she know Vinn? She knew the way he took his coffee and that he absolutely hated tea. She knew what books he liked to read and what movies he liked to watch. She knew he had a ticklish spot at the backs of his knees and that he always slept on the right side of the bed—no exceptions.

But how well did she *know* him?

Was his keeping her clothes a sentimental thing or a tactical thing? What if he wanted her to believe he

hadn't given up hope on her returning? What if this very minute she was being masterfully manipulated?

Anger prickled her skin like a rash. Vinn was ruthless—she had always known that about him. He detested failure. He saw it as a weakness, even as a character flaw. He wanted her back for three months to prove what, exactly? That she couldn't resist him?

Ailsa smiled a secret smile.

She would *show* him how well she could resist him.

Vinn paced his Milan office floor like a tiger on a treadmill. He wondered now if he should have stayed back at the villa in case Ailsa did another runner on him. She still hadn't signed the agreement. He might be considered a little ruthless at times but he could hardly force her to sign it. He could offer her more money but he had a feeling it wasn't about the money. It was about her wanting to stand up to him. She could stand up to him all she liked but he didn't want anything to compromise his grandfather's recovery.

He had to have her here with him, otherwise people would suspect it was all a ruse. He wanted his grandfather to believe he and Ailsa were back together. He'd seen the joy on Nonno's face when she'd walked into his hospital room. Vinn hadn't seen his grandfather so animated, so overjoyed since the day Vinn had presented Ailsa to him as his fiancée. His grandfather had always approved of Vinn's choice of bride, which had not surprised him because Ailsa was everything a man could want in a bride: beautiful and smart, accomplished and quick-witted—the downside of that being, of course,

she was a little sharp-tongued. His grandfather liked strong women and no one could describe Ailsa as anything but strong.

But Vinn hadn't chosen Ailsa as his bride to gain his grandfather's approval. He had chosen her because he couldn't imagine a time when he wouldn't feel attracted to her. He had never felt such powerful chemistry for a woman before. The sexual energy she triggered in him was shockingly primitive. No one had ever pushed his self-control to the edge the way she did. He wanted her with a fierce, burning ache that pulsed in his loins even now. He had tried for almost two years to rid his brain of the images of her going down on him, the way her lips and tongue could undo him until he was weak-kneed and shuddering. He knew she still wanted him as much as he wanted her. He could feel it in the air when they were in the same room together. It changed the atmosphere. Charged the atmosphere until the air all but crackled with tension.

Vinn couldn't settle to work—not with his grand-father still on the operating table and his almost-ex-wife no doubt searching through the bedroom they'd shared during their marriage. He'd heard Ailsa's foot-steps going up the stairs on his way out of the villa and knew it wouldn't take her long to see he had left her things in the wardrobe. It seemed a foolish oversight now that she was back. What would she make of it? Why hadn't he tossed the lot out? Or shipped it to her? *Damn it.* He could have got Carlotta to do it.

But no, he had left things as a reminder of what happened when he let his guard down. What they'd had

together was not something he'd had with anyone else and he'd expected it to continue. He'd had great sex before, yes. He'd even enjoyed some great relationships, and had even thought one or two might go the distance, but it wasn't until he'd met Ailsa that he'd realised what he'd been missing. She was feisty and opinionated and while it annoyed him at times, it also thrilled him. Because of his wealth and influence, he was used to people dancing around him—people-pleasers and sycophants all wanting to get on his good side.

But Ailsa wasn't afraid to stand up to him. She seemed to relish the opportunity to not just lock horns with him but to rip his horns off and stomp on them and smile sweetly while she was doing it. He'd always liked that about her. Her drive and determination rivalled his and it secretly impressed him as few others impressed him.

But she had left him and it still rankled. It rankled like the very devil. He couldn't countenance failure. Failure was for people who didn't try hard enough, who didn't work hard enough, who didn't *want* hard enough.

He hated surprises. He was a planner, an organiser, a goal-setter. Things didn't just happen—he *made* them happen. Success didn't come about by pure chance. Opportunity knocked on the door of preparation, and that was why, when Ailsa's younger brother had asked him for sponsorship, Vinn realised he had a chance to turn things around so he was back on the winner's podium.

Blackmail wasn't a word he was comfortable using but he would use it if he had to. He wanted Ailsa back for three months. Back in his house. Back in his life.

And, even more importantly, back in his bed.

He wouldn't have made an issue out of it if he hadn't seen the raw desire on her face, felt it in her body, felt it in her mouth as it was fused to his. She might baulk at signing the agreement but he had other ways to get her to change her mind. Much more satisfying ways.

He smiled and silently congratulated himself. *You've got this nailed.*

Ailsa waited for Vinn to come back that evening but he simply sent a text to say he had an urgent matter to see to and not to wait up. She hadn't realised how much she had been looking forward to another showdown with him until the opportunity for it was taken away. Wasn't he concerned she might leave and fly back to London? She hadn't signed his agreement. Yet. She couldn't get that ten million out of her mind.

She had never been the sort of person motivated by money. She enjoyed the good living she earned and was grateful she hadn't grown up in abject poverty. But the thought of all that money and the good she could do with it was tempting. Not just to build and expand her business but to help others. There must be other children born of rape out in the community. Perhaps she could set up a counselling service or a safe place where they could talk about their issues. She could even offer to pay for her mother to have counselling, something her mother had always shied away from. But if the prohibitive cost of long-term therapy were taken away, perhaps it would help her mother finally heal?

But signing the agreement would mean she would

be back in Vinn's life for three months. He thought he had her cornered. Wasn't that why he'd left her here unaccompanied tonight? He was confident she wouldn't leave. And if it hadn't been for his grandfather still undergoing surgery, she would have left.

Ailsa barely slept that night, not just because she was in one of the spare rooms instead of the bed she used to share with Vinn, but also because she was listening for his return. Every time there was a sound in the house she sprang upright, but each time it was just the villa creaking or a noise outside on the street. She kept glancing at her watch, her anger at him escalating as each hour passed. One o'clock. Two o'clock. Three. Four. Five. Why would he be at work at this hour? Or wasn't he at work? Was he with someone? Someone he had on standby to assuage his needs?

Needs Ailsa used to satisfy.

Her anger turned to hurt. Deep scoring hurt like someone had taken a blistering-hot blade to her belly. She curled up in a ball and rocked against the pain. Why had she allowed herself to get into this situation? Exposing herself to Vinn's power to hurt her like no one else had hurt her?

Somehow she must have slept but when she finally woke up around nine the next morning there was still no sign of Vinn. He texted her at about ten to let her know he was at the hospital with his grandfather. Had he been there all night? She wanted to believe he had been sitting by his grandfather's bed but would that be allowed? Wouldn't it be more likely he'd gone to spend the night with someone? Someone female?

It was later that following night when Ailsa realised she wasn't alone in the villa. She'd been listening out for the return of Vinn's car or the sound of the front door opening and closing, annoyed with herself for being on such tenterhooks. She had lost so much sleep over him and tied herself into such big choking emotional knots, she felt rattled to the core of her being. She was supposed to be over him. He wasn't supposed to have this sort of power over her now.

But when she heard sounds coming from within his study she realised he must have come back without telling her. It infuriated her that he was treating her as if she were a houseguest he had no desire to interact with unless it was absolutely necessary.

Ailsa didn't knock on Vinn's study door but barged right in and stalked over to his desk, where he was sitting. 'How long have you been back? I've been waiting for you since yesterday. Did you not think it would be polite to tell me you'd come back? I thought we had a burglar.'

He leaned back in his chair with a squeaking protest of expensive leather, his expression as inscrutable as a MI5 spy's. 'And what were you going to do if there had been a burglar in my office just now?'

Ailsa hated how he always criticised her impetuosity. So she was a little impulsive? He'd liked that about her in the bedroom. He'd been delighted and dazzled by it. *Stop thinking about you and him in bed.* She decided it was time for a change of subject. 'Why are my clothes still in your wardrobe?'

'I've been waiting for you to come back and collect them.'

She sucked in a breath, trying to contain her temper but it was like trying to stop a pot from boiling over while someone else was deliberately turning up the heat underneath. 'How long were you prepared to keep them?'

He picked up a gold ballpoint pen off his desk and clicked it on and off in a carefully measured sequence of clicks. On. Off. On. Off. 'As long as it took.'

Ailsa refused to back down from the challenge in his dark-as-night gaze. 'I might never have come back.'

Something glinted in the back of his eyes and his pen clicked again, acting as a punctuation mark. 'But you did.'

Ailsa ground her teeth so hard she was sure she would be on liquids for the rest of her life. 'You had no right to keep my things.'

'You didn't ask for them back.'

'That's beside the point.'

His gaze was unwavering on hers. 'Why didn't you?'

'I think you know why.'

'I don't.' Another click-click of the pen. 'Enlighten me.'

Ailsa compressed her lips. 'You bought me all that stuff. They were clothes to fit the role of trophy wife.'

'Are you saying you didn't like them?'

She had liked them too damn much. 'I'm not saying you haven't got good taste, I'm just saying you wanted me to act a role I was no longer prepared to play.'

He dropped the pen and pushed back his chair and

stood, coming around to sit on the corner of his desk right near where she was standing. She was conscious of his long strong legs within touching distance of hers and the way his eyes were almost level with hers because he was seated. She considered moving but didn't want to betray how vulnerable she felt around him. She put her game face on and stared back into his quietly assessing gaze.

'When did you change your mind?'

Ailsa tried to keep her expression under tight control but she could feel her left eyelid flickering. 'About what?'

'About not wanting to be a trophy wife, as you call it.'

She tucked a strand of hair back behind her ear for something to do with her hands. How could she tell him she had never been happy in the first place? That their marriage was not the fairy tale she had longed for since she was a little girl. That she had only accepted his offer of marriage because it made her feel marginally normal. The white dress and veil, the congregation-packed church, the vows, the hymns, the traditions that made her—for a short time at least—forget she was the daughter of a faceless monster. That for the first time in her life she had felt wanted and needed by someone. Someone who could have had anyone but had somehow chosen her. 'We should never have got married. We should have had a fling and left it at that. At least then we could have parted as friends.'

His eyes held hers for a long heart-chugging beat before his gaze went to her mouth. Then he lifted his hand and drew a line from the top of her cheekbone to

the centre of her chin, not touching her mouth but close enough for the sensitive nerves in her lips to get all excited in case he did. 'You don't think we could one day be friends, *cara?*'

Ailsa pressed her lips together to stop them from tingling. Her heart was thudding like a couch potato at a fun run and her resolve was nowhere to be seen. 'We've never been friends, Vinn. We were just two people who had sex and got married in a hurry and had more sex.'

His mouth shifted in a rueful manner and he slowly underscored her lower lip with his fingertip, just brushing along her vermillion border, creating a storm of longing in her flesh. His hand fell away from her face and his gaze met hers. 'Perhaps you're right.' He released a short sigh. 'But it was great sex, *sì?*'

Ailsa wished they weren't talking about sex. Talking about sex with Vinn was almost as good as doing it with him. Almost. The way he looked at her with those dark, sexily hooded eyes, the way his body was so close but not close enough, the way his hands kept touching her as if he couldn't help himself. Talking about sex—about *their* lovemaking—made her want him so badly it was like an unbearable itch taking over her entire body. 'Yes, but that doesn't mean I want it now. Or ever. From you, I mean. We're practically divorced and—'

His hands captured both of hers and drew her so close to him she was standing between his muscular thighs. Everything that was female in her started cheering like cheerleaders at a grand final. Her hands were flat against his chest, her breasts pushed so tightly against him she could feel the ridges of his muscles

against her nipples. 'You do want it. You want me. That's why you haven't had anyone since me.'

Ailsa made a vain effort to pull away. Well, maybe it was more of a token effort if she were to be perfectly honest. She didn't want to pull away. She wanted to smack her lips on his and rip off all his clothes and get down to business to assuage this treacherous need spiralling through her body. But some small vestige of her pride refused to allow her to capitulate so easily. 'I'm sure you've had dozens since me. How soon did you replace me? A week? Two? Or are we talking days or maybe even hours?'

His hands released her and he set her from him and stood from where he had perched on the corner of the desk. He went back around the other side of the desk as if he were putting a barricade between them. His expression was just as barricaded. 'Until our divorce is finalised, I consider myself still legally married.'

Ailsa looked at him in shock. 'What are you saying? That you haven't had anyone since me? No one at all? But I saw pictures of you in the press with...' She stopped before she betrayed her almost obsessional perusal of the press for any mention of him. She had even gone as far as buying Italian gossip magazines. Ridiculous. And expensive and practically useless since she couldn't read Italian.

'I have a social life, but I've refrained from getting involved with anyone until our divorce is done and dusted. I didn't think it would be fair to bring a new partner into such a complicated situation. Why are you looking so shocked?'

Ailsa tried to rearrange her features into blank impassivity. Tried but failed. 'I just thought you'd…you know…move on quickly.'

He straightened some papers on his desk that, as far as Ailsa could tell, didn't need straightening. His eyes met hers across the desk—dark and glinting and dangerously sexy. 'You mean for a man with my appetite for sex?'

The less she thought about his appetite for sex, the better. It was *her* appetite for sex that was the problem right now. She couldn't get it out of her mind. She couldn't get the ache out of her body. 'I never took you to be a man who'd be celibate for two days let alone almost two years.'

He gave a shrug. 'I've eased the tension in other ways. If nothing else, it's been good for business. All that redirected drive has paid off big time.'

Ailsa couldn't get her head around the fact he hadn't replaced her. Not with anyone. She'd spent the last two years torturing herself with images of him making love with other women, doing all the things he had done with her, saying all the things he had said to her, and yet…he hadn't.

He'd been celibate the whole time.

But why? What did it mean? He had more opportunity than most men to attract another lover. Many other lovers. And since they were officially separated and in the process of divorcing, then why wouldn't he have replaced her with someone else? Few people these days waited until the ink was dry on the divorce papers.

She had been celibate because having sex with some-

one else had never even crossed her mind. She'd looked at men in passing but mentally compared them to Vinn and found them lacking. No one came even close. No one stirred her senses the way he did. No one made her feel more like a woman than he did.

Ailsa slowly brought her gaze back to his, but somehow the knowledge that he had been celibate for so long only intensified the sexual energy that pulsated between them. She'd been aware of it before. Well aware. But now it was crackling in the air like static electricity. She ran her tongue over her suddenly dry lips, her chest fluttering as if there were a hummingbird trapped in one of her heart valves. Two hummingbirds. Possibly three. 'So…that explains why our kiss in the hallway got a little…heated…'

Vinn came back around from behind his desk and, standing right in front of her, slowly tucked a loose strand of her hair back behind her ear, just as she had done moments earlier. But her fingers brushing against her skin hadn't set her nerves abuzz like his did. Ailsa could feel her body drawn towards him as if he were an industrial-strength magnet and she was a tiny iron filing. 'Three months, *cara*. That's all I want. After that you can have your divorce.'

Ailsa watched his mouth as he spoke, her mind and her body seesawing over whether to accept his terms. If she didn't and left right now she would be divorced from him within weeks and free to move on with her life, leaving him free to move on with his. Isaac would miss out on his chance at a golfing career, but she could only hope that he would find another career. He was

young, and who didn't change career a couple of times these days anyway?

But if she accepted the three months arrangement she would be back in Vinn's life.

And even more tempting…back in his bed.

Could she do it? Could she risk three months with him just to get him out of her system once and for all? It wasn't as if she was committing to for ever. He didn't want for ever…or so he said.

Just three months.

She could have all the sex she wanted with him. She could indulge in a red-hot affair that had a time limit on it so she didn't have to feel trapped or worried he would suddenly start talking about making babies. It was risky. It was dangerous. But it was so tempting— especially since she'd found out he hadn't replaced her.

What did that mean?

Ailsa slowly brought her gaze back up to his. 'Why are you doing this?'

He slid a hand under the back of her hair, his fingers splaying through the strands, making her shiver in sensory delight. 'I told you—I want my grandfather to have a stress-free recovery.'

She swallowed back a whimper of pleasure as his fingers started a gentle massage at the nape of her tense-as-a-knotted-rope neck. 'This isn't just about your grandfather. It's about us. About this…this chemistry we have.'

He brought his mouth down to the side of hers, nudging against her lips without taking it further. 'So you feel it too, hmm?'

Ailsa couldn't deny it. Her body was betraying her second by second. She angled her head to give him greater access to her neck, where he was now leaving a blazing trail of fire as his lips moved over her skin, the slight graze of his stubble stirring her senses into a frenzy. Desire slithered in quicksilver streaks to all her secret places. 'I want it to go away.' Her voice was too soft and whispery but she couldn't seem to help it. 'It *has* to go away.'

His mouth came back to just above hers, his breath mingling with hers and making every reason to resist him slink away in defeat. 'Maybe three months together will burn it out of our systems.' He nudged her lips— an invitation to nudge him back.

Ailsa shuddered and slid her arms around his waist and placed her mouth on his, giving herself up to the flame of lust that threatened to consume them both. The heat of his mouth engulfed her, sending her senses spinning out of control. His tongue found hers in an erotic collision that made her inner core instantly contract with need. His lips moved on hers with an almost desperate hunger, as if he had been waiting for years for the chance to feed off her lips. She kissed him back with the same greedy fervour, her tongue darting and dancing with his, her body on fire, her blood racing, her heart giving a good impression of trying to pump its way out of her chest.

Vinn brought one of his hands to the front of her silky blouse, where her breasts were already aching for his touch. He skated his hands over her shape without undoing the buttons and her flesh leapt and peaked at

the promise of more of his touch. He tugged her blouse out of her skirt with an almost ruthless disregard for the price she'd paid for it. He slid his hands up her ribcage to just below her breasts, the slightly calloused pads of his fingers sending her into a paroxysm of pleasure.

His mouth continued its magic on hers, drawing from it a response that was just as feverish as his. Their tongues duelled and tangoed in a sexy combat that triggered a tug and release sensation between her thighs. He reached behind her back and deftly unclipped her bra, freeing her breasts to the caress of his hands. Delight rippled through her as he took possession of each breast in his hands, his thumb pads rolling over the budded nipples until she was breathless with need. He brought his mouth down to one breast, licking and stroking her areola with his tongue, sending her senses into raptures before he did the same to the other breast. His stubbly jaw abraded her tender flesh but she welcomed the rough caress, relishing the marks he would no doubt leave on her skin because it would prove that they were really doing this and it wasn't just her imagination playing tricks on her.

'I want you.' His admission was delivered with gruff urgency that made her blood pound all the harder.

Ailsa was beyond speech and began to work at his clothes, not caring that buttons were being popped. She had to get her hands on his body. She had to get her mouth on his hot skin. She had to get her desperate, unbearable desire for him sated.

A phone began to ring but she ignored it, too intent on freeing Vinn's belt from his trousers. But then his

hand came down and stalled her, and he reached past her to pick up his phone off his desk. 'Vinn Gagliardi.'

Even the way he said his own name made Ailsa want to swoon, especially with his desire-roughened voice making it sound all the more sexy. He continued the conversation in Italian and she gestured to him to see if it was news from the hospital but he simply shook his head and mouthed the word 'work' and turned slightly away to complete the call.

It made her feel shut out. Put aside. Put on pause, just like all the times in the past when his work took priority. Just like last night. Just like it would always be because she wasn't anything to him other than someone to have sex with when he wanted.

Ailsa did up her bra and tucked her blouse back into her skirt and finger-combed her hair into some semblance of order. She would have excused a call from the hospital, but a work-related call was a stinging reminder of where she stood on his list of priorities. She was a plaything, something he picked up and put down when it suited him. Hadn't it always been that way? She had fooled herself he would one day see her as more than a trophy wife. But he could have married anyone. She was nothing special and never had been.

Ailsa mouthed at him she would be waiting for him upstairs, feeling a glimmer of triumph when she saw the anticipatory gleam in his gaze. But she wasn't going to be upstairs waiting for him like the old days. She was going to leave while she still had the willpower and the sense to do so.

CHAPTER FIVE

AILSA SLIPPED OUT of the villa and once she'd walked a short distance she hailed a cab. 'The airport, thank you,' she said to the driver. She sat back against the seat and rummaged in her tote bag for her phone and her passport. She planned to book a flight on her phone on the way to the airport but when she looked at her screen she saw it was almost out of battery. Why hadn't she thought to charge it? Never mind. At least if she turned it off Vinn wouldn't be able to call her. She knew she should really be calling Isaac to explain and/or apologise about the bitter disappointment he was in for, but she couldn't face it just yet. She had to get a flight booked, which she would have to do once she got to the airport.

She dug deeper in her bag for her passport but she couldn't find it. She upended the bag and its contents spilled out onto the back seat of the taxi. She wanted to scream. She wanted to scream and pummel the seat until the stuffing came out. How could Vinn do this to her? It was virtually kidnap. He'd taken her passport. He'd actually taken it out of her bag without her permission. She had always known him to be ruthless but

this was getting ridiculous. Why was he so determined to make her stay with him? Was it just about his grandfather? Or was this about revenge?

'Is everything all right?' the driver asked.

Ailsa pasted a frozen smile on her face. 'Erm, I've changed my mind. I think I'll go to a hotel in the city instead.' She rattled off the first name she could think of, where she and Vinn had once had a drink after seeing a show. She would have no choice but to go back to his villa to demand he give back her passport but she wasn't going back until the morning. She wanted him to spend a sleepless night—like she had last night—worrying about where the hell she was.

It would serve him damn well right.

Vinn had only just got his work colleague off the phone when his phone rang again. His heart jumped when he saw it was the hospital calling. He'd spent the night before at the hospital, sitting in the waiting room, wanting to be on site when his grandfather came out of Theatre. But there had been a complication with the surgery and the operation had gone on well into the night. He had finally left the hospital after speaking to the surgeon, once his grandfather was transferred to Recovery, but he knew it was still way too early to be confident his grandfather was out of danger.

He mentally prepared himself for the worst this phone call might bring. His skin prickled from the top of his scalp to the soles of his feet, dread chugging through his veins at the anticipation of bad news. 'Vinn Gagliardi.'

'Signore Gagliardi, your grandfather is doing as well as can be expected and is now out of Recovery and in ICU. It's still early days but he's stable at the moment. We'll call you as soon as there is any change.'

'*Grazie.*' For a moment it was the only word Vinn could get past the sudden constriction in his throat. Emotions he hadn't visited since he was four years old were banked up there until he could scarcely draw a breath. 'Can I see him?'

'Best to leave it until tomorrow or even the day after,' the doctor said. 'He looks worse than he is and he won't know if you're there or not. We're keeping him on a ventilator for a couple of days to get him through the worst of it.'

Vinn put the phone down once the doctor had rung off. Things had changed a lot from thirty years ago, when relatives were often shielded from the truth out of a misguided sense of compassion. He wanted to know all there was to know about his grandfather's condition. He didn't want to be left in the dark like he had been as a child, expecting his mother to come home, excited at the thought of seeing her again, only to find out she was lying dead and cold in the morgue. Nothing could have prepared him for the shock and heartache, but he still believed if he'd been told earlier he would have handled it better. He hadn't even been given the chance to say goodbye to his mother. He hadn't been allowed to even see her. For years, too many torturous years, he had fooled himself into believing she wasn't actually dead. That she had simply gone away and would one

day walk back in the door and reach for him with one of her enveloping perfume-scented hugs.

But of course she hadn't come back. His childish mind had struggled to cope with the enormous loss the only way it could by conjuring up an explanation that was far more palatable than a young mother in her prime going into hospital for routine surgery only to die five days later from complications.

Vinn gave himself a mental shake. He hated thinking about his childhood. The loneliness of it. The sheer agony of it. The sickening realisation that at four years old he was without a reliable parent. His father had never been an involved father so Vinn couldn't excuse him on the basis of his grief. His father had grieved, certainly. But, within a month of the funeral, he had a new mistress, one of many who came and went over the years. Vinn had learned not to show his disapproval or his own ongoing grief for his mother. He'd buried it deep inside, locked it away with all his feelings and vulnerabilities because it was the only way he could cope. His grandfather and grandmother had understood, however. They'd never pressed him to talk about it but he knew they were conscious of his deep inner sadness and made every attempt to make up for his father's shortcomings by always being there as a solid, secure and steady influence in his life.

Vinn was suddenly conscious of the quietness of his villa. Had Ailsa given up on him joining her? He hadn't intended being away as long as he had the night before but he hadn't been able to tear himself away from the hospital until he'd spoken to the surgeon in

person. Was she still angry with him for leaving her so long? Wasn't her anger another sign she wanted him as much as he wanted her? He had been longer on the phone than he'd expected. Some smoking-hot sex with her was just what he needed to make himself forget the tragedy of the past. He smiled to himself, picturing her waiting for him, naked in the bed they had once shared. His body thickened at the thought of her silken golden limbs wrapping around him.

He took the stairs two at a time, anticipation making his heart race. But when he opened the master bedroom door, the bed and the room were empty. He swung to the en suite bathroom but it too was empty. He went through each of the spare rooms on that floor, wondering if she had chosen to wait for him in another room.

He went to the spare bedroom furthest from his that she'd apparently slept in the night before and that was when he saw her passport lying almost out of sight next to the bed. Had she dropped it and inadvertently kicked it further out of sight? He picked it up and flicked through the pages. She had been to Italy four times since their separation, but then he already knew that because he had sent her clients to make sure she came back. He'd liked the thought of her returning to the scene of the crime, so to speak. To remind her of everything she had thrown away by walking out on him.

Vinn slipped the passport into his pocket and took out his phone to call her. If she were still in the villa at least he would hear it ringing. He didn't hear it and within seconds it went through to the message service.

Before he could think what to do next a text message came through, but it wasn't from Ailsa. It was from an acquaintance of his who owned a luxury hotel in the centre of Milan, informing him that Ailsa had just checked in for the night. Nico Di Sante had heard the news of their reconciliation in the press the day before and wondered if anything was amiss. Vinn quickly replied, telling him everything was fine and that he would be joining Ailsa shortly, but to keep it a secret as he wanted to surprise her because she thought he was still caught up with work.

Vinn wanted to do more than surprise her. He was going to put the wedding and engagement rings she'd left behind two years ago back on her finger and that was where they would stay until he gave her permission to remove them. She knew the terms. If she didn't sign the agreement her brother's golfing career would be over before it began. He wouldn't sabotage her brother's career as he'd threatened. The boy deserved a chance even if Vinn wouldn't end up being the one to give it to him. Isaac was typical of other lads his age, dreaming of the big time without putting in the hard yards. He liked the boy and thought he had genuine potential but there was no way Vinn was going to get screwed around by Ailsa. Not again. Had he misjudged her love for her brother? Did she hate him more than she loved Isaac?

He didn't care if she hated him or not. A bit of hate never got in the way of good sex. As far as he was concerned, the more hate the better.

And right now he was damn near boiling with it.

* * *

Ailsa lay back in the luxury hotel bath that was as big as a swimming pool and sipped the complimentary champagne that had been delivered to the door a short time ago. It was a frightfully expensive show of defiance. She had never paid so much for a night's accommodation before but she figured it was worth it for one night of freedom before Vinn made her toe the line. Because, of course, she would have to do as he commanded.

Commanded, not asked. *Argh*.

She had thought about it long and hard. She couldn't let Isaac's chance slip away from him. After all, she knew what it felt like to give up on a dream. It hurt. The hurt and disappointment never went away. It sat like a weight in her chest, dragging her spirits down like a battleship's anchor.

You can't have what you want. You can never have what you want.

The words tortured her every time she heard them inside her head. Ailsa topped up her champagne glass. So what if she was getting tipsy and maudlin? So what if she felt sad and lonely and worthless? She was considering whether to have a good old self-pitying cry when the door of the bathroom suddenly opened and Vinn stood framed in the doorway. She gasped and drew her knees up to her chest, her heart knocking against her chest wall like a pendulum in an earthquake. 'How did you find me?'

His gaze raked her partially naked breasts—partially because of the amount of bubble bath she had poured into the water. 'Don't push me too far, *cara*. You know how it will end.'

Ailsa put up her chin and sent him a look as icy as the North Sea in winter. 'You stole my passport.'

'I did not steal your passport.' He took something out of his top pocket and handed it to her. 'I found it on the floor next to the bed in the spare bedroom.'

Ailsa took the passport with a bubble-coated hand and put it to one side on a marble shelf next to the bath. 'I don't believe you.'

He shrugged as if that didn't concern him. 'It's the truth whether you believe it or not.'

Ailsa wasn't sure what to think. She wouldn't put it past him to have taken her passport, but she also knew her tendency to lose things. She was clumsy and careless under stress and being anywhere near Vinn created more stress than she could handle.

He pulled out a folded document from his back pocket and, using one of the glossy magazines she'd brought into the bathroom as a firm backing, he unfolded it before handing her a pen. 'Sign it.'

Ailsa wished she had the courage to push the wretched document into the bathwater. She wanted to make it dissolve until it was nothing but flotsam floating around her. She wanted to take his stupid gold pen and stab him in the eyes with it. But instead she took the pen and, giving him a beady look, signed her name with an exaggerated flourish. 'Happy now?'

He folded the document and put it to one side and then put his hand back in his trouser pocket and took out the ring box she'd left behind two years ago. 'I want you to wear these until the three months is over.' There was something about his voice that warned her

she would be wise to put the rings back on her finger without an argument, even though it went against her nature to be told what to do.

She took the rings from the box and slipped them on her finger, shooting him another glare. She didn't want to let him know how much she'd missed wearing those rings. The engagement ring was the most beautiful she had ever seen. He'd had it designed specially for her and, while he had never told her how much it cost, she had a feeling it was more than what most people earned in a lifetime. But it wasn't the ring's value she loved. She would have been happy with a cheap ring if he had given it to her with his love. He started to undo his shirt buttons and she reared back in horror. 'What are you doing?'

'We were interrupted an hour or so ago.' His shirt dropped to the floor and his hands went to the waistband of his trousers. 'I was telling you how much I wanted you, remember?'

Ailsa wished she hadn't drunk so much champagne. Her willpower was never a match for Vinn's charm but with alcohol on board it was as good as useless. 'You were telling me how much you wanted me, yes. But, you might recall, I didn't say it back to you.'

Something tightened in his jaw and a guarded sheen hardened his gaze. 'You didn't have to say it. You were ripping my clothes off, and if it hadn't been for that phone call you'd be onto your second or third orgasm by now.'

Argh! How dare he remind her how many times he could make her come? She affected a scornful laugh.

'You think? I would have had to fake it because I do not want you, Vinn. Do you hear me? I. Do. Not. Want. You.'

He stripped off the rest of his clothes and stepped into the bath, sending a miniature tsunami over her body. 'How many times do you reckon you'll have to say it so you actually believe it, hmm?' There was a dangerously silky edge to his tone and he moved up close, capturing her chin between his finger and thumb.

Ailsa tried to brush off his hold like she was swatting an annoying insect. 'Stop touching me.'

His other hand slipped back under the curtain of her hair and he nudged his nose against hers in a playful bump that made her self-control fall over like a house of cards in a hurricane. 'You want me so bad you're shaking with it.'

'I'm shaking with anger and if you don't get your hands off me this instant I'll show you just how angry,' Ailsa said through gritted teeth.

He gave a deep chuckle and slowly but surely coiled a strand of her damp hair around one of his fingers, inexorably tethering her to him. 'I've missed your temper, *cara*. No one does angry quite as sexily as you. It turns me on.'

His pelvis was close enough for her to feel it—the swollen ridge of his arousal calling out to her feminine core like a primal drumbeat, sending an echo through her blood and through her body. 'No one makes me as angry as you do,' Ailsa said. 'I hate you for it. I hate you period.'

'You don't hate me, *cara*.' He slowly unwound her hair from around his finger. 'If you hated me you

wouldn't have come home with me from the hospital yesterday.'

Ailsa wrenched out of his hold with a strength she hadn't known she possessed, sending a wave of bath-water over the edge of the tub. 'I didn't have a flipping choice. You brought me there instead of to a hotel as I requested. It was basically abduction, that's what it was. Then you stole my passport and—'

'You know what your trouble is, *cara*? You don't trust yourself around me. That's why you have to paint me as the bad guy because you can't bear the thought that you're the one with the issue.'

How typical of him to make it seem as if *she* was the problem. It was her self-control that was the problem but that was beside the point. 'You think I can't resist you? Think again. I can and I will.' Dangerous words since his hairy legs were currently nudging hers under the soapy water and everything that was female in her was getting hot and bothered.

His smile was confident. I'll-have-you-eating-those-words-in-no-time confident. 'Come here.'

Ailsa sent him a look that would have withered a cactus. 'Dream on, buddy. The days when you could crook your little finger and I would come running are well and truly over.'

He laughed and moved closer, trailing a fingertip down between her soap-covered breasts. 'Then maybe I'll have to come to you, hmm?'

She suppressed a whimper of pleasure as his finger found her nipple beneath the bubbles. *Why wasn't she moving away?* The slow glide of his finger undid every

vertebra on her spine. Only he knew how to dismantle
her defences. She could feel her body moistening in
preparation, the signal of high arousal. The ache intensified, the need dragging at her, clawing at her, making
her desperate in a way that threatened her pride as it
had never been threatened before. She tried to think of
a way out of the tight corner Vinn had backed her into.
How could she satisfy him—*bad choice of word*—without compromising herself? Was there a way she could
get Isaac that sponsorship without committing to three
months of living with Vinn? 'What if we negotiated
the time frame a little?' she said. 'What if I stayed for
a week instead of—?'

'One month.'

She gave herself a mental high five. The old Vinn
would never negotiate over anything. There was hope
after all. 'I was thinking in days rather than—'

He shook his head and sent his finger down her
breastbone. 'No deal. One month or nothing. I realise
three months is a little long to be away from your business but a month is hardly more than a holiday. And,
from what I've heard from Isaac, you haven't had one
of those in a while.'

Like you can talk, Mr Workaholic. Ailsa chewed the
side of her mouth. One month was better than three
and she could catch up on all her Italian clients, giving
them the attention they deserved instead of fitting them
around her other work. Besides, Vinn's villa was huge.
Surely she could keep her distance from him in a house
that size? It was a win-win. Well, sort of… 'What have
you told Isaac about this…arrangement?'

'I told him the sponsorship would ultimately be up to you.'

Ailsa frowned. 'You told him you were effectively blackmailing me back into your bed?'

'No. I simply told him it was your decision whether I went ahead with the sponsorship.'

'So he'll blame *me* if it doesn't go ahead?'

He gave her an on-off smile that didn't involve his teeth. 'It would be a pity to disappoint him, *si*?'

Ailsa couldn't refuse. She had no room to refuse. If she refused, her relationship with her brother would end up like her relationship with her mother and stepfather. Damaged. Maybe even destroyed. Isaac would blame her for ever for not being able to follow his dream. It would be *her* fault. Vinn had cleverly orchestrated it so she had no choice but to agree. 'Okay. It's a deal.' She lifted her chin to a combative height. 'But I'm absolutely not sleeping with you.'

His eyes strayed to her mouth as if he couldn't stop himself. 'Who said anything about sleeping?' And then his mouth came crashing down on hers.

It was a kiss she had no way of resisting. No amount of self-control, no amount of anger, no amount of anything was going to be a match for the desire she felt for him. As soon as his lips met hers she was swept up in a maelstrom of lust that threatened to boil the water they were in.

Vinn's hands went to her breasts in a possessive movement that thrilled her as much as it annoyed her. How dare he think she was his for the asking? Not that he'd asked. He'd assumed and he'd assumed right, which

was even more annoying. Why did she have no will-power when it came to this man? Why him? What was it about him that made her so weak and needy?

His mouth left hers to suckle on her breasts in a way that lifted every hair on her scalp and sent shivers skating down her spine. No one knew her breasts like he did. No one handled them with such exquisite care and attention. He cradled them as if they were precious and tender, his touch evoking a fevered response from her that had her gasping and mewling like a wanton. His tongue circled her right nipple, rolling and grazing and teasing until she was mindless and limbless. Then he used his teeth in a gentle bite that made an arrow of lust shoot straight to her core. A possessive, you-are-mine-and-only-mine-bite that made her throw herself on his body, desperate for the release only he could give.

His fingers found her folds and within seconds she was flying, careening like an out of control vehicle, her gasps and cries so loud she was almost ashamed of them. She bit down on his shoulder to block the trai-torous sound, vaguely satisfied when he grunted and winced. She wanted him to feel pain. Why should it be just her who suffered for this crazy out of control need?

But within moments that was exactly what he seemed to want, for as soon as her stormy, tumultuous orgasm was over he withdrew and sat back against the edge of the bathtub, his arms draped either side, with a cat-standing-beside-an-empty-canary's-cage smile. 'Good?'

Ailsa glanced at the soapy water surrounding his groin that barely concealed his erection. 'Aren't you going to—?'

'Not right now.' He vaulted out of the bathtub in one effortless movement and reached for one of the fluffy white towels and began roughly drying himself.

Ailsa silently seethed at the way he was demonstrating his superior self-control. He'd made her come but he wasn't going to indulge his own pleasure just to show how he could resist her. *Damn it.* She would show him how hard it was to resist her. She got out of the bath and began drying herself with one of the towels, not roughly as he had done but with slow sensual strokes. She put one foot on the edge of the bath and leaned over to dry between her toes, feeling his eyes devour her derrière. She changed feet and swung her wet hair behind one shoulder and leaned forward again. He was the only man she had ever felt completely comfortable with being naked. She had the same hang-ups most women did about their bodies, but Vinn had always made her feel like a goddess.

She put her foot back down to the floor and turned to face him. 'Would you pass me that body moisturiser over there?'

He picked up a bottle of luxurious honeysuckle-scented creamy lotion. 'This one?'

Ailsa took it from him with a coy smile. 'Want me to rub your back for you?'

His eyes darkened with simmering lust. 'You're playing a dangerous game, *cara.*'

Ailsa squirted some lotion into one of her hands and then put the bottle aside to emulsify the lotion between her hands before smoothing some over her breasts. 'It's really important to moisturise after a hot bath. It keeps your skin supple and smooth.'

His eyes watched every movement of her hands moving over her breasts, the tension in the air at snapping point. When she reached for the bottle of lotion again his hand was already on it. He held her gaze while he poured some out into the middle of his palm. 'Turn around.'

Ailsa turned and shivered when his hand began a slow, sensual stroking motion from the tops of her shoulders to the base of her spine and then even further into the cleavage of her buttocks. Her body clenched tight with need, the sexy glide of his hands in the intimate spaces of her flesh making her forget everything but the desire that throbbed with every single beat of her pulse. He moved his hands to the front of her body, stroking over her breasts and down over her stomach before going lower. She could feel the brush of his body from behind, the hard ridge of his erection against her bottom making her need for him escalating to the point of pain.

He turned her in his arms and looked at her through sexily hooded eyes. 'You know I want you.'

Ailsa moved closer so the jut of his erection was pushed against her belly. 'Make love to me, Vinn.'

He framed her face in his hands, his eyes holding hers. 'That wasn't what you were saying a few minutes ago.'

'I'm saying it now.'

His eyes dipped to her mouth, lingering there for a pulsing moment. Then his mouth came down and covered hers in a searing kiss that inflamed her need like petrol on a fire. He held her body closer, the glide of

naked flesh against naked flesh stirring her senses into rapture. Ailsa linked her arms around his neck, stepping on tiptoe so she could feel the proud bulge of his arousal close to where she throbbed the most.

Vinn deepened the kiss, tangling his tongue with hers, making her whimper at the back of her throat. With his mouth still clamped to hers, they moved almost blindly to the bedroom where he laid her down on the bed and came down over her, propping his weight on his forearms with his legs in a sexy tangle with hers.

He lifted his mouth off hers, looking at her with a direct and probing gaze. 'Are you sure about this?'

Ailsa had never felt surer of anything. She would think about the implications of making love with Vinn again later. For now all she could think of was how wonderful it felt to be pinned to the bed with his weight, with his engorged length thick and heavy between her thighs. She traced a fingertip over his bottom lip, her stomach tilting when she encountered his prickly stubble just below. 'I want you. I don't want to want you, but I can't seem to help it.'

He pressed a brief hard kiss to her mouth. 'I feel the same.'

Ailsa moved beneath him, opening her legs to accommodate him, breathing in a quick sharp breath when he entered her swiftly and smoothly. Her body gripped him, welcoming him back with a tight clench of greedy muscles. He began a torturously slow rhythm but she egged him on by clutching him by the buttocks and bringing him closer with each slick thrust. She could feel the pressure building, the tension in her core so

intense but unable to finally let go without that extra bit of friction. He slipped a hand between their bodies, finding the swollen heart of her and caressing it with just the right amount of pressure to send her flying over the edge.

The orgasm smashed into her, rolling her over and over and over, sending waves and currents and eddies of pleasure through her body. It was almost too much and she tried to shrink back from it but Vinn wouldn't allow her to do so and kept on caressing her until she was in the middle of another orgasm, even more powerful than the first. She gasped and cried out as the storm broke over her, tossing her every which way like a shaken rag doll. She gained enough consciousness to feel Vinn pump his way through his own powerful orgasm, his guttural groan thrilling her because it made her feel wanted and needed and desired. She knew she could have been anybody, but he hadn't chosen anybody.

He had chosen her.

He hadn't made love with anyone since she'd left. It didn't mean he loved her. It meant he wanted to draw a line under their relationship once it was finally over, but she didn't want to think about that now. She closed her eyes and sighed as his arms gathered her close, just like the old days when she'd fooled herself this was a normal relationship with no secrets and hidden agendas.

Vinn stroked a hand down her thigh. 'I would have used a condom but since neither of us has been with anyone else I thought it'd be okay. I assume you've still got your contraceptive implant?'

Ailsa's stomach pitched. Her implant had been up for

renewal a couple of months ago but she'd put off making an appointment with her doctor. Why had she left it so late to get it changed? She knew exactly why—because she hadn't had sex with anyone.

Because she hadn't been able to even *think* about having sex with anyone other than Vinn.

Would the device still be working? She hoped and prayed…and yet a tiny part of her couldn't help thinking about a baby that looked exactly like Vinn. *No. No. No.* She mustn't think about it. *Must not. Must not. Must not think about it.* Allowing those thoughts into her head made it harder to ignore them the next time.

And there would be a next time.

There had been a lot of them lately. Thoughts. Treacherous thoughts of holding a baby in her arms. She was nearly thirty years old. Her mother had given birth to her at eighteen and to Isaac at twenty-eight. But how could Ailsa think of being a mother to a child?

She pushed those thoughts away and gave Vinn a you-know-me-so-well smile. 'Yep. I sure do.'

He traced a slow circle around her belly button. 'You're the only person I've ever made love to without a condom.'

'Because we were married, right?'

'Not just that…' His eyes went to her mouth for a moment before coming back to her gaze. 'I never felt any other relationship had the potential to work as ours did.'

Ailsa lowered her gaze to concentrate on the dark stubble on his chin. 'It would only have worked if I'd caved in to every one of your commands. I wasn't prepared to do that. I'm still not.'

He brushed the hair back from her forehead with a wistful look on his face. 'Maybe you're right. We should have had a fling and left it at that.'

Ailsa tiptoed her fingertip down from his sternum to his belly button. 'Changed your mind about that back rub?'

His eyes glinted. 'You've talked me into it.' And then his mouth came down and covered hers.

CHAPTER SIX

WHEN AILSA WOKE the next morning back at the villa there was no sign of Vinn. Well, apart from the indentation of his head on the pillow beside her and the little twinges in her intimate muscles, that was. He had taken her back to the villa late last night rather than spending the whole night at the hotel, and made love to her all over again. It made her wonder how she had gone so long without him making love to her. It made her wonder how she would cope once their 'reconciliation' was over.

She had a refreshing shower and, wrapping herself in a fluffy white bath towel, looked balefully at her creased clothes from the day before. There was any number of outfits in the walk-in wardrobe but somehow stepping back into the role of trophy wife—temporary as it was—was a little off-putting. Was she losing herself all over again? Capitulating to Vinn's demands as if she had no will and mind of her own?

But this was about his grandfather more than about her and Vinn. Dom was the one they were doing this for. She was still trying to make up her mind what to

do about her clothes when her phone rang from her handbag on the end of the bed. She took it out and saw it was a call from her brother. 'Hi Isaac.'

'Vinn told me you're okay with him sponsoring me,' Isaac said with such excitement in his voice it soothed some of her residual anger at Vinn. Some. Not all. 'I don't know how to thank you. I thought you'd be all dog-in-the-manger about it but he said you were amazing about it. Really amazing.'

'What else did he say about me?'

There was a little silence.

'He said you two were working on a reconciliation. Is it true? Are you back together?'

Ailsa hated lying to her brother but couldn't see any way out of it. If Isaac knew what was really going on he might refuse Vinn's sponsorship. She couldn't allow Isaac's one chance to hit the big time to be overshadowed by how Vinn had orchestrated things. 'It's true but it's only a trial reconciliation. Things might not work out so don't get your hopes up.'

'I'm happy for you, Ailsa. Really happy because you haven't been happy since you left him.'

'You don't have to worry about me, kiddo,' Ailsa said. 'I'm a big girl who can take care of herself.'

'What actually broke you guys up? You've always changed the subject when anyone mentions—'

'I'd rather not talk about it if you don't mind—'

'He didn't cheat on you, did he? I know he was a bit of a playboy before he met you but he wouldn't have married you if he didn't want to settle down.'

Ailsa let out a short sigh. 'No. He didn't cheat on me. We just…disagreed on stuff.'

'Like having kids?'

She was a little shocked at the direct way her brother was speaking. She had never overtly discussed her decision not to have children with him or with her mother and stepfather. It was something she didn't like discussing because it reminded her of why she'd made the decision in the first place. They knew her career was her top priority and she allowed them to think that was her main reason. Her only reason. 'Why would you say that?'

'I just wondered if you've been put off the idea of having kids because of Mum and Dad breaking up.'

Alisa knew the divorce had hit Isaac harder than it had her. She had moved out of home soon after but he had still been at school and had to move between two households for access visits. Their parents had done their best to keep things civil, but Ailsa knew there were times when things had been a little messy emotionally. 'Lots of people come from broken homes these days,' she said, skirting around the issue. 'It's the new normal.'

'So you do want kids?'

'For God's sake, Isaac.' Ailsa laughed but, to her chagrin, it sounded a little fake. 'I'm only twenty-nine. There's still plenty of time yet to decide if I want to go down that track.'

'Remember when you gave away all your childhood toys a few years back? All your dolls and stuff? I wondered why you would do that if you planned to have kids of your own some day.'

'I was doing a clean-up,' Ailsa said. 'All that stuff was taking up too much space at Mum's place after the divorce.'

'That wasn't the only thing,' Isaac said. 'You used to go all goochy-goochy-goo and embarrassing when you saw someone with a pram. Now you look the other way.'

No wonder her brother was an ace golfer. He had eyesight like an eagle's. 'Not every woman is cut out to be a mother. I have my career in any case and—'

'But you'd be a great mum, Ails.' He used his pet name for her, the name he had called her when he'd been too young to pronounce her name properly—except back then he'd had an adorable lisp. 'Sometimes I think you've been better at it than Mum. She's never been all that maternal, especially with you.'

'It's not going to happen,' Ailsa said. 'And certainly not with Vinn.'

'Oh… I didn't realise there were problems. But you can have IVF. It's not like Vinn couldn't afford it.'

'I do not need IVF.' And she could almost guarantee nor did Vinn. 'It's a choice I've made and I would appreciate it if everyone would damn well accept it.'

'Sorry. I didn't mean to upset you. I just wanted to call and say thanks for agreeing to the sponsorship. You have no idea what this means to me. I wouldn't be able to get anywhere near the pro circuit without Vinn's help. Three years all expenses paid. It's a dream offer.'

Ailsa wished she hadn't sounded so…so defensive. 'I'm sorry for biting your head off. I'm just feeling a little emotional right now. Vinn's grandfather is still in ICU and it's—'

'Yeah, he told me about that. It's kind of cool you're there with him, supporting him through such a tough time.'

I'm not here by choice. The words were on the tip of her tongue but she didn't say them out loud. Besides, she had made a choice. She had chosen to accept Vinn's deal and now she had to lie on the bed she had made.

Her only consolation was Vinn had joined her in it.

Vinn had left Ailsa to sleep in because he didn't trust himself not to reach for her again. And again and again and again. The need she awakened in him was ferocious. Ferocious and greedy and out of control, and the one thing he needed right now was to be in control. They could have a one-month fling. It would serve two purposes: get his grandfather through the danger period and draw a final line under Vinn's relationship with Ailsa.

He'd phoned the hospital first thing and the ICU specialist had informed him his grandfather was still stable. It was good news but he didn't feel he could relax until his grandfather was off the ventilator and conscious again and truly out of danger.

Vinn knew Ailsa had only slept with him to prove a point—to prove he couldn't resist her. Which was pretty much true. He couldn't. But in time he would be able to. He would make sure of it. He would have to because their relationship had a time limit on it and he was adamant about enforcing it. He would have liked three months with her because three months would have given his grandfather ample time to recuperate. But

he'd agreed to the compromise because three months was a long time for her to be away from her business. In the two years since she'd left him she had built up a successful interior decorating business that had enormous potential for expansion. It was a little unsettling to think she had only achieved that success once she'd left him. He hadn't intended to hold her back career-wise but she had seemed unhappy and unfulfilled in her previous job and he'd thought she would jump at the chance of being his wife, with all the benefits the position entailed.

Their affair had been so intense and passionate and he hadn't wanted to lose her...or at least not like that. He'd thought an offer of marriage would demonstrate his commitment even if he hadn't been in love with her. He had never been in love with anyone. He wasn't sure he had the falling in love gene. Maybe he was more like his father than he realised.

Although, unlike his father, he devoted himself to his work, to the business he had saved and rebuilt out of the ashes his father had left. He was proud of what he had achieved. It had taken guts and sacrifice and discipline to bring it back from the brink but he had done it. He'd owed it to his grandfather to restore the family business built over generations, to undo the damage his father had inflicted. He had built up the Gagliardi name to be something to be proud of again, instead of something of which to be ashamed.

But making love with Ailsa again reminded him of all the reasons why he'd wanted her in the first place. Would a month be enough to get her out of his system?

Or would it only feed the fire still smouldering deep inside him that he had relentlessly, ruthlessly tried to smother with work?

Ailsa came downstairs but was a little miffed to find Vinn had left the villa without speaking to her first. There was a note left on the kitchen bench informing her he had gone to visit his grandfather. Surely he could have walked upstairs to deliver the message in person? Why hadn't he? And why hadn't he taken her with him to the hospital? Wouldn't his grandfather be expecting her to be by Vinn's side? But then she recalled Vinn telling her his grandfather was being kept on a ventilator for a few days until he recovered from the surgery. It appeased her slightly, but still it was a chilling reminder of the charade they were playing. He would only want her 'on task' when his grandfather was awake and conscious.

And, of course, when Vinn had her in his bed. She was annoyed with herself for making love with him so soon. *Damn it.* Why hadn't she kept her distance? It was as if he had the upper hand again. He knew how much she wanted him. He wanted her too, which was some minor consolation, but she would be a fool to think he would always want her. Once their divorce was final he would move on. He would not spend weeks, months, almost two years remembering and missing and aching for every touch, every kiss, every passionate encounter. He wouldn't be curled up lonely in bed, wishing she were back in his arms. He would find someone else to have his babies for him and would not give her an-

other thought, while she would be left with her memories of him and her regrets over what she wanted but couldn't have.

Ailsa had finished making some calls to her assistant Brooke in her studio back in London when she heard the front door of the villa open. But the footsteps sounded nothing like Vinn's firm purposeful stride. She poked her head around the sitting room door to see the elderly housekeeper Carlotta shuffling in carrying some shopping.

'So you're back.' The old woman's tone could hardly be described as welcoming but Ailsa refused to be intimidated.

'Can I help you with those bags?'

Carlotta grudgingly allowed Ailsa to take the bags and carry them to the kitchen. Ailsa placed them on the bench and began unpacking them. 'Why are you here today? Vinn told me you had this week off.'

'How long are you staying?' The housekeeper's gaze was as sharp as her voice.

Ailsa shifted her lips from side to side, wondering if she should try a different tack with Vinn's housekeeper. In the past she had been quick to bite out of hurt, but she wondered now if that had been the wrong approach. 'I'm only staying a month. I presume Vinn told you his plan to keep me here until Dom is out of danger?'

Carlotta made a sound like a snort and glanced at the rings on Ailsa's hand. 'Long enough for you to get your hands on more expensive jewellery, no doubt. I'm surprised you didn't pawn those when you had the chance.'

Ailsa reined in her temper with an effort. 'I didn't

take them with me. I left them in Vinn's bedside drawer. I left everything he gave me behind—but surely you know that?'

Carlotta's expression flickered with puzzlement for a moment but then her features came back to her default position of haughty disapproval. 'Why are you back now if not for money? How much is he paying you?'

Ailsa could feel her cheeks giving her away. 'It's not about the money… It's about Dom's health and my brother's—'

'It was always about the money,' Carlotta said. 'You didn't love him. You've never loved Vinn. You just wanted to be married to a rich and powerful man to bolster your self-esteem.'

Ailsa bit the inside of her mouth to stop herself flinging back a retort. But, in a way, Carlotta had hit the nail on the head with startling accuracy. She had married Vinn for the wrong reasons. She had so wanted to be normal and acceptable, and what better way to prove it than to marry a man everyone looked up to and admired for his drive and focus and wealth? It had certainly helped that she'd found him irresistibly attractive. But she had grown to love him over the short time they were married, which was why she'd been so terrified when he'd brought up the topic of having a family.

How could *she* give him what he most wanted?

'If you cared about him you would have come back when his father died,' Carlotta said.

'I didn't know his father had died until he told me about it the day before yesterday.' Had it only been two days? It shamed Ailsa to think Vinn had managed to

lure her back into his bed in little more than forty-eight hours. Had she so little willpower? So little self-respect?

Carlotta gave her a disbelieving look and then made a business of unloading the shopping out of the bags. 'He wasn't close to his father but it brought back a lot of memories for him about when his mother died. And where was his wife when all this was going on? Living it up in London with not even the decency to call him or send a card and flowers.'

Ailsa decided to ignore the dig at her supposed lack of decency in order to pursue the subject of Vinn's mother's death and the impact it had on him. She'd tried to get him to talk about it but he'd always resisted. Should she try again? 'I didn't realise you were close to Vinn's mother. What was she like?'

Carlotta's expression lost some of its tightness. 'She was a wonderful person. Warm and friendly and loving and she loved Vinn so much. Motherhood suited her. Vinn was what she lived for. She should never have married Vinn's father but he was a charming suitor and she was shy and got swept off her feet before she realised what he was truly like.' She gave a heartfelt sigh and folded one of the shopping bags into a neat square. 'Vinn took her death hard, but then what four-year-old wouldn't? He used to be such a happy outgoing child but after his mother was taken from him he changed. Became more serious and hardly ever smiled. It was like he grew up overnight.'

'Her death must have hit you hard too,' Ailsa said.

Carlotta gave a sad twist of her mouth. 'I worked for her as a housekeeper but we became friends. When

Vinn moved in with his grandparents I came too. I've worked on and off for the Gagliardi family for most of my life. In some ways they *are* my family.'

'I can see now why you only wanted the best for Vinn,' Ailsa said, toying with an imaginary crumb on the kitchen bench. 'No wonder you didn't accept me.'

The elderly housekeeper looked at her for a long moment. 'I would have accepted you if I'd thought you loved him.'

'We didn't have that type of relationship,' Ailsa said. 'I know it's hard for you to understand but he didn't love me either so—'

'So you didn't have the courage to love him regardless.' The barb of disapproval was back in the old woman's tone.

Was loving Vinn a courageous or a crazy thing to do? Lusting after him was madness enough. Loving him would be emotional suicide because even if by some remote chance he grew to love her, what would he think of her once he found out she was the child of a ghastly criminal?

After spending the rest of the day reflecting on her conversation with Carlotta, Ailsa decided more could be served by drawing Vinn out about his childhood. She needed to try harder to understand him, to get to know the man he was behind the successful businessman. But she couldn't do that if she was constantly falling into bed with him. Making love with him within forty-eight hours of seeing him after a twenty-two month separation was a pathetic indictment on her part. How had

she succumbed so quickly? So readily? Why couldn't she have gone ahead with the charade without sleeping with him, as he'd first proposed?

Like that was ever going to work.

She had to get a grip on her self-control. Sex with Vinn was delightfully distracting but she needed to get to know him better. What motivated him to work so hard? What had made him marry a woman he didn't love when he could have had anyone? What was it about her that made him make such a commitment without love as the motivation?

She knew the more she slept with him the harder it would be to leave when the month was up. She had to keep reminding herself she was in the process of divorcing him. This was not a fairy tale where the handsome prince came riding back into town to claim his princess bride. This was a fake reconciliation in order to reduce the stress on an elderly man during a medical crisis.

Ailsa moved some of her clothes out of the walk-in wardrobe and into the bedroom she'd used the first night, further down the corridor from Vinn's. She was resetting her boundaries, making sure he got the message she wasn't the pushover he thought she was. Did he really think ten million pounds would buy her back into his bed? She'd scratched the itch and now the itch would have to go away. Or if it didn't she would damn well ignore it because it was time she made it absolutely clear to him that he didn't have the same hold over her as he had in the past. If they were going to sleep together then they would have to talk as well. Use not just their

bodies but also their minds. To connect in the way they should have done in the first place.

Ailsa came out of the en suite bathroom of the spare bedroom to find Vinn waiting for her.

'Why have you moved your things in here?' He waved a hand towards the pile of clothes on the bed she hadn't yet put away.

She tightened the towel she was wearing around her body. 'Because I think it's best if we keep things on a platonic basis for now.'

'Platonic?' The mockery in his tone was as jarring as the raking look he gave her towel-clad body. 'A bit late for that, don't you think?'

'I shouldn't have slept with you. You caught me in a weak moment. It won't be repeated. We need to talk to each other instead of having sex. Really talk.'

He came to stand in front of her. 'Such a stubborn little thing.' He stroked the upper curves of her breasts showing above the towel. 'You want me and yet you deny yourself because you think it will give me an edge.'

Ailsa wasn't too happy about being so transparent. 'The trouble with you, Vinn, is you're not used to someone saying no to you.'

He smiled a lazy smile and sent his finger on another slow journey, this time to her cleavage, dipping his finger into the space between her breasts. 'You say no with your words but your body says an emphatic yes.'

Ailsa trembled under his touch, the leisurely movement of his finger against the sensitive flesh of her breasts making her nipples tighten and ripples of plea-

sure flow through the rest of her body. Before she'd
met Vinn, her breasts were just breasts. Things that had
sprouted on her chest when she was thirteen. Things she
put in her bra and checked once a month for lumps. But
since his hands and mouth had explored and tasted and
tantalised them, she couldn't even look at her breasts
without thinking about his dark head bent over them
and his wickedly clever lips and tongue and teeth, and
the sensual havoc they could do to her.

She glanced at his tanned finger against the creamy
whiteness of her cleavage, her breath stalling in her
throat and rampant need spiralling through her body.
How could her body betray her like this? How could
it be so needy and hungry and greedy for his touch?
He slid his finger deeper into the valley of her cleavage. Well, *valley* was probably a bit of an exaggeration.
But, even though her breasts were on the small side,
that had never seemed to matter to Vinn. He made
her feel as if she could have been a lingerie model.
'Vinn… I…'

'Don't talk, *cara*.' He brought his mouth to the edge
of hers, playing with her lips with his in a teasing come-
and-play-with-me nudge. 'Just feel.'

Ailsa was pretty much incapable of speech. Saying
no or pretending she didn't want him seemed pointless when her body was on fire and red-hot need was
clawing at her insides with rapacious hunger. Had she
ever been able to say no to Vinn? 'I'm going to hate
myself for this tomorrow,' she said and bumped her
lips against his.

'It's just sex.' He gave her lips another nudge and

then followed it up with a bone-melting sweep of his tongue.

Ailsa glanced up into his eyes. 'Is it just sex?'

'What else could it be?' His mouth did another teasing movement against hers, making any thought of resisting him move even further out of her reach.

She braced herself against the surge of lust roaring through her body by placing one of her hands flat against his chest, the other somehow holding her towel in place. 'But why now? It seems so...so out of the blue. We've had zero contact other than through our lawyers for almost two years.'

His stubble grazed her cheek as he shifted position to go back to just below her ear. 'Because I've missed you.'

Ailsa shivered when his tongue found the shell of her ear. *He'd missed her?* Her old friend sarcasm came on duty before any romantic notions could take a foothold. She eased back a little to look at him eye to eye. 'But you knew where I was. There was nothing to stop you coming to see me in London. You didn't even call me or send a text. The only communication I got was through your lawyer a month later, once I'd instigated the divorce.'

His expression became rueful and his hands fell away from her body. He put some distance between them and then he rubbed one of his hands over the back of his neck as if trying to release a knot of tension. 'I had planned to come and see you but then I got caught up with—'

'Work has always been your first priority, hasn't it? And yet you won't allow it to be mine.'

His hand dropped back by his side and his mouth took on a grim line. 'My father died two days after you left.'

Ailsa was shocked into silence. She'd been under the impression Vinn's father had died a few months ago, not within two days of her leaving. She tried to think back to her conversation with Carlotta. Had the housekeeper said when Vinn's father had died? Was that why Carlotta was so convinced Ailsa didn't care about him? Had he been going to contact her and then got caught up in the tragedy of burying his father? When she hadn't heard from him after a week she'd instigated the divorce proceedings with her lawyer, figuring Vinn had had plenty of time to say what needed to be said. She'd taken his silence as his answer and yet now she realised there had been a good reason for that silence.

Remorse, regret, shame at her impetuosity rained down on her like stinging hail. Why hadn't she waited a few more days? Why hadn't *she* contacted him? Pride. Stubborn mulish pride had kept her in London with her phone mostly turned off because she'd wanted him to sweat it out. To miss her. To feel threatened he might lose her.

But *she* had lost him…

Vinn released a rough-edged breath. 'I probably should've contacted you to at least tell you he'd passed away but it was such a hideous time, with that poor family he'd nearly wiped out and his grieving girlfriend's family… I don't know…' He sighed again. 'I just had to get through each day. There wasn't time to think about my own stuff with the police and coroner's investiga-

tion and the distraught relatives threatening legal action, not to mention the constant press attention. And then, when I got your lawyer's letter informing me you were demanding a divorce, I figured it was too late to change your mind.'

It hadn't been too late. Ailsa swallowed the words behind a wall of regret. If only she had waited a few more days. A week or two…even a month. Why had she been so insistent on drawing that line in the sand so firmly it cut her off from him completely? But what was the point in admitting how immature and foolish she'd been? Their relationship was beyond salvage because they wanted different things out of life.

'I had no idea your father died so soon after I left… I'm so sorry. It must have been an awful time for you and Dom. I didn't see anything in the press back in London, otherwise I would have—'

'What? Sent flowers?' A note of sarcasm entered his voice. 'Just think—you could've sent two for the price of one. A wreath for my father and another one for the death of our marriage.'

For once, Ailsa refrained from flinging back an equally sarcastic response. She realised, shamefully for the first time, that he used sarcasm as she did. As a shield to keep people from discovering the truth about his emotional state. He might not have been close to his father, but a parent's death was still a huge event in one's life. Sometimes the death of a difficult parent was even trickier to deal with because of the ambiguity of feelings, and the nagging regret that those issues couldn't be resolved once death had placed its final stamp on things.

'I'm really sorry you had such a horrible time dealing with your dad's death and all the other stuff so soon after we…split up. But maybe if you'd contacted me straight away to tell me about your father's accident—'

'You would have come crawling back?' The dark light in his eyes warned her she was flirting with danger. 'You are assuming, of course, that I would've taken you back.'

Ailsa straightened her spine and forced herself to hold his gaze. 'I wouldn't have come back unless you apologised first for being such an arrogant chauvinist.'

'I see no need to apologise for wanting what most people want, and if you're honest with yourself you want it too. You're allowing your parents' divorce to dictate your life. That's crazy. And childish.'

'It's not about my parents' divorce,' Ailsa said. 'Why is it so hard for you to understand I don't want children? When a man says he doesn't want kids no one says anything. But when a woman does, everyone takes it upon themselves to talk her out of her decision as if she's being impossibly selfish.'

'Okay, so if it's not about your parents' divorce then what is it about?' His gaze was so direct she felt like a bug on a corkboard.

'I just told you.'

'You told me you didn't want children, but is it just about the interruption to your career?'

Ailsa shifted her gaze and made a business of securing the towel around her body. 'I'm not maternal. I never have been. My career is the most important thing to me.'

'Isaac once told me you were more of a mother to him than your mother was,' Vinn said. 'He said in many ways you still are.'

Ailsa wondered exactly how chummy her brother and Vinn were these days. But then she realised Isaac had always idolised Vinn from the moment she'd introduced them to each other. Vinn talked to her brother man to man, not man to child or even man to teenager. But how much of their childhood had Isaac shared with him?

'I'm ten years older than Isaac. I was just being a big sister. Mum did her best, but she found being a mother hard, with me especially, but with Isaac too.'

His frown brought his eyebrows together. 'Why you especially?'

Ailsa wished she'd kept her mouth shut but for some strange reason it was becoming more and more tempting to tell him about her background. When she'd first met him she hadn't wanted him to see her as anything other than a normal young woman. As the normal young woman she had been until the age of fifteen when she'd stumbled across the ugly truth. She didn't want to be a freak. She didn't want to be the outcome of a hideous crime. She wanted to be normal. 'I was a difficult, fractious baby who refused to take the breast and slept fitfully. She had trouble bonding with me. And she was young—only eighteen when she had me so it was hard for her.'

'But she still loved you and wanted you.'

She met his frowning gaze. Could she risk telling him the whole truth or would it be safer to give him a

cut-down version of it? She was tired of holding this dark secret inside.

Tired and lonely and utterly isolated.

No one but her mother and stepfather knew about the circumstances of her birth but they didn't like talking about it any more than she did. The lie was the elephant in the room quietly rotting in the corner. Wasn't it time to tell Vinn? He'd been her husband, her lover, and in some ways the first person who'd made her feel normal and acceptable. Then there would be one other person she could talk to about the shame that clung to her like grime. It wouldn't change the circumstances of her conception but it would mean she didn't have to keep it a secret from him any longer. It was too late to repair their marriage, mostly because they shouldn't have married in the first place, but surely she owed him the truth before the divorce was made final? 'She didn't want me, Vinn. That was the problem. She never wanted me.'

'Why do you say that? Surely she didn't say that to you?'

Ailsa gave him a tortured smile. 'Some things you don't have to say out loud, especially to kids. I was a mistake. I should never have been born.'

Vinn's expression was full of concern and he came up close to rest his hands on the top of her bare shoulders, his long tanned fingers warm and gentle on her flesh. 'But what about your dad, Michael? Does he make you feel the same as your mother?'

Ailsa knew she had come to a crossroads in her relationship with Vinn. If she took the truth turn, things would never be the same. If she took the white lie turn,

things would be the same but different. It was strange because she was dressed in nothing but a fluffy white bath towel and it felt as if the towel symbolised the white lie she was hiding behind. Once she stripped it away she would be naked.

Emotionally naked.

Vinn's hands gave her shoulders an encouraging squeeze. 'Talk to me, *cara*.' His voice was deep and gravelly, making her insides melt.

Ironic he should say that when she'd been the one to insist he talk to her. 'Vinn...' Ailsa sighed and placed her hands on his chest and suppressed a shiver as she felt his warm hard muscles flex beneath her palms, as if her touch shook him to the core as his did to her. 'The thing is... Michael isn't really my father. He's my stepfather.' She took a deep breath and went on. 'I have never met my real father and nor would I ever want to.'

'Why's that?' There was a note of unease in Vinn's tone and a gentling in the way his hands held her.

Ailsa swallowed tightly. 'My mother was raped at a party. She didn't tell anyone about the assault as she blamed herself for getting tipsy. By the time she realised she was pregnant it was too late to do anything about it. She eventually told my stepfather, who was her boyfriend at the time, and he insisted on marrying her and bringing me up as his own.'

Vinn's face was riven with shock but overlying that was concern—rich, dark concern that pulsed in his gaze as it held hers. 'Oh, *cara*... That's so... I don't know what to say. When did you find out? Was it recently? Did they tell you or—?'

'I found out when I was fifteen. They were never going to tell me. They'd made a pact about it.'

A heavy frown carved deep into his forehead. 'You've known since you were *fifteen*?'

Ailsa tried not to be daunted by the slightly accusatory tone of his voice. 'I overheard them arguing about it one day when I came home earlier than expected. My stepfather thought I should be told but Mum didn't. I confronted them about it and my mother reluctantly told me about the assault.'

'But Ailsa, why didn't you tell me?' His voice was hoarse and his hands fell away from her as if he couldn't bear to touch her. 'Why keep something like that from me? Your own husband, for God's sake.'

Ailsa tried to read his expression. Was it anger or disgust that made his eyes so dark and glittery? 'So this is suddenly all about you now, is it?' she said. 'I didn't tell you because I didn't want you to look at me like you're looking at me now. As something disgusting and freakish and ghastly.'

'I am not looking at you like—'

'Do you know what it's like to find out you're the child of rape?' Ailsa said, not giving him time to answer. 'It's disgusting and freakish and ghastly. Every time I look in the mirror I'm reminded of it. I look nothing like my mother, and of course I don't look like my stepfather. The face my mother sees when she sees me is the face of her rapist. A man who has never been charged and is probably out there with a wife and kids of his own by now. How could my mother ever love me? I'm the embodiment of her worst nightmare. She

thought she was doing the right thing in keeping me. Michael thought he was doing the right thing by marrying her and bringing me up as his own. But they wouldn't have got married if it hadn't been for me. Their relationship was doomed from the start and it was my fault. No surprise they got a divorce a few months after I found out. I've ruined so many lives.'

'*Cara...*' Vinn took a step towards her, his features still contorted with concern. 'You've done no such thing. You're the innocent victim here. Your mother too, and Michael. What happened was shocking. Even more shocking that justice hasn't been served.'

Ailsa turned away, frightened she might break down in front of him. Over the years she had taught herself not to cry. She vented her distress in other ways—tantrums, anger, sarcasm and put-downs.

She felt him come up behind her, his tall frame like a strong fortress. His hands went to her waist this time, resting there with such exquisite gentleness a ropey knot formed in her throat and she had to swallow furiously a couple of times to clear it.

Vinn rested his chin on the top of her head and cradled her against his body in a supportive embrace that stirred her body into feverish awareness. 'Thank you for telling me. It must have been difficult for you to keep that to yourself all this time.'

Ailsa slowly turned in his arms and somehow her arms were around his waist as if programmed to do so. The way their bodies fitted together felt so natural, so right, like two pieces of a complicated puzzle slotting together. She looked up into his gaze and was surprised

to see tenderness. 'You have to promise me something, Vinn. Please don't tell Isaac.'

His frown was back. 'He doesn't know?'

'No, and I don't want him to, nor do my mother or stepfather want him to find out.'

'Is that wise? I mean…keeping this a secret hasn't helped you or your mother or stepfather. In fact, it's made things so much worse.'

Ailsa dropped her arms from around his waist and stepped away. 'Don't make me regret telling you, Vinn. I absolutely insist Isaac doesn't find out. I couldn't bear it if he no longer saw me as his sister. I just couldn't bear it.'

There was a beat or two of silence.

'All right.' His tone was both resigned and reluctant. 'If that's what you insist. But will you tell your mother and Michael I now know?'

Ailsa hadn't thought that far ahead. She chewed at her lower lip, wondering if she'd done the right thing in telling Vinn after all. 'I don't see either of them much these days.' She chanced a glance at him and saw he was frowning again. 'They weren't too happy with me when I announced I was divorcing you. They thought I should've tried harder.'

'I'm the one who should have tried harder, *cara*.' His voice was weighted with regret and his expression rueful.

Ailsa was still thinking of something to say in response when his phone rang from where he'd left it on the bedside table. Vinn moved across to pick it up and, after a brief conversation, the lines of worry etched

into his face began to ease. 'Thank you for letting me know. *Ciao.*'

'Was that the hospital?'

Vinn nodded and let out a breath that sounded as if he'd been holding it for years. 'They've removed him from the ventilator. He's conscious and stable for the moment.'

Ailsa let out her own breath she hadn't realised she'd been holding. 'I'm so glad. Do you want to go and see him or is it too early?'

'I'll go in now but you stay here. It's just close relatives allowed at the moment.'

She tried not to feel shut out but how could she not? She wasn't close family any more. Strictly speaking, she was no longer Vinn's wife. She was nothing to him now. Sure, he might desire her but how long would that last? He'd set a time limit on their 'reconciliation'. She was little more than a mistress to him now. Someone to have sex with but not to build a future and a life together.

CHAPTER SEVEN

VINN DROVE LIKE a robot to the hospital to see his grand-father but it was Ailsa on his mind, not the frail old man. How could she have kept the secret of her background from him? Had he known her at all back then? Why had she felt she couldn't tell him something so important about her childhood? It explained so much about her reluctance to discuss having a family. He could only imagine what it must feel like, not knowing who her father was. He knew his all too well and, while deeply ashamed of the things his father had done and having been hurtfully and repeatedly let down by him, Vinn had still loved him.

While on one level he could understand Ailsa keep-ing her dark secret from him, another part was angry she hadn't trusted him with it earlier. There was a war going on inside him—a war between anger and compas-sion. One part of him recognised the trauma it must have been for Ailsa to find out her father was a criminal—a beast who'd taken advantage of her mother in the most despicable way. And yet another part of him felt angry Ailsa hadn't opened up to him. It was ironic but they

had shared so much sexually, been adventurous and open about what they liked and didn't like. How could she have shared her body so openly and yet not her heart?

Not that he had any right to sit in judgement. He knew there were things he hadn't shared either. Things that had shaped him, moulded him, changed him. Like losing his mother so unexpectedly and the grief and bone-deep sadness that followed—sadness that still clung to him, haunting him with a lingering feeling of isolation and loneliness. He had learned from an early age to be self-sufficient.

To rely on no one but himself.

Even though his grandparents had been as support-ive as they could, Vinn had still kept a part of himself contained, held back in case they too were snatched away from him.

Finding out about Ailsa's past now, when they were so close to divorcing, deepened his regret. Made it harder to grapple with because he had always blamed her for the breakup. He had given her everything money could buy, spoilt her as most women loved to be spoilt, but she had given nothing of herself but access to her body.

He felt shut out.

Locked out.

Lied to.

He'd made it his business to know every inch of her body. He had prided himself on their sex life—the frequency of it, the power and potency of it. The mon-umental satisfaction of it. But she had kept the most important information about herself from him.

It reminded him of how his father had kept the truth about his mother's death from him. But in the end it had only made things worse. He hadn't been adequately prepared for the blunt shock of the truth. He'd always wondered if his father had gently led him through that time with honesty instead of cowardly lies and cover-ups, he might have coped better with the loss of his mother.

Now he was left floundering again. Shocked. Stunned. Angry that Ailsa hadn't trusted him enough with the truth, as painful and heartbreaking as it was. If he had known earlier he might have been able to rescue their relationship, to tread more carefully over the issue of having a family. But he hadn't had all the information back then because she had wanted his body but not his trust.

Was it too late to come back from this? What did she want from him now?

A divorce. That was what she wanted. She was only with him now under sufferance in order to secure her brother's sponsorship.

He wanted her. That hadn't changed one iota. The desire he felt for her was as strong and powerful as ever—maybe even more so. She'd said she wanted to keep things platonic but he knew she still wanted him as much as he wanted her. He didn't want her to come back at him when the month was up and accuse him of coercing her into having sex with him. He wanted her to come to him because she owned and accepted her need of him. That she was fully engaged in their 'affair' because it was what *she* wanted.

His conscience gave him a prod about the use of the

word *affair*. An affair was temporary, but that was all he was prepared to offer now. Letting anyone, particularly Ailsa, have that much power over him was anathema to him. He was back to being an affair man again. Short-term and satisfying, that was how he'd liked his relationships in the past and he would learn to like them that way again. His relationships would run to his timetable and be conducted on his terms.

And his relationship with Ailsa would be no different.

Ailsa tried to settle with a book until Vinn came back from the hospital, but her mind was whirling and her body still restless, aching for the weight of his arms. She was annoyed with herself for not being able to switch off her desire for him. She felt guilty her restlessness came not from her worry over Dom's condition but for the aching need Vinn had awakened in her body. Every time he touched her it ramped up her desire another notch.

It was strange to admit it, but she knew if they hadn't got talking about his father's death so soon after her leaving him, and her confession about the secret she had been keeping all these years, they would have made love again by now. She had been so close to capitulating. She had resigned herself to another quick scratch of the itch. The itch he alone generated in her flesh.

But then he'd told her about his father's accident. They had actually talked. Not just talked but *communicated*. He had allowed her to see the difficult situation he'd been in back then. The situation she had placed him in with her childish storming off. For almost two

years she had seethed with anger at the way he had simply let her walk out of his life. Her anger had sustained her; it had motivated her to get her own business up and running. She had directed all those negative emotions into creating beauty and elegance in her clients' homes. Priding herself on how successful she had become in such a short time, not realising her most valuable clients had come her way via Vinn.

And now she had told him what she had told no one about her background. She had shared with him her pain and shame and he hadn't been revolted by her but rather by the situation. By the crime that was committed and the fact no justice was ever served.

You should have told him two years ago.

Ailsa closed her ears to the nudge of her conscience. She hadn't been ready two years ago. And anyway, they hadn't had that sort of relationship. They had communicated with their bodies but not their hearts and minds. She had allowed herself to be rushed into marriage because their lust for each other had been overwhelming. Vinn's passion for her had taken her by surprise, as had hers for him.

It had been like an explosion the first time they'd made love. Nothing in her experience could have prepared her for it. In the past, sex was something a partner did to her and, while she had sometimes enjoyed the physical closeness, until she'd made love with Vinn, full satisfying pleasure had mostly escaped her. But Vinn's expertise in bed had put an end to her orgasm drought. She'd become aware of her body's potential for pleasure and felt proud of the pleasure she brought to him. She

liked to think he hadn't felt such intense pleasure with anyone else, but she knew it was fanciful thinking on her part. As soon as they were officially divorced he would be off with another partner.

It still surprised her he hadn't already done so.

Was it more fanciful thinking to hope he cared for her? That he had in fact loved her and loved her still and wanted her back in his life? If so, why was he insisting it be a temporary affair? She'd convinced him to cut it down to one month instead of three. Surely if he wanted her back permanently he would have said so? He had enough bargaining power with Isaac's sponsorship. He knew she would do just about anything for her younger brother.

But what if this was a plan for revenge? What if Vinn wanted her back long enough to make her fall in love with him all over again? What if his plan was to hurt her pride, the way his pride was hurt when she'd walked out of their marriage? He might feel sorry for the circumstances of her background but she knew him well enough to know that wouldn't be enough to distract him from a goal. If he wanted revenge then what better tool than to have her fall for him, *properly* fall for him?

Not just in lust but in life-changing, long-lasting love.

Vinn sat by his grandfather's bedside in ICU for a couple of hours but, apart from a brief flicker of Nonno's eyelids and a weak grasp of his hand when he'd first arrived, the old man had been sleeping ever since. The transplant team were cautiously optimistic about his grandfather's condition but Vinn couldn't quite quell

a lingering sense of impending doom. The hospital sounds scraped at his nerves, bringing back memories he thought he had locked away. Even the squeak of a nurse's shoes along the corridor was enough to get his heart racing and his skin to break out in beads of sweat.

It wasn't that he didn't expect to lose his grandfather at some point. It was normal to outlive both your parents and grandparents, but still... Nonno was the only relative—the only person—Vinn trusted.

The only person he loved.

The only person he *allowed* himself to love.

What about Ailsa?

Vinn frowned at the thought of how he was fooling his grandfather about his relationship with Ailsa. Nonno had always liked her. He admired her spirit and feistiness and the way she stood up to Vinn. The only reason Vinn had orchestrated this charade was because of his grandfather's affection for Ailsa.

It had nothing to do with him—with *his* feelings for her, which right at this point in time were a little confusing, to say the least. For the last twenty-two months he'd been simmering and brooding with anger about the way she'd ended their relationship. He had concentrated on those negative feelings to the point of ignoring the presence of others. Other feelings he had ruthlessly suppressed because allowing himself to love someone exposed him to the potential for hurt.

For loss.

He was fine with the one-month plan. He had cut it down from three because he was not an unreasonable man. He was a business owner himself so he knew

the difficulties of running a business at arm's length. One month with Ailsa gave him enough time to get his grandfather out of danger and stable and well enough to cope with the truth about the state of their marriage.

Vinn didn't like thinking beyond the month ahead. But he did know one thing—he would be the one to call time because no way was he going to let Ailsa walk out on him again.

Ailsa was half asleep when she heard Vinn come back from the hospital just after midnight. Keen to find out how his grandfather was doing, she put aside her determination to keep her distance from Vinn and found him standing by the window in his study downstairs. He hadn't even bothered to turn on the lights and was silhouetted by the moonlight.

'Vinn?'

He turned from the window, his features cast in shadow giving him an intimidating air. 'Go back to bed.'

Ailsa stepped further into the room, the floorboards creaking eerily as she moved closer to his tall imposing figure. 'How is your grandfather? Were you able to speak to him?'

'Not really.' He pushed a hand back over his forehead, making his hair even more tousled as if it hadn't been the first time that night he'd done so. 'He was conscious for a bit but heavily dosed up with painkillers so went straight back to sleep.'

She moved closer so she could touch him on the arm. 'Are you okay?'

He gave her a vestige of a smile and a crooked one at that. 'It's tough...seeing him like that. So...so helpless, hovering between life and death.'

'Are the doctors happy with his progress so far?'

Vinn took her hand off his arm and, turning it over, began absently stroking the middle of her palm with his thumb. 'Yes, so far, but who can predict how these things will go? There are risks with any surgery and this is one hell of an operation, especially for a man that age.'

Ailsa began her own absent stroking of his hand, well, maybe it wasn't so absent for she couldn't resist the feel of his skin under her touch—the warmth of it, the way his fingers were so long and tanned compared to hers. 'Carlotta told me a little bit about your mother. How lovely she was and how much she loved you.'

He frowned. 'When did you see her? I thought she was having the week off.'

'She came earlier today when you were out,' Ailsa said. 'She brought in some shopping but she didn't stay long. I got the feeling she wanted to see if I was really back or not.'

'Did you argue with her?'

She tried not to be annoyed by the way he so readily took his housekeeper's side. 'No, not really.'

One of his eyebrows lifted. 'What's that supposed to mean?'

Ailsa blew out a small breath and pulled her hand out of his hold. 'Look, I understand your connection with her and I also understand hers to you. She genuinely cares about you and wants you to be happy. I guess she

realises, and did right from the start, that you would not be happy with me in the long-term.'

'Why would she think that?'

'Because… I don't love you.' Ailsa's mouth said the words but her heart wasn't in agreement. Why had it taken her so long to realise the depth of her feelings for him?

Something flickered across his features. 'Did you tell her that?'

'I didn't have to,' Ailsa said. 'She figured it out for herself. She thinks I married you to bolster my self-esteem.'

He took her left hand and ran the pad of his thumb over the setting of diamonds of her engagement ring. 'And is that why you married me, *cara*?' His voice was low and deep and with just the right amount of huski-ness to make her spine loosen.

Ailsa looked into his dark-as-pitch gaze and won-dered that he couldn't see it for himself. That along with her need to boost her self-esteem there had been another reason she had married him. A reason she had denied and disguised because if she admitted, even to herself, that she loved him it would make her decision to remain childless all the more heartbreaking. 'This is why I married you.' She stepped up on tiptoe and pressed her lips to his.

His hands settled on her hips, drawing her closer as he took control of the kiss. His tongue came in search of hers, making her whimper as his body stirred and thickened against hers. His stubble grazed her face as he changed position but she didn't care. She was hun-

gry for his touch. She was aching in every cell of her body for his possession. No one kissed her the way he did. No one made her senses sing the way he did. No one could trigger this torrent of lust the way he did. Her hands went to the buttons of his shirt, tearing at them with careless disregard for their welfare. She wanted him with a fierce need that clawed at her insides. And if the surging potency of him pressing against her was any indication, he wanted her just as badly. Just as ferociously.

Ailsa was only wearing a silky wrap and a slip of a nightgown and soon it was on the floor in a silken puddle at her feet. His ruined shirt joined it and then his trousers and underwear and socks and shoes. Then she was on the floor on her back without any real memory of how she got there as she was so intent on devouring his mouth and clutching at his hard male flesh.

'We should slow down or things will get out of—'

'Don't you dare slow down.' Ailsa dug her hands into the taut muscles of his buttocks and held him to her pulsing need. 'I want you. *Now*.'

He smiled against her mouth and drove into her with a gasp-inducing thrust that made every intimate muscle in her body weep with relief. He set a fast pace but she was with him all the way, panting and clawing and whimpering as the sensations built like a tornado approaching. She could feel the carpet burning the back of her shoulders but she was beyond caring. The need for release was so overwhelming she thought she might die if it didn't come soon.

And then she was there when he added that extra

friction with his fingers against her swollen clitoris. She came with a cry that sounded so primal and wild she could hardly believe it came from her throat. Her body bucked and thrashed beneath his with the force of her orgasm, waves and waves rolling through her. His release came on the tail-end of hers, the sheer power of it reverberating through her flesh, his deep agonised groan as primal-sounding as hers.

Ailsa lay panting on the floor under the press of his now relaxed body, her hands moving up and down his back and shoulders in the quiet of the afterglow. The moonlight shone in from the window, casting their entwined bodies in a ghostly light. It could well have been two years ago after one of their passionate lovemaking sessions…but this time somehow it felt different. She couldn't explain it… Perhaps it was because he knew about her background and the sheer relief of not having to hide that from him any more made her feel freer, less weighted. Less abnormal.

Vinn propped himself up on his arms and looked into her eyes. 'I didn't rush you too much?'

Ailsa gave him a lopsided smile and brushed some tousled strands of his hair back off his face. 'I'm fine apart from some mild carpet burn and stubble rash.'

Concern shadowed his gaze and he moved his weight off her and gently turned her so her back was facing him. He brought his mouth down to both of her shoulder blades in turn, pressing soft soothing kisses to the skin. She couldn't remember a time when he had been so tender, as if she were something precious and fragile and he couldn't bear to hurt her even if inadvertently.

He turned her back over so she was face up and then he softly ran a fingertip over the circle of skin on her chin. 'I keep forgetting how sensitive you are.'

'My skin might be but I'm certainly not.' It was a lie and she was sure he knew it.

His finger circled her still tingling mouth, his gaze thoughtful as it held hers. 'I'm not so sure you're as tough as you make everyone think.'

Ailsa worried he might see more than she wanted him to see, like how she was falling back in love with him. But maybe a part of her had always been in love with him. Now that part was growing, expanding, swelling inside her until there was no room for the hate she had claimed to feel for him.

She averted her gaze from his and focused her attention instead on the dip at the base of his neck between his clavicles, tracing her finger down from there to his sternum. 'Are we going to lie here on the floor all night or go up to bed?'

Vinn tipped up her chin so her gaze had to meet his. 'Which bed are you thinking of occupying? Mine or the spare bedroom?'

Ailsa gave him a rueful twist of her mouth. 'Do I have a choice?'

'That depends.' He brushed her lips with his, once, twice, three times.

She ran her tongue over her tingling lips and tasted his salt. 'On what?'

He wound a strand of her hair around one of his fingertips, his eyes still holding hers with quiet intensity. 'On whether we're talking about my willpower or yours?'

Ailsa sent her fingertip down his abdomen to the hardened length of him, circling him with her fingers, moving the pad of her thumb over the moist tip where his body was signalling its readiness to mate. 'How's yours doing so far?'

His dark eyes glinted. 'It's toast,' he said and his mouth came down on hers.

CHAPTER EIGHT

THE FOLLOWING EVENING on their way back from visiting his grandfather at the hospital, Vinn suggested a night out. 'Just like old times.'

Ailsa wasn't so sure she wanted to go back to the 'old times'. It had been fun going out for dinner at amazing restaurants were they were waited on like royalty and to nightclubs or exclusive bars, but when had they talked to each other on those occasions? She wanted to know more about his mother's death and how it had impacted on him. And even though it intensified her guilt over leaving him the way she had, she wanted to know more about his father's accident and how he'd juggled everything in the aftermath.

She waited until they were seated in one of the restaurants where they'd dined in the past, with drinks in front of them and their meals ordered, before she brought up the subject. 'Vinn… I've been wondering how you managed everything when your father died. Your work, your grandfather's grief. The other accident victims.'

His expression flickered like he was masking deep physical pain. He seemed to waver for a moment, as if

he was torn between wanting to change the subject and offloading some of the burden he'd gone through. 'It was difficult…' He paused for a beat. 'Different from when my mother died. I felt guilty about that, actually. That I wasn't grieving for my father the way I had for my mother. I don't miss him even now and yet not a day goes past without me thinking of her.'

Ailsa reached across the table and laid her hand on the top of his, her voice choking up as if it were her own mother she had lost. 'Oh, Vinn. You must have loved her so much and you were so terribly young.'

He turned over her hand and covered it with his. 'Even though I was young, I remember everything about her. Her smile, her hugs, the way she lit up a room when she walked into it.' His fingers began playing with hers. 'When my father injured those other innocent people I couldn't get them out of my mind. The kids, I mean, not just the parents, although that was bad enough. I couldn't bear the thought of those little kids growing up without their mother.'

Ailsa realised yet again how stupid and immature she had been to leave the way she had. Why hadn't she been there for him? Helping him, supporting him through such a harrowing time? 'I can't imagine how dreadful it must have been for you and for them. But they survived, yes?'

'Yes.' His hand briefly squeezed hers. 'I sent them presents at Christmas. I wasn't sure if they'd accept them, given it was my father who nearly destroyed their family, but they seem to like me contacting them. I

think it helps them put it behind them. Or at least I hope so.'

'I'm sure it helps enormously,' Ailsa said. 'It shows what a generous and caring person you are.'

He gave a stiff on-off smile and withdrew his hand. 'But it still doesn't change the fact my father almost killed them. But he did kill his girlfriend and no amount of Christmas presents or financial compensation will ever make up for that.'

Ailsa's heart squeezed at the way he carried such a burden of guilt and shame about his father even now. 'You weren't driving that car, Vinn. That was your father. You've done everything you can to help those poor people. So many people in your situation wouldn't have done half of what you've done for them.'

Their meals arrived and the conversation switched to less emotionally charged topics. But after their main meal and dessert was cleared, Vinn reached for her hand and began a gentle stroking of her fingers. 'Have you ever tried to talk to your mother about what happened to her? How it affected her and, consequently, her parenting of you?'

Ailsa began to chew at her lower lip. 'She doesn't like talking about it. Michael wanted her to get counselling but she always refused.' She looked at Vinn's tanned fingers entwined with hers. 'I never understood it as a little kid, but whenever I needed a hug from my mother she would pull away from me. It was as if she couldn't bear to touch me. It hurt so much so I taught myself not to need hugs.'

His fingers gave hers a brief squeeze. 'Can you see

it wasn't about you? That it was the trauma she associated with you that was the issue? That you're not personally to blame?'

Ailsa met his gaze. 'I do on an intellectual level but on an emotional level I still feel like that little kid needing a hug from her mum and being pushed away.'

Vinn cradled her hand so tenderly she felt like he was reaching back in time to her as that needy little child, offering her comfort and security. 'Do you think if you talked to your mother about your own issues with having a family it might help you and even her?'

Ailsa gave a non-committal shrug without speaking. What was the point of talking to her mother? It wouldn't change the fact she was the offspring of a criminal. No one could change that. She had to learn to live with it.

Vinn's fingers gently tapped her on the back of the hand as if to bring her out of her private reverie. 'Time to go home, or do you want coffee?'

Ailsa didn't want the evening to end. She had never felt so close to someone as she did right then. Not just a physical closeness, but an emotional closeness where walls had been lowered and screens and masks laid aside. Would this newfound intimacy between them last? What would happen when their month was up? What then? She gave him a tentative smile. 'No coffee for me.'

What I want is you.

Later, when they got home, Vinn reached for her without saying a word. His mouth came down on hers and his arms gathered her close. Their lovemaking was slow but intense, as if he was discovering her body's se-

crets all over again. There was an element of poignancy to his caresses and touches. They made her feel as if she was so much more than a woman he had wanted to marry because she ticked all the boxes. He made her feel as if she was the only woman he wanted to make love to. He might not love her the way she had grown to love him, but it was enough for her now to be held close enough for their hearts to beat against each other. Close enough for her to feel as if the last two painful years hadn't happened.

Close enough for her to feel as if she had finally come home.

Two weeks later, when Ailsa woke, she was starting to wonder how she would ever return to London and her former life of work, work and more work. Her days had formed a pattern of her sleeping in while Vinn rose early to see to his business commitments, then he would come back for her mid-morning so they could visit his grandfather together.

Dom was now fully awake and out of ICU and in a private room and, while he was still frail, at least he no longer had a jaundiced look about him. She was glad for him and for Vinn, for she could see the bond between them was strong and she couldn't help envying it. She had never felt close to her mother or stepfather and since both sets of grandparents had always lived abroad and two were now deceased, they hadn't been as involved with her and Isaac as much as other grandparents might have been. She was close to Isaac in that she loved him and would do anything for him

but he didn't know her as well as he might think. And she didn't want him to. She couldn't bear him finding out she was only his half-sister.

Another thing that had happened over the last few days was an unspoken truce between her and Carlotta. The elderly housekeeper came in the morning soon after Vinn left for his office and only stayed long enough to tidy whatever needed tidying. She didn't cook the evening meal as she used to before as Ailsa had insisted she and Vinn would eat out most evenings and any evening they didn't she would cook. If Carlotta was annoyed to find her services were not required in the same capacity as before, she certainly didn't show it. If anything, Ailsa thought Carlotta was privately pleased she had stepped up to the wifely role she had been resisting two years ago with such vehemence.

She lay back against the pillows on Vinn's bed and sighed. It was increasingly hard to find the strong-willed career girl who had fallen in lust with Vinn. In her place was a mellow version, a woman who was content to listen instead of spout an opinion, a woman who was dangerously close to wanting much more than she could ever have. She tried to console herself that once this month was up she would have ten million reasons to be content and happy with her lot in life. She was so much better off than most people. She had no right to be hankering after the fairy tale when she was not the daughter of royalty but the daughter of darkness.

Ailsa threw the covers off the bed and got to her feet but the room started to spin and she had to sit down again before she fell down. Her stomach had a queasy

feeling, a low-grade nausea that was annoying rather than debilitating. She waited for a moment or two before rising tentatively to her feet. *So far so good.* The room had stopped spinning but her stomach was still unsettled. She showered and dressed, deciding she'd better pull herself together before Vinn got back from the office, not wanting to add to his worries about his grandfather.

Carlotta was in the kitchen when Ailsa came downstairs and narrowed her bird-like gaze when Ailsa came in. 'Are you unwell? You look pale.'

Ailsa put a hand on her stomach. 'It must be something I ate last night when we went out for dinner. Too much rich food.'

Carlotta's expression was difficult to read, which was unusual because usually she had no qualms about showing what she felt, be it disapproval, censure or a grudging acceptance. 'Sit down, Signora Gagliardi,' she said, pulling out a chair. 'I will make you a cup of tea and some dry toast.'

Ailsa sat down but her mind kept tiptoeing around the reason why Carlotta would offer to make her tea and dry toast. There was no way she could be pregnant. She still had a contraceptive implant in her arm. Yes, it was a little overdue for a change but she hadn't had a normal period since she'd had it implanted so it must still be working. A flutter of panic beat inside her belly and she put a hand over her abdomen in an effort to quell it. It had to be still working.

It *had* to.

Carlotta turned from switching on the kettle and Ailsa wasn't quite quick enough to remove her hand

in time to escape the quick flick of the housekeeper's gaze. 'Will you tell him?'

Ailsa swallowed. 'Tell him what?'

'That you're having his *bambino*.'

She choked out a laugh. 'I'm not having his—'

'So it's not his child?'

Ailsa was struck dumb by the housekeeper's insinuation. She suddenly felt close to tears. This couldn't be happening. Not now. Not ever. She couldn't have Vinn's baby. She couldn't allow herself to dream of holding his child in her arms, of being with him permanently. He didn't want her for ever anyway. This was just for now, until his grandfather was well enough to handle the truth.

This was not part of the plan.

Carlotta came over with a steaming cup of tea and set in on the table in front of Ailsa. 'Drink it. The toast will be ready in a minute. Nibble on it slowly until your stomach settles.'

Ailsa wasn't sure if it was the nurturing the housekeeper was dishing out or the stress she was feeling about the possibility of being pregnant that made her emotions suddenly spill over. One sob rose in her throat and another closely followed it, then another and another until she sat with her head in her hands and with her shoulders shaking. 'This can't be happening... I can't do this... I can't have a baby. I just can't.'

Carlotta stroked the top of Ailsa's head with a touch so gentle it made her cry all the more. 'You are lucky to be with child. I would have given anything to have a *bambino* of my own but it wasn't to be. My husband left me because of it.'

Ailsa dragged her face out of her hands to look at the housekeeper's wistful expression. 'I'm sorry you weren't able to have children. I really am. But I've never wanted to have them. My career is too important to me.'

Carlotta brushed the hair back off Ailsa's face like she was a child, her gaze soft and full of wisdom. 'Have you really always not wanted to have children?'

Ailsa gave a shaky sigh and dropped her head back into her hands. 'Not always…but it's complicated and I don't want to talk about it.'

'He'll make a good father,' Carlotta said, still stroking the back of Ailsa's head. 'He won't be reckless and irresponsible like his father. He'll support you and the child—'

'But will he love me?' Ailsa looked up at her again.

Carlotta's expression became sombre. 'He might not say it the way other men would but he cares about you. Why else would he have asked you to come back to him?'

Ailsa got to her feet, holding onto the edge of the table in case she felt another wave of faintness. 'Please, I beg you. Don't tell him about this. I need to make sure first.'

'You're not going to get rid of—?'

'No,' Ailsa said, realising with a jolt it was true. 'No, I can't do that. It might be right for some people and I would never judge them for it, but it's not right for me.'

'But he has the right to know as soon as—'

'I'll cross that bridge if and when I come to it,' Ailsa said. 'This could be a false alarm. I don't want to get his hopes up. It would cause more hurt in the long run.'

Carlotta didn't look too convinced but she agreed to keep silent on the subject. 'Is there anything I can do for you, Signora Gagliardi?'

Ailsa attempted a smile but couldn't quite pull it off. 'Yes, call me Ailsa.'

Carlotta smiled back. 'Ailsa.'

Ailsa went back upstairs but, instead of going back to the master bedroom, she went to the one room she hadn't visited since she'd been back. The door was closed and she hadn't once been tempted to open it but now she held her breath and turned the doorknob and stepped inside. It was exactly the same as the last time she'd walked out of it with her ears stubbornly plugged against Vinn's suggestion they talk about having a family. It was the only room in the villa that was unfinished…incomplete, like an interrupted conversation. She looked at the room with new eyes, not seeing its potential as a reading room but as Vinn had seen it—as a nursery. A nursery for the child she might be carrying.

His child.

She looked at the empty space and in her mind's eye saw a white cradle with a pastel-coloured animal mobile dangling overhead. She saw soft toys—teddy bears and kittens and puppies and cute long-eared rabbits sitting on the shelf above the fireplace, next to a row of picture books and childhood classics. She saw neatly folded baby clothes—most of them handmade—in the chest of drawers.

And in the window…a rocking chair perfect for feeding or settling a baby…

Ailsa drew in a breath that pulled on something deep in her chest and turned and left the room, quietly closing the door behind her.

Vinn was late getting back to the villa to collect Ailsa to visit his grandfather. Work had been piling up while he'd been spending so much time with her and there were a few pressing meetings and some urgent paperwork he'd needed to see to. He was used to spending most of his time at work. Even during their marriage he had prioritised work over his time at home. He was always conscious of how close to losing everything he had been when his father had been convicted of fraud. It was a driving force inside him he had little or no control over. Working hard was in his blood as it was in his grandfather's and his great-grandfather's before him.

When he finally got back to the villa it was closer to lunch than he'd realised. He found Ailsa sitting outside in the garden with a magazine lying across her lap but she was staring into space rather than reading it. She gave a little start of surprise when she heard his footsteps on the flagstones and sprang out of the garden seat but then seemed to stumble and almost fell.

He rushed to stabilise her with a hand on her arm. '*Cara*, what's wrong?'

She squinted against the strong sunlight and leaned on him for support. 'It's hotter out here than I realised…'

It didn't feel hot to Vinn but then he was used to Milan in spring, which on balance was generally much warmer than what she'd be used to in London. 'Sit down for a bit here in the shade.' He guided her back to the

garden seat and crouched down in front of her with his hands resting on her knees. 'Feeling better now?'

She gave him a funny little smile and her gaze kept skipping away from his. 'Yep, much better now.'

She certainly didn't look it. She had a waxen look to her features and there were tiny beads of perspiration around her temples. Vinn placed a hand on her forehead to check if she had a temperature but, while she was clammy to touch, she wasn't burning with a fever that he could tell. 'Maybe you shouldn't come with me to visit Nonno today. You must have a virus or something.'

'Okay…'

He stood and held out his hand to help her to her feet. 'Come on, *tesoro*. Let's get you inside and resting. I'll call the doctor to come round and—'

'No!' There was a shrill note of panic in her tone. 'I… I don't need to see a doctor. It's just a bug or…or something…' She bit down on her lip and for a moment he thought she was going to cry.

He put his hands on the tops of her shoulders. 'Are you sure you're okay, *cara*?'

'I just need to lie down for a while…'

Vinn helped her upstairs and got her settled in bed with a long cool drink beside her. 'I won't be long. I'll just check in on Nonno and come back to see how you're feeling.'

'Okay…'

Ailsa waited until she heard the sound of Vinn's car leaving the driveway before she threw off the light bed-covers he had drawn over her moments ago. Sick or not,

she had to get her hands on a pregnancy test. Two or more tests. Possibly more. She felt a little guilty ducking out of the villa while he thought she was safely tucked up in bed but what else could she do?

She had to know, one way or the other.

The streets were crowded enough for her to blend in without being recognised…or so she hoped. She'd tied her hair back and pulled on a baseball cap and dressed in tracksuit pants and a T-shirt, making her look as if she was just out for a walk or a trip to the gym. She went into the first pharmacy she came to and bought two test kits, figuring if she bought too many from the one place it might draw too much attention to herself. She was about to walk into another pharmacy when she bumped into a man who was coming out. She mumbled an apology and went to sidestep him but he called her by name.

'Ailsa? I thought it was you hiding under that disguise.'

Ailsa looked up to see one of Vinn's acquaintances, Nico Di Sante, the owner of the hotel she had checked into on her first night in Milan two weeks ago. What quirk of fate had led her to that hotel and now to the very same pharmacy he was using? 'Oh…hi…'

His gaze narrowed. 'Are you okay?'

Ailsa tried to relax her tight features. 'Sure. I'm just trying to get some errands done without being recognised. You know what the paps are like.'

'Sure do.'

She shifted her weight from foot to foot, not wanting to extend their conversation past the greeting stage, but neither did she want to appear rude or draw unnec-

essary attention to herself. 'Well…it was nice seeing you again.'

'You too, Ailsa,' Nico said. 'Hey, I'm really glad you guys are back together. Vinn's really missed you.' He gave a short laugh. 'Not that he would ever admit it to anyone. He's too proud for that. Stubborn too.'

Ailsa managed a small smile. 'I missed him too.'

'Tell him to bring you in for cocktails in my new bar.' Nico smiled. 'On the house, of course.'

Ailsa stretched her mouth into an answering smile. 'Will do.'

But she had a horrible feeling it might be several months before she would be drinking alcohol again. Was this how her mother had felt, finding out she was pregnant? Feeling dread and shock and anguish instead of joy and excitement? She couldn't help feeling a wave of sadness for her mother. For how isolated and desperate she must have felt, unable to tell anyone what had happened to her and then the double blow of finding out she was pregnant. Her mother had said it had been too late to have a termination but why hadn't she put her up for adoption instead?

Maybe Vinn was right—she should try and talk to her mother. Even if she shut down the conversation, at least Ailsa would have tried instead of letting things go on the way they were for God knew how many more years.

She took out her phone on the walk back to Vinn's villa. She had never felt the need to talk to her mother as she did then and a wave of relief flooded her when she finally picked up on the seventh ring. 'Mum?'

'Ailsa…' Her mother sounded a little distracted and

Ailsa wondered if she had someone with her. A new man in her life perhaps?

'Is this a bad time to call?'

'No, of course not.'

'Mum…can I ask you something?'

'What's wrong? You sound upset. Is everything working out between you and—?'

Ailsa took a steadying breath. 'Why didn't you have me adopted? Did you ever think of—?'

'I did think of it…in the early days, but as the pregnancy went on I felt I couldn't do it.'

'So you…you *wanted* me?'

'I would be lying if I said I was completely happy about being pregnant,' her mother said. 'I wasn't the earth mother type. I wanted children but I probably wouldn't have been miserable without them either. But about six months into the pregnancy I knew I would never be able to let you go to someone else. But why are you asking me this now?'

'Mum, I think I'm pregnant,' Ailsa said. 'I don't know what to do.'

'Have you done a test?'

'Not yet. I just bought one. I just wanted to talk to someone…you, actually.'

'Oh, Ailsa…' Her mother gave a sigh. 'I'm probably not the best person to talk to. I felt so ambivalent about being pregnant with you and I know it's probably affected our relationship but—'

'I know and that's completely understandable,' Ailsa said. 'It must have been awful, so terrifying to know you had to carry a child you didn't want to term.'

'It wasn't just because of the...because of what happened,' her mother said. 'I was the same when I fell pregnant with Isaac. I'm not the nurturing type. I feel ashamed of it but I can't change it. It's hardwired into my personality. But it doesn't mean I don't love you and Isaac. I don't regret going ahead with the pregnancy. It was hard and I was in denial for a long time about how it affected me, but I'm glad I had you. I guess I'm not that good at showing it. But maybe you can help me work on that... I mean, if you'd like to?'

'I would love to,' Ailsa said, suddenly overcome with emotion. 'I'll do the test and let you know the results, okay?'

She ended the call with a bubble of hope expanding in her chest. Hope for a better relationship with her mother, hope for a future with Vinn.

Hope for a child.

Vinn's trip to the hospital to visit his grandfather was cut short because Nonno's specialists were doing a ward round. His grandfather had developed a slight temperature overnight and since Ailsa had some sort of virus, in spite of the thoroughness of the hygiene procedure on entering the ward, he thought it would be best to come back the following day when his grandfather was feeling better. His grandfather seemed more concerned about Ailsa than his own health when Vinn told him.

'Send her my love and tell her I hope she feels better soon,' Nonno said.

'Will do. Take care of yourself. I'll be in tomorrow and Ailsa will too if she's feeling well enough.'

Vinn decided to swing by a local florist on his way home and pick up some flowers for Ailsa. She'd looked so peaky and unwell and he thought a bunch of spring flowers would lift her spirits.

Two weeks had passed and he was becoming more and more conscious of the clock ticking on their relationship. It was way too early to know if his grandfather was out of danger—there were always things that could go wrong and he was still being closely monitored. Vinn wished now he'd insisted on the three months as he'd first proposed. That would have given him ample time to get his grandfather out of hospital and set up in the independent living apartment he'd bought for him so there would be twenty-four-hour medical care on hand.

Could he ask Ailsa to reconsider? They could come to some arrangement if she needed to go back to London for work. He could even go with her as he'd long thought about setting up a UK branch of his furniture business.

His mind started to run with the possibility of postponing the divorce, even taking it off the table altogether. They were a functional couple now. They communicated better than they ever had before and their sex life was as good, if not better, than when they were first married. And now that Ailsa had told him about her background, he realised how wrong it would have been to bring children into their marriage back then. But could he settle for a life without children? Could he take the risk that she might never change her mind?

His grandfather was in the winter of his life and his greatest wish was for a great-grandchild to hold before he died. But it was Vinn's wish too. He wanted to hold

his own child in his arms, to share the bond of a child with Ailsa because he couldn't imagine wanting a child with anyone else.

But she doesn't love you.

Vinn shoved the thought aside. What did romantic love have to do with it? That sort of love was fleeting anyway. It often didn't last beyond the honeymoon phase of a relationship. Caring for someone, providing for them, sharing your life with them and creating and raising a family with them required commitment and steadfastness and maturity.

Two years ago, he hadn't understood Ailsa's reluctance to commit to having a family. But he did now and he couldn't see any reason why they couldn't work through it and, even if they didn't end up having kids, at least they would have made that decision together. Their relationship had undergone a change, a remodelling that made him look forward to coming home to her. He might not love her in the Hollywood movie sense but he damn well cared about her and wanted her in his life.

Not just for a month. Not just for three months.

For ever.

CHAPTER NINE

AILSA WAS IN one of the guest bathrooms upstairs when she heard Vinn's footsteps on the stairs. Her heart began to race. She hadn't had time to do the test; she had barely had time to read the instructions. What was he doing home so soon? Normally he stayed a couple of hours at the hospital with his grandfather. She quickly bundled the test back into the paper bag and shoved it into the cupboard under the marble basin.

'Ailsa?' Vinn's knuckles rapped on the bathroom door. 'Are you okay?'

She took a calming breath. 'Yes…j-just finishing up in here.' She flushed the toilet and then turned on the taps in the guise of washing her hands. Her hand crept to her abdomen… She had always been so adamant about not wanting children but she had never been pregnant before, or even suspected she was pregnant.

What if Vinn's DNA was this very minute getting it on with hers? What if a tiny being was being fashioned inside her womb, a tiny embryo that would one day lift up its little chubby arms and call her Mummy?

Ailsa bit her lip so hard she thought she'd break the

skin. It wasn't supposed to happen like this. She'd been fine with her decision not to have kids when she wasn't pregnant. Falling pregnant changed everything.

It changed *her*.

'Ailsa. Open the door.'

Her heart leapt to her throat and pushed out the sob she'd been holding there. 'Go away. I'll be out in a minute.'

'No. I will not go away.' Vinn's voice had a steely edge to it that made her heart thump all the harder.

Ailsa blew out a breath, put on her game face and opened the door. 'What does a girl have to do around here to get a little privacy?'

His concerned gaze ran over her. 'Why have you locked yourself in here? Have you been sick?'

Ailsa found it hard to hold his gaze. How could she tell him before she knew for sure? Or should she tell him? It was a set of scales tipping back and forth inside her head—*Tell him. Don't tell him. Tell him. Don't tell him.* She let go of a breath she hadn't realised she'd been holding. 'I... I went to the pharmacy.'

'I have painkillers here if only you'd asked me to—'

'Not for painkillers.' She took another breath and let it out in a rush. 'For a pregnancy test.'

Shock rippled over his features, but then his eyes lit up and a broad smile broke over his face. 'You're pregnant? Really? But, *tesoro*, that's wonderful. I was on my way home to ask you to call off the divorce so we can start again.'

He wanted to start again? Oh, the irony of his timing. Had he made that decision before or just now when he

thought there was a chance she could be pregnant? How could she trust his offer was centred on his feelings for her, not his family-making plans? How could she accept knowing the one thing he wanted was a child, not the mother who came with it—her?

'I haven't done the test yet,' Ailsa said. 'I was about to when you started hammering on the door.'

He took her by the upper arms in a gentle hold, his face still wreathed in a smile. 'Sorry about that, *cara*. I was worried about you. Let's do the test now, shall we? It'll be fun doing it together—finding out at the same moment.'

Ailsa chewed at her lip. 'Don't get too excited, Vinn.'

His fingers tightened on her arms. 'You're not thinking about terminating?'

She pulled out of his hold and rubbed at her arms as if his touch had hurt her. 'Don't be ridiculous. Of course I'm not going to terminate.'

He reached for her again and his hands began a slow stroke of her arms. 'Let's do the test so we know one way or the other.'

Ailsa sighed and, pulling away, walked back to the bathroom where she'd stashed the test kits. He waited outside while she collected the sample of urine and then she opened the door again so he could join her as the test was processed.

'Is that two lines?' Vinn said, standing so close to her she could feel him all but shaking with excitement.

'No, it's too early.' Ailsa could feel her stomach doing cartwheels, her emotions in such turmoil she could barely breathe. It was as if she were holding her

destiny in her hands. Two lines would mean she was to become a mother. Two lines that would change her life for ever.

There weren't two lines.

The wand stayed negative.

Ailsa could feel Vinn's disappointment by the way his breath left his body. She could feel her own disappointment coursing through her, making it hard for her to process her emotions. She should be feeling relieved, not disappointed. This was good news...wasn't it?

No. Because the one thing she wanted was a baby. But not with a man who didn't love her, who only wanted her now because she was the one who got away.

She didn't just want a baby. She wanted Vinn to love her the way she loved him. The way she had always loved him. How could she settle for a rerun of their marriage when nothing had changed? Sure, he knew about her past and she knew a bit more about his, but it hadn't made him fall in love with her. He hadn't said anything about loving her.

'Don't worry, *cara*,' Vinn said, winding an arm around her waist. 'We'll keep trying for a baby. It'll happen sooner or later.'

Ailsa moved out of his hold. 'Vinn, stop. Stop planning my future for me without asking me what *I* want.'

His expression flickered and then reset itself to frowning. 'What are you saying? You wanted that baby. I know you did. I could see it in your eyes, damn it, I could feel it in your body. You're as disappointed as me. I know you are.'

She saw no reason to deny it, not even to herself.

The time for denial was over. She had to be clear about what she wanted and not settle for anything less. 'You're right. I do want a baby. But I want to have a baby with a man who loves me more than anything else. You're not that man. You've told me yourself you can never be that man.'

'But we'll be great parents, *cara*,' Vinn said. 'We're great together. So what if neither of us is in love with each other? We want each other, we respect each other. Surely that is something to build on?'

Ailsa let out a frustrated sigh. 'I can't be with a man who refuses to love me. Who fights against it as if it's some sort of deadly virus. I want to be loved for me, Vinn. For *me* with all my faults and foibles.'

'I care about you, Ailsa. You surely don't doubt that?'

'You can't say the words, can you? What is so terrifying about admitting you feel more for me than just caring about my welfare?'

'But I do care about you. I always have—'

She let out a laugh that was borderline hysterical. 'You "care" about me.' She put her fingers up in air quotes. 'What does "care" really mean? I'll tell you what it means. It means you don't love me. It means you won't love me. You're not capable or not willing to love me.'

'But you don't love me either so what's the problem?'

Ailsa shook her head at him, exasperated by his inability to see what was staring him in the face. But she wasn't going to say it. She wasn't going to tell him she loved him only for him to throw that love back in her face. To have him cheapen her love by offering a relationship that was loveless. 'I'm going back to London,

Vinn. Today. I'm sorry if it upsets your grandfather but I'm sure he'll understand I can't do this. I can't be in a marriage like this. I deserve more and so do you.'

Vinn's expression went through various makeovers. First it looked blank, then angry, then shocked and then back to angry again. 'So. You're leaving.' His tone was clipped as if he was making an enormous effort to control himself. 'You do happen to realise what will happen to your brother's sponsorship if you walk out that door?'

'Yes, but I'm hoping you won't punish Isaac because you and I can't be together,' Ailsa said. 'And as to the money you gave me…of course I'll give it back.'

'Keep it.' His lips were so tight it was as if he was spitting out lemon pips instead of words. 'You've earned it.'

'There's no need to be insulting,' Ailsa said, stung by his cruel words. 'But this is exactly why I'm calling it off now before we end up doing even worse to each other. I don't want our divorce to be long and drawn-out and uncivilised. We can be better than that.'

His look was so cutting Ailsa was surprised she didn't end up in little slices on the floor. 'Civilised you say? Then you married the wrong man.'

And, without another word, he turned and left her with just her regrets and heartbreak for company.

Vinn was so furious he wanted to punch a hole in the nearest wall. She was leaving. Again. She had called time on their relationship in the same half hour when he'd seen a glimpse of the future they could have had together.

A future with children.

A family.

The family he wanted more than he wanted success.

But no. She was leaving because she had never intended to come back. He had *made* her come back. Lured her and blackmailed her, hoping it would change her mind, hoping it would make her see how good they were together.

So she wanted to be civilised about their divorce, did she? He wasn't feeling too civilised right now. He felt every emotion he had locked down deep inside was about to explode out of him. Was it his fault he couldn't say the words she wanted to hear? Was it his fault he had taught himself not to feel love in case it was taken away? How could he switch the ability to love back on? The loss of his mother so young had permanently changed him. It had flicked a switch inside him and he could no longer find the control board to switch it back on again. Loving and losing were so inextricably linked inside his head that he couldn't untangle them, no matter how hard he tried.

He had been so looking forward to seeing his grandfather with the news of Ailsa's pregnancy. He had pictured it in his mind, imagining how delighted Nonno would be to hear the news of the baby. But there wasn't going to be a baby. There wasn't even going to be a marriage any more.

He had failed.

He had failed to win her back and he had failed his grandfather.

He would have to give Ailsa the divorce. He had no

choice, the law saw to that. The only consolation was she would have to wait another two years.

He hoped they would be as miserable for her as the last two had been for him.

Ailsa got off the plane in London with a raging temperature and a splitting headache. The bug that had been masquerading as a baby hit her during the flight and she'd curled up in her seat under a blanket and wondered if she had ever felt this miserable.

No. Never. Not even when she'd left Vinn the first time. This was much harder, much more painful because, along with losing Vinn, she'd lost the future she'd longed for. Why couldn't he love her? Was she so awful, so *abnormal* that he couldn't bring himself to love her?

Even as she'd boarded the plane in Milan she'd hoped he would come after her and tell her he'd made a mistake. But he hadn't. She'd stared at the entrance of the boarding gate as she had stared at the wand of that test kit. Wanting something to happen didn't make it happen. It either happened or it didn't.

Vinn didn't love her and she had best get over her disappointment. She'd done it before and she would do it again.

Even if it damn well killed her.

CHAPTER TEN

VINN WAS DREADING telling his grandfather that Ailsa had left him. He even considered not telling him, but that would be doing what his father had done, pretending everything was fine when it wasn't. Pathetic. But in a strange way now he could understand why his father had kept the news of his mother's condition under wraps. It was too painful to face. His father had tried to spare him from pain in the only way he knew how. By pretending. By lying. By hiding the truth until it could be hidden no longer.

But Vinn had to face Ailsa's leaving him just as he'd had to face his mother's death. It was just as permanent for there was nothing he could do to bring her back. Ailsa didn't love him. And all this time he had fooled himself she was the one with more invested in their relationship.

When Vinn went to the hospital the day after Ailsa had left for London, his grandfather still had a temperature and a change of antibiotic had been arranged. He couldn't help feeling concerned at the frailty of his grandfather's appearance. Would the news he was about

to break make things worse? How would he be able to live with himself if he sent Nonno over the edge? But how could he live with himself if he kept up the charade?

'Ailsa not coming in today?' Nonno said, glancing past Vinn's shoulders. 'Is she still feeling a little under the weather?'

Vinn pulled the visitor's chair closer to the bed and sat down and slowly released a breath. 'I don't know how to tell you this, Nonno, but she's gone back to London.'

'For work?'

How easy would it be to lie? All he had to say was yes and give his grandfather another day or two of peace before the ugly truth had to be faced. 'Not just for work,' Vinn said. 'The thing is…we weren't really back together.'

His grandfather put his gnarled hand on Vinn's forearm. 'You think I didn't know that?'

Vinn stared at his grandfather. 'You…*knew*?'

Nonno gave a single nod. 'I appreciate what you tried to do. I know you had my best interests at heart. But you have to want her back for you, not me. Because you can't live without her. Because no one else will fill the space she left.'

Vinn's throat was suddenly so constricted it felt as if he'd swallowed one of the pillows off his grandfather's bed. Two pillows. Plus the mattress. Ailsa had left a space so big and achingly empty his chest felt like it was being carved out with a rusty spoon. The inextricable knot was finally loosened inside him. He hadn't been

able to say the words but the feelings were there and could no longer be denied or ignored or masqueraded as anything else. His biggest fear hadn't been falling in love. His biggest fear was losing the only person he had loved with all his heart and soul and body. He had to have the courage to own those feelings. To embrace them and express them. 'I love her, Nonno. But I think I've ruined everything. Again.'

'Have you told her you love her?'

Vinn couldn't meet his grandfather's gaze and looked down at the wedding ring on his left hand instead. Why hadn't he taken it off by now? *Because you love her and can't bear the thought of never seeing her again.* He loved her. He loved her so damn much he hadn't been able to move on with his life. He hadn't taken off his wedding ring because taking it off would mean finally letting go of the hope. The hope that their marriage still had a chance. That was why he'd sent those Italian clients to her studio. He'd been unwilling to finally sever the connection. He'd clung to whatever thread he could to keep her in his life.

He brought his gaze back to his grandfather's. 'What if I've poisoned that love? What if it's too late?'

'You won't find out by sitting here talking to me,' Nonno said. 'The person you need to talk to is Ailsa.'

Vinn sprang to his feet. 'You're right. But I hate leaving you while you're still in ICU. That infection is worrying your specialists. What if you—?' He couldn't finish the sentence for the lump of emotion in his throat.

Nonno waved his hand towards the door. 'Go. I'll

be all right. I'm not ready to leave this world yet.' His eyes twinkled. 'I have one more thing to tick off on my bucket list.'

Ailsa got over her virus but her spirits were still so low she could barely drag herself through the day. Forty-eight hours had passed since she'd left Italy and she hadn't heard anything from Vinn. Not that she'd expected him to contact her. Their relationship was over and the sooner she moved on with her life the better. But, even so, every time the studio door opened, her heart would give an extra beat in the hope Vinn might walk through the door.

She'd sent a text to her mother to let her know there wasn't going to be a baby, and told both her mother and stepfather she had left Vinn because she didn't want them reading about it first in the press. Her mother had replied, saying she would come and see her as soon as she could.

It was lunchtime when the bell at the top of the door tinkled again and Ailsa looked up to see her mother and stepfather come in. Normally when her mother said she would drop by it could mean days and days before it actually happened. Was this a sign things were improving in her relationship with her mother? 'Mum? Dad? Why are you both here?'

Her mother spoke first. 'We were worried about you. And sad about your news about Vinn and you calling it quits. Are you okay? Is there anything we can do?'

Ailsa shook her head and sighed. 'No, there's nothing anyone can do.'

Her mother looked anxious and kept darting glances at Ailsa's stepfather. 'We feel so bad about everything. Me particularly. I know I haven't been the best mother to you. I tried but I was so messed-up after… Well, I should have got some help instead of bottling it up. But that's going to change now so—'

'Mum, it's fine, really. You don't have to apologise.'

'But I want to be closer to you,' her mother said. 'Since your father and I divorced… Sorry, I can't help calling Michael your father even though—'

'It's fine, Mum. Michael *is* my father.' Ailsa turned to face him. 'You're the only father I've ever known and ever wanted.'

Michael blinked back tears and reached for Ailsa's mother's hand. 'Thank you, sweetheart. What your mother is trying to say is we're working at some stuff. We're both having counselling.'

Ailsa looked at her parents' joined hands and the light shining in her mother's usually haunted and shadowed eyes. 'What's going on?'

Her mother gave a sheepish smile. 'I feel bad saying this when you're going through a relationship breakup, but your dad and I have realised we're not happy without each other.'

'But you weren't happy together.'

'That was because we weren't being honest with each other,' Michael said. 'We're learning how to do that now. I don't want to lose your mother. I don't want to lose the family we made together.'

Ailsa couldn't believe her ears. 'So you're getting remarried?'

'Maybe,' her mother said. 'We're not making any promises. But for now we're enjoying putting the past aside and moving forward.'

Ailsa hugged both her parents in turn. 'I'm happy for you.'

She just wished she could put the past aside and move forward too.

Ailsa was about to close the studio for the day when she saw Vinn walking towards the front door. Her breath stalled in her throat and her hand on the key in the door fell away and went to her chest, where her heart was threatening to leap out of her chest. He'd left his grandfather back in Milan to come and see her? What did it mean? 'Vinn?'

'Can we talk?' Vinn said.

Ailsa stepped back to let him enter and closed the door behind him. 'Why are you here? Is your grandfather okay? Oh, God...don't tell me something's happened.'

He smiled and reached for her hands, holding them within the cradle of his. 'Something has happened, *cara*. I've finally come to my senses and realised I love you. Can you forgive me for not telling you sooner?'

Ailsa did a rapid blink. 'You love me?'

He gave her hands a gentle squeeze, his dark eyes shining. 'So so much. I can't believe it's taken me this long to admit it. I was too frightened, too cowardly to admit I needed you, that I loved you so much I couldn't bear to take off my wedding ring because it was all I had left of you. That's why I fired Rosa. She told me I was

a fool to let the wife I was madly in love with go without a fight. I fired her rather than face up to the truth. And I let you go—twice. Please say you'll forgive me and come back to me.'

Ailsa was crying and laughing at the same time and threw herself against him, winding her arms around his neck. 'I love you too.'

'You do? You really do? Even after all the stupid mistakes I've made?'

She smiled. 'Of course I do. You don't have to say the words to show it, you know.'

He grinned back. 'True, but given how stubborn and blockheaded I am, I think it'd be wise if you did tell me now and again. At least once or twice a day.'

'I love you.' She pressed a kiss to his mouth. 'I love, love, love you.'

'That's a start.' He pressed a kiss to her lips. 'Stay married to me, *cara*? Please? We don't have to live all the time in Milan. I've been thinking about launching a showroom over here. Maybe you could send some clients my way.'

Ailsa grimaced in shame. 'I feel so bad I deliberately directed clients away from your beautiful designs out of spite. And all the while you were sending me clients. You're a much better person than I am.'

He stroked her face with a tender hand. 'You are a wonderful person, *cara*. Don't ever think you're not.'

Ailsa smiled again. 'I've come to some realisations of my own in the last little while. I am much more than my DNA. I might not know who my father is but I know who *I* am and that's all that matters.'

Vinn hugged her close. 'And I love who you are and can't wait to spend the rest of my life proving it to you.'

'I thought you only wanted me because you thought I was pregnant. I wouldn't have left the way I did if I'd known you loved me.'

He gave her a rueful smile. 'I'd actually bought you flowers on my way home that day. I planned to ask you to stay with me. I guess it was a roundabout way of expressing the feelings I hadn't yet admitted to myself.'

Ailsa stroked his jaw. 'We've been such fools wasting so much time. We've been making war instead of making love.'

His dark eyes shone with deep emotion. 'I want you in my life no matter what. Having children is not as important to me as you are. I love you and you'll be more than enough for me.'

Ailsa looked at him through a blurry sheen of tears. 'Oh, Vinn, I do want a baby. I didn't realise how much until I stood with you in that bathroom with that test wand in my hand.'

'You do? Really?' His hands gripped her so tightly it was almost painful. 'But I don't want you just saying that to appease me.'

'I want to make a family with you, darling,' Ailsa said and gave him a twinkling smile. 'How soon can we get started?'

He gave her an answering smile and brought his mouth down to hers. 'Now.'

EPILOGUE

Three months later...

IT WAS THE most unusual way to find out if a pregnancy test was positive or not but Ailsa didn't care. Unusual because instead of just her and Vinn peering at the test wand in the bathroom with expectant breaths held, Vinn's grandfather and Carlotta and Rosa were waiting in the sitting room downstairs for the results. Rosa had come back to work for Vinn and was such an enormous asset to the company that Vinn had been able to step back a little and spend more time with Ailsa and his grandfather.

Ailsa started to well up when she saw the positive lines appear and Vinn's arm around her waist tightened. 'That looks like a positive to me,' he said, grinning at her. 'What do you think?'

She turned in his embrace and linked her arms around his neck, smiling up at him with such joy filling her heart she thought it would burst. 'I think you are going to be the best father in the world. I love you. Do you have any idea how much?'

He pressed a gentle kiss to her mouth. 'I love you too, more than I can ever say, although it has to be said I'm pretty damn good at saying it now, don't you agree?'

'You are.' She kissed his mouth back. 'And I never get tired of hearing you say it.'

Vinn brushed back an imaginary hair from her face, his expression so tender and loving it made her chest expand as if her heart was searching for more room. 'I'm dying to spread the good news to Nonno and Carlotta and Rosa but there's something I have to do first.'

'What's that?'

'This,' he said, and covered her mouth with his.

* * * * *

CASTIGLIONE'S PREGNANT PRINCESS

LYNNE GRAHAM

First Published in Great Britain 2018
by Mills & Boon, an imprint of HarperCollins*Publishers*
1 London Bridge Street, London, SE1 9GF

Castiglione's Pregnant Princess © 2018 by Lynne Graham

Blackmailed into the Marriage Bed © 2018 by Melanie Milburne

ISBN: 978-0-263-93526-4

MIX
Paper from
responsible sources
FSC **C007454**

FSC
www.fsc.org

Printed and bound in Spain
by CPI, Barcelona

CASTIGLIONE'S PREGNANT PRINCESS

LYNNE GRAHAM

BLACKMAILED INTO THE MARRIAGE BED

MELANIE MILBURNE

MILLS & BOON

Also by Lynne Graham

Claimed for the Leonelli Legacy
His Queen by Desert Decree

Vows for Billionaires miniseries

The Secret Valtinos Baby
Castiglione's Pregnant Princess

Also by Melanie Milburne

Unwrapping His Convenient Fiancée
The Temporary Mrs Marchetti
Wedding Night with Her Enemy
A Ring for the Greek's Baby
The Tycoon's Marriage Deal
A Virgin for a Vow

Discover more at millsandboon.co.uk

Lynne Graham was born in Northern Ireland and has been a keen romance reader since her teens. She is very happily married to an understanding husband who has learned to cook since she started to write! Her five children keep her on her toes. She has a very large dog, who knocks everything over, a very small terrier, who barks a lot, and two cats. When time allows, Lynne is a keen gardener.

Melanie Milburne read her first Mills & Boon novel at the age of seventeen, in between studies for her final exams. After completing a master's degree in education she decided to write a novel, and thus her career as a romance author was born. Melanie is an ambassador for the Australian Childhood Foundation and a keen dog-lover and trainer. She enjoys long walks in the Tasmanian bush. In 2015 Melanie won the Holt Medallion—a prestigious award honouring outstanding literary talent.

CHAPTER ONE

TANYA could not believe her bad luck. The reason she had consistently put off visiting her sister in Tenerife was because she was afraid of bumping into Alejandro. And now, almost before she had set foot on foreign soil, he was here at the airport, instantly recognisable, instantly causing her heart to quicken its beats, instantly causing confusion in her mind.

He was as devastatingly handsome as she remembered, taller than most of his compatriots, his shiny black hair cut well above the collarline, his eyes — those soul-searching brown eyes which had frequently reduced her to jelly — enviably large and thickly fringed, his lips full and sensual. She would have lied had she said she did not feel anything, but her pain over the way they had parted, and the subsequent news that had filtered through to her that he was married, was a much more dominant emotion.

'Tanya! Tanya! Over here.'

Her sister's excited voice reached Tanya above the noise and general confusion of exiting passengers. She was not the only one to hear it. Alejandro turned his head and looked in Charlene's direction, and then from her to Tanya. It all happened in a split second; their eyes met and she saw the sudden narrowing in his before his attention was taken up by the beautiful woman who threw herself into his arms, a woman with jet-black hair piled on top of her head, perfectly applied make-up, elegantly dressed. Tanya's bitterness deepened. She had wondered what his wife looked like. Now she knew. And she would have given anything to be able to turn right round and catch the same plane back to England.

By this time Charlene had pushed her way to Tanya's side and was welcoming her sister enthusiastically. When Tanya next looked in Alejandro's direction he had gone. Maybe she had even imagined him? Although she knew she hadn't. It was all wishful thinking. She ought to have followed her instincts and never let Charlene persuade her to come here. The holiday was going to be a disaster. The next instant a card was being pushed into her hand and a well-remembered voice growled low in her ear, 'I would like to talk with you. Give me a ring.'

He disappeared as quickly as he had approached. Charlene looked at her sister in amazement. 'Was that who I thought it was?'

Tanya nodded. 'The very same.'

'I cannot believe it. In the two years I've been out here I've never seen him, not once.'

'I know, you told me,' muttered Tanya unhappily. 'It was what finally persuaded me to come. Hell, I wish I hadn't; he's going to ruin my holiday.'

'Rubbish, you won't see him again.' Charlene's tone was positive, her arm protectively around her younger sister. 'What did he want anyway?'

'He said he wanted to talk to me.'

'What a nerve.' Charlene was incensed. 'Is this his address?' She plucked the card from Tanya's hand and tore it into pieces, throwing them into the air where they fell like confetti.

Charlene was the elder of the two sisters, taller and heavier, and had always had more to say for herself. Not that Tanya was lacking in confidence; far from it. Having lost both their parents at a very tender age, they had been brought up separately by a succession of foster-parents, some not always happy experiences, and they had frequently needed to stand up for themselves.

Tanya's shoulder-length hair was a soft honey-gold, in complete contrast to Charlene's raven darkness. The only things they had in common were their eyes, sloe-shaped and a beautiful azure-blue.

'Come along.' Charlene picked up Tanya's case. 'My car's in the car park. Let's forget we ever saw that man; he's bad news without a doubt.'

Tanya followed her sister through the line of people waiting for taxis and over the road to the busy car park. The warmth of the day after England's freezing winter temperatures was blissful, and she shrugged off her jacket as she walked. Seeing Alejandro at the airport had put a damper on her spirits, but she was determined not to let it get her down. Charlene was probably right; they wouldn't see him again.

'Here we are.' Her sister's voice cut into her thoughts. She opened the boot of a smart white car and threw Tanya's case inside. 'Let's go.'

Alejandro was forgotten as they left the airport and hit the motorway. Tanya gazed with interest at her surroundings; the bare, jagged mountains in the distance, their tops draped in mist; the brown, barren countryside with just the odd shrub or clump of prickly pear growing tenaciously in the dry earth; the occasional flush of buildings, some industrial, some purpose-built holiday developments close to the shore.

It was all new and exciting, and she did not want to miss a thing. Charlene had recently moved in with a family whose daughter worked in the same hotel as Charlene, and they had become good friends. The girl's mother had agreed to Tanya's spending her holiday with them as well. Tanya found it difficult to believe the woman's generosity to a complete stranger.

They soon left the motorway and headed up into the hills, the road curving and climbing, bushes of white daisy-like flowers and clumps of spiny cactus adorning the roadside. They passed through a dusty village where old men sat outside bars and children kicked balls or rode BMXs, and passed several isolated houses on the outskirts; square, box-like dwellings built out of

blocks. Some had been whitewashed, some were still
bare concrete, looking, to Tanya's English eyes, as
though they were not finished. One or two had pantiled
roofs and looked more attractive, but when Charlene
turned off the road and pulled up beside one of the
unpainted buildings Tanya looked at her with a frown.
'Is this where you're living?'

Charlene smiled and nodded. 'It's not like it looks, I
assure you. It's heavenly inside; most of them are. You
can't go by external appearances. I was once told that
it was because the Canarians didn't care what a house
looked like on the outside, as we do — but I later
learned that the real reason is that they don't have to
pay taxes on unfinished buildings. The government run
campaigns sometimes to try to get people to paint their
walls white, but they're always a failure.'

Still looking doubtful, Tanya followed her sister. The
single-storey building was an odd shape, as though it
had had further rooms built on as and when the need
arose. There was a wall, built yet again out of grey
blocks, denoting the boundary of the property, but
there was no garden as such, just a few straggly plants
growing and a dog foraging. Coming from her smart
semi-detached house on the outskirts of Sheffield, with
its tidy green and abundant garden, Tanya found it
difficult to feel happy about spending a month here.

All the windows were shuttered — wooden, varnished
shutters — and the front door was wooden too. In fact
it was an ornately carved, expensive-looking door
which looked oddly out of place with its surroundings.
And once inside Tanya could see what Charlene meant.
The cool, clean hallway boasted a tiled floor, a polished
chair in the corner and a profusion of healthy plants
which hung and sat and filled every corner. It was like
an oasis in the desert.

In the shadowy living-room Charlene's friend's
mother waited to greet her. The tiny woman was
dressed all in black, her greying hair secured in a neat

bun. She smiled warmly as Charlene made the introductions in fluent Spanish and held out her hand. Tanya
smiled back. 'It's very kind of you to let me stay here.'
she said.

Through her sister she established that Señora
Guerra was very pleased to welcome her into their
house and she was to treat it as her home and come
and go as she pleased and not to worry about disturbing
them.

Tanya was grateful her sister spoke the language — it
had actually been a prerequisite of her job at the hotel.
In fact Charlene spoke several languages. Tanya, on
the other hand, spoke no more than schoolgirl French.

'She's a wonderful lady,' Charlene told her. 'Señor
Guerra died a few years ago, but she has coped
admirably. Maribel is her only child left at home. She
has three sons, but they are all married now, though
they frequently visit. She's delighted about it. The
house almost bursts at the seams when they all come.'

'I hope I won't be in the way,' said Tanya worriedly.

'Of course not. It was Señora Guerra's idea that you
stay here.' She turned and said something to the older
woman, who instantly smiled, speaking rapidly, gesturing eloquently, reassuring Tanya that she was not
putting them out in the least.

The room they were in amazed Tanya. It was like
going back a hundred years; it was like photographs
she had seen of days gone by. The furniture looked
like oak, big and solid, and the dresser packed with
plates and cups and saucers. There was a settee and
rocking-chairs with hand-embroidered cushions, pieces
of pottery, photographs and pictures on the walls and
more plants standing in big pots on the tiled floor or
hanging from the ceiling. Every inch of space was used.
It was cluttered but beautiful, and Tanya loved it.

She suddenly realised that her host was watching
her, and she gave an apologetic smile. 'I was admiring
your house. It's lovely.'

Charlene translated and the woman beamed, and then Tanya was taken to her room, which was next to Charlene's. Again, heavy oak furniture was dominant. The walls were painted a simple white, only the patchwork bedcover providing a bright splash of colour.

The first thing she did was open the windows and push back the shutters, allowing the bright sunlight to flood the room. The jagged outline of the mountains was up above them, the earlier mist having completely disappeared, the sky a clear, intense blue. Tanya was anxious to explore — so long as she did not bump into Alejandro! The thought of him being somewhere out there still festered in the back of her mind.

Her sister helped her unpack, and by the time she had freshened up and changed into a cotton sundress Señora Guerra had lunch waiting. A white cloth had been spread on the table in the living-room, and as soon as Tanya sat down her meal was set in front of her — white fish, potatoes cooked in their skins, carrots and peas.

'Bacalao,' confirmed Charlene with a smile, 'or codfish to you and me, and these —— ' indicating the potatoes, ' — are *papas arrugadas*, which, translated literally, means wrinkled potatoes. They're cooked in very salty water and allowed to boil dry, leaving a salty coating on their skins. The Canarians always cook them this way. I love them.'

Tanya's verdict later was one of approval too. It was a simple meal, yet filling and tasty, and when she was offered fresh fruit for dessert she had to refuse. They drank wine also, a sweet, local wine that was not really to Tanya's taste, though she was too polite to say so. Señora Guerra was a marvellous hostess, even with the language barrier, her actions and expressions when she was trying to get something across making Tanya laugh wholeheartedly.

After lunch Charlene took her for a short drive; once back she met Señora Guerra's daughter, ate another excellent meal — thinking she would be as fat as a pig when she went home if she went on like this — and now she lay in bed, her head sunk into a soft, sweet-smelling pillow. One way and another it had been quite a day, and she was desperately tired, yet thoughts of Alejandro kept her wide awake.

He had duped her all right. She had never dreamt that he was using her, that it was an affair he was after, a passionate fling before he went back to Tenerife to marry his childhood sweetheart. What a gullible fool she had been. He had even talked about bringing her here, had spoken of the pleasure he would get in showing her his beloved country — and she had believed him! What a silver-tongued swine he was. All the anger she had felt nine years ago came back with a vengeance, boiling, enraging, making her wish desperately and deeply that she had not let Charlene persuade her to come.

And why should he want to talk to her? What was there to say? Nothing! Not a thing. He had hurt her feelings immeasurably; she had given him all of her love, and for what? He was the last person she wanted to talk to now, and she hoped and prayed that she would never see him again.

Inevitably her thoughts went back to their first meeting. She had been eighteen at the time, and they had met at a friend's wedding. He had been working as a waiter in the hotel restaurant in which the reception was held, and there had been an instant mutual attraction. They had not spoken, Alejandro refusing to put his job in jeopardy by chatting to one of the guests, but the suggestion had been there in his eyes that he would like to see her again.

How he had found out where she worked Tanya did not know, but two days later he had been waiting outside the office block when she finished at five. For a few seconds all she could do was stare in amazement.

'Do forgive me,' he said, in heavily accented English,

'but I wanted to see you.' His teeth were white and even, his smile cautious.

'How did you know where to find me?' Her heart began to hammer and her blue eyes were wide as she looked at him. He was dressed in jeans and a black leather jacket with a roll-collared blue sweater beneath. He was fantastically handsome and a whole head taller than herself, which made him over six feet. He was a few years older as well, and she found him tremendously exciting.

'I have seen you many times as I live not far away from here, but I did not have the courage to speak,' he told her honestly. 'Then at the wedding I knew I had to make the effort. I hope you are not offended.'

Tanya shook her head, completely mesmerised by this fascinating stranger. She could not quite make up her mind from which part of the world he came — Spain or Italy, perhaps, judging by his colouring.

He held out his hand. 'My name is Alejandro Vázquez Herrera, and I believe you are Tanya? A beautiful name for a beautiful girl.'

'Tanya Elliott,' she confirmed, putting her slim hand into his, liking the feel of his firm handshake. 'How did you know?'

'By keeping my ears open at the wedding reception,' he confessed with an engaging smile. 'May I take you for a drink?'

'Perhaps a coffee?' she murmured. She felt a sudden shyness which was alien to her, and put it down to the fact that he wasn't English. He was really quite the most exciting person she had met in a long time.

She walked along at his side, aware of the curious glances of her colleagues. There would be plenty of questions tomorrow. 'Are you living in England permanently?' she ventured after they had walked a few yards in silence.

'No,' he said, shaking his head. 'I am here to study English. I am taking classes and doing a job at the same time to help pay for both them and my accommodation.'

'Your English sounds very good to me,' she said, hiding her disappointment that he would one day return to his home country.

'It has improved,' he agreed, lifting his shoulders in a modest gesture. 'I have been here twelve months now. I have enjoyed it very much.'

'How much longer do you plan to stay?' She waited with bated breath for his answer. It would be just her luck if he was planning to go home very shortly.

'I am in no hurry,' he told her.

Tanya's face broke into an involuntary smile of relief. 'Where do you come from?'

'The Canary Islands — Tenerife, to be exact. Have you ever been there?'

Tanya shook her head.

'Then you must; they are beautiful. Politically we belong to Spain, but we prefer to think of ourselves as independent.'

Tanya showed her ignorance. 'I'm not even sure where they are.'

He gave a slow, tolerant smile. 'In the Atlantic Ocean, just off the coast of Africa. The climate is superb. Ask a Canarian what the islands are unique for, and he will say the weather. It is our blessing. It encourages tourism and prospers our economy.'

'So what do you think of England?'

A grimace took the place of his smile. 'What do I think? I am used to it now, but it was so cold when I first came. I wondered how you put up with it. Now I think England is beautiful — not so much as Tenerife, of course, but. . .' He broke off and laughed. 'I am joking. Your country is — how do you say it? — on a par. Each has its own — advantages. Is that right?'

Tanya nodded, laughing also. He was being very diplomatic.

'Shall we take our coffee here?' He halted outside a

tearoom which had a good reputation and was not very busy at this time of day.

Afterwards Tanya had no idea what they talked about. She remembered him saying that his mother was no longer alive, that he had several brothers and sisters, all younger than himself, but apart from that she recalled nothing. She knew only that she had had a wonderful time and that Alejandro was no longer a stranger but a warm, humorous man who had kept her amused and happy and wormed his way just a little into her heart—even in that short space of time.

She could not sleep that night for thinking about him, and could not wait for their next date. He had only one evening free a week, he told her ruefully, but this week he had all day Sunday off and he would very much like to see her then.

Tanya lived in a small bed-sitter on the top floor of a converted Victorian house on the outskirts of Birmingham, found for her by the local council when she became of age and no longer qualified for foster care. Charlene had wanted her to move in to her much bigger and comfortable apartment, but Tanya craved her independence. She wanted to lead her own life.

In the weeks that followed Tanya saw as much of Alejandro as was possible, given that he worked unsociable hours and still took English lessons in his spare time. It was a passionate, intense affair, both feeling as though they had known each other forever, hating the hours they were forced to spend apart, never able to get enough of each other.

When her sister met him she was equally impressed. 'Lucky you,' she said, 'but be careful. Don't forget he'll be going home one day.'

'Yes, but he'll take me with him,' said Tanya confidently. 'He's already spoken about it.'

Charlene looked sceptical. 'Isn't that what they all say? I've lived longer than you, Tan; I know what men are like.'

But Tanya would listen to nothing detrimental about her beloved Alejandro, and for three months the affair raged. She grew more and more confident in her love for him, never actually declaring her feelings — and nor did he — but they both knew that it was there, and as far as Tanya was concerned she was happier than she had ever been in her life.

He showed his love in a dozen different ways; in his caring attitude, in the intense physical pleasure of their lovemaking, in the little gifts he bought her — nothing expensive — a single rose, chocolates, a glossy magazine, bath oils. None cost more than a pound or two, and yet they meant as much to Tanya as if he had bought her diamonds or gold.

Always he came to the flat for her; sometimes they went out, sometimes they stayed in, and once he had taken her back to his room at the hotel. Employees were actually not allowed to have members of the opposite sex in their rooms, but she had said so many times that she wanted to see where he lived, that in the end he had given in.

How many times since had she wished she had never gone there? It was as small and cramped as her own room, but far more untidy, and when she offered to make them a cup of coffee she could not help noticing the letter that had been left lying on the cupboard where the kettle stood.

Her eyes flicked over the boldly written page before she realised what she was doing, and once she had started she could not stop. It was from Alejandro's father, and surprisingly written in English — probably as a concession to his son's improving his knowledge of the language. Although his father's mastery of English was not very good, Tanya managed to make out that he was asking Alejandro when he was coming home, because Juanita was growing impatient. It was time he came back and made arrangements for his wedding, which had been put off long enough.

His wedding! Tanya felt the colour drain out of her
face, and without stopping to think she picked up the
letter and thrust it under Alejandro's nose. 'What the
hell is this all about?'

'You should not have read that, Tanya,' he said
quietly.

'But I have,' she cried, 'and I want to know about
this girl, this Juanita. Why have you never told me
about her? Why have you let me assume that it's me
you love? Hell, if I'd known all you were interested in
was an affair I——'

'That is not the case,' he interjected sharply.

'No?' Her eyes widened, full of scepticism. 'It looks
very much like that to me. Do you deny that there's
another girl in your life?'

'Yes, I do,' he announced strongly.

'So who is Juanita?'

'A lifelong friend, a family friend; we virtually grew
up together.'

'*A friend*?' Tanya's tone filled with disbelief. 'It
doesn't sound as though she's just a friend to me.'

'Maybe there was more in it once,' he admitted, 'but
that was over a long time ago. I have already written
and told her about you.'

Tanya shook her head, wanting to believe him, but
unable to. If he had written Juanita would surely have
told his father, especially if the families were close.
'You're lying,' she whispered. 'You're trying to get out
of it. Well, don't bother; it's over. I want nothing more
to do with you. You're nothing but a two-timing snake
in the grass. Juanita is welcome to you.' She picked up
her jacket and headed for the door.

'Tanya, stop!' Alejandro's voice came after her. 'Let
me explain; do not walk out on me like this.'

'What is there to explain?' she tossed over her
shoulder. 'Everything is as clear as tap water. You've
been using me; it's as simple as that. You've wanted a
girl to satisfy your basic male urges until you get back

to your true love. I feel sorry for her, do you know that? I wonder if she knows what type of man it is she's going to marry.'

'Do you really think I would behave so badly?' His dark eyes were cold, his whole body rigid.

'Yes, I do,' she yelled. 'I not only think it, there's proof in your father's letter. Goodbye, Alejandro.' She slammed the door and marched along the corridor, running down the steps and through the hotel grounds to the street. Not until she was long out of sight of the building did she slow down, but it was not until she reached the refuge of her bed-sitter that she let her tears fall.

Never had she felt so humiliated. She really had thought that she meant something to him. Her sister had been right. If only she had listened, if only she hadn't let herself get so deeply emotionally involved.

For two days Tanya did not leave her flat. Her face was so swollen by crying that she was too embarrassed to go to work, and she didn't even care whether she lost her job. Life was hell all of a sudden.

To begin with she had thought that Alejandro would contact her, that he would come round and explain everything, declare his love, say his father was mistaken, but she heard nothing, and the two days turned into a week, a week of intense misery. When she could stand it no longer she swallowed her pride and marched round to the hotel. It couldn't just end like this; she wouldn't let it. Maybe he had been right and she wrong. Maybe he had written to Juanita. Maybe she ought to give him the benefit of the doubt.

The news that he had gone back to Tenerife paralysed her, the shock of it almost greater than discovering that he had another girl. He had gone without a word, without trying to patch things up between them. It was over, all over, and when her sister announced that she had accepted a job as under-manager in a new, though relatively small hotel in Sheffield, Tanya readily accepted the invitation to go and live with her.

Several months went by, during which time Tanya gradually came back to life, settled down in a new job as a junior secretary with a computer software company, and resolutely pushed Alejandro out of her mind.

Until the day Charlene came home with the news that she had heard Alejandro was married. Tanya's mouth fell open and she felt as though someone had kicked her legs from beneath her. She dropped on to the nearest chair. 'To Juanita?' she managed to whisper.

Charlene nodded. 'I'm so sorry, Tan. But I thought it best you knew. Now you'll be able to get on with your life, accept some of those dates that you keep refusing.'

'But how — how did you find out?' Tanya's blue eyes were wide and troubled, her face pale.

'I got talking to one of the guests who hailed from Tenerife. I happened to mention Alejandro, and strangely enough he knew him — or at least he knew of him.'

Tanya swallowed hard. 'How long ago did he get married?'

Charlene shrugged. 'I don't know; he didn't say.'

So that definitely was the end of it, thought Tanya, as she lay in bed that night. Not even to herself had she admitted that she always hoped he might come back, that he would trace her and declare his love for her. Now there was no chance, none at all. It was definitely the end.

She still found it difficult to believe that he had been so warm and loving towards her when all the time there had been another girl in the background. She really had thought he was genuinely in love with her; she had never dreamt that it was all a game to him.

After this further blow to her pride Tanya decided

that she had stayed in long enough. She would go out on dates, enjoy male company, but she would never, ever, let herself become involved again. She would be like her sister, a dedicated career woman.

All went well until two years later when she met Peter. He was warm and wonderful and kind, and she fell in love. It was nothing like her love for Alejandro; this was a much gentler relationship, with none of the passion and hunger that had so inflamed her body, sent her soaring with the stars and flying with the eagles. But nevertheless she was content, and twelve months later they were married. Three years after that Peter died from a long and serious illness. Tanya was devastated. At the age of twenty-four she had suffered two terrible losses.

It took her time to pull herself together, but she managed it, and when she applied for promotion, and got the job of PA to the managing director of the software company, she put her heart and soul into her work, not minding that John Drake asked her to work long hours, that sometimes she dropped into bed so exhausted that she was sure she wouldn't wake with the alarm the next morning. But always she did, and somehow she survived.

When Charlene announced that she'd been offered a job running a large hotel in Tenerife Tanya could not believe the irony of it. Mention of Alejandro's native country brought painful memories back, and wild horses wouldn't drag her out there with her sister, although Charlene had done her best to persuade her.

'I have my own house now. I'm settled here; I like it,' Tanya insisted.

'And I suppose you're trying to tell me it has nothing to do with Alejandro Vázquez,' taunted Charlene.

'No, I'm not; it has everything to do with him. There's no way I want to meet that man again.'

'You're still hung up over him?' Charlene frowned.

'I thought all that had died when you married Peter. You haven't mentioned him for years.'

'He was my first love,' announced Tanya quietly. 'I'll never forget him.'

CHAPTER TWO

CHARLENE took a few days off work to show Tanya around, and there was far too much to see and enthuse over to worry herself about Alejandro, although she privately wished her sister hadn't torn up his card. Even though she would never, ever get in touch with him she was curious to know where he lived.

Señora Guerra was a dressmaker, with the reputation of being the finest one on the island, and with the start of Tenerife's annual *carnaval* only two weeks away she was busy finishing off the many costumes she had been asked to make. There was a constant stream of visitors to the house, all eagerly trying on and picking up their costumes. One room had been set aside for this purpose, and it was like an Aladdin's cave, filled with richly coloured fabrics, beads, sequins, feathers, each costume taking hours and hours of painstaking work to complete.

Tanya liked dressmaking herself and took a keen interest in all that was going on, and very often Señora Guerra — or Matilde, as she asked to be called — invited Tanya to see the dresses actually being tried on.

When a dark red, open-topped Mercedes pulled up outside one afternoon Tanya thought nothing of it, until she recognised the driver and his companion. Alejandro and his wife! It could not be! And yet it was. She could hardly believe her bad luck. Already she had told Matilde that she would like to see this particular dress tried on. There was no escape.

Her heart began to race at double-quick time, but as she watched from her window she saw Alejandro drive away, leaving his wife to walk alone into the house. It was a bitter sort of relief.

It took her all of five minutes to go down to Matilde's sewing-room, five minutes to calm her racing thoughts and still her trembling body. Although a confrontation with Alejandro had been avoided, meeting his wife would be as much of a trauma. How could she be civil to the woman who had married the man she, Tanya, loved?

Matilde smiled as she walked in and made introductions in her very rapid Spanish, as always speaking so quickly that one word ran into another and Tanya had no real idea what she had said the woman's name was — not that she needed to be told!

As Tanya watched the dress being pinned and adjusted she covertly studied Juanita. It was no wonder Alejandro loved her; she was beautiful. All the girls in Tenerife were beautiful, she had noticed, but this woman had a serene sort of beauty that came from within, that came with the confidence of being loved and in love. She stood tall and proud, and the purple and silver dress enhanced her dark Latin features, and Tanya hated her.

'You are English?' she said to Tanya, looking at her through the mirror, her smile wide, her teeth even and very white, and when Tanya nodded, 'My husband — he teach me a little English, but I do not use it often. I have never been to England. My husband — he say it is very cold there?'

Tanya smiled and nodded. 'Sometimes. It's our winter now, and it was snowing when I left.'

'It is our winter too.' Juanita laughed. 'It is not so warm, do you think?'

'To me it's very warm,' Tanya returned. 'You're so lucky to live in a place with such a wonderful climate.' And if it hadn't been for this attractive woman she might have been living here herself! Her mouth tightened at the thought.

The woman frowned and turned from the mirror to look directly at Tanya. 'Something is wrong?'

Tanya shook her head and forced a smile. 'It was just a thought, nothing important. I'm sorry. Your dress is so beautiful. Do you take part in the *carnaval* every year?'

'Yes—and sometimes my husband too, but this year he say he is too busy, too much work.'

Which accounted for the fact that he had dropped her off and not come in while the fitting took place. But he would be back, and Tanya was determined that she would not be here; she would shut herself away in her room until he had safely gone.

'You will come and see the *coso*? The *coso* is—how do you say it? The grand parade? Everything stops; even my husband, he take that day off. You can join him, if you like.'

An attack of panic quickened Tanya's heart, but somehow she managed to keep a smile pinned to her lips. 'You're very kind, but I expect I shall go with my sister.'

'Ah, your sister, yes. Matilde, she mentioned her. She lives here, is that right? She works in a hotel?'

Tanya nodded.

'She has been here in Tenerife a long time?'

'Two years, yes.'

'And you have not visited before. Why is that?'

Because the man I loved married you! The words were there inside her, aching to get out, but they would never be spoken. Surprisingly Tanya found herself liking this woman, liking her as a person in her own right, hating her only because of her association with Alejandro. 'I've been too busy,' she managed, and it was in part the truth—even if it was of her own making.

'And do you like Tenerife?'

'Very much, what little I've seen of it so far.'

'You must come and visit us. My husband and I, we will be very pleased.'

Tanya's smile grew weaker. 'You're very kind, thank

you, but I'm not sure that I'll have the time. There is so much to see and do.'

To her relief Matilde spoke, successfully putting an end to the conversation, and Juanita went behind a screen to take off the dress. Tanya wanted to make her escape, but Matilde indicated that she was going to make some coffee and would like her to join them.

For the next fifteen minutes Tanya was on tenterhooks, and just as she thought she could successfully make her excuses she heard Alejandro's car outside and his firm rap on the door.

Matilde went to open it and Juanita spoke, though Tanya had no idea what she said. All she could think of was that any second now she was going to come face to face with Alejandro. At least she was forewarned— he would have no idea that the girl he had once had a passionate affair with was sitting talking to his wife. It would be interesting to see his reaction.

To give him his due, there was little more than a sudden jerking muscle in his jaw to give away his surprise, and probably neither of the others even noticed.

His shoulders were broader than Tanya remembered, his black hair slightly longer, and, although he wore an open-necked shirt and plain grey trousers, they looked designer-made, his leather shoes too. In fact everything about him screamed money. He had told her that his father was a farmer, owning huge areas of land where he grew bananas and tomatoes, and that it was his ambition to follow in his footsteps. Was this from where his wealth came?

Matilde began to make introductions, but Alejandro stopped her and presumably announced that they were already acquainted. Certainly there was surprise in the woman's eyes as she looked briefly at Tanya and back to Alejandro.

But his attention was now on Tanya, and her heart began to panic as she looked at him—as she discovered that the attraction was still there! She had never expected to feel this kind of emotion; she had been filled with hate and disillusionment for so long that she had thought all other feelings dead. It was a shock to discover that he still had some sort of power over her.

'So we meet again, Tanya.' There was no warmth in his voice, no hint of pleasure. He was aloof, distancing himself from her, which was odd, considering that at the airport he had insisted that he wanted to talk to her.

She looked into the coldness of his eyes, matching the chill with her own. 'Unfortunately, yes, and if you'll excuse me I was just about to return to my room.'

A frown appeared. 'You're staying here — with Matilde?'

'That's right,' she answered sharply, 'And so is Charlene.'

'For how long?' It was almost an accusation.

'I'm here for a month — it's my holiday. Charlene lives here permanently.'

A slight pause. 'I didn't know. Matilde's never mentioned it.'

'There's no reason why she should.' Tanya lifted her hand to remove a stray strand of hair from her face, and as she did so Alejandro's eyes went to the wedding-ring that she still wore. There was a sudden narrowing, a start of surprise, though why he should be astonished she did not know. Nine years was a long time to remain single, to hold a torch for the man she had once loved. 'Goodbye, Alejandro,' she said quietly, coolly, and with a nod to his wife and to Matilde she left the room.

To her amazement he followed. 'I think after all there is much to be said, Tanya.'

She lifted her brows. 'Really?'

His snort of anger shocked her. 'I know you no longer have any feelings for me, but —'

'But nothing,' she cut in swiftly. 'It's the whole point,

isn't it? Neither of us have any feelings; it was all over
a long time ago, so what is there to say? I'm not the
sort of person who harbours feelings about the past, at
least not when we parted on such bad terms. I'd rather
leave things as they are.'

'I'd like to know what you've been doing.'

'Really?' Her fine, well-shaped brows rose.

'You're married!' It was a statement rather than a
question, almost an accusation.

Tanya was tempted to let him go on thinking it, but
an innate sense of honesty made her say quietly, 'I
was.'

A quick frown. 'You're divorced?'

'I'm a widow,' she replied flatly.

'Oh — I'm sorry.' His face shadowed. 'You have my
condolences.'

Tanya was not sure that he meant it, and she looked
at him coldly. 'Thank you.'

'And I'd still like to talk to you.'

She shook her head firmly. 'There's no point. It
would be a complete waste of time. Goodbye,
Alejandro.'

She did not expect him to let her go, but he did,
though she was conscious of him watching her as she
moved down the narrow enclosed corridor to her room.

Not until she closed the door behind her did Tanya
realise that she was holding her breath, and now she
dragged a deep gulp of air into her tortured lungs. It
was worse than she had imagined. Over the years her
anger had faded. Peter had restored her sanity, made
her see that she couldn't dwell on the past forever. But
what she hadn't remembered was the physical attraction. None of that had faded — he still had the power
to turn her limbs to jelly whether she liked it or not.

It really would be disastrous if she saw him again.
Notwithstanding the fact that he was married and
unavailable, it would be torture; her body wouldn't be
able to cope. Not even with Peter had she reached the

heights she had scaled with Alejandro — could again if she dared let it happen. Oh, no, she must never, ever let herself be coerced into any sort of one-to-one situation.

It actually amazed her that she still felt this magnetism, this strong pull towards him. It was unreal. Everything had been killed stone-dead nine years ago — or so she had thought!

She stood at the window, and less than five minutes later saw him opening the car door for his wife, pausing a moment before he got in himself, looking back at the house, almost as though he was aware of her there behind the shutters. Tanya knew he could not see her, but instinctively stepped back, and when he had gone she gave a sigh of relief and sat down on the edge of the bed.

Later, when Charlene came home, Tanya told her all about her meeting with Alejandro. 'I could not believe it when I saw him.'

'A cruel twist of fate, I agree,' said her sister. 'And what a nerve, wanting to see you again after the way he behaved. I hope you told him where to get off.'

Tanya nodded. 'I think I made myself clear.'

'And you say the dress isn't quite ready. Do you think he'll come again?'

'Goodness, I hope not,' said Tanya. 'I'm hoping his wife will pick it up herself.'

'Perhaps she doesn't drive.'

Tanya closed her eyes. 'Whatever happens, I'm going to keep well out of his way.'

But it didn't turn out like that. A few days later Matilde's daughter-in-law went into labour, complications set in, and Matilde was off like a shot to be with her family. And the very same afternoon Alejandro arrived to pick up his wife's dress.

Tanya opened the door without even thinking that it might be him, and when their eyes met her jaw sagged. 'I'm sorry; Señora Guerra's not at home.' She looked

at him coldly, her tone distant. 'You'll have to come
back some other time; I don't know whether the dress
is ready or not.'

'Fate moves in mysterious ways.'

Her brows rose characteristically. 'You think it's fate
that's throwing us together?'

'It would seem that way.'

She let out a little cry of fury. 'It seems more like a
curse to me. I'll tell Matilde you called.'

But his foot was inside the door before she could
stop him. 'Matilde wouldn't be very pleased if she
knew you were shutting me out of her house.' His jaw
was taut, his eyes glacial.

'Matilde doesn't know the circumstances.'

'I was compelled to tell her a little; she was puzzled
as to how we knew each other.'

And your wife, she wanted to ask, did she hear your
explanation too? Has she found out that I'm the girl
you once had an affair with? The one you wrote to her
about? Not that she had ever truly believed him. Her
mouth was tight, her eyes mutinous. 'I don't care what
Matilde might think. I don't want you here; I have
nothing to say to you.'

'Were you happy in your marriage?'

The question took her by surprise, and she relaxed
her grip on the door. Instantly Alejandro pushed his
way inside. Tanya followed, leaving the door open,
feeling that at least she had an escape route should she
need it.

'You haven't answered my question.' His abrupt
tone made her look at him sharply.

'Of course I was happy. I was very much in love with
Peter.'

'More than you loved me?'

The directness of his question made her gasp. 'I
never loved you.'

His eyes narrowed. 'You gave a very good imi-
tation of it.'

'Did I?' she asked coldly. 'You must have been mistaken. As far as I was concerned all we were having was a brief affair, fun while it lasted. I always knew you'd be coming back here.' Lies, all lies. Goodness, how could she say such a thing?

'So it meant nothing to you.'

'No.' The obsidian darkness of his eyes unnerved her, and her answer came out in a husky whisper. She covered her embarrassment by turning it into a cough.

'And the moment my back was turned you found yourself another man and got married?'

He made it sound as though she had done it the very next day, but she wasn't going to deny it. 'Something like that.'

He shook his head, looking at her with an intentness that cut right through her. 'I never thought you were that kind of girl.'

And she hadn't thought he was the sort of man who would use a girl and then let her down with no compunction whatsoever. 'It looks as though we never really knew each other.'

He nodded. 'It certainly does.'

'And now we've sorted that out perhaps you'll go. You'll have to call again for the dress.'

'What's the hurry?' He smiled faintly, grimly, and sat in Matilde's rocking-chair.

Alarm bells rang in Tanya's head. 'Aren't you a busy man?'

'Not so much that I can't spare the odd hour to talk to an old — flame.'

He said the word sneeringly, and Tanya bridled. At the same time she could not help noticing how much better his command of the English language was. He had scarcely an accent now, and she wondered whether he had been back to England or whether he had English friends here. Whatever, he was certainly very good.

'Perhaps the "old flame" doesn't want to talk to you,' she returned acidly.

'You have other plans? You're going out, is that it? Sightseeing all by yourself. What a pity your sister is working while you're here on holiday. It cannot be much fun.'

His derogatory tone needled Tanya, and she looked at him hotly. 'Charlene has already taken one week off. I'm not complaining; I have several trips organised and——'

'But none for today?' he cut in swiftly. 'Why don't you sit down?'

Tanya sat, not because she wanted to, but because she needed to. The effect of seeing Alejandro, talking to him, trying to ignore the very real sensations that churned inside, was very debilitating.

'Is your sister still in the hotel trade?'

'Indeed. She's managing a hotel in Playa de las Americas; that's why she came out here. It was too good an offer to miss, the first time she's been in complete charge. She loves it.' He confused her by flitting from subject to subject, although she knew she would far rather talk about Charlene than herself.

'And she has not married? Her career is more important to her?'

'Let's say she's never found the right man,' said Tanya, and at the age of thirty her sister was becoming more and more choosy. Tanya sometimes wondered if she would ever find anyone who would put up with her bossy, dominating nature and her strong, independent streak.

'Had you found the right man in Peter?'

Tanya swallowed hard. His questions were certainly hard-hitting, and always unexpected. 'I wouldn't have married him otherwise.' She looked at him as she spoke, trying to convince him, hiding the fact that Peter had been second-best. She hadn't admitted that at the time, but it was true. Not that she hadn't been happy—she had, very much so; he was a wonderful man—but the excitement of a strong physical relationship had been missing. If she hadn't met Alejandro she would never have known what she was capable of, what she needed, what her body needed. As it was, he had spoiled her for anyone else. She gave a tiny sigh, and Alejandro's mouth tightened, and she guessed he thought she was sighing for Peter.

'I thought I was seeing a ghost when I spotted you at the airport,' he said, with another complete turn in the conversation.

'I wasn't too happy about seeing you either,' she retorted.

'I didn't say I didn't want to see you.' The frown was there, grooving his brow, narrowing his eyes. 'It had been so long, I'd given up the idea that we'd ever meet again.'

And whose fault was that? she wanted to ask. You were the one who went away without a word; you were the one who ended it all. She lifted her shoulders in a tiny careless gesture. 'It's a small world. Would you like a cup of coffee?' She had to get out of the room, away from the stifling atmosphere. She had never known it would be like this.

'No, thank you,' he answered. 'I'd much prefer to sit and talk to you.'

Tanya groaned inwardly. 'About what? What is there to say? I'm sure you're not interested in every single little detail of my life since we parted, and neither do I want to hear about yours.'

Her bitter tone caused a further tightening of his features. 'You're making it pretty plain what you think about me.'

'There's no point in pretending.'

'I really misjudged you, Tanya.' He stood up suddenly, abruptly.

Good, he was going. Tanya rose too, but somehow they bumped into each other, and the next moment she was in his arms, his mouth on hers, and the years in between might never have been.

She was conscious of nothing except a rising hunger inside her, a desire that had lain buried for so many years. Nothing had changed. It was sheer insanity, she knew, but as her mouth clung to his the rights and wrongs of the situation did not seem to matter.

And she sensed in him the same voracity, felt him trembling slightly, felt the hammer beats of his heart, the urgency of his kisses. She began to soar, to forget the empty years. This was now, this was Alejandro, this was the man she. . .

Her thoughts tailed away. She had almost said 'loved', and that wasn't right. She did not love him. She desired him, that was all. It was a fatal attraction. Knowing him had brought her nothing but unhappiness. The trouble was she could not stop these feelings that overwhelmed her.

She had never thought of herself as being highly sexed; in fact it was only this man she responded to in such a way. Even as her thoughts ran along these lines her lips parted and their tongues entwined and she felt a powerful emotion tighten the pit of her stomach. She urged her body against his and found him equally excited, and the thought struck her that if they weren't careful they would end up making love.

It was enough to bring her to her senses, but almost as though the thought had hit him at the same time Alejandro let her go, pushing her away, and when she saw the harshness on his face she reeled back.

'What the hell's this all about, Tanya?' His voice rasped into the silence of the room. 'You declare you feel nothing for me, that you never have, and yet you kiss me like a thirsty woman who's found water in the desert. I'd like an explanation.'

Tanya closed her eyes. What could she say? She was horrified, mortified, totally ashamed of herself. What had come over her? How could she have been so wanton?

His hands snapped over her shoulders, fingers hurting, bruising. 'Look at me, Tanya. I want the truth.'

There was fire in his eyes, but ice also, a dangerous brilliance that sent a quiver of fear through her limbs. But she had no intention of letting him see that he intimidated her. 'I might ask the same of you,' she said fiercely, jerking herself free. Goodness, he was a married man; didn't that mean anything to him?

'I've always found you irresistible.'

'So that's what it was all those years ago?' she snapped. 'Sheer lust! The taking of a body that was only too willing!'

A shadow crossed his eyes, as though she had touched a raw nerve, gone in an instant, the accusation back. 'And how about you? Are you as guilty of the same feelings that you accuse me of? Is that why you responded now, why you responded to me when I was in England?'

'Unfortunately, yes,' she rasped, deciding honesty was the best policy. 'But it's not something I'm proud of, and I certainly have no intention of letting it happen again.'

'We might not be able to help ourselves.'

'You speak as though we're likely to meet again. I can assure you we will not; I shall make very certain of that.'

Again that narrowing of his eyes, an intent look that pierced right through her, a muscle jerking in his jaw. He shook his head slowly. 'You've changed, Tanya.'

'Doesn't life change us all? It deals some bitter blows; it's impossible to remain the same. My values have definitely changed.'

'It's sad to be widowed so young, certainly, but you shouldn't let it affect you forever. Life has to go on; you have to enjoy yourself again.' There was a sudden, surprising softness to his tone.

Tanya was glad he had misconstrued her words; no way did she want him to think that he was the one who had hurt her when he left England so suddenly and unexpectedly. 'I intend to,' she said, 'But in my own way — and that does not involve you. I'm not interested in rekindling our affair.'

The telephone ringing cut short their conversation.

'You'd better answer it,' said Tanya. 'I can't cope with the language.'

In the event it turned out to be Charlene. Tanya heard Alejandro explaining who he was and what he was doing there, and then Charlene must have given him a piece of her mind, because his face was grim when he turned back to Tanya and handed her the receiver. 'Your sister.' And when she had finished her conversation he said tightly, 'Is this a mutual hatred society? I was told in no uncertain terms to keep clear of you. What have you said to poison her mind against me?'

'I didn't have to say anything,' replied Tanya, her chin lifting haughtily. 'My sister is naturally very protective of me.'

His brows rose. 'I can assure you you need no protection; you're more than capable of looking after yourself.'

'I agree,' she said. 'And as a person who is very much in charge of her life, I'd like to ask you to leave.'

'What if I say I'd like that coffee now?'

'I'd say you were too late; the offer's withdrawn.'

'In that case,' he said with a shrug of his wide shoulders, 'I appear to have no choice, but this won't be the last time we meet, Tanya; I can guarantee that.'

CHAPTER THREE

IN THE days that followed Tanya was on tenterhooks. She did not want to see Alejandro again, but she did not see how she could avoid him if he came to the house. Matilde still had not returned, staying to look after her new grandchild while her daughter-in-law recovered from her ordeal, although Charlene had said that Matilde was using this as an excuse. The truth was she loved babies.

Tanya could have gone out every single moment of every single day, but she did not want to feel pushed into doing something simply because of Alejandro. When she had first said she was coming out here Charlene had said she would try and get the whole month off, but Carlos, her under-manager, had gone off sick and no one else was capable of taking over, and so Tanya was left to her own devices. She could have hired a car, but decided it wouldn't be very exciting driving around by herself.

It was a pity in one way that Charlene had chosen to live so far away from the beaches and the lively tourist areas. On the other hand, she saw the real Tenerife; she could wander into the village, where the pace of life was slow, watch the men talking over their drinks outside the local bar, the children playing, the dogs scavenging. Her disadvantage was the language barrier. The children could say hello and goodbye; their parents spoke no English at all.

Charlene had taken her into Playa de las Americas and Los Cristianos, and she had seen how the concrete jungle of tourism skirted the southern shore, and had experienced for herself the frenetic pace, even though people were supposed to be on holiday. At heart,

Tanya was a country lover and wanted to explore the unspoilt parts of the island, but not on her own.

One night Charlene drove her to a restaurant in the mountains high on the west coast, close to Masca. Tanya had been looking forward to it all day, but when their route took them along a series of extremely narrow and tight hairpin bends winding through the mountain like goat tracks, she began to wonder whether it was a good idea. And upon arrival she was horrified to discover Alejandro's dark red Mercedes parked outside. She wanted to turn right round and go home.

'Not on your life,' exclaimed Charlene. 'Not after I've driven all this way. Don't worry, I'll protect you.'

'I don't need your protection,' retorted Tanya. 'I'm twenty-seven, not seven. But this place is so out of the way; I cannot believe I'm about to bump into him again.'

'It has a good reputation,' informed her sister, 'And, judging by the number of cars, it's already busy. Perhaps with a bit of luck he won't even see us.'

But luck wasn't with them. The second they walked out on to the purple and red bougainvillaea-covered terrace perched on the mountainside Tanya saw Alejandro. Her heartbeats quickened, her throat tightened, and she looked across at his companion, giving a start of surprise when she discovered that it was not his wife.

The woman had black hair, the same, but it was short and thick and cut on a level with her chin. She wore a white low-cut dress and a chunky green necklace and was beautiful in a different sort of way to Juanita. She had eyes only for her companion, her hand touching his arm across the table in a proprietorial, familiar gesture.

Tanya felt her blood begin to boil. He was two-timing his wife *again*! Although he hadn't been married when he was in England, it amounted to the same thing. What a swine, what a cheat, what a bastard! How many other women had he had affairs with? At that moment he looked up and saw her.

If looks could kill he should have dropped dead; instead he offered her a surprised smile. Tanya glared icily and turned to her sister, who had been frantically looking for an empty table. 'There don't seem to be any,' she muttered. 'We ought to have booked.'

'Then let's get out of here,' hissed Tanya. 'I've just seen Alejandro — and he's with another woman.'

'Where?' Charlene scanned the room, and at the same time Alejandro rose from his table and came over to them.

His easy smile belied the fact that he had been caught deceiving his wife. 'As there are no tables perhaps you'd care to join us.'

'Like hell we would,' hurled Tanya. 'We'll find somewhere else to eat. It would be criminal to spoil your *pleasure*.'

Her deliberate emphasis on the last word caused a swift frown of annoyance. 'You're being extremely childish, Tanya. Inocente and I would be more than pleased to have your company.'

Inocente! Tanya glanced across at the black-haired girl and thought, Who are you trying to fool? This girl in no way wanted their presence at the table; it was there in her expression, in the hostility in her eyes, and Tanya could not believe it when Charlene accepted gracefully.

'Thank you, Alejandro. I really did want Tanya to experience this place.'

He gave a pleased smile and led the way back to their corner table. 'What did you do that for?' Tanya whispered fiercely to her sister as she trailed behind. 'This is the last thing I want.'

Charlene grinned. 'I thought it would be fun to ruin his evening.'

And ruin mine too, thought Tanya, though she relaxed a mite. Charlene's evil pleasure was infectious.

Introductions were made and the dark-haired girl smiled, though it was a surface smile only. She clearly wished them a thousand miles away, and must have wondered why her companion had insisted on inviting them to their table.

Inocente's English was good, and she listened attentively while Alejandro explained how he had met Tanya and Charlene, though her eyes were sharp as she looked from one sister to the other, evidently wondering whether either of them had been his lover.

A waiter came and set their places, handing each of them a menu, enquiring whether they would like an aperitif. Charlene declined, and Alejandro offered Tanya some of their wine. It was an excellent Marqués de Cáceres red, and Tanya drank half of it straight away, needing the courage it would give her to get through the rest of the evening. Alejandro raised an eyebrow and topped up her glass.

It was not easy to concentrate on the menu; she was far too aware of Alejandro at her side. She and her sister had effectively split him and his companion up. Inocente remained opposite him, while she and Charlene were opposite each other. Tanya knew that Alejandro always liked his girlfriend to sit facing him so that he could look at her while they ate and talked, but the way it had turned out this evening Tanya wished she hadn't been forced to sit so close.

'I certainly never expected to see you two here tonight,' said Alejandro.

I bet you didn't, she wanted to scream. I bet you thought you'd be nice and safe here in this out-of-the-way place. Her eyes flashed daggers, but somehow she managed to keep her tone even. 'We seem to be meeting a lot in unexpected circumstances.'

'Indeed we do.'

His leg brushed hers as he spoke, maybe accidentally, maybe not. Tanya quickly tucked her feet beneath her chair. He was the world's worst louse, she decided, and yet, despite her adverse feelings, she could not ignore the very real triggers of sensation that chased through her. Even knowing he was deceiving his wife, she still felt an incredible awareness. She was no better than the girl sitting next to her, she concluded angrily. 'It's strange that Charlene's been here for two years and you've not met, and now I've come we seem to be bumping into each other all the time.'

'Very strange,' he admitted, and then in a voice so low neither of the others heard, 'Or kismet.'

Tanya wanted to yell at him, to ask him what the devil he thought he was doing. Casanova had nothing on him. But she did not want to cause a scene in the restaurant and so she pretended not to have heard, and when the waiter came for their order she turned to him with relief.

It was a very long, tense next few hours. Inocente kept trying to dominate Alejandro's attention, but he insisted on bringing Tanya and Charlene into the conversation, and in the end the Tinerfeño girl lapsed into sullen silence.

Charlene insisted on talking about Tanya's husband, Peter. 'They were so much in love,' she concluded.

Tanya had tried to tell her sister to shut up by flashing her messages with her eyes, but Charlene either did not see or did not want to see, and by the end of the evening tempers were beginning to get short all round—except for Charlene's; she was thoroughly enjoying the situation. She could see by the tightening of Alejandro's face that he did not want to hear about Peter, but deliberately went on stressing his and Tanya's perfect relationship.

Tanya was glad when it was all over, when they pushed back their chairs and stood up to leave, though not so happy when Alejandro insisted on settling their bill. It made her feel indebted to him, and she did not want that; she did not want to feel any obligation whatsoever.

'I wish you hadn't said anything about Peter,' she said crossly to her sister as they made their way back down the mountain. Alejandro had sped off in front of them and was already well out of sight.

Charlene grimaced cheerfully. 'It's what he deserves. I hope it put him strictly in his place; the man's dissolute. I wonder if Inocente knows he's married. I felt like telling her, except that I didn't want to cause a scene, and I'm certainly glad that it all ended between you two. Imagine if you'd married him and he carried on like this.'

Tanya had already thought of that. The person she felt sorry for was Juanita. 'I guess that was never on the cards. I was just one of many.'

There must have been something in her voice that gave her away, because Charlene looked at her sharply. 'Hey, you're not still carrying a torch for him?'

'Charlene! Keep your eyes on the road,' screeched Tanya as they veered dangerously close towards the edge. The mountainside dropped sharply away and there were no barriers.

'Whoops!' exclaimed her sister, correcting the car. 'But if you do feel something for Alejandro, then you'd better get rid of it straight away. That man is bad news without a doubt.'

'You don't have to tell me,' replied Tanya, 'I know exactly what he's like, and don't worry, I have no intention of getting involved with him again. I learned my lesson a long time ago.' She closed her eyes as Charlene negotiated another sharp bend. This wasn't her idea of fun at all. She hadn't enjoyed it coming up, but it was even more scary going down, especially when all they had to guide them was the moon and the stars. Charlene seemed to have no qualms, but as far as she was concerned it was distinctly perilous.

They lapsed into silence, and she could not get

Alejandro out of her mind. She kept thinking of him with Inocente while his wife sat unsuspectingly at home. There was no doubt that he was having an affair with the girl; it was there in the way she looked at him, the way he spoke to her, the way they had walked out to his car with their arms around each other. Tanya felt quite sick at the thought.

When they got back home she feigned tiredness and went straight to her room. It had been bad enough discovering that she had meant nothing to Alejandro all those years ago, but to find out that he was still two-timing Juanita was devastating in the extreme. She had never thought in those early days that Alejandro was a womaniser. It was hard to believe that he had set out on this treacherous path of deceit at the early age of twenty-three. The saying that a leopard never changed its spots was certainly true where he was concerned. She wondered how many other girls there had been.

The next day Matilde came home and Alejandro turned up to collect the dress. This time Tanya had been half expecting him, knowing that he would want to make some sort of excuse for the night before.

She was outside when he came, sitting on a chair in the tiny square of back garden, soaking up the sunshine, Matilde's tan and white dog keeping her company, although he lay in the shade of the wall. She was out of sight of the front door, and although she had heard Alejandro's car had thought herself relatively safe. Until she heard him call her name.

Ought she to pretend not to hear? Her stomach muscles clenched involuntarily, pulses jerked, and she knew there was no way she could ignore him. Like him or hate him, it was all the same; the animal magnetism was there — getting stronger by the day!

Slowly she turned her head. 'Señora Guerra's in the house.' Her tone was hard, belying her tumultuous feelings.

'I'd like a word with you first.' He pushed open the
gate and strode the few feet to her side.

'If it's about last night I don't want to hear.' There
was irritation in her tone, and her sloe-shaped blue
eyes were cold and distant. 'You'll never change, will
you, Alejandro?' He loomed over her, tall and somehow threatening, putting her at a distinct disadvantage.
She jumped to her feet and faced him.

He frowned. 'What are you talking about?'

'Don't come the innocent with me,' she cried. 'How
many other women have there been?'

'Other women?'

'Yes, affairs on the side. It's a good job you didn't
bring your wife along today or I might have been
tempted to tell her.' Fury added strength to her words,
and she was speaking much more loudly than she
intended. Matilde popped her head out of the door,
frowned in their direction, and disappeared again.

Tanya was so uptight that she missed the shadow
that crossed Alejandro's face, saw only the tightening
of his jaw, the suppression of his anger. 'My words
have struck home, have they?'

'You don't know what you're talking about, Tanya.'
His normally generous lips were clamped thinly, his
dark eyes as hard as polished jet.

'Don't I?' She lifted her fine brows and eyed him
coldly. 'How can I not know when you flaunt your
girlfriends under everyone's nose?'

'You're talking about Inocente?'

'That's right.'

'And Beatriz, I presume?'

Tanya frowned. 'Beatriz? Who's she?'

'You seem to think that she's my girlfriend too,' he
rasped coldly. 'Can you tell me what gave you that
idea?'

'If you're talking about the woman whose dress
Matilde's making, I didn't think she was your girlfriend,' snapped Tanya. 'I thought she was your wife,

but if she isn't then you're simply confirming my already rock-bottom opinion of you.'

He looked at her sharply, questioningly. 'You'd heard I was married?'

'Yes, I had.' Tanya's tone was bitter. 'And I think what you're doing to her is diabolical. You want stringing up.'

'When did you hear? How did you hear?' He seemed not to notice her harsh words.

'Is it important?' she snapped.

'I'd like to know.' His eyes were narrowed on hers, his expression unreadable.

Tanya lifted her shoulders in a careless gesture. 'Someone Charlene met in the hotel told her. He came from Tenerife, knew you, apparently.'

'Was this before or after you'd married Peter?'

Suddenly she could see the way his mind was working. 'Heavens,' she cried sharply, 'I didn't marry him on the rebound, if that's what you're thinking. I didn't marry him because I'd heard you'd got married; it was a long time afterwards. And as Charlene said last night, we were extremely happy together. I would never have dreamt of seeing another man behind his back.'

She was so indignant that she was out of breath, her chest heaving as she looked at him belligerently and coldly, her fingers curled into her palms so tightly that her nails dug in and hurt, but she did nothing about it; in fact she welcomed the pain.

His eyes glittered with a cold light that Tanya had never seen before; his nostrils dilated. 'After all we had going for us, Tanya, I would never have believed that you could think so harshly of me.'

'All we had going for us?' she echoed loudly. 'We had nothing. It was a brief, glorious fling that was over the moment you left England.' And she was lying again! But what the hell — she refused to succumb to the indignity of confessing that she had spent hours and hours crying, pining, longing, wondering.

'You forgot me so instantly?'

His expression was so incredulous that she almost
laughed. 'Indeed I did. What did you expect? It was
fun while it lasted, I admit, but once you were out of
sight, Alejandro, you were out of mind. And why am I
telling you all this when it's your wife who's the person
I feel sorry for? You really are a swine, aren't you?
What do you tell her — that it's business keeping you
away from home? Or have you some other fancy
excuses?'

Alejandro looked at her long and hard. 'I hardly feel
you deserve the truth.'

'Truth?' Tanya's brows slid up. 'You mean a pack of
lies? Some way of attempting to absolve yourself? I
don't think I want to hear it.' He had lied by omission
nine years ago, proving he wasn't a man of integrity.
Why should she believe anything he tried to tell her
now? And lord, she wished he would move. Her
hostility was mixed with an awareness that was proving
a very real threat to her sanity.

'In that case there is nothing else I have to say.' He
turned abruptly and marched towards the house, and
perversely Tanya wished she hadn't been so sharp. It
would have been interesting to hear what sort of an
excuse he came up with. It was too late now, though.
Matilde had appeared in the doorway and was beaming
a smile of welcome. He was obviously a great favourite
of hers.

Tanya sat down again and closed her eyes. She
looked completely relaxed, as though she hadn't a care
in the world, no hint on her face of her rioting body
and mind. Not only was she battling with a desire to
know what he had been going to say, but she was
struggling with feelings that set her on fire, feelings she
had thought long since dead. Why, when she knew
only too well how immoral he was, did she respond
like this? What was there about him that drew her like
a moth to a flame?

He had said that it was kismet that drew them together and she had scorned the idea, but was there something in it? Why, after all these years apart, had they met again like this? Each occasion had been accidental — at the airport, the first time he came here, last night. Was there truly some hidden force behind it? Was it their destiny?

He obviously wasn't happy with his wife or he wouldn't be seeking the company of other women. On the other hand, he hadn't exactly been true to her before their marriage. He was a philanderer, a Don Juan, a man to be avoided at all costs. How many hearts he had broken she hated to think. Hers had been shattered. It had taken years to find the pieces and put it back together, and she was darn sure she wasn't going to risk it being damaged again.

It seemed an age that he remained indoors with the older woman. Tanya wondered whether he would come and speak to her once more or whether he would leave by the front door and that would be an end to it. She hoped for the latter, and since the costume was ready he would have no excuse for calling again.

She heard them talking, Matilde sounding excited, Alejandro's deep voice amused, and they were coming towards her. Tanya knew she could not pretend to be asleep, so she opened her eyes as they drew near.

Alejandro looked down at her. 'I've just given Matilde her usual invitation to our annual masked ball — well, maybe "ball" is too grand a word, it's a party really; everyone has them around *carnaval* time — and she thought it would be nice if you and your sister came too.'

Tanya's heartbeats grew heavy and rapid, her eyes widened, and she looked quickly from one to the other. Matilde was nodding and smiling, and Tanya could see that she genuinely wanted them to accompany her. Alejandro had no expression at all on his face.

'It's not really up to Matilde, is it?' she asked a trifle sharply.

Alejandro gave a wry smile. 'In that case, the invitation comes directly from me. Would you and Charlene do me the pleasure of attending?'

Tanya wanted to say no, definitely not, but she did not want to offend Matilde, who obviously thought it a brilliant idea. Besides, it would give her the opportunity to find out where Alejandro lived—she was curious about that—and what sort of a lifestyle he had, and—more interestingly—whether he had invited any other ex- or current girlfriends. 'I'll have to ask Charlene first,' she countered.

'Naturally, but I'm sure she won't refuse.'

'She might be working. When is it?'

'On Saturday—and I'm sure she'll be able to re-arrange her schedule if necessary.'

'Maybe,' Tanya said with a shrug.

'I think Matilde would welcome you accompanying her.'

'Do you always invite her?'

'Of course; my family have known her for many years.'

'Does she usually accept?'

He grimaced. 'Not always, which is a pity. It is one way we can repay her for all the long hours she puts in for us during the year. She not only makes costumes for our family for the *carnaval*, but she does all our dressmaking, and any necessary repairs and alterations. She is a—what do you say—a gem. One in a million.'

He was making it very hard for them to refuse, and probably knew it, because there was a confident smile on his lips.

'I'll still have to ask Charlene,' she said.

'As far as I'm concerned, her acceptance is a fore-gone conclusion. I'll expect you about eight-thirty. And don't forget to wear your mask—it's part of the fun.'

He kissed Matilde warmly on the cheek and made

his way back out of the gate. The tiny woman looked after him with admiration. '*Maravilloso, maravilloso*,' she said, but Tanya was wondering what he meant by 'fun'.

Charlene, as she might have known, was all for the idea; she enjoyed partying, though she did have one reservation. 'Whatever you do, steer clear of Alejandro—I don't want you getting upset all over again.'

'I don't need the warning,' replied Tanya, while privately thinking it might not be so easy. She somehow could not see herself being allowed to go through the whole evening without his seeking her out, and if she had to dance with him, if their bodies were pressed close together for any length of time, it would create total havoc with her senses.

They had three days to decide what to wear, for Matilde to make their masks, and for Tanya to worry herself sick about seeing Alejandro again. On the second day she accompanied Charlene into Playa de las Americas and spent her time looking round the shops for a suitable dress.

She was not sure what would be acceptable, but in the end chose an azure voile dress that complemented the colour of her eyes. The full, layered skirt felt pretty and feminine and the sleeveless, fitted top was held up by shoelace-thin straps. It was perfect for a party and she could wear it at other times as well, which did not make it feel such an extravagance.

The day of the party dawned, and apprehension tightened Tanya's nerves. Charlene came home from work early and Matilde ordered a taxi so that they would not have to worry about drinking and driving.

Alejandro's house was much further away than Tanya expected, on the outskirts of La Orotava in the north, and the winding mountain road took them through the beautiful, lush Orotava valley. In the taxi's headlamps Tanya could see that it was moist and fertile with trees and bushes lining the road. 'You must bring me here in the daytime,' she said impulsively to her sister. 'What an island of contrasts this is.'

Tanya did not know what she had expected Alejandro's house to look like — certainly not unfinished like Matilde's, but neither had she expected it to be this magnificent. She had vaguely imagined a large new house; instead it was a cream-painted mansion, hundreds of years old. She was extremely impressed, and more so when they walked through a wrought-iron gate into an inner tiled courtyard where a fountain played and people mingled. It was extraordinary.

He was certainly far wealthier than she had imagined, She stood there looking around her, completely awed. On each of the four sides were intricately carved wooden balconies, two tiers of them, and people were walking or talking, or looking down, and fairy-lights were strung along the length of them and between the shiny monster plants that grew in rich profusion in corners of the patio, different types of palms and ferns reaching for the sky, plants Tanya did not know the name of. It was like another world. And everyone wore masks and beautiful clothes, the women looking like brilliant butterflies, their dark-suited male counterparts a perfect foil.

On one section of the balcony a three-piece band played, softly, evocatively, although Tanya had no doubt that the volume would be turned up later on in the evening. She looked around her for Alejandro but could not see him. She had thought, mask or no, he would be instantly recognisable, but there were other tall, broad-shouldered males, and he could have been any one of them.

It was actually an exciting thought that she could stand next to him, brush by him, and not know it was him. On the other hand, he would not recognise her either, and it gave her a feeling of security. She was safe here; she could enjoy herself. She turned to speak to her sister, but Charlene had already disappeared into the crowd, Matilde too, and she was alone here in this gathering of happy people.

She looked for Inocente and Beatriz, wondered which of the women there was Alejandro's wife, and when a pretty girl came by with a tray of drinks Tanya took one and discovered it was champagne. Her nose wrinkled. Champagne held bittersweet memories. The very first time she had tasted it was on the day she had met Alejandro at her friend's wedding reception, and ever since it had brought back memories of that moment when their eyes met and she had known he was someone special.

'You shouldn't be standing alone.'

A deep voice in her ear startled her, and for a moment she thought it was Alejandro. Her heart began to patter, but when he spoke again she wondered how she could have been so wrong.

'I'm all right; I'm enjoying it. How did you know I was English?' He looked nothing like Alejandro really; his mouth was much thinner, his nose narrower.

'I didn't; it was a guess. Are you here alone?'

'I'm with my sister and my landlady actually, but they seem to have disappeared.'

'Are you a friend of Alejandro's?'

Tanya grimaced. 'I suppose you could say that. I knew him a long time ago in England. It's some house he has here.'

'It's been in his family for generations.'

'Oh?' Tanya had thought he and Juanita had bought it when they got married, that he had moved out of the family home. She wondered whether his brothers and sisters still lived here—or whether they were married too now and had moved out. There was a lot she did not know.

'Alejandro took over when his father died. You've not been here before?'

'No, I haven't. I'm here on holiday as a matter of

fact. I bumped into Alejandro accidentally, and he invited us to his party.'

'It's something that shouldn't be missed. Would you care to dance?'

Tanya looked around the crowded courtyard, saw other couples attempting it and failing because of the sheer number of people standing around, and shook her head. 'I don't think it's possible. Maybe later?'

'Can I show you my cousin's house, then?'

'Alejandro is your cousin?' Tanya felt a sharp shock of disbelief.

'Indeed he is; our fathers were brothers. May I introduce myself? Juan Vázquez Rodriquez.'

Tanya frowned. 'Vázquez *Rodriguez*? Alejandro is Vázquez Herrera. If your fathers are brothers you would surely have the same surname?' Was this man lying to her? Was he in fact no relation at all? Was he trying to make her feel safe when his intentions were perhaps strictly dishonourable?

'It can be confusing, I agree,' he said with a smile. 'We always have two surnames; didn't Alejandro tell you that? The first one our father's, the second our mother's — hence the difference. And you, my English rose, what is your name?'

'Tanya. Tanya Elliott.'

'A beautiful name for a beautiful girl.'

Unconsciously he had repeated Alejandro's own words, and Tanya wondered if all these Canario men were so profuse with their compliments.

At that moment Charlene came bustling up. 'There you are, Tanya; I wondered where you'd got to.' The older girl wore a brilliant red dress that offset her colouring beautifully. She had tucked a red hibiscus flower into her hair, and her delicate red mask was edged with glittering red sequins. She looked very exotic.

'Is this your sister?' Juan looked at the taller girl admiringly.

Tanya nodded. 'Yes, this is Charlene. Charlene, Alejandro's cousin, Juan.'

'Alejandro's cousin?'

Tanya knew that her sister's brows would be raised enquiringly, her eyes questioning. It was amazing how much of a person's expression these masks hid.

'Indeed I am,' Juan answered immediately. 'I was just about to show Tanya around the house. It would be my pleasure if you would accompany us as well.'

'Why don't you take Charlene while I stand around here a while longer?' suggested Tanya. The truth was she was scared of running into Alejandro. She wanted to stay here in the relative anonymity of a crowd. And she had seen Juan's sudden interest in her sister.

Charlene smiled, the suggestion pleasing her too. 'An excellent idea, Come along, Juan.' And she took hold of his arm.

Tanya gave a tiny inward smile. Charlene could be very dominant; Juan might not like it. On the other hand, she might be his type of girl. Who could tell?

She stood alone, thinking, dreaming, and through the murmur of voices all around her, the clink of glasses, the subtle blend of perfumes, Tanya could feel Alejandro's presence. It was as though he stood at her side, touching her, caressing her, and her skin shivered and she moved, but the feeling remained. He was there, somewhere, watching her. He had recognised her despite the blue mask with its painted-on eyes and beads and tiny feathers which obscured the whole of her face except her mouth.

She finished her champagne and took another glass off a passing girl and tried to bury herself deeper in the crowd. It was all in her mind, of course; he could not possibly identify her, could he?

Matilde approached and Tanya gave her a relieved smile. Matilde, in her black dress and gold mask, was nevertheless instantly recognisable because she was so tiny and her hair was still taken back in its relentless bun. Tanya wondered whether she ought to have fixed her own hair differently. Would it be a give-away? Ought she to have swept it up and dressed it with combs and jewels?

I'm becoming paranoid, she thought; I must stop this at once and begin to enjoy myself. She caught sight of Charlene up on the top balcony, Juan attentive at her side. Her sister was definitely enjoying herself — and she ought to be doing the same!

When a young man asked her to dance Tanya immediately accepted, and after that she was in constant demand. Most of them spoke only a few words of English, but it did not matter, and when one of them took her inside to a table groaning under the weight of carefully prepared food she discovered that she was actually enjoying herslf, that for the last hour she had forgotten Alejandro and was now completely relaxed.

The choice was staggering: smoked eel, deep-fried squid, snails, oysters, baby octopus — lots and lots of fish dishes — chicken breasts, chicken legs, hams and venison, various goats' cheeses — ewe's milk cheese, cream cheese, hard cheese — crusty bread, fruit, stuffed olives, asparagus tips, melon, an assortment of salads, paella, omelettes — and much, much more!

And afterwards it was back to the dancing. Tanya was whirled from partner to partner and she was laughing and happy — until she felt arms much stronger than the rest pull her against a body much harder than the rest. 'I think I've waited long enough,' came the deep-throated words.

CHAPTER FOUR

TANYA saw the glitter of brown eyes behind the black mask. She must have looked at Alejandro a dozen times tonight and not recognised him — yet he had known that she was the girl in the vibrant blue dress, the dancing butterfly whose feet had hardly touched the ground. 'How did you know it was me?' she asked huskily, her heart throbbing, suddenly, painfully, her throat aching and tightening.

'I saw you arrive,' he said simply.

'You've known for three hours and done nothing about it?' He had been watching her all this time?

'Did you want to dance with me?' came the curt question. Tanya shook her head firmly.

'I thought not, but I could not let the whole evening go by without at least one dance. You look ravishing, Tanya; has anyone told you that yet?'

'Everyone,' she announced airily.

His bark of laughter was surprising. 'Then they all have good taste, but don't forget I was the first to know you.'

'This is a splendid party,' she said in an attempt to move the conversation away from themselves.

'I'm glad you're enjoying it.'

'You have a wonderful house,'

'Have you seen around it yet?'

Tanya shook her head. 'Your cousin, Juan, offered to show me, but he took Charlene instead.'

'Yes, I've seen them together.'

He seemed to know who everyone was, despite their masks, and he looked exciting in his white dinner-jacket. In fact he was the only one in white; all the other men wore more traditional black.

'If you'd like to see it, I'll show you.'

'No, thanks,' she replied quickly. 'I'm enjoying your party, but I don't want to intrude into your—private life.'

'You think my—wife would have something to say about it?'

'If it was me I wouldn't be very happy if you took other girls all over the house,' she replied tartly. She tried to put a little space between them, but his arms were like bands of iron.

'Into the bedroom, you're thinking?'

Tanya lifted her shoulders. 'Not exactly, but I've no doubt it was in your mind.' Throb, throb, went her heart, and she hoped to goodness that Alejandro could not feel it against him.

'You have a very low opinion of me.'

'With just cause, wouldn't you think?' she asked, her tone deliberately cold. 'Which one is your wife?' She looked at the other dancers, as she had all evening, trying to guess which one was Juanita.

'Let's get out of this crowd,' he said abruptly, and, taking her wrist, he led her up a set of stairs to the first balcony. There he found a corner hidden by the palms creeping their way skyward.

Tanya felt her heart panicking and wondered at his sudden decision to get her alone — and alone they were! Although she could hear countless voices, the beat of insistent music, the peal of laughter, they were as alone as if they were locked in a room. Everyone was too busy having a good time to take any notice of them in this empty corner.

Breathless at the speed with which he had brought her here, Tanya leaned back against the wall. 'What's this all about?' Still her tone was distant; she did not want to give away by the slightest breath that she was drawn magnetically to him, that none of the feelings she had experienced all those years ago had faded.

'Your constant references to my wife.' There was a hardness in his tone too, and Tanya wondered.

'It hurts you, does it, that you've been caught out?' she asked scornfully. 'Or does everyone else know about your extra-marital affairs and out of loyalty say nothing?'

Alejandro's mouth tightened. 'There are no extra-marital affairs, Tanya. Juanita died six years ago.'

Tanya felt as though she had been delivered a body-blow. Her hands went to her mouth, and she was glad he could not see the swift, embarrassed colour suffusing her cheeks. This was the last thing she had expected. 'Oh, Alejandro, I'm sorry, so sorry; why didn't you——'

'Tell you?' he cut in harshly. 'Why, when you were so busy condemning me, so eager to think the worst?'

'Can you blame me?' she asked, busy doing some mental calculations. Six years ago, was about the time she had married Peter. She winced at the irony of it.

'You should have known I'm not the type to play around behind my wife's back.'

'That's rich,' she cried. 'What were you doing with me?'

'I wasn't married then.'

'No, but Juanita was at home waiting for you. I'm sorry that she died, but I still think you're an out-and-out swine. I've seen you with two different girls already, one of them married! I stupidly thought Beatriz was talking about you when she mentioned her husband. It's beyond belief the way you behave — and if I said I'd come out with you you'd probably have no qualms about that either. The way I see things, you've always enjoyed playing the field.'

Just below the edge of his mask she saw the spasmodic jerk of a muscle, his eyes glittering through the narrow slits in the plain black velvet — not for him the glitter of sequins — and she was glad she had angered him. He deserved it. He tried to give the image of

being an upper-class gentleman, but hell, he was
nothing of the sort! He used people for his own
perverse pleasure. God, she hated him.

'You jump to rash conclusions, Tanya. I ——'

'I'm not going to listen to any excuses,' she flared. 'I
know what I've seen and I don't like it, and when I get
back home to England I shall push all thoughts of you
out of my mind—forever.' Her chest heaved and her
eyes were as bright as his.

'You think that will be possible?' he asked, a much
quieter edge to his tone, a stillness about him that was
somehow threatening.

'I haven't thought about you for years; why should I
suddenly start thinking about you now?' she asked,
unaware of the desperation in her tone.

'Because of this.' And before she could stop him,
before she could even hazard a guess at his intentions,
he had enfolded her into the circle of his arms and
lowered his head until their two mouths met.

The last time it had happened, in Matilde's house,
Tanya had been unprepared and let herself respond
unthinkingly. Now she knew such a reaction would be
fatal, and although it took every ounce of will-power
and then some she managed to hold herself rigid. She
told herself the touch of his lips meant nothing, that
the racing of her heart meant nothing, that this man
meant nothing.

But Alejandro was not so easily put off. Instead of
letting her go, pushing her away in disgust, or even
making bruising demands, he slipped off her mask and
his mouth gentled, playing on hers expertly, sensually,
feather-light kisses on her cheeks, her eyes, her ears,
creating sensations, drawing out responses, slowly,
reluctantly, until finally she felt herself drowning and
could hold back no longer.

It was all and everything she remembered, sweet,
sweet agony, a drawing-out of her soul, every inch of
her sensitised, responsive, needing, hungering. Oh,

lord, why? *Why*! Against her own better judgement she pressed her body to his, felt his own pulsing need of her. Her lips parted, his tongue explored, she groaned, he groaned, neither spoke. It was a moment of intense physical pleasure.

When she unconsciously moved against him his arms tightened, his kiss deepened, and sheer animal hunger drove them both into a frenzy of kissing and touching and feeling and exciting. Tanya had forgotten how high he made her climb; the highest peak was not impossible where this man was concerned.

He slid the thin straps off her shoulders, exposing her firm, naked, aching breasts, stroking with electric fingertips, brushing a firm thumb over sensitised nipples. Aching, longing, washed over her. Desire spread like wildfire, her fingers threading through the wiry thickness of his hair, her mouth still pressed to his, drinking from him, taking all he offered. It was bliss, sheer, sweet heaven.

The party went on around them but neither was aware of it, and when his mouth left hers to burn a trail down the arch of her throat, to move with tantalising slowness to the aching curve of her breasts, and finally to take the throbbing heart of them, to taste and nip and suck thrusting nipples into his mouth, she did nothing to stop him. She was being lifted out of herself, transported to a place where physical pleasure knew no bounds.

And that was all it was — physical — she knew, and yet she could not stop him. It was a mutual hungering of like souls; it was the sweetest torture imaginable, setting her body on fire, pulses pounding, desire coursing through each and every one of her veins.

When he raised his head to look at her his mouth was soft and wet. At some time his mask had come off too and his eyes were glazed with desire. '*Mi cariño*, he muttered thickly, '*mi cariño*. Nothing has changed. Everything is as it always was between us.'

Tanya agreed. Nothing *had* changed on a physical level. In this respect they were still compatible, still able to arouse the utmost desire in each other's bodies. It was a marvel that her hatred hadn't killed it all stone-dead, but somehow it had survived, and at this moment in time she did not want to let him go.

His mouth met hers again and she clung to him, responding with a passion that had lain dormant for too long, her lips moving over his, her tongue touching and tasting and probing. Her groin ached and she gyrated against him, needing him, wanting him, desperately, *now*! Common sense had long since flown; this man had enticed her, drugged her, made her his in every sense of the word.

'Alejandro.' She breathed his name unconsciously. 'Oh, Alejandro. . .' And her kisses deepened and her body pressed even harder into his.

He gave a groan of anguish. 'Not here, not now, *amor mio*, I see my cousin approaching, but later, yes, later we will satisfy this hunger of ours.' Deftly he straightened her dress and they both pulled on their masks. Tanya was glad of something to hide her tumultuous feelings, and when her sister and Juan drew near there was nothing in their attitude to suggest that seconds earlier they had been in a passionate embrace.

'I've been looking all over for you,' complained Charlene, glancing swiftly from one to the other. 'What are you doing here?'

'Talking about old times,' Alejandro answered, and Tanya was surprised to hear that his tone was perfectly normal. She had been afraid to speak in case she gave herself away.

'It's almost midnight,' said Juan, his arm possessively about Charlene's waist. 'Isn't that when we all unmask?'

Alejandro inclined his head. 'Usually, although I've half a mind to dispense with that this evening, let everyone go home without knowing with whom they've been dancing.'

'*Maldito sea*, Alejandro, you cannot do that,' his cousin declared tersely. 'I've had this lovely woman in my arms all evening and haven't once seen her face.'

'You expect me to believe that?' asked Alejandro with a knowing smile. 'Don't think I didn't see you disappearing into one of the bedrooms.'

'But only to show her around,' Juan defended.

Charlene nodded her agreement. 'He's been a perfect gentleman.'

'Then you're lucky,' Alejandro quipped. 'It's certainly not like the Juan I know.'

Or the Alejandro she knew, thought Tanya. He hadn't even needed the protection of four walls and a door. Anyone could have walked up and seen them. She felt suddenly mortified. How could she have let herself get so carried away?

She was glad of the few minutes' respite, and when her sister and Juan began walking away she followed. Alejandro, however, had other ideas. His hand tightened around her wrist. 'Are you forgetting we have unfinished business?' The thickness was back in his voice.

Tanya shook her head, her eyes defensive. 'I got carried away; it was a mistake, and letting you make love to me would be an even worse one.'

Nostrils flared beneath the black mask. 'You cannot deny the chemistry between us.'

'I can't deny it,' she agreed, 'But I can fight it.'

'But why, when it gives us so much pleasure?'

'Because there's more to life than lust,' she slammed back, 'and that's all it is, all it has ever been. If you must know, I'm deeply ashamed. Just keep away from me, Alejandro. I don't want you, or your body, or any part of you.' She turned and raced after her sister, but Charlene was already out of sight.

Tanya could not find her way back. The stairs

seemed to have disappeared. She tried a couple of
doors, but they were locked; when she finally found
one open she tumbled inside—only to discover that it
was Alejandro's bedroom. At least she assumed it was
his. It was a male room anyway, with heavy dark
furniture and strong browns and greens in the décor.
An open adjoining door revealed a stark white bathroom and the unmistakable odour of Alejandro's
aftershave.

She had paused too long. Alejandro joined her, a
smile of satisfaction curving his lips. 'I'm glad to see
you've changed your mind.'

He knew she hadn't, he knew it was accidental her
being here, but nevertheless he intended to take full
advantage of the situation. At least that was Tanya's
interpretation, and she glared at him angrily. 'I would
never do anything so foolish. I'm trying to find my way
downstairs.'

'There's no rush,' he answered quietly, his hands on
her shoulders as he came up behind her.

Tanya tensed but did not move. She wanted to prove
to him that he could touch her without her melting in
his arms—or was it herself she wanted to convince?
Whatever, it was something she had to do.

He brushed away her hair from the back of her neck
and nuzzled her nape with his mouth, triggering off an
instant response. Tanya clenched her teeth and tried to
ignore the sensations surging through her, but when his
hands slid over her shoulders and down her arms, when
he turned her gently to face him, every good intention
faded.

He disposed of both their masks, his eyes never
leaving hers, and when he cupped her face between
firm brown hands her lips parted willingly for his kiss.
She was a weak-minded fool, and knew it, and yet
could do nothing about it. He had some fatal hold over
her; it was as though he had at some time hypnotised

her and whenever he gave the signal she was his to do with as he liked.

What would have happened had someone else not made the same mistake and come tripping into his room Tanya did not know, but she took the opportunity to make her escape, following the couple out to an inner landing and down the stairs to the courtyard below.

Relief made her limbs begin to tremble, and she was leaning against one of the wooden columns that supported the balconies, listening to the drum of her heartbeats, when Alejandro caught up with her yet again. But before he could retort a dainty hand touched his arm. 'Is that you, Alejandro? I've been looking for you all night.'

Tanya recognised Inocente the moment she spoke. The girl was wearing a silver lamé figure-hugging dress which flared out just below the knee. It was dramatic and sexy and her mask was silver too, her only touch of colour the blood-red of her lipstick and the matching polish on her nails.

Alejandro turned to the girl and smiled, easily, warmly, and draped his arm casually over her shoulders, 'You're not supposed to recognise me.'

'But I'm lonely; I want you. You haven't danced with me all evening.'

'You've not been short of partners.'

So he had recognised her as well, thought Tanya.

'No, but — they're not *you*.' There was a petulant pout to the girl's lips. 'Please dance with me now.'

She tugged him away, and Tanya told herself she was relieved, yet her body still ached for him. It was sheer contrariness, and she was intensely angry with herself for allowing these base feelings to take precedence, and made a silent vow never to let it happen again.

She looked at him now, dancing with Inocente, their bodies swaying together to the seductive music, the girl's head resting against Alejandro's shoulder, his arms about her, looking for all the world like two contented lovers.

From somewhere a clock struck midnight. Everyone stopped dancing, and Alejandro stepped into the middle of the floor by the fountain. Tanya had no idea what he was saying, but everyone listened attentively, and all of a sudden masks were taken off and there were oohs and aahs and looks of surprise.

Tanya caught sight of Charlene and Juan. He was looking at her sister in undisguised admiration, and he too was more handsome than Tanya had imagined. She hoped, for Charlene's sake, that he turned out to be a better catch than his cousin.

She looked for Alejandro, saw him once again with Inocente, the girl's eyes shining, happy now that she was in the arms of the man she loved. And over there was Beatriz with her husband; at least Tanya assumed it was her husband. Alejandro stopped and said a few words to them before carrying on with Inocente around the stone-paved floor.

He was so cool about it all, thought Tanya, flaunting one girl in front of another, heedless of hurt feelings, intent only on having a good time. She looked around for Matilde and Charlene. It was time to go; she had had enough. But her sister had disappeared and Matilde was huddled in a corner, talking to another couple, looking as though she would be there for some time.

At that moment she was asked if she would like to dance, and for the next hour she was swung from partner to partner, laughing and flirting, putting it on even more when she saw Alejandro watching. It was a convincing act, yet in truth she was as miserable as sin and wished she had stuck to her guns and not let herself be persuaded to come here.

All she had found out, apart from the fact that he was a widower, was that Alejandro was as lustful as ever and she — to her disgust — still responded to him. She was as bad as him in fact — except that she did not go around having affairs with several people at the same time. Since Peter there had been no one, at least no one of count. The odd date, yes, but nothing more than that.

It seemed like forever before Charlene and Matilde sought her out and said it was time they left. The crowd was thinning, several others having already gone, and Tanya would have liked it if they could have hopped into their taxi without seeing Alejandro again.

Of course that was impossible, and would have been extremely rude. In fact he approached them when he saw them all together. 'Not leaving already?'

'It's after two,' said Charlene. 'Matilde's almost dead on her feet, But it's been a wonderful party; thank you very much for inviting us.'

Wonderful because she had met Juan, thought Tanya. Matilde too was giving him her thanks, and finally he turned to her, taking both her hands in his. 'And thank you, too, Tanya, for coming.'

'It's been quite an experience,' she said with a faint smile. 'You certainly know how to do things in a big way.'

'The *carnaval* is the highlight of our year; everyone celebrates, and you certainly mustn't miss the grand parade. In fact you mustn't miss any of it. Next week the various dancing groups will be judged, and of course the *reina del carnaval*, the carnival queen, will be picked. I'm actually an honoured member of the jury this year. I'd like you to come and watch — the costumes they wear are out of this world. It's televised, of course, but it's much better to be present and feel the atmosphere.'

Tanya shook her head. 'I don't think so.'

'It's a woman's prerogative to change her mind.'

'You're asking too much.'

'It's for old times' sake.'

'Old times mean nothing to me,' she insisted.

His lips tightened in sudden anger. 'The choice is yours. I'll be in touch.'

CHAPTER FIVE

No ONE got up early on Sunday, not even Matilde, who was always an early riser. In fact Tanya was the first to get out of her bed, and only then because she'd had a restless night and could not stop thinking about Alejandro. In fact the longer she lay there, the more tormented her thoughts became.

She needed to be up and doing something, although there was very little to do in someone else's house when you were on holiday. She made herself a cup of coffee and took it outside, fussed Matilde's dog, refilled his bowl with water, and marvelled at yet another day with clear blue skies.

Charlene had suggested they go for a ride to Icod today to look at the three-thousand-year-old dragon tree and then on to Puerto de la Cruz. 'Puerto is much more sophisticated than Americas,' Charlene had told her, 'and although it has no beach as such it has a wonderful lido with a series of eight swimming-pools as well as a huge artificial lake.'

Tanya had agreed it sounded fascinating.

'And on an island in the middle of the lake is a subterranean nightclub,' Charlene had continued enthusiastically, 'All designed by César Manrique, Lanzarote's celebrated artist and architect. Everything he designs is made to look as natural as possible; the man's a genius.'

But when Charlene finally got up she announced that Juan was picking her up instead. 'I don't know why I forgot our plans,' she said apologetically. 'It must have been the drink — all that champagne, and I had a few gin and tonics as well. I don't know what I was thinking of, arranging to go out with him when you're here on holiday. Come with us; I'm sure he won't mind.'

But Tanya had no intention of playing gooseberry. She was glad Charlene had found herself a male friend, but she did wish her sister had thought more about her. In another two weeks she would be gone and Charlene could spend as much time as she liked with Juan Vázquez Rodriguez.

As it turned out Juan did not come alone; he brought with him his brother, Manuel. 'I could not let you sit here all day by yourself,' he said to Tanya as he introduced them, and the day turned out much better than she expected. Manuel was friendly and attentive, though younger than Tanya. He was a lot of fun and seemed attracted to her, even though she made it clear she was not looking for romance.

When he suggested taking her out the next day, saying it was his day off from work, she instantly accepted. A diversion like this was just what she needed to take her mind off Alejandro.

Much to Tanya's surprise he arrived on a motorbike, and her day turned out to be a hair-raising ride all around the island. It was fun, if a bit frantic at times, and she saw far more than she would have done had she waited for Charlene to take her. In fact she thoroughly enjoyed herself.

'Can I see you again?' he asked eagerly, when he finally dropped her off.

Tanya nodded. 'So long as you realise it's all just fun.' She had an idea this young man was getting serious about her. 'I don't wish to become involved.'

'There is someone else?' he asked with a frown. 'Juan said you were — what was the expression he used? Footloose and fancy-free. I am not sure what that means, but — '

'It means there is no man in my life at the moment,' Tanya informed him, 'and I want it to remain that way.'

'But why?'

'Losing my husband was painful; I'm not yet ready to start again with a new relationship.' It was a lie, but a necessary one. It was the kindest way to put this boy off.

'I understand,' he said, 'but I would still like to take you out again. I am working now until Sunday—can we go out then?'

'I can't promise,' said Tanya, 'I'm not sure what my arrangements are. I shall probably be going out with my sister, unless Juan claims her attention again.'

'I will come, just in case,' he said determinedly. 'I have enjoyed today very much.' He kissed her cheek briefly, shyly, '*Adiós*, Tanya, until Sunday.' With a roar of his engine he disappeared, leaving nothing but a cloud of dust behind.

Tanya had scarcely set foot in the house when Matilde said there was a phone call for her. It was Alejandro.

'Tanya,' he said abruptly, 'Matilde tells me you've been out all day with some boy. Who is he?'

It was a direct, no-beating-about-the-bush, question, and Tanya took offence at it. 'What business is it of yours?' she asked indignantly.

'I regard it very much as my business. You know no one here; I should hate you to get into the wrong company.'

That was rich, coming from him. If any man used a woman, it was Alejandro. 'You need have no fears in that respect,' she said tartly. 'He comes from a very good family.'

'What is his name?'

'Manuel.'

Alejandro snorted. 'There are dozens of Manuels in Tenerife. Did you find out his surname?'

'Yes, but I don't see that it's of any great importance. Why are you phoning me?' She heard his indrawn breath. He was angry with her for being evasive, but she did not care. He had no right at all to question her movements.

'I want you to come to Santa Cruz.'

It sounded like a mandate, and Tanya bridled. 'Just like that? You give the order and I run, is that what you're suggesting?'

'If that's how it sounded, I apologise,' he said stiffly. 'But it would be wrong of you to miss the *carnaval*, and I don't just mean the grand parade; I mean all of it — all the heats, all the dancing, all the excitement. I have an apartment in Santa Cruz; you can stay there.'

'No, thank you, I don't want to come.' Tanya deliberately hardened her voice.

'Your sister is at work, I presume?'

'Yes.'

'Then it is a ridiculous state of affairs,' he growled angrily. 'You cannot call sitting around there by yourself a holiday. Our *carnaval* is second only to Rio; it is the largest in Europe, and you should miss none of it.'

In truth Tanya thought it sounded pretty exciting, and it would be heaps better than amusing herself here, but to stay in Alejandro's apartment? It would be putting herself too much at risk.

'I am not using the apartment myself, Tanya, if that's what is worrying you.'

His astuteness surprised her.

'I would be with you during the day, naturally; most people take a week off work at this time of year. But I would return to my house in Orotava each evening. You'd have no need to feel threatened by my presence.'

'How thoughtful of you.' Tanya deliberately filled her tone with scorn.

Alejandro snorted his annoyance. '*Perdóneme*, I thought I was doing you a favour. If you don't want to enjoy the *carnaval*, then so be it. *Es tuya la perdida, no mía.*'

Tanya could just see in her mind's eye the arrogant

tilt to his head, the anger flashing in his eyes, but he deserved to be put down. Maybe it was because she had responded to his kiss that he thought she would jump at the opportunity. Maybe he did not know her as well as he thought!

'I didn't say I didn't want to come,' she said pointedly. In fact she thought it an excellent idea. Her holiday was beginning to pall, especially now Charlene had met Juan. He was all her sister could talk about. 'I'm merely suspicious about your motives.'

Another hiss of anger. 'You have made it very plain, *mi niña*, that you want nothing more to do with me. Our relationship will, I assure you, be strictly platonic — unless, of course, you change your mind.'

'I will never do that,' announced Tanya quickly. 'And in those circumstances I will be pleased to take you up on your offer, providing Charlene can stay with me if she gets any time off.'

'Naturally, she is very welcome — but — ' and his tone hardened ' — not your male friend.'

Tanya was glad he could not see her smile. He actually sounded jealous, which was ridiculous when he had so many girlfriends. 'Manuel will not like it,' she said, trying to make her voice sound regretful, 'but yes, I will conform with your wishes.'

'Good.' It was a curt response. 'I will pick you up first thing in the morning. It was my plan to escort you there today, but — since you were otherwise occupied — that is now impossible; it is far too late. *Buenas noches*, Tanya.'

The line went dead before she could respond, and as she put the receiver down she wondered whether she was making a big mistake. He had said he would behave, but, knowing Alejandro, how could he? He was an extremely sensual man. Right from the start of their relationship they had been unable to keep their hands off each other; how could they spend a whole week together without succumbing?

Charlene was equally uneasy when Tanya told her about Alejandro's invitation. 'Goodness, Tan, that's the craziest thing I've ever heard; you're playing right into his hands. You know what the guy's like—he's only after your body.'

'He assured me that our relationship would be strictly platonic,' Tanya told her, 'And he won't be there at night; I'll have the apartment to myself.'

'And you believed him?' asked her sister incredulously. 'You want your head reading if you believe anything that man says. Have you forgotten already how he treated you? And how about all these other girls we've seen him out with?'

'There are only two.'

'And two's too many if he's setting his cap at you again. Oh, Tan, darling, don't make a fool of yourself a second time.' Charlene hugged her sister tightly. 'You can't kid me; I know you're still attracted to him—but he's not worth it, really he isn't. He's not serious about you; I don't think he could be serious about anyone. I don't think he even loved his wife as a man should—otherwise he wouldn't have started an affair with you.'

Tanya heaved a sigh. 'You're right, I know you're right, but it seems too good an opportunity to miss.'

Charlene grimaced wryly. 'It's all my fault that you're being neglected. Trust Carlos to go off sick at a time like this. And I don't actually blame you for wanting to go to Santa Cruz. The *carnaval* really is something. If you're so determined, all I can say is, be careful.'

'I will, I promise. I'm older and wiser now. I'm going into this with my eyes wide open.'

'So long as you don't leave your heart wide open. Tan, darling, I love you. I don't want you hurt again. And if I can scrounge a day or two off I'll be up there like a shot. You will ring me as soon as you know the address?'

*   *   *

Matilde, not knowing the underlying tension between Alejandro and Tanya, was pleased that she was going to see all of the *carnaval*, though she insisted that Tanya come back to her for the final days of her holiday.

Not unnaturally, Tanya slept little that night, tossing and turning in her normally comfortable bed, worrying, wondering what she was letting herself in for, hoping it was not a terrible mistake — like going to his party had been!

She must remember at all times to keep her distance, not to let herself get into any compromising situations. It would be all too easy to give in to the dictates of her body. Although her mind agreed with her that she hated Alejandro, her body thought otherwise; it never listened to anything it was told.

Alejandro turned up at eight, much earlier than Tanya had expected. Although he was casually dressed in beige trousers and shirt, he still looked devastating, and despite every good resolution she had made Tanya's heartbeats quickened. He was so good-looking, so erotic! How could any woman resist him?

Her case was packed and stood ready by the door. She had put on a pair of white cotton trousers and T-shirt, and Alejandro looked her up and down, slowly, thoughtfully, his eyes finally coming to rest on her face. 'You look tired, Tanya. I trust you didn't lie awake half the night worrying about whether you're doing the right thing?'

'I didn't sleep well, that's true,' she answered, wishing he couldn't read her so accurately, 'but only because I was hot.'

He didn't believe her; it was there in his eyes. 'It's much cooler in the north,' he announced, his lips quirking. 'You should have no difficulty sleeping there.'

Oh, but she would. How could she possibly settle in Alejandro's apartment, knowing that he had slept in

the same bed, or, if not, in another room? His presence
would be stamped indelibly all over it, and she wished
too late that she had refused to go. Charlene was right;
she was making a mistake, a giant one.

It was on the tip of her tongue to say that she had
changed her mind when he said briskly, 'Right, if
you're ready, we'll go.'

'What's the rush?' she asked. 'Matilde has some
coffee on; wouldn't you like a cup?'

'Proscrastinating, Tanya?' The glint in his eye told
her that he had guessed her thoughts.

She turned swiftly away. 'I was being polite, that's
all.'

'Then we'll go.' He picked up her suitcase. '*Adiós*,
Matilde.' He was outside the house in a matter of
seconds, leaving Tanya to hurry after him. Her luggage
was stowed in his boot. They both got in and he started
the engine. Matilde waved them off.

It was as though she were going to another planet.
Tanya felt that she was leaving everything that was
comfortable and familiar behind her. She was going
away with this man who had once been her lover, she
was entrusting herself to him, believing him when he
said there would be nothing sexual between them —
and yet already it had started!

It was impossible to sit so close and not feel any
reaction. It was faintly better because the car had an
open top, but she was nevertheless still intensely aware
of him — and if it was like this now what was it going to
be like in a day or two's time?

She had thought he would drive south and pick up
the motorway, making the journey to Santa Cruz so
much quicker, but instead he headed in the opposite
direction. 'Where are we going?' she asked with a faint
frown.

'I thought I would take you to see my tomatoes. I
still grow them, you know, the same as my father did.'

He was completely relaxed, a smile playing about his lips.

'I suppose there's no hurry,' she said, trying to hide her annoyance. 'Is there nothing going on today in Santa Cruz? I thought the whole idea was for me to see all the events.'

'And so it is,' he agreed, still smiling, 'But in the main they do not start until late afternoon, and some, like the election of the *reina del carnaval*, do not start until after nine. They go on very late, I'm afraid.'

Tanya took a deep, angry breath and sat up a little straighter, her eyes over-bright as she glared at him. 'You've tricked me, Alejandro. My days will be just as empty as before.'

'Oh, no, they won't,' he said confidently, 'Because you'll have me. We can do whatever you want to do — see the sights, swim, sunbathe, go walking. The world is your oyster, *mi cariño* — and you have to admit it will be much more fun than being on your own.'

'I hate you.' She looked straight ahead, her hands clenched tightly in her lap. 'You set this whole thing up. You let me believe that all of the events took part in the daytime.'

'Would you have come if I'd told you the truth?'

'Most definitely not,' she cried. 'In fact I insist that you turn around right now and take me back to Matilde's.'

'Not on your life, Tanya.' His foot went down on the accelerator as if to confirm his intention. 'We need to spend time together, and this was the only way I could think of arranging it. You're mine now, Tanya, for the next seven days, completely mine.'

She looked across at him, her eyes narrowed coldly. 'I've never belonged to you, and I never will.' Her heart was panicking. What a situation! She had never dreamt that he would do this to her. She tilted her chin. 'Once you go back to your house at night there'll be nothing to stop me leaving. I refuse to be your prisoner.'

Still he smiled infuriatingly. 'Not a prisoner, Tanya, never that, and who's to say I'll go home?'

Her blue eyes widened. 'But you promised.' Her heart thudded.

'Promises are made to be broken.' His voice had gone down to its gravelly depths, the way it always did when there were things on his mind other than prosaic conversation.

Tanya's mind darted this way and that, trying to think of a way she could get out of this situation. Nothing came immediately. She was trapped, whether she liked it or not. She had never thought he would do this to her; she had trusted him. But never again. If she got out of this unscathed — and she had every intention of doing just that — then she would make very certain that Alejandro played no further part in her life.

'You've gone very quiet, *amor mío*.'

'I am not your love,' she retorted furiously.

'You could be.'

'Along with Inocente and Beatriz?' Her eyes blazed as she looked at him.

'Beatriz is my *cuñada*, my sister-in-law.'

Again Tanya was stunned. She really was making quite a fool of herself. Her voice was little more than a whisper when she said, 'Why didn't you tell me?'

'Because I thought Matilde would have said.'

Tanya shook her head. 'She did introduce us, but you know how quickly she speaks. I caught the name Vázquez, but that was all.'

'So you assumed she was my wife, and then later, when I knocked that little theory on the head, you thought she was my mistress? What an opinion you have of me.'

'I'm sorry, Alejandro.'

'*Sorry*?' It was his turn to be angry. 'I seem to be

getting the blame for all sorts of things I haven't done, and I'm not sure that I like it.'

Tanya wanted to tell him that if he hadn't done the dirty on her in the first place she would never have jumped to such conclusions, but he wouldn't listen, she knew, not in the mood he was in at this moment, and she could hardly blame him. And there was still Inocente, who was apparently his current girlfriend, and if that was the case why was he insisting on spending time with her, Tanya? It was a whole mixed-up situation.

'Have you nothing more to say for yourself?' Gone were the low, sensual tones, replaced by a cold hardness that made Tanya squirm.

'It was a legitimate mistake, one anyone could have made,' she returned defensively. 'And you haven't told me about Inocente; what does she mean to you?'

'Inocente is my friend.'

'Your *friend*?' asked Tanya, her tone derisive. 'She looks far more than that to me. The girl's in love with you.'

'We are close, yes,' he admitted.

More than close, thought Tanya. Lovers might be a more accurate description.

'You are jealous of Inocente?'

Tanya tossed him a swift, sceptical glance. 'That's the very last thing I'd feel. You're welcome to her; you're welcome to as many girls as you like. Just don't try and add me to your list.'

His hands clenched the wheel suddenly, knuckles white, and Tanya guessed she had struck a raw nerve. He hated to think that he had once had her in the palm of his hand and then lost her; he hated the thought that she might never really have had any deep affection for him. He needed to try and prove himself. He had a massive male ego, and she had bruised it.

Within half an hour they had reached his tomato *finca*, and Tanya was extremely impressed. There were acres and acres of tomato plants growing in serried ranks, much bigger and thicker than any she had seen in England. They were supported by twigs and taller than a person, and women were between the rows, picking the tomatoes, putting them into baskets, in which they would eventually be transferred to the packing plant.

'What surprises me,' said Tanya, 'is that the Canary tomatoes we have in England are very small, and yet I've seen no small ones here. Why is that? Are there different sorts?'

'No, they're all the same,' he said, shaking his head. 'It's just that the English specify small tomatoes. You will see later how they're graded on conveyors. Such places as Holland and Belgium, Mexico, the USA, they all want big ones.'

'They're certainly much tastier,' agreed Tanya.

Some of the tomatoes, growing on higher ground, were sheltered from the strong winds that sometimes blew on the island by walls of strong nylon sheeting stretched between posts.

They did not stay long; the tension between them was too great. It was a brief, whistle-stop tour, and then they were on their way again. The road through the mountains climbed higher and higher, and Tanya caught occasional glimpses of Teide in the distance, snow-peaked and dramatic against an unbelievably deep blue sky. They passed through a village where purple and red bougainvillaea made a brilliant splash of colour against the white walls of the houses.

He drove a little too quickly round dangerous hairpin bends, the wind blew through her hair, and the higher they climbed the colder it became, and the silence between them was tangible. Stopping to look at his tomatoes being grown had done nothing to lessen the tension.

When they reached the road that took them past Mount Teide he finally spoke. 'Do you want to stop and take a closer look? Take a ride in the cable car, maybe?'

Tanya shook her head. 'I went up with Charlene, but I could do with a jumper out of my case.' If she had known when they set off that he was going to bring her this way she would have been prepared. There was frozen snow on the lava either side of the road, frozen snow on the shrubs and plants. She knew it was frozen because she and Charlene had tried to make snowballs. It amazed her that the sun didn't melt it more quickly; she had learned that it took months for it to disappear off the top of the mountain.

Alejandro stopped the car and opened the boot, waiting while she unsnapped her case and took out a thick jumper. He shrugged into a jacket himself, and then they were on their way again. Neither spoke.

They dropped slowly down out of the mountains, through town after town, until finally, thankfully, they reached the outskirts of the capital.

'Where is your apartment?' Tanya spoke without thinking, and it was as though her voice had cracked the silence, for Alejandro looked at her and faintly smiled. 'Not far now.'

Tanya had not been to Santa Cruz before and found it was not quite what she had expected. She had always thought that all capitals were beautiful, but this one wasn't. And as if knowing what she was thinking, Alejandro said, 'It might not have great looks, but it has great people. It's nicknamed "Capital de la Amabilidad", the Capital of Kindness. The Santacruceros are a warm, friendly people, as you'll find out.'

If I stay long enough, thought Tanya.

His apartment was at the top of a high-rise block, not very far from the commercial centre. A high-speed lift took them up, and once inside Tanya was staggered by its opulence. She had expected a tiny bachelor apartment, furnished with only the essentials for infre-

quent visits; instead it was a veritable home from home.
It wanted for nothing; it was as luxurious as his house
in Orotava.

'Do you stay here often?' she asked. Perhaps he used
it as his love-nest, entertained his lady-friends here.

'I used to, when Juanita was alive,' he told her. 'She
loved it here. I'm afraid I only stay now when business
dictates.'

Instantly Tanya felt ashamed of her traitorous
thoughts and was glad she had not voiced them aloud.

'If you're hungry there's plenty of food in the
kitchen,' he said.

Tanya frowned. 'Does that mean you're leaving?'

'Isn't it what you want?' His tone was clipped, his
face expressionless.

'Of course not. You can't bring me to a strange place
and then just dump me. I might as well have stayed
where I was. Take me back if you're not happy with
the situation.'

'I don't want to do that, Tanya, and you know it.'

Their eyes met and warred for several long, painful
seconds, then he heaved a sigh and pulled her into his
arms. 'Oh, Tanya *mio*, why do we argue like this?'

She did not answer; she simply allowed the warmth
of him to flood into her, allowed feelings to rise, and
marvelled that she could feel like this when seconds
earlier she had wished herself a million miles away.

'It is not what I want at all,' he murmured in her ear.
'I want this to be an enjoyable week for you, for us, I
want us to get to know one another all over again —
and, of course, I also want you to enjoy our *carnaval*.'
He said the word proudly. This annual event meant a
lot to him, as it did to most Tinerfeños.

But that was a secondary consideration, she realised
now. His main aim was for them to resume their
relationship of nine years ago. She ought to have
known, ought to have guessed what he had in mind.
Or perhaps she had known, and that was why she had

agreed to come. Perhaps deep down she *wanted* to carry on where they had left off. Didn't her body still crave his? Wasn't it still as wonderful between them?

'Tanya?' He lifted her chin, compelling her to look at him, and desire flared within her.

'I want to enjoy it too,' she whispered.

CHAPTER SIX

TANYA woke the next morning to rain and grey skies, and she could not believe it. This was the first time since she had been out here that she had seen rain. Some days had been cloudy, yes, but they had always cleared quickly, leaving blue skies behind. Now the sky looked as though it would remain like this for the rest of the day, and it was much cooler too than in the south, suggesting it would be sensible to wear sweater and trousers, not suntop and shorts.

She yawned and stretched and looked around the bedroom. The furniture here was not quite so over-powering as in Matilde's house. It still had a fairly heavy look to it, but it was in a pine shade rather than dark oak, and the rugs at the side of the bed were in a sea-green and cream weave which matched the bedspread.

It was the largest of the three bedrooms, and Alejandro had insisted that she take it. She guessed it was the one that he and Juanita had shared, and no doubt it held too many memories for him ever to use it again. But it hadn't helped her, sleeping in the same bed as he had, and she had spent half the night wishing he were there beside her.

Through the window she could see clouds boiling around the peaks of the Anaga mountains, stormy and dramatic, a very stirring background to the city.

Yesterday had turned out all right after all. She had fixed them a salad after they had finally made their peace, and then they had walked around Santa Cruz. She had told him about Manuel, who he really was, assuring him that there was nothing between them, and he had accepted her word, though she had seen for a moment his anger when she brought up the boy's name.

They spent some time standing on the promenade along the outer sea walls, watching the big ships come and go. 'Santa Cruz is a major port as well as an administrative and commercial centre,' Alejandro told her.

However, it was the preparations for the *carnaval* that impressed her most. There was a huge stage and backdrop in the main square, the Plaza de España. 'This is where all the judging takes place,' Alejandro informed her, 'where the groups of dancers and singers perform, where the heats for the carnival queen, both children and adults, are held, and where the grand final for the *reina del carnaval* is played out to its conclusive and glorious moments,' He was very enthusiastic about it, and Tanya could not help feeling some excitement too.

Later, much later, they found a quiet little restaurant, and then he took her back to the apartment. Half expecting him to say that he was going to stay the night, Tanya was surprised when, after a disappointing kiss on her brow, he announced his intention of leaving.

'It is best,' he said. 'You are too beautiful; you arouse in me great desire. If I do not go now, *mi cariño*, I will be unable to go at all.'

Tanya felt great excitement at the thought of him spending the night in her bed, but she knew it would be insanity, and something she would deeply regret later. She must never forget that it would mean nothing to him. 'And you would be breaking your promise,' she pointed out.

'Indeed, but I will think of you, alone here in your bed. Perhaps you will think of me a little too?'

'Oh, I expect I shall think of you,' she said, 'But not in exactly the same way. I shall be thinking how relieved I am that you've gone home. And I've no doubt Inocente would be relieved too, if she knew of the situation.' It helped her to bring in the other girl's name, helped her remember what a swine he was. It was all too easy to forget; he could be so charming, so attentive; he could make her feel that she meant everything to him.

The last few hours of peace might never have been. He drew in a harsh, angry breath, mentally withdrawing from her, his eyes a hard core of jet. 'I thought I had convinced you that Inocente is no more than a good friend. It seems I was mistaken.'

'No, you didn't convince me,' retorted Tanya. 'You can say what you like, I know only what my eyes tell me, and when she finds out that you've installed me here I guess she'll be one very angry lady. Unless you don't tell her.'

'Of course I shall tell her,' he said. 'I have nothing to hide. You are grossly mistaken in thinking that she would be hurt. She understands what my relationship with you is.'

Tanya looked at him, her head on one side. 'Really? Then she knows more than me. What did you tell her, that *we're* just good friends as well? I should be interested to hear what you consider our relationship is.'

'It doesn't matter what I told her,' he answered sharply. 'What is of importance, is why are you being particularly difficult.'

'Am I?' Tanya feigned innocence. 'I hadn't realised.'

'*Maldito sea*, Tanya, you know very well you are. Why do you keep harping on about Inocente? Why cannot we forget her, enjoy ourselves, recapture some of our past magic?'

Past magic? Yes, it had been that all right, until she had seen his father's letter about Juanita and the nightmare had begun. She would never forget that moment, or the way Alejandro had left England without so much as a word. How could they ever get back on to any sort of footing after that? 'It is not possible,' she said faintly.

'Not possible because you are being stubborn,' he growled, gripping her shoulders so hard that he hurt. 'If you relaxed and let go a little you would see that there is still a lot of pleasure to be had.'

'Maybe I don't want pleasure of that sort.' She eyed him stonily, bravely.

'Why?' he snarled, and then, as a sudden thought struck him, 'Is it because of Peter? Do you have some sort of hang-up where he is concerned? Do you feel it would be disloyal to let yourself get close to another man?'

'Of course not,' Tanya cried, 'but you're living under a delusion. You and I were never that close; there is nothing to recapture.'

'Pardon me.' His eyes grew steely. 'I thought there was.' And as if to add emphasis to his words he slid his hands down to her bottom and pulled her hard against him.

It was impossible to stop the flood of feelings, especially when he lowered his head and touched his lips to hers. It was like putting a match to a dry piece of paper — she ignited immediately. 'Actually, the magic *is* still there,' he muttered against her mouth. 'All it needs is a little encouragement.'

Tanya could not answer him. Her lips were parted against his, her whole body throbbing, and every thought of denying or rejecting him had fled. It took no more than a touch to have her melt in his arms, the briefest brush of his lips, the feel of his hard body against hers.

However much hatred she might feel, there was no denying the strong physical chemistry that bonded them together, or at least bonded her to him. Alejandro had no sense of loyalty. He had played around with her even though he had another girl back home, and now he was doing the very same thing, pushing Inocente into the background while he renewed his affair with her. Probably, once she had gone back to England, he would marry Inocente—that seemed to be the way he worked.

Yet even while her mind admitted all this her body still craved his. She hadn't the strength to reject him. Her mouth moved against his and her hands slid upwards to cradle his head. She put her all into the kiss, drinking eagerly from his mouth, feeling her whole body pulse and race and grow warm.

It was Alejandro who called a halt, who finally, gently, put her from him. There was a question in his eyes. 'Unless you want me to stay the night?'

Yes, yes, yes, her heart clamoured. No, no, no, insisted her mind. She shook her head, not trusting herself to speak.

'Then I'll leave now, while I still have the will-power. But I'll be round early tomorrow.' He cupped her face between strong brown hands. 'You are still as lovely as I remember, still my beautiful Tanya. Hell, I missed you. I wish. . .' He broke off suddenly. '*Buenas noches, amor mio*; miss me a little bit.'

He had gone then, leaving Tanya wondering what he had been going to say. What did he wish? Was it something to do with their breaking up? Had he been about to offer explanations? Whatever, she wouldn't have accepted them. There was no possible reason he could give for leaving her, other than he thought it time to put an end to their relationship.

Today she would be strong, she decided the next morning as she stood beneath the refreshing jets of the shower; today she would not let him kiss her. It spelled disaster; it fuelled the very real desire that, much to her disgust, still lay buried deep inside her.

He had not said exactly what time he would come. 'Early' to Tanya meant perhaps ten or eleven or even early afternoon, certainly not before nine, which was when he came hammering on the door.

Inevitably her heartbeats quickened, and she checked her appearance in the mirror by the door before opening it. Her smile of welcome faded somewhat when she saw that Alejandro was accompanied by a small boy.

'We have company today,' he said as he moved inside. 'Tanya, this is my son, Manolo. Manolo, *esta es la señora de quien hablé.*'

Very correctly the boy held out his hand and Tanya took it, all the time thinking, Alejandro's *son*! Alejandro had a son! She wa. shocked to the very core. 'It is good to meet you, Manolo,' she said, her tone faint.

The boy did not speak, merely looking at her shyly. She judged him to be about seven, dark-haired, slim and with big brown eyes like his father's. Other than that he looked nothing like him. Tanya guessed that the boy took after his mother, with his fine straight nose and slightly pointed chin.

'The children's *carnaval* queen gala is being held this afternoon and Manolo wants to see it,' Alejandro informed her. 'His favourite cousin has entered; isn't that right, Manolo?'

The boy frowned. '*No comprendo*, Papá.'

Tanya expected Alejandro to speak to his son in his native language; instead he said patiently in much slower English, 'You want to see Doña?'

Manolo smiled widely, his even white teeth shining. '*Sí*, Papá, *sí. Espero que ella gane.*'

Alejandro frowned. 'Manolo, please speak in English. Tanya will not understand what you are saying.'

'I am sorry, Papá,' said the boy at once, and hesitatingly to Tanya, 'I did not know you could not speak my language.'

'It's all right,' she said with a careful smile, admiring the fact that he could speak English so well. He made her feel very inadequate.

'Papá, *puede* — I mean, can I have a look around?'

'Of course,' Alejandro said, 'except in the room Tanya is using; it is the big bedroom. You must not go in there; it would be very rude.'

'OK, Papá.' And he skipped off happily.

'I trust you slept well.' Alejandro looked at Tanya and smiled warmly.

She nodded. 'Very well, thank you. Why didn't you tell me you had a son?'

He shrugged. 'The need never arose, and as a matter of fact I don't know whether you have any children either. We seem not to have had any deep, meaningful conversations. Perhaps it is time.'

'No, I haven't any children, and no, I don't want any in-depth talks,' answered Tanya tartly.

'You're angry with me for not telling you about Manolo?'

'Not really; it has nothing to do with me, has it? It's a surprise, though, I must admit.' More than a surprise, a shock of the highest order.

'You wish I hadn't brought him today?'

'Heavens, no!' exclaimed Tanya at once. 'He's — he's very welcome. It will be nice to have — other company.'

'You mean a chaperon?' His brows rose and he looked at her quizzically, but there was a quirk to his lips, and Tanya knew that he had been thinking the same thing.

'Things do seem to get a bit tense between us,' she agreed. 'It might help having him with us. What time does the judging start?'

'Not until four. I thought we might take Manolo to the beach.'

Tanya nodded. Amazingly the rain, which had looked set in for the whole day, had cleared, and although the skies weren't particularly clear the sun shone at this moment. 'An excellent idea.' A beach meant crowds, no chance of their getting close. Yes, it was a superb suggestion.

'I guess you haven't done much swimming since you've been here.'

Tanya confessed that she hadn't. 'But it's my own choice. A boy pushed me in a lake when I was little, and I've been terrified of water since. Charlene made me learn to swim, but I'm not very good and I don't enjoy it.'

'That's a pity.' Alejandro frowned. 'Manolo swims like a fish; I taught him myself at an extremely early age. But never mind; today you need not be afraid. I will personally keep my eye on you.'

Tanya was not sure whether she liked the reassurance. She would much prefer to sunbathe while Alejandro and his son enjoyed the water.

'Have you eaten?' he asked next.

'I've had a bread roll and some marmalade,' she said, 'and there's still some coffee in the pot if you'd like one.'

By this time Manolo had finished his tour of the apartment and was bouncing up and down on the white leather settee. 'I think we should go,' said Alejandro, 'before I have no furniture left. We'll show Manolo the ships first. They are a passion of his. It's his ambition to join the Navy when he grows up. He wants to be an admiral. Or he might be an explorer like Christopher Columbus,' he added with a laugh. 'He has big ideas for so small a boy.'

It was about twelve by the time they reached Las Teresitas, and Tanya could not believe what she saw. Tenerife being a volcanic island, almost all of its beaches were black sand, at least the ones she had seen. Here it was white.

'Am I seeing things?' she asked Alejandro.

He spread his hands expansively. 'The biggest man-made beach in the world. Four million sacks of sand were shipped here from the Spanish Sahara.'

'I'm impressed,' said Tanya.

'It's a favourite bathing spot for all Santacruceros,'

he told her. It was dotted with palms and an occasional stand that sold cold drinks, et cetera. There was parking along the road for hundreds of cars, and Manolo was out like a flash and down on to the sand. Alejandro smiled fondly. 'Let's join him.'

Manolo was already pulling off his shirt and trousers, anxious to get in the water, and Alejandro followed suit. In fact they seemed to be having a race, and Tanya watched them, smiling, thinking what a wonderful relationship they had.

They both had their swimming-trunks on underneath, and the moment they were ready they dashed towards the sea. The skies had cleared altogether now, and the water was a wonderful blue-green. Father and son played together like porpoises.

Tanya spread her towel and stripped off her own sweater and cotton trousers. She too had put on her bikini before coming out, and now she smoothed in sun-cream before lying back to enjoy the warmth of the sun. It did not feel quite so hot as in the south, but it was hot enough. She closed her eyes and relaxed, listening to the sound of youths shouting, children squealing, mothers consoling, and then she felt cold water dripping on to her stomach.

When she opened her eyes both Alejandro and Manolo were standing over her, laughing, shaking their wet hands over her body. 'We've come to get you,' said Alejandro.

'Yes,' said the boy.

'We refuse to let you lie here.'

'We want you to join us.'

'Do I have any choice?' asked Tanya, sitting up.

'None at all,' answered Alejandro.

'Is the water cold?'

'Not once you're used to it.' He held out his hands and she took them, allowing him to pull her to her feet. Contact, even something as innocent as this, triggered a sudden warmth through her body, but she knew she had to be careful because of Manolo. What his father had told him about her, she was not sure, but it could be nothing more than that they had met in England, certainly not that he was after some sort of affair with her now.

Tanya walked reluctantly with them towards the ocean which had looked so beautiful from her position on the sand but which now looked positively menacing. There was so much of it, and it was so deep and so strong, and she was so afraid.

Sensing her hesitation, Alejandro took her hand. 'I'll be with you every inch of the way.' And to his son, 'Tanya does not swim very well; we must look after her.' So Manolo took her other hand, and between them they led her into the water.

It was cold, icy cold, and when they were a few feet out Alejandro suggested she dip herself completely into the water. 'The quicker you do it, the better it will be.' And because she did not want to make a fool of herself, Tanya obeyed. It took her breath away at first, but then she began to discover that it wasn't so cold after all.

They waded out another couple of yards until it was up to her breasts. 'Now let's see what you can do,' said Alejandro.

'I can't do anything.' Tanya was suddenly terrified of taking her feet off the bottom. 'I'm scared. I can't do it, Alejandro. I want to go back.'

But he would hear none of it. 'Try floating. I'll put my hand under your back; you have nothing to fear.' And more softly, 'Trust me, *mi cariño*.'

His hand was solid and comforting behind her, and gradually she allowed herself to fall backwards, her feet coming up, until finally she was floating on the surface of the water, Alejandro's hand still beneath her.

'Relax,' he murmured mesmerically. 'Close your eyes and think of something nice.' And because she knew he was there, because she knew he would let nothing happen to her, Tanya did so, and when Alejandro moved his hand away she remained floating, and she marvelled that she was doing it without feeling any fear. That was the main thing, not her achievement. Alejandro was giving her confidence.

Manolo too floated at her side, and when she opened her eyes and looked at him he grinned. 'It is easy, yes?'

Within half an hour Tanya found herself actually swimming and enjoying it — for the first time in her life she was enjoying it. Alejandro never moved away from her; he swam at her side, or stood and watched, and always he was there at the ready in case she should panic, always offering her words of encouragement.

Manolo had joined a group of boys his own age, and she and Alejandro were alone. They were floating again now, side by side, and he said quietly, 'Tanya, you are driving me crazy, do you know that? You are as irresistible to me now as you were nine years ago.'

She wished he hadn't said that, because nine years ago he had left England without contacting her again. In less than a week after their argument he had gone. She couldn't have been that irresistible! 'You have a smooth tongue, Alejandro.'

'You do not believe me?'

'Once I would have believed you, but not any longer. Now I suspect you say the same sort of thing to every girl.'

He gave a snort of anger and rolled off his back to tread water at her side. 'That was uncalled for.'

'Was it?' she asked, looking into the angry dark depths of his eyes. 'Not from this side of the fence. In any case, a lot's happened since then. I'm not quite the gullible young girl I was. We had a good time while it lasted, but it's over, forgotten, and that's how I'd like it to remain.'

'I'm not getting through to you, am I, Tanya?'

'No.' She rolled off her back too and began to swim

towards the shore, and this time she did not need him to give her confidence; she was swimming automatically, capably — and she amazed herself.

He easily caught her up. 'Haven't I made myself clear that I'd like to begin all over again?'

Tanya's feet touched the bottom. 'Perfectly, but I don't happen to feel the same way.'

'Because there's someone else in your life?'

She started to wade out of the water. 'No.'

'Then why?' He was walking with her, looking at her, trying to make her see his point of view.

'Let's say that when I walked out of your hotel room all those years ago it was a decision I've never regretted. I've never wished to undo it, to resume a relationship with you. It didn't work then; it wouldn't work now.' Hell, why was she lying, why did she consistently push him away from her? The answer was simple — she did not trust him.

'It could work, Tanya.'

'No.' She shook her head determinedly. 'I refuse to even give it a try. You're wasting your time.'

'Papá, Papá, wait for me.' Manolo had spotted his father leaving.

Alejandro turned but Tanya carried on, and when they joined her she was lying face down on her towel.

'I think Tanya is tired,' said Manolo.

'I think so too,' said Alejandro.

'I would like a drink, Papá.'

'Then we will go and get you one.'

Silence reigned as they moved away, and Tanya squinted at them through half-closed eyes. Manolo was trying to match his stride to his father's, his head tilted at exactly the same angle, his hands clasped similarly behind his back. He clearly adored his father and, what was more important, was extremely well-behaved.

When they returned she was still lying in the same position, but sat up instantly when Manolo said, 'Wake up, Tanya; we have a Coke for you.'

'Thank you.' She took the can from the boy and they
both sat down on their towels beside her, and there
was silence as they all drank thirstily through their
straws. Manolo was the first to finish, noisily, happily.
'Can we swim again now?'

'I'll stay here with Tanya,' said Alejandro. 'You go
and play with your new friends. Don't go out too far.'

'No, Papá.'

The boy ran off happily enough, and Tanya said,
'He's a nice boy, well-behaved and well-adjusted.
You've done a good job on him.'

'It was no hardship,' he said with a shrug of his wide
shoulders. 'We were always close, even before Juanita
died.'

'Was she ill long?' asked Tanya, recalling Peter's
lengthy period of poor health.

'No, no, it was an accident. A hit-and-run affair.
They never caught the person who did it.' A shadow
chased across his face, and Tanya could see his mind
going back to that painful time.

'I'm so sorry.' Unthinkingly she laid her hand on his
arm.

He put his much bigger hand over hers. 'Manolo was
just over two at the time. The poor little fellow could
not understand what had happened. He needed me
then and he's clung to me ever since.'

Which made him just turned eight now, not seven as
she had thought. Which meant——

Alejandro's voice cut into her thoughts. 'It was a
long time ago, Tanya.' He had evidently mistaken her
sudden tension for sympathy over his loss.

Her eyes flashed. 'I was actually thinking that if
Manolo is eight you didn't waste much time in marrying
Juanita.' Her tone was sharply critical, and she
snatched her hand away from beneath his.

'You were the one who put an end to our relationship, Tanya,' he pointed out coldly.

Was that what he really thought? Hadn't it occurred

to him that if he'd come after her she would have said how much she loved him, admitted she had been wrong not to believe his declaration that he did not love Juanita? Now that she had met Manolo she knew that she had been right. 'I'm glad that I did,' she spat savagely. 'If I wasn't sure before that I had done the right thing, I am now.'

'You had doubts?' he asked sharply.

Tanya shrugged. 'Only in my weaker moments.'

'And were there many of those?' His eyes were intent upon hers.

'For the first few days, that's all,' she cried. 'After that I put you right out of my mind.'

Her harsh words fuelled Alejandro's anger and he jerked himself furiously to his feet. 'I am wasting my time. I will get my son and take him to see the *eleccion de la reina infantil*. You can please yourself whether you come or not.'

CHAPTER SEVEN

TANYA went to the election of the juvenile queen, but only because Manolo insisted. When she declared, after they had eaten their lunch in a side-street restaurant, that she was going back to the apartment he caught her hand anxiously. 'No, no, Tanya, you must come with us. Papá, tell her; make her come.' He seemed to have taken an instant liking to her, and actually the feeling was mutual. Tanya was fond of him too.

Banks of seats were erected in the square for the audience, and Manolo sat between her and Alejandro. They looked like an average happy family, thought Tanya; how deceptive appearances could be. Manolo was disappointed when his cousin did not win, although slightly appeased when she was selected as one of the queen's entourage.

On their drive back to the apartment the boy went to sleep, and once they got there Alejandro said he was taking his son home.

'Do you usually stay here?' asked Tanya.

Alejandro nodded.

'I'm sorry.' But if he thought she would suggest they did so now he was mistaken. The more time they spent together the less easy it was to pretend indifference.

Once indoors she sat down on the white leather couch and pondered over her discovery that Alejandro and Juanita had got married almost immediately he came home from England. It was a hard fact to take in. And twelve months later — probably less than that, depending on when his birthday was — Manolo had been born!

It proved beyond any shadow of doubt that she,

Tanya, had meant nothing to him. He had needed female company while he was in England and she had proved the perfect companion, giving him her all. He must have thought his luck was in. And then the instant things had gone a little wrong between them he had turned tail and fled, without giving her another thought!

She wished now that she had never let him cajole her into coming here to Santa Cruz. Everything was worse than she had imagined. She got up and paced the room, looked out through the window at the receding shape of the mountains, at the pinpoints of light beginning to appear in the buildings climbing their slopes, looked down at the cars in the street below, turned and looked at the room with its white tiled floor and pine furniture and the glossy green leaves of exotic plants which added to its still coolness.

She shivered and suddenly thought longingly of England with its carpeted floors and central heating or cosy coal fires. She wanted to go back to her house where she felt safe and secure; she did not want to stay here where Alejandro unsettled her.

The telephone rang, and it startled her in the silence of the room. Alejandro! Her heart pattered as she picked it up. 'Hello?'

But it was her sister, ringing to ask where she had been. 'I was going to come and see you,' she said accusingly.

Tanya explained about their day out, and the discovery of Alejandro's son, and had only just set the phone down when it rang again. This time it *was* Alejandro. 'Get yourself ready,' he told her. 'We're having supper out.'

Although she was hungry Tanya said sharply, 'Oh, no, we're not. Besides, it's much too far for you to keep travelling backwards and forwards from Orotava.'

'That's my problem, not yours,' he told her gruffly. 'I'll be there in half an hour.'

The phone went dead before she could speak again, and Tanya was left with no choice. He had sounded as though he was only making the offer because he thought it was the right thing to do. He needn't have bothered; she would have much preferred to spend the evening alone.

No, that wasn't strictly true; she did not want to be alone, but her own company would certainly be better than Alejandro's. They had nothing in common any more, except perhaps an unwanted animal attraction. Maybe this was what they'd had all along. Maybe she had never loved him. Maybe she had mistaken physical pleasure for love. He was the only man who had ever stimulated her to the extreme in this way.

Peter's lovemaking had been gentle and certainly less than innovative, but she had been happy and satisfied because he had been loving in other ways too, her friend as well as her lover, her right arm when she had needed him, always obliging, always happy and generous and thoughtful.

Alejandro had some of these traits too, but it had been the physical side of their relationship that had been dominant, and, looking back, she could see that she had put this before everything else. She had hungered for his body but not his soul and his mind — and those feelings were still there, unfortunately.

He turned up in thirty minutes exactly, and Tanya was waiting. She was given a thorough appraisal, starting at the tip of her pink-painted toenails, at her strappy white sandals, right up the slender length of her legs to the curve of her hips and the swell of her breasts beneath her pink linen dress, finally coming to rest on her face, their eyes meeting, but his giving nothing away.

Tanya felt uncomfortably warm, and she expected some comment, a compliment perhaps, but all he said was, 'Good, you're ready. Let's go.'

With a mental shrug she slipped into her white

jacket, picked up her bag, and followed him out to the
lift. There was still an atmosphere between them, and
she wished he had not suggested they go out. It was
going to be a tense, difficult evening.

They sat in silence in his Mercedes, the soft cover
pulled over on this cool February evening, and instead
of taking her to a restaurant in Santa Cruz, as she had
expected, he drove along the La Cuesta highway to the
university town of La Laguna. It was only a matter of
eight kilometres, and once there he pulled up outside a
big house in one of the narrow streets in the old part
of the town. Tanya looked at him in surprise.

'Where are we?'

'At my brother's.'

'But——'

'It is all right; you've been invited.'

Tanya shook her head, feeling a little bemused. She
had no wish to meet any members of his family. Why
had he invited her? What had he said? How about
Inocente—where did she fit into all of this? Wasn't she
Alejandro's girlfriend? Oughtn't she to have been
asked instead?

He pushed open a huge, carved wooden door and
they stepped into a plant-filled patio along similar lines
to his own. It amazed Tanya that there was this oasis
of green just the other side of an innocent-looking wall.
It must be, she thought, that all the older houses had
these private, beautiful courtyards.

Immediately a side-door opened, and to Tanya's
surprise Beatriz came forward to greet them.
'Alejandro, welcome.' They embraced and kissed
warmly, as they had at the airport when Tanya had
mistaken her for his wife. 'And Tanya, I am so glad
you have at last come.' She kissed Tanya on each
cheek. 'I keep asking Alejandro to bring you; he say
you are always doing something else. Come inside and
meet my husband. He is looking forward to seeing you.'

Alejandro's brother looked nothing like him, much shorter and with a paunch, his dark hair already receding even though he was a few years younger. 'Crisógono, meet Tanya. Tanya, my husband,' introduced Beatriz.

'So you are the mysterious Tanya.' Crisógono gave her a warm, welcoming smile and a bear-like hug. 'We heard about you when Alejandro came back from his time spent in England and couldn't believe it when he said he'd met you again recently.' His English was as perfect as Alejandro's and Tanya remembered Beatriz saying that her husband too had been to England.

Alejandro had told his family about her all those years ago! Tanya was shocked, and wondered exactly what he had said—especially since Juanita had been waiting at home for him. He could not have told them that they'd had a sizzling affair; he must have hinted that she was someone he'd met—a platonic friend, no more. On the other hand, he had declared that he'd written to Juanita, telling the girl about her. Perhaps they did know. Perhaps everyone knew. Perhaps they thought that they might get back together again now that he was a widower. Heavens, it was so embarrassing.

'It's very kind of you to invite me,' she said with a faint smile. 'You must forgive me if I seem confused. Alejandro did not tell me we were coming here.'

'Alejandro!' exclaimed his sister-in-law at once. 'You are very naughty.'

'I thought it would be a nice surprise,' he insisted, smiling at Beatriz, looking at Tanya speculatively.

She did not respond. She was, in fact, not sure how to behave. She had no idea what sort of a relationship she was supposed to be having with Alejandro.

'You are very welcome,' announced Crisógono. 'Come and sit down; I will pour you a drink.'

They were in a large room filled to overflowing with large pieces of furniture and the inevitable pot plants, and Tanya chose a deep, comfortable armchair. Alejandro lowered himself into the chair next to her, separated only by a small, square, black-carved table with a beautiful figurine of the madonna standing on it.

Tanya wished he had chosen to sit somewhere else. It made them seem like a couple, which they were most definitely not.

Crisógono handed her a glass with just a drop of wine in the bottom which he proudly announced was from his own vineyard. 'Taste it and tell me what you think.'

Tanya sipped the golden liquid and tried not to grimace when she found it too sweet, like the one Matilde usually gave her. Perhaps all the local wines were sweet. But Crisógono, who had been watching her closely, said at once, 'You do not like it? Drink no more; I have another.' Within a matter of seconds her glass was replaced. 'Smell the bouquet,' he said proudly. 'Savour it. You will like this one, I am sure.'

Tanya smiled. He was being very dramatic. But when she tasted the wine it was much more to her taste, and she nodded enthusiastically. 'Yes, I like this one, thank you.' She held out her glass so that he could fill it.

'And you, Alejandro, my brother, what will you have to drink — your usual whisky?'

Alejandro inclined his head.

'My brother does not like my wine,' Crisógono told Tanya, shaking his head sadly. 'He has far more sophisticated tastes.'

It was true, thought Tanya. Crisógono was very much more down to earth than Alejandro, despite the fact that they were both farmers — in different ways; both worked the land, and in fact the younger man's produce went through quite a sophisticated process once the grapes were picked, whereas Alejandro's tomatoes were simply picked and sold. It was an odd parallel.

'Of course he has,' said Beatriz, 'when you consider the company he keeps.'

Tanya frowned.

'He has not told you of his other interest?' asked Beatriz.

She shook her head. 'No.'

'Alejandro, shame on you. Have you not taken her out on your yacht?'

'No, I haven't, Beatriz,' answered Alejandro sharply. 'We do not have the close relationship you are insinuating. Tanya is someone I once knew very briefly, that is all.'

'What do you mean "knew briefly"? asked his sister-in-law, equally sharply. 'Were you not lovers in England?'

'That was a long time ago,' answered Alejandro calmly. 'We are now both older and wiser. We are not so close.'

Tanya felt her cheeks colouring — so he *had* told them! She pasted a brilliant smile to her lips and pretended she was not disturbed by this discussion about their relationship. 'What is this, Alejandro, about a yacht? Goodness, how could you keep something so exciting to yourself?'

He looked at her then, smiling slowly. 'There is no mystery; it is a business interest. I charter it — to the rich and famous, complete with crew, though sometimes I captain it myself; it all depends. *Zafra* — that is the tomato season — is from late October to the end of April. The rest of the year there is not much to do except prepare the ground for the following year's crop. It is a sideline, that's all.'

'And an extremely profitable one,' added Crisógono.

'But not so satisfying as growing tomatoes, Cris,' pointed out Alejandro. 'It is fun, yes, but there is no end-product. It is like one big holiday, and after a while it becomes tedious.'

He said it so matter-of-factly that Tanya laughed out loud. 'If that's tedium, what is my job?'

'What do you do?' asked Beatriz with interest

'I'm a PA.' And when the woman frowned, 'I'm sorry, I'm a personal assistant — to the managing director of a computer software company.'

'That sounds very important,' said the other woman.

'My boss depends on me a lot, I suppose,' confessed Tanya.

'And he has let you come away on a month's holiday?'

Tanya smiled. 'He owes it me. I haven't taken my full quota of holidays for the last few years.' Ever since Peter died, in fact. There seemed no point when she had no one to go away with.

'How much longer have you left?'

'Just under two weeks.'

'Enough time to see our *carnaval*,' concluded Beatriz happily. 'I am so glad Alejandro persuaded you to use his apartment. So many tourists go to Santa Cruz just for the *coso*. There is so much they miss. You met Manolo today, is that right? What do you think of my handsome *sobrino*?'

'He is a fine boy,' replied Tanya. 'We got on very well.'

'He is missing a mother. I keep telling Alejandro, it is time he married again.'

Alejandro looked at his sister-in-law sharply. 'And you talk too much about matters that are of no importance to Tanya.'

'Oh, but I am interested,' Tanya said. 'I agree with Beatriz that Manolo needs a mother. Have you and Inocente made any plans to get married?' She made it sound like a perfectly innocent question.

'Inocente is a friend, nothing else,' snorted Alejandro. 'I will never marry her; what put that idea into your head?'

And Beatriz looked at her in horror. 'That girl, I do

not like her, and nor does Manolo. She will not make good mother.'

Even Crisógono shook his head. 'She is not my brother's type; I do not know what he sees in her or why he ever takes her out. She is a selfish one.'

Tanya held up her hands as if trying to stop their comments. 'I'm sorry, I wasn't aware that you all had such strong feelings. I assumed——'

'You assume too much,' growled Alejandro.

'I think it is time to eat,' said Beatriz.

Despite the uproar she had caused the meal was a relaxed affair, even if Alejandro did glower at her at times, apparently still angry over her remarks about Inocente.

They started with an unusual fish soup, served carefully by a pretty girl who obviously worked for them. Tanya was impressed. Beatriz told her that the soup was made from a very old Canarian recipe. This was followed by salty pork ribs boiled together with potatoes and corn on the cob—washed down with plenty of Crisógono's *vino*.

During the course of the meal Tanya discovered that their two children were already in bed, as they, like Manolo, had missed their siesta. 'Normally, they would join us,' said Beatriz. 'It is a pity you will not see them, but—it is much quieter,' she added with a laugh.

Too full for any pudding, Tanya accepted a brandy with her coffee, which was served in a glass and was strong and black and liberally sweetened. The Canarians had a great love of sugar, she discovered—they even sugared freshly squeezed orange juice. Alejandro told her that it dated back to the islands' first export industry of sugar-cane.

Tanya was so enjoying herself that she was disappointed when Alejandro said it was time to leave—until she looked at her watch and realised it was already half-past eleven. How the time had flown! Considering she had not wanted to come out this evening, it had been extremely pleasant — probably because Beatriz and her husband were so friendly and welcoming. 'You must come again before you go back to England,' they both said as she left.

Once on their way Alejandro said sharply, 'What was all that about Inocente? you know she means nothing to me.'

'I know that's what you've told me,' she said, 'but it's not what Inocente herself feels. Surely you know that?' Or was he always blind where his women were concerned? Had he not known that she, Tanya, had once been madly in love with him? And Juanita, she too must have been in love when he left for England — yet it hadn't stopped him having an affair. And now Inocente — he was treating her with equal disregard. What type of a man was he, for goodness' sake?

'And how would you know what Inocente's feelings for me are?' he asked coldly.

Tanya lifted her shoulders. 'I've seen the way she looks at you — and the way *you* treat her,' she added scathingly. 'When you're together she means everything to you. There's more to your relationship than you're admitting.'

'If I was in love with Inocente, would I be spending my time with you?' he rasped.

Tanya eyed him coldly, although she knew he couldn't see her expression in the darkness of the car. 'I don't think you're the type of man who'll ever remain true to one woman for long.'

'Your opinion of me continues to sink, doesn't it?' he asked harshly. 'No matter how much I put myself out for you it makes no difference.'

'Why should it?' she countered. 'It's what you're like beneath the surface that counts.'

'And you think you know the true me?'

'I not only think it, I know it. You're a cheating swine, Alejandro. You cheat me, you cheat your family, you cheat Inocente, you cheated Juanita. Shall

I tell you who I feel sorry for? Manolo! Beatriz is right: he does need a mother.'

'You said earlier today that I had done a very good job in bringing him up.'

'Yes, you have, but he is still young; he should have the love of two parents. It is unfair to deprive him of a mother's love.'

'Are you suggesting yourself for the role model?' There was a sudden stillness to him, although his attention was to all outward appearances on his driving.

'Heavens, no!' Tanya cried at once. 'You're the last person I'd marry; and, according to your family, Inocente wouldn't be a very suitable candidate either. Perhaps you should look around for someone else.'

'Perhaps I don't want to look around.'

'Meaning you're happy in your single state? That you enjoy flitting from girlfriend to girlfriend, that you would be stifled if you had to settle down with one woman?' Tanya did not realise that her tone had risen, that she sounded almost shrill in the close confines of the car — not until he slammed the brakes on and brought the car to a skidding halt.

'That is enough.' He half turned in his seat towards her. 'I will not be spoken to like this.'

'The truth hurts, does it?' she taunted, her eyes locked into the glittering depths of his, feeling the full extent of his anger. But instead of being intimidated she was excited, conscious only that his sex appeal had never been stronger.

'You know nothing,' he snarled.

Tanya touched the tip of her tongue to suddenly dry lips.

'And you're certainly not the sweet, friendly girl I met in England. You're. . .' His voice tailed off, and it was almost possible to hear the hammer throb of their heartbeats. 'Hell, Tanya,' he growled thickly.

They gravitated towards each other, slowly, pain-fully, their eyes never leaving each other's faces, until

in one final, aching, groaning moment their mouths
met.

It was a deeply passionate, mutually hungry kiss, an
animal hunger, a hunger born of deep-seated, unslaked
desire. Tanya had never felt such an intense need, and
she moved her mouth against Alejandro's, their
tongues entwining, tasting, demanding.

She wanted more than this constricted place allowed;
she wanted their whole bodies to meet, not just their
lips. Her hands went to his head, fingers curling into
the thickness of his hair, holding him, pulling, hurting,
wanting, needing.

Alejandro too groaned his frustration, one hand on
her chin, thumb pulling down her lower lip so that he
could explore her mouth more deeply, his other hand
on her back, trying to urge her closer to him.

He muttered something in Spanish beneath his
breath, and then, still barely audibly, 'This is no good,
Tanya, not here. We must get home, and quickly.
Promise you won't go cold on me?'

'I promise.' Her eyes were like luminous blue orbs,
moist, glowing, soft, reflecting her feelings, telling him
without words that her need was as great as his.

Reluctantly he dragged himself away, turned the key
and started the engine, put it into drive, and pulled
back out on to the road. With one hand on the wheel
and one hand on her thigh, her own hand covering it,
he drove the rest of the way home, slowly, carefully,
not wanting to break the bond that had sprung into
fragile existence.

In the lift they fell upon each other again, not able
to wait until they reached privacy. Lips meeting, sucking, tasting; bodies swaying, pressing, urging. Throb,
throb, throb, went their hearts. Pulses raced; adrenalin
ran high. Out of the lift and into the apartment, more
kissing, tasting, inciting. Clothes dragged off, bodies
meeting, skin inflaming.

This was what she needed, what she had ached for

since meeting him again. Tanya held nothing back —
she could not; she was out of control, drugged by this
man she had loved so many years ago. Excitement
tortured, fuelled, burned. She could hear a pounding in
her head as well as her heart, such energy, such heat.

Mouths moved to kiss and taste, to explore eyes and
ears and noses and chins. Whatever he did she did,
unthinkingly, urgently. He kissed her nipples; she
kissed his. He nipped them with his fine white teeth;
she bit his. It was an agony of hurt and pain and loving.

At what stage he carried her to the bed she did not
know, but they were lying down and he was touching
and kissing every secret inch of her, and when the
moment arrived she arched her body against his,
breathing deeply, painfully, enjoying, urging, sensing.

They both cried out at the same time, an explosion
of feeling rocking her to the very core, clinging now,
tightly, emotionally, then relaxing and lying close side
by side, holding, sighing, smiling, and finally —
sleeping.

Tanya dreamed that she was married to Alejandro,
that as well as Manolo they had children of their own,
four of them, three girls and a boy. All Canarians
loved children, she had learned, and Alejandro told
her that he wanted many. There had been no interven-
ing years; she had not married Peter. She had followed
him out to Tenerife and there had been no Juanita
waiting for him. They had been blissfully happy until
one day she had caught him with another woman in his
arms — Inocente — and her whole world collapsed.

She had gone up to the other woman and tried to
drag them apart. 'He's mine; you cannot have him.
Get away.'

'Tanya, what is wrong?' It was Alejandro's voice,
soft and puzzled.

'What are you doing with Inocente? You're mine;
she can't have you.'

'*Amor mio, amor mio*, you are dreaming.'

Tanya dragged open her heavy eyelids, and for a moment could not think where she was. Alejandro was looking at her, his expression tender and concerned. Alejandro in bed beside her! Alejandro naked! And she remembered, and colour flooded her cheeks. Last night she had drank too much of Crisógono's *vino*; last night she had let Alejandro make love to her. This morning she felt embarrassed.

'It is all right, *mi cariño*,' he murmured, stroking her hair back from her forehead. 'It was a dream, nothing more, nothing to feel worried about.'

'Oh, yes, there is. You shouldn't be here, I shouldn't have let you——'

'Shh.' He put a silencing finger to her lips. 'I am here, and it's all right, and you were right in your dream when you said I am yours. We belong together, Tanya, you and I. We should never have parted. We——'

It was Tanya's turn to interrupt. 'No, Alejandro, we do not belong. I made a mistake last night, a grave mistake.'

'How can you say that?' His fingertips brushed the soft skin of her cheek, creating a fresh surge of sensation. 'How can you say that after what we have been through together?'

'I should never have let you make love to me,' she protested. 'It was wrong; it was——'

'Hush, *bebé*, hush.' His lips covered hers, gentle this morning, his impatient hunger of the night before gone.

Instantly Tanya was lost. The old magic was back; there was nothing she could do about it. 'Oh, Alejandro,' she sighed.

'Tanya.'

They made love again, taking their time now, no hurry, just long, lazy moments of sensual pleasure, and then Tanya suddenly remembered. 'Manolo!' she exclaimed, sitting up. 'He'll wonder where you are. You must go home at once.'

'Manolo is all right,' he told her softly. 'He has a nanny, a live-in nanny; she will look after him. I told her where I was going. She would not expect me home; she knows that my brother always plies me with drink.'

Tanya relaxed again and then jumped when the telephone rang.

'I will get it,' he said. 'You lie there and look beautiful.'

He padded out of the bedroom, completely unself-conscious about his nudity, and when he returned he was smiling. 'That was Charlene. She had quite a shock when she heard my voice. She rang to say that she has managed to—er—wangle, I believe was her word, a day off, and is coming to spend it with you. What a pity. I was looking forward to a day spent together, now that we have rediscovered our feelings for each other.'

CHAPTER EIGHT

'THERE's no need to panic,' said Alejandro, catching Tanya's arm, pulling her back as she tried to scramble out of bed. 'Your sister won't be here for another hour at least.'

'But I must be ready. I must have time to pull myself together.' She did not want Charlene seeing her with this look of love on her face. She had not seen herself in the mirror, but she knew that she was glowing; she could feel it—she could feel her eyes sparkling, her face soft and relaxed, her whole body tingling with well-being.

The love she had felt for Alejandro nine years ago had come back with a vengeance. She was a woman satisfied, a woman who knew she had satisfied her man. It was a wonderful sensation.

She allowed Alejandro to hold her for a few minutes, feeling peaceful and happy and content. Alejandro too looked relaxed and completely in tune with the world. 'Now we have rediscovered our feelings', he had said— whatever those feelings were! She still had no real idea whether he loved her or whether it was purely a physical thing on his part. She had never known, and unless he told her she never would; and it was too big a risk to take to let herself get deeply involved with him again.

She could never forget that while he had been making love to her in England Juanita had been waiting for him here. And this time it was Inocente who was waiting. The sudden note of discord in her thoughts made her wriggle uneasily.

'*Enamorada*, sweetheart, something is wrong?' His arms tightened around her, and the pressure of his body against hers was almost more than she could bear. Once more she was lost; she wanted to touch him, stroke him, make love all over again. Her heartbeats grew stronger and her throat seemed to close up, and she looked at him with her luminous blue eyes.

She could not tell him what she had been thinking, not in this moment of closeness. They were fleeting thoughts, unwanted thoughts. She loved Alejandro; that was enough, for now at least. She wanted to savour this happy feeling; she did not want to spoil it or lose it. Whatever else happened, it would be there to add to her memories of almost nine years ago.

'It's all right,' she whispered.

They lay together for another ten minutes, Alejandro leaning up on one elbow, looking at her face, stroking her nose, her eyelids, her lips, the contour of her cheeks, pushing back stray wisps of hair, murmuring soft words in his native language. Tanya hoped they were words of love; she hoped so, so very much.

At length he was the one who made the move, though he furthered the moments of intimacy by joining her in the shower, and they had only just got dressed when the doorbell rang, announcing Charlene's presence.

Tanya hugged her sister, but Charlene was looking across the room. 'I didn't expect to find you still here Alejandro.'

Tanya gasped at her insensitivity, but Alejandro merely raised an eyebrow. 'I'm sorry if I've disappointed you.'

'I hope you're going soon. It took a lot of organising to get this day off.' Charlene never believed in holding back; if she thought something, she said it.

'Don't worry, I won't spoil your day with your sister.' He spoke easily, but his mouth was suddenly grim, and Tanya knew he was thinking that Charlene had no such compunction about spoiling *his* day.

She sighed unhappily and went into the kitchen to

make coffee; Charlene followed. 'I'd have to be blind not to see what you two have been up to,' she said in a loud whisper. 'How could you, Tan, after the way he treated you?'

Tanya smiled ruefully. 'I can't help it.'

'You can't help it? He's the guy who broke your heart, for heaven's sake. Don't you remember?'

'Of course I remember, but — oh, Charlene, I know you won't understand, but the old magic's still there. I only have to look at him and I go weak at the knees.'

Charlene shook her head. 'You're going to get hurt again. He has another girlfriend, in case you'd forgotten.'

'He says she means nothing to him.'

'Nothing, my eye. You surely don't believe him?'

'I don't know. All I know is that I love him and there's nothing I can do about it.'

'Of course there is,' cried Charlene. 'You can get out of here for a start. You ought to have known he wouldn't leave you alone. The guy's a womaniser of the highest order. I wouldn't trust him as far as I could throw him.'

'You say the sweetest things, Charlene.' Alejandro had come into the kitchen behind them. 'Don't you think you should leave Tanya to make up her own mind?'

'Not where you're concerned,' snapped the older girl. 'You did the dirty on her once; I don't want it happening again.'

'*I* did the dirty?' A frown scoured his brow. 'As I recall, Tanya was the one who walked out on me.'

'And you——'

'Oh, shut up, you two,' interrupted Tanya. 'You're spoiling my holiday.'

Her sister grimaced. 'I'm sorry; it's just that I'm disappointed in you.'

'I think, Charlene,' said Alejandro, walking over to

Tanya and putting his arm about her shoulders, 'that your sister is capable of making up her own mind.'

It was going to be a difficult day, thought Tanya wearily. She wished Charlene hadn't come. She wished she could have spent it alone with Alejandro. Before her sister arrived she had been on top of the world; now she was slowly sliding down, and she did not want to. She wanted to stay up there; she wanted to retain these feelings, savour them, remember them.

She made the coffee strong, the way Alejandro liked it, and got out rolls and butter.

'Can you imagine Peter eating something like this for breakfast?' asked Charlene with a wicked laugh. 'He was an egg and bacon man, Alejandro, very much a traditionalist.'

'Is that so?' he asked, and there was a sudden edge to his tone.

Tanya wished her sister had not brought Peter's name into the conversation.

But Charlene was not finished yet. 'Oh, yes, he was a stickler for all things proper, wasn't he, Tan?'

Tanya smiled weakly and nodded.

'For instance he would never have stayed the night with Tanya before they were married. He loved her too much; he wouldn't have thought it proper.'

Alejandro pushed back his chair and stood up, dark eyes savage. 'I think I should go.'

'What's wrong?' taunted Charlene. 'Can't you bear to hear me talk about Peter? He was a fine man without a doubt, and Tanya was devastated when he died. They were so much in love.'

'Charlene, shut up,' hissed Tanya through grated teeth.

'Why, when it's the truth? Don't you ever talk about Peter to Alejandro? Don't you ever tell him what a good marriage you had? You'll never find another man as good as he was.'

Tanya knew why Charlene was saying these things,

but that did not stop her being appalled, and when Alejandro spun round on his heel and left the room, his face tense, she followed him out to the lift. 'I apologise for Charlene's outspokenness,' she said. 'She had no right saying those things.'

'But I've no doubt they were true.' Gone was the gentleness, the caring, replaced by a stone-cold anger. 'I hadn't realised how much you loved your husband. I think I should perhaps be grateful to Charlene for opening my eyes.'

'It's perfectly natural I should love the man I married,' she told him, feeling a rising anger too. Why should it make any difference? People could love again, couldn't they?

'It sounds as though your feelings for Peter went far deeper than they ever did for me.' His eyes blazed coldly into hers, testing, questioning, awaiting her response.

Tanya turned away, disappointed and confused. In a matter of seconds the magic spell had been broken.

His hand on her shoulder spun her round. 'I'm waiting, Tanya.' And his clipped tones were like a knife in her heart. 'Don't be afraid to tell me the truth.'

'There is more than one kind of love,' she said huskily. 'What I felt for Peter —— '

'Was so strong that you cannot forget it,' he snarled. 'Is that what you were going to say? Could I be right in thinking that last night and this morning your thoughts were with Peter and not me, that it was his body you were drowning in, not mine, that you only gave yourself to me because you still ache with love for this man I did not know? I think I have a lot to thank Charlene for. It would appear I was in danger of making a fool of myself for the second time.'

The lift came, and without another word he stepped into it. Tanya walked slowly back to the apartment, feeling rejected and disappointed and hurt, and extremely angry with her sister.

'I guess that put him in his place,' said Charlene with satisfaction.

Tanya glared, her blue eyes fierce. 'You had no right talking about Peter like that.'

'It needed something to get that star-struck look out of your eyes. Really, Tan, you need your head examining for falling for Alejandro all over again. I know he's got charm, oodles of it, but the truth is he's a two-timing creep. I've actually done you a favour. He didn't like it, did he? He didn't like hearing about Peter.'

'Nor did I,' snapped Tanya.

'Surely you're not trying to forget him?' Charlene frowned. 'You're not trying to replace him with Alejandro?'

'I'll never forget Peter,' she replied. 'He'll always have a special place in my heart. But there's nothing to stop me falling in love again.'

'With that swine?'

'You don't know him, Charlene.'

'I know what he did to you, and I'll never forgive him — and nor should you. He's not serious, you know. He's duping you again; he's playing with you. Can't you see what he's like?'

Tanya closed her eyes. This was a side to Alejandro that she had blacked out of her mind for the last twelve hours. She did not want to think about it. He had seemed to be genuinely fond of her; it had gone further than simple attraction, hadn't it? It was why he was so hurt; he felt let down by Charlene's deliberate comments. And there hadn't been time to talk to him, to tell him that he meant more to her than Peter ever had. *More to her*! The thought stood out in her mind in neon lights. It was true. She was deeply and irrevocably in love. It had never gone away.

'Tanya?'

'I see him differently from you, Charlene. I know I was hurt and upset all those years ago, and I said I hated him, but — well, I don't any more, and nothing you can say will make any difference.'

'The real question, then, is, does he love you?' Charlene looked at her sister with concern in her eyes. 'And I think we both know the answer to that. He isn't capable of loving. When I said he was a womaniser I meant it. He might let you think he loves you, but I expect he does that to all the girls he takes out. Be careful, Tanya, please. I don't want you hurt again.'

There was no more said after that. They went to the same beach as yesterday, they had lunch at the apartment, they strolled around Santa Cruz, idly watching the election of the old-age pensioner *carnaval* queen. They went back to the apartment and changed, and Charlene took her to a popular restaurant in Esperanza.

It had been a long day, thought Tanya, when she finally went to bed. Charlene had tried to persuade her to return to Matilde's, but she had been adamant. 'I came up here to see the *carnaval*, every little bit of it, I'm not going to miss out now.'

And so, with an admonition to be careful, Charlene had left, driving away in her smart white car.

The bed felt empty without Alejandro, the night never-ending. Tanya kept hoping he might ring, but the phone remained silent, and she woke the next morning feeling thoroughly dejected. Even the weather reflected her mood, the jagged peaks of the mountains hidden behind a grey curtain of rain.

She stayed in all day, alone, miserable, willing Alejandro to contact her, wanting to make amends, to explain her feelings, to repair the rift Charlene had torn in their delicate relationship.

He had left her a programme of events for the *carnaval*, and tonight was the *carnaval* queen gala heats — and if Alejandro was a member of the jury, as he put it, then she wouldn't be seeing him tonight either!

She toyed with the idea of going anyway, but as there was no sign of the rain letting up there was really no sense in getting wet when she probably wouldn't even see Alejandro. She decided to watch it on television instead.

It was late afternoon when the skies cleared, when the fangs of the Anaga Mountains stood out in sharp relief against a haze of blue. She would go for a walk; she had had enough of sitting indoors, beautiful though the apartment was.

Before she had even fetched her jacket from the wardrobe a knock came on the door, a loud, peremptory knock, and she knew it was Alejandro, still sounding as though he was in a bad mood. But at least he was here; she could talk to him, explain, make him understand that Charlene had been deliberately trying to cause mischief.

Her heartbeats drummed painfully and she pinned a smile of welcome to her lips as she opened the door, and even though Alejandro's face looked like thunder she still kept smiling as she stood back for him to enter. 'I'm so glad you've come.' He had on a crisp white shirt and dark trousers, as though he'd been out on business all day. He looked devastatingly handsome, and triggered everything inside her into vibrant life.

'The only reason I'm here,' he said, the moment the door closed, 'is because I feel responsible for you.' He walked across to the wide window with its panoramic views over the capital.

'You don't have to feel guilty,' Tanya flared in sudden anger. She had been hoping for an apology, at least a suggestion they talk. 'I don't mind being alone.'

He turned round slowly and faced her, his brown eyes cool, a faint frown between his brows. 'Have you been out today?'

'No,' she admitted, 'but only because of the weather. As a matter of fact I was just about to go for a walk.'

'Then I'll join you. I think we should talk.' Still no hint that he was pleased to see her.

'What about?' asked Tanya.

'Us. You and me. You and Peter. Your feelings.'

'How about yours?' she countered sharply.

'Mine too, if you like,' he replied with an indifferent lift of his shoulders.

Tanya felt a faint surge of hope. He was prepared to discuss *his* feelings. Maybe now they would get somewhere.

They left the apartment in silence, descended to the ground floor in silence, Alejandro standing straight and tall and unapproachable, Tanya's heartbeats hurried, every one of her senses alert and responsive. How could he ignore her like this after the passion of their lovemaking? How could he turn his feelings on and off because of a few ill-chosen words?

The lift doors opened and they walked out into the sunshine, but Alejandro's reserve did not melt. They strolled side by side, mingling with happy, voluble Santacruceros, all in party mood. They were probably the only two who weren't smiling. *Carnaval* fever had taken over everyone during this pre-Lenten festival. Banks and shops were closed; the whole city was out celebrating.

Tanya thought they were heading towards the port, but instead he led the way into a park, which was a welcome oasis of greenery among all the offices and apartment blocks. Tropical trees and flowers grew in abundance: bottlebrush, with its racemes of scarlet flowers, jacaranda vivid with clusters of purple, yellow mimosa, even a red poinsettia as tall as herself, which she found totally amazing, because she had only ever seen it as a houseplant.

'Why, Tanya, why?' he asked as they walked slowly along the path.

'Why what?' She turned to look at him, saw the

disapproving frown between his brows, the grimness to his lips, and she ached for the rapport of two days ago.

'Why did you let me make love to you?'

It was a loaded question, and Tanya knew a lot depended on her answer. 'Because—I couldn't help myself,' she said slowly, hesitantly. 'Because I wanted to.'

'Were you thinking of Peter?' He looked straight ahead as he spoke, and she saw a muscle jerking in his jaw, a sure sign of inner tension.

'Did I behave as though I was thinking of another man?' She wanted him to believe that she had been genuine in her response without her having to put it into words.

'I suppose not, but who really understands the vagaries of a woman's mind?'

'I am what you see,' she told him. 'I don't know what type of woman you normally associate with, but I can assure you that I don't hide behind anything.'

They paused to look at a statue of a solidly built woman with large, pendulous breasts and a scrap of material covering her loins. She was half hidden in the mist from a fountain and was somewhat the worse for wear, but nevertheless her nudity managed to arouse in Tanya some of the feelings she had felt the night before last.

There had been no coyness, no embarrassment at stripping off in front of him—it had all seemed so natural, so right, and yet now he was accusing her of having false emotions.

'I wouldn't like to think that you did, Tanya, but after what your sister said——'

She stopped him with a sharp outburst. 'Charlene was out to cause trouble, that's all. If you prefer to believe her, then this conversation is pointless.' She swung round on her heel and began to walk back the way they had come. She was disappointed in him, outraged in fact that he still thought the worst of her.

She had never questioned *him*, even though thoughts of Juanita were often uppermost in her mind.

He caught up with her. 'There are so many unanswered questions, Tanya.'

'And do any of them really matter?' she riposted, her eyes the same vivid blue as the sky. 'Why can't we accept that things have happened in our lives that neither of us were happy about at the time? Why can't we accept that the past is just that, over and done with? Why can't we forget everything and — and begin all over again?' She was baring her soul here, letting him know that she was still attracted to him.

'You mean that?'

Tanya nodded.

'You're willing to forget that I've been married?'

'Yes.'

'You're willing to forget Inocente?'

Tanya paused. 'That depends on whether you see her again.'

'I'll naturally have to see her to tell her it's all over between us.'

'So there was something?' she accused, eyes narrowing.

'Inocente thought so.'

'But you didn't; you were playing her along?' The same as he had her all those years ago? Was she making a terrible mistake in suggesting they start to see each other again? Could Charlene be right — he was not to be trusted?

Alejandro's breath came out on a surge of impatience. 'I am not "playing her along", as you put it. Inocente knows what my feelings for her are; she's simply hoping that they'll change.'

'And meantime she's pleasant company? Have you ever taken her to bed?' The moment the question was out Tanya wished she could retract it. She was the one who had said let bygones be bygones, and yet here she was asking questions that she had no right asking. But she wanted to know. This was too immediate. It wasn't like Peter or Juanita; this was now, a girl in his present life. She had a right to know what was going on between them.

'As a matter of fact, no,' he answered, 'though I don't expect you'll believe me. You seem to have it firmly fixed in your mind that we're having a raging affair.'

'Inocente has always given that impression, but nevertheless, if you tell me it's not so, then I believe you.'

They had left the park now and were strolling between high-rise apartments. It was not such a relaxing atmosphere, and Tanya regretted turning back. She would have liked to seal their new agreement with a kiss but there was no chance of that here, there were far too many people milling around.

'Let's go back to the apartment,' he said gruffly, and Tanya remembered the last time he had said that — and where it had led! It was as though someone had suddenly put a match to her, lighting her up from inside, and there was a lift to her step as hand in hand they retraced their steps. Suddenly the future looked rosy.

As they stood waiting for the lift he took her face between his palms and gently kissed her. The doors opened and they turned together — and Inocente stood watching them! The woman's eyes were filled with pure hatred as they turned upon Tanya. She was wearing a tight, cream, linen suit which showed off her sensual body, and extremely high-heeled shoes which made her legs look very long.

Alejandro was the first to speak. 'Inocente, what are you doing here?' He spoke in English, forcing her to do the same.

'What does it look like?' Her eyes softened as she looked at him. 'I came to see you, *amor mio*. I knew you were one of the jury this evening. I guessed I

would find you here, but I did not expect to find you—
otherwise engaged. What is—Tanya doing here?' She
somehow managed to make her name sound like a
dirty word.

'Tanya is my guest for the duration of the *carnaval*,'
he answered patiently.

'She is staying in your apartment?' Inocente's wide
eyes opened even further.

'That is right. Would you care to come up and join
us for afternoon tea? It's a little late, I'm afraid,
because——'

'No, I would not,' snapped the dark-haired girl
viciously, 'but I would like to talk to you.'

'For a few minutes,' he agreed, and, turning to
Tanya, said softly, 'Would you mind very much going
up alone? I won't be long, I promise.' He touched her
chin in a gentle, affectionate gesture.

What if she said no? What would he say then? Tanya
was furious. Just as they had started to get back on a
sound footing this woman had turned up and spoiled
everything. But she kept her feelings well-hidden,
smiling at him warmly, touching his face too. 'I'll look
forward to it,' she said huskily.

She entered the lift without a glance at Inocente,
trying to look every inch a woman in love, a woman
confident of her man. In actual truth she wasn't, not at
all. This woman was clever and probably knew
Alejandro far better than she did. She would know
how to wind him round her little finger. He had said he
would tell her it was all over, but Tanya doubted
whether Inocente would accept it. This was probably
the end. He would come up and tell her that he could
not keep his word—Inocente might even come with
him to make sure that she got her marching orders.

Dejectedly she sat down on the beautiful soft leather
settee, thinking that she would never see a white settee
again without remembering this moment. What hurt
most was that Inocente had come to his apartment to

find him, and yet Alejandro had told her that he had
invited no one here. So how had she known about it?
It was clear she could believe nothing he said.

It was an age before he returned. Tanya was even
toying with the idea of packing her suitcase and
demanding that he take her back to Matilde's. None of
it was worth the heartache. Then he walked in the
door. 'Tanya, *mi cariño*, I am so sorry to have kept
you waiting. Inocente was not so easy to handle as I
imagined.'

'You mean she wouldn't accept the fact that you
want to finish with her?' Tanya rose and faced him, no
warmth or pleasure in her face. 'I didn't really think
she would; she's the clinging vine type. But you don't
have to worry. I've had time to sit and think. It
wouldn't have worked; we're completely incompatible,
you and I.'

'Incompatible?' He looked baffled by this sudden
attack.

'Except where things physical are concerned, of
course, but where would that get us? Nowhere at all.
Once you'd got it out of your system I'd be dumped
again. No, Alejandro, I think it would be better all
round if I went back to Matilde's for the rest of my
holiday.'

'You're not serious?' His frown was deep, his eyes
darkly incredulous. 'Tanya—you have it all wrong.
Inocente has gone. It is over, finished; she finally
accepted it.'

Tanya swallowed hard. She wanted to believe him
but was not sure if she could. It was all so delicate, this
relationship of theirs. She felt as though she were
poised on a knife-edge all the time.

'You do not believe me?' He looked troubled by her
attitude.

'I'd like to, but from what little I've seen of Inocente
I didn't think she'd give you up that easily.'

'It wasn't easy, I agree,' he said 'but it's done now;

you can forget her.' He took her into his arms and held
her for several long moments, stroking the honey-gold
of her hair, soothing, relaxing, instilling peace into her,
until finally Tanya lifted her head and smiled into his
face.

'That's better,' he murmured, and he lifted her chin,
pressing a kiss to her mouth. 'My beautiful Tanya,
don't ever doubt anything I tell you. I would never lie.'

Except by omission, she thought. He had never told
her about Juanita, and she would not have found out if
she hadn't seen the letter from his father. But she
believed now that he had told Inocente the truth, and
she was happy in his arms, accepting his kiss, responding, holding him too, letting him see by actions rather
than words that she believed him.

The gala heats began at nine-thirty, and Alejandro
told her that Beatriz and Crisógono were coming so
she would not be alone. They had a light meal of an
omelette beforehand and, even though they thought
they had plenty of time, when they got to the square it
was almost time for the event to start.

Alejandro spotted his brother on the second row and
left Tanya to make her way to them. 'I'll see you later
when it's all over,' he murmured, his mouth close to
hers, one last, intimate kiss exchanged.

Tanya felt on top of the world again, watching him
walk away. Lord, he was magnificent: tall, imposing,
exciting, standing out from the crowd. And he was
hers! There had been no words of love exchanged as
yet, and he hadn't made love to her again, but she was
confident now. It was all coming together. She loved
him and——

A hand tapping her shoulder made her spin around,
and there was Inocente, black eyes blazing, two spots
of high colour in her cheeks. 'You are looking very
sure of yourself, but I can guarantee that whatever
Alejandro told you it is not true.'

'Really?' Tanya lifted her chin, trying her hardest to

look disdainful, even though her heart was stammering uneasily. 'And why would he lie?'

'To keep you happy—until you go back to England. And then——' she paused to add emphasis to her words, '—he will be mine again.'

CHAPTER NINE

INOCENTE sounded so confident that Tanya felt like
believing her, but Alejandro had been adamant that it
was all over. The girl was lying; she had to be. 'I think
you're wrong,' she said coldly. 'Alejandro and I have
reached an understanding. You're no longer a part of
his life, and he told you that. Why won't you accept
it?'

'Because I know what he feels for you will not last.
He has had other girls before, but always he has come
back to me, and he always will. So you see, you are
wasting your time.'

This sounded dangerously close to the truth—it was
exactly what had happened to her in England—but
surely Alejandro wouldn't do the dirty on her a second
time? Surely she could believe that his feelings for her
were genuine, that this time it was going to be a
permanent relationship?

'You're lying,' she said sharply. 'It's yourself you're
trying to convince, not me.' There were crowds all
around them, but she was conscious of nothing except
this woman with bright red lips and fingernails like
talons.

Inocente gave a shrug of her narrow shoulders. 'If
you do not believe me, wait and see. It will happen, I
can promise you. Alejandro and I go back a long way;
we are close, *very* close. I have spent many happy
hours here in his apartment, as well as at his home in
Orotava. There is nothing I do not know about him,
and it is a fact that one day soon you will be—how do
you say it in England?—you will be history.'

There was contempt in the woman's tone, a curl to
her lips, and Tanya felt cold inside. She was strongly

127

inclined to believe Inocente — it went along with everything she knew about Alejandro, but still she kept her chin high. 'You can say what you like; I shall not believe you. Alejandro and I — '

'Tanya! *Tanya!*' Beatriz's voice, loud and clear, reached her from her seat several yards away. 'Come along; you will miss the beginning.'

Relief shuddered through her as she caught Beatriz's eye. 'Excuse me,' she said to Inocente. 'I must go.'

'Don't think you are going to win,' spat the other girl, 'just because you have got his family on your side. Alejandro loves me, and it will not be long now before he asks me to marry him.' With a toss of her head, her thick black hair swinging across her face, she turned and marched away.

Tanya felt herself trembling, though whether it was with anger or relief that the confrontation was over, she did not know. Damn Inocente and her vicious tongue. Again she was left feeling extremely unsure of herself.

She squeezed past a row of people to the vacant seat Beatriz had kept for her, sinking into it with relief, unaware that her face had gone deathly pale.

'What was Inocente saying to you?' Beatriz's face was full of concern.

Tanya grimaced. 'She was warning me off your brother-in-law. Thank you for rescuing me.'

A torrent of angry Spanish flowed from the woman's lips, finishing finally, 'That girl, she is bad. You must not listen. Alejandro is a fool for getting involved with her. I tell him so, many times, but he take no notice. What it is about her I do not know, but she is evil. She has her — what do you say? — she has her nails stuck in him and she will not let go.'

Crisógono nodded his agreement. 'Beatriz is right; Inocente is no good. I wonder what she's doing here.'

'She came to see Alejandro,' Tanya told him. 'We met her earlier outside his apartment.'

'And she didn't take kindly to seeing you with him?' Crisógono nodded his understanding. 'That explains her attack. Don't let it worry you, Tanya. It's very clear to both Beatriz and me whom he prefers. We said so the other night after you'd gone, didn't we?' he asked his wife. 'I haven't seen my brother so happy in a long time.'

And then the proceedings started and there was no time for further conversation.

Tanya was enthralled by it all, and absolutely astounded by the lavishness and size of the costumes. Beatriz told her that they took many, many months to complete. 'They are made by top dress designers who guard their creations with their life. The dresses have to be hinged so that they can get through the stage doors, because the designers will not even tell the organisers their dimensions. Sometimes it is difficult even for the girl to walk.'

Tanya could see this for herself as each girl paraded about the stage. On occasions, as the contestant turned to walk this way and that, male assistants had to lift the dress and turn it for her. The girl herself was almost hidden inside a startling creation of feathers and sequins and silks of all hues and shapes.

Even with the girl's arms outstretched, the skirt of the costume was still at least another metre each side of her, and her striking head-dress was so tall and unwieldy that it was a wonder it stayed in place, or that her neck was strong enough to stand the weight. Each design was different, resembling a fine bird of paradise, a peacock, a butterfly, a dragon, a tree, or nothing at all, just a glittering display that took your breath away.

'To make, they cost millions of pesetas,' Beatriz informed her. 'Different Canarian companies sponsor them, and the girls, they spend many hours in the *gimnasio* preparing themselves for the weight of the dresses.'

Tanya could well believe this. She had never seen

anything so extravagant as these 'dresses' in all her life; they made the dresses sewn by Matilde look very simple indeed.

The girls were beautiful also. Tanya had a sudden image of Alejandro watching them, eyeing them up and down. How could he not be attracted? From the waist up the girls were virtually naked, except for a spangly creation barely covering their breasts. They swayed gently to the music — as far as the weight of their outfits would let them — smiling all the time, their eyes sparkling, inviting.

Jealousy seared through her. Would he be tempted by any of them? Would any of them be his next victim? *Victim*! Was that how she saw herself? The word had crept into her mind unawares, but it showed how little she trusted him, how Inocente had poisoned her mind. But so too had Charlene. Both, in their own way, had warned her off Alejandro. Shouldn't she take some notice at least?

'Something is wrong?'

Tanya discovered that Beatriz was watching her face, seeing the conflicting emotions.

'You are not enjoying it?'

'Yes, yes, of course I am,' Tanya answered immediately. 'It was just a thought — nothing to do with the gala.'

'It is Inocente who has upset you, yes?'

Tanya lifted her shoulders, 'A little.'

Beatriz shook her head angrily. 'More than a little, I would say; you must try to forget her. Do you love Alejandro?'

Beatriz's direct question shocked Tanya, and she looked at the other woman, wide-eyed. 'Is it obvious?'

'To me, yes,' said the woman, smiling softly. 'Because I love him too, as a brother-in-law, of course. He is a fine man, if a little stupid sometimes where the female sex is concerned — and I do not mean you, Tanya. You are different; you would be good for him.

You are not interested in him for his money, like a lot of other girls, like Inocente. That is all she is after, I am sure.'

'I've never thought much about money,' Tanya agreed. She hadn't even known that Alejandro was wealthy. Oh, he had the trappings now all right, but there had been no expensive car or designer clothes all those years ago. What did money matter where love was concerned? It certainly didn't matter to her.

'Are you seeing Alejandro later, when the judging is over?' asked Beatriz.

'He said so,' Tanya acknowledged. Unless Inocente waylaid him first! She could see the other girl standing several yards away, apparently intent on the beautiful girls and their floating dresses, but frequently glancing in Tanya's direction. Occasionally their eyes met, and there was such venom on the dark girl's face that Tanya felt as though she were being beaten to the ground.

'Then we will have to make sure that you get to him before Inocente.' Beatriz glanced fiercely across at where the other girl was standing.

Tanya had not realised that Beatriz had spotted Inocente, but now the girl looked across and saw both pairs of eyes in her direction. Her chin came up, her black hair was tossed, and a supremely confident smile curved her lips. I know what you're thinking, she seemed to say, but I shall get to him first, don't worry.

Beatriz swore beneath her breath and her hand caught hold of Tanya's, squeezing tightly. The heats drew to an end, there was a surge of movement from the audience, and Tanya lost sight of Inocente. Beatriz swept her along and whether it was by good luck or genuine management, Alejandro was suddenly at their side.

'Did you enjoy that, *mi cariño*?' he asked with a gentle smile, his hand finding hers and holding it firmly.

'Yes, it was most enjoyable. They were wonderful creations.'

'Weren't they indeed? How the girls manage to walk in them I don't know.'

'They were very pretty girls. Have you made up your mind who's to be in the finals?'

'You didn't hear it announced?' He frowned faintly.

Tanya shook her head. 'I'm afraid Beatriz and I were talking.'

'I should have known.' His face lightened. 'Beatriz likes to talk, and always at the wrong time. Never mind, you will see the finalists tomorrow. I have already made up my mind who I would like to win, but, of course, I am not the only member of the jury.'

Tanya tried to imagine which girl it was he had decided would make a suitable queen of the *carnaval*, and in so doing felt another stab of jealousy. It was silly, she knew, but she could not help it. She simply did not trust him. And how could a relationship succeed without trust?

As they followed the crowds Tanya caught a glimpse of an evil-looking Inocente. Her eyes were on Alejandro and she did not even notice Tanya watching her, and Alejandro, Tanya was pleased to note, did not even see the girl. Beatriz did, though, and carefully steered their small party in a different direction, and very soon Inocente was out of sight.

'Are you coming back to the apartment, Cris?' Alejandro asked his brother.

But both he and his wife shook their head. 'We must get home; besides, I'm sure you'd much prefer to be alone with Tanya.'

Tanya was suddenly not sure that she wanted to be alone with Alejandro. It was this thing called trust that was bothering her. Inocente had sounded so very sure that they would get back together once she, Tanya, had returned to England. And he had said nothing about seeing her again once her holiday was over, nothing about a continued relationship. It really did seem as though he was interested only in the here and now.

They strolled hand in hand through the streets, and everywhere people were laughing and talking excitedly. 'You're very quiet,' remarked Alejandro as they ascended in the high-speed lift to his apartment.

'I'm tired,' she lied.

'Then I won't keep you up any longer. You have enjoyed tonight?'

'Yes.'

'Beatriz and Cris looked after you?'

'Of course.'

'I thought you looked a bit strained.'

Tanya shrugged. 'There's nothing wrong that a good night's sleep won't put right.' Except that she doubted she would sleep. Her mind was too active, too distressed.

At the apartment door he hesitated. 'I want to come in, but I know that if I do it will be impossible to leave, and I promised Manolo I would be there in the morning to tell him all about tonight.'

He took her face between his palms and kissed first her forehead, then the tip of her nose, and finally her lips.

Tanya felt the usual flood of sensations, but she could not respond. Inocente's confident words, and her vindictive expression, were too vivid in her mind.

Alejandro held her from him and frowned. 'There *is* something wrong. Tanya, you must tell me; I want no more barriers between us.'

She wanted to tell him what Inocente had said, she wanted to hear him deny it, but what if he didn't? Perhaps tomorrow she would feel better. She would have sorted out the conflict in her mind, she might even feel able to give him the benefit of the doubt, but not now, not tonight, not while Inocente's malevolent face loomed large in her mind's eye.

'Alejandro, I promise you, it's just tiredness. It's not been an easy day.'

'My fault because I was angry with you,' he said sorrowfully. He slid his hand beneath the fall of her hair to her nape, his thumb caressing the soft skin behind her ear. 'I neglected you; left you here all alone. I apologise. The truth is I was jealous of your husband, and the love you felt for him. I could not think of you without picturing you together, you in his arms making love.'

And now *she* was jealous of Inocente and all those other girls he had been watching so closely tonight. Not Juanita; Juanita was his past. But he was, after all, a healthy, full-blooded male, more sensual than most. How could he fail to be attracted by them? By any girl? She already knew that he could not remain faithful to one girl at a time; always he had two on the go. How could she have faith in him?

He bent and kissed her again, his lips brushing hers gently. '*Buenas noches, mi corazón.* Tomorrow we will spend the whole day together, I promise you. Go now and get your beauty sleep.'

Tanya nodded, smiling weakly. 'Goodnight, Alejandro.'

As she had known, sleep did not come easily, and when she did manage to drop off she had nightmarish dreams about Inocente. She woke soon after seven, feeling that she had not slept at all.

She had just made herself a strong cup of coffee when the telephone rang. 'Tanya, I have bad news.' Alejandro's deep voice sounded in her ear. 'There is some sort of trouble at the packing plant; I must go and sort it out.'

In one way she felt relieved, in another desperate because she had another day to get through alone. She pulled a wry face to herself. 'It's all right, Alejandro; you do whatever you have to do.'

'Did you not sleep well, Tanya? You still sound weary.'

'I suppose I am,' she agreed. 'I was over-tired actually. I hardly slept at all.'

'Have I woken you, *mi cariño*?'

'No, no, I was making myself a drink.'

'Then I suggest you take it to bed with you and try to get a few more hours. You'll have another late night tonight at the finals.'

Tanya was not sure whether she wanted to go again. Was the pleasure of seeing the scintillating costumes worth the torment of visualising Alejandro with these girls? 'Will Beatriz be there again?' she asked.

'But of course. It is an annual event for them, notwithstanding the fact that one of the finalists is Beatriz's cousin.'

'Really? She never said.' On the other hand, they had been talking about Inocente so much that they had discussed little else. Was this the one he favoured? Was she as beautiful as Beatriz? Actually, all the girls were beautiful, and she could not blame him for showing an interest in these lovely Canarian girls, Inocente included. With her own fair complexion and golden hair she felt quite pale and uninteresting beside them.

And why was she getting paranoid? He had chosen her; he had been attracted to her in England; he had, he said, given up Inocente. Why was she worrying? 'I'll be ready when you come,' she said, but her voice was strained.

When the doorbell sounded later in the morning she sprang up to open it. When she saw Inocente she could not believe her eyes. Not this woman again.

'If you've come looking for Alejandro he's not here,' she said sharply.

'Yes, I know, I've just left him,' announced Inocente with satisfaction.

Tanya felt a fierce pain stab her heart. So Alejandro had been lying when he said it was business keeping

him away. It was Inocente, this girl he insisted he had
finished with! This was the type of business he meant.

'He asked me to tell you that he won't be able to
make it today after all. He said you might as well go
out and enjoy the sunshine instead of sitting around.'

A chill stole down Tanya's spine. He had asked
Inocente to pass on this message instead of ringing her
again himself! 'Will he be here for the gala queen final
tonight?' Her voice was little more than a whisper.

Inocente lifted her slender shoulders. 'I expect so;
he takes his duties as a member of the jury seriously,
but I imagine he will be leaving straight away again
afterwards.'

Meaning he would not have time for her! How much
of this was true and how much Inocente had made up
Tanya was not sure. Only of one thing was she sure: he
would not be coming here today.

'Thank you for telling me,' she said, her chin high,
trying not to show her distress.

'It is my pleasure.' With a satisfied smile the girl
turned and headed back towards the lift.

Tanya closed the door quietly, fighting the urge to
slam it. Damn Inocente! Damn Alejandro! Between
them they were playing some kind of game with her.
Well she *would* go out; she would go out all day and
she wouldn't go to the finals. If he looked for her she
wouldn't find her, and, if he didn't like it, too bad. He
should have apologised himself instead of letting
Inocente pass on his message.

If it hadn't been for the fact that she wanted to see
the grand parade on Shrove Tuesday, and the firework
display afterwards, she would have taken a bus back to
Matilde's right there and then, and if he thought he
was going to come to her tomorrow and console her
with apologies he could think again.

The telephone rang but she did not answer; it could
only be Charlene, and she did not want to speak to
her. She picked up her bag and left the apartment, this

time getting a great deal of satisfaction out of slamming the door.

It was a long day and an even longer evening. In the end she did go to the gala queen finals, but she stood well out of sight and melted into the crowd the instant the decision was announced.

She did not want to go back to the apartment yet in case Alejandro came looking for her, but where was there to go at this time of night? Until suddenly she heard her name called. 'Tanya, it is you, isn't it?' She looked across and saw Juan smiling at her. 'What are you doing here alone?' he asked. 'Where is Alejandro?'

'I've no idea,' she answered with a shrug of her shoulders

Juan frowned. 'But I thought you and my cousin were very close. I thought ——'

'You thought wrong,' she interrupted sharply.

'Charlene told me that you had resumed your relationship of however many years ago it was.'

'Charlene must have got the wrong impression.'

'But you are staying in Alejandro's apartment?'

'It doesn't mean a thing. It was a generous gesture on his part, that's all.'

'In that case you won't have any objections to joining me for a drink?'

'Not at all.' Tanya smiled easily. This was the answer to her prayers.

Juan spent the next hour talking about Charlene, extolling her virtues, leaving Tanya in no doubt that he had fallen for her sister very badly, and when he finally took her back to the apartment she felt that she was safe from Alejandro.

At the door Juan bade her goodnight, and she did not put the light on until she had closed it behind her. She had the shock of her life when she saw Alejandro standing in the middle of the floor waiting for her, his face thunderous, his whole body rigid with anger.

'Where the devil have you been?' The furious words

were thrust across the room. 'Do you not care that I
have been out of my mind with worry?' I rang Matilde,
I rang your sister, I was thinking of telephoning the
police.'

'What do you mean, where have I been?' demanded
Tanya crossly. 'A more pertinent question would be,
what are you doing here? I understood I wouldn't be
seeing you today.'

'I said I was busy this morning.' A black scowl
darkened his features. 'I telephoned; I came. You were
missing, gone; no message, nothing.' His eyes were
piercingly sharp. 'I even thought you might have left
altogether until I checked your clothes. Where the hell
have you been, and whose voice was that I heard?
Someone you picked up? *Maldito sea*, Tanya, how can
you do this to me?'

She lifted her chin in her usual defensive manner. 'It
wasn't a stranger, as a matter of fact; it was your
cousin.'

'Manuel again? I thought you said there was nothing
going on there.'

'Not Manuel, Juan.'

'Juan?' he asked with a frown.

'That's right,' she agreed coolly. 'It isn't a crime, is
it, to have a drink with someone else?' Lord, why was
he so angry when all this was his doing?

'Have you been with him all day?' The questions
were fired at her like bullets from a gun.

'Goodness, no. I only met him an hour ago in the
square.'

'You were there? But Cris said they hadn't seen
you.'

'I didn't sit with them.'

'But why?'

'You should know the answer to that,' she returned
bitterly.

His frown deepened. 'You'd better explain.'

'What is there to say, expect that I would have

thought more of you if you'd given me your excuses in person?'

'You're not making sense, Tanya.'

She sighed impatiently and moved further into the room. 'I'm talking about Inocente. Why send a message with her? Why didn't you tell me yourself that you couldn't make it?'

'You've seen Inocente?' His eyes narrowed questioningly.

'It would appear that so did you,' she riposted. 'And to think that I believed your excuse.'

'Tanya.' He took her by the shoulders and looked deep into her eyes. 'I have not seen Inocente today.'

She ripped herself free before his nearness could destroy her. 'Don't lie to me, Alejandro.'

'It is the truth,' he insisted. 'Tanya, look at me.' He caught hold of her again. 'Why would I lie about something like that?'

'You tell me,' she spat, avoiding his eyes. They would be her undoing.

'I wouldn't lie to you.'

'No?' Her brows rose sceptically. 'I'm afraid I don't believe you.'

'But you believed Inocente?'

'Why would she tell lies?' Tanya asked. 'Why would she say *you* had sent her? She must have known I would find out whether she was speaking the truth.'

'She would lie to split us up, Tanya.'

Tanya eyed him coldly. 'If you haven't seen her today, then explain how she knew that you'd already phoned me. It made perfect sense when she said that you wouldn't be able to make it after all.'

He shook his head. 'I do not know how she knew, but rest assured I will find out.' Then his tone softened. '*Mi cariño*, how could you think this of me?'

Quite easily, thought Tanya. It was difficult to trust him completely when he had let her down so badly in the past. 'Inocente sounded very sincere.'

'Inocente was extremely angry when I finished with
her. I did not realise it at the time, but it is obvious she
will go to any lengths to put an end to our relationship.
She sees you as the person who has come between me
and her. The truth of the matter is that I never had any
serious intentions where Inocente was concerned.'

The same as he had never had any serious intentions
about her all those years ago. The question was, had
he now? Or was she as much a game to him as Inocente
had been? Was this how he treated all his women?
When someone else took his fancy was the last one
dumped? Maybe she ought to ask him.

But before she could put her thoughts into words
Alejandro's arms tightened around her and his mouth
sought hers. 'Let's not talk about Inocente any more,'
he muttered thickly. '*Dios*, Tanya, how I have suffered
today. Do not do this to me again.'

'You think I haven't suffered too?' She tried to pull
away, but his arms tightened.

'*Querida*, I am sure you have, but I will make it up
to you, I promise.' His mouth closed over hers, and
instantly Tanya was lost. Whatever this man did,
whatever he said, contact with him was always explosive. In this respect at least nothing had changed.

The kiss deepened, but when he tried to take their
lovemaking further Tanya wrenched herself away. 'No,
Alejandro, not tonight.' Not any night, in fact, not
until she was very, very sure of his feelings.

His frown grew harsh. 'This is because of Inocente?'

Tanya nodded, but it was only partly true. She
wanted to know where she stood before she continued
any sort of intimate relationship; she wanted to know
what he felt, what the future held in store for her.

He muttered beneath his breath. 'I am sorry this has
happened, Tanya, and I am even more sorry that I
cannot stay and put matters right between us, but I
must get home to Manolo.' He looked angry at his
commitment. 'I want you to promise me, Tanya, that

tomorrow you will be here when I come. No more running away?'

'I promise,' she said quietly, almost uninterestedly.

His lips tightened. 'And if Inocente turns up again do not speak to her; send her away and let me deal with her. *Buenas noches, amor mío*. I am sorry you have been so troubled.

'*Buenas noches*, Alejandro.'

He did not kiss her again, for which Tanya was grateful, because she doubted whether she would have been able to stop herself responding, and when he had gone her mind was a maelstrom. She needed proof that he wanted more from her than her body, proof that his intentions were serious, and until that time came she had to hold him off, no matter how difficult she found it.

CHAPTER TEN

To TANYA'S relief the next few days were so hectic that there was no time for intimacies, no time for indepth conversations. There was so much going on, every day something different: the opening parade, the *comparsas* show, the dancers, the fancy dress contest, the songs of the *rondallas* — street musicians — the *murgas* — groups of musical critics poking fun at local dignitaries and politicians — the orchestral musical festival, and, of course, the grand procession.

Manolo came for that, and all Alejandro's brothers and sisters and aunts and uncles and nephews and nieces who were not taking part in the parade. Tanya had learned that La Orotava's own *carnaval* was taking place this week too, but because most members of Alejandro's family lived nearer to Santa Cruz, it was the custom for them all to come here.

It took four hours for the parade to pass by. Alejandro found her a vantage point where she could see everything clearly, and she waved enthusiastically at Beatriz, looking beautiful and elegant in her silver and purple costume.

Alejandro had even persuaded Tanya to paint her face — her eyes were outlined dramatically, and glitter and jewels stuck to her cheeks. Everyone entered into the spirit of the *carnaval*, he told her.

The television cameras were there, beaming the proceedings out live all over the Canaries and mainline Spain, positioned high on a scaffold where they got the best view, arc lights illuminating the parading men, women and children when night fell. The locals were there, the tourists with their cameras and camcorders; everyone but everyone was at the *coso*.

It was vibrant, gaudy, magnificent, brash, smelly, crowded, frenetic. It was everything. Tanya had never seen a parade before on such a lavish scale. Refreshment kiosks did a roaring trade. Pampero rum and Cola was the traditional drink, Alejandro told her as he handed her a glass later on when the parade had finished and the street party began.

The words 'fast food' took on a new meaning when Tanya saw the speed with which stallholders made up hot-dogs and hamburgers. Then there were the stalls that sold sweets and popcorn and balloons. Everywhere was noisy and crowded and aggressive and gaudy. She loved it.

The fireworks display was something else too, and Manolo's face was a picture of wonder. Tropical salsa music beat out into the early hours. There were people dancing, drinking, eating, laughing, shouting, children crying, mothers soothing. Manolo kept going for much longer than Tanya expected, but finally Alejandro said it was time to take his son home.

Tanya did not want the day to end either; she had never enjoyed a party so much in her life. And although Alejandro had been fun these last few days he had left her strictly alone. Contrarily she resented it, her whole body constantly throbbing with need of him.

On Ash Wednesday it was the Burial of the Sardine — a ritual in which a huge papier mâché sardine filled with fireworks, was pulled through the streets, followed by lamenting women dressed in black. It was then dropped into the sea, and exploded. 'It's a traditional way of wishing good fishing for the coming year,' explained Alejandro when Tanya questioned him.

Afterwards there was a further fireworks display, and for another two days there were celebrations of one sort or another. And then it was all over — in Santa Cruz at least.

'Now is the time,' Alejandro told her, 'for other towns to have their own carnivals. It is unfortunate Orotava held theirs this week — it would have been an excuse for you to stay at my house — but if you want to go to any of the others?' There was a glint in his eye as he spoke, and Tanya felt her heartbeats quicken, her pulses race all out of time with themselves.

It was late and they were in his apartment, sitting lingering over a meal Tanya had cooked them, the first time they had spent any real time alone since Inocente had ruined things for her.

'I don't think I could stand the pace,' she said with a short laugh. 'I'm going back to Matilde's tomorrow to recover.' There was still something of an atmosphere between them; she still did not know what his true feelings for her were, so she intended to distance herself from him now that the *carnaval* was over. It was the perfect excuse. And if he was seriously interested, then it would be up to him to make a move.

'And what if I say I don't want you to go?'

Her heart quickened its beat, and she paused a moment before answering in case he had something further to add, but when he remained silent, she said, 'I'm going home to England in a few days. I want to see some more of my sister before then.'

Alejandro frowned in surprise. 'Your holiday is almost over? Tanya, that cannot be; you must stay longer.'

She shook her head. 'It's not possible; I have a job to go to and a house to look after. I must get back.' She hoped he would tell her to give up her job, to sell her house, and come to live with him here in Tenerife. She hoped he would ask her to marry him.

But all he said was, 'Then let us spend at least one more day together.'

Tanya felt a lump of disappointment well in her throat; she had her answer. One more day and it would be over. He did not love her; his feelings were, as she had guessed, purely physical. 'What good will one more day do?' she asked, hoping her voice would not give her away.

'I thought we could go out on my yacht. It's rarely free for my own personal use, so when it is I like to make the most of it. Will you come?'

Tanya was sorely tempted. It was an opportunity too good to miss, but would she be doing the right thing? You've spent the whole week with him; what does one more day matter? asked a little voice inside her. Nothing, she supposed, except that it would make parting all the harder, and except that she could be in danger of giving herself away. She had managed to distance herself from him these last few days, but being alone on his yacht would be very different from mixing with thousands of people at the *carnaval*.

'Is it such a difficult decision?' he asked softly, his dark eyes ever watchful on hers.

'I'm torn between loyalty to my sister and the thought of a day out at sea. I've never been on a yacht before.'

'Then you have no choice,' he urged insistently. 'Charlene will be at work in any case, and I promise to take you straight back to Matilde's afterwards.'

Tanya gave in reluctantly. 'Ok, I'll come.' The thought of it accelerated her heartbeats. It could be what they both needed, a day free of interruptions, away from other people. Maybe he would tell her how he felt; maybe this was his plan.

Tanya was ready when Alejandro came to pick her up the next morning. She wore white cotton trousers, rubber-soled shoes, and a navy and white striped jumper. In her bag she had put her bikini, sun-cream, sunglasses, a towel—and a jacket. She still hadn't got over how much cooler this northern tip of the island was.

He appraised her silently, nodding his approval. He had on a navy sweatshirt and jeans, and Tanya could

not remember ever seeing him dressed so casually. Not
that he looked less attractive; far from it. Already her
pulses were racing, and she had high hopes for the
outcome of today. She had spent most of the night
worrying, but in the end had decided that only good
could come out of it. She would relax and enjoy herself
and let things take their natural course.

His yacht, named *Water Dancer*, was much bigger
than she expected, and Tanya was very impressed. 'I
love it,' she said excitedly. 'I love the name; I love
everything about it.'

'I'm glad you approve,' he said solemnly.

'What do you want me to do?'

'Nothing, just stand around and look beautiful.' His
tone was deep and sensual, and Tanya felt her adrenalin begin to flow.

He untied the boat, started the engine, and slowly
and steadily steered her out of the harbour. Tanya
watched him, admiring the ease with which he handled
the vessel, and as they left Tenerife behind, as the
island became smaller and smaller until it was no more
than a dot on the horizon, her excitement grew. She
felt confident that today she would find out exactly
what Alejandro's feelings were.

'I had a word with Inocente,' he said, after they had
been going for about an hour. Up until then they had
spoken about nothing except the boat, the glorious
weather, everything in fact except themselves. She had
explored *Water Dancer*, admired the layout, the ultra-
smart galley, the luxurious cabins, the sumptuous
lounge, and now she was beside him again, watching
his strong, capable hands on the wheel.

'What did she say?' Her heart skipped an uneasy
beat. She did not want to talk about Inocente today;
she wanted nothing to spoil this rare occasion.

'She admitted she had deliberately tried to break us
up.'

'Did she really?' Tanya did not altogether believe

him. 'And did she also tell you how she'd found out that I wasn't seeing you on that particular morning?'

'From Cecilia, my daily housekeeper,' he said with a wry twist to his lips. 'Inocente came round to my house; the woman told her in all innocence.'

'I see, and why did she come round to your house when you were supposed to have finished with her?' It sounded to Tanya as though he had not done a very good job of it.

'She does not give up easily, unfortunately.'

'So it would seem,' she snapped. 'And there's also the fact that you said she had never been to your apartment when she told me she had. One of you is lying.'

'Tanya, *amor mío*, I can assure you she has not, not ever. She got that address also from Cecilia. The woman was particularly indiscreet. I have already spoken to her. And if it will put your mind at rest, I gave Inocente a piece of my mind also for telling such outrageous lies. I do not think she will be troubling us again.'

Tanya smiled weakly. Maybe not, but the damage was already done. There was still a thin thread of suspicion that would not go away.

They dropped anchor round about one o'clock, and Alejandro produced a bottle of champagne and a superb cold buffet lunch, and afterwards she put on her bikini and lay on the deck in the warm sunshine. Earlier it had been chilly, but now it was still and warm and she closed her eyes.

Alejandro changed into his swimming-trunks too and sat down beside her, and the next second she felt his hands on her legs, applying her sun-cream. 'It is far too easy to get burnt in this African sun,' he told her.

It was an excuse to touch her, and Tanya knew it, and she felt fire course through her limbs. When suddenly he stopped she opened her eyes and he was looking at her intently, desire darkening his eyes.

'Tanya, *querida*,' he said hoarsely, 'I can resist you no longer.' And his mouth came down on hers, hesitantly at first, until he met with no resistance, and then it was a kiss of mutual hunger.

They had both been building up to it all morning and, despite their talk about Inocente, neither could hold anything back. Tongues entwined; bodies pressed. Tanya's hands reached up into the thick blackness of his hair; his hands explored the curves of her body, disposing with indecent haste of her spotted bikini top, teasing her already erect nipples between thumb and forefinger.

Tanya arched her body into his, excitement running like quicksilver through her limbs. Any second now she expected his whispered words of love. This was the moment she had been waiting for.

'*Mi corazón*, Tanya mine.' His fingers trailed over the flatness of her stomach, inching inside the edge of her bikini bottom, easing it down over her hips, exploring, inciting, sending her soaring sky-high.

But when he began to take off his own swimming-trunks too she knew she had to stop him. Disappointment washed over her, engulfing her, saddening her, angering her. If this was all he wanted, then he could take a running jump. She was not his plaything; this wasn't the reason she had come out with him today. It was words of love she wanted, not the physical act.

'No, Alejandro.' She rolled away from and sat up, her hands around her knees, her whole body tense.

'No?' His voice sounded loud out here where all was still and quiet, save for the swishing of the waves against the side of his boat.

'No.'

He swore violently and jerked himself to his feet where he stood looking down at her, his face harshly critical. '*Maldito sea*! Tanya, I have waited patiently. I have waited for you to be ready, for you to make the first move, to give me some form of encouragement. I did not want to rush you. I thought this was the moment. It is obvious I was wrong; it is obvious I am wasting my time.' He gave a snort of anger and hurled himself towards the cabin.

Tanya closed her eyes, tears squeezing through her lids and rolling down her cheeks. This was it. It was all over; there was no hope left. Alejandro had proved that all he wanted was her body, an affair, a physical relationship. It was all he had ever wanted. He had no feelings for her, not real feelings, not like the ones she had for him.

Today had been a mistake; she ought to have gone back to Matilde's, as she had planned. Except that then she would have kept wondering and hoping, and now she knew that there was no hope. She shivered and rubbed her arms and wanted to go into the cabin to get her clothes, but because Alejandro was there she refrained.

Not until he came back out, fully dressed, and restarted the engine did she get to her feet. She glanced across at him, but his face was set, his eyes straight ahead, and she spun on her heel and marched inside.

Her hands were trembling as she pulled on her trousers and jumper, and her head was held high when she walked back out to the deck. She had been tempted, for a moment, to stay there out of sight, but that was the coward's way out. If he wanted to be offended because she wouldn't let him make love, then that was his bad luck, not hers. Why shouldn't she enjoy the rest of the voyage?

'Enjoy' was perhaps the wrong word. The atmosphere was so thick that it could be cut with a knife. 'I don't know why you're behaving like this,' she snapped, when she could bear the silence no longer. 'Surely I'm not the first woman to say no to you?' Or maybe she was; maybe that was what was annoying him.

His eyes were cold on hers. 'That isn't the issue,

Tanya; surely you know that? Surely you know what is wrong?'

She knew he didn't love her, but if it wasn't because she had rejected him that was making him so cold then she didn't know what was. But she had no intention of admitting her ignorance, and she lifted her shoulders in an indifferent shrug. 'So you're going to spoil the rest of the day because of it?'

His fingers clenched the wheel so tightly that his knuckles shone white. 'You make it sound as though it means nothing.'

'What is to be will be,' she said. 'You can't make things happen.'

'You're damn right you can't.' Her words seemed to anger him more and more, and the boat was going so fast that it seemed to be almost skimming the waves.

Maybe it would be best after all if she kept out of his way. She returned to the main cabin and sat on one of the grey velvet seats. To her relief he eased off the throttle slightly, and the journey back to Tenerife was accomplished in reasonable comfort — of the body if not the mind!

They reached the harbour and he steered the boat skilfully back into its berth. Tanya climbed off, not looking forward to the ride home. This was the end, apparently, of their relationship. His feelings had never been as great as hers, and now it was all over.

She wished that she had never let Charlene persuade her to come to Tenerife. In the nine years since she had first loved and lost Alejandro she had pushed him right out of her mind. Not completely — it was impossible ever to forget a person you had loved so deeply — but she had resigned herself to a life without him. . . and now all the old heartache had come back. There would be months and months spent thinking about him, wishing that things had been different.

Suddenly she remembered that she had left her bag on the deck where she had been standing as he tied up.

At the exact moment she turned she saw Alejandro pitch forward, try to save himself, and then hit the deck with a resounding thud. She had never run so quickly in her life, and her heart was thumping desperately when she scrambled on board. He made no move to get up.

'Alejandro.' Her voice rose shrilly. '*Alejandro*!' Panic began to set in. What if he was dead? She put her fingers to the side of his neck, feeling for his pulse. To her relief she found it. But he was still unconscious. She mustn't try to move him; she must get help. Off the boat again she jumped, and to her relief saw the harbour master. She ran up to him. 'Please, you must help. My friend's tripped and knocked himself out. He needs an ambulance.'

'*Ambulancia? Si*. I do it at once.'

The next few minutes were agonising. Alejandro was still unconscious when the ambulance arrived. They let her ride with him to the private clinic, and she waited while he was X-rayed and examined. He had apparently hit his head when he fell, and although there appeared to be no serious injury they could not be one hundred per cent sure until he regained consciousness. No one could tell her how long that would be.

Tanya had never felt so devastated in her life. She was finally allowed to see Alejandro when he was put in his hospital bed, and she could have cried when she saw how pale and still he looked. . .and it was all her fault. She had realised when she got back to the yacht that he must have caught his foot in the strap of her bag. By her own forgetfulness she had put his life in danger. How could she live with it if he died?

Crisógono, as the closest relative Tanya knew, was informed and he turned up at the clinic just as Tanya thought of leaving. 'Oh, Cris,' she cried, flinging herself into his arms. 'Please let him be all right.'

'My brother's tough.' He told her with a smile that

she knew was forced. 'We must all hope and pray, but I'm sure he'll pull through.'

'I hope so,' she whispered brokenly.

'How did it happen?'

She felt her face colouring as she told him about the bag, but he insisted that she must not blame herself. 'Alejandro should have looked where he was walking,' he said, but she could see the strain in his face.

'Manolo!' she exclaimed suddenly. 'Alejandro told me his nanny is off on a week's holiday. He was going to friends straight after school, and they're bringing him home at six. Someone must be there to tell him about his father, to stay with him. Oh, Cris, what are we going to do? Shall I go?' It was the very least she could do. 'Manolo likes me; he knows we were going out together today.' Goodness, what did you tell an eight-year-old child?

'I think that's a good idea,' said Crisógono. 'I'd like to stay here a while with Alejandro, just in case he regains consciousness, but I'll tell Beatriz when I get home and I've no doubt she'll come to see you.'

He found her the house key in Alejandro's trouser pocket and Tanya took a taxi to La Orotava, after first directing the driver to the apartment in Santa Cruz so that she could pick up her clothes; Cris said he would arrange to fetch Alejandro's car later. It felt strange entering the house by herself; she felt almost guilty. And as she walked through the rooms she could sense Alejandro, almost as though he were there with her.

She found the kitchen, a large room looking as though it had recently been modernised, and made herself a cup of coffee, but before she had taken even one sip of it she heard Manolo's excited voice. 'Papá, Papá, *donde estás*?'

The boy stopped short when he saw Tanya instead of his father, but he grinned easily. '*Hola*, Tanya.'

'Hello, Manolo,' she answered gravely.

'*Dónde está* Papá?' He looked around the kitchen

expectantly. 'Oh, I am sorry. I forget you do not speak Spanish. Where is Papá? I have a lot to tell him.'

'Manolo,' Tanya went down on one knee front of him and took his small hands into hers, wondering how on earth she was going to break the news. 'I am afraid your daddy is not here. He is poorly; he is — in hospital.'

Manolo's already large eyes widened considerably and his face grew pale. 'Papá is in hospital?' Tears began to well. 'But I want my *papá*. Tanya, I want him here. He must come home; I want him.'

'That is not possible, my darling.' She pulled him into her arms. 'He is not very well.'

'What is wrong with him? Papá is never sick, never.'

'He fell, Manolo. He fell and hurt his head, as you fall sometimes.'

'But I do not go to the hospital.'

'Because you are never badly hurt.'

'Papá is hurting a lot?'

'He is asleep at the moment.'

'I want to go to him.'

The tears were falling fast now, and Tanya produced a handkerchief, mopping his face, but no sooner had she dried one lot of tears than another instantly followed. 'Your daddy wouldn't know you were there,' she told him softly. 'Tomorrow, perhaps, you can go; he will be much better then.' She mentally crossed her fingers that she was right.

'Will you stay with me, Tanya?' He raised his little tear-stained face to hers.

'Of course, my darling. Of course I will.'

'All night?'

'Yes, Manolo.'

'Will you sleep with me?'

Tanya was not sure that his father would approve of that; he had brought his son up to be much older than his years.

'I'll sleep in the next room, and we'll leave the doors open.'

'And the light on?'

'Just a little one.'

'How did Papá fall? What was he doing?'

'He tripped and fell on his yacht. We had just come back. He banged his head.' Manolo was a sensible boy; she did not see why she should not tell him the truth.

'I hurt my head once. Papá bandaged it up. Does he have a bandage on?'

Tanya shook her head. 'No, he hasn't.'

The news seemed to reassure Manolo. He obviously thought it couldn't be too bad if he wasn't bandaged. 'I am hungry, Tanya.'

'Then you tell me what you would like and we'll do it together.'

Later, when Manolo was in bed, she telephoned Charlene to explain why she wouldn't be back.

'But it's not your place to look after his son,' said her sister resentfully. 'He has family; why can't they do it?'

'Because I want to. It's my fault he's in hospital; it's the very least I can do.'

'I think you're crazy.'

'You don't understand.'

'Don't forget you're flying home on Friday.'

'I won't. How's Juan? I saw him the other day.'

'Yes, he told me; he's fine. I'll explain about his cousin. Maybe he'll be able to organise someone else to look after Manolo.'

Tanya felt like screaming, and after a few more words with her sister she put down the phone. She ought to have known Charlene would not understand.

And then Beatriz came, flustered, anxious, concerned both about her brother-in-law and his son. 'This is terrible.' she said, hugging Tanya, and holding her for many long seconds. 'Poor Alejandro.'

'Have you been to the clinic?'

'Not yet. Cris, he tell me all about it.'

'Alejandro has not regained consciousness?'

'No.'

The two women went on talking and worrying, and Beatriz asked Tanya if she would continue to look after Manolo. 'We all have families of our own,' she explained. 'He could come to one of us, of course, but he would worry that his father might come home and he would not be here. He will be happier in his own home. It is unfortunate that his nanny is away.'

'I'll stay for as long as I'm needed,' said Tanya. Even if it meant extending her holiday she would stay. This was the man she loved. Looking after his son was the very least she could do, especially as the accident had been her fault.

The thought would not go away, keeping her awake all through the night, and when she heard Manolo call out she was at his side immediately.

He was dreaming, thrashing about in the bed, calling for his father. Tanya put a soothing hand on his forehead, murmuring softly, encouragingly, trying to relax and comfort him, having no idea whether she got through, but finally he lay still, his breathing deep and normal.

For the rest of the night Tanya sat in his room. She saw no point in going back to bed when she would not sleep. The armchair was deep and comfortable, and she imagined Manolo curled up in it with his father while he read him a story. She had always regretted that she and Peter had no children. If she'd had a little boy she would have wanted him to be like Manolo, polite and well-behaved, a genuine joy to be with and to take out anywhere.

The next thing she knew it was daylight and Manolo was tugging her arm. 'Wake up, Tanya, wake up. I want to go and see Papá.'

It took Tanya a second or two to realise where she was and what had happened, and when she did she hugged Manolo closely. This precious child was the son of the man she loved and he was worried about him, the same as she was. It was a bond they shared at this moment in time.

'I think your daddy would insist that you go to school. When you come out I will take you, I promise.'

'I don't want to go to school.' Tears began to roll down his cheeks again.

'Oh, Manolo, I know you don't. There are lots of things in life that we don't want to do, but we have to. Please be a brave boy for your daddy's sake.'

He buried his face in her chest and she let him cry, stroking his thick black hair, so like his father's, and in a minute or two he had pulled himself together. 'If you think it is what Papá would want me to do, then I will go.' He was trying very hard to be brave.

Tanya hugged him. 'You're a good boy, Manolo.

'And you will take me when I come out?'

'Yes, of course, I promise.'

'At lunchtime?'

Tanya shook her head. 'Oh, no, you must have your siesta. I will take you after you have finished for the day.' Cris had explained to her that his brother's housekeeper would be there to keep her eye on him. 'And now I think you should get washed and dressed while I see to your breakfast.'

She found out that Manolo normally went to school with a friend who lived near by, so after she had taken him there, Manolo explaining to the boy's mother what had happened, because the woman did not speak English, she took a taxi to the hospital.

She kept her fingers mentally crossed that Alejandro would have come out of his coma, hurrying down the ward, not bothering to ask whether it would be all right; no one would have stopped her anyway. When she saw the empty bed, every vestige of colour drained from Tanya's face, Oh, no, please, no. There was some mistake. She was in the wrong ward; this couldn't have happened. Oh, please, God, no. 'No!' The word came out in a thin wail.

CHAPTER ELEVEN

THE next thing Tanya knew she was sitting on the bed, surrounded by nurses, a glass of water being pushed into her hand. 'Alejandro,' she managed to gasp. 'What has happened to him?'

There was much gesticulating and talking, but Tanya did not know what they were saying. 'English,' she said. 'Please speak in English.' But no one spoke her language and she began to feel desperate, until another nurse, seeing the commotion, stopped to see what was going on, and to Tanya's relief he spoke English.

'Where is Alejandro Vázquez?' she asked. 'He was in this bed last night.'

After a brief discussion with the nurses he told her that Alejandro had been moved earlier that morning to a clinic in Santa Cruz.

Intense relief washed over her.

'His brother organised it,' went on the doctor. 'He did not tell you?'

Tanya shook her head. 'I was so afraid that Alejandro. . .' Her voice was too choked to speak her thoughts.

'I will give you the address,' said the doctor kindly. 'This man is your husband?' He had noticed the ring on her finger.

'No, my—er—friend. I was with him when the accident happened.'

'I see; I understand your concern. You have a car?'

'No.'

'Then I will get someone to order you a taxi. Come, come with me.'

At the clinic Tanya was taken to Alejandro's room. She had no idea what to expect and was deeply distressed when she saw that he was still unconscious. There were tubes and wires monitoring his every breath. He did not look ill or pale or anything like that, he looked just as though he were naturally asleep, and when Tanya was left alone she took his hand in hers.

'Oh, Alejandro, please get better. I love you so much. I can't bear the thought that you're hurt, and all because of my stupidity in forgetting my bag. If we hadn't argued it wouldn't have happened. I should never have stopped you making love to me. I love you desperately. Oh, my darling, please speak, please open your eyes, *please*.' But there was nothing, no response, not even the flicker of an eyelid.

She continued to talk to him, to tell him her innermost feelings, to hold his hand, to stroke it, to look at him, to study every line on his face. He was so handsome, so beautiful, so everything. She touched his face, his eyelids, his nose, his mouth, his infinitely kissable lips. She leaned forward and pressed her lips to his. 'I love you, Alejandro. I love you with all my heart.' Her tears fell on his cheeks and she wiped them away with a gentle finger.

And then a noise behind made her turn, and there was Beatriz, her own eyes moist. Tanya wondered how long she had stood there, but she did not feel embarrassed.

'You found him, I see. I telephoned to tell you he had been moved, but no answer. I not think you come this early.'

'I took Manolo to his friend's and then went straight to the hospital,' Tanya told her. 'I don't mind telling you I thought the worst when I saw his bed empty.'

'I am sorry you were worried,' said Beatriz, her hand coming over Tanya's. 'We thought it better to have him nearer home. Alejandro, he will pull through, I am sure. He is strong. He will be all right. How is Manolo?'

'He wanted to come,' said Tanya with a wry smile.

'He wanted to see his father last night. I've promised he can see him when he finishes school.'

'What have you told him?'

'I told him about the accident, but I just said he was asleep last night. I haven't told him that he hasn't woken at all.'

Beatriz nodded. 'He adores Alejandro. I am so proud of the way he has brought the boy up.'

'He does him credit,' agreed Tanya.

'*Sí*, very much so.' She glanced fondly at her brother-in-law. 'I do not know any other man who would do this for a boy who was not his own.'

Tanya looked sharply at Beatriz. 'What do you——'

Her question was cut off as a nurse hurried into the ward, followed closely by a man in a white coat who she presumed was the doctor.

'We had better get out,' said Beatriz, 'and I must go. I came to check you had found Alejandro, and to see how he was, of course. I'll be back later. You will still be here?'

'Yes,' agreed Tanya. 'I shall stay all day if they'll let me.'

But that was not possible, she was told afterwards. She ought not to be here now. She could come back later in the morning and then again this afternoon.

In the taxi Tanya's thoughts were in chaos. What had Beatriz meant when she said Manolo wasn't Alejandro's? If he wasn't Alejandro's son, then whose boy was he? Perhaps he was adopted. Was that what she had meant? Perhaps Juanita hadn't been able to have children. But why hadn't Alejandro told her? On the other hand, why should he? He clearly regarded Manolo as his own, and probably saw no reason to tell anyone that he wasn't actually his own flesh and blood.

Back at Alejandro's house Tanya met his house-keeper, who had no idea that her employer was in hospital. To begin with she had been suspicious of this strange girl who had come walking into the house, but once Tanya explained what had happened — with mime and careful use of words, because she also could speak no English — she accepted her. Cecilia was very distressed when she learned what had happened.

Alejandro's car had turned up in her absence, and Tanya decided to use it to go back and forth to the hospital. It was costing her a small fortune in taxi fares. She wished there were some change in him; she wished he would come round. She talked and talked, pouring out her heart and soul, but all to no avail.

Cris came, and other brothers and sisters of Alejandro, all looking suitably solemn, and Tanya felt sure they must be blaming her. She had told Crisógono that it was her bag he had fallen over, and she felt sure he must have passed the word on. Even the fact that they were friendly towards her made no difference to her guilt.

When Manolo arrived home from school his first words were that he wanted to visit his father, and, true to her promise, Tanya took him. She prayed that Alejandro would be awake, but he wasn't. Manolo stood and looked with great interest at all the tubes and instruments, but he did not say anything. He seemed to take for granted the fact that when you were ill in hospital they did all sorts of things to you.

'Papá doesn't look poorly,' he whispered to Tanya.

'No, he doesn't,' she agreed. 'But he's hurting inside, and that's why he's sleeping all the time.'

'He does not feel the hurt when he is asleep?'

'That's right, Manolo. You can talk to him if you like; he might hear you.'

'Like as if it is a dream?' he asked, his eyes wide.

Tanya nodded.

'I dreamt about Papá last night.'

'Yes, I know, I heard you.'

'I cried; I was frightened. I thought Papá was going to die.'

'No, Manolo.' Tanya gathered him to her. 'Your

papá is going to get well. You tell him now that he must get better; tell him you want him home.'

They spent an hour at the hospital, and at the end of it she could see that Manolo was beginning to get agitated. Then Beatriz and Crisógono came again with their two children, and he was happy when he had someone his own age to talk to. He ran off with his cousins, and Tanya said to Cris, 'How long do you think he will be like this?'

Cris shook his head sadly. 'I do not know; the doctors do not know either. We have to be patient.'

Being patient was the hardest thing Tanya had ever had to do. She slept that night, but only because her body insisted, and the next day she was at the clinic as soon as it was allowed. Manolo came with her again after school, and Tanya began to worry that his father's continuing sleep might have some detrimental effect on him.

'Why doesn't Papá wake up?' he kept asking, and Tanya had to tell him that it was because of his illness. 'But he can hear us talking,' she assured him.

'I could sing to him,' said Manolo hopefully. 'Papá likes to me to sing.'

'That's a wonderful idea,' she agreed at once. 'I'd like to hear you sing as well.'

And so, in a clear, high voice, without any sign of self-consciousness, Manolo began to sing. Tanya had no idea what it was, because he sang in his native language, but it sounded very cheerful, and as she watched Alejandro she thought she saw his eyelids flicker, and a tiny movement of his fingers. Manolo did too, because he halted and then went on with renewed vigour, and this time Alejandro definitely showed signs of hearing his son's voice.

It was with a struggle that his eyes eventually opened, as though his lids were glued together and he was having to prise them apart. 'Papá! Papá!' Manolo threw himself at his father before Tanya could restrain him, and Alejandro's arms came about his son.

Tanya felt tears well, and wondered whether she ought to go out the room. Alejandro would not want her here, not after their argument. She was the very last person he would wish to speak to.

But already Alejandro' s eyes were on her. At first he frowned, as if trying to recollect what had happened, and then he let go of his son and held out his hand to Tanya. 'Come here,' he said faintly.

But at that moment a nurse came into the room to make one of her routine checks, and, upon seeing Alejandro conscious, she let out a cry of pleasure. 'It is good; it is good. I will fetch the doctor.'

Hanging back then, in case the doctor came immediately Tanya was surprised when Alejandro said more strongly, 'Tanya, I want to hold you.'

With a faint smile she joined Manolo, and the two of them held on to him for a few poignant moments. Perhaps he hadn't yet remembered their argument, she thought, clinging to these few precious moments. And then the doctor came and they were ushered out and more tests and examinations were made over the next hour or so, until finally the medical staff pronounced they could find nothing wrong. 'But we will keep him in for a few days' observation,' the doctor told her.

Beatriz and Crisógono and their children came after that and Tanya left, feeling that she was in the way. Beatriz promised to bring Manolo home.

Tomorrow was the day she should be flying back to England, and that evening Charlene phoned her. 'I'm not going,' said Tanya at once, 'not until Alejandro's out of hospital. Manolo needs me. I've already cancelled my flight.'

'You're a fool. What if you lose your job?'

'No, I won't. I've telephoned John Drake and explained the position. He's going to keep the temp on until I get back.'

Charlene grumbled some more, but Tanya would
not change her mind, and in bed that night she wondered if she was doing the right thing. She had not had
a chance to tell Alejandro that she was looking after
his son, though she had no doubt that Beatriz had done
so. Would he appreciate it, or would he be angry and
say she was pushing her nose in where it was not
wanted?

Because she was not sure of the reception she would
get Tanya almost did not go to visit him the next
morning, until Manolo asked her to tell his daddy he
would visit him after school; then she knew she had to
go, for his son's sake. Manolo had clung to her these
last few days. It was amazing how easily he had
accepted her. They had built up a rapport that would
be difficult to break, and she hoped the boy would not
be too upset when she went back to England.

She would be upset herself, there was no doubt
about it. Leaving Alejandro would be hard, devastating
in fact, and it would be very difficult to carry on her
life as though he had not happened. Though she knew
she must. This had been just another interlude, exciting
while it lasted but destined for failure.

When she got to the hospital, Alejandro, wearing a
pair of deep blue Paisley pyjamas, was sitting in a chair
near the wide-open window. He turned when he heard
her footsteps, and Tanya held her breath, wondering
what sort of reception she would get. He needed a
shave; three days of growth had darkened his chin.
'Designer stubble', they called it, and actually it suited
him; he would look very handsome with a beard, she
thought. Not that he didn't already. His dark good
looks had attracted her right from the very beginning,
from the day she had seen him at her friend's wedding.
Her heart had quickened its beats then, and it did the
same now.

'Tanya.' His smile was welcoming but wary.

'Hello, Alejandro, how are you feeling?' She went

up to him, but not too close, because she knew if she did so she would want to throw herself into his arms.

'I'm anxious to get out of here,' he grumbled. 'I don't see why I can't leave now. I'm perfectly fit.'

'They need to make sure there are no after-effects, nothing they've missed.' She twisted her fingers uneasily. 'It was my fault you fell. If I hadn't forgotten my bag it wouldn't have been lying around. I'm sorry.'

'Hell, don't apologise. I should have looked where I was going. I was so damn mad at you, but I've done a lot of thinking since I came round. It was wrong of me to be angry simply because you said no. Will you ever forgive me?'

Tanya was startled by his apology, startled but pleased. 'I already have,' she said softly. 'I've done a lot of thinking too, Alejandro. I should never have let you kiss me when I knew I'd put a stop to it if you went too far.'

He looked as though he agreed. 'What I can't understand, Tanya, is that only two weeks ago we spent a wonderful night together, and now you're virtually holding me at arm's length. Why is that?'

Tanya drew in a deep breath and avoided looking at him. 'It was a mistake.'

'A mistake?' He frowned. 'Some mistake when you actively enjoyed it. And don't say you didn't, because no woman can act like that.'

'I did enjoy it,' she said with a rueful grimace, 'but it is something I have no intention of repeating.'

'Ever?' His dark eyes were watchful on hers.

Tanya drew in a deep breath and exhaled it slowly. 'If the circumstances were right I might,' she ventured, choosing her words carefully.

'And what would those circumstances be?' He pushed himself up from his chair and came to stand beside her, not touching, but close enough for her to feel the utter maleness of him, close enough to drive her insane.

She closed her eyes, and her voice was no more than a husky whisper. 'Mutual love. A one-sided affair is worse than no affair at all.'

'I agree,' he said to her surprise. 'Loving someone who doesn't love you can be torture.'

Tanya looked at him in astonishment. He knew! Oh, lord, he knew! Had Beatriz told him? Or had he guessed? Had she given herself away? She must change the subject quickly now, before it become too embarrassing. Inching away from him, she made a show of smelling the red roses that stood on his bedside table. Flowers for a man! She did not know who had sent them, but could only guess that it was Inocente. Her fingers curled.

As if he too had had enough of talking about themselves he said gruffly, 'I want to thank you for looking after Manolo. Things are bit hazy in my mind, but isn't it today you should be flying home?'

Tanya inclined her head. 'I cancelled it. I'll go once you're fit and well. Manolo asked me to tell you that he'll be in to see you when he comes out of school. He's been every day, talking to you, singing, praying. He loves you totally. Why didn't you tell me that he wasn't your real son?'

Alejandro looked at her sharply, and as if the surprise of her knowing was too great for him he sat down again. 'Who told you that?'

'Beatriz let it slip.' Tanya perched herself on the edge of the bed. 'She was admiring you. He really does you credit, Alejandro. Is he adopted?'

'No, not exactly.'

Tanya frowned. 'Then I don't understand. I presumed Juanita couldn't have children so you adopted.'

'Beatriz didn't tell you the circumstances?'

'No.'

He sighed heavily. 'It's quite a story.'

'If you're not up to it. . .' she said at once, half rising to leave.

He stayed her with his hand. 'I'd like you to know—if you really want to hear, that is.'

'I do,' she whispered. She wanted to hear anything to do with this man.

'It all began the day I wrote to Juanita telling her I'd fallen in love with you.'

He had actually told Juanita he loved her? Tanya was not convinced she could accept that. Maybe he had written to the girl, but surely not to say that he loved her? If he had loved her he would never have left England so suddenly.

'She was terribly distressed, because she had always thought that one day we would get married. Oh, we'd talked about it when we were young, I admit, but as I got older my feelings changed. I thought I'd made it clear to her, but obviously not, because on the rebound she went out with some other guy. He got her pregnant and then didn't want to know about it. When I got back here she was on the verge of suicide.'

'So you married her after all?'

Alejandro nodded.

He had certainly wasted no time, thought Tanya. One argument they'd had, and he'd married his child-hood sweetheart. She admired his selflessness; it made her see him in a whole new light. She hadn't realised he had such a caring side to him. But—would he have done it if he hadn't genuinely loved Juanita? That was the crucial question.

'And when she died you brought up Manolo as your own? That was very generous of you.' And further proof that he had loved Juanita. Why else would he want to bring up someone else's child?

'I could do no less. Manolo and I had grown very close.'

'He always called you Papá?'

'Yes.'

'Does he know the truth?'

'No, although one day I expect I shall tell him.'

'Juanita's death must have been very traumatic for you.' She remembered when Peter died she had been inconsolable.

'Juanita was a very dear friend.'

'You are still claiming you did not love her?'

His brows lifted. 'It is the truth, Tanya.'

Tanya eyed him in bewilderment. 'You did that — married a woman you did not love, simply to give her respectability?'

'More than that: a shoulder to lean on, a friend in time of need, a companion.'

Tanya wished she could believe him. 'But she still loved you?'

He heaved a sigh. 'I guess so.'

Tanya wanted to ask whether he had ever made love to her; but it was too personal a question. She guessed he had; no man could live with a woman for six years and remain celibate. Unless of course he had married her on the understanding that he was free to indulge in other relationships. It was a saddening thought.

'And now you are still looking after Manolo, even though you don't have to.' What a large heart this man had. A pity none of it was extended towards her. 'Didn't Juanita have any family who could have taken him in?'

'No one knew in her family that he wasn't mine. Beatriz is the only one who knows, because Juanita used to be a friend of hers. I trusted her to tell no one.'

'You mustn't blame her,' said Tanya at once. 'She was upset; she spoke without thinking. She probably thought you'd already told me. You're a remarkable man, Alejandro. You amaze me, in fact.'

'I did what I wanted to do. I love Manolo as much as if he were my own. In fact I regard him as mine.'

'He's certainly a fine boy.'

'You get on well with him?'

Tanya nodded. 'He seems to have taken to me. I hope you didn't think I was being frightfully cheeky, staying at your house. Cris seemed to think it would be best.

'I'm glad you did.' His voice dropped an octave. 'I like the thought of you in my house. Did you like sleeping there?'

'Yes,' she said huskily, her pulses beginning a stampede. It was incredible the way he could set her on fire with just the tone of his voice.

'Did you think of me a little?' His brown eyes were narrowed and watchful.

'More than a little,' she confessed. 'I was desperately worried.'

That wasn't the answer he wanted, and it showed in his eyes. 'You were worried because you felt the accident was your fault? Or was there another reason?'

Tanya closed her eyes. Did she tell him? Could she risk declaring her love at the cost of being spurned?

'Tanya?' He had risen without her being aware of it and was now standing in front of her. 'Tanya, I need to know what your real feelings are.'

'My feelings have never changed from the moment I first met you,' she said huskily, still not looking at him, studying her hands instead.

She heard his swiftly indrawn breath. 'So it's never been anything more than a physical attraction — and now you're fighting it because your conscience tells you it's wrong.'

'*No!*' Her head shot up in quick denial.

'No?' He frowned. 'Then what do you feel?'

'Damn you, Alejandro,' she cried, 'why are you putting me through this? What's the point when we both know what your feelings are?'

'When a man loves a woman as much as I love you he likes to know where he stands,' he said quietly.

Tanya felt her mouth drop open. She had not heard him right; she couldn't have. Alejandro did not love her. He wanted no more from her than a sexual relationship; it was all he had ever wanted.

'You look surprised.' He sat down on the bed beside her, taking her hands into his own.

'Don't play games with me, Alejandro.'

'*Mi corazón*, I would never do that.' He lifted her hands to his mouth, kissing her fingers, stroking them. 'You see, like yours, *my* feelings have never changed. I hoped, *amor mío*, that you would one day love me too. It saddens me that this will never be.'

Tanya felt a deep joy well up from the pit of her stomach, spreading and growing until it engulfed her whole body. *Alejandro loved her*! The impossible had happened—and if what he said was true he had loved her all along. Yet why had he never said? Why had he let her think his feelings went no deeper than a surface attraction? 'I didn't know that you loved me,' she said so softly that he only just caught her words.

'Tanya, Tanya, how can that be? Haven't I shown by my actions, by my need of you, by every word I've said, that I love you?'

'You never put it into words,' she reproached quietly.

'Did I have to? My sweet, sweet girl, I thought my body said it all. Are you telling me that you never knew?'

She gave an almost imperceptible nod.

With a groan he gathered her to him, and for the very first time Tanya felt his love flow into her. She knew happiness such as she had never known before. She lifted her face towards his, expecting him to kiss her, disappointed when he did no more than brush his lips against her forehead.

Very gently he put her from him. 'But as you said earlier, for one person to love is worse than not loving at all.'

Now she could tell him; now she could open her heart without fear of making a fool of herself. Her eyes shone as she looked at him; her whole body sang. 'Alejandro, it is not one-sided.'

There was a sudden stillness about him, and his dark handsome eyes looked at her at first in wonder and then in growing disbelief.

'I love you too, Alejandro,' she said huskily.

He frowned. 'Is this a sudden decision?'

'Goodness, no,' she replied, shaking her head vigorously. 'I have always loved you, from the very moment we first met.'

'I want to believe you,' he said slowly. 'I want desperately to believe you, but how can it be when you turned your back on me nine years ago, when you disappeared out of my life as though you had gone off the face of the earth? And how can it be when you do not let me make love to you? No, Tanya, I do not believe you.' He got up suddenly and went over to the window, staring out at the gardens with their brilliant exotic flowers.

Tanya felt sudden bewilderment. How could he not believe her? What did she have to do to prove it? She had accepted his word; why did he not accept hers? She went over to him and touched his shoulders, and was surprised at how tense he was. 'Alejandro, it is true. I do love you. Please, you must believe me.'

He turned and his eyes were shuttered, as though he had pulled a mask down over his emotions. 'I am sorry; I cannot believe you. You are mistaking a chemical attraction for love, that is all, all it has ever been.'

'No, Alejandro, no. I *do* love you. I do.' She put her arms around him and pressed her lips to his, but it was like kissing a statue, and she stepped back in utter confusion.

'I think you should leave.' His voice was dead, lifeless, and she could not believe he was doing this to her.

'But Alejandro. . .' Her voice trailed off as to her dismay a nurse came into the room, followed by the doctor doing his daily rounds. Of all the inopportune moments. She gave him one last pleading glance as she left, but he was not even looking at her.

She stood outside for several long minutes, trying to decide whether to wait or leave the hospital altogether. What point was there in protesting her love when he had made up his mind? She kept shaking her head. It was unreal the way he had reacted. She would have thought that when he discovered their mutual love he would be overjoyed. Exactly why didn't he believe her?

Because she had walked out on him, he had said. That was a laugh for a start; *he* was the one who had left England. And because she wouldn't let him make love to her. Again, another inexcusable statement. He was out of his mind. The accident had done more to him than anyone realised. She would go; there was no point in continuing their conversation while he was so adamant. She would give him time to think, hopefully to accept the fact that she was telling the truth. Lord, it didn't bear thinking about. They had both admitted their love, and yet she was still as far away from him as ever.

CHAPTER TWELVE

WHEN Manolo came home from school he was eager to go and see his father, but Tanya insisted that he have something to eat first. This, she had discovered via Alejandro's housekeeper, was his normal routine, but she had let it slide while his father was in hospital, giving him a piece of fruit to keep him going until his meal when they got home.

Today, though, she wanted to put off the moment when she went back. Not that there would be any time for conversation — Manolo always monopolised his father, and usually other members of the family came too. It was generally only in the mornings that Tanya had Alejandro to herself.

Her plan did not really work, because Manolo wolfed down his sandwich and orange juice and pronounced himself ready in three minutes flat, and they were at the hospital at their usual time. To Tanya's intense relief Beatriz was already there, welcoming her warmly, and not seeming to notice the tension between her and Alejandro.

When visiting finished at seven Tanya had still not spoken to him privately, and as he let her go with a faint, regretful smile Tanya did not know whether she would be welcome again.

Outside Beatriz had a quiet word with her. 'I thought Alejandro seemed a little subdued. Do you know why?'

'I didn't notice,' lied Tanya, shaking her head. Not for anything was she prepared to disclose their earlier conversation.

'I hope he is not suffering in silence. I hope there is nothing wrong that he isn't telling us.'

'I shouldn't think so.' said Tanya.

'Please ask when you see him tomorrow. I know he will talk to you.'

Tanya grimaced. 'He doesn't tell me everything, Beatriz.'

'Then you must insist. If not I will see the doctor.'

Tanya spent an almost sleepless night. It was impossible to accept that now she had discovered Alejandro loved her he would not believe that she loved him. There must be some way she could make him see the truth, but how, if words alone would not do it?

She was no nearer a solution when she got up the next morning, and once she had taken Manolo to his friend's home she could not make up her mind whether to go to the hospital or not. She went back to the house, and was still debating when Cecilia came. The woman looked pleased to see her still there, pushing a carefully wrapped parcel into her hand. 'Alejandro, you give?' Tanya's decision was made for her.

It was with some trepidation that Tanya walked into Alejandro's ward. Today he was not sitting; he was pacing the room. He looked pale, and was not as well as yesterday, although his jaw was freshly shaven and he had on a clean pair of pyjamas.

'*Buenos días*,' Tanya.' It was a curt, almost uninterested greeting.

'*Buenos días*,' she replied quietly, swallowing the lump which had risen in her throat. She loved this man so much that it crucified her to be treated so distantly. How could he do it when he had confessed he loved her? 'Your housekeeper's sent this for you.' She handed him the parcel, which was obviously a book, careful not to let their fingers touch. Contact would be both explosive and disastrous; already she was brimming over with conflicting emotions.

'Thank you.' He put it on the windowsill, ready to be opened later, and when he said nothing further Tanya turned to leave. She had reached the doorway before he spoke. 'The doctor says I can go home tomorrow.'

She suddenly felt as though a heavy weight were sitting in the bottom of her stomach. Once he was home she would no longer be needed. It would be the end. She would go back to England and never see Alejandro again. She felt tears welling, and desperately tried to stop them. 'That's good news.' Lord, was that thin, wavery sound her own voice?

'You don't look particularly elated. I thought you'd be pleased. You can go home now without having to pretend any more.'

'Pretend?' she asked, shocked. 'My love for you is not pretence, Alejandro, nor is it purely physical. I don't know how you can think that.'

'I think maybe you do not even know that you are pretending. I think you are deceived by your feelings. I think you are mistaking desire for real emotions.'

'Damn you, Alejandro.' Tanya glared at him furiously. He was out of his mind; he had to be. The accident had affected his brain. But if that was the way he wanted to play it she wasn't going to beg and plead. She would pack her bags and go the moment he was discharged, and if he truly loved her he would come after her. If he didn't. . . She did not dare think about that.

She swung around on her heel without saying any more, hoping against hope that he would call her back as she marched down the corridor, but her footsteps echoed alone.

She did not go back to the house straight away, going down to the harbour instead and standing watching the ships coming and going. When she did finally return Cecilia had left and she went up to her room to pack her case. One more night she would stay, then the second he set foot inside tomorrow she would be gone. If he couldn't believe her, then he wasn't worth loving.

She sat forlornly outside in the courtyard, listening to the bird-song, looking up at the palms reaching as high as the building. Usually she loved the quiet serenity, but today her mind was in too much turmoil to feel anything but distress.

She could have been happy here with Alejandro, with Manolo, with their own children. Now she realised it had never been anything more than a pipe-dream. She and Alejandro were not destined for each other.

It was a long day. When Manolo came home she told him that she was not feeling well and could not take him to the hospital.

'But I want to see Papá,' he protested.

'Your daddy is coming home tomorrow,' she told him.

'He is?'

Tanya nodded.

Manolo's face broke into a big smile. 'I am so happy. I have missed my *papá*.'

There was no doubt, she thought, of the love this child had for the man who had brought him up as his own. Alejandro's love, too, for Manolo was undeniable. There was some good in him somewhere, even though at times she found it very hard to find.

She wondered what Inocente thought of it all; whether she would be willing to marry Alejandro and accept Manolo as well. And what did Manolo think of Inocente? Would he accept her as a mother? Would Alejandro marry Inocente? It was very possible. Even though he had professed to love her, he had married Juanita, so what was to say he wouldn't do it a second time? Lord, how she hurt inside.

Not surprisingly, Tanya had a terrible night, tossing and turning, worrying and wondering, crying, despairing, telling herself not to be stupid, getting up and walking about the room, making herself a hot drink, going back to bed, still not sleeping. Damn Alejandro, she kept telling herself, damn the man. He wasn't worth loving; he wasn't worth all this heartache.

She fell asleep as dawn broke, and was woken by Manolo jumping on her bed. 'Wake up, Tanya, wake up. What time is Papá coming? I do not have to go to school today, do I?' He was so excited that Tanya hadn't the heart to say yes.

'Of course you don't, my darling. It's the weekend.' In any case, it would probably be better if Manolo was here. She would be able to make her escape while the two of them were greeting each other. Manolo definitely wouldn't leave his father alone, and Alejandro would be pleased to see his so-called son too.

All day they waited. Cecilia came and went. Manolo began to get fretful 'I want my *papá*. Why doesn't he come, Tanya? Is he hurting again?'

Tanya was worried too, though she tried not to show it. 'Of course not. I expect he's waiting for the doctor to say he can come. The doctors are very busy. They have a lot of other people to look at.'

'I want to go to him,' sobbed Manolo, tears welling in his big brown eyes.

Tanya took him into her arms. 'He'll be here any minute now, I assure you.' She rocked him as though he were a baby, murmuring words of comfort, and, curled up in a corner of the settee, they both went to sleep.

'Papá, Papá.'

Tanya was woken by Manolo's excited cry. He leapt up and straight into Alejandro's waiting arms. How she wished that she could have greeted Alejandro so eagerly herself, so warmly, so lovingly. She was almost jealous of Manolo. And her time had come to leave. It was going to be the biggest wrench of her life.

Quietly she slipped out of the room. Neither saw her go. Upstairs she picked up her suitcase and took one last look around. She had grown to love this old house, could have been completely happy living here, looking after it for Alejandro. She had thought about it a lot, had entertained such high hopes, until he had dashed them to the ground like a leaf in a storm, taken her heart and tossed it mercilessly away.

When she finally turned he was standing in the doorway. 'What are you doing?' he asked gruffly.

'What does it look like?' she retorted. 'I'm leaving. There's no place for me here any more.' She did not realise how despairing she sounded.

'I don't want you to go.'

Tanya turned surprised eyes on Alejandro's face. He was deadly serious, no hint of a smile, nothing to say, Tanya, I've made a mistake; I know you love me, and I want us to be together for always. Nothing like that, but nevertheless he was serious.

'Why?' She mouthed the word without any actual sound coming out.

'Because—because I—I need you.'

'You're prepared to let me stay on here even though you think I don't love you?'

'We both want you to stay.' Manolo appeared from behind his father.

Tanya suddenly knew why Alejandro had asked her. It was for his son's sake; Manolo did not want her to go. But it would be too much of a strain living under the same roof as Alejandro while not sharing his bed. She could not do it.

She shook her head. 'I'm sorry, Manolo, but I have to go home to England. I have a job and a house. . .' And she was saying the same things she had said to his father.

'But I love you, Tanya,' wailed the boy, and, 'Papá loves you too, don't you Papá?'

Alejandro put his hand on Manolo's shoulder. 'The point is, Tanya does not love us. We cannot force her to stay.'

'Tanya does love me,' cried Manolo. 'I know she does; she told me so.'

Tanya remembered; she had been comforting him yesterday when he couldn't go to visit his father, and she had hugged him close and said, 'Oh, Manolo, I love you so much.'

'And she loves you too, Papá, I am sure. Don't you, Tanya?' The boy looked at her imploringly.

Tanya nodded slowly, 'Yes, Manolo, I love your *papá*.'

'Manolo, I think you should leave the room.' Alejandro's voice was hoarse. 'I want to talk to Tanya alone.'

'You are going to ask her to stay?'

Alejandro inclined his head.

Manolo smiled. 'Then I will go. But please don't be long. I have waited all day for you, Papá.'

When he had gone Alejandro stepped into the room and closed the door behind him. His eyes searched her face. 'Would you lie to my son, Tanya?'

'Of course not.' Her eyes never wavered from his. Something told her that this was the testing time. Her heart beat louder.

'You told Manolo you loved me.'

'I also told *you* that I loved you.'

'It is the truth?'

'The choice is yours whether you believe me or not.' She was not going to beg him to accept her word.

His eyes flickered uncertainly. 'I want to believe you, Tanya.'

He had already said that to her.

'But I was hurt once before, I thought you loved me nine years ago and then ——' he made a sound like air escaping from a balloon '—it was all over. You walked out of my life and disappeared without a trace.'

'We have already had this conversation,' railed Tanya. 'And I was not the one who did the walking out. OK, we argued, and I left, but I came after you — and what did I find? That you'd gone back to Tenerife.

And that was it, the end, no further word from you. So how the hell can you say that *I* walked out on you?'

Alejandro frowned, a deep frown that cut into his forehead and pulled his brows together until they almost looked like one line across his face. 'You came after me?'

'That's right.'

'Who did you speak to? Were you given no message?'

'Hell, I don't know who I spoke to; everyone at the hotel, I think. And no, I wasn't given a message. All I was told was that you had gone home to Tenerife.' She saw the changing expressions on his face. 'Are you saying that you left a note for me?'

'Not a note, no; it was verbal. I didn't have time for writing letters. My father was dying; I had to get home, and quickly. But I tried to get in touch with you later. . . Oh I don't know how long—a couple of weeks, or more, maybe. My father had died before I even got here, and his affairs were in such a mess there was much to do; he had left no will, nothing. But I thought you would have my message and understand. I thought you would wait for me.'

'I got no message,' she said, shaking her head, but hope suddenly riding high in her heart, 'and when I found you missing I was devastated. When my sister was offered a job in Sheffield I went with her. I could see no point in staying around Birmingham any longer. There were too many memories.'

He shook his head, his eyes full of pain. 'I tried to find you. I rang everyone I could think of. I even came back over to England, but you had disappeared without trace. I assumed you did not want me to find you.'

Tanya shuddered. If only she had known. 'So you married Juanita?' she asked quietly.

He nodded.

Tanya sighed, and they came together of mutual accord. His arms crushed her against him; his mouth found hers. Time stood still. Hearts throbbed, bodies pulsed, and Tanya felt as though she were being lifted to another planet. Life had turned full circle and she was back in the arms of the man she loved. And what was more, he loved her. Her happiness was complete.

'How much did you love Peter?' he asked when they finally drew apart. There was a faint frown on his brow, and he had obviously been thinking about this man who had been her husband.

'Not as much as I love you.' She looked at him, her eyes shining with honesty. 'We were happy enough together, but there was none of the magic I feel with you.'

'I'm glad,' he said huskily, 'because what I feel for you is very special too. When I came round in the hospital and saw you standing there I thought I was dreaming. After you'd rejected me on the yacht I really thought it was all over. Why did you do it?'

'Why did I reject you?' Her smile was wry. 'Because I thought all you were after was my body, and I couldn't handle that any longer. You'll never know how hard it was.'

'It looks as though we both made the same mistake.'

Tanya nodded sadly. 'Why didn't you ever mention that you'd tried to get in touch with me?'

He grimaced. 'Believe me, I wanted to, many times, but usually when things were running smoothly between us, and then I'd be afraid of rocking the boat by mentioning the past. If I'd known what I know now. . .'

She finished the sentence for him. 'We would have saved ourselves a lot of heartache.'

Alejandro nodded. 'I entirely agree.'

'And do you believe me now that I love you?'

'*Dios*, Tanya, I need my head examining for ever disbelieving you.' He drew her to him and kissed her. '*Mi corazón*, I promise I will never doubt anything you say to me again.'

'Alejandro, can I tell you that I think you are wonderful?'

He smiled. 'You are pretty fantastic yourself.'

'I don't mean that,' she said, knowing he was referring to the night they had spent together. 'I was thinking about the way you've brought Manolo up as your own. Not many men would do that. I've misjudged you. I thought you were a selfish womaniser. I thought you were stringing me along when it was really Juanita you loved. And I thought you were playing me off against Inocente. I didn't think you were capable of loving one woman alone.'

'Tanya, Tanya.' He cupped her face between his hands. 'There has never been anyone else for me but you. You were my first lover, and you will be my last. We will forget all the years between. I love you, Manolo loves you, and you love us. What more could a man ask for — except perhaps children of our own?'

Tanya nodded. 'I would like that too.'

'Will you marry me, Tanya?'

'Yes, Alejandro.'

'You will be happy living here?'

'Blissfully so.'

'We will get married on March the twenty-eighth, my saint's day.'

Tanya frowned. 'Your saint's day? What do you mean?'

He smiled. 'Every single day is a saint's day, and when it is your namesake then you celebrate also. It is a much bigger occasion than even your own birthday. So why not make it our wedding-day? You have three weeks to prepare yourself. Will that be enough?'

'More than enough. I'd readily marry you tomorrow.'

'And do my family out of all the excitement? I don't think we dare.' He kissed her again, and it was many minutes later when he said, 'Manolo will be growing impatient. Let us go and tell him that he is going to get a new *mamá*.'

Welcome to Europe

TENERIFE — 'the land of eternal spring'

Tenerife is quite simply a holiday paradise, combining all the comforts of home with touches of the exotic — such as the banana plantations you'll find. With its long beaches and sunny climate, and its relaxed, friendly atmosphere, it's the ideal destination for couples of all ages. Go to the top of Mount Teide, the highest mountain in Spain, or simply relax on the beach with a cool drink. . . The choice is yours.

THE ROMANTIC PAST

There is much debate about the history of the Canary Islands — how they came into being, where their early inhabitants came from, and how they got their name. Contrary to what you might think, the name seems to have nothing to do with canaries! Apparently there was an expedition to the islands in 30 BC, and large dogs were seen roaming around. As the Latin word for dog is *canis*, the lands became known as the Canis Islands.

The Spaniards arrived in the fifteenth century and found that the islands were inhabited by a primitive people known as the **Guanches**, who had blond hair and blue eyes, lived in caves and dressed in animal hide.

The Spanish started their conquest of the Canary Islands in 1402. This expedition was led by Béthencourt, who was so happy when he first saw the islands that he named the first two he came across Alegranza (Joy) and Graciosa (the Beautiful). Tenerife was the last of the islands to be conquered, falling to the Spanish in 1494, despite brave resistance by the Guanches.

A famous name associated with the Canary Islands is **Christopher Columbus**. Columbus might not actually have stayed on Tenerife, but his log book reveals that while he was sailing past it he saw an eruption of Mount Teide. . .which might explain why he didn't decide to stop there! However, he did stay on two of the other Canary Islands — on Gran Canaria and on Gomera, where it is rumoured that he had a love-affair with Beatriz de Bobadilla. Perhaps this is why he returned to the small island of Gomera on two further voyages!

Nelson probably had less pleasant memories of the Canary Islands. . . He lost an arm in Tenerife during the unsuccessful British attempt to conquer the islands in 1797.

THE ROMANTIC PRESENT — pastimes for lovers. . .

If you're going to Tenerife to enjoy a beach holiday you'll probably head for the south of the island, to a resort like **Playa de las Americas** or **Los Cristianos**. Of the two, Los Cristianos, which used to be a fishing village, is quieter and probably more attractive, with

Mount Teide making a spectacular backdrop. The large beach is an ideal place to sunbathe and relax with your partner.

There's no shortage of things to do in the evenings — Los Cristianos is well supplied with bars and restaurants, including many to make you feel you're 'home from home' with names like the British Bar and menus offering you English breakfasts and fish and chips. But if you want to try more typical Canarian cuisine, try exploring some of the back streets.

If you prefer smaller, less crowded beaches than those in Los Cristianos, try visiting **Abades**, on the south-east coast of the island, or Poris, which is just slightly further up.

If you want to do more than just lie on a beach, there are plenty of other parts of Tenerife just waiting to be explored. The capital of the island is **Santa Cruz**, where nearly a third of the island's population live. If you enjoy shopping, that alone is a good enough reason for a visit here — the shopping facilities are the best in Tenerife, with both small shops and larger stores with better quality goods. Start at the **Plaza de España**, and shop until you drop. . .

And if you're exhausted after that, why not visit the beautiful **Parque Municipal García Sanabria**? Wandering along its shady paths and admiring the sub-tropical plants and water gardens is guaranteed to relax you. Don't miss the well known floral clock at the entrance, or the impressive fountain at the centre.

If you're visiting the north of the island, you may well decide to stay in **Puerto de la Cruz**, the longest-established tourist resort and one which has its own distinctive character, with traditional old houses, cobbled roads and a seafront promenade.

Puerto de la Cruz and the surrounding area offer lots of activities. Visit the **Bananera El Guanche**, where you can learn all about how the banana grows and enjoy a banana and a taste of banana liqueur at the end of your tour. Don't miss a visit to the **Botanical Gardens**, where the exotic plants and trees include cinnamon trees, coffee plants and a rubber tree which is almost two hundred years old. Another interesting place to visit is **Loro Parque**. *Loro* is the Spanish word for parrot, and you will see parrots everywhere here. Some of them have even been trained to roller skate and ride tricycles!

Wherever you are on Tenerife, you can't fail to miss the majestic height of **Mount Teide**. A visit here is bound to be one of the highlights of your trip. You can take a cable car ride to just below the summit and, once there, enjoy a *lumumba* — a brandy-laced chocolate drink. If you're feeling active, it will take you about three quarters of an hour to walk to the summit from here, where you can admire the spectacular views.

If you want to discover 'traditional' Tenerife, rather than the places where all the tourists go, visit the tiny rustic villages of **La Sobrera** and **La Zarza** in the east of the island.

Or if history fascinates you, visit **Masca** in the northwest of the island. It is inland and set away from the road, and legend has it that it was discovered by a fisherman who was marooned on the beach at the foot of the valley. Walking inland, he came across this attractive area, went back to collect his family, and founded Masca. Today it is a tranquil, serene place with interesting architecture and narrow streets.

Try to make time to see the famous dragon tree — **El Drago** — in the north-west of the island. The tree is apparently over 3,000 years old. If it is cut it bleeds a red sap, or 'dragon's blood', which is how it got its name.

Whether you've spent the day exploring or sunning yourself, the evening is a time to go out and eat. Try a Canarian soup for a starter. *Sopa de berros* — water-cress soup with herbs — is particularly recommended. Fish is usually good — why not try *cazuela canaria*, fish stew? To accompany your main meal, you might like to try a local dish called *papas arrugadas*. The literal translation of this — wrinkled potatoes — might not sound too appetising, but they're actually new potatoes cooked in their skin in well salted water, usually served with mojo sauce, made of oil, vinegar and local herbs.

And to drink, you can enjoy beer or wine. It's worth trying the well known *malvasia* and *moscatel* wines. You might also like to try *cobana* — a banana liqueur — and the local rum, called *ron*, which is sold everywhere and is quite strong! And if you don't feel like alcohol, the local mineral water is said to be excellent.

It's the end of your holiday, and after your stay here you're likely to have trouble packing all the **souvenirs** you've acquired into your suitcase! Choose from **hem-stitch embroidery** — *calados* — which you might see local craftsmen at work on, **basketwork** — including palm-leaf baskets — and the **banana liqueur**, *cobana*. And if you really can't squeeze everything into your luggage, why not do as so many visitors have done. . .and return as soon as you can?

DID YOU KNOW THAT. . .?

* Tenerife is the largest of the Canary Islands.

* Mount Teide in Tenerife is the **highest mountain** in Spain.

* you can throw **snowballs** on Mount Teide while people **sunbathe** twenty miles away.

* the unit of currency in Tenerife is the **peseta**.

* if you want to say 'I love you' when you're in Tenerife you can whisper '*Te quiero*'.

Full of Eastern Passion...

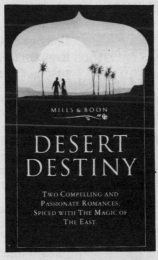

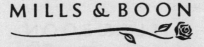

SUMMER SPECIAL!

Four exciting new Romances for the price of three

Each Romance features British heroines and their encounters with dark and desirable Mediterranean men. *Plus, a free Elmlea recipe booklet inside every pack.*

So sit back and enjoy your sumptuous summer reading pack and indulge yourself with the free Elmlea recipe ideas.

Available July 1994   Price £5.70

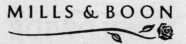

MILLS & BOON

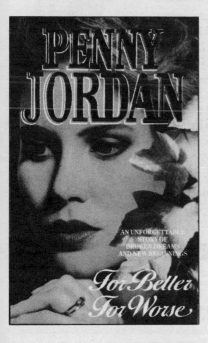